breaking dawn

STEPHENIE MEYER

Megan Tingley Books

LITTLE, BROWN AND COMPANY
New York   Boston

Little, Brown and Company
Hachette Book Group USA
237 Park Avenue, New York, NY 10017
Visit our Web site at www.lb-teens.com

First International Edition: August 2008
First published in hardcover in August 2008 by Little, Brown and Company.

Little, Brown and Company is a division of Hachette Book Group USA, Inc.
The Little, Brown name and logo are trademarks of Hachette Book Group USA, Inc.

Epigraph on page 365 from *Empire* by Orson Scott Card. A Tor Book. Published by
Tom Doherty Associates, LLC. Copyright © 2006 by Orson Scott Card.
Reprinted with permission of the author.

The characters and events portrayed in this book are fictitious. Any similarity
to real persons, living or dead, is coincidental and not intended by the author.

ISBN 978-0-316-03214-8

Library of Congress Control Number: 2008928027

10 9 8
RRD-C

Printed in the United States of America

This book is dedicated to my ninja/agent, Jodi Reamer.
Thank you for keeping me off the ledge.

And thanks also to my favorite band,
the very aptly named Muse,
for providing a saga's worth of inspiration.

‑‑‑ ‑‑‑

BOOK ONE

❧ ❧

bella

CONTENTS

-+- -+-

Childhood is not from birth to a certain age and at a certain age
The child is grown, and puts away childish things.
Childhood is the kingdom where nobody dies.

Edna St. Vincent Millay

PREFACE

I'd had more than my fair share of near-death experiences; it wasn't something you ever really got used to.

It seemed oddly inevitable, though, facing death again. Like I really *was* marked for disaster. I'd escaped time and time again, but it kept coming back for me.

Still, this time was so different from the others.

You could run from someone you feared, you could try to fight someone you hated. All my reactions were geared toward those kinds of killers—the monsters, the enemies.

When you loved the one who was killing you, it left you no options. How could you run, how could you fight, when doing so would hurt that beloved one? If your life was all you had to give your beloved, how could you not give it?

If it was someone you truly loved?

1. ENGAGED

NO ONE IS STARING AT YOU, I PROMISED MYSELF. *NO ONE IS staring at you. No one is staring at you.*

But, because I couldn't lie convincingly even to myself, I had to check.

As I sat waiting for one of the three traffic lights in town to turn green, I peeked to the right—in her minivan, Mrs. Weber had turned her whole torso in my direction. Her eyes bored into mine, and I flinched back, wondering why she didn't drop her gaze or look ashamed. It was still considered rude to stare at people, wasn't it? Didn't that apply to me anymore?

Then I remembered that these windows were so darkly tinted that she probably had no idea if it was even me in here, let alone that I'd caught her looking. I tried to take some comfort in the fact that she wasn't really staring at me, just the car.

My car. Sigh.

I glanced to the left and groaned. Two pedestrians were frozen on the sidewalk, missing their chance to cross as they stared. Behind them, Mr. Marshall was gawking through the plate-glass window of his little souvenir shop. At least he didn't have his nose pressed up against the glass. Yet.

The light turned green and, in my hurry to escape, I stomped on the gas pedal without thinking—the normal way I would have punched it to get my ancient Chevy truck moving.

Engine snarling like a hunting panther, the car jolted forward so fast that my body slammed into the black leather seat and my stomach flattened against my spine.

"Arg!" I gasped as I fumbled for the brake. Keeping my head, I merely tapped the pedal. The car lurched to an absolute standstill anyway.

I couldn't bear to look around at the reaction. If there had been any doubt as to who was driving this car before, it was gone now. With the toe of my shoe, I gently nudged the gas pedal down one half millimeter, and the car shot forward again.

I managed to reach my goal, the gas station. If I hadn't been running on vapors, I wouldn't have come into town at all. I was going without a lot of things these days, like Pop-Tarts and shoelaces, to avoid spending time in public.

Moving as if I were in a race, I got the hatch open, the cap off, the card scanned, and the nozzle in the tank within seconds. Of course, there was nothing I could do to make the numbers on the gauge pick up the pace. They ticked by sluggishly, almost as if they were doing it just to annoy me.

It wasn't bright out—a typical drizzly day in Forks, Washington—but I still felt like a spotlight was trained on me, drawing attention to the delicate ring on my left hand. At times like this, sensing the eyes on my back, it felt as if the ring were pulsing like a neon sign: *Look at me, look at me.*

It was stupid to be so self-conscious, and I knew that. Besides my dad and mom, did it really matter what people were saying about my engagement? About my new car? About my mysterious acceptance into an Ivy League college? About the shiny black credit card that felt red-hot in my back pocket right now?

"Yeah, who cares what they think," I muttered under my breath.

"Um, miss?" a man's voice called.

I turned, and then wished I hadn't.

Two men stood beside a fancy SUV with brand-new kayaks tied to the top. Neither of them was looking at me; they both were staring at the car.

Personally, I didn't get it. But then, I was just proud I could distinguish between the symbols for Toyota, Ford, and Chevy. This car was glossy black, sleek, and pretty, but it was still just a car to me.

"I'm sorry to bother you, but could you tell me what kind of car you're driving?" the tall one asked.

"Um, a Mercedes, right?"

"Yes," the man said politely while his shorter friend rolled his eyes at my answer. "I know. But I was wondering, is that . . . are you driving a Mercedes *Guardian*?" The man said the name with reverence. I had a feeling this guy would get along well with Edward Cullen, my . . . my fiancé (there really was no getting around that truth with the wedding just days away). "They aren't supposed to be available in Europe yet," the man went on, "let alone here."

While his eyes traced the contours of my car—it didn't look much different from any other Mercedes sedan to me, but what did I know?—I briefly contemplated my issues with words like *fiancé*, *wedding*, *husband*, etc.

I just couldn't put it together in my head.

On the one hand, I had been raised to cringe at the very thought of poofy white dresses and bouquets. But more than that, I just couldn't reconcile a staid, respectable, dull concept like *husband* with my concept of *Edward*. It was like casting an archangel as an accountant; I couldn't visualize him in any commonplace role.

Like always, as soon as I started thinking about Edward I was caught up in a dizzy spin of fantasies. The stranger had to clear his throat to get my attention; he was still waiting for an answer about the car's make and model.

"I don't know," I told him honestly.

"Do you mind if I take a picture with it?"

It took me a second to process that. "Really? You want to take a picture with the car?"

"Sure—nobody is going to believe me if I don't get proof."

"Um. Okay. Fine."

I swiftly put away the nozzle and crept into the front seat to hide while the enthusiast dug a huge professional-looking camera out of his backpack. He and his friend took turns posing by the hood, and then they went to take pictures at the back end.

"I miss my truck," I whimpered to myself.

Very, very convenient—too convenient—that my truck would wheeze its last wheeze just weeks after Edward and I had agreed to our lopsided compromise, one detail of which was that he be allowed to replace my truck when it passed on. Edward swore it was only to be expected; my truck had lived a long, full life and then expired of natural causes. According to him. And, of course, I had no way to verify his story or to try to raise my truck from the dead on my own. My favorite mechanic—

I stopped that thought cold, refusing to let it come to a conclusion. Instead, I listened to the men's voices outside, muted by the car walls.

". . . went at it with a flamethrower in the online video. Didn't even pucker the paint."

"Of course not. You could roll a tank over this baby. Not much of a market for one over here. Designed for Middle East diplomats, arms dealers, and drug lords mostly."

"Think *she's* something?" the short one asked in a softer voice. I ducked my head, cheeks flaming.

"Huh," the tall one said. "Maybe. Can't imagine what you'd need missile-proof glass and four thousand pounds of body armor for around here. Must be headed somewhere more hazardous."

Body armor. *Four thousand pounds* of body armor. And *missile*-proof glass? Nice. What had happened to good old-fashioned bulletproof?

Well, at least this made some sense—if you had a twisted sense of humor.

It wasn't like I hadn't expected Edward to take advantage of our deal, to weight it on his side so that he could give so much more than he would receive. I'd agreed that he could replace my truck when it needed replacing, not expecting that moment to come quite so soon, of course. When I'd been forced to admit that the truck had become no more than a still-life tribute to classic Chevys on my curb, I knew his idea of a replacement was probably going to embarrass me. Make me the focus of stares and whispers. I'd been right about that part. But even in my darkest imaginings I had not foreseen that he would get me *two* cars.

The "before" car and the "after" car, he'd explained when I'd flipped out.

This was just the "before" car. He'd told me it was a loaner and promised that he was returning it after the wedding. It all had made absolutely no sense to me. Until now.

Ha ha. Because I was so fragilely human, so accident-prone, so much a victim to my own dangerous bad luck, apparently I needed a tank-resistant car to keep me safe. Hilarious. I was sure he and his brothers had enjoyed the joke quite a bit behind my back.

Or maybe, just maybe, a small voice whispered in my head, it's not a joke, silly. Maybe he's really that worried about you. This wouldn't be the first time he's gone a little overboard trying to protect you.

I sighed.

I hadn't seen the "after" car yet. It was hidden under a sheet in the deepest corner of the Cullens' garage. I knew most people would have peeked by now, but I really didn't want to know.

Probably no body armor on that car—because I wouldn't need it after the honeymoon. Virtual indestructibility was just one of the many perks I was looking forward to. The best parts about being a Cullen were not expensive cars and impressive credit cards.

"Hey," the tall man called, cupping his hands to the glass in an effort to peer in. "We're done now. Thanks a lot!"

"You're welcome," I called back, and then tensed as I started the engine and eased the pedal—ever so gently—down. . . .

No matter how many times I drove down the familiar road home, I still couldn't make the rain-faded flyers fade into the background. Each one of them, stapled to telephone poles and taped to street signs, was like a fresh slap in the face. A well-deserved slap in the face. My mind was sucked back into the thought I'd interrupted so immediately before. I couldn't avoid it on this road. Not with pictures of *my favorite mechanic* flashing past me at regular intervals.

My best friend. My Jacob.

The HAVE YOU SEEN THIS BOY? posters were not Jacob's father's idea. It had been *my* father, Charlie, who'd printed up the flyers and spread them all over town. And not just Forks, but Port Angeles and Sequim and Hoquiam and Aberdeen and every other town in the Olympic Peninsula. He'd made sure that all the police stations in the state of Washington had the same flyer hanging on the wall, too. His own station had a whole corkboard dedicated to finding Jacob. A corkboard that was mostly empty, much to his disappointment and frustration.

My dad was disappointed with more than the lack of response. He was most disappointed with Billy, Jacob's father—and Charlie's closest friend.

For Billy's not being more involved with the search for his sixteen-year-old "runaway." For Billy's refusing to put up the flyers in La Push, the reservation on the coast that was Jacob's home. For his seeming resigned to Jacob's disappearance, as if there was nothing he could do. For his saying, "Jacob's grown up now. He'll come home if he wants to."

And he was frustrated with me, for taking Billy's side.

I wouldn't put up posters, either. Because both Billy and I knew where Jacob was, roughly speaking, and we also knew that no one had seen this *boy*.

The flyers put the usual big, fat lump in my throat, the usual stinging tears in my eyes, and I was glad Edward was out hunting this Saturday. If Edward saw my reaction, it would only make him feel terrible, too.

Of course, there were drawbacks to it being Saturday. As I turned slowly and carefully onto my street, I could see my dad's police cruiser in the driveway of our home. He'd skipped fishing again today. Still sulking about the wedding.

So I wouldn't be able to use the phone inside. But I *had* to call. . . .

I parked on the curb behind the Chevy sculpture and pulled the cell phone Edward had given me for emergencies out of the glove compartment. I dialed, keeping my finger on the "end" button as the phone rang. Just in case.

"Hello?" Seth Clearwater answered, and I sighed in relief. I was way too chicken to speak to his older sister, Leah. The phrase "bite my head off" was not entirely a figure of speech when it came to Leah.

"Hey, Seth, it's Bella."

"Oh, hiya, Bella! How are you?"

Choked up. Desperate for reassurance. "Fine."

"Calling for an update?"

"You're psychic."

"Not hardly. I'm no Alice—you're just predictable," he joked. Among the Quileute pack down at La Push, only Seth was comfortable even mentioning the Cullens by name, let alone joking about things like my nearly omniscient sister-in-law-to-be.

"I know I am." I hesitated for a minute. "How is he?"

Seth sighed. "Same as ever. He won't talk, though we know he hears us. He's trying not to think *human*, you know. Just going with his instincts."

"Do you know where he is now?"

"Somewhere in northern Canada. I can't tell you which province. He doesn't pay much attention to state lines."

"Any hint that he might . . ."

"He's not coming home, Bella. Sorry."

I swallowed. "S'okay, Seth. I knew before I asked. I just can't help wishing."

"Yeah. We all feel the same way."

"Thanks for putting up with me, Seth. I know the others must give you a hard time."

"They're not your hugest fans," he agreed cheerfully. "Kind of lame, I think. Jacob made his choices, you made yours. Jake doesn't like their attitude about it. 'Course, he isn't super thrilled that you're checking up on him, either."

I gasped. "I thought he wasn't talking to you?"

"He can't hide everything from us, hard as he's trying."

So Jacob knew I was worried. I wasn't sure how I felt about that. Well, at least he knew I hadn't skipped off into the sunset and forgotten him completely. He might have imagined me capable of that.

"I guess I'll see you at the . . . wedding," I said, forcing the word out through my teeth.

"Yeah, me and my mom will be there. It was cool of you to ask us."

I smiled at the enthusiasm in his voice. Though inviting the Clearwaters had been Edward's idea, I was glad he'd thought of it. Having Seth there would be nice—a link, however tenuous, to my missing best man. "It wouldn't be the same without you."

"Tell Edward I said hi, 'kay?"

"Sure thing."

I shook my head. The friendship that had sprung up between Edward and Seth was something that still boggled my mind. It was proof, though, that things didn't have to be this way. That vampires and werewolves could get along just fine, thank you very much, if they were of a mind to.

Not everybody liked this idea.

"Ah," Seth said, his voice cracking up an octave. "Er, Leah's home."

"Oh! Bye!"

The phone went dead. I left it on the seat and prepared myself mentally to go inside the house, where Charlie would be waiting.

My poor dad had so much to deal with right now. Jacob-the-runaway was just *one* of the straws on his overburdened back. He was almost as worried about me, his barely-a-legal-adult daughter who was about to become a Mrs. in just a few days' time.

I walked slowly through the light rain, remembering the night we'd told him. . . .

*　　*　　*

As the sound of Charlie's cruiser announced his return, the ring suddenly weighed a hundred pounds on my finger. I wanted to shove my left hand in a pocket, or maybe sit on it, but Edward's cool, firm grasp kept it front and center.

"Stop fidgeting, Bella. Please try to remember that you're not confessing to a murder here."

"Easy for you to say."

I listened to the ominous sound of my father's boots clomping up the sidewalk. The key rattled in the already open door. The sound reminded me of that part of the horror movie when the victim realizes she's forgotten to lock her deadbolt.

"Calm down, Bella," Edward whispered, listening to the acceleration of my heart.

The door slammed against the wall, and I flinched like I'd been Tasered.

"Hey, Charlie," Edward called, entirely relaxed.

"No!" I protested under my breath.

"What?" Edward whispered back.

"Wait till he hangs his gun up!"

Edward chuckled and ran his free hand through his tousled bronze hair.

Charlie came around the corner, still in his uniform, still armed, and tried not to make a face when he spied us sitting together on the loveseat. Lately, he'd been putting forth a lot of effort to like Edward more. Of course, this revelation was sure to end that effort immediately.

"Hey, kids. What's up?"

"We'd like to talk to you," Edward said, so serene. "We have some good news."

Charlie's expression went from strained friendliness to black suspicion in a second.

"Good news?" Charlie growled, looking straight at me.

"Have a seat, Dad."

He raised one eyebrow, stared at me for five seconds, then stomped to the recliner and sat down on the very edge, his back ramrod straight.

"Don't get worked up, Dad," I said after a moment of loaded silence. "Everything's okay."

Edward grimaced, and I knew it was in objection to the word *okay*. He probably would have used something more like *wonderful* or *perfect* or *glorious*.

"Sure it is, Bella, sure it is. If everything is so great, then why are you sweating bullets?"

"I'm not sweating," I lied.

I leaned away from his fierce scowl, cringing into Edward, and instinctively wiped the back of my right hand across my forehead to remove the evidence.

"You're pregnant!" Charlie exploded. "You're pregnant, aren't you?"

Though the question was clearly meant for me, he was glaring at Edward now, and I could have sworn I saw his hand twitch toward the gun.

"No! Of course I'm not!" I wanted to elbow Edward in the ribs, but I knew that move would only give me a bruise. I'd *told* Edward that people would immediately jump to this conclusion! What other possible reason would sane people have for getting married at eighteen? (His answer then had made me roll my eyes. *Love*. Right.)

Charlie's glower lightened a shade. It was usually pretty clear on my face when I was telling the truth, and he believed me now. "Oh. Sorry."

"Apology accepted."

There was a long pause. After a moment, I realized everyone was waiting for *me* to say something. I looked up at Edward, panic-stricken. There was no way I was going to get the words out.

He smiled at me and then squared his shoulders and turned to my father.

"Charlie, I realize that I've gone about this out of order. Traditionally, I should have asked you first. I mean no disrespect, but since Bella has already said yes and I don't want to diminish her choice in the matter, instead of asking you for her hand, I'm asking you for your blessing. We're getting married, Charlie. I love her more than anything in the world, more than my own life, and—by some miracle—she loves me that way, too. Will you give us your blessing?"

He sounded so sure, so calm. For just an instant, listening to the absolute confidence in his voice, I experienced a rare moment of insight. I could see, fleetingly, the way the world looked to him. For the length of one heartbeat, this news made perfect sense.

And then I caught sight of the expression on Charlie's face, his eyes now locked on the ring.

I held my breath while his skin changed colors—fair to red, red to purple, purple to blue. I started to get up—I'm not sure what I planned to do; maybe use the Heimlich maneuver to make sure he wasn't choking—but Edward squeezed my hand and murmured "Give him a minute" so low that only I could hear.

The silence was much longer this time. Then, gradually, shade by shade, Charlie's color returned to normal. His lips pursed, and his eyebrows furrowed; I recognized his "deep in thought" expression. He studied the two of us for a long moment, and I felt Edward relax at my side.

"Guess I'm not that surprised," Charlie grumbled. "Knew I'd have to deal with something like this soon enough."

I exhaled.

"You sure about this?" Charlie demanded, glaring at me.

"I'm one hundred percent sure about Edward," I told him without missing a beat.

"Getting married, though? What's the rush?" He eyed me suspiciously again.

The rush was due to the fact that I was getting closer to nineteen every stinking day, while Edward stayed frozen in all his seventeen-year-old perfection, as he had for over ninety years. Not that this fact necessitated *marriage* in my book, but the wedding was required due to the delicate and tangled compromise Edward and I had made to finally get to this point, the brink of my transformation from mortal to immortal.

These weren't things I could explain to Charlie.

"We're going away to Dartmouth together in the fall, Charlie," Edward reminded him. "I'd like to do that, well, the right way. It's how I was raised." He shrugged.

He wasn't exaggerating; they'd been big on old-fashioned morals during World War I.

Charlie's mouth twisted to the side. Looking for an angle to argue from. But what could he say? *I'd prefer you live in sin first?* He was a dad; his hands were tied.

"Knew this was coming," he muttered to himself, frowning. Then, suddenly, his face went perfectly smooth and blank.

"Dad?" I asked anxiously. I glanced at Edward, but I couldn't read his face, either, as he watched Charlie.

"Ha!" Charlie exploded. I jumped in my seat. "Ha, ha, ha!"

I stared incredulously as Charlie doubled over in laughter; his whole body shook with it.

I looked at Edward for a translation, but Edward had his lips pressed tightly together, like he was trying to hold back laughter himself.

"Okay, fine," Charlie choked out. "Get married." Another roll of laughter shook through him. "But . . ."

"But what?" I demanded.

"But *you* have to tell your mom! I'm not saying one word to Renée! That's all yours!" He busted into loud guffaws.

*   *   *

I paused with my hand on the doorknob, smiling. Sure, at the time, Charlie's words had terrified me. The ultimate doom: telling Renée. Early marriage was higher up on her blacklist than boiling live puppies.

Who could have foreseen her response? Not me. Certainly not Charlie. Maybe Alice, but I hadn't thought to ask her.

"Well, Bella," Renée had said after I'd choked and stuttered out the impossible words: *Mom, I'm marrying Edward.* "I'm a little miffed that you waited so long to tell me. Plane tickets only get more expensive. Oooh," she'd fretted. "Do you think Phil's cast will be off by then? It will spoil the pictures if he's not in a tux—"

"Back up a second, Mom." I'd gasped. "What do you mean, waited so long? I just got en-en . . ."—I'd been unable to force out the word *engaged*—"things settled, you know, today."

"Today? Really? That *is* a surprise. I assumed . . ."

"What did you assume? *When* did you assume?"

"Well, when you came to visit me in April, it looked like things were pretty much sewn up, if you know what I mean. You're not very hard to read, sweetie. But I didn't say anything because I knew it wouldn't do any good. You're exactly like Charlie." She'd sighed, resigned. "Once you make up your mind, there is no reasoning with you. Of course, exactly like Charlie, you stick by your decisions, too."

And then she'd said the last thing that I'd ever expected to hear from my mother.

"You're not making my mistakes, Bella. You sound like you're scared silly, and I'm guessing it's because you're afraid of *me*." She'd giggled. "Of what I'm going to think. And I know I've said a lot of things about marriage and stupidity—and I'm not taking them back—but you need to realize that those things specifically applied to *me*. You're a completely different person than I am. You make your own kinds of mistakes, and I'm sure you'll have your share of regrets in life. But commitment was never your problem, sweetie. You have a better chance of making this work than most forty-year-olds I know." Renée had laughed again. "My little middle-aged child. Luckily, you seem to have found another old soul."

"You're not . . . mad? You don't think I'm making a humongous mistake?"

"Well, sure, I wish you'd wait a few more years. I mean, do I look old enough to be a mother-in-law to you? Don't answer that. But this isn't about me. This is about you. Are you happy?"

"I don't know. I'm having an out-of-body experience right now."

Renée had chuckled. "Does he make you happy, Bella?"

"Yes, but—"

"Are you ever going to want anyone else?"

"No, but—"

"But what?"

"But aren't you going to say that I sound exactly like every other infatuated teenager since the dawn of time?"

"You've never been a teenager, sweetie. You know what's best for *you*."

For the last few weeks, Renée had unexpectedly immersed herself in wedding plans. She'd spent hours every day on the phone with Edward's mother, Esme—no worries about the in-laws getting along. Renée *adored* Esme, but then, I doubted anyone could help responding that way to my lovable almost-mother-in-law.

It let me right off the hook. Edward's family and my family were taking care of the nuptials together without my having to do or know or think too hard about any of it.

Charlie was furious, of course, but the sweet part was that he wasn't furious at *me*. Renée was the traitor. He'd counted on her to play the heavy. What could he do now, when his ultimate threat—telling Mom—had turned out to be utterly empty? He had nothing, and he knew it. So he moped around the house, muttering things about not being able to trust anyone in this world. . . .

"Dad?" I called as I pushed open the front door. "I'm home."

"Hold on, Bells, stay right there."

"Huh?" I asked, pausing automatically.

"Gimme a second. Ouch, you got me, Alice."

Alice?

"Sorry, Charlie," Alice's trilling voice responded. "How's that?"

"I'm bleeding on it."

"You're fine. Didn't break the skin—trust me."

"What's going on?" I demanded, hesitating in the doorway.

"Thirty seconds, please, Bella," Alice told me. "Your patience will be rewarded."

"Humph," Charlie added.

I tapped my foot, counting each beat. Before I got to thirty, Alice said, "Okay, Bella, come in!"

Moving with caution, I rounded the little corner into our living room.

"Oh," I huffed. "Aw. Dad. Don't you look—"

"Silly?" Charlie interrupted.

"I was thinking more like *debonair*."

Charlie blushed. Alice took his elbow and tugged him around into a slow spin to showcase the pale gray tux.

"Now cut that out, Alice. I look like an idiot."

"No one dressed by me *ever* looks like an idiot."

"She's right, Dad. You look fabulous! What's the occasion?"

Alice rolled her eyes. "It's the final check on the fit. For both of you."

I peeled my gaze off the unusually elegant Charlie for the first time and saw the dreaded white garment bag laid carefully across the sofa.

"Aaah."

"Go to your happy place, Bella. It won't take long."

I sucked in a deep breath and closed my eyes. Keeping them shut, I stumbled my way up the stairs to my room. I stripped down to my underwear and held my arms straight out.

"You'd think I was shoving bamboo splinters under your nails," Alice muttered to herself as she followed me in.

I paid no attention to her. I was in my happy place.

In my happy place, the whole wedding mess was over and done. Behind me. Already repressed and forgotten.

We were alone, just Edward and me. The setting was fuzzy and constantly in flux—it morphed from misty forest to cloud-covered city to arctic night—because Edward was keeping the location of our honeymoon a secret to surprise me. But I wasn't especially concerned about the *where* part.

Edward and I were together, and I'd fulfilled my side of our compromise perfectly. I'd married him. That was the big one. But I'd also accepted all his outrageous gifts and was registered, however futilely, to attend Dartmouth College in the fall. Now it was his turn.

Before he turned me into a vampire—his big compromise—he had one other stipulation to make good on.

Edward had an obsessive sort of concern over the human things that I would be giving up, the experiences he didn't want me to miss. Most of them—like the prom, for example—seemed silly to me. There was only one human experience I worried about missing. Of course it would be the one he wished I would forget completely.

Here was the thing, though. I knew a little about what I was going to be like when I wasn't human anymore. I'd seen newborn vampires firsthand, and I'd heard all my family-to-be's stories about those wild early days. For several years, my biggest personality trait was going to be *thirsty*. It would take some time before I could be *me* again. And even when I was in control of myself, I would never feel exactly the way I felt now.

Human . . . and passionately in love.

I wanted the complete experience before I traded in my warm, breakable, pheromone-riddled body for something beautiful, strong . . . and unknown. I wanted a *real* honeymoon with Edward. And, despite the danger he feared this would put me in, he'd agreed to try.

I was only vaguely aware of Alice and the slip and slide of satin over my skin. I didn't care, for the moment, that the whole town was talking about me. I didn't think about the spectacle I would have to star in much too soon. I didn't worry about tripping on my train or giggling at the wrong moment or being too young or the staring audience or even the empty seat where my best friend should be.

I was with Edward in my happy place.

2. LONG NIGHT

"I MISS YOU ALREADY."

"I don't need to leave. I can stay. . . ."

"Mmm."

It was quiet for a long moment, just the thud of my heart hammering, the broken rhythm of our ragged breathing, and the whisper of our lips moving in synchronization.

Sometimes it was so easy to forget that I was kissing a vampire. Not because he seemed ordinary or human—I could never for a second forget that I was holding someone more angel than man in my arms—but because he made it seem like nothing at all to have his lips against my lips, my face, my throat. He claimed he was long past the temptation my blood used to be for him, that the idea of losing me had cured him of any desire for it. But I knew the smell of my blood still caused him pain—still burned his throat like he was inhaling flames.

I opened my eyes and found his open, too, staring at my face. It made no sense when he looked at me that way. Like I was the prize rather than the outrageously lucky winner.

Our gazes locked for a moment; his golden eyes were so deep that I imagined I could see all the way into his soul. It seemed silly that this fact—the existence of his soul—had ever been in question, even if he *was* a vampire. He had the most beautiful soul, more beautiful than his brilliant mind or his incomparable face or his glorious body.

He looked back at me as if he could see my soul, too, and as if he liked what he saw.

He couldn't see into my mind, though, the way he saw into everyone else's. Who knew why—some strange glitch in my brain that made it immune to all the extraordinary and frightening things some immortals could do. (Only my mind was immune; my body was still subject to vampires with abilities that worked in ways other than Edward's.) But I was seriously grateful to whatever malfunction it was that kept my thoughts a secret. It was just too embarrassing to consider the alternative.

I pulled his face to mine again.

"Definitely staying," he murmured a moment later.

"No, no. It's your bachelor party. You have to go."

I said the words, but the fingers of my right hand locked into his bronze hair, my left pressed tighter against the small of his back. His cool hands stroked my face.

"Bachelor parties are designed for those who are sad to

see the passing of their single days. I couldn't be more eager to have mine behind me. So there's really no point."

"True." I breathed against the winter-cold skin of his throat.

This was pretty close to my happy place. Charlie slept obliviously in his room, which was almost as good as being alone. We were curled up on my small bed, intertwined as much as it was possible, considering the thick afghan I was swathed in like a cocoon. I hated the necessity of the blanket, but it sort of ruined the romance when my teeth started chattering. Charlie would notice if I turned the heat on in August. . . .

At least, if *I* had to be bundled up, Edward's shirt was on the floor. I never got over the shock of how perfect his body was—white, cool, and polished as marble. I ran my hand down his stone chest now, tracing across the flat planes of his stomach, just marveling. A light shudder rippled through him, and his mouth found mine again. Carefully, I let the tip of my tongue press against his glass-smooth lip, and he sighed. His sweet breath washed—cold and delicious—over my face.

He started to pull away—that was his automatic response whenever he decided things had gone too far, his reflex reaction whenever he most wanted to keep going. Edward had spent most of his life rejecting any kind of physical gratification. I knew it was terrifying to him trying to change those habits now.

"Wait," I said, gripping his shoulders and hugging myself close to him. I kicked one leg free and wrapped it around his waist. "Practice makes perfect."

He chuckled. "Well, we should be fairly close to perfection

by this point, then, shouldn't we? Have you slept at all in the last month?"

"But this is the dress rehearsal," I reminded him, "and we've only practiced certain scenes. It's no time for playing safe."

I thought he would laugh, but he didn't answer, and his body was motionless with sudden stress. The gold in his eyes seemed to harden from a liquid to a solid.

I thought over my words, realized what he would have heard in them.

"Bella . . . ," he whispered.

"Don't start this again," I said. "A deal's a deal."

"I don't know. It's too hard to concentrate when you're with me like this. I—I can't think straight. I won't be able to control myself. You'll get hurt."

"I'll be fine."

"Bella . . ."

"Shh!" I pressed my lips to his to stop his panic attack. I'd heard it before. He wasn't getting out of this deal. Not after insisting I marry him first.

He kissed me back for a moment, but I could tell he wasn't as into it as before. Worrying, always worrying. How different it would be when he didn't need to worry about me anymore. What would he do with all his free time? He'd have to get a new hobby.

"How are your feet?" he asked.

Knowing he didn't mean that literally, I answered, "Toasty warm."

"Really? No second thoughts? It's not too late to change your mind."

"Are you trying to ditch me?"

He chuckled. "Just making sure. I don't want you to do anything you're not sure about."

"I'm sure about you. The rest I can live through."

He hesitated, and I wondered if I'd put my foot in my mouth again.

"Can you?" he asked quietly. "I don't mean the wedding—which I am positive you will survive despite your qualms—but afterward . . . what about Renée, what about Charlie?"

I sighed. "I'll miss them." Worse, that they would miss me, but I didn't want to give him any fuel.

"Angela and Ben and Jessica and Mike."

"I'll miss my friends, too." I smiled in the darkness. "Especially Mike. Oh, Mike! How will I go on?"

He growled.

I laughed but then was serious. "Edward, we've been through this and through this. I know it will be hard, but this is what I want. I want you, and I want you forever. One lifetime is simply not enough for me."

"Frozen forever at eighteen," he whispered.

"Every woman's dream come true," I teased.

"Never changing . . . never moving forward."

"What does that mean?"

He answered slowly. "Do you remember when we told Charlie we were getting married? And he thought you were . . . pregnant?"

"And he thought about shooting you," I guessed with a laugh. "Admit it—for one second, he honestly considered it."

He didn't answer.

"What, Edward?"

"I just wish . . . well, I wish that he'd been right."

"Gah," I gasped.

"More that there was some way he *could* have been. That we had that kind of potential. I *hate* taking that away from you, too."

It took me a minute. "I know what I'm doing."

"How could you know that, Bella? Look at my mother, look at my sister. It's not as easy a sacrifice as you imagine."

"Esme and Rosalie get by just fine. If it's a problem later, we can do what Esme did—we'll adopt."

He sighed, and then his voice was fierce. "It's not *right*! I don't want you to have to make sacrifices for me. I want to give you things, not take things away from you. I don't want to steal your future. If I were human—"

I put my hand over his lips. "*You* are my future. Now stop. No moping, or I'm calling your brothers to come and get you. Maybe you *need* a bachelor party."

"I'm sorry. I am moping, aren't I? Must be the nerves."

"Are *your* feet cold?"

"Not in that sense. I've been waiting a century to marry you, Miss Swan. The wedding ceremony is the one thing I can't wait—" He broke off mid-thought. "Oh, for the love of all that's holy!"

"What's wrong?"

He gritted his teeth. "You don't have to call my brothers. Apparently Emmett and Jasper are not going to let me bow out tonight."

I clutched him closer for one second and then released him. I didn't have a prayer of winning a tug-of-war with Emmett. "Have fun."

There was a squeal against the window—someone

deliberately scraping their steel nails across the glass to make a horrible, cover-your-ears, goose-bumps-down-your-spine noise. I shuddered.

"If you don't send Edward out," Emmett—still invisible in the night—hissed menacingly, "we're coming in after him!"

"Go," I laughed. *"Before* they break my house."

Edward rolled his eyes, but he got to his feet in one fluid movement and had his shirt back on in another. He leaned down and kissed my forehead.

"Get to sleep. You've got a big day tomorrow."

"Thanks! That's sure to help me wind down."

"I'll meet you at the altar."

"I'll be the one in white." I smiled at how perfectly blasé I sounded.

He chuckled, said, "Very convincing," and then suddenly sank into a crouch, his muscles coiled like a spring. He vanished—launching himself out my window too swiftly for my eyes to follow.

Outside, there was a muted thud, and I heard Emmett curse.

"You'd better not make him late," I murmured, knowing they could hear.

And then Jasper's face was peering in my window, his honey hair silver in the weak moonlight that worked through the clouds.

"Don't worry, Bella. We'll get him home in plenty of time."

I was suddenly very calm, and my qualms all seemed unimportant. Jasper was, in his own way, just as talented as Alice with her uncannily accurate predictions. Jasper's medium was moods rather than the future, and it was impossible to resist feeling the way he wanted you to feel.

I sat up awkwardly, still tangled in my blanket. "Jasper? What do vampires do for bachelor parties? You're not taking him to a strip club, are you?"

"Don't tell her anything!" Emmett growled from below. There was another thud, and Edward laughed quietly.

"Relax," Jasper told me—and I did. "We Cullens have our own version. Just a few mountain lions, a couple of grizzly bears. Pretty much an ordinary night out."

I wondered if I would ever be able to sound so cavalier about the "vegetarian" vampire diet.

"Thanks, Jasper."

He winked and dropped from sight.

It was completely silent outside. Charlie's muffled snores droned through the walls.

I lay back against my pillow, sleepy now. I stared at the walls of my little room, bleached pale in the moonlight, from under heavy lids.

My last night in my room. My last night as Isabella Swan. Tomorrow night, I would be Bella Cullen. Though the whole marriage ordeal was a thorn in my side, I had to admit that I liked the sound of that.

I let my mind wander idly for a moment, expecting sleep to take me. But, after a few minutes, I found myself more alert, anxiety creeping back into my stomach, twisting it into uncomfortable positions. The bed seemed too soft, too warm without Edward in it. Jasper was far away, and all the peaceful, relaxed feelings were gone with him.

It was going to be a very long day tomorrow.

I was aware that most of my fears were stupid—I just had to get over myself. Attention was an inevitable part of life. I couldn't always blend in with the scenery. However, I did have a few specific worries that were completely valid.

First there was the wedding dress's train. Alice clearly had let her artistic sense overpower practicalities on that one. Maneuvering the Cullens' staircase in heels and a train sounded impossible. I should have practiced.

Then there was the guest list.

Tanya's family, the Denali clan, would be arriving sometime before the ceremony.

It would be touchy to have Tanya's family in the same room with our guests from the Quileute reservation, Jacob's father and the Clearwaters. The Denalis were no fans of the werewolves. In fact, Tanya's sister Irina was not coming to the wedding at all. She still nursed a vendetta against the werewolves for killing her friend Laurent (just as he was about to kill me). Thanks to that grudge, the Denalis had abandoned Edward's family in their worst hour of need. It had been the unlikely alliance with the Quileute wolves that had saved all our lives when the horde of newborn vampires had attacked. . . .

Edward had promised me it wouldn't be dangerous to have the Denalis near the Quileutes. Tanya and all her family—besides Irina—felt horribly guilty for that defection. A truce with the werewolves was a small price to make up some of that debt, a price they were prepared to pay.

That was the big problem, but there was a small problem, too: my fragile self-esteem.

I'd never seen Tanya before, but I was sure that meeting

her wouldn't be a pleasant experience for my ego. Once upon a time, before I was born probably, she'd made her play for Edward—not that I blamed her or anyone else for wanting him. Still, she would be beautiful at the very least and magnificent at best. Though Edward clearly—if inconceivably—preferred me, I wouldn't be able to help making comparisons.

I had grumbled a little until Edward, who knew my weaknesses, made me feel guilty.

"We're the closest thing they have to family, Bella," he'd reminded me. "They still feel like orphans, you know, even after all this time."

So I'd conceded, hiding my frown.

Tanya had a big family now, almost as big as the Cullens. There were five of them; Tanya, Kate, and Irina had been joined by Carmen and Eleazar much the same way the Cullens had been joined by Alice and Jasper, all of them bonded by their desire to live more compassionately than normal vampires did.

For all the company, though, Tanya and her sisters were still alone in one way. Still in mourning. Because a very long time ago, they'd had a mother, too.

I could imagine the hole that loss would leave, even after a thousand years; I tried to visualize the Cullen family without their creator, their center, and their guide—their father, Carlisle. I couldn't see it.

Carlisle had explained Tanya's history during one of the many nights I'd stayed late at the Cullens' home, learning as much as I could, preparing as much as was possible for the future I'd chosen. Tanya's mother's story was one among many, a cautionary tale illustrating just one of the rules

I would need to be aware of when I joined the immortal world. Only one rule, actually—one law that broke down into a thousand different facets: *Keep the secret.*

Keeping the secret meant a lot of things—living inconspicuously like the Cullens, moving on before humans could suspect they weren't aging. Or keeping clear of humans altogether—except at mealtime—the way nomads like James and Victoria had lived; the way Jasper's friends, Peter and Charlotte, still lived. It meant keeping control of whatever new vampires you created, like Jasper had done when he'd lived with Maria. Like Victoria had failed to do with her newborns.

And it meant not creating some things in the first place, because some creations were uncontrollable.

"I don't know Tanya's mother's name," Carlisle had admitted, his golden eyes, almost the exact shade of his fair hair, sad with remembering Tanya's pain. "They never speak of her if they can avoid it, never think of her willingly.

"The woman who created Tanya, Kate, and Irina—who loved them, I believe—lived many years before I was born, during a time of plague in our world, the plague of the immortal children.

"What they were thinking, those ancient ones, I can't begin to understand. They created vampires out of humans who were barely more than infants."

I'd had to swallow back the bile that rose in my throat as I'd pictured what he was describing.

"They were very beautiful," Carlisle had explained quickly, seeing my reaction. "So endearing, so enchanting, you can't imagine. You had but to be near them to love them; it was an automatic thing.

"However, they could not be taught. They were frozen at whatever level of development they'd achieved before being bitten. Adorable two-year-olds with dimples and lisps that could destroy half a village in one of their tantrums. If they hungered, they fed, and no words of warning could restrain them. Humans saw them, stories circulated, fear spread like fire in dry brush. . . .

"Tanya's mother created such a child. As with the other ancients, I cannot fathom her reasons." He'd taken a deep, steadying breath. "The Volturi became involved, of course."

I'd flinched as I always did at that name, but of course the legion of Italian vampires—royalty in their own estimation—was central to this story. There couldn't be a law if there was no punishment; there couldn't be a punishment if there was no one to deliver it. The ancients Aro, Caius, and Marcus ruled the Volturi forces; I'd only met them once, but in that brief encounter, it seemed to me that Aro, with his powerful mind-reading gift—one touch, and he knew every thought a mind had ever held—was the true leader.

"The Volturi studied the immortal children, at home in Volterra and all around the world. Caius decided the young ones were incapable of protecting our secret. And so they had to be destroyed.

"I told you they were loveable. Well, covens fought to the last man—were utterly decimated—to protect them. The carnage was not as widespread as the southern wars on this continent, but more devastating in its own way. Long-established covens, old traditions, friends . . . Much was lost. In the end, the practice was completely eliminated. The immortal children became unmentionable, a taboo.

"When I lived with the Volturi, I met two immortal children, so I know firsthand the appeal they had. Aro studied the little ones for many years after the catastrophe they'd caused was over. You know his inquisitive disposition; he was hopeful that they could be tamed. But in the end, the decision was unanimous: the immortal children could not be allowed to exist."

I'd all but forgotten the Denali sisters' mother when the story returned to her.

"It is unclear precisely what happened with Tanya's mother," Carlisle had said. "Tanya, Kate, and Irina were entirely oblivious until the day the Volturi came for them, their mother and her illegal creation already their prisoners. It was ignorance that saved Tanya's and her sisters' lives. Aro touched them and saw their total innocence, so they were not punished with their mother.

"None of them had ever seen the boy before, or dreamed of his existence, until the day they watched him burn in their mother's arms. I can only guess that their mother had kept her secret to protect them from this exact outcome. But why had she created him in the first place? Who was he, and what had he meant to her that would cause her to cross this most uncrossable of lines? Tanya and the others never received an answer to any of these questions. But they could not doubt their mother's guilt, and I don't think they've ever truly forgiven her.

"Even with Aro's perfect assurance that Tanya, Kate, and Irina were innocent, Caius wanted them to burn. Guilty by association. They were lucky that Aro felt like being merciful that day. Tanya and her sisters were pardoned, but left with unhealing hearts and a very healthy respect for the law. . . ."

I'm not sure where exactly the memory turned into a dream. One moment it seemed that I was listening to Carlisle in my memory, looking at his face, and then a moment later I was looking at a gray, barren field and smelling the thick scent of burning incense in the air. I was not alone there.

The huddle of figures in the center of the field, all shrouded in ashy cloaks, should have terrified me—they could only be Volturi, and I was, against what they'd decreed at our last meeting, still human. But I knew, as I sometimes did in dreams, that I was invisible to them.

Scattered all around me were smoking heaps. I recognized the sweetness in the air and did not examine the mounds too closely. I had no desire to see the faces of the vampires they had executed, half afraid that I might recognize someone in the smoldering pyres.

The Volturi soldiers stood in a circle around something or someone, and I heard their whispery voices raised in agitation. I edged closer to the cloaks, compelled by the dream to see whatever thing or person they were examining with such intensity. Creeping carefully between two of the tall hissing shrouds, I finally saw the object of their debate, raised up on a little hillock above them.

He was beautiful, adorable, just as Carlisle had described. The boy was a toddler still, maybe two years of age. Light brown curls framed his cherubic face with its round cheeks and full lips. And he was trembling, his eyes closed as if he was too frightened to watch death coming closer every second.

I was struck with such a powerful need to save the lovely, terrified child that the Volturi, despite all their devastating menace, no longer mattered to me. I shoved past them, not caring if they realized my presence. Breaking free of them altogether, I sprinted toward the boy.

Only to stagger to a halt as I got a clear view of the hillock that he sat upon. It was not earth and rock, but a pile of human bodies, drained and lifeless. Too late not to see these faces. I knew them all—Angela, Ben, Jessica, Mike. . . . And directly beneath the adorable boy were the bodies of my father and my mother.

The child opened his bright, bloodred eyes.

3. BIG DAY

MY OWN EYES FLEW OPEN.

I lay shivering and gasping in my warm bed for several minutes, trying to break free of the dream. The sky outside my window turned gray and then pale pink while I waited for my heart to slow.

When I was fully back to the reality of my messy, familiar room, I was a little annoyed with myself. What a dream to have the night before my wedding! That's what I got for obsessing over disturbing stories in the middle of the night.

Eager to shake off the nightmare, I got dressed and headed down to the kitchen long before I needed to. First I cleaned the already tidy rooms, and then when Charlie was up I made him pancakes. I was much too keyed up to have any interest in eating breakfast myself—I sat bouncing in my seat while he ate.

"You're picking up Mr. Weber at three o'clock," I reminded him.

"I don't have that much to do today besides bring the minister, Bells. I'm not likely to forget my only job." Charlie had taken the entire day off for the wedding, and he was definitely at loose ends. Now and then, his eyes flickered furtively to the closet under the stairs, where he kept his fishing gear.

"That's not your only job. You also have to be dressed and presentable."

He scowled into his cereal bowl and muttered the words "monkey suit" under his breath.

There was a brisk tapping on the front door.

"You think you have it bad," I said, grimacing as I rose. "Alice will be working on me all day long."

Charlie nodded thoughtfully, conceding that he did have the lesser ordeal. I ducked in to kiss the top of his head as I passed—he blushed and *harrumph*ed—and then continued on to get the door for my best girlfriend and soon-to-be sister.

Alice's short black hair was not in its usual spiky do—it was smoothed into sleek pin curls around her pixie face, which wore a contrastingly businesslike expression. She dragged me from the house with barely a "Hey, Charlie" called over her shoulder.

Alice appraised me as I got into her Porsche.

"Oh, hell, look at your eyes!" She *tsk*ed in reproach. "What did you *do*? Stay up all night?"

"Almost."

She glowered. "I've only allotted so much time to make you stunning, Bella—you might have taken better care of my raw material."

"No one expects me to be stunning. I think the bigger problem is that I might fall asleep during the ceremony and not be able to say 'I do' at the right part, and then Edward will make his escape."

She laughed. "I'll throw my bouquet at you when it gets close."

"Thanks."

"At least you'll have plenty of time to sleep on the plane tomorrow."

I raised one eyebrow. *Tomorrow*, I mused. If we were heading out tonight after the reception, and we would still be on a plane tomorrow . . . well, we weren't going to Boise, Idaho. Edward hadn't dropped a single hint. I wasn't too stressed about the mystery, but it *was* strange not knowing where I would be sleeping tomorrow night. Or hopefully *not* sleeping . . .

Alice realized that she'd given something away, and she frowned.

"You're all packed and ready," she said to distract me.

It worked. "Alice, I wish you would let me pack my own things!"

"It would have given too much away."

"And denied you an opportunity to shop."

"You'll be my sister officially in ten short hours . . . it's about time to get over this aversion to new clothes."

I glowered groggily out the windshield until we were almost to the house.

"Is he back yet?" I asked.

"Don't worry, he'll be there before the music starts. But you don't get to see him, no matter when he gets back. We're doing this the traditional way."

I snorted. "Traditional!"

"Okay, aside from the bride and groom."

"You know he's already peeked."

"Oh no—that's why I'm the only one who's seen you in the dress. I've been very careful to not think about it when he's around."

"Well," I said as we turned into the drive, "I see you got to reuse your graduation decorations." Three miles of drive were once again wrapped in hundreds of thousands of twinkle lights. This time, she'd added white satin bows.

"Waste not, want not. Enjoy this, because you don't get to see the inside decorations until it's time." She pulled into the cavernous garage north of the main house; Emmett's big Jeep was still gone.

"Since when is the bride not allowed to see the decorations?" I protested.

"Since she put me in charge. I want you to get the full impact coming down the stairs."

She clapped her hand over my eyes before she let me inside the kitchen. I was immediately assailed by the scent.

"What is *that*?" I wondered as she guided me into the house.

"Is it too much?" Alice's voice was abruptly worried. "You're the first human in here; I hope I got it right."

"It smells wonderful!" I assured her—almost intoxicating,

but not at all overwhelming, the balance of the different fragrances was subtle and flawless. "Orange blossoms . . . lilac . . . and something else—am I right?"

"Very good, Bella. You only missed the freesia and the roses."

She didn't uncover my eyes until we were in her oversized bathroom. I stared at the long counter, covered in all the paraphernalia of a beauty salon, and began to feel my sleepless night.

"Is this really necessary? I'm going to look plain next to him no matter what."

She pushed me down into a low pink chair. "No one will dare to call you plain when I'm through with you."

"Only because they're afraid you'll suck their blood," I muttered. I leaned back in the chair and closed my eyes, hoping I'd be able to nap through it. I did drift in and out a little bit while she masked, buffed, and polished every surface of my body.

It was after lunchtime when Rosalie glided past the bathroom door in a shimmery silver gown with her golden hair piled up in a soft crown on top of her head. She was so beautiful it made me want to cry. What was even the point of dressing up with Rosalie around?

"They're back," Rosalie said, and immediately my childish fit of despair passed. Edward was home.

"Keep him out of here!"

"He won't cross you today," Rosalie reassured her. "He values his life too much. Esme's got them finishing things up out back. Do you want some help? I could do her hair."

My jaw fell open. I floundered around in my head, trying to remember how to close it.

I had never been Rosalie's favorite person in the world. Then, making things even more strained between us, she was personally offended by the choice I was making now. Though she had her impossible beauty, her loving family, and her soul mate in Emmett, she would have traded it all to be human. And here I was, callously throwing away everything she wanted in life like it was garbage. It didn't exactly warm her to me.

"Sure," Alice said easily. "You can start braiding. I want it intricate. The veil goes here, underneath." Her hands started combing through my hair, hefting it, twisting it, illustrating in detail what she wanted. When she was done, Rosalie's hands replaced hers, shaping my hair with a feather-light touch. Alice moved back to my face.

Once Rosalie received Alice's commendation on my hair, she was sent off to retrieve my dress and then to locate Jasper, who had been dispatched to pick up my mother and her husband, Phil, from their hotel. Downstairs, I could faintly hear the door opening and closing over and over. Voices began to float up to us.

Alice made me stand so that she could ease the dress over my hair and makeup. My knees shook so badly as she fastened the long line of pearl buttons up my back that the satin quivered in little wavelets down to the floor.

"Deep breaths, Bella," Alice said. "And try to lower your heart rate. You're going to sweat off your new face."

I gave her the best sarcastic expression I could manage. "I'll get right on that."

"I have to get dressed now. Can you hold yourself together for two minutes?"

"Um . . . maybe?"

She rolled her eyes and darted out the door.

I concentrated on my breathing, counting each movement of my lungs, and stared at the patterns that the bathroom light made on the shiny fabric of my skirt. I was afraid to look in the mirror—afraid the image of myself in the wedding dress would send me over the edge into a full-scale panic attack.

Alice was back before I had taken two hundred breaths, in a dress that flowed down her slender body like a silvery waterfall.

"Alice—wow."

"It's nothing. No one will be looking at me today. Not while you're in the room."

"Har har."

"Now, are you in control of yourself, or do I have to bring Jasper up here?"

"They're back? Is my mom here?"

"She just walked in the door. She's on her way up."

Renée had flown in two days ago, and I'd spent every minute I could with her—every minute that I could pry her away from Esme and the decorations, in other words. As far as I could tell, she was having more fun with this than a kid locked inside Disneyland overnight. In a way, I felt almost as cheated as Charlie. All that wasted terror over her reaction . . .

"Oh, Bella!" she squealed now, gushing before she was all the way through the door. "Oh, honey, you're so beautiful! Oh, I'm going to cry! Alice, you're amazing! You and Esme should go into business as wedding planners. Where did you find this dress? It's gorgeous! So graceful, so elegant. Bella, you look like you just stepped out of an Austen movie." My mother's voice sounded a little distance away, and everything in the room was slightly blurry. "Such a creative idea, designing the theme around Bella's ring. So romantic! To think it's been in Edward's family since the eighteen hundreds!"

Alice and I exchanged a brief conspiratorial look. My mom was off on the dress style by more than a hundred years. The wedding wasn't actually centered around the ring, but around Edward himself.

There was a loud, gruff throat-clearing in the doorway.

"Renée, Esme said it's time you got settled down there," Charlie said.

"Well, Charlie, don't you look dashing!" Renée said in a tone that was almost shocked. That might have explained the crustiness of Charlie's answer.

"Alice got to me."

"Is it really time already?" Renée said to herself, sounding almost as nervous as I felt. "This has all gone so fast. I feel dizzy."

That made two of us.

"Give me a hug before I go down," Renée insisted. "Carefully now, don't tear anything."

My mother squeezed me gently around the waist, then wheeled for the door, only to complete the spin and face me again.

"Oh goodness, I almost forgot! Charlie, where's the box?"

My dad rummaged in his pockets for a minute and then produced a small white box, which he handed to Renée. Renée lifted the lid and held it out to me.

"Something blue," she said.

"Something old, too. They were your Grandma Swan's," Charlie added. "We had a jeweler replace the paste stones with sapphires."

Inside the box were two heavy silver hair combs. Dark blue sapphires were clustered into intricate floral shapes atop the teeth.

My throat got all thick. "Mom, Dad . . . you shouldn't have."

"Alice wouldn't let us do anything else," Renée said. "Every time we tried, she all but ripped our throats out."

A hysterical giggle burst through my lips.

Alice stepped up and quickly slid both combs into my hair under the edge of the thick braids. "That's something old and something blue," Alice mused, taking a few steps back to admire me. "And your dress is new . . . so here—"

She flicked something at me. I held my hands out automatically, and the filmy white garter landed in my palms.

"That's mine and I want it back," Alice told me.

I blushed.

"There," Alice said with satisfaction. "A little color— that's all you needed. You are officially perfect." With a little self-congratulatory smile, she turned to my parents. "Renée, you need to get downstairs."

"Yes, ma'am." Renée blew me a kiss and hurried out the door.

"Charlie, would you grab the flowers, please?"

While Charlie was out of the room, Alice hooked the garter out of my hands and then ducked under my skirt. I gasped and tottered as her cold hand caught my ankle; she yanked the garter into place.

She was back on her feet before Charlie returned with the

two frothy white bouquets. The scent of roses and orange blossom and freesia enveloped me in a soft mist.

Rosalie—the best musician in the family next to Edward—began playing the piano downstairs. Pachelbel's Canon. I began hyperventilating.

"Easy, Bells," Charlie said. He turned to Alice nervously. "She looks a little sick. Do you think she's going to make it?"

His voice sounded far away. I couldn't feel my legs.

"She'd better."

Alice stood right in front of me, on her tiptoes to better stare me in the eye, and gripped my wrists in her hard hands.

"Focus, Bella. Edward is waiting for you down there."

I took a deep breath, willing myself into composure.

The music slowly morphed into a new song. Charlie nudged me. "Bells, we're up to bat."

"Bella?" Alice asked, still holding my gaze.

"Yes," I squeaked. "Edward. Okay." I let her pull me from the room, with Charlie tagging along at my elbow.

The music was louder in the hall. It floated up the stairs along with the fragrance of a million flowers. I concentrated on the idea of Edward waiting below to get my feet to shuffle forward.

The music was familiar, Wagner's traditional march surrounded by a flood of embellishments.

"It's my turn," Alice chimed. "Count to five and follow me." She began a slow, graceful dance down the staircase. I should have realized that having Alice as my only bridesmaid was a mistake. I would look that much more uncoordinated coming behind her.

A sudden fanfare trilled through the soaring music. I recognized my cue.

"Don't let me fall, Dad," I whispered. Charlie pulled my hand through his arm and then grasped it tightly.

One step at a time, I told myself as we began to descend to the slow tempo of the march. I didn't lift my eyes until my feet were safely on the flat ground, though I could hear the murmurs and rustling of the audience as I came into view. Blood flooded my cheeks at the sound; of course I could be counted on to be the blushing bride.

As soon as my feet were past the treacherous stairs, I was looking for him. For a brief second, I was distracted by the profusion of white blossoms that hung in garlands from everything in the room that wasn't alive, dripping with long lines of white gossamer ribbons. But I tore my eyes from the bowery canopy and searched across the rows of satin-draped chairs—blushing more deeply as I took in the crowd of faces all focused on me—until I found him at last, standing before an arch overflowing with more flowers, more gossamer.

I was barely conscious that Carlisle stood by his side, and Angela's father behind them both. I didn't see my mother where she must have been sitting in the front row, or my new family, or any of the guests—they would have to wait till later.

All I really saw was Edward's face; it filled my vision and overwhelmed my mind. His eyes were a buttery, burning gold; his perfect face was almost severe with the depth of his emotion. And then, as he met my awed gaze, he broke into a breathtaking smile of exultation.

Suddenly, it was only the pressure of Charlie's hand

on mine that kept me from sprinting headlong down the aisle.

The march was too slow as I struggled to pace my steps to its rhythm. Mercifully, the aisle was very short. And then, at last, at last, I was there. Edward held out his hand. Charlie took my hand and, in a symbol as old as the world, placed it in Edward's. I touched the cool miracle of his skin, and I was home.

Our vows were the simple, traditional words that had been spoken a million times, though never by a couple quite like us. We'd asked Mr. Weber to make only one small change. He obligingly traded the line "till death do us part" for the more appropriate "as long as we both shall live."

In that moment, as the minister said his part, my world, which had been upside down for so long now, seemed to settle into its proper position. I saw just how silly I'd been for fearing this—as if it were an unwanted birthday gift or an embarrassing exhibition, like the prom. I looked into Edward's shining, triumphant eyes and knew that I was winning, too. Because nothing else mattered but that I could stay with him.

I didn't realize I was crying until it was time to say the binding words.

"I do," I managed to choke out in a nearly unintelligible whisper, blinking my eyes clear so I could see his face.

When it was his turn to speak, the words rang clear and victorious.

"I do," he vowed.

Mr. Weber declared us husband and wife, and then Edward's hands reached up to cradle my face, carefully, as if it were as delicate as the white petals swaying above our heads. I tried to comprehend, through the film of tears blinding me, the surreal fact that this amazing person was *mine*. His golden eyes looked as if they would have tears, too, if such a thing were not impossible. He bent his head toward mine, and I stretched up on the tips of my toes, throwing my arms—bouquet and all—around his neck.

He kissed me tenderly, adoringly; I forgot the crowd, the place, the time, the reason . . . only remembering that he loved me, that he wanted me, that I was his.

He began the kiss, and he had to end it; I clung to him, ignoring the titters and the throat-clearing in the audience. Finally, his hands restrained my face and he pulled back— too soon—to look at me. On the surface his sudden smile was amused, almost a smirk. But underneath his momentary entertainment at my public exhibition was a deep joy that echoed my own.

The crowd erupted into applause, and he turned our bodies to face our friends and family. I couldn't look away from his face to see them.

My mother's arms were the first to find me, her tear-streaked face the first thing I saw when I finally tore my eyes unwillingly from Edward. And then I was handed through the crowd, passed from embrace to embrace, only vaguely aware of who held me, my attention centered on Edward's hand clutched tightly in my own. I did recognize the difference between the soft, warm hugs of my human friends and the gentle, cool embraces of my new family.

One scorching hug stood out from all the others—Seth Clearwater had braved the throng of vampires to stand in for my lost werewolf friend.

4. GESTURE

THE WEDDING FLOWED INTO THE RECEPTION PARTY smoothly—proof of Alice's flawless planning. It was just twilight over the river; the ceremony had lasted exactly the right amount of time, allowing the sun to set behind the trees. The lights in the trees glimmered as Edward led me through the glass back doors, making the white flowers glow. There were another ten thousand flowers out here, serving as a fragrant, airy tent over the dance floor set up on the grass under two of the ancient cedars.

Things slowed down, relaxed as the mellow August evening surrounded us. The little crowd spread out under the soft shine of the twinkle lights, and we were greeted again by the friends we'd just embraced. There was time to talk now, to laugh.

"Congrats, guys," Seth Clearwater told us, ducking his head under the edge of a flower garland. His mother, Sue, was tight by his side, eyeing the guests with wary intensity. Her face was thin and fierce, an expression that was accented by her short, severe hairstyle; it was as short as her daughter Leah's—I wondered if she'd cut it the same way in a show of solidarity. Billy Black, on Seth's other side, was not as tense as Sue.

When I looked at Jacob's father, I always felt like I was seeing two people rather than just one. There was the old man in the wheelchair with the lined face and the white smile that everyone else saw. And then there was the direct descendant of a long line of powerful, magical chieftains, cloaked in the authority he'd been born with. Though the magic had—in the absence of a catalyst—skipped his generation, Billy was still a part of the power and the legend. It flowed straight through him. It flowed to his son, the heir to the magic, who had turned his back on it. That left Sam Uley to act as the chief of legends and magic now. . . .

Billy seemed oddly at ease considering the company and the event—his black eyes sparkled like he'd just gotten some good news. I was impressed by his composure. This wedding must have seemed a very bad thing, the worst thing that could happen to his best friend's daughter, in Billy's eyes.

I knew it wasn't easy for him to restrain his feelings, considering the challenge this event foreshadowed to the ancient treaty between the Cullens and the Quileutes— the treaty that prohibited the Cullens from ever creating another vampire. The wolves knew a breach was coming, but the Cullens had no idea how they would react. Before the alliance, it would have meant an immediate attack. A war. But now that they knew each other better, would there be forgiveness instead?

As if in response to that thought, Seth leaned toward Edward, arms extended. Edward returned the hug with his free arm.

I saw Sue shudder delicately.

"It's good to see things work out for you, man," Seth said. "I'm happy for you."

"Thank you, Seth. That means a lot to me." Edward pulled away from Seth and looked at Sue and Billy. "Thank you, as well. For letting Seth come. For supporting Bella today."

"You're welcome," Billy said in his deep, gravelly voice, and I was surprised at the optimism in his tone. Perhaps a stronger truce was on the horizon.

A bit of a line was forming, so Seth waved goodbye and wheeled Billy toward the food. Sue kept one hand on each of them.

Angela and Ben were the next to claim us, followed by Angela's parents and then Mike and Jessica—who were, to my surprise, holding hands. I hadn't heard that they were together again. That was nice.

Behind my human friends were my new cousins-in-law, the Denali vampire clan. I realized I was holding my breath as the vampire in front—Tanya, I assumed from the strawberry tint in her blond curls—reached out to embrace Edward. Next to her, three other vampires with golden eyes stared at me with open curiosity. One woman had long, pale blond hair, straight as corn silk. The other woman and the man beside her were both black-haired, with a hint of an olive tone to their chalky complexions.

And they were all four so beautiful that it made my stomach hurt.

Tanya was still holding Edward.

"Ah, Edward," she said. "I've missed you."

Edward chuckled and deftly maneuvered out of the hug, placing his hand lightly on her shoulder and stepping back, as if to get a better look at her. "It's been too long, Tanya. You look well."

"So do you."

"Let me introduce you to my wife." It was the first time Edward had said that word since it was officially true; he seemed like he would explode with satisfaction saying it now. The Denalis all laughed lightly in response. "Tanya, this is my Bella."

Tanya was every bit as lovely as my worst nightmares had predicted. She eyed me with a look that was much more speculative than it was resigned, and then reached out to take my hand.

"Welcome to the family, Bella." She smiled, a little rueful. "We consider ourselves Carlisle's extended family, and I *am* sorry about the, er, recent incident when we did not behave as such. We should have met you sooner. Can you forgive us?"

"Of course," I said breathlessly. "It's so nice to meet you."

"The Cullens are all evened up in numbers now. Perhaps it will be our turn next, eh, Kate?" She grinned at the blonde.

"Keep the dream alive," Kate said with a roll of her

golden eyes. She took my hand from Tanya's and squeezed it gently. "Welcome, Bella."

The dark-haired woman put her hand on top of Kate's. "I'm Carmen, this is Eleazar. We're all so very pleased to finally meet you."

"M-me, too," I stuttered.

Tanya glanced at the people waiting behind her— Charlie's deputy, Mark, and his wife. Their eyes were huge as they took in the Denali clan.

"We'll get to know each other later. We'll have *eons* of time for that!" Tanya laughed as she and her family moved on.

All the standard traditions were kept. I was blinded by flashbulbs as we held the knife over a spectacular cake—too grand, I thought, for our relatively intimate group of friends and family. We took turns shoving cake in each other's faces; Edward manfully swallowed his portion as I watched in disbelief. I threw my bouquet with atypical skill, right into Angela's surprised hands. Emmett and Jasper howled with laughter at my blush while Edward removed my borrowed garter—which I'd shimmied down nearly to my ankle— *very* carefully with his teeth. With a quick wink at me, he shot it straight into Mike Newton's face.

And when the music started, Edward pulled me into his arms for the customary first dance; I went willingly, despite my fear of dancing—especially dancing in front of an audience—just happy to have him holding me. He did all the work, and I twirled effortlessly under the glow of a canopy of lights and the bright flashes from the cameras.

"Enjoying the party, Mrs. Cullen?" he whispered in my ear.

I laughed. "That will take a while to get used to."

"We have a while," he reminded me, his voice exultant, and he leaned down to kiss me while we danced. Cameras clicked feverishly.

The music changed, and Charlie tapped on Edward's shoulder.

It wasn't nearly as easy to dance with Charlie. He was no better at it than I was, so we moved safely from side to side in a tiny square formation. Edward and Esme spun around us like Fred Astaire and Ginger Rogers.

"I'm going to miss you at home, Bella. I'm already lonely."

I spoke through a tight throat, trying to make a joke of it. "I feel just horrible, leaving you to cook for yourself—it's practically criminal negligence. You could arrest me."

He grinned. "I suppose I'll survive the food. Just call me whenever you can."

"I promise."

It seemed like I danced with everyone. It was good to see all my old friends, but I really wanted to be with Edward more than anything else. I was happy when he finally cut in, just half a minute after a new dance started.

"Still not that fond of Mike, eh?" I commented as Edward whirled me away from him.

"Not when I have to listen to his thoughts. He's lucky I didn't kick him out. Or worse."

"Yeah, right."

"Have you had a chance to look at yourself?"

"Um. No, I guess not. Why?"

"Then I suppose you don't realize how utterly, heart-breakingly beautiful you are tonight. I'm not surprised

Mike's having difficulty with improper thoughts about a married woman. I *am* disappointed that Alice didn't make sure you were forced to look in a mirror."

"You are very biased, you know."

He sighed and then paused and turned me around to face the house. The wall of glass reflected the party back like a long mirror. Edward pointed to the couple in the mirror directly across from us.

"Biased, am I?"

I caught just a glimpse of Edward's reflection—a perfect duplicate of his perfect face—with a dark-haired beauty at his side. Her skin was cream and roses, her eyes were huge with excitement and framed with thick lashes. The narrow sheath of the shimmering white dress flared out subtly at the train almost like an inverted calla lily, cut so skillfully that her body looked elegant and graceful—while it was motionless, at least.

Before I could blink and make the beauty turn back into me, Edward suddenly stiffened and turned automatically in the other direction, as if someone had called his name.

"Oh!" he said. His brow furrowed for an instant and then smoothed out just as quickly.

Suddenly, he was smiling a brilliant smile.

"What is it?" I asked.

"A surprise wedding gift."

"Huh?"

He didn't answer; he just started dancing again, spinning me the opposite way we'd been headed before, away from the lights and then into the deep swath of night that ringed the luminous dance floor.

He didn't pause until we reached the dark side of one

of the huge cedars. Then Edward looked straight into the blackest shadow.

"Thank you," Edward said to the darkness. "This is very . . . kind of you."

"Kind is my middle name," a husky familiar voice answered from the black night. "Can I cut in?"

My hand flew up to my throat, and if Edward hadn't been holding me I would have collapsed.

"Jacob!" I choked as soon as I could breathe. "Jacob!"

"Hey there, Bells."

I stumbled toward the sound of his voice. Edward kept his grip under my elbow until another set of strong hands caught me in the darkness. The heat from Jacob's skin burned right through the thin satin dress as he pulled me close. He made no effort to dance; he just hugged me while I buried my face in his chest. He leaned down to press his cheek to the top of my head.

"Rosalie won't forgive me if she doesn't get her official turn on the dance floor," Edward murmured, and I knew he was leaving us, giving me a gift of his own—this moment with Jacob.

"Oh, Jacob." I was crying now; I couldn't get the words out clearly. "Thank you."

"Stop blubbering, Bella. You'll ruin your dress. It's just me."

"Just? Oh, Jake! Everything is perfect now."

He snorted. "Yeah—the party can start. The best man finally made it."

"Now *everyone* I love is here."

I felt his lips brush my hair. "Sorry I'm late, honey."

"I'm just so happy you came!"

"That was the idea."

I glanced toward the guests, but I couldn't see through the dancers to the spot where I'd last seen Jacob's father. I didn't know if he'd stayed. "Does Billy know you're here?" As soon as I asked, I knew that he must have—it was the only way to explain his uplifted expression before.

"I'm sure Sam's told him. I'll go see him when . . . when the party's over."

"He'll be so glad you're home."

Jacob pulled back a little bit and straightened up. He left one hand on the small of my back and grabbed my right hand with the other. He cradled our hands to his chest; I could feel his heart beat under my palm, and I guessed that he hadn't placed my hand there accidentally.

"I don't know if I get more than just this one dance," he said, and he began pulling me around in a slow circle that didn't match the tempo of the music coming from behind us. "I'd better make the best of it."

We moved to the rhythm of his heart under my hand.

"I'm glad I came," Jacob said quietly after a moment. "I didn't think I would be. But it's good to see you . . . one more time. Not as sad as I'd thought it would be."

"I don't want you to feel sad."

"I know that. And I didn't come tonight to make you feel guilty."

"No—it makes me very happy that you came. It's the best gift you could have given me."

He laughed. "That's good, because I didn't have time to stop for a real present."

My eyes were adjusting, and I could see his face now, higher up than I expected. Was it possible that he was still growing? He had to be closer to seven feet than to six. It was a relief to see his familiar features again after all this time—his deep-set eyes shadowed under his shaggy black brows, his high cheekbones, his full lips stretched over his bright teeth in the sarcastic smile that matched his tone. His eyes were tight around the edges—careful; I could see that he was being *very* careful tonight. He was doing all he could to make me happy, to not slip and show how much this cost him.

I'd never done anything good enough to deserve a friend like Jacob.

"When did you decide to come back?"

"Consciously or subconsciously?" He took a deep breath before he answered his own question. "I don't really know. I guess I've been wandering back this direction for a while, and maybe it's because I was headed here. But it wasn't until this morning that I really started *running*. I didn't know if I could make it." He laughed. "You wouldn't believe how weird this feels—walking around on two legs again. And clothes! And then it's more bizarre *because* it feels weird. I didn't expect that. I'm out of practice with the whole human thing."

We revolved steadily.

"It would have been a shame to miss seeing you like this, though. That's worth the trip right there. You look unbelievable, Bella. So beautiful."

"Alice invested a lot of time in me today. The dark helps, too."

"It's not so dark for me, you know."

"Right." Werewolf senses. It was easy to forget all the

things he could do, he seemed so human. Especially right now.

"You cut your hair," I noted.

"Yeah. Easier, you know. Thought I'd better take advantage of the hands."

"It looks good," I lied.

He snorted. "Right. I did it myself, with rusty kitchen shears." He grinned widely for a moment, and then his smile faded. His expression turned serious. "Are you happy, Bella?"

"Yes."

"Okay." I felt his shoulders shrug. "That's the main thing, I guess."

"How are you, Jacob? Really?"

"I'm fine, Bella, really. You don't need to worry about me anymore. You can stop bugging Seth."

"I'm not just bugging him because of you. I *like* Seth."

"He's a good kid. Better company than some. I tell you, if I could get rid of the voices in my head, being a wolf would be about perfect."

I laughed at the way it sounded. "Yeah, I can't get mine to shut up, either."

"In your case, that would mean you're insane. Of course, I already knew that you were insane," he teased.

"Thanks."

"Insanity is probably easier than sharing a pack mind. Crazy people's voices don't send babysitters to watch them."

"Huh?"

"Sam's out there. And some of the others. Just in case, you know."

"In case of what?"

"In case I can't keep it together, something like that. In case I decide to trash the party." He flashed a quick smile at what was probably an appealing thought to him. "But I'm not here to ruin your wedding, Bella. I'm here to . . ." He trailed off.

"To make it perfect."

"That's a tall order."

"Good thing you're so tall."

He groaned at my bad joke and then sighed. "I'm just here to be your friend. Your best friend, one last time."

"Sam should give you more credit."

"Well, maybe I'm being oversensitive. Maybe they'd be here anyway, to keep an eye on Seth. There are a *lot* of vampires here. Seth doesn't take that as seriously as he should."

"Seth knows that he's not in any danger. He understands the Cullens better than Sam does."

"Sure, sure," Jacob said, making peace before it could turn into a fight.

It was strange to have him being the diplomat.

"Sorry about those voices," I said. "Wish I could make it better." In so many ways.

"It's not that bad. I'm just whining a little."

"You're . . . happy?"

"Close enough. But enough about me. You're the star today." He chuckled. "I bet you're just *loving* that. Center of attention."

"Yeah. Can't get enough attention."

He laughed and then stared over my head. With pursed lips, he studied the shimmering glow of the reception party, the graceful whirl of the dancers, the fluttering petals falling from the garlands; I looked with him. It all seemed very distant from this black, quiet space. Almost like watching the white flurries swirling inside a snow globe.

"I'll give them this much," he said. "They know how to throw a party."

"Alice is an unstoppable force of nature."

He sighed. "Song's over. Do you think I get another one? Or is that asking too much?"

I tightened my hand around his. "You can have as many dances as you want."

He laughed. "That would be interesting. I think I'd better stick with two, though. Don't want to start talk."

We turned in another circle.

"You'd think I'd be used to telling you goodbye by now," he murmured.

I tried to swallow the lump in my throat, but I couldn't force it down.

Jacob looked at me and frowned. He wiped his fingers across my cheek, catching the tears there.

"You're not supposed to be the one crying, Bella."

"Everyone cries at weddings," I said thickly.

"This is what you want, right?"

"Right."

"Then smile."

I tried. He laughed at my grimace.

"I'm going to try to remember you like this. Pretend that . . ."

"That what? That I died?"

He clenched his teeth. He was struggling with himself— with his decision to make his presence here a gift and not a judgment. I could guess what he wanted to say.

"No," he finally answered. "But I'll see you this way in my head. Pink cheeks. Heartbeat. Two left feet. All of that."

I deliberately stomped on his foot as hard as I could.

He smiled. "That's my girl."

He started to say something else and then snapped his mouth closed. Struggling again, teeth gritted against the words he didn't want to say.

My relationship with Jacob used to be so easy. Natural as breathing. But since Edward had come back into my life, it was a constant strain. Because—in Jacob's eyes—by choosing Edward, I was choosing a fate that was worse than death, or at least equivalent to it.

"What is it, Jake? Just tell me. You can tell me anything."

"I—I . . . I don't have anything to tell you."

"Oh please. Spit it out."

"It's true. It's not . . . it's—it's a question. It's something I want *you* to tell *me*."

"Ask me."

He struggled for another minute and then exhaled. "I shouldn't. It doesn't matter. I'm just morbidly curious."

Because I knew him so well, I understood.

"It's not tonight, Jacob," I whispered.

Jacob was even more obsessed with my humanity than Edward. He treasured every one of my heartbeats, knowing that they were numbered.

"Oh," he said, trying to smother his relief. "Oh."

A new song started playing, but he didn't notice the change this time.

"When?" he whispered.

"I don't know for sure. A week or two, maybe."

His voice changed, took on a defensive, mocking edge. "What's the holdup?"

"I just didn't want to spend my honeymoon writhing in pain."

"You'd rather spend it how? Playing checkers? Ha ha."

"Very funny."

"Kidding, Bells. But, honestly, I don't see the point. You can't have a real honeymoon with your vampire, so why go through the motions? Call a spade a spade. This isn't the first time you've put this off. That's a *good* thing, though," he said, suddenly earnest. "Don't be embarrassed about it."

"I'm not putting anything off," I snapped. "And *yes I can* have a real honeymoon! I can do anything I want! Butt out!"

He stopped our slow circling abruptly. For a moment, I wondered if he'd finally noticed the music change, and I scrambled in my head for a way to patch up our little tiff before he said goodbye to me. We shouldn't part on this note.

And then his eyes bulged wide with a strange kind of confused horror.

"What?" he gasped. "What did you say?"

"About what . . . ? Jake? What's wrong?"

"What do you mean? Have a real honeymoon? While you're still *human*? Are you kidding? That's a sick joke, Bella!"

I glared at him. "I said butt out, Jake. This is *so* not your business. I shouldn't have . . . we shouldn't even be talking about this. It's private—"

His enormous hands gripped the tops of my arms, wrapping all the way around, fingers overlapping.

"Ow, Jake! Let go!"

He shook me.

"Bella! Have you lost your mind? You can't be that stupid! Tell me you're joking!"

He shook me again. His hands, tight as tourniquets, were quivering, sending vibrations deep into my bones.

"Jake—stop!"

The darkness was suddenly very crowded.

"Take your hands off her!" Edward's voice was cold as ice, sharp as razors.

Behind Jacob, there was a low snarl from the black night, and then another, overlapping the first.

"Jake, bro, back away," I heard Seth Clearwater urge. "You're losing it."

Jacob seemed frozen as he was, his horrified eyes wide and staring.

"You'll hurt her," Seth whispered. "Let her go."

"Now!" Edward snarled.

Jacob's hands dropped to his sides, and the sudden gush of blood through my waiting veins was almost painful. Before I could register more than that, cold hands replaced the hot ones, and the air was suddenly whooshing past me.

I blinked, and I was on my feet a half dozen feet away from where I'd been standing. Edward was tensed in front of me. There were two enormous wolves braced between him and Jacob, but they did not seem aggressive to me. More like they were trying to prevent the fight.

And Seth—gangly, fifteen-year-old Seth—had his long arms around Jacob's shaking body, and he was tugging him away. If Jacob phased with Seth so close . . .

"C'mon, Jake. Let's go."

"I'll kill you," Jacob said, his voice so choked with rage that it was low as a whisper. His eyes, focused on Edward, burned with fury. "I'll kill you myself! I'll do it now!" He shuddered convulsively.

The biggest wolf, the black one, growled sharply.

"Seth, get out of the way," Edward hissed.

Seth tugged on Jacob again. Jacob was so bewildered with rage that Seth was able to yank him a few feet farther back. "Don't do it, Jake. Walk away. C'mon."

Sam—the bigger wolf, the black one—joined Seth then. He put his massive head against Jacob's chest and shoved.

The three of them—Seth towing, Jake trembling, Sam pushing—disappeared swiftly into the darkness.

The other wolf stared after them. I wasn't sure, in the weak light, about the color of his fur—chocolate brown, maybe? Was it Quil, then?

"I'm sorry," I whispered to the wolf.

"It's all right now, Bella," Edward murmured.

The wolf looked at Edward. His gaze was not friendly. Edward gave him one cold nod. The wolf huffed and then turned to follow the others, vanishing as they had.

"All right," Edward said to himself, and then he looked at me. "Let's get back."

"But Jake—"

"Sam has him in hand. He's gone."

"Edward, I'm so sorry. I was stupid—"

"You did nothing wrong—"

"I have such a big mouth! Why would I . . . I shouldn't have let him get to me like that. What was I thinking?"

"Don't worry." He touched my face. "We need to get back to the reception before someone notices our absence."

I shook my head, trying to reorient myself. Before someone noticed? Had anyone *missed* that?

Then, as I thought about it, I realized the confrontation that had seemed so catastrophic to me had, in reality, been very quiet and short here in the shadows.

"Give me two seconds," I pleaded.

My insides were chaotic with panic and grief, but that didn't matter—only the outside mattered right now. Putting on a good show was something I knew I had to master.

"My dress?"

"You look fine. Not a hair out of place."

I took two deep breaths. "Okay. Let's go."

He put his arms around me and led me back to the light. When we passed under the twinkle lights, he spun me gently onto the dance floor. We melted in with the other dancers as if our dance had never been interrupted.

I glanced around at the guests, but no one seemed shocked or frightened. Only the very palest faces there showed any signs of stress, and they hid it well. Jasper and Emmett were on the edge of the floor, close together, and I guessed that they had been nearby during the confrontation.

"Are you—"

"I'm fine," I promised. "I can't believe I did that. What's wrong with me?"

"Nothing is wrong with *you*."

I'd been so glad to see Jacob here. I knew the sacrifice it had taken him. And then I'd ruined it, turned his gift into a disaster. I should be quarantined.

But my idiocy would not ruin anything else tonight. I would put this away, shove it in a drawer and lock it up to deal with later. There would be plenty of time to flagellate myself for this, and nothing I could do now would help.

"It's over," I said. "Let's not think of it again tonight."

I expected a quick agreement from Edward, but he was silent.

"Edward?"

He closed his eyes and touched his forehead to mine. "Jacob is right," he whispered. "What *am* I thinking?"

"He is not." I tried to keep my face smooth for the watching crowd of friends. "Jacob is way too prejudiced to see anything clearly."

He mumbled something low that sounded almost like "*should* let him kill me for even thinking . . ."

"Stop it," I said fiercely. I grabbed his face in my hands and waited until he opened his eyes. "You and me. That's the only thing that matters. The only thing you're allowed to think about now. Do you hear me?"

"Yes," he sighed.

"Forget Jacob came." I could do that. I *would* do that. "For me. Promise that you'll let this go."

He stared into my eyes for a moment before answering. "I promise."

"Thank you. Edward, I'm not afraid."

"I am," he whispered.

"Don't be." I took a deep breath and smiled. "By the way, I love you."

He smiled just a little in return. "That's why we're here."

"You're monopolizing the bride," Emmett said, coming up behind Edward's shoulder. "Let me dance with my little sister. This could be my last chance to make her blush."

He laughed loudly, as unaffected as he usually was by any serious atmosphere.

It turned out there were actually lots of people I hadn't danced with yet, and that gave me a chance to truly compose and resolve myself. When Edward claimed me again, I found that the Jacob-drawer was shut nice and tight. As he wrapped his arms around me, I was able to unearth my earlier sense of joy, my certainty that everything in my life was in the right place tonight. I smiled and laid my head against his chest. His arms tightened.

"I could get used to this," I said.

"Don't tell me you've gotten over your dancing issues?"

"Dancing isn't so bad—with you. But I was thinking more of this,"—and I pressed myself to him even tighter—"of never having to let you go."

"Never," he promised, and he leaned down to kiss me.

It was a serious kind of kiss—intense, slow but building. . . .

I'd pretty much forgotten where I was when I heard Alice call, "Bella! It's time!"

I felt a brief flicker of irritation with my new sister for the interruption.

Edward ignored her; his lips were hard against mine, more urgent than before. My heart broke into a sprint and my palms were slick against his marble neck.

"Do you want to miss your plane?" Alice demanded, right next to me now. "I'm sure you'll have a lovely honeymoon camped out in the airport waiting for another flight."

Edward turned his face slightly to murmur, "Go away, Alice," and then pressed his lips to mine again.

"Bella, do you want to wear that dress on the airplane?" she demanded.

I wasn't really paying much attention. At the moment, I simply didn't care.

Alice growled quietly. "I'll tell her where you're taking her, Edward. So help me, I will."

He froze. Then he lifted his face from mine and glared at his favorite sister. "You're awfully small to be so hugely irritating."

"I didn't pick out the perfect going-away dress to have it wasted," she snapped back, taking my hand. "Come with me, Bella."

I tugged against her hold, stretching up on my toes to kiss him one more time. She jerked my arm impatiently, hauling me away from him. There were a few chuckles from the watching guests. I gave up then and let her lead me into the empty house.

She looked annoyed.

"Sorry, Alice," I apologized.

"I don't blame you, Bella." She sighed. "You don't seem to be able to help yourself."

I giggled at her martyred expression, and she scowled.

"Thank you, Alice. It was the most beautiful wedding anyone ever had," I told her earnestly. "Everything was exactly right. You're the best, smartest, most talented sister in the whole world."

That thawed her out; she smiled a huge smile. "I'm glad you liked it."

Renée and Esme were waiting upstairs. The three of them quickly had me out of my dress and into Alice's deep blue going-away ensemble. I was grateful when someone pulled the pins out of my hair and let it fall loose down my back, wavy from the braids, saving me from a hairpin headache later. My mother's tears streamed without a break the entire time.

"I'll call you when I know where I'm going," I promised as I hugged her goodbye. I knew the honeymoon secret was probably driving her crazy; my mother hated secrets, unless she was in on them.

"I'll tell you as soon as she's safely away," Alice outdid me, smirking at my wounded expression. How unfair, for me to be the last to know.

"You have to visit me and Phil very, very soon. It's your turn to go south—see the sun for once," Renée said.

"It didn't rain today," I reminded her, avoiding her request.

"A miracle."

"Everything's ready," Alice said. "Your suitcases are in the car—Jasper's bringing it around." She pulled me back toward the stairs with Renée following, still halfway embracing me.

"I love you, Mom," I whispered as we descended. "I'm so glad you have Phil. Take care of each other."

"I love you, too, Bella, honey."

"Goodbye, Mom. I love you," I said again, my throat thick.

Edward was waiting at the bottom of the stairs. I took his outstretched hand but leaned away, scanning the little crowd that was waiting to see us off.

"Dad?" I asked, my eyes searching.

"Over here," Edward murmured. He pulled me through

the guests; they made a pathway for us. We found Charlie leaning awkwardly against the wall behind everyone else, looking a little like he was hiding. The red rims around his eyes explained why.

"Oh, Dad!"

I hugged him around the waist, tears streaming again— I was crying so much tonight. He patted my back.

"There, now. You don't want to miss your plane."

It was hard to talk about love with Charlie—we were so much alike, always reverting to trivial things to avoid embarrassing emotional displays. But this was no time for being self-conscious.

"I love you forever, Dad," I told him. "Don't forget that."

"You, too, Bells. Always have, always will."

I kissed his cheek at the same time that he kissed mine.

"Call me," he said.

"Soon," I promised, knowing this was *all* I could promise. Just a phone call. My father and my mother could not be allowed to see me again; I would be too different, and much, much too dangerous.

"Go on, then," he said gruffly. "Don't want to be late."

The guests made another aisle for us. Edward pulled me close to his side as we made our escape.

"Are you ready?" he asked.

"I am," I said, and I knew that it was true.

Everyone applauded when Edward kissed me on the doorstep. Then he rushed me to the car as the rice storm began. Most of it went wide, but someone, probably Emmett, threw with uncanny precision, and I caught a lot of the ricochets off Edward's back.

The car was decorated with more flowers that trailed in streamers along its length, and long gossamer ribbons that were tied to a dozen shoes—designer shoes that looked brand-new—dangling behind the bumper.

Edward shielded me from the rice while I climbed in, and then he was in and we were speeding away as I waved out the window and called "I love you" to the porch, where my families waved back.

The last image I registered was one of my parents. Phil had both arms wrapped tenderly around Renée. She had one arm tight around his waist but had her free hand reached out to hold Charlie's. So many different kinds of love, harmonious in this one moment. It seemed a very hopeful picture to me.

Edward squeezed my hand.

"I love you," he said.

I leaned my head against his arm. "That's why we're here," I quoted him.

He kissed my hair.

As we turned onto the black highway and Edward really hit the accelerator, I heard a noise over the purr of the engine, coming from the forest behind us. If I could hear it, then he certainly could. But he said nothing as the sound slowly faded in the distance. I said nothing, either.

The piercing, heartbroken howling grew fainter and then disappeared entirely.

5. ISLE ESME

"Houston?" I asked, raising my eyebrows when we reached the gate in Seattle.

"Just a stop along the way," Edward assured me with a grin.

It felt like I'd barely fallen asleep when he woke me. I was groggy as he pulled me through the terminals, struggling to remember how to open my eyes after every blink. It took me a few minutes to catch up with what was going on when we stopped at the international counter to check in for our next flight.

"Rio de Janeiro?" I asked with slightly more trepidation.

"Another stop," he told me.

The flight to South America was long but comfortable in the wide first-class seat, with Edward's arms cradled around me. I slept myself out and awoke unusually alert as we circled toward the airport with the light of the setting sun slanting through the plane's windows.

We didn't stay in the airport to connect with another flight as I'd expected. Instead we took a taxi through the dark, teeming, living streets of Rio. Unable to understand a word of Edward's Portuguese instructions to the driver, I guessed that we were off to find a hotel before the next leg of our journey. A sharp twinge of something very close to stage fright twisted in the pit of my stomach as I considered that. The taxi continued through the swarming crowds until they thinned somewhat, and we appeared to be nearing the extreme western edge of the city, heading into the ocean.

We stopped at the docks.

Edward led the way down the long line of white yachts moored in the night-blackened water. The boat he stopped at was smaller than the others, sleeker, obviously built for speed instead of space. Still luxurious, though, and more graceful than the rest. He leaped in lightly, despite the heavy bags he carried. He dropped those on the deck and turned to help me carefully over the edge.

I watched in silence while he prepared the boat for departure, surprised at how skilled and comfortable he seemed, because he'd never mentioned an interest in boating before. But then again, he was good at just about everything.

As we headed due east into the open ocean, I reviewed basic geography in my head. As far as I could remember, there wasn't much east of Brazil . . . until you got to Africa.

But Edward sped forward while the lights of Rio faded and ultimately disappeared behind us. On his face was a familiar exhilarated smile, the one produced by any form of speed. The boat plunged through the waves and I was showered with sea spray.

Finally the curiosity I'd suppressed so long got the best of me.

"Are we going much farther?" I asked.

It wasn't like him to forget that I was human, but I wondered if he planned for us to live on this small craft for any length of time.

"About another half hour." His eyes took in my hands, clenched on the seat, and he grinned.

Oh well, I thought to myself. He was a vampire, after all. Maybe we were going to Atlantis.

Twenty minutes later, he called my name over the roar of the engine.

"Bella, look there." He pointed straight ahead.

I saw only blackness at first, and the moon's white trail across the water. But I searched the space where he pointed until I found a low black shape breaking into the sheen of moonlight on the waves. As I squinted into the darkness, the silhouette became more detailed. The shape grew into a squat, irregular triangle, with one side trailing longer than the other before sinking into the waves. We drew closer, and I could see the outline was feathery, swaying to the light breeze.

And then my eyes refocused and the pieces all made sense: a small island rose out of the water ahead of us, waving with palm fronds, a beach glowing pale in the light of the moon.

"Where are we?" I murmured in wonder while he shifted course, heading around to the north end of the island.

He heard me, despite the noise of the engine, and smiled a wide smile that gleamed in the moonlight.

"This is Isle Esme."

The boat slowed dramatically, drawing with precision into position against a short dock constructed of wooden planks, bleached into whiteness by the moon. The engine cut off, and the silence that followed was profound. There was nothing but the waves, slapping lightly against the boat, and the rustle of the breeze in the palms. The air was warm, moist, and fragrant—like the steam left behind after a hot shower.

"Isle *Esme*?" My voice was low, but it still sounded too loud as it broke into the quiet night.

"A gift from Carlisle—Esme offered to let us borrow it."

A gift. Who gives an island as a gift? I frowned. I hadn't realized that Edward's extreme generosity was a learned behavior.

He placed the suitcases on the dock and then turned back, smiling his perfect smile as he reached for me. Instead of taking my hand, he pulled me right up into his arms.

"Aren't you supposed to wait for the threshold?" I asked, breathless, as he sprung lightly out of the boat.

He grinned. "I'm nothing if not thorough."

Gripping the handles of both huge steamer trunks in one hand and cradling me in the other arm, he carried me up the dock and onto a pale sand pathway through the dark vegetation.

For a short while it was pitch black in the jungle-like growth, and then I could see a warm light ahead. It was about at the point when I realized the light was a house—the two bright, perfect squares were wide windows framing a front door—that the stage fright attacked again, more forcefully than before, worse than when I'd thought we were headed for a hotel.

My heart thudded audibly against my ribs, and my breath seemed to get stuck in my throat. I felt Edward's eyes on my face, but I refused to meet his gaze. I stared straight ahead, seeing nothing.

He didn't ask what I was thinking, which was out of character for him. I guessed that meant that he was just as nervous as I suddenly was.

He set the suitcases on the deep porch to open the doors—they were unlocked.

Edward looked down at me, waiting until I met his gaze before he stepped through the threshold.

He carried me through the house, both of us very quiet, flipping on lights as he went. My vague impression of the house was that it was quite large for a tiny island, and oddly familiar. I'd gotten used to the pale-on-pale color scheme preferred by the Cullens; it felt like home. I couldn't focus on any specifics, though. The violent pulse beating behind my ears made everything a little blurry.

Then Edward stopped and turned on the last light.

The room was big and white, and the far wall was mostly glass—standard décor for my vampires. Outside, the moon was bright on white sand and, just a few yards away from the house, glistening waves. But I barely noted that part. I was more focused on the absolutely *huge* white bed in the center of the room, hung with billowy clouds of mosquito netting.

Edward set me on my feet.

"I'll . . . go get the luggage."

The room was too warm, stuffier than the tropical night outside. A bead of sweat dewed up on the nape of my neck. I walked slowly forward until I could reach out and touch the foamy netting. For some reason I felt the need to make sure everything was real.

I didn't hear Edward return. Suddenly, his wintry finger caressed the back of my neck, wiping away the drop of perspiration.

"It's a little hot here," he said apologetically. "I thought . . . that would be best."

"Thorough," I murmured under my breath, and he chuckled. It was a nervous sound, rare for Edward.

"I tried to think of everything that would make this . . . easier," he admitted.

I swallowed loudly, still facing away from him. Had there ever been a honeymoon like this before?

I knew the answer to that. No. There had not.

"I was wondering," Edward said slowly, "if . . . first . . . maybe you'd like to take a midnight swim with me?" He took a deep breath, and his voice was more at ease when he spoke again. "The water will be very warm. This is the kind of beach you approve of."

"Sounds nice." My voice broke.

"I'm sure you'd like a human minute or two. . . . It was a long journey."

I nodded woodenly. I felt barely human; maybe a few minutes alone would help.

His lips brushed against my throat, just below my ear. He chuckled once and his cool breath tickled my overheated skin. "Don't take *too* long, Mrs. Cullen."

I jumped a little at the sound of my new name.

His lips brushed down my neck to the tip of my shoulder. "I'll wait for you in the water."

He walked past me to the French door that opened right onto the beach sand. On the way, he shrugged out of his shirt, dropping it on the floor, and then slipped through the door into the moonlit night. The sultry, salty air swirled into the room behind him.

Did my skin burst into flames? I had to look down to check. Nope, nothing was burning. At least, not visibly.

I reminded myself to breathe, and then I stumbled toward the giant suitcase that Edward had opened on top of a low white dresser. It must be mine, because my familiar bag of toiletries was right on top, and there was a lot of pink in there, but I didn't recognize even one article of clothing. As I pawed through the neatly folded piles—looking for something familiar and comfortable, a pair of old sweats maybe—it came to my attention that there was an awful lot of sheer lace and skimpy satin in my hands. Lingerie. Very lingerie-ish lingerie, with French tags.

I didn't know how or when, but someday, Alice was going to pay for this.

Giving up, I went to the bathroom and peeked out

through the long windows that opened to the same beach as the French doors. I couldn't see him; I guessed he was there in the water, not bothering to come up for air. In the sky above, the moon was lopsided, almost full, and the sand was bright white under its shine. A small movement caught my eye—draped over a bend in one of the palm trees that fringed the beach, the rest of his clothes were swaying in the light breeze.

A rush of heat flashed across my skin again.

I took a couple of deep breaths and then went to the mirrors above the long stretch of counters. I looked exactly like I'd been sleeping on a plane all day. I found my brush and yanked it harshly through the snarls on the back of my neck until they were smoothed out and the bristles were full of hair. I brushed my teeth meticulously, twice. Then I washed my face and splashed water on the back of my neck, which was feeling feverish. That felt so good that I washed my arms as well, and finally I decided to just give up and take the shower. I knew it was ridiculous to shower before swimming, but I needed to calm down, and hot water was one reliable way to do that.

Also, shaving my legs again seemed like a pretty good idea.

When I was done, I grabbed a huge white towel off the counter and wrapped it under my arms.

Then I was faced with a dilemma I hadn't considered. What was I supposed to put on? Not a swimsuit, obviously. But it seemed silly to put my clothes back on, too. I didn't even want to think about the things Alice had packed for me.

My breathing started to accelerate again and my hands

trembled—so much for the calming effects of the shower. I started to feel a little dizzy, apparently a full-scale panic attack on the way. I sat down on the cool tile floor in my big towel and put my head between my knees. I prayed he wouldn't decide to come look for me before I could pull myself together. I could imagine what he would think if he saw me going to pieces this way. It wouldn't be hard for him to convince himself that we were making a mistake.

And I wasn't freaking out because I thought we were making a mistake. Not at all. I was freaking out because I had no idea how to do this, and I was afraid to walk out of this room and face the unknown. Especially in French lingerie. I knew I wasn't ready for *that* yet.

This felt exactly like having to walk out in front of a theater full of thousands with no idea what my lines were.

How did people do this—swallow all their fears and trust someone else so implicitly with every imperfection and fear they had—with less than the absolute commitment Edward had given me? If it weren't Edward out there, if I didn't know in every cell of my body that he loved me as much as I loved him—unconditionally and irrevocably and, to be honest, irrationally—I'd never be able to get up off this floor.

But it *was* Edward out there, so I whispered the words "Don't be a coward" under my breath and scrambled to my feet. I hitched the towel tighter under my arms and marched determinedly from the bathroom. Past the suitcase full of lace and the big bed without looking at either. Out the open glass door onto the powder-fine sand.

Everything was black-and-white, leached colorless by the moon. I walked slowly across the warm powder, pausing beside the curved tree where he had left his clothes. I laid my hand against the rough bark and checked my breathing to make sure it was even. Or even enough.

I looked across the low ripples, black in the darkness, searching for him.

He wasn't hard to find. He stood, his back to me, waist deep in the midnight water, staring up at the oval moon. The pallid light of the moon turned his skin a perfect white, like the sand, like the moon itself, and made his wet hair black as the ocean. He was motionless, his hands resting palms down against the water; the low waves broke around him as if he were a stone. I stared at the smooth lines of his back, his shoulders, his arms, his neck, the flawless shape of him. . . .

The fire was no longer a flash burn across my skin— it was slow and deep now; it smoldered away all my awkwardness, my shy uncertainty. I slipped the towel off without hesitation, leaving it on the tree with his clothes, and walked out into the white light; it made me pale as the snowy sand, too.

I couldn't hear the sound of my footsteps as I walked to the water's edge, but I guessed that he could. Edward did not turn. I let the gentle swells break over my toes, and found that he'd been right about the temperature—it was very warm, like bath water. I stepped in, walking carefully across the invisible ocean floor, but my care was unnecessary; the sand continued perfectly smooth, sloping gently toward Edward. I waded through the weightless current till I was at his side, and then I placed my hand lightly over his cool hand lying on the water.

"Beautiful," I said, looking up at the moon, too.

"It's all right," he answered, unimpressed. He turned slowly to face me; little waves rolled away from his movement and broke against my skin. His eyes looked silver in his ice-colored face. He twisted his hand up so that he could twine our fingers beneath the surface of the water. It was warm enough that his cool skin did not raise goose bumps on mine.

"But I wouldn't use the word *beautiful*," he continued. "Not with you standing here in comparison."

I half-smiled, then raised my free hand—it didn't tremble now—and placed it over his heart. White on white; we matched, for once. He shuddered the tiniest bit at my warm touch. His breath came rougher now.

"I promised we would *try*," he whispered, suddenly tense. "If . . . if I do something wrong, if I hurt you, you must tell me at once."

I nodded solemnly, keeping my eyes on his. I took another step through the waves and leaned my head against his chest.

"Don't be afraid," I murmured. "We belong together."

I was abruptly overwhelmed by the truth of my own words. This moment was so perfect, so right, there was no way to doubt it.

His arms wrapped around me, holding me against him, summer and winter. It felt like every nerve ending in my body was a live wire.

"Forever," he agreed, and then pulled us gently into deeper water.

The sun, hot on the bare skin of my back, woke me in the morning. Late morning, maybe afternoon, I wasn't sure.

Everything besides the time was clear, though; I knew exactly where I was—the bright room with the big white bed, brilliant sunlight streaming through the open doors. The clouds of netting would soften the shine.

I didn't open my eyes. I was too happy to change anything, no matter how small. The only sounds were the waves outside, our breathing, my heartbeat. . . .

I was comfortable, even with the baking sun. His cool skin was the perfect antidote to the heat. Lying across his wintry chest, his arms wound around me, felt very easy and natural. I wondered idly what I'd been so panicky about last night. My fears all seemed silly now.

His fingers softly trailed down the contours of my spine, and I knew that he knew I was awake. I kept my eyes shut and tightened my arms around his neck, holding myself closer to him.

He didn't speak; his fingers moved up and down my back, barely touching it as he lightly traced patterns on my skin.

I would have been happy to lie here forever, to never disturb this moment, but my body had other ideas. I laughed at my impatient stomach. It seemed sort of prosaic to be hungry after all that had passed last night. Like being brought back down to earth from some great height.

"What's funny?" he murmured, still stroking my back. The sound of his voice, serious and husky, brought with it a deluge of memories from the night, and I felt a blush color my face and neck.

To answer his question, my stomach growled. I laughed again. "You just can't escape being human for very long."

I waited, but he did not laugh with me. Slowly, sinking

through the many layers of bliss that clouded my head, came the realization of a different atmosphere outside my own glowing sphere of happiness.

I opened my eyes; the first thing I saw was the pale, almost silvery skin of his throat, the arc of his chin above my face. His jaw was taut. I propped myself up on my elbow so I could see his face.

He was staring at the frothy canopy above us, and he didn't look at me as I studied his grave features. His expression was a shock—it sent a physical jolt through my body.

"Edward," I said, a strange little catch in my throat, "what is it? What's wrong?"

"You have to ask?" His voice was hard, cynical.

My first instinct, the product of a lifetime of insecurities, was to wonder what I had done wrong. I thought through everything that had happened, but I couldn't find any sour note in the memory. It had all been simpler than I'd expected; we'd fit together like corresponding pieces, made to match up. This had given me a secret satisfaction—we were compatible physically, as well as all the other ways. Fire and ice, somehow existing together without destroying each other. More proof that I belonged with him.

I couldn't think of any part that would make him look like this—so severe and cold. What had I missed?

His finger smoothed the worried lines on my forehead.

"What are you thinking?" he whispered.

"You're upset. I don't understand. Did I . . . ?" I couldn't finish.

His eyes tightened. "How badly are you hurt, Bella? The truth—don't try to downplay it."

"Hurt?" I repeated; my voice came out higher than usual because the word took me so by surprise.

He raised one eyebrow, his lips a tight line.

I made a quick assessment, stretching my body automatically, tensing and flexing my muscles. There was stiffness, and a lot of soreness, too, it was true, but mostly there was the odd sensation that my bones all had become unhinged at the joints, and I had changed halfway into the consistency of a jellyfish. It was not an unpleasant feeling.

And then I was a little angry, because he was darkening this most perfect of all mornings with his pessimistic assumptions.

"Why would you jump to that conclusion? I've never been better than I am now."

His eyes closed. "Stop that."

"Stop *what?*"

"Stop acting like I'm not a monster for having agreed to this."

"Edward!" I whispered, really upset now. He was pulling my bright memory through the darkness, staining it. "Don't ever say that."

He didn't open his eyes; it was like he didn't want to see me.

"Look at yourself, Bella. Then tell me I'm not a monster."

Wounded, shocked, I followed his instruction unthinkingly and then gasped.

What had happened to me? I couldn't make sense of the fluffy white snow that clung to my skin. I shook my head, and a cascade of white drifted out of my hair.

I pinched one soft white bit between my fingers. It was a piece of down.

"Why am I covered in feathers?" I asked, confused.

He exhaled impatiently. "I bit a pillow. Or two. That's not what I'm talking about."

"You . . . bit a pillow? *Why?*"

"Look, Bella!" he almost growled. He took my hand—very gingerly—and stretched my arm out. "Look at *that*."

This time, I saw what he meant.

Under the dusting of feathers, large purplish bruises were beginning to blossom across the pale skin of my arm. My eyes followed the trail they made up to my shoulder, and then down across my ribs. I pulled my hand free to poke at a discoloration on my left forearm, watching it fade where I touched and then reappear. It throbbed a little.

So lightly that he was barely touching me, Edward placed his hand against the bruises on my arm, one at a time, matching his long fingers to the patterns.

"Oh," I said.

I tried to remember this—to remember pain—but I couldn't. I couldn't recall a moment when his hold had been too tight, his hands too hard against me. I only remembered wanting him to hold me tighter, and being pleased when he did. . . .

"I'm . . . so sorry, Bella," he whispered while I stared at the bruises. "I knew better than this. I should not have—" He made a low, revolted sound in the back of his throat. "I am more sorry than I can tell you."

He threw his arm over his face and became perfectly still.

I sat for one long moment in total astonishment, trying

to come to terms—now that I understood it—with his misery. It was so contrary to the way that I felt that it was difficult to process.

The shock wore off slowly, leaving nothing in its absence. Emptiness. My mind was blank. I couldn't think of what to say. How could I explain it to him in the right way? How could I make him as happy as I was—or as I *had* been, a moment ago?

I touched his arm, and he didn't respond. I wrapped my fingers around his wrist and tried to pry his arm off his face, but I could have been yanking on a sculpture for all the good it did me.

"Edward."

He didn't move.

"Edward?"

Nothing. So, this would be a monologue, then.

"*I'm* not sorry, Edward. I'm . . . I can't even tell you. I'm *so* happy. That doesn't cover it. Don't be angry. Don't. I'm really f—"

"Do not say the word *fine*." His voice was ice cold. "If you value my sanity, do not say that you are fine."

"But I *am*," I whispered.

"Bella," he almost moaned. "Don't."

"No. *You* don't, Edward."

He moved his arm; his gold eyes watched me warily.

"Don't ruin this," I told him. "I. Am. Happy."

"I've already ruined this," he whispered.

"Cut it out," I snapped.

I heard his teeth grind together.

"Ugh!" I groaned. "Why can't you just read my mind already? It's so *inconvenient* to be a mental mute!"

His eyes widened a little bit, distracted in spite of himself.

"That's a new one. You love that I can't read your mind."

"Not today."

He stared at me. "Why?"

I threw my hands up in frustration, feeling an ache in my shoulder that I ignored. My palms fell back against his chest with a sharp smack. "Because all this angst would be completely unnecessary if you could see how I feel right now! Or five minutes ago, anyway. I *was* perfectly happy. Totally and completely blissed out. Now—well, I'm sort of pissed, actually."

"You *should* be angry at me."

"Well, I am. Does that make you feel better?"

He sighed. "No. I don't think anything could make me feel better now."

"*That,*" I snapped. "That right there is why I'm angry. You are *killing my buzz*, Edward."

He rolled his eyes and shook his head.

I took a deep breath. I was feeling more of the soreness now, but it wasn't that bad. Sort of like the day after lifting weights. I'd done that with Renée during one of her fitness obsessions. Sixty-five lunges with ten pounds in each hand. I couldn't walk the next day. This was not as painful as that had been by half.

I swallowed my irritation and tried to make my voice soothing. "We knew this was going to be tricky. I thought that was assumed. And then—well, it was a lot easier than I thought it would be. And this is really nothing." I brushed my fingers along my arm. "I think for a first time, not knowing what to expect, we did amazing. With a little practice—"

His expression was suddenly so livid that I broke off mid-sentence.

"Assumed? Did you *expect* this, Bella? Were you anticipating that I would hurt you? Were you thinking it would be worse? Do you consider the experiment a success because you can walk away from it? No broken bones—that equals a victory?"

I waited, letting him get it all out. Then I waited some more while his breathing went back to normal. When his eyes were calm, I answered, speaking with slow precision.

"I didn't know what to expect—but I definitely did not expect how . . . how . . . just wonderful and perfect it was." My voice dropped to a whisper, my eyes slipped from his face down to my hands. "I mean, I don't know how it was for you, but it was like that for me."

A cool finger pulled my chin back up.

"Is that what you're worried about?" he said through his teeth. "That I didn't *enjoy* myself?"

My eyes stayed down. "I know it's not the same. You're not human. I just was trying to explain that, for a human, well, I can't imagine that life gets any better than that."

He was quiet for so long that, finally, I had to look up. His face was softer now, thoughtful.

"It seems that I have more to apologize for." He frowned. "I didn't dream that you would construe the way I feel about what I did to you to mean that last night wasn't . . . well, the best night of my existence. But I don't want to think of it that way, not when you were . . ."

My lips curved up a little at the edges. "Really? The best ever?" I asked in a small voice.

He took my face between his hands, still introspective. "I spoke to Carlisle after you and I made our bargain, hoping he could help me. Of course he warned me that this would be very dangerous for you." A shadow crossed his expression. "He had faith in me, though—faith I didn't deserve."

I started to protest, and he put two fingers over my lips before I could comment.

"I also asked him what *I* should expect. I didn't know what it would be for me . . . what with my being a vampire." He smiled halfheartedly. "Carlisle told me it was a very powerful thing, like nothing else. He told me physical love was something I should not treat lightly. With our rarely changing temperaments, strong emotions can alter us in permanent ways. But he said I did not need to worry about that part—you had already altered me so completely." This time his smile was more genuine.

"I spoke to my brothers, too. They told me it was a very great pleasure. Second only to drinking human blood." A line creased his brow. "But I've tasted your blood, and there could be no blood more potent than *that*. . . . I don't think they were wrong, really. Just that it was different for us. Something more."

"It *was* more. It was everything."

"That doesn't change the fact that it was wrong. Even if it were possible that you really did feel that way."

"What does *that* mean? Do you think I'm making this up? Why?"

"To ease my guilt. I can't ignore the evidence, Bella. Or

your history of trying to let me off the hook when I make mistakes."

I grabbed his chin and leaned forward so that our faces were inches apart. "You listen to me, Edward Cullen. I am not pretending anything for your sake, okay? I didn't even know there was a reason to make you feel better until you started being all miserable. *I've* never been so happy in all my life—I wasn't this happy when you decided that you loved me more than you wanted to kill me, or the first morning I woke up and you were there waiting for me. . . . Not when I heard your voice in the ballet studio"— he flinched at the old memory of my close call with a hunting vampire, but I didn't pause—"or when you said 'I do' and I realized that, somehow, I get to keep you forever. Those are the happiest memories I have, and this is better than any of it. So just deal with it."

He touched the frown line between my eyebrows. "I'm making you unhappy now. I don't want to do that."

"Then don't *you* be unhappy. That's the only thing that's wrong here."

His eyes tightened, then he took a deep breath and nodded. "You're right. The past is past and I can't do anything to change it. There's no sense in letting my mood sour this time for you. I'll do whatever I can to make you happy now."

I examined his face suspiciously, and he gave me a serene smile.

"Whatever makes me happy?"

My stomach growled at the same time that I asked.

"You're hungry," he said quickly. He was swiftly out of

the bed, stirring up a cloud of feathers. Which reminded me.

"So, why exactly did you decide to ruin Esme's pillows?" I asked, sitting up and shaking more down from my hair.

He had already pulled on a pair of loose khaki pants, and he stood by the door, rumpling his hair, dislodging a few feathers of his own.

"I don't know if I *decided* to do anything last night," he muttered. "We're just lucky it was the pillows and not you." He inhaled deeply and then shook his head, as if shaking off the dark thought. A very authentic-looking smile spread across his face, but I guessed it took a lot of work to put it there.

I slid carefully off the high bed and stretched again, more aware, now, of the aches and sore spots. I heard him gasp. He turned away from me, and his hands balled up, knuckles white.

"Do I look that hideous?" I asked, working to keep my tone light. His breath caught, but he didn't turn, probably to hide his expression from me. I walked to the bathroom to check for myself.

I stared at my naked body in the full-length mirror behind the door.

I'd definitely had worse. There was a faint shadow across one of my cheekbones, and my lips were a little swollen, but other than that, my face was fine. The rest of me was decorated with patches of blue and purple. I concentrated on the bruises that would be the hardest to hide—my arms and my shoulders. They weren't so bad. My skin marked up easily. By the time a bruise showed I'd usually forgotten how I'd come by it. Of course, these were just developing. I'd look even worse tomorrow. That would not make things any easier.

I looked at my hair, then, and groaned.

"Bella?" He was right there behind me as soon as I'd made a sound.

"I'll *never* get this all out of my hair!" I pointed to my head, where it looked like a chicken was nesting. I started picking at the feathers.

"You *would* be worried about your hair," he mumbled, but he came to stand behind me, pulling out the feathers much more quickly.

"How did you keep from laughing at this? I look ridiculous."

He didn't answer; he just kept plucking. And I knew the answer anyway—there was nothing that would be funny to him in this mood.

"This isn't going to work," I sighed after a minute. "It's all dried in. I'm going to have to try to wash it out." I turned around, wrapping my arms around his cool waist. "Do you want to help me?"

"I'd better find some food for you," he said in a quiet voice, and he gently unwound my arms. I sighed as he disappeared, moving too fast.

It looked like my honeymoon was over. The thought put a big lump in my throat.

When I was mostly feather-free and dressed in an unfamiliar white cotton dress that concealed the worst of the violet blotches, I padded off barefoot to where the smell of eggs and bacon and cheddar cheese was coming from.

Edward stood in front of the stainless steel stove, sliding an omelet onto the light blue plate waiting on the counter. The scent of the food overwhelmed me. I felt like I could eat the plate and the frying pan, too; my stomach snarled.

"Here," he said. He turned with a smile on his face and set the plate on a small tiled table.

I sat in one of the two metal chairs and started snarfing down the hot eggs. They burned my throat, but I didn't care.

He sat down across from me. "I'm not feeding you often enough."

I swallowed and then reminded him, "I was asleep. This is really good, by the way. Impressive for someone who doesn't eat."

"Food Network," he said, flashing my favorite crooked smile.

I was happy to see it, happy that he seemed more like his normal self.

"Where did the eggs come from?"

"I asked the cleaning crew to stock the kitchen. A first, for this place. I'll have to ask them to deal with the feathers. . . . " He trailed off, his gaze fixed on a space above my head. I didn't respond, trying to avoid saying anything that would upset him again.

I ate everything, though he'd made enough for two.

"Thank you," I told him. I leaned across the table to kiss him. He kissed me back automatically, and then suddenly stiffened and leaned away.

I gritted my teeth, and the question I meant to ask came out sounding like an accusation. "You aren't going to touch me again while we're here, are you?"

He hesitated, then half-smiled and raised his hand to stroke my cheek. His fingers lingered softly on my skin, and I couldn't help leaning my face into his palm.

"You know that's not what I meant."

He sighed and dropped his hand. "I know. And you're right." He paused, lifting his chin slightly. And then he spoke again with firm conviction. "I will not make love with you until you've been changed. I will never hurt you again."

6. DISTRACTIONS

M Y ENTERTAINMENT BECAME THE NUMBER-ONE PRIOR-
ity on Isle Esme. We snorkeled (well, I snorkeled while he
flaunted his ability to go without oxygen indefinitely). We
explored the small jungle that ringed the rocky little peak.
We visited the parrots that lived in the canopy on the south
end of the island. We watched the sunset from the rocky
western cove. We swam with the porpoises that played in
the warm, shallow waters there. Or at least I did; when
Edward was in the water, the porpoises disappeared as if a
shark was near.

I knew what was going on. He was trying to keep
me busy, distracted, so that I wouldn't continue badger-
ing him about the sex thing. Whenever I tried to talk him

into taking it easy with one of the million DVDs under the big-screen plasma TV, he would lure me out of the house with magic words like *coral reefs* and *submerged caves* and *sea turtles*. We were going, going, going all day, so that I found myself completely famished and exhausted when the sun eventually set.

I drooped over my plate after I finished dinner every night; once I'd actually fallen asleep right at the table and he'd had to carry me to bed. Part of it was that Edward always made too much food for one, but I was so *hungry* after swimming and climbing all day that I ate most of it. Then, full and worn out, I could barely keep my eyes open. All part of the plan, no doubt.

Exhaustion didn't help much with my attempts at persuasion. But I didn't give up. I tried reasoning, pleading, and grouching, all to no avail. I was usually unconscious before I could really press my case far. And then my dreams felt so real—nightmares mostly, made more vivid, I guessed, by the too-bright colors of the island—that I woke up tired no matter how long I slept.

About a week or so after we'd gotten to the island, I decided to try compromise. It had worked for us in the past.

I was sleeping in the blue room now. The cleaning crew wasn't due until the next day, and so the white room still had a snowy blanket of down. The blue room was smaller, the bed more reasonably proportioned. The walls were dark, paneled in teak, and the fittings were all luxurious blue silk.

I'd taken to wearing some of Alice's lingerie collection to sleep in at night—which weren't so revealing compared to the scanty bikinis she'd packed for me when it came right down to it. I wondered if she'd seen a vision of why I would want such things, and then shuddered, embarrassed by that thought.

I'd started out slow with innocent ivory satins, worried that revealing more of my skin would be the opposite of helpful, but ready to try anything. Edward seemed to notice nothing, as if I were wearing the same ratty old sweats I wore at home.

The bruises were much better now—yellowing in some places and disappearing altogether in others—so tonight I pulled out one of the scarier pieces as I got ready in the paneled bathroom. It was black, lacy, and embarrassing to look at even when it wasn't on. I was careful not to look in the mirror before I went back to the bedroom. I didn't want to lose my nerve.

I had the satisfaction of watching his eyes pop open wide for just a second before he controlled his expression.

"What do you think?" I asked, pirouetting so that he could see every angle.

He cleared his throat. "You look beautiful. You always do."

"Thanks," I said a bit sourly.

I was too tired to resist climbing quickly into the soft bed. He put his arms around me and pulled me against his chest, but this was routine—it was too hot to sleep without his cool body close.

"I'll make you a deal," I said sleepily.

"I will not make any deals with you," he answered.

"You haven't even heard what I'm offering."

"It doesn't matter."

I sighed. "Dang it. And I really wanted . . . Oh well."
He rolled his eyes.

I closed mine and let the bait sit there. I yawned.

It took only a minute—not long enough for me to zonk
out.

"All right. What is it you want?"

I gritted my teeth for a second, fighting a smile. If there
was one thing he couldn't resist, it was an opportunity to
give me something.

"Well, I was thinking . . . I know that the whole
Dartmouth thing was just supposed to be a cover story, but
honestly, one semester of college probably wouldn't kill me,"
I said, echoing his words from long ago, when he'd tried to
persuade me to put off becoming a vampire. "Charlie would
get a thrill out of Dartmouth stories, I bet. Sure, it might
be embarrassing if I can't keep up with all the brainiacs. Still
. . . eighteen, nineteen. It's really not such a big difference.
It's not like I'm going to get crow's feet in the next year."

He was silent for a long moment. Then, in a low voice,
he said, "You would wait. You would stay human."

I held my tongue, letting the offer sink in.

"Why are you *doing* this to me?" he said through his
teeth, his tone suddenly angry. "Isn't it hard enough without
all of this?" He grabbed a handful of lace that was ruffled
on my thigh. For a moment, I thought he was going to rip
it from the seam. Then his hand relaxed. "It doesn't matter.
I won't make any deals with you."

"I want to go to college."

"No, you don't. And there is nothing that is worth
risking your life again. That's worth hurting you."

"But I *do* want to go. Well, it's not college as much as it's that I want—I want to be human a little while longer."

He closed his eyes and exhaled through his nose. "You are making me insane, Bella. Haven't we had this argument a million times, you always begging to be a vampire without delay?"

"Yes, but . . . well, I have a reason to be human that I didn't have before."

"What's that?"

"Guess," I said, and I dragged myself off the pillows to kiss him.

He kissed me back, but not in a way that made me think I was winning. It was more like he was being careful not to hurt my feelings; he was completely, maddeningly in control of himself. Gently, he pulled me away after a moment and cradled me against his chest.

"You are *so* human, Bella. Ruled by your hormones." He chuckled.

"That's the whole point, Edward. I *like* this part of being human. I don't want to give it up yet. I don't want to wait through years of being a blood-crazed newborn for some part of this to come back to me."

I yawned, and he smiled.

"You're tired. Sleep, love." He started humming the lullaby he'd composed for me when we first met.

"I wonder why I'm so tired," I muttered sarcastically. "That couldn't be part of your scheme or anything."

He just chuckled once and went back to humming.

"For as tired as I've been, you'd think I'd sleep better."

The song broke off. "You've been sleeping like the dead,

Bella. You haven't said a word in your sleep since we got here. If it weren't for the snoring, I'd worry you were slipping into a coma."

I ignored the snoring jibe; I didn't snore. "I haven't been tossing? That's weird. Usually I'm all over the bed when I'm having nightmares. And shouting."

"You've been having nightmares?"

"Vivid ones. They make me so tired." I yawned. "I can't believe I haven't been babbling about them all night."

"What are they about?"

"Different things—but the same, you know, because of the colors."

"Colors?"

"It's all so bright and real. Usually, when I'm dreaming, I know that I am. With these, I don't know I'm asleep. It makes them scarier."

He sounded disturbed when he spoke again. "What is frightening you?"

I shuddered slightly. "Mostly . . ." I hesitated.

"Mostly?" he prompted.

I wasn't sure why, but I didn't want to tell him about the child in my recurring nightmare; there was something private about that particular horror. So, instead of giving him the full description, I gave him just one element. Certainly enough to frighten me or anyone else.

"The Volturi," I whispered.

He hugged me tighter. "They aren't going to bother us anymore. You'll be immortal soon, and they'll have no reason."

I let him comfort me, feeling a little guilty that he'd misunderstood. The nightmares weren't like that, exactly.

It wasn't that I was afraid for myself—I was afraid for the boy.

He wasn't the same boy as that first dream—the vampire child with the bloodred eyes who sat on a pile of dead people I loved. This boy I'd dreamed of four times in the last week was definitely human; his cheeks were flushed and his wide eyes were a soft green. But just like the other child, he shook with fear and desperation as the Volturi closed in on us.

In this dream that was both new and old, I simply *had* to protect the unknown child. There was no other option. At the same time, I knew that I would fail.

He saw the desolation on my face. "What can I do to help?"

I shook it off. "They're just dreams, Edward."

"Do you want me to sing to you? I'll sing all night if it will keep the bad dreams away."

"They're not all bad. Some are nice. So . . . colorful. Underwater, with the fish and the coral. It all seems like it's really happening—I don't know that I'm dreaming. Maybe this island is the problem. It's really *bright* here."

"Do you want to go home?"

"No. No, not yet. Can't we stay awhile longer?"

"We can stay as long as you want, Bella," he promised me.

"When does the semester start? I wasn't paying attention before."

He sighed. He may have started humming again, too, but I was under before I could be sure.

Later, when I awoke in the dark, it was with shock. The dream had been so very real . . . so vivid, so sensory. . . .

I gasped aloud, now, disoriented by the dark room. Only a second ago, it seemed, I had been under the brilliant sun.

"Bella?" Edward whispered, his arms tight around me, shaking me gently. "Are you all right, sweetheart?"

"Oh," I gasped again. Just a dream. Not real. To my utter astonishment, tears overflowed from my eyes without warning, gushing down my face.

"Bella!" he said—louder, alarmed now. "What's wrong?" He wiped the tears from my hot cheeks with cold, frantic fingers, but others followed.

"It was only a dream." I couldn't contain the low sob that broke in my voice. The senseless tears were disturbing, but I couldn't get control of the staggering grief that gripped me. I wanted so badly for the dream to be real.

"It's okay, love, you're fine. I'm here." He rocked me back and forth, a little too fast to soothe. "Did you have another nightmare? It wasn't real, it wasn't real."

"Not a nightmare." I shook my head, scrubbing the back of my hand against my eyes. "It was a *good* dream." My voice broke again.

"Then why are you crying?" he asked, bewildered.

"Because I woke up," I wailed, wrapping my arms around his neck in a chokehold and sobbing into his throat.

He laughed once at my logic, but the sound was tense with concern.

"Everything's all right, Bella. Take deep breaths."

"It was so real," I cried. "I *wanted* it to be real."

"Tell me about it," he urged. "Maybe that will help."

"We were on the beach. . . ." I trailed off, pulling back to look with tear-filled eyes at his anxious angel's face, dim in the darkness. I stared at him broodingly as the unreasonable grief began to ebb.

"And?" he finally prompted.

I blinked the tears out of my eyes, torn. "Oh, Edward . . ."

"Tell me, Bella," he pleaded, eyes wild with worry at the pain in my voice.

But I couldn't. Instead I clutched my arms around his neck again and locked my mouth with his feverishly. It wasn't desire at all—it was need, acute to the point of pain. His response was instant but quickly followed by his rebuff.

He struggled with me as gently as he could in his surprise, holding me away, grasping my shoulders.

"No, Bella," he insisted, looking at me as if he was worried that I'd lost my mind.

My arms dropped, defeated, the bizarre tears spilling in a fresh torrent down my face, a new sob rising in my throat. He was right—I must be crazy.

He stared at me with confused, anguished eyes.

"I'm s-s-s-orry," I mumbled.

But he pulled me to him then, hugging me tightly to his marble chest.

"I can't, Bella, I can't!" His moan was agonized.

"Please," I said, my plea muffled against his skin. "Please, Edward?"

I couldn't tell if he was moved by the tears trembling in my voice, or if he was unprepared to deal with the suddenness of my attack, or if his need was simply as unbearable in that moment as my own. But whatever the reason, he pulled my lips back to his, surrendering with a groan.

And we began where my dream had left off.

I stayed very still when I woke up in the morning and tried to keep my breathing even. I was afraid to open my eyes.

I was lying across Edward's chest, but he was very still and his arms were not wrapped around me. That was a bad sign. I was afraid to admit I was awake and face his anger— no matter whom it was directed at today.

Carefully, I peeked through my eyelashes. He was staring up at the dark ceiling, his arms behind his head. I pulled myself up on my elbow so that I could see his face better. It was smooth, expressionless.

"How much trouble am I in?" I asked in a small voice.

"Heaps," he said, but turned his head and smirked at me.

I breathed a sigh of relief. "I *am* sorry," I said. "I didn't mean . . . Well, I don't know exactly what that *was* last night." I shook my head at the memory of the irrational tears, the crushing grief.

"You never did tell me what your dream was about."

"I guess I didn't—but I sort of *showed* you what it was about." I laughed nervously.

"Oh," he said. His eyes widened, and then he blinked. "Interesting."

"It was a very good dream," I murmured. He didn't comment, so a few seconds later I asked, "Am I forgiven?"

"I'm thinking about it."

I sat up, planning to examine myself—there didn't seem to be any feathers, at least. But as I moved, an odd wave of vertigo hit. I swayed and fell back against the pillows.

"Whoa . . . head rush."

His arms were around me then. "You slept for a long time. Twelve hours."

"*Twelve?*" How strange.

I gave myself a quick once-over while I spoke, trying to be inconspicuous about it. I looked fine. The bruises on my arms were still a week old, yellowing. I stretched experimentally. I felt fine, too. Well, better than fine, actually.

"Is the inventory complete?"

I nodded sheepishly. "The pillows all appear to have survived."

"Unfortunately, I can't say the same for your, er, nightgown." He nodded toward the foot of the bed, where several scraps of black lace were strewn across the silk sheets.

"That's too bad," I said. "I liked that one."

"I did, too."

"Were there any other casualties?" I asked timidly.

"I'll have to buy Esme a new bed frame," he confessed, glancing over his shoulder. I followed his gaze and was shocked to see that large chunks of wood had apparently been gouged from the left side of the headboard.

"Hmm." I frowned. "You'd think I would have heard that."

"You seem to be extraordinarily unobservant when your attention is otherwise involved."

"I was a bit absorbed," I admitted, blushing a deep red.

He touched my burning cheek and sighed. "I'm really going to miss that."

I stared at his face, searching for any signs of the anger or remorse I feared. He gazed back at me evenly, his expression calm but otherwise unreadable.

"How are *you* feeling?"

He laughed.

"What?" I demanded.

"You look so guilty—like you've committed a crime."

"I *feel* guilty," I muttered.

"So you seduced your all-too-willing husband. That's not a capital offense."

He seemed to be teasing.

My cheeks got hotter. "The word *seduced* implies a certain amount of premeditation."

"Maybe that was the wrong word," he allowed.

"You're not angry?"

He smiled ruefully. "I'm not angry."

"Why not?"

"Well . . ." He paused. "I didn't hurt you, for one thing. It was easier this time, to control myself, to channel the excesses." His eyes flickered to the damaged frame again. "Maybe because I had a better idea of what to expect."

A hopeful smile started to spread across my face. "I *told* you that it was all about practice."

He rolled his eyes.

My stomach growled, and he laughed. "Breakfast time for the human?" he asked.

"Please," I said, hopping out of bed. I moved too quickly, though, and had to stagger drunkenly to regain my balance. He caught me before I could stumble into the dresser.

"Are you all right?"

"If I don't have a better sense of equilibrium in my next life, I'm demanding a refund."

I cooked this morning, frying up some eggs—too hungry

to do anything more elaborate. Impatient, I flipped them onto a plate after just a few minutes.

"Since when do you eat eggs sunny-side up?" he asked.

"Since now."

"Do you know how many eggs you've gone through in the last week?" He pulled the trash bin out from under the sink—it was full of empty blue cartons.

"Weird," I said after swallowing a scorching bite. "This place is messing with my appetite." And my dreams, and my already dubious balance. "But I like it here. We'll probably have to leave soon, though, won't we, to make it to Dartmouth in time? Wow, I guess we need to find a place to live and stuff, too."

He sat down next to me. "You can give up the college pretense now—you've gotten what you wanted. And we didn't agree to a deal, so there are no strings attached."

I snorted. "It wasn't a pretense, Edward. I don't spend *my* free time plotting like some people do. *What can we do to wear Bella out today?*" I said in a poor impression of his voice. He laughed, unashamed. "I really do want a little more time being human." I leaned over to run my hand across his bare chest. "I have not had enough."

He gave me a dubious look. "For *this*?" he asked, catching my hand as it moved down his stomach. "Sex was the key all along?" He rolled his eyes. "Why didn't I think of that?" he muttered sarcastically. "I could have saved myself a lot of arguments."

I laughed. "Yeah, probably."

"You are *so* human," he said again.

"I know."

A hint of a smile pulled at his lips. "We're going to Dartmouth? Really?"

"I'll probably fail out in one semester."

"I'll tutor you." The smile was wide now. "You're going to love college."

"Do you think we can find an apartment this late?"

He grimaced, looking guilty. "Well, we sort of already have a house there. You know, just in case."

"You bought a house?"

"Real estate is a good investment."

I raised one eyebrow and then let it go. "So we're ready, then."

"I'll have to see if we can keep your 'before' car for a little longer. . . ."

"Yes, heaven forbid I not be protected from tanks."

He grinned.

"How much longer can we stay?" I asked.

"We're fine on time. A few more weeks, if you want. And then we can visit Charlie before we go to New Hampshire. We could spend Christmas with Renée. . . ."

His words painted a very happy immediate future, one free of pain for everyone involved. The Jacob-drawer, all but forgotten, rattled, and I amended the thought—for *almost* everyone.

This wasn't getting any easier. Now that I'd discovered *exactly* how good being human could be, it was tempting to let my plans drift. Eighteen or nineteen, nineteen or twenty . . . Did it really matter? I wouldn't change so much in a year. And being human with Edward . . . The choice got trickier every day.

"A few weeks," I agreed. And then, because there never

seemed to be enough time, I added, "So I was thinking—you know what I was saying about practice before?"

He laughed. "Can you hold on to that thought? I hear a boat. The cleaning crew must be here."

He wanted me to hold on to that thought. So did that mean he was not going to give me any more trouble about practicing? I smiled.

"Let me explain the mess in the white room to Gustavo, and then we can go out. There's a place in the jungle on the south—"

"I don't want to go out. I am not hiking all over the island today. I want to stay here and watch a movie."

He pursed his lips, trying not to laugh at my disgruntled tone. "All right, whatever you'd like. Why don't you pick one out while I get the door?"

"I didn't hear a knock."

He cocked his head to the side, listening. A half second later, a faint, timid rap on the door sounded. He grinned and turned for the hallway.

I wandered over to the shelves under the big TV and started scanning through the titles. It was hard to decide where to begin. They had more DVDs than a rental store.

I could hear Edward's low, velvet voice as he came back down the hall, conversing fluidly in what I assumed was perfect Portuguese. Another, harsher, human voice answered in the same tongue.

Edward led them into the room, pointing toward the kitchen on his way. The two Brazilians looked incredibly short and dark next to him. One was a round man, the other a slight female, both their faces creased with lines. Edward gestured to me with a proud smile, and I heard my name mixed in with a flurry of unfamiliar words. I flushed a little as I thought of the downy mess in the white room, which they would soon encounter. The little man smiled at me politely.

But the tiny coffee-skinned woman didn't smile. She stared at me with a mixture of shock, worry, and most of all, wide-eyed *fear*. Before I could react, Edward motioned for them to follow him toward the chicken coop, and they were gone.

When he reappeared, he was alone. He walked swiftly to my side and wrapped his arms around me.

"What's with her?" I whispered urgently, remembering her panicked expression.

He shrugged, unperturbed. "Kaure's part Ticuna Indian. She was raised to be more superstitious—or you could call it more aware—than those who live in the modern world. She suspects what I am, or close enough." He still didn't sound worried. "They have their own legends here. The *Libishomen*—a blood-drinking demon who preys exclusively on beautiful women." He leered at me.

Beautiful women only? Well, that was kind of flattering.

"She looked terrified," I said.

"She is—but mostly she's worried about you."

"Me?"

"She's afraid of why I have you here, all alone." He chuckled darkly and then looked toward the wall of movies. "Oh well, why don't you choose something for us to watch? That's an acceptably human thing to do."

"Yes, I'm sure a movie will convince her that you're human." I laughed and clasped my arms securely around his neck, stretching up on my tiptoes. He leaned down so that I could kiss him, and then his arms tightened around me, lifting me off the floor so he didn't have to bend.

"Movie, schmovie," I muttered as his lips moved down my throat, twisting my fingers in his bronze hair.

Then I heard a gasp, and he put me down abruptly. Kaure stood frozen in the hallway, feathers in her black hair, a large sack of more feathers in her arms, an expression of horror on her face. She stared at me, her eyes bugging out, as I blushed and looked down. Then she recovered herself and murmured something that, even in an unfamiliar language, was clearly an apology. Edward smiled and answered in a friendly tone. She turned her dark eyes away and continued down the hall.

"She was thinking what I think she was thinking, wasn't she?" I muttered.

He laughed at my convoluted sentence. "Yes."

"Here," I said, reaching out at random and grabbing a movie. "Put this on and we can pretend to watch it."

It was an old musical with smiling faces and fluffy dresses on the front.

"Very honeymoonish," Edward approved.

While actors on the screen danced their way through a perky introduction song, I lolled on the sofa, snuggled into Edward's arms.

"Will we move back into the white room now?" I wondered idly.

"I don't know. . . . I've already mangled the headboard in the other room beyond repair—maybe if we limit the destruction to one area of the house, Esme might invite us back someday."

I smiled widely. "So there will be more destruction?"

He laughed at my expression. "I think it might be safer if it's premeditated, rather than if I wait for you to assault me again."

"It would only be a matter of time," I agreed casually, but my pulse was racing in my veins.

"Is there something the matter with your heart?"

"Nope. Healthy as a horse." I paused. "Did you want to go survey the demolition zone now?"

"Maybe it would be more polite to wait until we're alone. *You* may not notice me tearing the furniture apart, but it would probably scare them."

In truth, I'd already forgotten the people in the other room. "Right. Drat."

Gustavo and Kaure moved quietly through the house while I waited impatiently for them to finish and tried to pay attention to the happily-ever-after on the screen. I was starting to get sleepy—though, according to Edward, I'd slept half the day—when a rough voice startled me. Edward sat up, keeping me cradled against him, and answered Gustavo in flowing Portuguese. Gustavo nodded and walked quietly toward the front door.

"They're finished," Edward told me.

"So that would mean that we're alone now?"

"How about lunch first?" he suggested.

I bit my lip, torn by the dilemma. I *was* pretty hungry.

With a smile, he took my hand and led me to the kitchen. He knew my face so well, it didn't matter that he couldn't read my mind.

"This is getting out of hand," I complained when I finally felt full.

"Do you want to swim with the dolphins this afternoon—burn off the calories?" he asked.

"Maybe later. I had another idea for burning calories."

"And what was that?"

"Well, there's an awful lot of headboard left—"

But I didn't finish. He'd already swept me up into his arms, and his lips silenced mine as he carried me with inhuman speed to the blue room.

7. UNEXPECTED

THE LINE OF BLACK ADVANCED ON ME THROUGH THE shroud-like mist. I could see their dark ruby eyes glinting with desire, lusting for the kill. Their lips pulled back over their sharp, wet teeth—some to snarl, some to smile.

I heard the child behind me whimper, but I couldn't turn to look at him. Though I was desperate to be sure that he was safe, I could not afford any lapse in focus now.

They ghosted closer, their black robes billowing slightly with the movement. I saw their hands curl into bone-colored claws. They started to drift apart, angling to come at us from all sides. We were surrounded. We were going to die.

And then, like a burst of light from a flash, the whole

scene was different. Yet nothing changed—the Volturi still stalked toward us, poised to kill. All that really changed was how the picture looked to me. Suddenly, I was hungry for it. I *wanted* them to charge. The panic changed to bloodlust as I crouched forward, a smile on my face, and a growl ripped through my bared teeth.

I jolted upright, shocked out of the dream.

The room was black. It was also steamy hot. Sweat matted my hair at the temples and rolled down my throat.

I groped the warm sheets and found them empty.

"Edward?"

Just then, my fingers encountered something smooth and flat and stiff. One sheet of paper, folded in half. I took the note with me and felt my way across the room to the light switch.

The outside of the note was addressed to Mrs. Cullen.

I'm hoping you won't wake and notice my absence, but, if you should, I'll be back very soon. I've just gone to the mainland to hunt. Go back to sleep and I'll be here when you wake again. I love you.

I sighed. We'd been here about two weeks now, so I should have been expecting that he would have to leave, but I hadn't been thinking about time. We seemed to exist outside of time here, just drifting along in a perfect state.

I wiped the sweat off my forehead. I felt absolutely wide awake, though the clock on the dresser said it was after one. I knew I would never be able to sleep as hot and sticky as

I felt. Not to mention the fact that if I shut off the light and closed my eyes, I was sure to see those prowling black figures in my head.

I got up and wandered aimlessly through the dark house, flipping on lights. It felt so big and empty without Edward there. Different.

I ended up in the kitchen and decided that maybe comfort food was what I needed.

I poked around in the fridge until I found all the ingredients for fried chicken. The popping and sizzling of the chicken in the pan was a nice, homey sound; I felt less nervous while it filled the silence.

It smelled so good that I started eating it right out of the pan, burning my tongue in the process. By the fifth or sixth bite, though, it had cooled enough for me to taste it. My chewing slowed. Was there something off about the flavor? I checked the meat, and it was white all the way through, but I wondered if it was completely done. I took another experimental bite; I chewed twice. Ugh—definitely bad. I jumped up to spit it into the sink. Suddenly, the chicken-and-oil smell was revolting. I took the whole plate and shook it into the garbage, then opened the windows to chase away the scent. A coolish breeze had picked up outside. It felt good on my skin.

I was abruptly exhausted, but I didn't want to go back to the hot room. So I opened more windows in the TV room and lay on the couch right beneath them. I turned on the same movie we'd watched the other day and quickly fell asleep to the bright opening song.

When I opened my eyes again, the sun was halfway up the sky, but it was not the light that woke me. Cool arms were around me, pulling me against him. At the same time, a sudden pain twisted in my stomach, almost like the aftershock of catching a punch in the gut.

"I'm sorry," Edward was murmuring as he wiped a wintry hand across my clammy forehead. "So much for thoroughness. I didn't think about how hot you would be with me gone. I'll have an air conditioner installed before I leave again."

I couldn't concentrate on what he was saying. "Excuse me!" I gasped, struggling to get free of his arms.

He dropped his hold automatically. "Bella?"

I streaked for the bathroom with my hand clamped over my mouth. I felt so horrible that I didn't even care—at first—that he was with me while I crouched over the toilet and was violently sick.

"Bella? What's wrong?"

I couldn't answer yet. He held me anxiously, keeping my hair out of my face, waiting till I could breathe again.

"Damn rancid chicken," I moaned.

"Are you all right?" His voice was strained.

"Fine," I panted. "It's just food poisoning. You don't need to see this. Go away."

"Not likely, Bella."

"Go away," I moaned again, struggling to get up so I could rinse my mouth out. He helped me gently, ignoring the weak shoves I aimed at him.

After my mouth was clean, he carried me to the bed and sat me down carefully, supporting me with his arms.

"Food poisoning?"

"Yeah," I croaked. "I made some chicken last night. It tasted off, so I threw it out. But I ate a few bites first."

He put a cold hand on my forehead. It felt nice. "How do you feel now?"

I thought about that for a moment. The nausea had passed as suddenly as it had come, and I felt like I did any other morning. "Pretty normal. A little hungry, actually."

He made me wait an hour and keep down a big glass of water before he fried me some eggs. I felt perfectly normal, just a little tired from being up in the middle of the night. He put on CNN—we'd been so out of touch, world war three could have broken out and we wouldn't have known—and I lounged drowsily across his lap.

I got bored with the news and twisted around to kiss him. Just like this morning, a sharp pain hit my stomach when I moved. I lurched away from him, my hand tight over my mouth. I knew I'd never make it to the bathroom this time, so I ran to the kitchen sink.

He held my hair again.

"Maybe we should go back to Rio, see a doctor," he suggested anxiously when I was rinsing my mouth afterward.

I shook my head and edged toward the hallway. Doctors meant needles. "I'll be fine right after I brush my teeth."

When my mouth tasted better, I searched through my suitcase for the little first-aid kit Alice had packed for me, full of human things like bandages and painkillers and— my object now—Pepto-Bismol. Maybe I could settle my stomach and calm Edward down.

But before I found the Pepto, I happened across something else that Alice had packed for me. I picked up the small blue box and stared at it in my hand for a long moment, forgetting everything else.

Then I started counting in my head. Once. Twice. Again.

The knock startled me; the little box fell back into the suitcase.

"Are you well?" Edward asked through the door. "Did you get sick again?"

"Yes and no," I said, but my voice sounded strangled.

"Bella? Can I please come in?" Worriedly now.

"O . . . kay?"

He came in and appraised my position, sitting cross-legged on the floor by the suitcase, and my expression, blank and staring. He sat next to me, his hand going to my forehead at once.

"What's wrong?"

"How many days has it been since the wedding?" I whispered.

"Seventeen," he answered automatically. "Bella, what is it?"

I was counting again. I held up a finger, cautioning him to wait, and mouthed the numbers to myself. I'd been wrong about the days before. We'd been here longer than I'd thought. I started over again.

"Bella!" he whispered urgently. "I'm losing my mind over here."

I tried to swallow. It didn't work. So I reached into the suitcase and fumbled around until I found the little blue box of tampons again. I held them up silently.

He stared at me in confusion. "What? Are you trying to pass this illness off as PMS?"

"No," I managed to choke out. "No, Edward. I'm trying to tell you that my period is five days late."

His facial expression didn't change. It was like I hadn't spoken.

"I don't think I have food poisoning," I added.

He didn't respond. He had turned into a sculpture.

"The dreams," I mumbled to myself in a flat voice. "Sleeping so much. The crying. All that food. Oh. Oh. *Oh.*"

Edward's stare seemed glassy, as if he couldn't see me anymore.

Reflexively, almost involuntarily, my hand dropped to my stomach.

"Oh!" I squeaked again.

I lurched to my feet, slipping out of Edward's unmoving hands. I'd never changed out of the little silk shorts and camisole I'd worn to bed. I yanked the blue fabric out of the way and stared at my stomach.

"Impossible," I whispered.

I had absolutely no experience with pregnancy or babies or any part of that world, but I wasn't an idiot. I'd seen enough movies and TV shows to know that this wasn't how it worked. I was only five days late. If I *was* pregnant, my body wouldn't even have registered that fact. I would not have morning sickness. I would not have changed my eating or sleeping habits.

And I most definitely would not have a small but defined bump sticking out between my hips.

I twisted my torso back and forth, examining it from every angle, as if it would disappear in exactly the right light. I ran my fingers over the subtle bulge, surprised by how rock hard it felt under my skin.

"Impossible," I said again, because, bulge or no bulge,

period or no period (and there was definitely no period, though I'd never been late a day in my life), there was no way I could be *pregnant*. The only person I'd ever had sex with was a vampire, for crying out loud.

A vampire who was still frozen on the floor with no sign of ever moving again.

So there had to be some other explanation, then. Something wrong with me. A strange South American disease with all the signs of pregnancy, only accelerated . . .

And then I remembered something—a morning of internet research that seemed a lifetime ago now. Sitting at the old desk in my room at Charlie's house with gray light glowing dully through the window, staring at my ancient, wheezing computer, reading avidly through a web site called "Vampires A–Z." It had been less than twenty-four hours since Jacob Black, trying to entertain me with the Quileute legends he didn't believe in yet, had told me that Edward was a vampire. I'd scanned anxiously through the first entries on the site, which was dedicated to vampire myths around the world. The Filipino *Danag*, the Hebrew *Estrie*, the Romanian *Varacolaci*, the Italian *Stregoni benefici* (a legend actually based on my new father-in-law's early exploits with the Volturi, not that I'd known anything about that at the time) . . . I'd paid less and less attention as the stories had grown more and more implausible. I only remembered vague bits of the later entries. They mostly seemed like excuses dreamed up to explain things like infant mortality rates—and infidelity. *No, honey, I'm not having an affair! That sexy woman you saw sneaking out of the house was an evil succubus. I'm lucky I escaped with my life!* (Of course, with what I knew now about Tanya and her sisters, I suspected that some of those excuses had been nothing but fact.) There had been one for the ladies, too. *How can you accuse me of cheating on you—just because you've come home from a two-year sea voyage and I'm pregnant? It was the incubus. He hypnotized me with his mystical vampire powers.* . . .

That had been part of the definition of the incubus—the ability to father children with his hapless prey.

I shook my head, dazed. But . . .

I thought of Esme and especially Rosalie. Vampires couldn't have children. If it were possible, Rosalie would have found a way by now. The incubus myth was nothing but a fable.

Except that . . . well, there *was* a difference. Of course Rosalie could not conceive a child, because she was frozen in the state in which she passed from human to inhuman. Totally unchanging. And human women's bodies had to *change* to bear children. The constant change of a monthly cycle for one thing, and then the bigger changes needed to accommodate a growing child. Rosalie's body couldn't change.

But mine could. Mine did. I touched the bump on my stomach that had not been there yesterday.

And human men—well, they pretty much stayed the same from puberty to death. I remembered a random bit of trivia, gleaned from who knows where: Charlie Chaplin was in his seventies when he fathered his youngest child. Men had no such thing as child-bearing years or cycles of fertility.

Of course, how would anyone know if vampire men could father children, when their partners were not able? What vampire on earth would have the restraint necessary to test the theory with a human woman? Or the inclination?

I could think of only one.

Part of my head was sorting through fact and memory and speculation, while the other half—the part that controlled the ability to move even the smallest muscles—was stunned beyond the capacity for normal operations. I couldn't move my lips to speak, though I wanted to ask Edward to *please* explain to me what was going on. I needed to go back to where he sat, to touch him, but my body wouldn't follow instructions. I could only stare at my shocked eyes in the mirror, my fingers gingerly pressed against the swelling on my torso.

And then, like in my vivid nightmare last night, the scene abruptly transformed. Everything I saw in the mirror looked completely different, though nothing actually *was* different.

What happened to change everything was that a soft little nudge bumped my hand—from inside my body.

In the same moment, Edward's phone rang, shrill and demanding. Neither of us moved. It rang again and again. I tried to tune it out while I pressed my fingers to my stomach, waiting. In the mirror my expression was no longer bewildered—it was wondering now. I barely noticed when the strange, silent tears started streaming down my cheeks.

The phone kept ringing. I wished Edward would answer it—I was having a moment. Possibly the biggest of my life.

Ring! Ring! Ring!

Finally, the annoyance broke through everything else. I got down on my knees next to Edward—I found myself moving more carefully, a thousand times more aware of the way each motion felt—and patted his pockets until I found the phone. I half-expected him to thaw out and answer it himself, but he was perfectly still.

I recognized the number, and I could easily guess why she was calling.

"Hi, Alice," I said. My voice wasn't much better than before. I cleared my throat.

"Bella? Bella, are you okay?"

"Yeah. Um. Is Carlisle there?"

"He is. What's the problem?"

"I'm not . . . one hundred percent . . . sure. . . ."

"Is Edward all right?" she asked warily. She called Carlisle's name away from the phone and then demanded, "Why didn't he pick up the phone?" before I could answer her first question.

"I'm not sure."

"Bella, what's going on? I just saw—"

"What did you see?"

There was a silence. "Here's Carlisle," she finally said.

It felt like ice water had been injected in my veins. If Alice had seen a vision of me with a green-eyed, angel-faced child in my arms, she would have answered me, wouldn't she?

While I waited through the split second it took for Carlisle to speak, the vision I'd imagined for Alice danced behind my lids. A tiny, beautiful little baby, even more beautiful than the boy in my dream—a tiny Edward in my arms. Warmth shot through my veins, chasing the ice away.

"Bella, it's Carlisle. What's going on?"

"I—" I wasn't sure how to answer. Would he laugh at my

conclusions, tell me I was crazy? Was I just having another colorful dream? "I'm a little worried about Edward. . . . Can vampires go into shock?"

"Has he been harmed?" Carlisle's voice was suddenly urgent.

"No, no," I assured him. "Just . . . taken by surprise."

"I don't understand, Bella."

"I think . . . well, I think that . . . maybe . . . I might be . . ." I took a deep breath. "Pregnant."

As if to back me up, there was another tiny nudge in my abdomen. My hand flew to my stomach.

After a long pause, Carlisle's medical training kicked in.

"When was the first day of your last menstrual cycle?"

"Sixteen days before the wedding." I'd done the mental math thoroughly enough just before to be able to answer with certainty.

"How do you feel?"

"Weird," I told him, and my voice broke. Another trickle of tears dribbled down my cheeks. "This is going to sound crazy—look, I know it's way too early for any of this. Maybe I *am* crazy. But I'm having bizarre dreams and eating all the time and crying and throwing up and . . . and . . . I swear something *moved* inside me just now."

Edward's head snapped up.

I sighed in relief.

Edward held his hand out for the phone, his face white and hard.

"Um, I think Edward wants to talk to you."

"Put him on," Carlisle said in a strained voice.

Not entirely sure that Edward *could* talk, I put the phone in his outstretched hand.

He pressed it to his ear. "Is it possible?" he whispered.

He listened for a long time, staring blankly at nothing.

"And Bella?" he asked. His arm wrapped around me as he spoke, pulling me close into his side.

He listened for what seemed like a long time and then said, "Yes. Yes, I will."

He pulled the phone away from his ear and pressed the "end" button. Right away, he dialed a new number.

"What did Carlisle say?" I asked impatiently.

Edward answered in a lifeless voice. "He thinks you're pregnant."

The words sent a warm shiver down my spine. The little nudger fluttered inside me.

"Who are you calling now?" I asked as he put the phone back to his ear.

"The airport. We're going home."

Edward was on the phone for more than an hour without a break. I guessed that he was arranging our flight home, but I couldn't be sure because he wasn't speaking English. It sounded like he was arguing; he spoke through his teeth a lot.

While he argued, he packed. He whirled around the room like an angry tornado, leaving order rather than destruction in his path. He threw a set of my clothes on the bed without looking at them, so I assumed it was time for me to get dressed. He continued with his argument while I changed, gesturing with sudden, agitated movements.

When I could no longer bear the violent energy radiating out of him, I quietly left the room. His manic concentration made me sick to my stomach—not like the morning sickness, just uncomfortable. I would wait somewhere else for his mood to pass. I couldn't talk to this icy, focused Edward who honestly frightened me a little.

Once again, I ended up in the kitchen. There was a bag of pretzels in the cupboard. I started chewing on them absently, staring out the window at the sand and rocks and trees and ocean, everything glittering in the sun.

Someone nudged me.

"I know," I said. "I don't want to go, either."

I stared out the window for a moment, but the nudger didn't respond.

"I don't understand," I whispered. "What is *wrong* here?"

Surprising, absolutely. Astonishing, even. But *wrong*?

No.

So why was Edward so *furious*? He was the one who had actually wished out loud for a shotgun wedding.

I tried to reason through it.

Maybe it wasn't so confusing that Edward wanted us to go home right away. He'd want Carlisle to check me out, make sure my assumption was right—though there was absolutely no doubt in my head at this point. Probably they'd want to figure out why I was already *so* pregnant, with the bump and the nudging and all of that. That wasn't normal.

Once I thought of this, I was sure I had it. He must be so worried about the baby. I hadn't gotten around to freaking out yet. My brain worked slower than his—it was still stuck marveling over the picture it had conjured up before: the tiny child with Edward's eyes—green, as his had been when he was human—lying fair and beautiful in my arms. I hoped he would have Edward's face exactly, with no interference from mine.

It was funny how abruptly and entirely necessary this vision had become. From that first little touch, the whole world had shifted. Where before there was just one thing I could not live without, now there were two. There was no division—my love was not split between them now; it wasn't like that. It was more like my heart had grown, swollen up to twice its size in that moment. All that extra space, already filled. The increase was almost dizzying.

I'd never really understood Rosalie's pain and resentment before. I'd never imagined myself a mother, never wanted that. It had been a piece of cake to promise Edward that I didn't care about giving up children for him, because I truly didn't. Children, in the abstract, had never appealed to me. They seemed to be loud creatures, often dripping some form of goo. I'd never had much to do with them. When I'd dreamed of Renée providing me with a brother, I'd always imagined an *older* brother. Someone to take care of me, rather than the other way around.

This child, Edward's child, was a whole different story.

I wanted him like I wanted air to breathe. Not a choice— a necessity.

Maybe I just had a really bad imagination. Maybe that was why I'd been unable to imagine that I would *like* being married until after I already was—unable to see that I would want a baby until after one was already coming. . . .

As I put my hand on my stomach, waiting for the next nudge, tears streaked down my cheeks again.

"Bella?"

I turned, made wary by the tone of his voice. It was too cold, too careful. His face matched his voice, empty and hard.

And then he saw that I was crying.

"Bella!" He crossed the room in a flash and put his hands on my face. "Are you in pain?"

"No, no—"

He pulled me against his chest. "Don't be afraid. We'll be home in sixteen hours. You'll be fine. Carlisle will be ready when we get there. We'll take care of this, and you'll be fine, you'll be fine."

"Take care of this? What do you mean?"

He leaned away and looked me in the eye. "We're going to get that thing out before it can hurt any part of you. Don't be scared. I *won't* let it hurt you."

"That *thing*?" I gasped.

He looked sharply away from me, toward the front door. "Dammit! I forgot Gustavo was due today. I'll get rid of him and be right back." He darted out of the room.

I clutched the counter for support. My knees were wobbly.

Edward had just called my little nudger a *thing*. He said Carlisle would get it out.

"No," I whispered.

I'd gotten it wrong before. He didn't care about the baby at all. He wanted to *hurt* him. The beautiful picture in my head shifted abruptly, changed into something dark. My pretty baby crying, my weak arms not enough to protect him. . . .

What could I do? Would I be able to reason with them?

What if I couldn't? Did this explain Alice's strange silence on the phone? Is that what she'd seen? Edward and Carlisle killing that pale, perfect child before he could live?

"No," I whispered again, my voice stronger. That could *not* be. I would not allow it.

I heard Edward speaking Portuguese again. Arguing again. His voice got closer, and I heard him grunt in exasperation. Then I heard another voice, low and timid. A woman's voice.

He came into the kitchen ahead of her and went straight to me. He wiped the tears from my cheeks and murmured in my ear through the thin, hard line of his lips.

"She's insisting on leaving the food she brought—she made us dinner." If he had been less tense, less furious, I knew he would have rolled his eyes. "It's an excuse—she wants to make sure I haven't killed you yet." His voice went ice cold at the end.

Kaure edged nervously around the corner with a covered dish in her hands. I wished I could speak Portuguese, or that my Spanish was less rudimentary, so that I could try to thank this woman who had dared to anger a vampire just to check on me.

Her eyes flickered between the two of us. I saw her measuring the color in my face, the moisture in my eyes. Mumbling something I didn't understand, she put the dish on the counter.

Edward snapped something at her; I'd never heard him be so impolite before. She turned to go, and the whirling motion of her long skirt wafted the smell of the food into my face. It was strong—onions and fish. I gagged and whirled for the sink. I felt Edward's hands on my forehead and heard his soothing murmur through the roaring in my ears. His hands disappeared for a second, and I heard the refrigerator slam shut. Mercifully, the smell disappeared with the sound, and Edward's hands were cooling my clammy face again. It was over quickly.

I rinsed my mouth in the tap while he caressed the side of my face.

There was a tentative little nudge in my womb.

It's okay. We're okay, I thought toward the bump.

Edward turned me around, pulling me into his arms. I rested my head on his shoulder. My hands, instinctively, folded over my stomach.

I heard a little gasp and I looked up.

The woman was still there, hesitating in the doorway with her hands half-outstretched as if she had been looking for some way to help. Her eyes were locked on my hands, popping wide with shock. Her mouth hung open.

Then Edward gasped, too, and he suddenly turned to face the woman, pushing me slightly behind his body. His arm wrapped across my torso, like he was holding me back.

Suddenly, Kaure was shouting at him—loudly, furiously, her unintelligible words flying across the room like knives. She raised her tiny fist in the air and took two steps forward, shaking it at him. Despite her ferocity, it was easy to see the terror in her eyes.

Edward stepped toward her, too, and I clutched at his arm, frightened for the woman. But when he interrupted her tirade, his voice took me by surprise, especially considering how sharp he'd been with her when she *wasn't* screeching at him. It was low now; it was pleading. Not only that, but the sound was different, more guttural, the cadence off. I didn't think he was speaking Portuguese anymore.

For a moment, the woman stared at him in wonder, and then her eyes narrowed as she barked out a long question in the same alien tongue.

I watched as his face grew sad and serious, and he nodded once. She took a quick step back and crossed herself.

He reached out to her, gesturing toward me and then resting his hand against my cheek. She replied angrily again, waving her hands accusingly toward him, and then gestured to him. When she finished, he pleaded again with the same low, urgent voice.

Her expression changed—she stared at him with doubt plain on her face as he spoke, her eyes repeatedly flashing to my confused face. He stopped speaking, and she seemed to be deliberating something. She looked back and forth between the two of us, and then, unconsciously it seemed, took a step forward.

She made a motion with her hands, miming a shape like a balloon jutting out from her stomach. I started—did her legends of the predatory blood-drinker include *this*? Could she possibly know something about what was growing inside me?

She walked a few steps forward deliberately this time and asked a few brief questions, which he responded to tensely. Then he became the questioner—one quick query. She hesitated and then slowly shook her head. When he spoke again, his voice was so agonized that I looked up at him in shock. His face was drawn with pain.

In answer, she walked slowly forward until she was

close enough to lay her small hand on top of mine, over my stomach. She spoke one word in Portuguese.

"Morte," she sighed quietly. Then she turned, her shoulders bent as if the conversation had aged her, and left the room.

I knew enough Spanish for that one.

Edward was frozen again, staring after her with the tortured expression fixed on his face. A few moments later, I heard a boat's engine putter to life and then fade into the distance.

Edward did not move until I started for the bathroom. Then his hand caught my shoulder.

"Where are you going?" His voice was a whisper of pain.

"To brush my teeth again."

"Don't worry about what she said. It's nothing but legends, old lies for the sake of entertainment."

"I didn't understand anything," I told him, though it wasn't entirely true. As if I could discount something because it was a legend. My life was circled by legend on every side. They were all true.

"I packed your toothbrush. I'll get it for you."

He walked ahead of me to the bedroom.

"Are we leaving soon?" I called after him.

"As soon as you're done."

He waited for my toothbrush to repack it, pacing silently around the bedroom. I handed it to him when I was finished.

"I'll get the bags into the boat."

"Edward—"

He turned back. "Yes?"

I hesitated, trying to think of some way to get a few seconds alone. "Could you . . . pack some of the food? You know, in case I get hungry again."

"Of course," he said, his eyes suddenly soft. "Don't worry about anything. We'll get to Carlisle in just a few hours, really. This will all be over soon."

I nodded, not trusting my voice.

He turned and left the room, one big suitcase in each hand.

I whirled and scooped up the phone he'd left on the counter. It was very unlike him to forget things—to forget that Gustavo was coming, to leave his phone lying here. He was so stressed he was barely himself.

I flipped it open and scrolled through the preprogrammed numbers. I was glad he had the sound turned off, afraid that he would catch me. Would he be at the boat now? Or back already? Would he hear me from the kitchen if I whispered?

I found the number I wanted, one I had never called before in my life. I pressed the "send" button and crossed my fingers.

"Hello?" the voice like golden wind chimes answered.

"Rosalie?" I whispered. "It's Bella. Please. You have to help me."

BOOK TWO

<< >>

jacob

And yet, to say the truth,
reason and love keep little company together nowadays.

William Shakespeare
A Midsummer Night's Dream
Act III, Scene i

PREFACE

Life sucks, and then you die.

Yeah, I should be so lucky.

8. WAITING FOR THE DAMN FIGHT TO START ALREADY

"JEEZ, PAUL, DON'T YOU FREAKING HAVE A HOME OF YOUR *own?*"

Paul, lounging across *my* whole couch, watching some stupid baseball game on *my* crappy TV, just grinned at me and then—real slow—he lifted one Dorito from the bag in his lap and wedged it into his mouth in one piece.

"You better've brought those with you."

Crunch. "Nope," he said while chewing. "Your sister said to go ahead and help myself to anything I wanted."

I tried to make my voice sound like I wasn't about to punch him. "Is Rachel here now?"

It didn't work. He heard where I was going and shoved

the bag behind his back. The bag crackled as he smashed it into the cushion. The chips crunched into pieces. Paul's hands came up in fists, close to his face like a boxer.

"Bring it, kid. I don't need Rachel to protect me."

I snorted. "Right. Like you wouldn't go crying to her first chance."

He laughed and relaxed into the sofa, dropping his hands. "I'm not going to go tattle to a girl. If you got in a lucky hit, that would be just between the two of us. And vice versa, right?"

Nice of him to give me an invitation. I made my body slump like I'd given up. "Right."

His eyes shifted to the TV.

I lunged.

His nose made a very satisfying crunching sound of its own when my fist connected. He tried to grab me, but I danced out of the way before he could find a hold, the ruined bag of Doritos in my left hand.

"You broke my nose, idiot."

"Just between us, right, Paul?"

I went to put the chips away. When I turned around, Paul was repositioning his nose before it could set crooked. The blood had already stopped; it looked like it had no source as it trickled down his lips and off his chin. He cussed, wincing as he pulled at the cartilage.

"You are such a pain, Jacob. I swear, I'd rather hang out with Leah."

"Ouch. Wow, I bet Leah's really going to love to hear that you want to spend some quality time with her. It'll just warm the cockles of her heart."

"You're going to forget I said that."

"Of course. I'm sure it won't slip out."

"Ugh," he grunted, and then settled back into the couch, wiping the leftover blood on the collar of his t-shirt. "You're fast, kid. I'll give you that." He turned his attention back to the fuzzy game.

I stood there for a second, and then I stalked off to my room, muttering about alien abductions.

Back in the day, you could count on Paul for a fight pretty much whenever. You didn't have to hit him then—any mild insult would do. It didn't take a lot to flip him out of control. Now, of course, when I really *wanted* a good snarling, ripping, break-the-trees-down match, he had to be all mellow.

Wasn't it bad enough that yet another member of the pack had imprinted—because, really, that made four of ten now! When would it stop? Stupid myth was supposed to be *rare,* for crying out loud! All this mandatory love-at-first-sight was completely sickening!

Did it have to be *my* sister? Did it have to be *Paul?*

When Rachel'd come home from Washington State at the end of the summer semester—graduated early, the nerd—my biggest worry'd been that it would be hard keeping the secret around her. I wasn't used to covering things up in my own home. It made me real sympathetic to kids like Embry and Collin, whose parents didn't know they were werewolves. Embry's mom thought he was going through some kind of rebellious stage. He was permanently grounded for constantly sneaking out, but, of course, there wasn't much he could do about that. She'd check his room every night, and every night it would be empty again. She'd yell and he'd take it in silence, and then go through it all again the next day. We'd tried to talk Sam into giving Embry a break and letting his mom in on the gig, but Embry'd said he didn't mind. The secret was too important.

So I'd been all geared up to be keeping that secret. And then, two days after Rachel got home, Paul ran into her on the beach. Bada bing, bada boom—true love! No secrets necessary when you found your other half, and all that imprinting werewolf garbage.

Rachel got the whole story. And I got Paul as a brother-in-law someday. I knew Billy wasn't much thrilled about it, either. But he handled it better than I did. 'Course, he did escape to the Clearwaters' more often than usual these days. I didn't see where that was so much better. No Paul, but plenty of Leah.

I wondered—would a bullet through my temple actually kill me or just leave a really big mess for me to clean up?

I threw myself down on the bed. I was tired—hadn't slept since my last patrol—but I knew I wasn't going to sleep. My head was too crazy. The thoughts bounced around inside my skull like a disoriented swarm of bees. Noisy. Now and then they stung. Must be hornets, not bees. Bees died after one sting. And the same thoughts were stinging me again and again.

This waiting was driving me insane. It had been almost four weeks. I'd expected, one way or another, the news would have come by now. I'd sat up nights imagining what form it would take.

Charlie sobbing on the phone—Bella and her husband lost in an accident. A plane crash? That would be hard to fake. Unless the leeches didn't mind killing a bunch of bystanders to authenticate it, and why would they? Maybe a small plane instead. They probably had one of those to spare.

Or would the murderer come home alone, unsuccessful in his attempt to make her one of them? Or not even getting that far. Maybe he'd smashed her like a bag of chips in his drive to get some? Because her life was less important to him than his own pleasure . . .

The story would be so tragic—Bella lost in a horrible accident. Victim of a mugging gone wrong. Choking to death at dinner. A car accident, like my mom. So common. Happened all the time.

Would he bring her home? Bury her here for Charlie? Closed-casket ceremony, of course. My mom's coffin had been nailed shut. . . .

I could only hope that he'd come back here, within my reach.

Maybe there would be no story at all. Maybe Charlie would call to ask my dad if he'd heard anything from Dr. Cullen, who just didn't show up to work one day. The house abandoned. No answer on any of the Cullens' phones. The mystery picked up by some second-rate news program, foul play suspected . . .

Maybe the big white house would burn to the ground, everyone trapped inside. Of course, they'd need bodies for that one. Eight humans of roughly the right size. Burned beyond recognition—beyond the help of dental records.

Either of those would be tricky—for me, that is. It would be hard to find them if they didn't want to be found. Of course, I had forever to look. If you had forever, you could check out every single piece of straw in the haystack, one by one, to see if it was the needle.

Right now, I wouldn't mind dismantling a haystack. At least that would be something to *do*. I hated knowing that I could be losing my chance. Giving the bloodsuckers the time to escape, if that was their plan.

We could go tonight. We could kill every one of them that we could find.

I liked that plan because I knew Edward well enough to know that, if I killed any one of his coven, I would get my chance at him, too. He'd come for revenge. And I'd give it to him—I wouldn't let my brothers take him down as a pack. It would be just him and me. May the better man win.

But Sam wouldn't hear of it. *We're not going to break the treaty. Let them make the breach.* Just because we had no proof that the Cullens had done anything wrong. Yet. You had to add the yet, because we all knew it was inevitable. Bella was either coming back one of them, or not coming back. Either way, a human life had been lost. And that meant game on.

In the other room, Paul brayed like a mule. Maybe he'd switched to a comedy. Maybe the commercial was funny. Whatever. It grated on my nerves.

I thought about breaking his nose again. But it wasn't Paul I wanted to fight with. Not really.

I tried to listen to other sounds, the wind in the trees. It wasn't the same, not through human ears. There were a million voices in the wind that I couldn't hear in this body.

But these ears were sensitive enough. I could hear past the trees, to the road, the sounds of the cars coming around that last bend where you could finally see the beach—the vista of the islands and the rocks and the big blue ocean stretching to the horizon. The La Push cops liked to hang out right around there. Tourists never noticed the reduced speed limit sign on the other side of the road.

I could hear the voices outside the souvenir shop on the beach. I could hear the cowbell clanging as the door opened and closed. I could hear Embry's mom at the cash register, printing out a receipt.

I could hear the tide raking across the beach rocks. I could hear the kids squeal as the icy water rushed in too fast for them to get out of the way. I could hear the moms complain about the wet clothes. And I could hear a familiar voice. . . .

I was listening so hard that the sudden burst of Paul's donkey laugh made me jump half off the bed.

"Get out of my house," I grumbled. Knowing he wouldn't pay any attention, I followed my own advice. I wrenched open my window and climbed out the back way so that I wouldn't see Paul again. It would be too tempting. I knew I would hit him again, and Rachel was going to be pissed enough already. She'd see the blood on his shirt, and she'd blame me right away without waiting for proof. Of course, she'd be right, but still.

I paced down to the shore, my fists in my pockets. Nobody looked at me twice when I went through the dirt lot by First Beach. That was one nice thing about summer—no one cared if you wore nothing but shorts.

I followed the familiar voice I'd heard and found Quil easy enough. He was on the south end of the crescent, avoiding the bigger part of the tourist crowd. He kept up a constant stream of warnings.

"Keep out of the water, Claire. C'mon. No, don't. Oh! *Nice*, kid. Seriously, do you want Emily to yell at me? I'm not bringing you back to the beach again if you don't—Oh yeah? Don't—ugh. You think that's funny, do you? Hah! Who's laughing now, huh?"

He had the giggling toddler by the ankle when I reached them. She had a bucket in one hand, and her jeans were drenched. He had a huge wet mark down the front of his t-shirt.

"Five bucks on the baby girl," I said.

"Hey, Jake."

Claire squealed and threw her bucket at Quil's knees. "Down, down!"

He set her carefully on her feet and she ran to me. She wrapped her arms around my leg.

"Unca Jay!"

"How's it going, Claire?"

She giggled. "Qwil *aaaaawl* wet now."

"I can see that. Where's your mama?"

"Gone, gone, gone," Claire sang, "Cwaire pway wid Qwil *aaaawl* day. Cwaire nebber gowin home." She let go of me and ran to Quil. He scooped her up and slung her onto his shoulders.

"Sounds like somebody's hit the terrible twos."

"Threes actually," Quil corrected. "You missed the party. Princess theme. She made me wear a crown, and then Emily suggested they all try out her new play makeup on me."

"Wow, I'm *really* sorry I wasn't around to see that."

"Don't worry, Emily has pictures. Actually, I look pretty hot."

"You're such a patsy."

Quil shrugged. "Claire had a great time. That was the point."

I rolled my eyes. It was hard being around imprinted people. No matter what stage they were in—about to tie the knot like Sam or just a much-abused nanny like Quil— the peace and certainty they always radiated was downright puke-inducing.

Claire squealed on his shoulders and pointed at the ground. "Pity wock, Qwil! For me, for me!"

"Which one, kiddo? The red one?"

"No wed!"

Quil dropped to his knees—Claire screamed and pulled his hair like a horse's reigns.

"This blue one?"

"No, no, no . . . ," the little girl sang, thrilled with her new game.

The weird part was, Quil was having just as much fun as she was. He didn't have that face on that so many of the tourist dads and moms were wearing—the when-is-nap-time? face. You never saw a real parent so jazzed to play whatever stupid kiddie sport their rugrat could think up. I'd seen Quil play peekaboo for an hour straight without getting bored.

And I couldn't even make fun of him for it—I envied him too much.

Though I did think it sucked that he had a good fourteen years of monk-i-tude ahead of him until Claire was his age—for Quil, at least, it was a good thing werewolves didn't get older. But even all that time didn't seem to bother him much.

"Quil, you ever think about dating?" I asked.

"Huh?"

"No, no yewwo!" Claire crowed.

"You know. A real girl. I mean, just for now, right? On your nights off babysitting duty."

Quil stared at me, his mouth hanging open.

"Pity wock! Pity wock!" Claire screamed when he didn't offer her another choice. She smacked him on the head with her little fist.

"Sorry, Claire-bear. How about this pretty purple one?"

"No," she giggled. "No poopoh."

"Give me a clue. I'm begging, kid."

Claire thought it over. "Gween," she finally said.

Quil stared at the rocks, studying them. He picked four rocks in different shades of green, and offered them to her.

"Did I get it?"

"Yay!"

"Which one?"

"*Aaaaawl* ob dem!!"

She cupped her hands and he poured the small rocks into them. She laughed and immediately clunked him on the head with them. He winced theatrically and then got to his feet and started walking back up toward the parking lot. Probably worried about her getting cold in her wet clothes. He was worse than any paranoid, overprotective mother.

"Sorry if I was being pushy before, man, about the girl thing," I said.

"Naw, that's cool," Quil said. "It kind of took me by surprise is all. I hadn't thought about it."

"I bet she'd understand. You know, when she's grown up. She wouldn't get mad that you had a life while she was in diapers."

"No, I know. I'm sure she'd understand that."

He didn't say anything else.

"But you won't do that, will you?" I guessed.

"I can't see it," he said in a low voice. "I can't imagine. I just don't . . . see anyone that way. I don't notice girls anymore, you know. I don't see their faces."

"Put that together with the tiara and makeup, and maybe Claire will have a different kind of competition to worry about."

Quil laughed and made kissing noises at me. "You available this Friday, Jacob?"

"You wish," I said, and then I made a face. "Yeah, guess I am, though."

He hesitated a second and then said, "You ever think about dating?"

I sighed. Guess I'd opened myself up for that one.

"You know, Jake, maybe you should think about getting a life."

He didn't say it like a joke. His voice was sympathetic. That made it worse.

"I don't see them, either, Quil. I don't see their faces."

Quil sighed, too.

Far away, too low for anyone but just us two to hear it over the waves, a howl rose out of the forest.

"Dang, that's Sam," Quil said. His hands flew up to touch Claire, as if making sure she was still there. "I don't know where her mom's at!"

"I'll see what it is. If we need you, I'll let you know." I raced through the words. They came out all slurred together. "Hey, why don't you take her up to the Clearwaters'? Sue and Billy can keep an eye on her if they need to. They might know what's going on, anyway."

"Okay—get outta here, Jake!"

I took off running, not for the dirt path through the weedy hedge, but in the shortest line toward the forest. I hurdled the first line of driftwood and then ripped my way through the briars, still running. I felt the little tears as the thorns cut into my skin, but I ignored them. Their sting would be healed before I made the trees.

I cut behind the store and darted across the highway. Somebody honked at me. Once in the safety of the trees, I ran faster, taking longer strides. People would stare if I was out in the open. Normal people couldn't run like this. Sometimes I thought it might be fun to enter a race—you know, like the Olympic trials or something. It would be cool to watch the expressions on those star athletes' faces when I blew by them. Only I was pretty sure the testing they did to make sure you weren't on steroids would probably turn up some really freaky crap in my blood.

As soon as I was in the true forest, unbound by roads or houses, I skidded to a stop and kicked my shorts off. With quick, practiced moves, I rolled them up and tied them to the leather cord around my ankle. As I was still pulling the ends tight, I started shifting. The fire trembled down my spine, throwing tight spasms out along my arms and legs. It only took a second. The heat flooded through me, and I felt the silent shimmer that made me something else. I threw my heavy paws against the matted earth and stretched my back in one long, rolling extension.

Phasing was very easy when I was centered like this. I didn't have issues with my temper anymore. Except when it got in the way.

For one half second, I remembered the awful moment at that unspeakable joke of a wedding. I'd been so insane with fury that I couldn't make my body work right. I'd been trapped, shaking and burning, unable to make the change and kill the monster just a few feet away from me. It had been so confusing. Dying to kill him. Afraid to hurt her. My friends in the way. And then, when I was finally able to take the form I wanted, the order from my leader. The edict from the Alpha. If it had been just Embry and Quil there that night without Sam . . . would I have been able to kill the murderer, then?

I hated it when Sam laid down the law like that. I hated the feeling of having no choice. Of having to obey.

And then I was conscious of an audience. I was not alone in my thoughts.

So self-absorbed all the time, Leah thought.

Yeah, no hypocrisy there, Leah, I thought back.

Can it, guys, Sam told us.

We fell silent, and I felt Leah's wince at the word *guys.* Touchy, like always.

Sam pretended not to notice. *Where's Quil and Jared?*

Quil's got Claire. He's taking her to the Clearwaters'.

Good. Sue will take her.

Jared was going to Kim's, Embry thought. *Good chance he didn't hear you.*

There was a low grumble through the pack. I moaned along with them. When Jared finally showed up, no doubt he'd still be thinking about Kim. And nobody wanted a replay of what they were up to right now.

Sam sat back on his haunches and let another howl rip into the air. It was a signal and an order in one.

The pack was gathered a few miles east of where I was. I loped through the thick forest toward them. Leah,

Embry, and Paul all were working in toward them, too. Leah was close—soon I could hear her footfalls not far into the woods. We continued in a parallel line, choosing not to run together.

Well, we're not waiting all day for him. He'll just have to catch up later.

'Sup, boss? Paul wanted to know.

We need to talk. Something's happened.

I felt Sam's thoughts flicker to me—and not just Sam's, but Seth's and Collin's and Brady's as well. Collin and Brady—the new kids—had been running patrol with Sam today, so they would know whatever he knew. I didn't know why Seth was already out here, and in the know. It wasn't his turn.

Seth, tell them what you heard.

I sped up, wanting to be there. I heard Leah move faster, too. She hated being outrun. Being the fastest was the only edge she claimed.

Claim this, moron, she hissed, and then she really kicked it into gear. I dug my nails into the loam and shot myself forward.

Sam didn't seem in the mood to put up with our usual crap. *Jake, Leah, give it a rest.*

Neither of us slowed.

Sam growled, but let it go. *Seth?*

Charlie called around till he found Billy at my house.

Yeah, I talked to him, Paul added.

I felt a jolt go through me as Seth thought Charlie's name. This was it. The waiting was over. I ran faster, forcing myself to breathe, though my lungs felt kinda stiff all of a sudden.

Which story would it be?

So he's all flipped out. Guess Edward and Bella got home last week, and . . .

My chest eased up.

She was alive. Or she wasn't *dead* dead, at least.

I hadn't realized how much difference it would make to me. I'd been thinking of her as dead this whole time, and I only saw that now. I saw that I'd never believed that he would bring her back alive. It shouldn't matter, because I knew what was coming next.

Yeah, bro, and here's the bad news. Charlie talked to her, said she sounded bad. She told him she's sick. Carlisle got on and told Charlie that Bella picked up some rare disease in South America. Said she's quarantined. Charlie's going crazy, 'cause even he's not allowed to see her. He says he doesn't care if he gets sick, but Carlisle wouldn't bend. No visitors. Told Charlie it was pretty serious, but that he's doing everything he can. Charlie's been stewing about it for days, but he only called Billy now. He said she sounded worse today.

The mental silence when Seth finished was profound. We all understood.

So she would die of this disease, as far as Charlie knew. Would they let him view the corpse? The pale, perfectly still, unbreathing white body? They couldn't let him touch the cold skin—he might notice how hard it was. They'd have to wait until she could hold still, could keep from killing Charlie and the other mourners. How long would that take?

Would they bury her? Would she dig herself out, or would the bloodsuckers come for her?

The others listened to my speculating in silence. I'd put a lot more thought into this than any of them.

Leah and I entered the clearing at nearly the same time. She was sure her nose led the way, though. She dropped onto her haunches beside her brother while I trotted forward to stand at Sam's right hand. Paul circled and made room for me in my place.

Beatcha again, Leah thought, but I barely heard her.

I wondered why I was the only one on my feet. My fur stood up on my shoulders, bristling with impatience.

Well, what are we waiting for? I asked.

No one said anything, but I heard their feelings of hesitation.

Oh, come on! The treaty's broken!

We have no proof—maybe she is sick. . . .

OH, PLEASE!

Okay, so the circumstantial evidence is pretty strong. Still . . .

Jacob. Sam's thought came slow, hesitant. *Are you sure this is what you want? Is it really the right thing? We all know what she wanted.*

The treaty doesn't mention anything about victim preferences, Sam!

Is she really a victim? Would you label her that way?

Yes!

Jake, Seth thought, *they aren't our enemies.*

Shut up, kid! Just 'cause you've got some kind of sick hero worship thing going on with that bloodsucker, it doesn't change the law. They are our enemies. They are in our territory. We take them out. I don't care if you had fun fighting alongside Edward Cullen once upon a time.

So what are you going to do when Bella fights with them, Jacob? Huh? Seth demanded.

She's not Bella anymore.

You gonna be the one to take her down?

I couldn't stop myself from wincing.

No, you're not. So, what? You gonna make one of us do it? And then hold a grudge against whoever it is forever?

I wouldn't. . . .

Sure you won't. You're not ready for this fight, Jacob.

Instinct took over and I crouched forward, snarling at the gangly sand-colored wolf across the circle.

Jacob! Sam cautioned. *Seth, shut up for a second.*

Seth nodded his big head.

Dang, what'd I miss? Quil thought. He was running for the gathering place full-out. *Heard about Charlie's call. . . .*

We're getting ready to go, I told him. *Why don't you swing by Kim's and drag Jared out with your teeth? We're going to need everyone.*

Come straight here, Quil, Sam ordered. *We've decided nothing yet.*

I growled.

Jacob, I have to think about what's best for this pack. I have to choose the course that protects you all best. Times have changed since our ancestors made that treaty. I . . . well, I don't honestly believe that the Cullens are a danger to us. And we know that they will not be here much longer. Surely once they've told their story, they will disappear. Our lives can return to normal.

Normal?

If we challenge them, Jacob, they will defend themselves well.

Are you afraid?

Are you so ready to lose a brother? He paused. *Or a sister?* he tacked on as an afterthought.

I'm not afraid to die.

I know that, Jacob. It's one reason I question your judgment on this.

I stared into his black eyes. *Do you intend to honor our fathers' treaty or not?*

I honor my pack. I do what's best for them.

Coward.

His muzzle tensed, pulling back over his teeth.

Enough, Jacob. You're overruled. Sam's mental voice changed, took on that strange double timbre that we could not disobey. The voice of the Alpha. He met the gaze of every wolf in the circle.

The pack is not attacking the Cullens without provocation. The spirit of the treaty remains. They are not a danger to our people, nor are they a danger to the people of Forks. Bella Swan made an informed choice, and we are not going to punish our former allies for her choice.

Hear, hear, Seth thought enthusiastically.

I thought I told you to shut it, Seth.

Oops. Sorry, Sam.

Jacob, where do you think you're going?

I left the circle, moving toward the west so that I could turn my back on him. *I'm going to tell my father goodbye. Apparently there was no purpose in me sticking around this long.*

Aw, Jake—don't do that again!

Shut up, Seth, several voices thought together.

We don't want you to leave, Sam told me, his thought softer than before.

So force me to stay, Sam. Take away my will. Make me a slave.

You know I won't do that.

Then there's nothing more to say.

I ran away from them, trying very hard not to think about what was next. Instead, I concentrated on my memories of the long wolf months, of letting the humanity bleed out of me until I was more animal than man. Living in the moment, eating when hungry, sleeping when tired, drinking when thirsty, and running—running just to run. Simple desires, simple answers to those desires. Pain came in easily managed forms. The pain of hunger. The pain of cold ice under your paws. The pain of cutting claws when dinner got feisty. Each pain had a simple answer, a clear action to end that pain.

Not like being human.

Yet, as soon as I was in jogging distance of my house, I shifted back into my human body. I needed to be able to think in privacy.

I untied my shorts and yanked them on, already running for the house.

I'd done it. I'd hidden what I was thinking and now it was too late for Sam to stop me. He couldn't hear me now.

Sam had made a very clear ruling. The pack would not attack the Cullens. Okay.

He hadn't mentioned an individual acting alone.

Nope, the pack wasn't attacking anyone today.

But I was.

9. SURE AS HELL DIDN'T SEE
THAT ONE COMING

I DIDN'T REALLY PLAN TO SAY GOODBYE TO MY FATHER.

After all, one quick call to Sam and the game would be up. They'd cut me off and push me back. Probably try to make me angry, or even hurt me—somehow force me to phase so that Sam could lay down a new law.

But Billy was expecting me, knowing I'd be in some kind of state. He was in the yard, just sitting there in his wheelchair with his eyes right on the spot where I came through the trees. I saw him judge my direction—headed straight past the house to my homemade garage.

"Got a minute, Jake?"

I skidded to a stop. I looked at him and then toward the garage.

"C'mon kid. At least help me inside."

I gritted my teeth but decided that he'd be more likely to cause trouble with Sam if I didn't lie to him for a few minutes.

"Since when do you need help, old man?"

He laughed his rumbling laugh. "My arms are tired. I pushed myself all the way here from Sue's."

"It's downhill. You coasted the whole way."

I rolled his chair up the little ramp I'd made for him and into the living room.

"Caught me. Think I got up to about thirty miles per hour. It was great."

"You're gonna wreck that chair, you know. And then you'll be dragging yourself around by your elbows."

"Not a chance. It'll be your job to carry me."

"You won't be going many places."

Billy put his hands on the wheels and steered himself to the fridge. "Any food left?"

"You got me. Paul was here all day, though, so probably not."

Billy sighed. "Have to start hiding the groceries if we're gonna avoid starvation."

"Tell Rachel to go stay at his place."

Billy's joking tone vanished, and his eyes got soft. "We've only had her home a few weeks. First time she's been here in a long time. It's hard—the girls were older than you when your mom passed. They have more trouble being in this house."

"I know."

Rebecca hadn't been home once since she got married, though she did have a good excuse. Plane tickets from Hawaii were pretty pricey. Washington State was close enough that Rachel didn't have the same defense. She'd taken classes straight through the summer semesters, working double shifts over the holidays at some café on campus. If it hadn't been for Paul, she probably would have taken off again real quick. Maybe that was why Billy wouldn't kick him out.

"Well, I'm going to go work on some stuff. . . ." I started for the back door.

"Wait up, Jake. Aren't you going to tell me what happened? Do I have to call Sam for an update?"

I stood with my back to him, hiding my face.

"Nothing happened. Sam's giving them a bye. Guess we're all just a bunch of leech lovers now."

"Jake . . ."

"I don't want to talk about it."

"Are you leaving, son?"

The room was quiet for a long time while I decided how to say it.

"Rachel can have her room back. I know she hates that air mattress."

"She'd rather sleep on the floor than lose you. So would I."

I snorted.

"Jacob, please. If you need . . . a break. Well, take it. But not so long again. Come back."

"Maybe. Maybe my gig will be weddings. Make a cameo at Sam's, then Rachel's. Jared and Kim might come first, though. Probably ought to have a suit or something."

"Jake, look at me."

I turned around slowly. "What?"

He stared into my eyes for a long minute. "Where are you going?"

"I don't really have a specific place in mind."

He cocked his head to the side, and his eyes narrowed. "Don't you?"

We stared each other down. The seconds ticked by.

"Jacob," he said. His voice was strained. "Jacob, don't. It's not worth it."

"I don't know what you're talking about."

"Leave Bella and the Cullens be. Sam is right."

I stared at him for a second, and then I crossed the room in two long strides. I grabbed the phone and disconnected the cable from the box and the jack. I wadded the gray cord up in the palm of my hand.

"Bye, Dad."

"Jake, wait—," he called after me, but I was out the door, running.

The motorcycle wasn't as fast as running, but it was more discreet. I wondered how long it would take Billy to wheel himself down to the store and then get someone on the phone who could get a message to Sam. I'd bet Sam was still in his wolf form. The problem would be if Paul came back to our place anytime soon. He could phase in a second and let Sam know what I was doing. . . .

I wasn't going to worry about it. I would go as fast as I could, and if they caught me, I'd deal with that when I had to.

I kicked the bike to life and then I was racing down the muddy lane. I didn't look behind me as I passed the house.

The highway was busy with tourist traffic; I wove in and

out of the cars, earning a bunch of honks and a few fingers. I took the turn onto the 101 at seventy, not bothering to look. I had to ride the line for a minute to avoid getting smeared by a minivan. Not that it would have killed me, but it would have slowed me down. Broken bones—the big ones, at least—took *days* to heal completely, as I had good cause to know.

The freeway cleared up a little, and I pushed the bike to eighty. I didn't touch the brake until I was close to the narrow drive; I figured I was in the clear then. Sam wouldn't come this far to stop me. It was too late.

It wasn't until that moment—when I was sure that I'd made it—that I started to think about what exactly I was going to do now. I slowed down to twenty, taking the twists through the trees more carefully than I needed to.

I knew they would hear me coming, bike or no bike, so surprise was out. There was no way to disguise my intentions. Edward would hear my plan as soon as I was close enough. Maybe he already could. But I thought this would still work out, because I had his ego on my side. He'd *want* to fight me alone.

So I'd just walk in, see Sam's precious evidence for myself, and then challenge Edward to a duel.

I snorted. The parasite'd probably get a kick out of the theatrics of it.

When I finished with him, I'd take as many of the rest of them as I could before they got me. Huh—I wondered if Sam would consider my death *provocation*. Probably say I got what I deserved. Wouldn't want to offend his bloodsucker BFFs.

The drive opened up into the meadow, and the smell hit

me like a rotten tomato to the face. Ugh. Reeking vampires. My stomach started churning. The stench would be hard to take this way—undiluted by the scent of humans as it had been the other time I'd come here—though not as bad as smelling it through my wolf nose.

I wasn't sure what to expect, but there was no sign of life around the big white crypt. Of course they knew I was here.

I cut the engine and listened to the quiet. Now I could hear tense, angry murmurs from just the other side of the wide double doors. Someone was home. I heard my name and I smiled, happy to think I was causing them a little stress.

I took one big gulp of air—it would only be worse inside—and leaped up the porch stairs in one bound.

The door opened before my fist touched it, and the doctor stood in the frame, his eyes grave.

"Hello, Jacob," he said, calmer than I would have expected. "How are you?"

I took a deep breath through my mouth. The reek pouring through the door was overpowering.

I was disappointed that it was Carlisle who answered. I'd rather Edward had come through the door, fangs out. Carlisle was so . . . just *human* or something. Maybe it was the house calls he made last spring when I got busted up. But it made me uncomfortable to look into his face and know that I was planning to kill him if I could.

"I heard Bella made it back alive," I said.

"Er, Jacob, it's not really the best time." The doctor seemed uncomfortable, too, but not in the way I expected. "Could we do this later?"

I stared at him, dumbfounded. Was he asking to post-pone the death match for a more convenient time?

And then I heard Bella's voice, cracked and rough, and I couldn't think about anything else.

"Why not?" she asked someone. "Are we keeping secrets from Jacob, too? What's the point?"

Her voice was not what I was expecting. I tried to remember the voices of the young vampires we'd fought in the spring, but all I'd registered was snarling. Maybe those newborns hadn't had the piercing, ringing sound of the older ones, either. Maybe all new vampires sounded hoarse.

"Come in, please, Jacob," Bella croaked more loudly.

Carlisle's eyes tightened.

I wondered if Bella was thirsty. My eyes narrowed, too.

"Excuse me," I said to the doctor as I stepped around him. It was hard—it went against all my instincts to turn my back to one of them. Not impossible, though. If there was such a thing as a safe vampire, it was the strangely gentle leader.

I would stay away from Carlisle when the fight started. There were enough of them to kill without including him.

I sidestepped into the house, keeping my back to the wall. My eyes swept the room—it was unfamiliar. The last time I'd been in here it had been all done up for a party. Everything was bright and pale now. Including the six vampires standing in a group by the white sofa.

They were all here, all together, but that was not what froze me where I stood and had my jaw dropping to the floor.

It was Edward. It was the expression on his face.

I'd seen him angry, and I'd seen him arrogant, and once I'd seen him in pain. But this—this was beyond agony. His eyes were half-crazed. He didn't look up to glare at me. He stared down at the couch beside him with an expression like someone had lit him on fire. His hands were rigid claws at his side.

I couldn't even enjoy his anguish. I could only think of one thing that would make him look like that, and my eyes followed his.

I saw her at the same moment that I caught her scent.

Her warm, clean, human scent.

Bella was half-hidden behind the arm of the sofa, curled up in a loose fetal position, her arms wrapped around her knees. For a long second I could see nothing except that she was still the Bella that I loved, her skin still a soft, pale peach, her eyes still the same chocolate brown. My heart thudded a strange, broken meter, and I wondered if this was just some lying dream that I was about to wake up from.

Then I really saw her.

There were deep circles under her eyes, dark circles that jumped out because her face was all haggard. Was she thinner? Her skin seemed tight—like her cheekbones might break right through it. Most of her dark hair was pulled away from her face into a messy knot, but a few strands stuck limply to her forehead and neck, to the sheen of sweat that covered her skin. There was something about her fingers and wrists that looked so fragile it was scary.

She *was* sick. Very sick.

Not a lie. The story Charlie'd told Billy was not a story. While I stared, eyes bugging, her skin turned light green.

The blond bloodsucker—the showy one, Rosalie—bent over her, cutting into my view, hovering in a strange, protective way.

This was wrong. I knew how Bella felt about almost everything—her thoughts were so obvious; sometimes it was like they were printed on her forehead. So she didn't have to tell me every detail of a situation for me to get it. I knew that Bella didn't like Rosalie. I'd seen it in the set of her lips when she talked about her. Not just that she didn't like her. She was *afraid* of Rosalie. Or she had been.

There was no fear as Bella glanced up at her now. Her expression was . . . apologetic or something. Then Rosalie snatched a basin from the floor and held it under Bella's chin just in time for Bella to throw up noisily into it.

Edward fell to his knees by Bella's side—his eyes all tortured-looking—and Rosalie held out her hand, warning him to keep back.

None of it made sense.

When she could raise her head, Bella smiled weakly at me, sort of embarrassed. "Sorry about that," she whispered to me.

Edward moaned real quiet. His head slumped against Bella's knees. She put one of her hands against his cheek. Like she was comforting *him*.

I didn't realize my legs had carried me forward until Rosalie hissed at me, suddenly appearing between me and the couch. She was like a person on a TV screen. I didn't care she was there. She didn't seem real.

"Rose, don't," Bella whispered. "It's fine."

Blondie moved out of my way, though I could tell she hated to do it. Scowling at me, she crouched by Bella's head, tensed to spring. She was easier to ignore than I ever would have dreamed.

"Bella, what's wrong?" I whispered. Without thinking about it, I found myself on my knees, too, leaning over the back of the couch across from her . . . husband. He didn't seem to notice me, and I barely glanced at him. I reached out for her free hand, taking it in both of mine. Her skin was icy. "Are you all right?"

It was a stupid question. She didn't answer it.

"I'm so glad you came to see me today, Jacob," she said.

Even though I knew Edward couldn't hear her thoughts, he seemed to hear some meaning I didn't. He moaned again, into the blanket that covered her, and she stroked his cheek.

"What is it, Bella?" I insisted, wrapping my hands tight around her cold, fragile fingers.

Instead of answering, she glanced around the room like she was searching for something, both a plea and a warning in her look. Six pairs of anxious yellow eyes stared back at her. Finally, she turned to Rosalie.

"Help me up, Rose?" she asked.

Rosalie's lips pulled back over her teeth, and she glared up at me like she wanted to rip my throat out. I was sure that was exactly the case.

"Please, Rose."

The blonde made a face, but leaned over her again, next to Edward, who didn't move an inch. She put her arm carefully behind Bella's shoulders.

"No," I whispered. "Don't get up. . . ." She looked so weak.

"I'm answering your question," she snapped, sounding a little bit more like the way she usually talked to me.

Rosalie pulled Bella off the couch. Edward stayed where he was, sagging forward till his face was buried in the cushions. The blanket fell to the ground at Bella's feet.

Bella's body was swollen, her torso ballooning out in a strange, sick way. It strained against the faded gray sweatshirt that was way too big for her shoulders and arms. The rest of her seemed thinner, like the big bulge had grown out of what it had sucked from her. It took me a second to realize what the deformed part was—I didn't understand until she folded her hands tenderly around her bloated stomach, one above and one below. Like she was cradling it.

I saw it then, but I still couldn't believe it. I'd seen her just a month ago. There was no way she could be pregnant. Not *that* pregnant.

Except that she was.

I didn't want to see this, didn't want to think about this. I didn't want to imagine him inside her. I didn't want to know that something I hated so much had taken root in the body I loved. My stomach heaved, and I had to swallow back vomit.

But it was worse than that, so much worse. Her distorted body, the bones jabbing against the skin of her face. I could only guess that she looked like this—so pregnant, so sick— because whatever was inside her was taking her life to feed its own. . . .

Because it was a monster. Just like its father.

I always knew he would kill her.

His head snapped up as he heard the words inside mine. One second we were both on our knees, and then he was on his feet, towering over me. His eyes were flat black, the circles under them dark purple.

"Outside, Jacob," he snarled.

I was on my feet, too. Looking down on him now. This was why I was here.

"Let's do this," I agreed.

The big one, Emmett, pushed forward on Edward's other side, with the hungry-looking one, Jasper, right behind him. I really didn't care. Maybe my pack would clean up the scraps when they finished me off. Maybe not. It didn't matter.

For the tiniest part of a second my eyes touched on the two standing in the back. Esme. Alice. Small and distractingly feminine. Well, I was sure the others would kill me before I had to do anything about them. I didn't want to kill girls . . . even vampire girls.

Though I might make an exception for that blonde.

"No," Bella gasped, and she stumbled forward, out of balance, to clutch at Edward's arm. Rosalie moved with her, like there was a chain locking them to each other.

"I just need to talk to him, Bella," Edward said in a low voice, talking only to her. He reached up to touch her face, to stroke it. This made the room turn red, made me see fire—that, after all he'd done to her, he was still allowed to touch her that way. "Don't strain yourself," he went on, pleading. "Please rest. We'll both be back in just a few minutes."

She stared at his face, reading it carefully. Then she nodded and drooped toward the couch. Rosalie helped lower her back onto the cushions. Bella stared at me, trying to hold my eyes.

"Behave," she insisted. "And then come back."

I didn't answer. I wasn't making any promises today. I looked away and then followed Edward out the front door.

A random, disjointed voice in my head noted that separating him from the coven hadn't been so difficult, had it?

He kept walking, never checking to see if I was about to spring at his unprotected back. I supposed he didn't need to check. He would know when I decided to attack. Which meant I'd have to make that decision very quickly.

"I'm not ready for you to kill me yet, Jacob Black," he whispered as he paced quickly away from the house. "You'll have to have a little patience."

Like I cared about his schedule. I growled under my breath. "Patience isn't my specialty."

He kept walking, maybe a couple hundred yards down the drive away from the house, with me right on his heels. I was all hot, my fingers trembling. On the edge, ready and waiting.

He stopped without warning and pivoted to face me. His expression froze me again.

For a second I was just a kid—a kid who had lived all of his life in the same tiny town. Just a child. Because I knew I would have to live a lot more, suffer a lot more, to ever understand the searing agony in Edward's eyes.

He raised a hand as if to wipe sweat from his forehead, but his fingers scraped against his face like they were going to rip his granite skin right off. His black eyes burned in their sockets, out of focus, or seeing things that weren't there. His mouth opened like he was going to scream, but nothing came out.

This was the face a man would have if he were burning at the stake.

For a moment I couldn't speak. It was too real, this face—I'd seen a shadow of it in the house, seen it in her eyes and his, but this made it final. The last nail in her coffin.

"It's killing her, right? She's dying." And I knew when I said it that my face was a watered-down echo of his. Weaker, different, because I was still in shock. I hadn't wrapped my head around it yet—it was happening too fast. He'd had time to get to this point. And it was different because I'd already lost her so many times, so many ways, in my head. And different because she was never really mine to lose.

And different because this wasn't my fault.

"My fault," Edward whispered, and his knees gave out. He crumpled in front of me, vulnerable, the easiest target you could imagine.

But I felt cold as snow—there was no fire in me.

"Yes," he groaned into the dirt, like he was confessing to the ground. "Yes, it's killing her."

His broken helplessness irritated me. I wanted a fight, not an execution. Where was his smug superiority now?

"So why hasn't Carlisle done anything?" I growled. "He's a doctor, right? Get it out of her."

He looked up then and answered me in a tired voice. Like he was explaining this to a kindergartener for the tenth time. "She won't let us."

It took a minute for the words to sink in. Jeez, she was running true to form. Of course, die for the monster spawn. It was so *Bella*.

"You know her well," he whispered. "How quickly you see. . . . I didn't see. Not in time. She wouldn't talk to me

on the way home, not really. I thought she was frightened—
that would be natural. I thought she was angry with me for
putting her through this, for endangering her life. Again.
I never imagined what she was really thinking, what she
was *resolving*. Not until my family met us at the airport
and she ran right into Rosalie's arms. Rosalie's! And then I
heard what Rosalie was thinking. I didn't understand until
I heard that. Yet *you* understand after one second. . . ." He
half-sighed, half-groaned.

"Just back up a second. She won't *let* you." The sarcasm
was acid on my tongue. "Did you ever notice that she's exactly
as strong as a normal hundred-and-ten-pound human girl?
How stupid are you vamps? Hold her down and knock her
out with drugs."

"I wanted to," he whispered. "Carlisle would have. . . ."

What, too noble were they?

"No. Not noble. Her bodyguard complicated things."

Oh. His story hadn't made much sense before, but it fit
together now. So that's what Blondie was up to. What was
in it for her, though? Did the beauty queen want Bella to
die so bad?

"Maybe," he said. "Rosalie doesn't look at it quite that
way."

"So take the blonde out first. Your kind can be put back
together, right? Turn her into a jigsaw and take care of
Bella."

"Emmett and Esme are backing her up. Emmett would
never let us . . . and Carlisle won't help me with Esme against
it. . . ." He trailed off, his voice disappearing.

"You should have left Bella with me."

"Yes."

It was a bit late for that, though. Maybe he should have thought about all this *before* he knocked her up with the life-sucking monster.

He stared up at me from inside his own personal hell, and I could see that he agreed with me.

"We didn't know," he said, the words as quiet as a breath. "I never dreamed. There's never been anything like Bella and I before. How could we know that a human was able to conceive a child with one of us—"

"When the human should get ripped to shreds in the process?"

"Yes," he agreed in a tense whisper. "They're out there, the sadistic ones, the incubus, the succubus. They exist. But the seduction is merely a prelude to the feast. No one *survives.*" He shook his head like the idea revolted him. Like he was any different.

"I didn't realize they had a special name for what you are," I spit.

He stared up at me with a face that looked a thousand years old.

"Even you, Jacob Black, cannot hate me as much as I hate myself."

Wrong, I thought, too enraged to speak.

"Killing me now doesn't save her," he said quietly.

"So what does?"

"Jacob, you have to do something for me."

"The *hell* I do, parasite!"

He kept staring at me with those half-tired, half-crazy eyes. "For her?"

I clenched my teeth together hard. "I did everything I could to keep her away from you. Every single thing. It's too late."

"You know her, Jacob. You connect to her on a level that I don't even understand. You are part of her, and she is part of you. She won't listen to me, because she thinks I'm underestimating her. She thinks she's strong enough for this. . . ." He choked and then swallowed. "She might listen to you."

"Why would she?"

He lurched to his feet, his eyes burning brighter than before, wilder. I wondered if he was really going crazy. Could vampires lose their minds?

"Maybe," he answered my thought. "I don't know. It feels like it." He shook his head. "I have to try to hide this in front of her, because stress makes her more ill. She can't keep anything down as it is. I have to be composed; I can't make it harder. But that doesn't matter now. She has to listen to you!"

"I can't tell her anything you haven't. What do you want me to do? Tell her she's stupid? She probably already knows that. Tell her she's going to die? I bet she knows that, too."

"You can offer her what she wants."

He wasn't making any sense. Part of the crazy?

"I don't care about anything but keeping her alive," he said, suddenly focused now. "If it's a child she wants, she can have it. She can have half a dozen babies. Anything she wants." He paused for one beat. "She can have puppies, if that's what it takes."

He met my stare for a moment and his face was frenzied under the thin layer of control. My hard scowl crumbled as I processed his words, and I felt my mouth pop open in shock.

"But not this way!" he hissed before I could recover. "Not this *thing* that's sucking the life from her while I stand there helpless! Watching her sicken and waste away. Seeing it *hurting* her." He sucked in a fast breath like someone had punched him in the gut. "You *have* to make her see reason, Jacob. She won't listen to me anymore. Rosalie's always there, feeding her insanity—encouraging her. Protecting her. No, protecting *it*. Bella's life means nothing to her."

The noise coming from my throat sounded like I was choking.

What was he saying? That Bella should, what? Have a baby? With *me*? What? How? Was he giving her up? Or did he think she wouldn't mind being shared?

"Whichever. Whatever keeps her alive."

"That's the craziest thing you've said yet," I mumbled.

"She loves you."

"Not enough."

"She's ready to die to have a child. Maybe she'd accept something less extreme."

"Don't you know her at all?"

"I know, I know. It's going to take a lot of convincing. That's why I need you. You know how she thinks. Make her see sense."

I couldn't think about what he was suggesting. It was too much. Impossible. Wrong. Sick. Borrowing Bella for the weekends and then returning her Monday morning like a rental movie? So messed up.

So tempting.

I didn't want to consider, didn't want to imagine, but

the images came anyway. I'd fantasized about Bella that way too many times, back when there was still a possibility of *us*, and then long after it was clear that the fantasies would only leave festering sores because there was no possibility, none at all. I hadn't been able to help myself then. I couldn't stop myself now. Bella in *my* arms, Bella sighing *my* name . . .

Worse still, this new image I'd never had before, one that by all rights shouldn't have existed for me. Not yet. An image I knew I wouldn't've suffered over for *years* if he hadn't shoved it in my head now. But it stuck there, winding threads through my brain like a weed—poisonous and unkillable. Bella, healthy and glowing, so different than now, but something the same: her body, not distorted, changed in a more natural way. Round with *my* child.

I tried to escape the venomous weed in my mind. "Make *Bella* see sense? What universe do you live in?"

"At least try."

I shook my head fast. He waited, ignoring the negative answer because he could hear the conflict in my thoughts.

"Where is this psycho crap coming from? Are you making this up as you go?"

"I've been thinking of nothing but ways to save her since I realized what she was planning to do. What she would die to do. But I didn't know how to contact you. I knew you wouldn't listen if I called. I would have come to find you soon, if you hadn't come today. But it's hard to leave her, even for a few minutes. Her condition . . . it changes so fast. The thing is . . . growing. Swiftly. I can't be away from her now."

"What *is* it?"

"None of us have any idea. But it is stronger than she is. Already."

I could suddenly see it then—see the swelling monster in my head, breaking her from the inside out.

"Help me stop it," he whispered. "Help me stop this from happening."

"*How?* By offering my stud services?" He didn't even flinch when I said that, but I did. "You're really sick. She'll never listen to this."

"Try. There's nothing to lose now. How will it hurt?"

It would hurt me. Hadn't I taken enough rejection from Bella without this?

"A little pain to save her? Is it such a high cost?"

"But it won't work."

"Maybe not. Maybe it will confuse her, though. Maybe she'll falter in her resolve. One moment of doubt is all I need."

"And then you pull the rug out from under the offer? 'Just kidding, Bella'?"

"If she wants a child, that's what she gets. I won't rescind."

I couldn't believe I was even thinking about this. Bella would punch me—not that I cared about that, but it would probably break her hand again. I shouldn't let him talk to me, mess with my head. I should just kill him now.

"Not now," he whispered. "Not yet. Right or wrong, it would destroy her, and you know it. No need to be hasty. If she won't listen to you, you'll get your chance. The moment Bella's heart stops beating, I will be begging for you to kill me."

"You won't have to beg long."

The hint of a worn smile tugged at the corner of his mouth. "I'm very much counting on that."

"Then we have a deal."

He nodded and held out his cold stone hand.

Swallowing my disgust, I reached out to take his hand. My fingers closed around the rock, and I shook it once.

"We have a deal," he agreed.

10. WHY DIDN'T I JUST WALK AWAY? OH RIGHT, BECAUSE I'M AN IDIOT.

I FELT LIKE—LIKE I DON'T KNOW WHAT. LIKE THIS WASN'T real. Like I was in some Goth version of a bad sitcom. Instead of being the A/V dweeb about to ask the head cheerleader to the prom, I was the finished-second-place werewolf about to ask the vampire's wife to shack up and procreate. Nice.

No, I wouldn't do it. It was twisted and wrong. I was going to forget all about what he'd said.

But I would talk to her. I'd try to make her listen to me.

And she wouldn't. Just like always.

Edward didn't answer or comment on my thoughts as he led the way back to the house. I wondered about the place that he'd chosen to stop. Was it far enough from the house that the others couldn't hear his whispers? Was that the point?

Maybe. When we walked through the door, the other Cullens' eyes were suspicious and confused. No one looked disgusted or outraged. So they must not have heard either favor Edward had asked me for.

I hesitated in the open doorway, not sure what to do now. It was better right there, with a little bit of breathable air blowing in from outside.

Edward walked into the middle of the huddle, shoulders stiff. Bella watched him anxiously, and then her eyes flickered to me for a second. Then she was watching him again.

Her face turned a grayish pale, and I could see what he meant about the stress making her feel worse.

"We're going to let Jacob and Bella speak privately," Edward said. There was no inflection at all in his voice. Robotic.

"Over my pile of ashes," Rosalie hissed at him. She was still hovering by Bella's head, one of her cold hands placed possessively on Bella's sallow cheek.

Edward didn't look at her. "Bella," he said in that same empty tone. "Jacob wants to talk to you. Are you afraid to be alone with him?"

Bella looked at me, confused. Then she looked at Rosalie.

"Rose, it's fine. Jake's not going to hurt us. Go with Edward."

"It might be a trick," the blonde warned.

"I don't see how," Bella said.

"Carlisle and I will always be in your sight, Rosalie,"

Edward said. The emotionless voice was cracking, showing the anger through it. "We're the ones she's afraid of."

"No," Bella whispered. Her eyes were glistening, her lashes wet. "No, Edward. I'm not. . . ."

He shook his head, smiling a little. The smile was painful to look at. "I didn't mean it that way, Bella. I'm fine. Don't worry about me."

Sickening. He was right—she was beating herself up about hurting his feelings. The girl was a classic martyr. She'd totally been born in the wrong century. She should have lived back when she could have gotten herself fed to some lions for a good cause.

"Everyone," Edward said, his hand stiffly motioning toward the door. "Please."

The composure he was trying to keep up for Bella was shaky. I could see how close he was to that burning man he'd been outside. The others saw it, too. Silently, they moved out the door while I shifted out of the way. They moved fast; my heart beat twice, and the room was cleared except for Rosalie, hesitating in the middle of the floor, and Edward, still waiting by the door.

"Rose," Bella said quietly. "I want you to go."

The blonde glared at Edward and then gestured for him to go first. He disappeared out the door. She gave me a long warning glower, and then she disappeared, too.

Once we were alone, I crossed the room and sat on the floor next to Bella. I took both her cold hands in mine, rubbing them carefully.

"Thanks, Jake. That feels good."

"I'm not going to lie, Bells. You're hideous."

"I know," she sighed. "I'm scary-looking."

"Thing-from-the-swamp scary," I agreed.

She laughed. "It's so good having you here. It feels nice to smile. I don't know how much more drama I can stand."

I rolled my eyes.

"Okay, okay," she agreed. "I bring it on myself."

"Yeah, you do. What're you thinking, Bells? Seriously!"

"Did he ask you to yell at me?"

"Sort of. Though I can't figure why he thinks you'd listen to me. You never have before."

She sighed.

"I told you—," I started to say.

"Did you know that '*I told you so*' has a brother, Jacob?" she asked, cutting me off. "His name is '*Shut the hell up.*'"

"Good one."

She grinned at me. Her skin stretched tight over the bones. "I can't take credit—I got it off a rerun of *The Simpsons.*"

"Missed that one."

"It was funny."

We didn't talk for a minute. Her hands were starting to warm up a little.

"Did he really ask you to talk to me?"

I nodded. "To talk some sense into you. *There's* a battle that's lost before it starts."

"So why did you agree?"

I didn't answer. I wasn't sure I knew.

I did know this—every second I spent with her was only going to add to the pain I would have to suffer later. Like a junkie with a limited supply, the day of reckoning was coming for me. The more hits I took now, the harder it would be when my supply ran out.

"It'll work out, you know," she said after a quiet minute. "I believe that."

That made me see red again. "Is dementia one of your symptoms?" I snapped.

She laughed, though my anger was so real that my hands were shaking around hers.

"Maybe," she said. "I'm not saying things will work out *easily*, Jake. But how could I have lived through all that I've lived through and not believe in magic by this point?"

"*Magic?*"

"Especially for you," she said. She was smiling. She pulled one of her hands away from mine and pressed it against my cheek. Warmer than before, but it felt cool against my skin, like most things did. "More than anyone else, you've got some magic waiting to make things right for you."

"What are you babbling about?"

Still smiling. "Edward told me once what it was like— your imprinting thing. He said it was like *A Midsummer Night's Dream*, like magic. You'll find who you're really looking for, Jacob, and maybe then all of this will make sense."

If she hadn't looked so fragile I would've been screaming.

As it was, I *did* growl at her.

"If you think that imprinting could ever make sense of this *insanity* . . ." I struggled for words. "Do you really think that just because I might someday imprint on some stranger it would make this right?" I jabbed a finger toward her swollen body. "Tell me what the point was then,

Bella! What was the point of me loving you? What was the point of *you* loving *him*? When you die"—the words were a snarl—"how is that ever right again? What's the point to all the pain? Mine, yours, his! You'll kill him, too, not that I care about that." She flinched, but I kept going. "So what was the point of your twisted love story, in the end? If there is *any* sense, please show me, Bella, because I don't see it."

She sighed. "I don't know yet, Jake. But I just . . . feel . . . that this is all going somewhere good, hard to see as it is now. I guess you could call it *faith*."

"You're dying for *nothing*, Bella! Nothing!"

Her hand dropped from my face to her bloated stomach, caressed it. She didn't have to say the words for me to know what she was thinking. She was dying for *it*.

"I'm not going to die," she said through her teeth, and I could tell she was repeating things she'd said before. "I *will* keep my heart beating. I'm strong enough for that."

"That's a load of crap, Bella. You've been trying to keep up with the supernatural for too long. No normal person can do it. You're *not* strong enough." I took her face in my hand. I didn't have to remind myself to be gentle. Everything about her screamed *breakable*.

"I can do this. I can do this," she muttered, sounding a lot like that kids' book about the little engine that could.

"Doesn't look like it to me. So what's your plan? I hope you have one."

She nodded, not meeting my eyes. "Did you know Esme jumped off a cliff? When she was human, I mean."

"So?"

"So she was close enough to dead that they didn't even

bother taking her to the emergency room—they took her right around to the morgue. Her heart was still beating, though, when Carlisle found her. . . ."

That's what she'd meant before, about keeping her heart beating.

"You're not planning on surviving this human," I stated dully.

"No. I'm not stupid." She met my stare then. "I guess you probably have your own opinion on that point, though."

"Emergency vampirization," I mumbled.

"It worked for Esme. And Emmett, and Rosalie, and even Edward. None of them were in such great shape. Carlisle only changed them because it was that or death. He doesn't end lives, he saves them."

I felt a sudden twinge of guilt about the good vampire doctor, like before. I shoved the thought away and started in on the begging.

"Listen to me, Bells. Don't do it that way." Like before, when the call from Charlie had come, I could see how much difference it really made to me. I realized I needed her to stay alive, in some form. In any form. I took a deep breath. "Don't wait until it's too late, Bella. Not that way. Live. Okay? Just live. Don't do this to me. Don't do it to him." My voice got harder, louder. "You know what he's going to do when you die. You've seen it before. You want him to go back to those Italian killers?" She cringed into the sofa.

I left out the part about how that wouldn't be necessary this time.

Struggling to make my voice softer, I asked, "Remember when I got mangled up by those newborns? What did you tell me?"

I waited, but she wouldn't answer. She pressed her lips together.

"You told me to be good and listen to Carlisle," I reminded her. "And what did I do? I listened to the vampire. For you."

"You listened because it was the right thing to do."

"Okay—pick either reason."

She took a deep breath. "It's not the right thing now." Her gaze touched her big round stomach and she whispered under her breath, "I won't kill him."

My hands shook again. "Oh, I hadn't heard the great news. A bouncing baby boy, huh? Shoulda brought some blue balloons."

Her face turned pink. The color was so beautiful—it twisted in my stomach like a knife. A serrated knife, rusty and ragged.

I was going to lose this. Again.

"I don't know he's a boy," she admitted, a little sheepish. "The ultrasound wouldn't work. The membrane around the baby is too hard—like their skin. So he's a little mystery. But I always see a boy in my head."

"It's not some pretty baby in there, Bella."

"We'll see," she said. Almost smug.

"*You* won't," I snarled.

"You're very pessimistic, Jacob. There is definitely a chance that I might walk away from this."

I couldn't answer. I looked down and breathed deep and slow, trying to get a grip on my fury.

"Jake," she said, and she patted my hair, stroked my cheek. "It's going to be okay. Shh. It's okay."

I didn't look up. "No. It will not be okay."

She wiped something wet from my cheek. "Shh."

"What's the deal, Bella?" I stared at the pale carpet. My bare feet were dirty, leaving smudges. Good. "I thought the whole point was that you wanted your vampire more than anything. And now you're just giving him up? That doesn't make any sense. Since when are you desperate to be a mom? If you wanted that so much, why did you marry a vampire?"

I was dangerously close to that offer he wanted me to make. I could see the words taking me that way, but I couldn't change their direction.

She sighed. "It's not like that. I didn't really care about having a baby. I didn't even think about it. It's not just having a baby. It's . . . well . . . *this* baby."

"It's a killer, Bella. Look at yourself."

"He's not. It's me. I'm just weak and human. But I can tough this out, Jake, I can—"

"Aw, *come on!* Shut up, Bella. You can spout this crap to your bloodsucker, but you're not fooling me. You know you're not going to make it."

She glared at me. "I do not *know* that. I'm worried about it, sure."

"*Worried* about it," I repeated through my teeth.

She gasped then and clutched at her stomach. My fury vanished like a light switch being turned off.

"I'm fine," she panted. "It's nothing."

But I didn't hear; her hands had pulled her sweatshirt to the side, and I stared, horrified, at the skin it exposed. Her stomach looked like it was stained with big splotches of purple-black ink.

She saw my stare, and she yanked the fabric back in place.

"He's strong, that's all," she said defensively.

The ink spots were bruises.

I almost gagged, and I understood what he'd said, about watching it hurt her. Suddenly, I felt a little crazy myself.

"Bella," I said.

She heard the change in my voice. She looked up, still breathing heavy, her eyes confused.

"Bella, don't do this."

"Jake—"

"Listen to me. Don't get your back up yet. Okay? Just listen. What if . . . ?"

"What if what?"

"What if this wasn't a one-shot deal? What if it wasn't all or nothing? What if you just listened to Carlisle like a good girl, and kept yourself alive?"

"I won't—"

"I'm not done yet. So you stay alive. Then you can start over. This didn't work out. Try again."

She frowned. She raised one hand and touched the place where my eyebrows were mashing together. Her fingers smoothed my forehead for a moment while she tried to make sense of it.

"I don't understand. . . . What do you mean, try again? You can't think Edward would let me . . . ? And what difference would it make? I'm sure any baby—"

"Yes," I snapped. "Any kid *of his* would be the same."

Her tired face just got more confused. "What?"

But I couldn't say any more. There was no point. I would never be able to save her from herself. I'd never been able to do that.

Then she blinked, and I could see she got it.

"Oh. Ugh. *Please*, Jacob. You think I should kill my baby and replace it with some generic substitute? Artificial insemination?" She was mad now. "Why would I want to have some stranger's baby? I suppose it just doesn't make a difference? Any baby will do?"

"I didn't mean that," I muttered. "Not a stranger."

She leaned forward. "Then what are you saying?"

"Nothing. I'm saying nothing. Same as ever."

"Where did that come from?"

"Forget it, Bella."

She frowned, suspicious. "Did *he* tell you to say that?"

I hesitated, surprised that she'd made that leap so quick. "No."

"He did, didn't he?"

"No, really. He didn't say anything about artificial whatever."

Her face softened then, and she sank back against the pillows, looking exhausted. She stared off to the side when she spoke, not talking to me at all. "He would do anything for me. And I'm hurting him so much. . . . But what is he thinking? That I would trade this"—her hand traced across her belly—"for some stranger's . . ." She mumbled the last part, and then her voice trailed off. Her eyes were wet.

"You don't have to hurt him," I whispered. It burned like poison in my mouth to beg for him, but I knew this angle was probably my best bet for keeping her alive. Still a thousand-to-one odds. "You could make him happy again, Bella. And I really think he's losing it. Honestly, I do."

She didn't seem to be listening; her hand made small circles on her battered stomach while she chewed on her lip.

It was quiet for a long time. I wondered if the Cullens were very far away. Were they listening to my pathetic attempts to reason with her?

"Not a stranger?" she murmured to herself. I flinched. "What exactly did Edward say to you?" she asked in a low voice.

"Nothing. He just thought you might listen to me."

"Not that. About trying again."

Her eyes locked on mine, and I could see that I'd already given too much away.

"Nothing."

Her mouth fell open a little. "Wow."

It was silent for a few heartbeats. I looked down at my feet again, unable to meet her stare.

"He really would do *anything*, wouldn't he?" she whispered.

"I told you he was going crazy. Literally, Bells."

"I'm surprised you didn't tell on him right away. Get him in trouble."

When I looked up, she was grinning.

"Thought about it." I tried to grin back, but I could feel the smile mangle on my face.

She knew what I was offering, and she wasn't going to think twice about it. I'd known that she wouldn't. But it still stung.

"There isn't much you wouldn't do for me, either, is there?" she whispered. "I really don't know why you bother. I don't deserve either of you."

"It makes no difference, though, does it?"

"Not this time." She sighed. "I wish I could explain it to you right so that you would understand. I can't hurt him"—she pointed to her stomach—"any more than I could pick up a gun and shoot you. I love him."

"Why do you always have to love the wrong things, Bella?"

"I don't think I do."

I cleared the lump out of my throat so that I could make my voice hard like I wanted it. "Trust me."

I started to get to my feet.

"Where are you going?"

"I'm not doing any good here."

She held out her thin hand, pleading. "Don't go."

I could feel the addiction sucking at me, trying to keep me near her.

"I don't belong here. I've got to get back."

"Why did you come today?" she asked, still reaching limply.

"Just to see if you were really alive. I didn't believe you were sick like Charlie said."

I couldn't tell from her face whether she bought that or not.

"Will you come back again? Before . . ."

"I'm not going to hang around and watch you die, Bella."

She flinched. "You're right, you're right. You *should* go."

I headed for the door.

"Bye," she whispered behind me. "Love you, Jake."

I almost went back. I almost turned around and fell down on my knees and started begging again. But I knew that I had to quit Bella, quit her cold turkey, before she killed me, like she was going to kill him.

"Sure, sure," I mumbled on my way out.

I didn't see any of the vampires. I ignored my bike, standing all alone in the middle of the meadow. It wasn't fast enough for me now. My dad would be freaked out—Sam, too. What would the pack make of the fact that they hadn't heard me phase? Would they think the Cullens got me before I'd had the chance? I stripped down, not caring who might be watching, and started running. I blurred into wolf mid-stride.

They were waiting. Of course they were.

Jacob, Jake, eight voices chorused in relief.

Come home now, the Alpha voice ordered. Sam was furious.

I felt Paul fade out, and I knew Billy and Rachel were waiting to hear what had happened to me. Paul was too anxious to give them the good news that I wasn't vampire chow to listen to the whole story.

I didn't have to tell the pack I was on my way—they could see the forest blurring past me as I sprinted for home. I didn't have to tell them that I was half-past crazy, either. The sickness in my head was obvious.

They saw all the horror—Bella's mottled stomach; her raspy voice: *he's strong, that's all*; the burning man in Edward's face: *watching her sicken and waste away . . . seeing it hurting her*; Rosalie crouched over Bella's limp body: *Bella's life means nothing to her*—and for once, no one had anything to say.

Their shock was just a silent shout in my head. Wordless.

!!!!

I was halfway home before anyone recovered. Then they all started running to meet me.

It was almost dark—the clouds covered the sunset completely. I risked darting across the freeway and made it without being seen.

We met up about ten miles out of La Push, in a clearing left by the loggers. It was out of the way, wedged between two spurs of the mountain, where no one would see us. Paul found them when I did, so the pack was complete.

The babble in my head was total chaos. Everyone shouting at once.

Sam's hackles were sticking straight up, and he was growling in an unbroken stream as he paced back and forth around the top of the ring. Paul and Jared moved like shadows behind him, their ears flat against the sides of their head. The whole circle was agitated, on their feet and snarling in low bursts.

At first their anger was undefined, and I thought I was in for it. I was too messed up to care about that. They could do whatever they wanted to me for circumventing orders.

And then the unfocused confusion of thoughts began to move together.

How can this be? What does it mean? What will it be?

Not safe. Not right. Dangerous.

Unnatural. Monstrous. An abomination.

We can't allow it.

The pack was pacing in synchronization now, thinking in synchronization, all but myself and one other. I sat beside whichever brother it was, too dazed to look over with either my eyes or my mind and see who was next to me, while the pack circled around us.

The treaty does not cover this.

This puts everyone in danger.

I tried to understand the spiraling voices, tried to follow the curling pathway the thoughts made to see where they were leading, but it wasn't making sense. The pictures in the center of their thoughts were *my* pictures—the very worst of them. Bella's bruises, Edward's face as he burned.

They fear it, too.

But they won't do anything about it.

Protecting Bella Swan.

We can't let that influence us.

The safety of our families, of everyone here, is more important than one human.

If they won't kill it, we have to.

Protect the tribe.

Protect our families.

We have to kill it before it's too late.

Another of my memories, Edward's words this time: *The thing is growing. Swiftly.*

I struggled to focus, to pick out individual voices.

No time to waste, Jared thought.

It will mean a fight, Embry cautioned. *A bad one.*

We're ready, Paul insisted.

We'll need surprise on our side, Sam thought.

If we catch them divided, we can take them down separately. It will increase our chances of victory, Jared thought, starting to strategize now.

I shook my head, rising slowly to my feet. I felt unsteady there—like the circling wolves were making me dizzy. The wolf beside me got up, too. His shoulder pushed against mine, propping me up.

Wait, I thought.

The circling paused for one beat, and then they were pacing again.

There's little time, Sam said.

But—what are you thinking? You wouldn't attack them for breaking the treaty this afternoon. Now you're planning an ambush, when the treaty is still intact?

This is not something our treaty anticipated, Sam said. *This is a danger to every human in the area. We don't know what kind of creature the Cullens have bred, but we know that it is strong and fast-growing. And it will be too young to follow any treaty. Remember the newborn vampires we fought? Wild, violent, beyond the reach of reason or restraint. Imagine one like that, but protected by the Cullens.*

We don't know— I tried to interrupt.

We don't know, he agreed. *And we can't take chances with the unknown in this case. We can only allow the Cullens to exist while we're absolutely sure that they can be trusted not to cause harm. This . . . thing cannot be trusted.*

They don't like it any more than we do.

Sam pulled Rosalie's face, her protective crouch, from my mind and put it on display for everyone.

Some are ready to fight for it, no matter what it is.

It's just a baby, for crying out loud.

Not for long, Leah whispered.

Jake, buddy, this is a big problem, Quil said. *We can't just ignore it.*

You're making it into something bigger than it is, I argued. *The only one who's in danger here is Bella.*

Again by her own choice, Sam said. *But this time her choice affects us all.*

I don't think so.

We can't take that chance. We won't allow a blood drinker to hunt on our lands.

Then tell them to leave, the wolf who was still supporting me said. It was Seth. Of course.

And inflict the menace on others? When blood drinkers cross our land, we destroy them, no matter where they plan to hunt. We protect everyone we can.

This is crazy, I said. *This afternoon you were afraid to put the pack in danger.*

This afternoon I didn't know our families were at risk.

I can't believe this! How're you going to kill this creature without killing Bella?

There were no words, but the silence was full of meaning.

I howled. *She's human, too! Doesn't our protection apply to her?*

She's dying anyway, Leah thought. *We'll just shorten the process.*

That did it. I leaped away from Seth, toward his sister, with my teeth bared. I was about to catch her left hind leg when I felt Sam's teeth cut into my flank, dragging me back.

I howled in pain and fury and turned on him.

Stop! he ordered in the double timbre of the Alpha.

My legs seemed to buckle under me. I jerked to a halt, only managing to keep on my feet by sheer willpower.

He turned his gaze away from me. *You will not be cruel to him, Leah,* he commanded her. *Bella's sacrifice is a heavy price, and we will* all *recognize that. It is against everything we stand for to take a human life. Making an exception to that code is a bleak thing. We will* all *mourn for what we do tonight.*

Tonight? Seth repeated, shocked. *Sam—I think we should*

talk about this some more. Consult with the Elders, at least. You can't seriously mean for us to—

We can't afford your tolerance for the Cullens now. There is no time for debate. You will *do as you are told, Seth.*

Seth's front knees folded, and his head fell forward under the weight of the Alpha's command.

Sam paced in a tight circle around the two of us.

We need the whole pack for this. Jacob, you are our strongest fighter. You will *fight with us tonight. I understand that this is hard for you, so you will concentrate on their fighters—Emmett and Jasper Cullen. You don't have to be involved with the . . . other part. Quil and Embry will fight with you.*

My knees trembled; I struggled to hold myself upright while the voice of the Alpha lashed at my will.

*Paul, Jared, and I will take on Edward and Rosalie. I think, from the information Jacob has brought us, they will be the ones guarding Bella. Carlisle and Alice will also be close, possibly Esme. Brady, Collin, Seth, and Leah will concentrate on them. Whoever has a clear line on—*we all heard him mentally stutter over Bella's name—*the creature will take it. Destroying the creature is our first priority.*

The pack rumbled in nervous agreement. The tension had everyone's fur standing on end. The pacing was quicker, and the sound of the paws against the brackish floor was sharper, toenails tearing into the soil.

Only Seth and I were still, the eye in the center of a storm of bared teeth and flattened ears. Seth's nose was almost touching the ground, bowed under Sam's commands. I felt his pain at the coming disloyalty. For him this was a betrayal—during that one day of alliance, fighting beside Edward Cullen, Seth had truly become the vampire's friend.

There was no resistance in him, however. He would obey no matter how much it hurt him. He had no other choice.

And what choice did I have? When the Alpha spoke, the pack followed.

Sam had never pushed his authority this far before; I knew he honestly hated to see Seth kneeling before him like a slave at the foot of his master. He wouldn't force this if he didn't believe that he had no other choice. He couldn't lie to us when we were linked mind to mind like this. He really believed it was our duty to destroy Bella and the monster she carried. He really believed we had no time to waste. He believed it enough to die for it.

I saw that he would face Edward himself; Edward's ability to read our thoughts made him the greatest threat in Sam's mind. Sam would not let someone else take on that danger.

He saw Jasper as the second-greatest opponent, which is why he'd given him to me. He knew that I had the best chance of any of the pack to win that fight. He'd left the easiest targets for the younger wolves and Leah. Little Alice was no danger without her future vision to guide her, and we knew from our time of alliance that Esme was not a fighter. Carlisle would be more of a challenge, but his hatred of violence would hinder him.

I felt sicker than Seth as I watched Sam plan it out, trying to work the angles to give each member of the pack the best chance of survival.

Everything was inside out. This afternoon, I'd been chomping at the bit to attack them. But Seth had been right—it wasn't a fight I'd been ready for. I'd blinded myself with that hate. I hadn't let myself look at it carefully, because I must have known what I would see if I did.

Carlisle Cullen. Looking at him without that hate clouding my eyes, I couldn't deny that killing him was murder. He was good. Good as any human we protected. Maybe better. The others, too, I supposed, but I didn't feel as strongly about them. I didn't know them as well. It was Carlisle who would hate fighting back, even to save his own life. That's why we would be able to kill him—because he wouldn't want *us*, his enemies, to die.

This was wrong.

And it wasn't just because killing Bella felt like killing *me*, like suicide.

Pull it together, Jacob, Sam ordered. *The tribe comes first.*

I was wrong today, Sam.

Your reasons were wrong then. But now we have a duty to fulfill.

I braced myself. *No.*

Sam snarled and stopped pacing in front of me. He stared into my eyes and a deep growl slid between his teeth.

Yes, the Alpha decreed, his double voice blistering with the heat of his authority. *There are no loopholes tonight. You, Jacob, are going to fight the Cullens with us. You, with Quil and Embry, will take care of Jasper and Emmett. You are obligated to protect the tribe. That is why you exist. You will perform this obligation.*

My shoulders hunched as the edict crushed me. My legs collapsed, and I was on my belly under him.

No member of the pack could refuse the Alpha.

11. THE TWO THINGS AT THE VERY TOP OF MY THINGS-I-NEVER-WANT-TO-DO LIST

SAM STARTED MOVING THE OTHERS INTO FORMATION while I was still on the ground. Embry and Quil were at my sides, waiting for me to recover and take the point.

I could feel the drive, the need, to get on my feet and lead them. The compulsion grew, and I fought it uselessly, cringing on the ground where I was.

Embry whined quietly in my ear. He didn't want to think the words, afraid that he would bring me to Sam's attention again. I felt his wordless plea for me to get up, for me to get this over with and be done with it.

There was fear in the pack, not so much for self but for the whole. We couldn't imagine that we would all make it out alive tonight. Which brothers would we lose? Which minds would leave us forever? Which grieving families would we be consoling in the morning?

My mind began to work with theirs, to think in unison, as we dealt with these fears. Automatically, I pushed up from the ground and shook out my coat.

Embry and Quil huffed in relief. Quil touched his nose to my side once.

Their minds were filled with our challenge, our assignment. We remembered together the nights we'd watched the Cullens practicing for the fight with the newborns. Emmett Cullen was strongest, but Jasper would be the bigger problem. He moved like a lightning strike—power and speed and death rolled into one. How many centuries' experience did he have? Enough that all the other Cullens looked to him for guidance.

I'll take point, if you want flank, Quil offered. There was more excitement in his mind than most of the others. When Quil had watched Jasper's instruction those nights, he'd been dying to test his skill against the vampire's. For him, this would be a contest. Even knowing it was his life on the line, he saw it that way. Paul was like that, too, and the kids who had never been in battle, Collin and Brady. Seth probably would've been the same—if the opponents were not his friends.

Jake? Quil nudged me. *How do you want to roll?*

I just shook my head. I couldn't concentrate—the compulsion to follow orders felt like puppet strings hooked into all of my muscles. One foot forward, now another.

Seth was dragging behind Collin and Brady—Leah had assumed point there. She ignored Seth while planning with the others, and I could see that she'd rather leave him out of the fight. There was a maternal edge to her feelings for her younger brother. She wished Sam would send him home. Seth didn't register Leah's doubts. He was adjusting to the puppet strings, too.

Maybe if you stopped resisting . . . , Embry whispered.

Just focus on our part. The big ones. We can take them down. We own them! Quil was working himself up—like a pep talk before a big game.

I could see how easy it would be—to think about nothing more than my part. It wasn't hard to imagine attacking Jasper and Emmett. We'd been close to that before. I'd thought of them as enemies for a very long time. I could do that now again.

I just had to forget that they were protecting the same thing I would protect. I had to forget the reason why I might want them to win. . . .

Jake, Embry warned. *Keep your head in the game.*

My feet moved sluggishly, pulling against the drag of the strings.

There's no point fighting it, Embry whispered again.

He was right. I would end up doing what Sam wanted, if he was willing to push it. And he was. Obviously.

There was a good reason for the Alpha's authority. Even a pack as strong as ours wasn't much of a force without a leader. We had to move together, to think together, in order to be effective. And that required the body to have a head.

So what if Sam was wrong now? There was nothing anyone could do. No one could dispute his decision.

Except.

And there it was—a thought I'd never, never wanted to have. But now, with my legs all tied up in strings, I recognized the exception with relief—more than relief, with a fierce joy.

No one could dispute the Alpha's decision—except for *me*.

I hadn't earned anything. But there were things that had been born in me, things that I'd left unclaimed.

I'd never wanted to lead the pack. I didn't want to do it now. I didn't want the responsibility for all our fates resting on my shoulders. Sam was better at that than I would ever be.

But he was wrong tonight.

And I had not been born to kneel to him.

The bonds fell off my body the second that I embraced my birthright.

I could feel it gathering in me, both a freedom and also a strange, hollow power. Hollow because an Alpha's power came from his pack, and I had no pack. For a second, loneliness overwhelmed me.

I had no pack now.

But I was straight and strong as I walked to where Sam stood, planning with Paul and Jared. He turned at the sound of my advance, and his black eyes narrowed.

No, I told him again.

He heard it right away, heard the choice that I'd made in the sound of the Alpha voice in my thoughts.

He jumped back a half step with a shocked yelp.

Jacob? What have you done?

I won't follow you, Sam. Not for something so wrong.

He stared at me, stunned. *You would . . . you would choose your enemies over your family?*

They aren't—I shook my head, clearing it—*they aren't*

our enemies. They never have been. Until I really thought about destroying them, thought it through, I didn't see that.

This isn't about them, he snarled at me. *This is about Bella. She has never been the one for you, she has never chosen you, but you continue to destroy your life for her!*

They were hard words, but true words. I sucked in a big gulp of air, breathing them in.

Maybe you're right. But you're going to destroy the pack over her, Sam. No matter how many of them survive tonight, they will always have murder on their hands.

We have to protect our families!

I know what you've decided, Sam. But you don't decide for me, not anymore.

Jacob—you can't turn your back on the tribe.

I heard the double echo of his Alpha command, but it was weightless this time. It no longer applied to me. He clenched his jaw, trying to *force* me to respond to his words.

I stared into his furious eyes. *Ephraim Black's son was not born to follow Levi Uley's.*

Is this it, then, Jacob Black? His hackles rose and his muzzle pulled back from his teeth. Paul and Jared snarled and bristled at his sides. *Even if you can defeat me, the pack will never follow you!*

Now *I* jerked back, a surprised whine escaping my throat.

Defeat you? I'm not going to fight you, Sam.

Then what's your plan? I'm not stepping aside so that you can protect the vampire spawn at the tribe's expense.

I'm not telling you to step aside.

If you order them to follow you—

I'll never *take anyone's will away from him.*

His tail whipped back and forth as he recoiled from the judgment in my words. Then he took a step forward so that we were toe to toe, his exposed teeth inches from mine. I hadn't noticed till this moment that I'd grown taller than him.

There cannot be more than one Alpha. The pack has chosen me. Will you rip us apart tonight? Will you turn on your brothers? Or will you end this insanity and join us again? Every word was layered with command, but it couldn't touch me. Alpha blood ran undiluted in my veins.

I could see why there was never more than one Alpha male in a pack. My body was responding to the challenge. I could feel the instinct to defend my claim rising in me. The primitive core of my wolf-self tensed for the battle of supremacy.

I focused all my energy to control that reaction. I would not fall into a pointless, destructive fight with Sam. He was my brother still, even though I was rejecting him.

There is only one Alpha for this pack. I'm not contesting that. I'm just choosing to go my own way.

Do you belong to a coven now, Jacob?

I flinched.

I don't know, Sam. But I do know this—

He shrunk back as he felt the weight of the Alpha in my tone. It affected him more than his touched me. Because I *had* been born to lead him.

I will stand between you and the Cullens. I won't just watch while the pack kills innocent—it was hard to apply that word to vampires, but it was true—*people. The pack is better than that. Lead them in the right direction, Sam.*

I turned my back on him, and a chorus of howls tore into the air around me.

Digging my nails into the earth, I raced away from the uproar I'd caused. I didn't have much time. At least Leah was the only one with a prayer of outrunning me, and I had a head start.

The howling faded with the distance, and I took comfort as the sound continued to rip apart the quiet night. They weren't after me yet.

I had to warn the Cullens before the pack could get it together and stop me. If the Cullens were prepared, it might give Sam a reason to rethink this before it was too late. I sprinted toward the white house I still hated, leaving my home behind me. Home didn't belong to me anymore. I'd turned my back on it.

Today had begun like any other day. Made it home from patrol with the rainy sunrise, breakfast with Billy and Rachel, bad TV, bickering with Paul . . . How did it change so completely, turn all surreal? How did everything get messed up and twisted so that I was here now, all alone, an unwilling Alpha, cut off from my brothers, choosing vampires over them?

The sound I'd been fearing interrupted my dazed thoughts—it was the soft impact of big paws against the ground, chasing after me. I threw myself forward, rocketing through the black forest. I just had to get close enough so that Edward could hear the warning in my head. Leah wouldn't be able to stop me alone.

And then I caught the mood of the thoughts behind me. Not anger, but enthusiasm. Not chasing . . . but following.

My stride broke. I staggered two steps before it evened out again.

Wait up. My legs aren't as long as yours.

SETH! What do you think you're DOING? GO HOME!

He didn't answer, but I could feel his excitement as he kept right on after me. I could see through his eyes as he could see through mine. The night scene was bleak for me—full of despair. For him, it was hopeful.

I hadn't realized I was slowing down, but suddenly he was on my flank, running in position beside me.

I am not joking, Seth! This is no place for you. Get out of here.

The gangly tan wolf snorted. *I've got your back, Jacob. I think you're right. And I'm not going to stand behind Sam when—*

Oh yes you are the hell going to stand behind Sam! Get your furry butt back to La Push and do what Sam tells you to do.

No.

Go, Seth!

Is that an order, Jacob?

His question brought me up short. I skidded to a halt, my nails gouging furrows in the mud.

I'm not ordering anyone to do anything. I'm just telling you what you already know.

He plopped down on his haunches beside me. *I'll tell you what I know—I know that it's awful quiet. Haven't you noticed?*

I blinked. My tail swished nervously as I realized what he was thinking underneath the words. It wasn't quiet in one sense. Howls still filled the air, far away in the west.

They haven't phased back, Seth said.

I knew that. The pack would be on red alert now. They would be using the mind link to see all sides clearly. But I couldn't hear what they were thinking. I could only hear Seth. No one else.

Looks to me like separate packs aren't linked. Huh. Guess there was no reason for our fathers to know that before. 'Cause there was no reason for separate packs before. Never enough wolves for two. Wow. It's really quiet. Sort of eerie. But also kinda nice, don't you think? I bet it was easier, like this, for Ephraim and Quil and Levi. Not such a babble with just three. Or just two.

Shut up, Seth.

Yes, sir.

Stop that! There are not two packs. There is THE pack, and then there is me. That's all. So you can go home now.

If there aren't two packs, then why can we hear each other and not the rest? I think that when you turned your back on Sam, that was a pretty significant move. A change. And when I followed you away, I think that was significant, too.

You've got a point, I conceded. *But what can change can change right back.*

He got up and started trotting toward the east. *No time to argue about it now. We should be moving right along before Sam . . .*

He was right about that part. There was no time for this argument. I fell into a run again, not pushing myself quite as hard. Seth stayed on my heels, holding the Second's traditional place on my right flank.

I can run somewhere else, he thought, his nose dipping a little. *I didn't follow you because I was after a promotion.*

Run wherever you want. Makes no difference to me.

There was no sound of pursuit, but we both stepped it

up a little at the same time. I was worried now. If I couldn't tap into the pack's mind, it was going to make this more difficult. I'd have no more advance warning of attack than the Cullens.

We'll run patrols, Seth suggested.

And what do we do if the pack challenges us? My eyes tightened. *Attack our brothers? Your sister?*

No—we sound the alarm and fall back.

Good answer. But then what? I don't think . . .

I know, he agreed. Less confident now. *I don't think I can fight them, either. But they won't be any happier with the idea of attacking us than we are with attacking them. That might be enough to stop them right there. Plus, there're only eight of them now.*

Stop being so . . . Took me a minute to decide on the right word. *Optimistic. It's getting on my nerves.*

No problem. You want me to be all doom and gloom, or just shut up?

Just shut up.

Can do.

Really? Doesn't seem like it.

He was finally quiet.

And then we were across the road and moving through the forest that ringed the Cullens' house. Could Edward hear us yet?

Maybe we should be thinking something like, "We come in peace."

Go for it.

Edward? He called the name tentatively. *Edward, you there? Okay, now I feel kinda stupid.*

You sound stupid, too.

Think he can hear us?

We were less than a mile out now. *I think so. Hey, Edward. If you can hear me—circle the wagons, bloodsucker. You've got a problem.*

We've *got a problem,* Seth corrected.

Then we broke through the trees into the big lawn. The house was dark, but not empty. Edward stood on the porch between Emmett and Jasper. They were snow white in the pale light.

"Jacob? Seth? What's going on?"

I slowed and then paced back a few steps. The smell was so sharp through this nose that it felt like it was honestly burning me. Seth whined quietly, hesitating, and then he fell back behind me.

To answer Edward's question, I let my mind run over the confrontation with Sam, moving through it backward. Seth thought with me, filling in the gaps, showing the scene from another angle. We stopped when we got to the part about the "abomination," because Edward hissed furiously and leaped off the porch.

"They want to kill Bella?" he snarled flatly.

Emmett and Jasper, not having heard the first part of the conversation, took his inflectionless question for a statement. They were right next to him in a flash, teeth exposed as they moved on us.

Hey, now, Seth thought, backing away.

"Em, Jazz—not *them*! The others. The pack is coming."

Emmett and Jasper rocked back on their heels; Emmett turned to Edward while Jasper kept his eyes locked on us.

"What's *their* problem?" Emmett demanded.

"The same one as mine," Edward hissed. "But they have their own plan to handle it. Get the others. Call Carlisle! He and Esme have to get back here now."

I whined uneasily. They *were* separated.

"They aren't far," Edward said in the same dead voice as before.

I'm going to go take a look, Seth said. *Run the western perimeter.*

"Will you be in danger, Seth?" Edward asked.

Seth and I exchanged a glance.

Don't think so, we thought together. And then I added, *But maybe I should go. Just in case . . .*

They'll be less likely to challenge me, Seth pointed out. *I'm just a kid to them.*

You're just a kid to me, kid.

I'm outta here. You need to coordinate with the Cullens.

He wheeled and darted into the darkness. I wasn't going to order Seth around, so I let him go.

Edward and I stood facing each other in the dark meadow. I could hear Emmett muttering into his phone. Jasper was watching the place where Seth had vanished into the woods. Alice appeared on the porch and then, after staring at me with anxious eyes for a long moment, she flitted to Jasper's side. I guessed that Rosalie was inside with Bella. Still guarding her—from the wrong dangers.

"This isn't the first time I've owed you my gratitude, Jacob," Edward whispered. "I would never have asked for this from you."

I thought of what he'd asked me for earlier today. When it came to Bella, there were no lines he wouldn't cross. *Yeah, you would.*

He thought about it and then nodded. "I suppose you're right about that."

I sighed heavily. *Well, this isn't the first time that I didn't do it for you.*

"Right," he murmured.

Sorry I didn't do any good today. Told you she wouldn't listen to me.

"I know. I never really believed she would. But . . ."

You had to try. I get it. She any better?

His voice and eyes went hollow. "Worse," he breathed.

I didn't want to let that word sink in. I was grateful when Alice spoke.

"Jacob, would you mind switching forms?" Alice asked. "I want to know what's going on."

I shook my head at the same time Edward answered.

"He needs to stay linked to Seth."

"Well, then would *you* be so kind as to tell me what's happening?"

He explained in clipped, emotionless sentences. "The pack thinks Bella's become a problem. They foresee potential danger from the . . . from what she's carrying. They feel it's their duty to remove that danger. Jacob and Seth disbanded from the pack to warn us. The rest are planning to attack tonight."

Alice hissed, leaning away from me. Emmett and Jasper exchanged a glance, and then their eyes ranged across the trees.

Nobody out here, Seth reported. *All's quiet on the western front.*

They may go around.

I'll make a loop.

"Carlisle and Esme are on their way," Emmett said. "Twenty minutes, tops."

"We should take up a defensive position," Jasper said.

Edward nodded. "Let's get inside."

I'll run perimeter with Seth. If I get too far for you to hear my head, listen for my howl.

"I will."

They backed into the house, eyes flickering everywhere. Before they were inside, I turned and ran toward the west.

I'm still not finding much, Seth told me.

I'll take half the circle. Move fast—we don't want them to have a chance to sneak past us.

Seth lurched forward in a sudden burst of speed.

We ran in silence, and the minutes passed. I listened to the noises around him, double-checking his judgment.

Hey—something coming up fast! he warned me after fifteen minutes of silence.

On my way!

Hold your position—I don't think it's the pack. It sounds different.

Seth—

But he caught the approaching scent on the breeze, and I read it in his mind.

Vampire. Bet it's Carlisle.

Seth, fall back. It might be someone else.

No, it's them. I recognize the scent. Hold up, I'm going to phase to explain it to them.

Seth, I don't think—

But he was gone.

Anxiously, I raced along the western border. Wouldn't it be just peachy if I couldn't take care of Seth for one freaking night? What if something happened to him on my watch? Leah would shred me into kibble.

At least the kid kept it short. It wasn't two minutes later when I felt him in my head again.

Yep, Carlisle and Esme. Boy, were they surprised to see me! They're probably inside by now. Carlisle said thanks.

He's a good guy.

Yeah. That's one of the reasons why we're right about this.

Hope so.

Why're you so down, Jake? I'll bet Sam won't bring the pack tonight. He's not going to launch a suicide mission.

I sighed. It didn't seem to matter, either way.

Oh. This isn't about Sam so much, is it?

I made the turn at the end of my patrol. I caught Seth's scent where he'd turned last. We weren't leaving any gaps.

You think Bella's going to die anyway, Seth whispered.

Yeah, she is.

Poor Edward. He must be crazy.

Literally.

Edward's name brought other memories boiling to the surface. Seth read them in astonishment.

And then he was howling. *Oh, man! No way! You did not! That just plain ol' sucks rocks, Jacob! And you know it, too! I can't believe you said you'd kill him. What is that? You have to tell him no.*

Shut up, shut up, you idiot! They're going to think the pack is coming!

Oops! He cut off mid-howl.

I wheeled and started loping in toward the house. *Just keep out of this, Seth. Take the whole circle for now.*

Seth seethed and I ignored him.

False alarm, false alarm, I thought as I ran closer in. *Sorry. Seth is young. He forgets things. No one's attacking. False alarm.*

When I got to the meadow, I could see Edward staring out of a dark window. I ran in, wanting to be sure he got the message.

There's nothing out there—you got that?

He nodded once.

This would be a lot easier if the communication wasn't one way. Then again, I was kinda glad I wasn't in *his* head.

He looked over his shoulder, back into the house, and I saw a shudder run through his whole frame. He waved me away without looking in my direction again and then moved out of my view.

What's going on?

Like I was going to get an answer.

I sat very still in the meadow and listened. With these ears, I could almost hear Seth's soft footfalls, miles out into the forest. It was easy to hear every sound inside the dark house.

"It was a false alarm," Edward was explaining in that dead voice, just repeating what I'd told him. "Seth was upset about something else, and he forgot we were listening for a signal. He's very young."

"Nice to have toddlers guarding the fort," a deeper voice grumbled. Emmett, I thought.

"They've done us a great service tonight, Emmett," Carlisle said. "At great personal sacrifice."

"Yeah, I know. I'm just jealous. Wish I was out there."

"Seth doesn't think Sam will attack now," Edward said mechanically. "Not with us forewarned, and lacking two members of the pack."

"What does Jacob think?" Carlisle asked.

"He's not as optimistic."

No one spoke. There was a quiet dripping sound that I couldn't place. I heard their low breathing—and I could separate Bella's from the rest. It was harsher, labored. It hitched and broke in strange rhythms. I could hear her heart. It seemed . . . too fast. I paced it against my own heartbeat, but I wasn't sure if that was any measure. It wasn't like I was normal.

"Don't touch her! You'll wake her up," Rosalie whispered.

Someone sighed.

"Rosalie," Carlisle murmured.

"Don't start with me, Carlisle. We let you have your way earlier, but that's all we're allowing."

It seemed like Rosalie and Bella were both talking in plurals now. Like they'd formed a pack of their own.

I paced quietly in front of the house. Each pass brought me a little closer. The dark windows were like a TV set running in some dull waiting room—it was impossible to keep my eyes off them for long.

A few more minutes, a few more passes, and my fur was brushing the side of the porch as I paced.

I could see up through the windows—see the top of the walls and the ceiling, the unlit chandelier that hung there. I was tall enough that all I would have to do was stretch my neck a little . . . and maybe one paw up on the edge of the porch. . . .

I peeked into the big, open front room, expecting to see something very similar to the scene this afternoon. But it had changed so much that I was confused at first. For a second I thought I'd gotten the wrong room.

The glass wall was gone—it looked like metal now. And the furniture was all dragged out of the way, with Bella curled up awkwardly on a narrow bed in the center of the open space. Not a normal bed—one with rails like in a hospital. Also like a hospital were the monitors strapped to her body, the tubes stuck into her skin. The lights on the monitors flashed, but there was no sound. The dripping noise was from the IV plugged into her arm—some fluid that was thick and white, not clear.

She choked a little in her uneasy sleep, and both Edward and Rosalie moved in to hover over her. Her body jerked, and she whimpered. Rosalie smoothed her hand across Bella's forehead. Edward's body stiffened—his back was to me, but his expression must have been something to see, because Emmett wrenched himself between them before there was time to blink. He held his hands up to Edward.

"Not tonight, Edward. We've got other things to worry about."

Edward turned away from them, and he was the burning man again. His eyes met mine for one moment, and then I dropped back to all fours.

I ran back into the dark forest, running to join Seth, running away from what was behind me.

Worse. Yes, she was worse.

12. SOME PEOPLE JUST DON'T GRASP THE CONCEPT OF "UNWELCOME"

I WAS RIGHT ON THE EDGE OF SLEEP.

The sun had risen behind the clouds an hour ago—the forest was gray now instead of black. Seth'd curled up and passed out around one, and I'd woken him at dawn to trade off. Even after running all night, I was having a hard time making my brain shut up long enough to fall asleep, but Seth's rhythmic run was helping. One, two-three, four, one, two-three, four—*dum dum-dum dum*—dull paw thuds against the damp earth, over and over as he made the wide circuit surrounding the Cullens' land. We were already wearing a trail into the ground. Seth's thoughts were empty, just a blur of green and gray as the woods flew past him.

It was restful. It helped to fill my head with what he saw rather than letting my own images take center stage.

And then Seth's piercing howl broke the early morning quiet.

I lurched up from the ground, my front legs pulling toward a sprint before my hind legs were off the ground. I raced toward the place where Seth had frozen, listening with him to the tread of paws running in our direction.

Morning, boys.

A shocked whine broke through Seth's teeth. And then we both snarled as we read deeper into the new thoughts.

Oh, man! Go away, Leah! Seth groaned.

I stopped when I got to Seth, head thrown back, ready to howl again—this time to complain.

Cut the noise, Seth.

Right. Ugh! Ugh! Ugh! He whimpered and pawed at the ground, scratching deep furrows in the dirt.

Leah trotted into view, her small gray body weaving through the underbrush.

Stop whining, Seth. You're such a baby.

I growled at her, my ears flattening against my skull. She skipped back a step automatically.

What do you think you're doing, Leah?

She huffed a heavy sigh. *It's pretty obvious, isn't it? I'm joining your crappy little renegade pack. The vampires' guard dogs.* She barked out a low, sarcastic laugh.

No, you're not. Turn around before I rip out one of your hamstrings.

Like you could catch me. She grinned and coiled her body for launch. *Wanna race, O fearless leader?*

I took a deep breath, filling my lungs until my sides bulged. Then, when I was sure I wasn't going to scream, I exhaled in a gust.

Seth, go let the Cullens know that it's just your stupid sister— I thought the words as harshly as possible. *I'll deal with this.*

On it! Seth was only too happy to leave. He vanished toward the house.

Leah whined, and she leaned after him, the fur on her shoulders rising. *You're just going to let him run off to the vampires* alone?

I'm pretty sure he'd rather they took him out than spend another minute with you.

Shut up, Jacob. Oops, I'm sorry—I meant, shut up, most high Alpha.

Why the hell *are you here?*

You think I'm just going to sit home while my little brother volunteers as a vampire chew toy?

Seth doesn't want or need your protection. In fact, no one wants you here.

Oooh, ouch, that's gonna leave a huge *mark. Ha,* she barked. *Tell me who* does *want me around, and I'm outta here.*

So this isn't about Seth at all, is it?

Of course it is. I'm just pointing out that being unwanted is not a first for me. Not really a motivating factor, if you know what I mean.

I gritted my teeth and tried to get my head straight.

Did Sam send you?

If I was here on Sam's errand, you wouldn't be able to hear me. My allegiance is no longer with him.

I listened carefully to the thoughts mixed in with the

words. If this was a diversion or a ploy, I had to be alert enough to see through it. But there was nothing. Her declaration was nothing but the truth. Unwilling, almost despairing truth.

You're loyal to me now? I asked with deep sarcasm. *Uh-huh. Right.*

My choices are limited. I'm working with the options I've got. Trust me, I'm not enjoying this any more than you are.

That wasn't true. There was an edgy kind of excitement in her mind. She was unhappy about this, but she was also riding some weird high. I searched her mind, trying to understand.

She bristled, resenting the intrusion. I usually tried to tune Leah out—I'd never tried to make sense of her before.

We were interrupted by Seth, thinking his explanation at Edward. Leah whined anxiously. Edward's face, framed in the same window as last night, showed no reaction to the news. It was a blank face, dead.

Wow, he looks bad, Seth muttered to himself. The vampire showed no reaction to that thought, either. He disappeared into the house. Seth pivoted and headed back out to us. Leah relaxed a little.

What's going on? Leah asked. *Catch me up to speed.*

There's no point. You're not staying.

Actually, Mr. Alpha, I am. Because since apparently I have to belong to someone—and don't think I haven't tried breaking off on my own, you know yourself how well that doesn't work—I choose you.

Leah, you don't like me. I don't like you.

Thank you, Captain Obvious. That doesn't matter to me. I'm staying with Seth.

You don't like vampires. Don't you think that's a little conflict of interest right there?

You don't like vampires either.

But I am committed to this alliance. You aren't.

I'll keep my distance from them. I can run patrols out here, just like Seth.

And I'm supposed to trust you with that?

She stretched her neck, leaning up on her toes, trying to be as tall as me as she stared into my eyes. *I will not betray my pack.*

I wanted to throw my head back and howl, like Seth had before. *This isn't your pack! This isn't even a pack. This is just me, going off on my own! What is it with you Clearwaters? Why can't you leave me alone?*

Seth, just coming up behind us now, whined; I'd offended him. Great.

I've been helpful, haven't I, Jake?

You haven't made too much a nuisance of yourself, kid, but if you and Leah are a package deal—if the only way to get rid of her is for you to go home. . . . Well, can you blame me for wanting you gone?

Ugh, Leah, you ruin everything!

Yeah, I know, she told him, and the thought was loaded with the heaviness of her despair.

I felt the pain in the three little words, and it was more than I would've guessed. I didn't want to feel that. I didn't want to feel bad for her. Sure, the pack was rough on her, but she brought it all on herself with the bitterness that tainted her every thought and made being in her head a nightmare.

Seth was feeling guilty, too. *Jake . . . You're not really*

gonna send me away, are you? Leah's not so bad. Really. I mean,
with her here, we can push the perimeter out farther. And this puts
Sam down to seven. There's no way he's going to mount an attack
that outnumbered. It's probably a good thing. . . .

You know I don't want to lead a pack, Seth.

So don't lead us, Leah offered.

I snorted. *Sounds perfect to me. Run along home now.*

Jake, Seth thought. *I belong here. I do like vampires. Cullens,*
anyway. They're people to me, and I'm going to protect them, 'cause
that's what we're supposed to do.

Maybe you belong, kid, but your sister doesn't. And she's going
to go wherever you are—

I stopped short, because I saw something when I said
that. Something Leah had been trying not to think.

Leah wasn't going anywhere.

Thought this was about Seth, I thought sourly.

She flinched. *Of course I'm here for Seth.*

And to get away from Sam.

Her jaw clenched. *I don't have to explain myself to you. I just*
have to do what I'm told. I belong to your pack, Jacob. The end.

I paced away from her, growling.

Crap. I was never going to get rid of her. As much as she
disliked me, as much as she loathed the Cullens, as happy as
she'd be to go kill all the vampires right now, as much as it
pissed her off to have to protect them instead—none of that
was *anything* compared to what she felt being free of Sam.

Leah didn't like me, so it wasn't such a chore having me
wish she would disappear.

She loved Sam. Still. And having *him* wish she would
disappear was more pain than she was willing to live with,
now that she had a choice. She would have taken any other

option. Even if it meant moving in with the Cullens as their lapdog.

I don't know if I'd go that far, she thought. She tried to make the words tough, aggressive, but there were big cracks in her show. *I'm sure I'd give killing myself a few good tries first. Look, Leah . . .*

No, you look, *Jacob. Stop arguing with me, because it's not going to do any good. I'll stay out of your way, okay? I'll do anything you want. Except go back to Sam's pack and be the pathetic ex-girlfriend he can't get away from. If you want me to leave—* she sat back on her haunches and stared straight into my eyes—*you're going to have to* make *me.*

I snarled for a long, angry minute. I was beginning to feel some sympathy for Sam, despite what he had done to me, to Seth. No wonder he was always ordering the pack around. How else would you ever get anything done?

Seth, are you gonna get mad at me if I kill your sister?

He pretended to think about it for a minute. *Well . . . yeah, probably.*

I sighed.

Okay, then, Ms. Do-Anything-I-Want. Why don't you make yourself useful by telling us what you know? What happened after we left last night?

Lots of howling. But you probably heard that part. It was so loud that it took us a while to figure out that we couldn't hear either of you anymore. Sam was . . . Words failed her, but we could see it in our head. Both Seth and I cringed. *After that, it was clear pretty quick that we were going to have to rethink things. Sam was planning to talk to the other Elders first thing this morning. We were supposed to meet up and figure out a game plan. I could tell he wasn't going to mount another attack right away, though. Suicide at this point, with you and Seth AWOL and the bloodsuckers forewarned. I'm not sure what they'll do, but I wouldn't be wandering the forest alone if I was a leech. It's open season on vamps now.*

You decided to skip the meeting this morning? I asked.

When we split up for patrols last night, I asked permission to go home, to tell my mother what had happened—

Crap! You told Mom? Seth growled.

Seth, hold off on the sibling stuff for a sec. Go on, Leah.

So once I was human, I took a minute to think things through. Well, actually, I took all night. I bet the others think I fell asleep. But the whole two-separate-packs, two-separate-pack-minds thing gave me a lot to sift through. In the end, I weighed Seth's safety and the, er, other benefits against the idea of turning traitor and sniffing vampire stink for who knows how long. You know what I decided. I left a note for my mom. I expect we'll hear it when Sam finds out. . . .

Leah cocked an ear to the west.

Yeah, I expect we will, I agreed.

So that's everything. What do we do now? she asked.

She and Seth both looked at me expectantly.

This was exactly the kind of thing I didn't want to have to do.

I guess we just keep an eye out for now. That's all we can *do. You should probably take a nap, Leah.*

You've had as much sleep as I have.

Thought you were going to do what you were told?

Right. That's going to get old, she grumbled, and then she yawned. *Well, whatever. I don't care.*

I'll run the border, Jake. I'm not tired at all. Seth was so glad I hadn't forced them home, he was all but prancing with excitement.

Sure, sure. I'm going to go check in with the Cullens.

Seth took off along the new path worn into the damp earth. Leah looked after him thoughtfully.

Maybe a round or two before I crash. . . . Hey Seth, wanna see how many times I can lap you?

NO!

Barking out a low chuckle, Leah lunged into the woods after him.

I growled uselessly. So much for peace and quiet.

Leah was trying—for Leah. She kept her jibes to a minimum as she raced around the circuit, but it was impossible not to be aware of her smug mood. I thought of the whole "two's company" saying. It didn't really apply, because *one* was plenty to my mind. But if there *had* to be three of us, it was hard to think of anyone that I wouldn't trade her for.

Paul? she suggested.

Maybe, I allowed.

She laughed to herself, too jittery and hyper to get offended. I wondered how long the buzz from dodging Sam's pity would last.

That will be my goal, then—to be less annoying than Paul.

Yeah, work on that.

I changed into my other form when I was a few yards from the lawn. I hadn't been planning to spend much time human here. But I hadn't been planning to have Leah in my head, either. I pulled on my ragged shorts and started across the lawn.

The door opened before I got to the steps, and I was surprised to see Carlisle rather than Edward step outside to meet me—his face looked exhausted and defeated. For a second, my heart froze. I faltered to a stop, unable to speak.

"Are you all right, Jacob?" Carlisle asked.

"Is Bella?" I choked out.

"She's . . . much the same as last night. Did I startle you? I'm sorry. Edward said you were coming in your human form, and I came out to greet you, as he didn't want to leave her. She's awake."

And Edward didn't want to lose any time with her, because he didn't have much time left. Carlisle didn't say the words out loud, but he might as well have.

It had been a while since I'd slept—since before my last patrol. I could really feel that now. I took a step forward, sat down on the porch steps, and slumped against the railing.

Moving whisper-quiet as only a vampire could, Carlisle took a seat on the same step, against the other railing.

"I didn't get a chance to thank you last night, Jacob. You don't know how much I appreciate your . . . compassion. I know your goal was to protect Bella, but I owe you the safety of the rest of my family as well. Edward told me what you had to do. . . ."

"Don't mention it," I muttered.

"If you prefer."

We sat in silence. I could hear the others in the house. Emmett, Alice, and Jasper, speaking in low, serious voices upstairs. Esme humming tunelessly in another room. Rosalie and Edward breathing close by—I couldn't tell which was which, but I could hear the difference in

Bella's labored panting. I could hear her heart, too. It seemed . . . uneven.

It was like fate was out to make me do everything I'd ever sworn I wouldn't in the course of twenty-four hours. Here I was, hanging around, waiting for her to die.

I didn't want to listen anymore. Talking was better than listening.

"She's family to you?" I asked Carlisle. It had caught my notice before, when he'd said I'd helped the *rest* of his family, too.

"Yes. Bella is already a daughter to me. A beloved daughter."

"But you're going to let her die."

He was quiet long enough that I looked up. His face was very, very tired. I knew how he felt.

"I can imagine what you think of me for that," he finally said. "But I can't ignore her will. It wouldn't be right to make such a choice for her, to force her."

I wanted to be angry with him, but he was making it hard. It was like he was throwing my own words back at me, just scrambled up. They'd sounded right before, but they couldn't be right now. Not with Bella dying. Still . . . I remembered how it felt to be broken on the ground under Sam—to have no choice but be involved in the murder of someone I loved. It wasn't the same, though. Sam was wrong. And Bella loved things she shouldn't.

"Do you think there's any chance she'll make it? I mean, as a vampire and all that. She told me about . . . about Esme."

"I'd say there's an even chance at this point," he answered quietly. "I've seen vampire venom work miracles, but there are conditions that even venom cannot overcome. Her heart is working too hard now; if it should fail . . . there won't be anything for me to do."

Bella's heartbeat throbbed and faltered, giving an agonizing emphasis to his words.

Maybe the planet had started turning backward. Maybe that would explain how everything was the opposite of what it had been yesterday—how I could be hoping for what had once seemed like the very worst thing in the world.

"What is that thing doing to her?" I whispered. "She was so much worse last night. I saw . . . the tubes and all that. Through the window."

"The fetus isn't compatible with her body. Too strong, for one thing, but she could probably endure that for a while. The bigger problem is that it won't allow her to get the sustenance she needs. Her body is rejecting every form of nutrition. I'm trying to feed her intravenously, but she's just not absorbing it. Everything about her condition is accelerated. I'm watching her—and not just her, but the fetus as well—starve to death by the hour. I can't stop it and I can't slow it down. I can't figure out what it *wants*." His weary voice broke at the end.

I felt the same way I had yesterday, when I'd seen the black stains across her stomach—furious, and a little crazy.

I clenched my hands into fists to control the shaking. I hated the thing that was hurting her. It wasn't enough for the monster to beat her from the inside out. No, it was starving her, too. Probably just looking for something to sink its teeth into—a throat to suck dry. Since it wasn't big enough to kill anyone else yet, it settled for sucking Bella's life from her.

I could tell them exactly what it wanted: death and blood, blood and death.

My skin was all hot and prickly. I breathed slowly in and out, focusing on that to calm myself.

"I wish I could get a better idea of what exactly it is," Carlisle murmured. "The fetus is well protected. I haven't been able to produce an ultrasonic image. I doubt there is any way to get a needle through the amniotic sac, but Rosalie won't agree to let me try, in any case."

"A needle?" I mumbled. "What good would that do?"

"The more I know about the fetus, the better I can estimate what it will be capable of. What I wouldn't give for even a little amniotic fluid. If I knew even the chromosomal count . . ."

"You're losing me, Doc. Can you dumb it down?"

He chuckled once—even his laugh sounded exhausted. "Okay. How much biology have you taken? Did you study chromosomal pairs?"

"Think so. We have twenty-three, right?"

"Humans do."

I blinked. "How many do you have?"

"Twenty-five."

I frowned at my fists for a second. "What does that mean?"

"I thought it meant that our species were almost completely different. Less related than a lion and a house cat. But this new life—well, it suggests that we're more genetically compatible than I'd thought." He sighed sadly. "I didn't know to warn them."

I sighed, too. It had been easy to hate Edward for the same ignorance. I still hated him for it. It was just hard to feel the same way about Carlisle. Maybe because I wasn't ten shades of jealous in Carlisle's case.

"It might help to know what the count was—whether the fetus was closer to us or to her. To know what to expect." Then he shrugged. "And maybe it wouldn't help anything. I guess I just wish I had something to study, anything to do."

"Wonder what my chromosomes are like," I muttered randomly. I thought of those Olympic steroids tests again. Did they run DNA scans?

Carlisle coughed self-consciously. "You have twenty-four pairs, Jacob."

I turned slowly to stare at him, raising my eyebrows.

He looked embarrassed. "I was . . . curious. I took the liberty when I was treating you last June."

I thought about it for a second. "I guess that should piss me off. But I don't really care."

"I'm sorry. I should have asked."

"S'okay, Doc. You didn't mean any harm."

"No, I promise you that I did *not* mean you any harm. It's just that . . . I find your species fascinating. I suppose that the elements of vampiric nature have come to seem commonplace to me over the centuries. Your family's divergence from humanity is much more interesting. Magical, almost."

"Bibbidi-Bobbidi-Boo," I mumbled. He was just like Bella with all the magic garbage.

Carlisle laughed another weary laugh.

Then we heard Edward's voice inside the house, and we both paused to listen.

"I'll be right back, Bella. I want to speak with Carlisle for a moment. Actually, Rosalie, would you mind accompany-ing me?" Edward sounded different. There was a little life in his dead voice. A spark of something. Not hope exactly, but maybe the *desire* to hope.

"What is it, Edward?" Bella asked hoarsely.

"Nothing you need to worry about, love. It will just take a second. Please, Rose?"

"Esme?" Rosalie called. "Can you mind Bella for me?"

I heard the whisper of wind as Esme flitted down the stairs.

"Of course," she said.

Carlisle shifted, twisting to look expectantly at the door. Edward was through the door first, with Rosalie right on his heels. His face was, like his voice, no longer dead. He seemed intensely focused. Rosalie looked suspicious.

Edward shut the door behind her.

"Carlisle," he murmured.

"What is it, Edward?"

"Perhaps we've been going about this the wrong way. I was listening to you and Jacob just now, and when you were speaking of what the . . . fetus wants, Jacob had an interesting thought."

Me? What had *I* thought? Besides my obvious hatred for the thing? At least I wasn't alone in that. I could tell that Edward had a difficult time using a term as mild as *fetus.*

"We haven't actually addressed *that* angle," Edward went on. "We've been trying to get Bella what she needs. And her body is accepting it about as well as one of ours would. Perhaps we should address the needs of the . . . fetus first.

Maybe if we can satisfy it, we'll be able to help her more effectively."

"I'm not following you, Edward," Carlisle said.

"Think about it, Carlisle. If that creature is more vampire than human, can't you guess what it craves—what it's not getting? Jacob did."

I did? I ran through the conversation, trying to remember what thoughts I'd kept to myself. I remembered at the same time that Carlisle understood.

"Oh," he said in a surprised tone. "You think it is . . . thirsty?"

Rosalie hissed under her breath. She wasn't suspicious anymore. Her revoltingly perfect face was all lit up, her eyes wide with excitement. "Of course," she muttered. "Carlisle, we have all that type O negative laid aside for Bella. It's a good idea," she added, not looking at me.

"Hmm." Carlisle put his hand to his chin, lost in thought. "I wonder . . . And then, what would be the best way to administer. . . ."

Rosalie shook her head. "We don't have time to be creative. I'd say we should start with the traditional way."

"Wait a minute," I whispered. "Just hold on. Are you—are you talking about making Bella drink *blood*?"

"It was your idea, dog," Rosalie said, scowling at me without ever quite looking at me.

I ignored her and watched Carlisle. That same ghost of hope that had been in Edward's face was now in the doctor's eyes. He pursed his lips, speculating.

"That's just . . ." I couldn't find the right word.

"Monstrous?" Edward suggested. "Repulsive?"

"Pretty much."

"But what if it helps her?" he whispered.

I shook my head angrily. "What are you gonna do, shove a tube down her throat?"

"I plan to ask her what she thinks. I just wanted to run it past Carlisle first."

Rosalie nodded. "If you tell her it might help the baby, she'll be willing to do anything. Even if we do have to feed them through a tube."

I realized then—when I heard how her voice got all lovey-dovey as she said the word *baby*—that Blondie would be in line with anything that helped the little life-sucking monster. Was that what was going on, the mystery factor that was bonding the two of them? Was Rosalie after the kid?

From the corner of my eye, I saw Edward nod once, absently, not looking in my direction. But I knew he was answering my questions.

Huh. I wouldn't have thought the ice-cold Barbie would have a maternal side. So much for protecting Bella—Rosalie'd probably jam the tube down Bella's throat herself.

Edward's mouth mashed into a hard line, and I knew I was right again.

"Well, we don't have time to sit around discussing this," Rosalie said impatiently. "What do you think, Carlisle? Can we try?"

Carlisle took a deep breath, and then he was on his feet. "We'll ask Bella."

Blondie smiled smugly—sure that, if it was up to Bella, she would get her way.

I dragged myself up from the stairs and followed after

them as they disappeared into the house. I wasn't sure why. Just morbid curiosity, maybe. It was like a horror movie. Monsters and blood all over the place.

Maybe I just couldn't resist another hit of my dwindling drug supply.

Bella lay flat on the hospital bed, her belly a mountain under the sheet. She looked like wax—colorless and sort of see-through. You'd think she was already dead, except for the tiny movement of her chest, her shallow breathing. And then her eyes, following the four of us with exhausted suspicion.

The others were at her side already, flitting across the room with sudden darting motions. It was creepy to watch. I ambled along at a slow walk.

"What's going on?" Bella demanded in a scratchy whisper. Her waxy hand twitched up—like she was trying to protect her balloon-shaped stomach.

"Jacob had an idea that might help you," Carlisle said. I wished he would leave me out of it. I hadn't suggested anything. Give the credit to her bloodsucking husband, where it belonged. "It won't be . . . pleasant, but—"

"But it will help the baby," Rosalie interrupted eagerly. "We've thought of a better way to feed him. Maybe."

Bella's eyelids fluttered. Then she coughed out a weak chuckle. "Not pleasant?" she whispered. "Gosh, that'll be such a change." She eyed the tube stuck into her arm and coughed again.

Blondie laughed with her.

The girl looked like she only had hours left, and she had to be in pain, but she was making jokes. So Bella. Trying to ease the tension, make it better for everyone else.

Edward stepped around Rosalie, no humor touching his intense expression. I was glad for that. It helped, just a little bit, that he was suffering worse than me. He took her hand, not the one that was still protecting her swollen belly.

"Bella, love, we're going to ask you to do something monstrous," he said, using the same adjectives he'd offered me. "Repulsive."

Well, at least he was giving it to her straight.

She took a shallow, fluttery breath. "How bad?"

Carlisle answered. "We think the fetus might have an appetite closer to ours than to yours. We think it's thirsty."

She blinked. "Oh. *Oh.*"

"Your condition—both of your conditions—are deteriorating rapidly. We don't have time to waste, to come up with more palatable ways to do this. The fastest way to test the theory—"

"I've got to drink it," she whispered. She nodded slightly —barely enough energy for a little head bob. "I can do that. Practice for the future, right?" Her colorless lips stretched into a faint grin as she looked at Edward. He didn't smile back.

Rosalie started tapping her toe impatiently. The sound was really irritating. I wondered what she would do if I threw her through a wall right now.

"So, who's going to catch me a grizzly bear?" Bella whispered.

Carlisle and Edward exchanged a quick glance. Rosalie stopped tapping.

"What?" Bella asked.

"It will be a more effective test if we don't cut corners, Bella," Carlisle said.

"*If* the fetus is craving blood," Edward explained, "it's not craving animal blood."

"It won't make a difference to you, Bella. Don't think about it," Rosalie encouraged.

Bella's eyes widened. "Who?" she breathed, and her gaze flickered to me.

"I'm not here as a donor, Bells," I grumbled. "'Sides, it's human blood that thing's after, and I don't think mine applies—"

"We have blood on hand," Rosalie told her, talking over me before I'd finished, like I wasn't there. "For you—just in case. Don't worry about anything at all. It's going to be fine. I have a good feeling about this, Bella. I think the baby will be so much better."

Bella's hand ran across her stomach.

"Well," she rasped, barely audible. "*I'm* starving, so I'll bet he is, too." Trying to make another joke. "Let's go for it. My first vampire act."

13. GOOD THING I'VE GOT A STRONG STOMACH

CARLISLE AND ROSALIE WERE OFF IN A FLASH, DARTING upstairs. I could hear them debating whether they should warm it up for her. Ugh. I wondered what all house-of-horrors stuff they kept around here. Fridge full of blood, check. What else? Torture chamber? Coffin room?

Edward stayed, holding Bella's hand. His face was dead again. He didn't seem to have the energy to keep up even that little hint of hope he'd had before. They stared into each other's eyes, but not in a gooey way. It was like they were having a conversation. Kind of reminded me of Sam and Emily.

No, it wasn't gooey, but that only made it harder to watch.

I knew what it was like for Leah, having to see that all the time. Having to hear it in Sam's head. Of course we all felt bad for her, we weren't monsters—in that sense, anyway. But I guess we'd blamed her for how she handled it. Lashing out at everyone, trying to make us all as miserable as she was.

I would never blame her again. How could anyone help spreading this kind of misery around? How could anyone *not* try to ease some of the burden by shoving a little piece of it off on someone else?

And if it meant that I had to have a pack, how could I blame her for taking my freedom? I would do the same. If there was a way to escape this pain, I'd take it, too.

Rosalie darted downstairs after a second, flying through the room like a sharp breeze, stirring up the burning smell. She stopped inside the kitchen, and I heard the creak of a cupboard door.

"Not *clear*, Rosalie," Edward murmured. He rolled his eyes.

Bella looked curious, but Edward just shook his head at her.

Rosalie blew back through the room and disappeared again.

"This was your idea?" Bella whispered, her voice rough as she strained to make it loud enough for me to hear. Forgetting that I could hear just fine. I kind of liked how, a lot of the time, she seemed to forget that I wasn't completely human. I moved closer, so that she wouldn't have to work so hard.

"Don't blame me for this one. Your vampire was just picking snide comments out of my head."

She smiled a little. "I didn't expect to see you again."

"Yeah, me, either," I said.

It felt weird just standing here, but the vampires had shoved all the furniture out of the way for the medical setup. I imagined that it didn't bother them—sitting or standing didn't make much difference when you were stone. Wouldn't bother me much, either, except that I was so exhausted.

"Edward told me what you had to do. I'm sorry."

"S'okay. It was probably only a matter of time till I snapped over something Sam wanted me to do," I lied.

"And Seth," she whispered.

"He's actually happy to help."

"I hate causing you trouble."

I laughed once—more a bark than a laugh.

She breathed a faint sigh. "I guess that's nothing new, is it?"

"No, not really."

"You don't have to stay and watch this," she said, barely mouthing the words.

I could leave. It was probably a good idea. But if I did, with the way she looked right now, I could be missing the last fifteen minutes of her life.

"I don't really have anywhere else to go," I told her, trying to keep the emotion out of my voice. "The wolf thing is a lot less appealing since Leah joined up."

"Leah?" she gasped.

"You didn't tell her?" I asked Edward.

He just shrugged without moving his eyes from her face. I could see it wasn't very exciting news to him, not something worth sharing with the more important events that were going down.

Bella didn't take it so lightly. It looked like it was bad news to her.

"Why?" she breathed.

I didn't want to get into the whole novel-length version. "To keep an eye on Seth."

"But Leah hates us," she whispered.

Us. Nice. I could see that she was afraid, though.

"Leah's not going to bug anyone." But me. "She's in my pack"—I grimaced at the words—"so she follows my lead." Ugh.

Bella didn't look convinced.

"You're scared of *Leah*, but you're best buds with the psychopath blonde?"

There was a low hiss from the second floor. Cool, she'd heard me.

Bella frowned at me. "Don't. Rose . . . understands."

"Yeah," I grunted. "She understands that you're gonna die and she doesn't care, s'long as she gets her mutant spawn out of the deal."

"Stop being a jerk, Jacob," she whispered.

She looked too weak to get mad at. I tried to smile instead. "You say that like it's possible."

Bella tried not to smile back for a second, but she couldn't help it in the end; her chalky lips pulled up at the corners.

And then Carlisle and the psycho in question were there. Carlisle had a white plastic cup in his hand—the kind with a lid and a bendy straw. Oh—*not clear*; now I got it. Edward didn't want Bella to have to think about what she was doing any more than necessary. You couldn't see what was in the cup at all. But I could smell it.

Carlisle hesitated, the hand with the cup half-extended. Bella eyed it, looking scared again.

"We could try another method," Carlisle said quietly.

"No," Bella whispered. "No, I'll try this first. We don't have time. . . ."

At first I thought she'd finally gotten a clue and was worried about herself, but then her hand fluttered feebly against her stomach.

Bella reached out and took the cup from him. Her hand shook a little, and I could hear the sloshing from inside. She tried to prop herself up on one elbow, but she could barely lift her head. A whisper of heat brushed down my spine as I saw how frail she'd gotten in less than a day.

Rosalie put her arm under Bella's shoulders, supporting her head, too, like you did with a newborn. Blondie was all about the babies.

"Thanks," Bella whispered. Her eyes flickered around at us. Still aware enough to feel self-conscious. If she wasn't so drained, I'd bet she'd've blushed.

"Don't mind them," Rosalie murmured.

It made me feel awkward. I should've left when Bella'd offered the chance. I didn't belong here, being part of this. I thought about ducking out, but then I realized a move like that would only make this worse for Bella—make it harder for her to go through with it. She'd figure I was too disgusted to stay. Which was almost true.

Still. While I wasn't going to claim responsibility for this idea, I didn't want to jinx it, either.

Bella lifted the cup to her face and sniffed at the end of the straw. She flinched, and then made a face.

"Bella, sweetheart, we can find an easier way," Edward said, holding his hand out for the cup.

"Plug your nose," Rosalie suggested. She glared at Edward's hand like she might take a snap at it. I wished she would. I bet Edward wouldn't take *that* sitting down, and I'd love to see Blondie lose a limb.

"No, that's not it. It's just that it—" Bella sucked in a deep breath. "It smells good," she admitted in a tiny voice.

I swallowed hard, fighting to keep the disgust off my face.

"That's a good thing," Rosalie told Bella eagerly. "That means we're on the right track. Give it a try." Given Blondie's new expression, I was surprised she didn't break into a touchdown dance.

Bella shoved the straw between her lips, squeezed her eyes shut, and wrinkled her nose. I could hear the blood slopping around in the cup again as her hand shook. She sipped at it for a second, and then moaned quietly with her eyes still closed.

Edward and I stepped forward at the same time. He touched her face. I clenched my hands behind my back.

"Bella, love—"

"I'm okay," she whispered. She opened her eyes and stared up at him. Her expression was . . . apologetic. Pleading. Scared. "It *tastes* good, too."

Acid churned in my stomach, threatening to overflow. I ground my teeth together.

"That's good," Blondie repeated, still jazzed. "A good sign."

Edward just pressed his hand to her cheek, curling his fingers around the shape of her fragile bones.

Bella sighed and put her lips to the straw again. She took a real pull this time. The action wasn't as weak as everything else about her. Like some instinct was taking over.

"How's your stomach? Do you feel nauseated?" Carlisle asked.

Bella shook her head. "No, I don't feel sick," she whispered. "There's a first, eh?"

Rosalie beamed. "Excellent."

"I think it's a bit early for that, Rose," Carlisle murmured.

Bella gulped another mouthful of blood. Then she flashed a look at Edward. "Does this screw my total?" she whispered. "Or do we start counting *after* I'm a vampire?"

"No one is counting, Bella. In any case, no one died for this." He smiled a lifeless smile. "Your record is still clean."

They'd lost me.

"I'll explain later," Edward said, so low the words were just a breath.

"What?" Bella whispered.

"Just talking to myself," he lied smoothly.

If he succeeded with this, if Bella lived, Edward wasn't going to be able to get away with so much when her senses were as sharp as his. He'd have to work on the honesty thing.

Edward's lips twitched, fighting a smile.

Bella chugged a few more ounces, staring past us toward the window. Probably pretending we weren't here. Or maybe just me. No one else in this group would be disgusted by what she was doing. Just the opposite—they were probably having a tough time not ripping the cup away from her.

Edward rolled his eyes.

Jeez, how did anyone stand living with him? It was really too bad he couldn't hear Bella's thoughts. Then he'd annoy the crap out of her, too, and she'd get tired of him.

Edward chuckled once. Bella's eyes flicked to him immediately, and she half-smiled at the humor in his face. I would guess that wasn't something she'd seen in a while.

"Something funny?" she breathed.

"Jacob," he answered.

She looked over with another weary smile for me. "Jake's a crack-up," she agreed.

Great, now I was the court jester. "Bada *bing*," I mumbled in weak rim-shot impression.

She smiled again, and then took another swig from the cup. I flinched when the straw pulled at empty air, making a loud sucking sound.

"I did it," she said, sounding pleased. Her voice was clearer—rough, but not a whisper for the first time today. "If I keep this down, Carlisle, will you take the needles out of me?"

"As soon as possible," he promised. "Honestly, they aren't doing that much good where they are."

Rosalie patted Bella's forehead, and they exchanged a hopeful glance.

And anyone could see it—the cup full of human blood had made an immediate difference. Her color was returning—there was a tiny hint of pink in her waxy cheeks. Already she didn't seem to need Rosalie's support so much anymore. Her breathing was easier, and I would swear her heartbeat was stronger, more even.

Everything accelerated.

That ghost of hope in Edward's eyes had turned into the real thing.

"Would you like more?" Rosalie pressed.

Bella's shoulders slumped.

Edward flashed a glare at Rosalie before he spoke to Bella. "You don't have to drink more right away."

"Yeah, I know. But . . . I *want* to," she admitted glumly.

Rosalie pulled her thin, sharp fingers through Bella's lank hair. "You don't need to be embarrassed about that, Bella. Your body has cravings. We all understand that." Her tone was soothing at first, but then she added harshly, "Anyone who doesn't understand shouldn't be here."

Meant for me, obviously, but I wasn't going to let Blondie get to me. I was glad Bella felt better. So what if the means grossed me out? It wasn't like I'd said anything.

Carlisle took the cup from Bella's hand. "I'll be right back."

Bella stared at me while he disappeared.

"Jake, you look awful," she croaked.

"Look who's talking."

"Seriously—when's the last time you slept?"

I thought about that for a second. "Huh. I'm not actually sure."

"Aw, Jake. Now I'm messing with your health, too. Don't be stupid."

I gritted my teeth. She was allowed to kill herself for a monster, but I wasn't allowed to miss a few nights' sleep to watch her do it?

"Get some rest, please," she went on. "There're a few beds upstairs—you're welcome to any of them."

The look on Rosalie's face made it clear that I wasn't welcome to one of them. It made me wonder what Sleepless Beauty needed a bed for anyway. Was she that possessive of her props?

"Thanks, Bells, but I'd rather sleep on the ground. Away from the stench, you know."

She grimaced. "Right."

Carlisle was back then, and Bella reached out for the blood, absentminded, like she was thinking of something else. With the same distracted expression, she started sucking it down.

She really was looking better. She pulled herself forward, being careful of the tubes, and scooted into a sitting position. Rosalie hovered, her hands ready to catch Bella if she sagged. But Bella didn't need her. Taking deep breaths in between swallows, Bella finished the second cup quickly.

"How do you feel now?" Carlisle asked.

"Not sick. Sort of hungry . . . only I'm not sure if I'm hungry or *thirsty*, you know?"

"Carlisle, just look at her," Rosalie murmured, so smug she should have canary feathers on her lips. "This is obviously what her body wants. She should drink more."

"She's still human, Rosalie. She needs food, too. Let's give her a little while to see how this affects her, and then maybe we can try some food again. Does anything sound particularly good to you, Bella?"

"Eggs," she said immediately, and then she exchanged a look and a smile with Edward. His smile was brittle, but there was more life on his face than before.

I blinked then, and almost forgot how to open my eyes again.

"Jacob," Edward murmured. "You really should sleep. As Bella said, you're certainly welcome to the accommodations here, though you'd probably be more comfortable outside. Don't worry about anything—I promise I'll find you if there's a need."

"Sure, sure," I mumbled. Now that it appeared Bella had a few more hours, I could escape. Go curl up under a tree somewhere. . . . Far enough away that the smell couldn't reach me. The bloodsucker would wake me up if something went wrong. He owed me.

"I do," Edward agreed.

I nodded and then put my hand on Bella's. Hers was icy cold.

"Feel better," I said.

"Thanks, Jacob." She turned her hand over and squeezed mine. I felt the thin band of her wedding ring riding loose on her skinny finger.

"Get her a blanket or something," I muttered as I turned for the door.

Before I made it, two howls pierced the still morning air. There was no mistaking the urgency of the tone. No misunderstanding this time.

"Dammit," I snarled, and I threw myself through the door. I hurled my body off the porch, letting the fire rip me apart midair. There was a sharp tearing sound as my shorts shredded. *Crap.* Those were the only clothes I had. Didn't matter now. I landed on paws and took off toward the west.

What is it? I shouted in my head.

Incoming, Seth answered. *At least three.*

Did they split up?

I'm running the line back to Seth at the speed of light, Leah promised. I could feel the air huffing through her lungs as she pushed herself to an incredible velocity. The forest whipped around her. *So far, no other point of attack.*

Seth, do not *challenge them. Wait for me.*

They're slowing. Ugh—it's so off not *being able to hear them. I think . . .*

What?

I think they've stopped.

Waiting for the rest of the pack?

Shh. Feel that?

I absorbed his impressions. The faint, soundless shimmer in the air.

Someone's phasing?

Feels like it, Seth agreed.

Leah flew into the small open space where Seth waited. She raked her claws into the dirt, spinning out like a race car.

Got your back, bro.

They're coming, Seth said nervously. *Slow. Walking.*

Almost there, I told them. I tried to fly like Leah. It felt horrible being separated from Seth and Leah with potential danger closer to their end than mine. Wrong. I should be with them, between them and whatever was coming.

Look who's getting all paternal, Leah thought wryly.

Head in the game, Leah.

Four, Seth decided. Kid had good ears. *Three wolves, one man.*

I made the little clearing then, moving immediately to the point. Seth sighed with relief and then straightened up, already in place at my right shoulder. Leah fell in on my left with a little less enthusiasm.

So now I rank under Seth, she grumbled to herself.

First come, first served, Seth thought smugly. *'Sides, you were never an Alpha's Third before. Still an upgrade.*

Under my baby brother is not an upgrade.

Shh! I complained. *I don't care where you stand. Shut up and get ready.*

They came into view a few seconds later, walking, as Seth had thought. Jared in the front, human, hands up. Paul and Quil and Collin on four legs behind him. There was no aggression in their postures. They hung back behind Jared, ears up, alert but calm.

But . . . it was weird that Sam would send Collin rather than Embry. That wasn't what I would do if I were sending a diplomacy party into enemy territory. I wouldn't send a kid. I'd send the experienced fighter.

A diversion? Leah thought.

Were Sam, Embry, and Brady making a move alone? That didn't seem likely.

Want me to check? I can run the line and be back in two minutes.

Should I warn the Cullens? Seth wondered.

What if the point was to divide us? I asked. *The Cullens know something's up. They're ready.*

Sam wouldn't be so stupid . . . , Leah whispered, fear jagged in her mind. She was imagining Sam attacking the Cullens with only the two others beside him.

No, he wouldn't, I assured her, though I felt a little sick at the image in her head, too.

All the while, Jared and the three wolves stared at us,

waiting. It was eerie not to hear what Quil and Paul and Collin were saying to one another. Their expressions were blank—unreadable.

Jared cleared his throat, and then he nodded to me. "White flag of truce, Jake. We're here to talk."

Think it's true? Seth asked.

Makes sense, but . . .

Yeah, Leah agreed. *But.*

We didn't relax.

Jared frowned. "It would be easier to talk if I could hear you, too."

I stared him down. I wasn't going to phase back until I felt better about this situation. Until it made sense. Why Collin? That was the part that had me most worried.

"Okay. I guess I'll just talk, then," Jared said. "Jake, we want you to come back."

Quil let out a soft whine behind him. Seconding the statement.

"You've torn our family apart. It's not meant to be this way."

I wasn't exactly in disagreement with that, but it was hardly the point. There were a few unresolved differences of opinion between me and Sam at the moment.

"We know that you feel . . . strongly about the situation with the Cullens. We know that's a problem. But this is an overreaction."

Seth growled. *Overreaction? And attacking our allies without warning* isn't?

Seth, you ever heard of a poker face? Cool it.

Sorry.

Jared's eyes flickered to Seth and back to me. "Sam is

willing to take this slowly, Jacob. He's calmed down, talked to the other Elders. They've decided that immediate action is in no one's best interest at this point."

Translation: They've already lost the element of surprise, Leah thought.

It was weird how distinct our joint thinking was. The pack was already Sam's pack, was already "them" to us. Something outside and other. It was especially weird to have Leah thinking that way—to have her be a solid part of the "us."

"Billy and Sue agree with you, Jacob, that we can wait for Bella . . . to be separated from the problem. Killing her is not something any of us feel comfortable with."

Though I'd just given Seth crap for it, I couldn't hold back a small snarl of my own. So they didn't quite *feel comfortable* with murder, huh?

Jared raised his hands again. "Easy, Jake. You know what I mean. The point is, we're going to wait and reassess the situation. Decide later if there's a problem with the . . . thing."

Ha, Leah thought. *What a load.*

You don't buy it?

I know what they're thinking, Jake. What Sam's *thinking. They're betting on Bella dying anyway. And then they figure you'll be so mad . . .*

That I'll lead the attack myself. My ears pressed against my skull. What Leah was guessing sounded pretty spot-on. And very possible, too. When . . . if that thing killed Bella, it was going to be easy to forget how I felt about Carlisle's family right now. They would probably look like enemies—like no more than bloodsucking leeches—to me all over again.

I'll remind you, Seth whispered.

I know you will, kid. Question is whether I'll listen to you.

"Jake?" Jared asked.

I huffed a sigh.

Leah, make a circuit—just to be sure. I'm going to have to talk to him, and I want to be positive there isn't anything else going on while I'm phased.

Give me a break, Jacob. You can phase in front of me. Despite my best efforts, I've seen you naked before—doesn't do much for me, so no worries.

I'm not trying to protect the innocence of your eyes, I'm trying to protect our backs. Get out of here.

Leah snorted once and then launched herself into the forest. I could hear her claws cutting into the soil, pushing her faster.

Nudity was an inconvenient but unavoidable part of pack life. We'd all thought nothing of it before Leah came along. Then it got awkward. Leah had average control when it came to her temper—it took her the usual length of time to stop exploding out of her clothes every time she got pissed. We'd all caught a glimpse. And it wasn't like she wasn't worth looking at; it was just that it was so *not* worth it when she caught you thinking about it later.

Jared and the others were staring at the place where she'd disappeared into the brush with wary expressions.

"Where's she going?" Jared asked.

I ignored him, closing my eyes and pulling myself together again. It felt like the air was trembling around me, shaking out from me in small waves. I lifted myself up on my hind legs, catching the moment just right so that I was fully upright as I shimmered down into my human self.

"Oh," Jared said. "Hey, Jake."

"Hey, Jared."

"Thanks for talking to me."

"Yeah."

"We want you to come back, man."

Quil whined again.

"I don't know if it's that easy, Jared."

"Come home," he said, leaning forward. Pleading. "We can sort this out. You don't belong here. Let Seth and Leah come home, too."

I laughed. "Right. Like I haven't been begging them to do that from hour one."

Seth snorted behind me.

Jared assessed that, his eyes cautious again. "So, what now, then?"

I thought that over for a minute while he waited.

"I don't know. But I'm not sure things could just go back to normal anyway, Jared. I don't know how it works—it doesn't feel like I can just turn this Alpha thing off and on as the mood strikes. It feels sort of permanent."

"You still belong with us."

I raised my eyebrows. "Two Alphas can't belong in the same place, Jared. Remember how close it got last night? The instinct is too competitive."

"So are you all just going to hang out with the parasites for the rest of your lives?" he demanded. "You don't have a home here. You're already out of clothes," he pointed out.

"You gonna stay wolf all the time? You know Leah doesn't like eating that way."

"Leah can do whatever she wants when she gets hungry. She's here by her own choice. *I'm* not telling anyone what to do."

Jared sighed. "Sam is sorry about what he did to you."

I nodded. "I'm not angry anymore."

"But?"

"But I'm not coming back, not now. We're going to wait and see how it plays out, too. And we're going to watch out for the Cullens for as long as that seems necessary. Because, despite what you think, this isn't just about Bella. We're protecting those who should be protected. And that applies to the Cullens, too." At least a fair number of them, anyway.

Seth yelped softly in agreement.

Jared frowned. "I guess there's nothing I can say to you, then."

"Not now. We'll see how things go."

Jared turned to face Seth, concentrating on him now, separate from me. "Sue asked me to tell you—no, to *beg* you—to come home. She's brokenhearted, Seth. All alone. I don't know how you and Leah can do this to her. Abandon her this way, when your dad just barely died—"

Seth whimpered.

"Ease up, Jared," I warned.

"Just letting him know how it is."

I snorted. "Right." Sue was tougher than anyone I knew. Tougher than my dad, tougher than me. Tough enough to play on her kids' sympathies if that's what it took to get them home. But it wasn't fair to work Seth that way. "Sue's known about this for how many hours now? And most of that time spent with Billy and Old Quil and Sam? Yeah, I'm sure she's just perishing of loneliness. 'Course you're free to go if you want, Seth. You know that."

Seth sniffed.

Then, a second later, he cocked an ear to the north. Leah must be close. Jeez, she was fast. Two beats, and Leah skidded to a stop in the brush a few yards away. She trotted in, taking the point in front of Seth. She kept her nose in the air, very obviously not looking in my direction.

I appreciated that.

"Leah?" Jared asked.

She met his gaze, her muzzle pulling back a little over her teeth.

Jared didn't seem surprised by her hostility. "Leah, you *know* you don't want to be here."

She snarled at him. I gave her a warning glance she didn't see. Seth whined and nudged her with his shoulder.

"Sorry," Jared said. "Guess I shouldn't assume. But you don't have any ties to the bloodsuckers."

Leah very deliberately looked at her brother and then at me.

"So you want to watch out for Seth, I get that," Jared said. His eyes touched my face and then went back to hers. Probably wondering about that second look—just like I was. "But Jake's not going to let anything happen to him, and he's not afraid to be here." Jared made a face. "Anyway, *please*, Leah. We want you back. Sam wants you back."

Leah's tail twitched.

"Sam told me to beg. He told me to literally get down

on my knees if I have to. He wants you home, Lee-lee, where you belong."

I saw Leah flinch when Jared used Sam's old nickname for her. And then, when he added those last three words, her hackles rose and she was yowling a long stream of snarls through her teeth. I didn't have to be in her head to hear the cussing-out she was giving him, and neither did he. You could almost hear the exact words she was using.

I waited till she was done. "I'm going to go out on a limb here and say that Leah belongs wherever she wants to be."

Leah growled, but, as she was glaring at Jared, I figured it was in agreement.

"Look, Jared, we're still family, okay? We'll get past the feud, but, until we do, you probably ought to stick to your land. Just so there aren't misunderstandings. Nobody wants a family brawl, right? Sam doesn't want that, either, does he?"

"Of course, not," Jared snapped. "We'll stick to our land. But where is *your* land, Jacob? Is it vampire land?"

"No, Jared. Homeless at the moment. But don't worry—this isn't going to last forever." I had to take a breath. "There's not that much time . . . left. Okay? Then the Cullens will probably go, and Seth and Leah will come home."

Leah and Seth whined together, their noses turning my direction in synchronization.

"And what about you, Jake?"

"Back to the forest, I think. I can't really stick around La Push. Two Alphas means too much tension. 'Sides, I was headed that way anyway. Before this mess."

"What if we need to talk?" Jared asked.

"Howl—but watch the line, 'kay? We'll come to you.

And Sam doesn't need to send so many. We aren't looking for a fight."

Jared scowled, but nodded. He didn't like me setting conditions for Sam. "See you around, Jake. Or not." He waved halfheartedly.

"Wait, Jared. Is Embry okay?"

Surprise crossed his face. "Embry? Sure, he's fine. Why?"

"Just wondering why Sam sent Collin."

I watched his reaction, still suspicious that something was going on. I saw knowledge flash in his eyes, but it didn't look like the kind I was expecting.

"That's not really your business anymore, Jake."

"Guess not. Just curious."

I saw a twitch from the corner of my eye, but I didn't acknowledge it, because I didn't want to give Quil away. He was reacting to the subject.

"I'll let Sam know about your . . . instructions. Goodbye, Jacob."

I sighed. "Yeah. Bye, Jared. Hey, tell my dad that I'm okay, will you? And that I'm sorry, and that I love him."

"I'll pass that along."

"Thanks."

"C'mon, guys," Jared said. He turned away from us, heading out of sight to phase because Leah was here. Paul and Collin were right on his heels, but Quil hesitated. He yelped softly, and I took a step toward him.

"Yeah, I miss you, too, bro."

Quil jogged over to me, his head hanging down morosely. I patted his shoulder.

"It'll be okay."

He whined.

"Tell Embry I miss having you two on my flanks."

He nodded and then pressed his nose to my forehead. Leah snorted. Quil looked up, but not at her. He looked back over his shoulder at where the others had gone.

"Yeah, go home," I told him.

Quil yelped again and then took off after the others. I'd bet Jared wasn't waiting super-patiently. As soon as he was gone, I pulled the warmth from the center of my body and let it surge through my limbs. In a flash of heat, I was on four legs again.

Thought you were going to make out with him, Leah snickered.

I ignored her.

Was that okay? I asked them. It worried me, speaking *for* them that way, when I couldn't hear exactly what they were thinking. I didn't want to assume anything. I didn't want to be like Jared that way. *Did I say anything you didn't want me to? Did I not say something I should have?*

You did great, Jake! Seth encouraged.

You could have hit Jared, Leah thought. *I wouldn't have minded that.*

I guess we know why Embry wasn't allowed to come, Seth thought.

I didn't understand. *Not allowed?*

Jake, didya see Quil? He's pretty torn up, right? I'd put ten to one that Embry's even more upset. And Embry doesn't have a Claire. There's no way Quil can just pick up and walk away from La Push. Embry might. So Sam's not going to take any chances on him getting convinced to jump ship. He doesn't want our pack any bigger than it is now.

Really? You think? I doubt Embry would mind shredding some Cullens.

But he's your best friend, Jake. He and Quil would rather stand behind you than face you in a fight.

Well, I'm glad Sam kept him home, then. This pack is big enough. I sighed. *Okay, then. So we're good, for now. Seth, you mind keeping an eye on things for a while? Leah and I both need to crash. This felt on the level, but who knows? Maybe it was a distraction.*

I wasn't always so paranoid, but I remembered the feel of Sam's commitment. The total one-track focus on destroying the danger he saw. Would he take advantage of the fact that he could lie to us now?

No problem! Seth was only too eager to do whatever he could. *You want me to explain to the Cullens? They're probably still kinda tense.*

I got it. I want to check things out anyway.

They caught the whir of images from my fried brain.

Seth whimpered in surprise. *Ew.*

Leah whipped her head back and forth like she was trying to shake the image out of her mind. *That is easily the freakin' grossest thing I've heard in my life. Yuck. If there was anything in my stomach, it would be coming back.*

They are vampires, I guess, Seth allowed after a minute, compensating for Leah's reaction. *I mean, it makes sense. And if it helps Bella, it's a good thing, right?*

Both Leah and I stared at him.

What?

Mom dropped him a lot when he was a baby, Leah told me. *On his head, apparently.*

He used to gnaw on the crib bars, too.

Lead paint?

Looks like it, she thought.

Seth snorted. *Funny. Why don't you two shut up and sleep?*

14. YOU KNOW THINGS ARE BAD WHEN YOU FEEL GUILTY FOR BEING RUDE TO VAMPIRES

WHEN I GOT BACK TO THE HOUSE, THERE WAS NO ONE waiting outside for my report. Still on alert?

Everything's cool, I thought tiredly.

My eyes quickly caught a small change in the now-familiar scene. There was a stack of light-colored fabric on the bottom step of the porch. I loped over to investigate. Holding my breath, because the vampire smell stuck to the fabric like you wouldn't believe, I nudged the stack with my nose.

Someone had laid out clothes. Huh. Edward must have caught my moment of irritation as I'd bolted out the door. Well. That was . . . nice. And weird.

I took the clothes gingerly between my teeth—ugh—

and carried them back to the trees. Just in case this was some joke by the blond psychopath and I had a bunch of girls' stuff here. Bet she'd love to see the look on my human face as I stood there naked, holding a sundress.

In the cover of the trees, I dropped the stinking pile and shifted back to human. I shook the clothes out, snapping them against a tree to beat some of the smell from them. They were definitely guy's clothes—tan pants and a white button-down shirt. Neither of them long enough, but they looked like they'd fit around me. Must be Emmett's. I rolled the cuffs up on the shirtsleeves, but there wasn't much I could do about the pants. Oh well.

I had to admit, I felt better with some clothes to my name, even stinky ones that didn't quite fit. It was hard not being able to just jet back home and grab another pair of old sweatpants when I needed them. The homeless thing again—not having anyplace to go *back* to. No possessions, either, which wasn't bothering me too bad now, but would probably get annoying soon.

Exhausted, I walked slowly up the Cullens' porch steps in my fancy new secondhand clothes but hesitated when I got to the door. Did I knock? Stupid, when they knew I was here. I wondered why no one acknowledged that—told me either to *come in* or *get lost*. Whatever. I shrugged and let myself in.

More changes. The room had shifted back to normal—almost—in the last twenty minutes. The big flat-screen was on, low volume, showing some chick flick that no one seemed to be watching. Carlisle and Esme stood by the back windows, which were open to the river again. Alice, Jasper, and Emmett were out of sight, but I heard them murmuring upstairs. Bella was on the couch like yesterday, with just one tube still hooked into her, and an IV hanging behind the back of the sofa. She was wrapped up like a burrito in a couple of thick quilts, so at least they'd listened to me before. Rosalie was cross-legged on the ground by her head. Edward sat at the other end of the couch with Bella's burrito'ed feet in his lap. He looked up when I came in and smiled at me—just a little twitch of his mouth—like something pleased him.

Bella didn't hear me. She only glanced up when he did, and then she smiled, too. With real energy, her whole face lighting up. I couldn't remember the last time she'd looked so excited to see me.

What was *with* her? For crying out loud, she was *married*! Happily married, too—there was no question that she was in love with her vampire past the boundaries of sanity. And hugely pregnant, to top it off.

So why did she have to be so damn thrilled to see me? Like I'd made her whole freakin' day by walking through the door.

If she would just not care . . . Or more than that—really not want me around. It would be so much easier to stay away.

Edward seemed to be in agreement with my thoughts—we were on the same wavelength so much lately it was crazy. He was frowning now, reading her face while she beamed at me.

"They just wanted to talk," I mumbled, my voice dragging with exhaustion. "No attack on the horizon."

"Yes," Edward answered. "I heard most of it."

That woke me up a little. We'd been a good three miles out. "How?"

"I'm hearing you more clearly—it's a matter of familiarity and concentration. Also, your thoughts are slightly easier to pick up when you're in your human form. So I caught most of what passed out there."

"Oh." It bugged me a little, but for no good reason, so I shrugged it off. "Good. I hate repeating myself."

"I'd tell you to go get some sleep," Bella said, "but my guess is that you're going to pass out on the floor in about six seconds, so there's probably no point."

It was amazing how much better she sounded, how much stronger she looked. I smelled fresh blood and saw that the cup was in her hands again. How much blood would it take to keep her going? At some point, would they start trotting in the neighbors?

I headed for the door, counting off the seconds for her as I walked. "One Mississippi . . . two Mississippi . . ."

"Where's the flood, mutt?" Rosalie muttered.

"You know how you drown a blonde, Rosalie?" I asked without stopping or turning to look at her. "Glue a mirror to the bottom of a pool."

I heard Edward chuckle as I pulled the door shut. His mood seemed to improve in exact correlation to Bella's health.

"I've already heard that one," Rosalie called after me.

I trudged down the steps, my only goal to drag myself far enough into the trees that the air would be pure again. I planned to ditch the clothes a convenient distance from the house for future use rather than tying them to my leg, so I wouldn't be smelling them, either. As I fumbled with the buttons on the new shirt, I thought randomly about how buttons would never be in style for werewolves.

I heard the voices while I slogged across the lawn.

"Where are you going?" Bella asked.

"There was something I forgot to say to him."

"Let Jacob sleep—it can wait."

Yes, *please*, let Jacob sleep.

"It will only take a moment."

I turned slowly. Edward was already out the door. He had an apology in his expression as he approached me.

"Jeez, what *now?*"

"I'm sorry," he said, and then he hesitated, like he didn't know how to phrase what he was thinking.

What's on your mind, mind reader?

"When you were speaking to Sam's delegates earlier," he murmured, "I was giving a play-by-play for Carlisle and Esme and the rest. They were concerned—"

"Look, we're not dropping our guard. You don't have to believe Sam like we do. We're keeping our eyes open regardless."

"No, no, Jacob. Not about that. We trust your judgment. Rather, Esme was troubled by the hardships this is putting your pack through. She asked me to speak to you privately about it."

That took me off guard. "Hardships?"

"The *homeless* part, particularly. She's very upset that you are all so . . . bereft."

I snorted. Vampire mother hen—bizarre. "We're tough. Tell her not to worry."

"She'd still like to do what she can. I got the impression that Leah prefers not to eat in her wolf form?"

"And?" I demanded.

"Well, we do have normal human food here, Jacob. Keeping up appearances, and, of course, for Bella. Leah is welcome to anything she'd like. All of you are."

"I'll pass that along."

"Leah hates us."

"So?"

"So try to pass it along in such a way as to make her consider it, if you don't mind."

"I'll do what I can."

"And then there's the matter of clothes."

I glanced down at the ones I was wearing. "Oh yeah. Thanks." It probably wouldn't be good manners to mention how bad they reeked.

He smiled, just a little. "Well, we're easily able to help out with any needs there. Alice rarely allows us to wear the same thing twice. We've got piles of brand-new clothes that are destined for Goodwill, and I'd imagine that Leah is fairly close to Esme's size. . . ."

"Not sure how she'll feel about bloodsucker castoffs. She's not as practical as I am."

"I trust that you can present the offer in the best possible light. As well as the offer for any other physical object you might need, or transportation, or anything else at all. And showers, too, since you prefer to sleep outdoors. Please . . . don't consider yourselves without the benefits of a home."

He said the last line softly—not trying to keep quiet this time, but with some kind of real emotion.

I stared at him for a second, blinking sleepily. "That's, er, nice of you. Tell Esme we appreciate the, uh, thought. But the perimeter cuts through the river in a few places, so we stay pretty clean, thanks."

"If you would pass the offer on, regardless."

"Sure, sure."

"Thank you."

I turned away from him, only to stop cold when I heard the low, pained cry from inside the house. By the time I looked back, he was already gone.

What *now*?

I followed after him, shuffling like a zombie. Using about the same number of brain cells, too. It didn't feel like I had a choice. Something was wrong. I would go see what it was. There would be nothing I could do. And I would feel worse.

It seemed inevitable.

I let myself in again. Bella was panting, curled over the bulge in the center of her body. Rosalie held her while Edward, Carlisle, and Esme all hovered. A flicker of motion caught my eye; Alice was at the top of the stairs, staring down into the room with her hands pressed to her temples. It was weird—like she was barred from entering somehow.

"Give me a second, Carlisle," Bella panted.

"Bella," the doctor said anxiously, "I heard something crack. I need to take a look."

"Pretty sure"—pant—"it was a rib. Ow. Yep. Right here." She pointed to her left side, careful not to touch.

It was breaking her *bones* now.

"I need to take an X-ray. There might be splinters. We don't want it to puncture anything."

Bella took a deep breath. "Okay."

Rosalie lifted Bella carefully. Edward seemed like he

was going to argue, but Rosalie bared her teeth at him and growled, "I've already got her."

So Bella was stronger now, but the thing was, too. You couldn't starve one without starving the other, and healing worked just the same. No way to win.

Blondie carried Bella swiftly up the big staircase with Carlisle and Edward right on her heels, none of them taking any notice of me standing dumbstruck in the doorway.

So they had a blood bank *and* an X-ray machine? Guess the doc brought his work home with him.

I was too tired to follow them, too tired to move. I leaned back against the wall and then slid to the ground. The door was still open, and I pointed my nose toward it, grateful for the clean breeze blowing in. I leaned my head against the jamb and listened.

I could hear the sound of the X-ray machinery upstairs. Or maybe I just assumed that's what it was. And then the lightest of footsteps coming down the stairs. I didn't look to see which vampire it was.

"Do you want a pillow?" Alice asked me.

"No," I mumbled. What was with the pushy hospitality? It was creeping me out.

"That doesn't look comfortable," she observed.

"S'not."

"Why don't you move, then?"

"Tired. Why aren't you upstairs with the rest of them?" I shot back.

"Headache," she answered.

I rolled my head around to look at her.

Alice was a tiny little thing. 'Bout the size of one of my

arms. She looked even smaller now, sort of hunched in on herself. Her small face was pinched.

"Vampires get headaches?"

"Not the normal ones."

I snorted. Normal vampires.

"So how come you're never with Bella anymore?" I asked, making the question an accusation. It hadn't occurred to me before, because my head had been full of other crap, but it was weird that Alice was never around Bella, not since I'd been here. Maybe if Alice were by her side, Rosalie *wouldn't* be. "Thought you two were like this." I twisted two of my fingers together.

"Like I said"—she curled up on the tile a few feet from me, wrapping her skinny arms around her skinny knees—"headache."

"Bella's giving you a headache?"

"Yes."

I frowned. Pretty sure I was too tired for riddles. I let my head roll back around toward the fresh air and closed my eyes.

"Not Bella, really," she amended. "The . . . fetus."

Ah, someone else who felt like I did. It was pretty easy to recognize. She said the word grudgingly, the way Edward did.

"I can't see it," she told me, though she might have been talking to herself. For all she knew, I was already gone. "I can't see anything about it. Just like you."

I flinched, and then my teeth ground together. I didn't like being compared to the creature.

"Bella gets in the way. She's all wrapped around it, so she's . . . blurry. Like bad reception on a TV—like trying to focus your eyes on those fuzzy people jerking around on the screen. It's killing my head to watch her. And I can't see more than a few minutes ahead, anyway. The . . . fetus is too much a part of her future. When she first decided . . . when she knew she wanted it, she blurred right out of my sight. Scared me to death."

She was quiet for a second, and then she added, "I have to admit, it's a relief having you close by—in spite of the wet-dog smell. Everything goes away. Like having my eyes closed. It numbs the headache."

"Happy to be of service, ma'am," I mumbled.

"I wonder what it has in common with you . . . why you're the same that way."

Sudden heat flashed in the center of my bones. I clenched my fists to hold off the tremors.

"I have nothing in common with that life-sucker," I said through my teeth.

"Well, there's *something* there."

I didn't answer. The heat was already burning away. I was too dead tired to stay furious.

"You don't mind if I sit here by you, do you?" she asked.

"Guess not. Stinks anyway."

"Thanks," she said. "This is the best thing for it, I guess, since I can't take aspirin."

"Could you keep it down? Sleeping, here."

She didn't respond, immediately lapsing into silence. I was out in seconds.

I was dreaming that I was really thirsty. And there was a big glass of water in front of me—all cold, you could see the condensation running down the sides. I grabbed the cup and took a huge gulp, only to find out pretty quick that it wasn't water—it was straight bleach. I choked it back out, spewing it everywhere, and a bunch of it blew out of my nose. It burned. My nose was on fire. . . .

The pain in my nose woke me up enough to remember where I'd fallen asleep. The smell was pretty fierce, considering that my nose wasn't actually inside the house. Ugh. And it was noisy. Someone was laughing too loud. A familiar laugh, but one that didn't go with the smell. Didn't belong.

I groaned and opened my eyes. The skies were dull gray—it was daytime, but no clue as to when. Maybe close to sunset—it was pretty dark.

"About time," Blondie mumbled from not too far away. "The chainsaw impersonation was getting a little tired."

I rolled over and wrenched myself into a sitting position. In the process, I figured out where the smell was coming from. Someone had stuffed a wide feather pillow under my face. Probably *trying* to be nice, I'd guess. Unless it'd been Rosalie.

Once my face was out of the stinking feathers, I caught other scents. Like bacon and cinnamon, all mixed up with the vampire smell.

I blinked, taking in the room.

Things hadn't changed too much, except that now Bella was sitting up in the middle of the sofa, and the IV was gone. Blondie sat at her feet, her head resting against Bella's knees. Still gave me chills to see how casually they touched her, though I guess that was pretty brain-dead, all things considered. Edward was on one side of her, holding her hand. Alice was on the floor, too, like Rosalie. Her face wasn't pinched up now. And it was easy to see why—she'd found another painkiller.

"Hey, Jake's coming around!" Seth crowed.

He was sitting on Bella's other side, his arm slung carelessly over her shoulders, an overflowing plate of food on his lap.

What the hell?

"He came to find you," Edward said while I got to my feet. "And Esme convinced him to stay for breakfast."

Seth took in my expression, and he hurried to explain. "Yeah, Jake—I was just checking to see if you were okay 'cause you didn't ever phase back. Leah got worried. I *told* her you probably just crashed human, but you know how she is. Anyway, they had all this food and, dang,"—he turned to Edward—"man, you can *cook*."

"Thank you," Edward murmured.

I inhaled slowly, trying to unclench my teeth. I couldn't take my eyes off Seth's arm.

"Bella got cold," Edward said quietly.

Right. None of my business, anyway. She didn't belong to me.

Seth heard Edward's comment, looked at my face, and suddenly he needed both hands to eat with. He took his arm off Bella and dug in. I walked over to stand a few feet from the couch, still trying to get my bearings.

"Leah running patrol?" I asked Seth. My voice was still thick with sleep.

"Yeah," he said as he chewed. Seth had new clothes on, too. They fit him better than mine fit me. "She's on it. No worries. She'll howl if there's anything. We traded off around midnight. I ran twelve hours." He was proud of that, and it showed in his tone.

"Midnight? Wait a minute—what time is it now?"

"'Bout dawn." He glanced toward the window, checking.

Well, *damn*. I'd slept through the rest of the day and the whole night—dropped the ball. "Crap. Sorry about that, Seth. Really. You shoulda kicked me awake."

"Naw, man, you needed some serious sleep. You haven't taken a break since when? Night before your last patrol for Sam? Like forty hours? Fifty? You're not a machine, Jake. 'Sides, you didn't miss anything at all."

Nothing at all? I glanced quickly at Bella. Her color was back to the way I remembered it. Pale, but with the rose undertone. Her lips were pink again. Even her hair looked better—shinier. She saw me appraising and gave me a grin.

"How's the rib?" I asked.

"Taped up nice and tight. I don't even feel it."

I rolled my eyes. I heard Edward grind his teeth together, and I figured her blow-it-off attitude bugged him as much at it bugged me.

"What's for breakfast?" I asked, a little sarcastic. "O negative or AB positive?"

She stuck her tongue out at me. Totally herself again. "Omelets," she said, but her eyes darted down, and I saw that her cup of blood was wedged between her leg and Edward's.

"Go get some breakfast, Jake," Seth said. "There's a bunch in the kitchen. You've got to be empty."

I examined the food in his lap. Looked like half a cheese

omelet and the last fourth of a Frisbee-sized cinnamon roll. My stomach growled, but I ignored it.

"What's Leah having for breakfast?" I asked Seth critically.

"Hey, I took food to her before I ate *anything*," he defended himself. "She said she'd rather eat roadkill, but I bet she caves. These cinnamon rolls . . . " He seemed at a loss for words.

"I'll go hunt with her, then."

Seth sighed as I turned to leave.

"A moment, Jacob?"

It was Carlisle asking, so when I turned around again, my face was probably less disrespectful than it would have been if anyone else had stopped me.

"Yeah?"

Carlisle approached me while Esme drifted off toward the other room. He stopped a few feet away, just a little bit farther away than the normal space between two humans having a conversation. I appreciated him giving me my space.

"Speaking of hunting," he began in a somber tone. "That's going to be an issue for my family. I understand that our previous truce is inoperative at the moment, so I wanted your advice. Will Sam be hunting for us outside of the perimeter you've created? We don't want to take a chance with hurting any of your family—or losing any of ours. If you were in our shoes, how would you proceed?"

I leaned away, a little surprised, when he threw it back at me like that. What would I know about being in a bloodsucker's expensive shoes? But, then again, I did know Sam.

"It's a risk," I said, trying to ignore the other eyes I felt on me and to talk only to him. "Sam's calmed down some, but I'm pretty sure that in his head, the treaty is void. As long as he thinks the tribe, or any other human, is in real danger, he's not going to ask questions first, if you know what I mean. But, with all that, his priority is going to be La Push. There really aren't enough of them to keep a decent watch on the people while putting out hunting parties big enough to do much damage. I'd bet he's keeping it close to home."

Carlisle nodded thoughtfully.

"So I guess I'd say, go out together, just in case. And probably you should go in the day, 'cause we'd be expecting night. Traditional vampire stuff. You're fast—go over the mountains and hunt far enough away that there's no chance he'd send anyone that far from home."

"And leave Bella behind, unprotected?"

I snorted. "What are we, chopped liver?"

Carlisle laughed, and then his face was serious again. "Jacob, you can't fight against your brothers."

My eyes tightened. "I'm not saying it wouldn't be hard, but if they were really coming to kill her—I would be able to stop them."

Carlisle shook his head, anxious. "No, I didn't mean that you would be . . . incapable. But that it would be very wrong. I can't have that on my conscience."

"It wouldn't be on yours, Doc. It would be on mine. And I can take it."

"No, Jacob. We will make sure that our actions don't make that a necessity." He frowned thoughtfully "We'll go three at a time," he decided after a second. "That's probably the best we can do."

"I don't know, Doc. Dividing down the middle isn't the best strategy."

"We've got some extra abilities that will even it up. If Edward is one of the three, he'll be able to give us a few miles' radius of safety."

We both glanced at Edward. His expression had Carlisle backtracking quickly.

"I'm sure there are other ways, too," Carlisle said. Clearly, there was no physical need strong enough to get Edward away from Bella now. "Alice, I would imagine you could see which routes would be a mistake?"

"The ones that disappear," Alice said, nodding. "Easy."

Edward, who had gone all tense with Carlisle's first plan, loosened up. Bella was staring unhappily at Alice, that little crease between her eyes that she got when she was stressed out.

"Okay, then," I said. "That's settled. I'll just be on my way. Seth, I'll expect you back on at dusk, so get a nap in there somewhere, all right?"

"Sure, Jake. I'll phase back soon as I'm done. Unless . . ." he hesitated, looking at Bella. "Do you need me?"

"She's got blankets," I snapped at him.

"I'm fine, Seth, thanks," Bella said quickly.

And then Esme flitted back in the room, a big covered dish in her hands. She stopped hesitantly just behind Carlisle's elbow, her wide, dark gold eyes on my face. She held the dish out and took a shy step closer.

"Jacob," she said quietly. Her voice wasn't quite so piercing as the others'. "I know it's . . . unappetizing to you, the idea of eating here, where it smells so unpleasant. But I would feel much better if you would take some food with you when you go. I know you can't go home, and that's because of us. Please—ease some of my remorse. Take something to eat." She held the food out to me, her face all soft and pleading. I don't know how she did it, because she didn't look older than her mid-twenties, and she was bone pale, too, but something about her expression suddenly reminded me of my mom.

Jeez.

"Uh, sure, sure," I mumbled. "I guess. Maybe Leah's still hungry or something."

I reached out and took the food with one hand, holding it away, at arm's length. I'd go dump it under a tree or something. I didn't want her to feel bad.

Then I remembered Edward.

Don't you say anything to her! Let her think I ate it.

I didn't look at him to see if he was in agreement. He'd *better* be in agreement. Bloodsucker owed me.

"Thank you, Jacob," Esme said, smiling at me. How did a stone face have *dimples*, for crying out loud?

"Um, thank you," I said. My face felt hot—hotter than usual.

This was the problem with hanging out with vampires— you got used to them. They started messing up the way you saw the world. They started feeling like friends.

"Will you come back later, Jake?" Bella asked as I tried to make a run for it.

"Uh, I don't know."

She pressed her lips together, like she was trying not to smile. "Please? I might get cold."

I inhaled deeply through my nose, and then realized, too late, that that was not a good idea. I winced. "Maybe."

"Jacob?" Esme asked. I backed toward the door as she continued; she took a few steps after me. "I left a basket of clothes on the porch. They're for Leah. They're freshly washed—I tried to touch them as little as possible." She frowned. "Do you mind taking them to her?"

"On it," I muttered, and then I ducked out the door before anyone could guilt me into anything else.

15. TICK TOCK TICK TOCK
TICK TOCK

HEY, JAKE, THOUGHT YOU SAID YOU WANTED ME AT DUSK. How come you didn't have Leah wake me up before she crashed?

'Cause I didn't need you. I'm still good.

He was already picking up the north half of the circle. *Anything?*

Nope. Nothing but nothing.

You did some scouting?

He'd caught the edge of one of my side trips. He headed up the new trail.

Yeah—I ran a few spokes. You know, just checking. If the Cullens are going to make a hunting trip . . .

Good call.

Seth looped back toward the main perimeter.

It was easier to run with him than it was to do the same with Leah. Though she was trying—trying hard—there was always an edge to her thoughts. She didn't want to be here. She didn't want to feel the softening toward the vampires that was going on in my head. She didn't want to deal with Seth's cozy friendship with them, a friendship that was only getting stronger.

Funny, though, I'd've thought her biggest issue would just be *me*. We'd always gotten on each other's nerves when ·we were in Sam's pack. But there was no antagonism toward me now at all, just the Cullens and Bella. I wondered why. Maybe it was simply gratitude that I wasn't forcing her to leave. Maybe it was because I understood her hostility better now. Whichever, running with Leah wasn't nearly as bad as I'd expected.

Of course, she hadn't eased up *that* much. The food and clothes Esme had sent for her were all taking a trip down-river right now. Even after I'd eaten my share—not because it smelled nearly irresistible away from the vampire burn, but to set a good example of self-sacrificing tolerance for Leah— she'd refused. The small elk she'd taken down around noon had not totally satisfied her appetite. Did make her mood worse, though. Leah hated eating raw.

Maybe we should run a sweep east? Seth suggested. *Go deep, see if they're out there waiting.*

I was thinking about that, I agreed. *But let's do it when we're all awake. I don't want to let down our guard. We should do it before the Cullens give it a try, though. Soon.*

Right.

That got me thinking.

If the Cullens were able to get out of the immediate area

safely, they really ought to keep on going. They probably should have taken off the second we'd come to warn them. They had to be able to afford other digs. And they had friends up north, right? Take Bella and run. It seemed like an obvious answer to their problems.

I probably ought to suggest that, but I was afraid they would listen to me. And I didn't want to have Bella disappear—to never know whether she'd made it or not.

No, that was stupid. I would tell them to go. It made no sense for them to stay, and it would be better—not less painful, but healthier—for me if Bella left.

Easy to say now, when Bella wasn't right there, looking all thrilled to see me and also clinging to life by her fingernails at the same time . . .

Oh, I already asked Edward about that, Seth thought.

What?

I asked him why they hadn't taken off yet. Gone up to Tanya's place or something. Somewhere too far for Sam to come after them.

I had to remind myself that I'd just decided to give the Cullens that exact advice. That it was best. So I shouldn't be mad at Seth for taking the chore out of my hands. Not mad at all.

So what did he say? Are they waiting for a window?

No. They're not leaving.

And that shouldn't sound like good news.

Why not? That's just stupid.

Not really, Seth said, defensive now. *It takes some time to build up the kind of medical access that Carlisle has here. He's got all the stuff he needs to take care of Bella, and the credentials to get more. That's one of the reasons they want to make a hunting run. Carlisle thinks they're going to need more blood for Bella soon.*

She's using up all the O negative they stored for her. He doesn't like depleting the stockpile. He's going to buy some more. Did you know you can buy *blood? If you're a doctor.*

I wasn't ready to be logical yet. *Still seems stupid. They could bring most of it with them, right? And steal what they need wherever they go. Who cares about legal crap when you're the undead?*

Edward doesn't want to take any risks moving her.

She's better than she was.

Seriously, Seth agreed. In his head, he was comparing my memories of Bella hooked up to the tubes with the last time he'd seen her as he'd left the house. She'd smiled at him and waved. *But she can't move around much, you know. That thing is kicking the hell out of her.*

I swallowed back the stomach acid in my throat. *Yeah, I know.*

Broke another of her ribs, he told me somberly.

My stride faltered, and I staggered a step before I regained my rhythm.

Carlisle taped her up again. Just another crack, he said. Then Rosalie said something about how even normal human babies have been known to crack ribs. Edward looked like he was gonna rip her head off.

Too bad he didn't.

Seth was in full report mode now—knowing it was all vitally interesting to me, though I'd never've asked to hear it. *Bella's been running a fever off and on today. Just low grade— sweats and then chills. Carlisle's not sure what to make of it—she might just be sick. Her immune system can't be in peak form right now.*

Yeah, I'm sure it's just a coincidence.

She's in a good mood, though. She was chatting with Charlie, laughing and all—

Charlie! What?! *What do you mean, she was talking to Charlie?!*

Now Seth's pace stuttered; my fury surprised him. *Guess he calls every day to talk to her. Sometimes her mom calls, too. Bella sounds so much better now, so she was reassuring him that she was on the mend—*

On the mend? *What the* hell *are they thinking?! Get Charlie's hopes up just so that he can be destroyed even worse when she dies? I thought they were getting him ready for that! Trying to prepare him! Why would she set him up like this?*

She might not die, Seth thought quietly.

I took a deep breath, trying to calm myself. *Seth. Even if she pulls through this, she's not doing it human. She knows that, and so do the rest of them. If she doesn't die, she's going to have to do a pretty convincing impersonation of a corpse, kid. Either that, or disappear. I thought they were trying to make this easier on Charlie. Why . . . ?*

Think it's Bella's idea. No one said anything, but Edward's face kinda went right along with what you're thinking now.

On the same wavelength with the bloodsucker yet again.

We ran in silence for a few minutes. I started off along a new line, probing south.

Don't get too far.

Why?

Bella asked me to ask you to stop by.

My teeth locked together.

Alice wants you, too. She says she's tired of hanging out in the attic like the vampire bat in the belfry. Seth snorted a laugh.

I was switching off with Edward before. Trying to keep Bella's temperature stable. Cold to hot, as needed. I guess, if you don't want to do it, I could go back—

No. I got it, I snapped.

Okay. Seth didn't make any more comments. He concentrated very hard on the empty forest.

I kept my southern course, searching for anything new. I turned around when I got close to the first signs of habitation. Not near the town yet, but I didn't want to get any wolf rumors going again. We'd been nice and invisible for a long while now.

I passed right through the perimeter on my way back, heading for the house. As much as I knew it was a stupid thing to do, I couldn't stop myself. I must be some kind of masochist.

There's nothing wrong with you, Jake. This isn't the most normal situation.

Shut up, please, Seth.

Shutting.

I didn't hesitate at the door this time; I just walked through like I owned the place. I figured that would piss Rosalie off, but it was a wasted effort. Neither Rosalie or Bella were anywhere in sight. I looked around wildly, hoping I'd missed them somewhere, my heart squeezing against my ribs in a weird, uncomfortable way.

"She's all right," Edward whispered. "Or, the same, I should say."

Edward was on the couch with his face in his hands; he hadn't looked up to speak. Esme was next to him, her arm wrapped tight around his shoulders.

"Hello, Jacob," she said. "I'm so glad you came back."

"Me, too," Alice said with a deep sigh. She came prancing down the stairs, making a face. Like I was late for an appointment.

"Uh, hey," I said. It felt weird to try to be polite.

"Where's Bella?"

"Bathroom," Alice told me. "Mostly fluid diet, you know. Plus, the whole pregnancy thing does that to you, I hear."

"Ah."

I stood there awkwardly, rocking back and forth on my heels.

"Oh, wonderful," Rosalie grumbled. I whipped my head around and saw her coming from a hall half-hidden behind the stairway. She had Bella cradled gently in her arms, a harsh sneer on her face for me. "I knew I smelled something nasty."

And, just like before, Bella's face lit up like a kid's on Christmas morning. Like I'd brought her the greatest gift ever.

It was so unfair.

"Jacob," she breathed. "You came."

"Hi, Bells."

Esme and Edward both got up. I watched how carefully Rosalie laid Bella out on the couch. I watched how, despite that, Bella turned white and held her breath—like she was set on not making any noise no matter how much it hurt.

Edward brushed his hand across her forehead and then along her neck. He tried to make it look as if he was just sweeping her hair back, but it looked like a doctor's examination to me.

"Are you cold?" he murmured.

"I'm fine."

"Bella, you know what Carlisle told you," Rosalie said. "Don't downplay *anything*. It doesn't help us take care of either of you."

"Okay, I'm a little cold. Edward, can you hand me that blanket?"

I rolled my eyes. "Isn't that sort of the point of me being here?"

"You just walked in," Bella said. "After running all day, I'd bet. Put your feet up for a minute. I'll probably warm up again in no time."

I ignored her, going to sit on the floor next the sofa while she was still telling me what to do. At that point, though, I wasn't sure how. . . . She looked pretty brittle, and I was afraid to move her, even to put my arms around her. So I just leaned carefully against her side, letting my arm rest along the length of hers, and held her hand. Then I put my other hand against her face. It was hard to tell if she felt colder than usual.

"Thanks, Jake," she said, and I felt her shiver once.

"Yeah," I said.

Edward sat on the arm of the sofa by Bella's feet, his eyes always on her face.

It was too much to hope, with all the super-hearing in the room, that no one would notice my stomach rumbling.

"Rosalie, why don't you get Jacob something from the kitchen?" Alice said. She was invisible now, sitting quietly behind the back of the sofa.

Rosalie stared at the place Alice's voice had come from in disbelief.

"Thanks, anyway, Alice, but I don't think I'd want to

eat something Blondie's spit in. I'd bet my system wouldn't take too kindly to venom."

"Rosalie would never embarrass Esme by displaying such a lack of hospitality."

"Of *course* not," Blondie said in a sugar-sweet voice that I immediately distrusted. She got up and breezed out of the room.

Edward sighed.

"You'd tell me if she poisoned it, right?" I asked.

"Yes," Edward promised.

And for some reason I believed him.

There was a lot of banging in the kitchen, and—weirdly—the sound of metal protesting as it was abused. Edward sighed again, but smiled just a little, too. Then Rosalie was back before I could think much more about it. With a pleased smirk, she set a silver bowl on the floor next to me.

"Enjoy, mongrel."

It had once probably been a big mixing bowl, but she'd bent the bowl back in on itself until it was shaped almost exactly like a dog dish. I had to be impressed with her quick craftsmanship. And her attention to detail. She'd scratched the word *Fido* into the side. Excellent handwriting.

Because the food looked pretty good—steak, no less, and a big baked potato with all the fixings—I told her, "Thanks, Blondie."

She snorted.

"Hey, do you know what you call a blonde with a brain?" I asked, and then continued on the same breath, "a golden retriever."

"I've heard that one, too," she said, no longer smiling.

"I'll keep trying," I promised, and then I dug in.

She made a disgusted face and rolled her eyes. Then she sat in one of the armchairs and started flicking through channels on the big TV so fast that there was no way she could really be surfing for something to watch.

The food was good, even with the vampire stink in the air. I was getting really used to that. Huh. Not something I'd been wanting to do, exactly . . .

When I was finished—though I was considering licking the bowl, just to give Rosalie something to complain about—I felt Bella's cold fingers pulling softly through my hair. She patted it down against the back of my neck.

"Time for a haircut, huh?"

"You're getting a little shaggy," she said. "Maybe—"

"Let me guess, someone around here used to cut hair in a salon in Paris?"

She chuckled. "Probably."

"No thanks," I said before she could really offer. "I'm good for a few more weeks."

Which made me wonder how long *she* was good for. I tried to think of a polite way to ask.

"So . . . um . . . what's the, er, date? You know, the due date for the little monster."

She smacked the back of my head with about as much force as a drifting feather, but didn't answer.

"I'm serious," I told her. "I want to know how long I'm gonna have to be here." *How long you're gonna be here*, I added in my head. I turned to look at her then. Her eyes were thoughtful; the stress line was there between her brows again.

"I don't know," she murmured. "Not exactly. Obviously, we're not going with the nine-month model here, and we can't get an ultrasound, so Carlisle is guesstimating from how big I am. Normal people are supposed to be about forty centimeters here"—she ran her finger right down the middle of her bulging stomach—"when the baby is fully grown. One centimeter for every week. I was thirty this morning, and I've been gaining about two centimeters a day, sometimes more. . . ."

Two weeks to a day, the days flying by. Her life speeding by in fast-forward. How many days did that give her, if she was counting to forty? Four? It took me a minute to figure out how to swallow.

"You okay?" she asked.

I nodded, not really sure how my voice would come out.

Edward's face was turned away from us as he listened to my thoughts, but I could see his reflection in the glass wall. He was the burning man again.

Funny how having a deadline made it harder to think about leaving, or having her leave. I was glad Seth'd brought that up, so I knew they were staying here. It would be intolerable, wondering if they were about to go, to take away one or two or three of those four days. My four days.

Also funny how, even knowing that it was almost over, the hold she had on me only got harder to break. Almost like it was related to her expanding belly—as if by getting bigger, she was gaining gravitational force.

For a minute I tried to look at her from a distance, to separate myself from the pull. I knew it wasn't my imagination that my need for her was stronger than ever. Why was that? Because she was dying? Or knowing that even if she didn't, still—best case scenario—she'd be changing into something else that I wouldn't know or understand?

She ran her finger across my cheekbone, and my skin was wet where she touched it.

"It's going to be okay," she sort of crooned. It didn't matter that the words meant nothing. She said it the way people sang those senseless nursery rhymes to kids. Rock-a-bye, baby.

"Right," I muttered.

She curled against my arm, resting her head on my shoulder. "I didn't think you would come. Seth said you would, and so did Edward, but I didn't believe them."

"Why not?" I asked gruffly.

"You're not happy here. But you came anyway."

"You wanted me here."

"I know. But you didn't have to come, because it's not fair for me to want you here. I would have understood."

It was quiet for a minute. Edward'd put his face back together. He looked at the TV as Rosalie went on flipping through the channels. She was into the six hundreds. I wondered how long it would take to get back to the beginning.

"Thank you for coming," Bella whispered.

"Can I ask you something?" I asked.

"Of course."

Edward didn't look like he was paying attention to us at all, but he knew what I was about to ask, so he didn't fool me.

"Why *do* you want me here? Seth could keep you warm, and he's probably easier to be around, happy little punk. But when *I* walk in the door, you smile like I'm your favorite person in the world."

"You're one of them."

"That sucks, you know."

"Yeah." She sighed. "Sorry."

"Why, though? You didn't answer that."

Edward was looking away again, like he was staring out the windows. His face was blank in the reflection.

"It feels . . . *complete* when you're here, Jacob. Like all my family is together. I mean, I guess that's what it's like—I've never had a big family before now. It's nice." She smiled for half a second. "But it's just not whole unless you're here."

"I'll never be part of your family, Bella."

I could have been. I would have been good there. But that was just a distant future that died long before it had a chance to live.

"You've always been a part of my family," she disagreed.

My teeth made a grinding sound. "That's a crap answer."

"What's a good one?"

"How about, 'Jacob, I get a kick out of your pain.'"

I felt her flinch.

"You'd like that better?" she whispered.

"It's easier, at least. I could wrap my head around it. I could deal with it."

I looked back down at her face then, so close to mine. Her eyes were shut and she was frowning. "We got off track, Jake. Out of balance. You're supposed to be part of my life—I can feel that, and so can you." She paused for a second without opening her eyes—like she was waiting for me to deny it. When I didn't say anything, she went on.

"But not like this. We did something wrong. No. I did. I did something wrong, and we got off track. . . ."

Her voice trailed off, and the frown on her face relaxed until it was just a little pucker at the corner of her lips. I waited for her to pour some more lemon juice into my paper cuts, but then a soft snore came from the back of her throat.

"She's exhausted," Edward murmured. "It's been a long day. A hard day. I think she would have gone to sleep earlier, but she was waiting for you."

I didn't look at him.

"Seth said it broke another of her ribs."

"Yes. It's making it hard for her to breathe."

"Great."

"Let me know when she gets hot again."

"Yeah."

She still had goose bumps on the arm that wasn't touching mine. I'd barely raised my head to look for a blanket when Edward snagged one draped over the arm of the sofa and flung it out so that it settled over her.

Occasionally, the mind-reading thing saved time. For example, maybe I wouldn't have to make a big production out of the accusation about what was going on with Charlie. That mess. Edward would just *hear* exactly how furious—

"Yes," he agreed. "It's not a good idea."

"Then why?" Why was Bella telling her father she was *on the mend* when it would only make him more miserable?

"She can't bear his anxiety."

"So it's better—"

"No. It's *not* better. But I'm not going to force her to do anything that makes her unhappy now. Whatever happens, this makes her feel better. I'll deal with the rest afterward."

That didn't sound right. Bella wouldn't just shuffle Charlie's pain off to some later date, for someone else to face. Even dying. That wasn't her. If I knew Bella, she had to have some other plan.

"She's very sure she's going to live," Edward said.

"But not human," I protested.

"No, not human. But she hopes to see Charlie again, anyway."

Oh, this just got better and better.

"See. Charlie." I finally looked at him, my eyes bugging. "Afterwards. See Charlie when she's all sparkly white with the bright red eyes. I'm not a bloodsucker, so maybe I'm missing something, but *Charlie* seems like kind of a strange choice for her first meal."

Edward sighed. "She knows she won't be able to be near him for at least a year. She thinks she can stall. Tell Charlie she has to go to a special hospital on the other side of the world. Keep in contact through phone calls. . . ."

"That's insane."

"Yes."

"Charlie's not stupid. Even if she doesn't kill him, he's going to notice a difference."

"She's sort of banking on that."

I continued to stare, waiting for him to explain.

"She wouldn't be aging, of course, so that would set a time limit, even if Charlie accepted whatever excuse she comes up with for the changes." He smiled faintly. "Do you remember when you tried to tell her about your transformation? How you made her guess?"

My free hand flexed into a fist. "She told you about that?"

"Yes. She was explaining her . . . idea. You see, she's not allowed to tell Charlie the truth—it would be very dangerous for him. But he's a smart, practical man. She thinks he'll come up with his own explanation. She assumes he'll get it wrong." Edward snorted. "After all, we hardly adhere to vampire canon. He'll make some wrong assumption about us, like she did in the beginning, and we'll go along with it. She thinks she'll be able to see him . . . from time to time."

"Insane," I repeated.

"Yes," he agreed again.

It was weak of him to let her get her way on this, just to keep her happy now. It wouldn't turn out well.

Which made me think that he probably wasn't expecting her to live to try out her crazy plan. Placating her, so that she could be happy for a little while longer.

Like four more days.

"I'll deal with whatever comes," he whispered, and he turned his face down and away so that I couldn't even read his reflection. "I won't cause her pain now."

"Four days?" I asked.

He didn't look up. "Approximately."

"Then what?"

"What do you mean, exactly?"

I thought about what Bella had said. About the thing being wrapped up nice and tight in something strong, something like vampire skin. So how did that work? How did it get out?

"From what little research we've been able to do, it

would appear the creatures use their own teeth to escape the womb," he whispered.

I had to pause to swallow back the bile.

"Research?" I asked weakly.

"That's why you haven't seen Jasper and Emmett around. That's what Carlisle is doing now. Trying to decipher ancient stories and myths, as much as we can with what we have to work with here, looking for anything that might help us predict the creature's behavior."

Stories? If there were myths, then . . .

"Then is this thing not the first of its kind?" Edward asked, anticipating my question. "Maybe. It's all very sketchy. The myths could easily be the products of fear and imagination. Though . . ."—he hesitated—"your myths are true, are they not? Perhaps these are, too. They do seem to be localized, linked. . . ."

"How did you find . . . ?"

"There was a woman we encountered in South America. She'd been raised in the traditions of her people. She'd heard warnings about such creatures, old stories that had been passed down."

"What were the warnings?" I whispered.

"That the creature must be killed immediately. Before it could gain too much strength."

Just like Sam thought. Was he right?

"Of course, their legends say the same of us. That we must be destroyed. That we are soulless murderers."

Two for two.

Edward laughed one hard chuckle.

"What did their stories say about the . . . mothers?"

Agony ripped across his face, and, as I flinched away

from his pain, I knew he wasn't going to give me an answer. I doubted he could talk.

It was Rosalie—who'd been so still and quiet since Bella'd fallen asleep that I'd nearly forgotten her—who answered.

She made a scornful noise in the back of her throat. "Of course there were no survivors," she said. *No survivors*, blunt and uncaring. "Giving birth in the middle of a disease-infested swamp with a medicine man smearing sloth spit across your face to drive out the evil spirits was never the safest method. Even the normal births went badly half the time. None of them had what this baby has—caregivers with an idea of what the baby needs, who try to meet those needs. A doctor with a totally unique knowledge of vampire nature. A plan in place to deliver the baby as safely as possible. Venom that will repair anything that goes wrong. The baby will be fine. And those other mothers would probably have survived if they'd had that—if they even existed in the first place. Something I am not convinced of." She sniffed disdainfully.

The baby, the baby. Like that was all that mattered. Bella's life was a minor detail to her—easy to blow off.

Edward's face went white as snow. His hands curved into claws. Totally egotistical and indifferent, Rosalie twisted in her chair so that her back was to him. He leaned forward, shifting into a crouch.

Allow me, I suggested.

He paused, raising one eyebrow.

Silently, I lifted my doggy bowl off the floor. Then, with a quick, powerful flip of my wrist, I threw it into the back of Blondie's head so hard that—with an earsplitting *bang*—it smashed flat before it ricocheted across the room and snapped the round top piece off the thick newel post at the foot of the stairs.

Bella twitched but didn't wake up.

"Dumb blonde," I muttered.

Rosalie turned her head slowly, and her eyes were blazing.

"You. Got. Food. In. My. Hair."

That did it.

I busted up. I pulled away from Bella so that I wouldn't shake her, and laughed so hard that tears ran down my face. From behind the couch, I heard Alice's tinkling laugh join in.

I wondered why Rosalie didn't spring. I sort of expected it. But then I realized that my laughing had woken Bella up, though she'd slept right through the real noise.

"What's so funny?" she mumbled.

"I got food in her hair," I told her, chortling again.

"I'm not going to forget this, dog," Rosalie hissed.

"S'not so hard to erase a blonde's memory," I countered. "Just blow in her ear."

"Get some new jokes," she snapped.

"C'mon, Jake. Leave Rose alo—" Bella broke off midsentence and sucked in a sharp breath. In the same second, Edward was leaning over the top of me, ripping the blanket out of the way. She seemed to convulse, her back arching off the sofa.

"He's just," she panted, "stretching."

Her lips were white, and she had her teeth locked together like she was trying to hold back a scream.

Edward put both hands on either side of her face.

"Carlisle?" he called in a tense, low voice.

"Right here," the doctor said. I hadn't heard him come in.

"Okay," Bella said, still breathing hard and shallow. "Think it's over. Poor kid doesn't have enough room, that's all. He's getting so big."

It was really hard to take, that adoring tone she used to describe the thing that was tearing her up. Especially after Rosalie's callousness. Made me wish I could throw something at Bella, too.

She didn't pick up on my mood. "You know, he reminds me of you, Jake," she said—affectionate tone—still gasping.

"Do *not* compare me to that thing," I spit out through my teeth.

"I just meant your growth spurt," she said, looking like I'd hurt her feelings. Good. "You shot right up. I could watch you getting taller by the minute. He's like that, too. Growing so fast."

I bit my tongue to keep from saying what I wanted to say—hard enough that I tasted blood in my mouth. Of course, it would heal before I could swallow. That's what Bella needed. To be strong like me, to be able to heal. . . .

She took an easier breath and then relaxed back into the sofa, her body going limp.

"Hmm," Carlisle murmured. I looked up, and his eyes were on me.

"What?" I demanded.

Edward's head leaned to one side as he reflected on whatever was in Carlisle's head.

"You know that I was wondering about the fetus's genetic makeup, Jacob. About his chromosomes."

"What of it?"

"Well, taking your similarities into consideration—"

"Similar*ties*?" I growled, not appreciating the plural.

"The accelerated growth, and the fact that Alice cannot see either of you."

I felt my face go blank. I'd forgotten about that other one.

"Well, I wonder if that means that we have an answer. If the similarities are gene-deep."

"Twenty-four pairs," Edward muttered under his breath.

"You don't know that."

"No. But it's interesting to speculate," Carlisle said in a soothing voice.

"Yeah. Just *fascinating*."

Bella's light snore started up again, accenting my sarcasm nicely.

They got into it then, quickly taking the genetics conversation to a point where the only words I could understand were the *the*'s and the *and*'s. And my own name, of course. Alice joined in, commenting now and then in her chirpy bird voice.

Even though they were talking about me, I didn't try to figure out the conclusions they were drawing. I had other things on my mind, a few facts I was trying to reconcile.

Fact one, Bella'd said that the creature was protected by something as strong as vampire skin, something that was too impenetrable for ultrasounds, too tough for needles. Fact two, Rosalie'd said they had a plan to deliver the creature safely. Fact three, Edward'd said that—in myths—other monsters like this one would chew their way out of their own mothers.

I shuddered.

And that made a sick kind of sense, because, fact four, not many things could cut through something as strong as vampire skin. The half-creature's teeth—according to myth—were strong enough. My teeth were strong enough.

And vampire teeth were strong enough.

It was hard to miss the obvious, but I sure wished I could. Because I had a pretty good idea exactly how Rosalie planned to get that thing "safely" out.

16. TOO-MUCH-INFORMATION
ALERT

I TOOK OFF EARLY, LONG BEFORE SUNRISE WAS DUE. I'd gotten just a little bit of uneasy sleep leaning against the side of the sofa. Edward woke me when Bella's face was flushed, and he took my spot to cool her back down. I stretched and decided I was rested enough to get some work done.

"Thank you," Edward said quietly, seeing my plans. "If the route is clear, they'll go today."

"I'll let you know."

It felt good to get back to my animal self. I was stiff from sitting still for so long. I extended my stride, working out the kinks.

Morning, Jacob, Leah greeted me.

Good, you're up. How long's Seth been out?

Not out yet, Seth thought sleepily. *Almost there. What do you need?*

You think you got another hour in you?

Sure thing. No problem. Seth got to his feet right away, shaking out his fur.

Let's make the deep run, I told Leah. *Seth, take the perimeter.*

Gotcha. Seth broke into an easy jog.

Off on another vampire errand, Leah grumbled.

You got a problem with that?

Of course not. I just love to coddle those darling leeches.

Good. Let's see how fast we can run.

Okay, I'm definitely up for that!

Leah was on the far western rim of the perimeter. Rather than cut close to the Cullens' house, she stuck to the circle as she raced around to meet me. I sprinted off straight east, knowing that even with the head start, she'd be passing me soon if I took it easy for even a second.

Nose to the ground, Leah. This isn't a race, it's a reconnaissance mission.

I can do both and still kick your butt.

I gave her that one. *I know.*

She laughed.

We took a winding path through the eastern mountains. It was a familiar route. We'd run these mountains when the vampires had left a year ago, making it part of our patrol route to better protect the people here. Then we'd pulled back the lines when the Cullens returned. This was their treaty land.

But that fact would probably mean nothing to Sam now.

The treaty was dead. The question today was how thin he was willing to spread his force. Was he looking for stray Cullens to poach on their land or not? Had Jared spoken the truth or taken advantage of the silence between us?

We got deeper and deeper into the mountains without finding any trace of the pack. Fading vampire trails were everywhere, but the scents were familiar now. I was breathing them in all day long.

I found a heavy, somewhat recent concentration on one particular trail—all of them coming and going here except for Edward. Some reason for gathering that must have been forgotten when Edward brought his dying pregnant wife home. I gritted my teeth. Whatever it was, it had nothing to do with me.

Leah didn't push herself past me, though she could have now. I was paying more attention to each new scent than I was to the speed contest. She kept to my right side, running with me rather than racing against me.

We're getting pretty far out here, she commented.

Yeah. If Sam was hunting strays, we should have crossed his trail by now.

Makes more sense right now for him to bunker down in La Push, Leah thought. *He knows we're giving the bloodsuckers three extra sets of eyes and legs. He's not going to be able to surprise them.*

This was just a precaution, really.

Wouldn't want our precious parasites taking unnecessary chances.

Nope, I agreed, ignoring the sarcasm.

You've changed so much, Jacob. Talk about one-eighties.

You're not exactly the same Leah I've always known and loved, either.

True. Am I less annoying than Paul now?

Amazingly . . . yes.

Ah, sweet success.

Congrats.

We ran in silence again then. It was probably time to turn around, but neither of us wanted to. It felt nice to run like this. We'd been staring at the same small circle of a trail for too long. It felt good to stretch our muscles and take the rugged terrain. We weren't in a huge hurry, so I thought maybe we should hunt on the way back. Leah was pretty hungry.

Yum, yum, she thought sourly.

It's all in your head, I told her. *That's the way wolves eat. It's natural. It tastes fine. If you didn't think about it from a human perspective—*

Forget the pep talk, Jacob. I'll hunt. I don't have to like it.

Sure, sure, I agreed easily. It wasn't my business if she wanted to make things harder for herself.

She didn't add anything for a few minutes; I started thinking about turning back.

Thank you, Leah suddenly told me in a much different tone.

For?

For letting me be. For letting me stay. You've been nicer than I had any right to expect, Jacob.

Er, no problem. Actually, I mean that. I don't mind having you here like I thought I would.

She snorted, but it was a playful sound. *What a glowing commendation!*

Don't let it go to your head.

Okay—if you don't let this go to yours. She paused for a

second. *I think you make a good Alpha. Not in the same way Sam does, but in your own way. You're worth following, Jacob.*

My mind went blank with surprise. It took me a second to recover enough to respond.

Er, thanks. Not totally sure I'll be able to stop that one from going to my head, though. Where did that come from?

She didn't answer right away, and I followed the wordless direction of her thoughts. She was thinking about the future—about what I'd said to Jared the other morning. About how the time would be up soon, and then I'd go back to the forest. About how I'd promised that she and Seth would return to the pack when the Cullens were gone. . . .

I want to stay with you, she told me.

The shock shot through my legs, locking my joints. She blew past me and then put on the brakes. Slowly, she walked back to where I was frozen in place.

I won't be a pain, I swear. I won't follow you around. You can go wherever you want, and I'll go where I want. You'll only have to put up with me when we're both wolves. She paced back and forth in front of me, swishing her long gray tail nervously. *And, as I'm planning on quitting as soon as I can manage it . . . maybe that won't be so often.*

I didn't know what to say.

I'm happier now, as a part of your pack, than I have been in years.

I want to stay, too, Seth thought quietly. I hadn't realized he'd been paying much attention to us as he ran the perimeter. *I like this pack.*

Hey, now! Seth, this isn't going to be a pack much longer. I tried to put my thoughts together so they would convince him. *We've got a purpose now, but when . . . after that's over, I'm just going to go wolf. Seth, you need a purpose. You're a good kid. You're the kind of person who always has a crusade. And there's no way you're leaving La Push now. You're going to graduate from high school and do something with your life. You're going to take care of Sue. My issues are not going to mess up your future.*

But—

Jacob is right, Leah seconded.

You're agreeing with me?

Of course. But none of that applies to me. *I was on my way out, anyway. I'll get a job somewhere away from La Push. Maybe take some courses at a community college. Get into yoga and meditation to work on my temper issues. . . . And stay a part of this pack for the sake of my mental well-being. Jacob—you can see how that makes sense, right? I won't bother you, you won't bother me, everyone is happy.*

I turned back and started loping slowly toward the west.

This is a bit much to deal with, Leah. Let me think about it, 'kay?

Sure. Take your time.

It took us longer to make the run back. I wasn't trying for speed. I was just trying to concentrate enough that I wouldn't plow headfirst into a tree. Seth was grumbling a little bit in the back of my head, but I was able to ignore him. He knew I was right. He wasn't going to abandon his mom. He would go back to La Push and protect the tribe like he should.

But I couldn't see Leah doing that. And that was just plain scary.

A pack of the two of us? No matter the physical distance,

I couldn't imagine the . . . the *intimacy* of that situation. I wondered if she'd really thought it through, or if she was just desperate to stay free.

Leah didn't say anything as I chewed it over. It was like she was trying to prove how easy it would be if it was just us.

We ran into a herd of black-tailed deer just as the sun was coming up, brightening the clouds a little bit behind us. Leah sighed internally but didn't hesitate. Her lunge was clean and efficient—graceful, even. She took down the largest one, the buck, before the startled animal fully understood the danger.

Not to be outdone, I swooped down on the next largest deer, snapping her neck between my jaws quickly, so she wouldn't feel unnecessary pain. I could feel Leah's disgust warring with her hunger, and I tried to make it easier for her by letting the wolf in me have my head. I'd lived all-wolf for long enough that I knew how to be the animal completely, to see his way and think his way. I let the practical instincts take over, letting her feel that, too. She hesitated for a second, but then, tentatively, she seemed to reach out with her mind and try to see my way. It felt very strange—our minds were more closely linked than they had ever been before, because we both were *trying* to think together.

Strange, but it helped her. Her teeth cut through the fur and skin of her kill's shoulder, tearing away a thick slab of streaming flesh. Rather than wince away as her human thoughts wanted to, she let her wolf-self react instinctively. It was kind of a numbing thing, a thoughtless thing. It let her eat in peace.

It was easy for me to do the same. And I was glad I hadn't forgotten this. This would be my life again soon.

Was Leah going to be a part of that life? A week ago, I would've found that idea beyond horrifying. I wouldn't've been able to stand it. But I knew her better now. And, relieved from the constant pain, she wasn't the same wolf. Not the same girl.

We ate together until we both were full.

Thanks, she told me later as she was cleaning her muzzle and paws against the wet grass. I didn't bother; it had just started to drizzle and we had to swim the river again on our way back. I'd get clean enough. *That wasn't so bad, thinking your way.*

You're welcome.

Seth was dragging when we hit the perimeter. I told him to get some sleep; Leah and I would take over the patrol. Seth's mind faded into unconsciousness just seconds later.

You headed back to the bloodsuckers? Leah asked.

Maybe.

It's hard for you to be there, but hard to stay away, too. I know how that feels.

You know, Leah, you might want to think a little bit about the future, about what you really want to do. My head is not going to be the happiest place on earth. And you'll have to suffer right along with me.

She thought about how to answer me. *Wow, this is going to sound bad. But, honestly, it will be easier to deal with your pain than face mine.*

Fair enough.

I know it's going to be bad for you, Jacob. I understand that— maybe better than you think. I don't like her, but . . . she's your Sam. She's everything you want and everything you can't have.

I couldn't answer.

I know it's worse for you. At least Sam is happy. At least he's alive and well. I love him enough that I want that. I want him to have what's best for him. She sighed. *I just don't want to stick around to watch.*

Do we need to talk about this?

I think we do. Because I want you to know that I won't make it worse for you. Hell, maybe I'll even help. I wasn't born *a compassionless shrew. I used to be sort of nice, you know.*

My memory doesn't go that far back.

We both laughed once.

I'm sorry about this, Jacob. I'm sorry you're in pain. I'm sorry it's getting worse and not better.

Thanks, Leah.

She thought about the things that were worse, the black pictures in my head, while I tried to tune her out without much success. She was able to look at them with some distance, some perspective, and I had to admit that this was helpful. I could imagine that maybe I would be able to see it that way, too, in a few years.

She saw the funny side of the daily irritations that came from hanging out around vampires. She liked my ragging on Rosalie, chuckling internally and even running through a few blonde jokes in her mind that I might be able to work in. But then her thoughts turned serious, lingering on Rosalie's face in a way that confused me.

You know what's crazy? she asked.

Well, almost everything is crazy right now. But what do you mean?

That blond vampire you hate so much—I totally get her perspective.

For a second I thought she was making a joke that was in

very poor taste. And then, when I realized she was serious, the fury that ripped through me was hard to control. It was a good thing we'd spread out to run our watch. If she'd been within *biting* distance . . .

Hold up! Let me explain!

Don't want to hear it. I'm outta here.

Wait! Wait! she pleaded as I tried to calm myself enough to phase back. *C'mon, Jake!*

Leah, this isn't really the best way to convince me that I want to spend more time with you in the future.

Yeesh! What an overreaction. You don't even know what I'm talking about.

So what are you talking about?

And then she was suddenly the pain-hardened Leah from before. *I'm talking about being a genetic dead end, Jacob.*

The vicious edge to her words left me floundering. I hadn't expected to have my anger trumped.

I don't understand.

You would, if you weren't just like the rest of them. If my "female stuff"—she thought the words with a hard, sarcastic tone—*didn't send you running for cover just like any stupid male, so you could actually pay attention to what it all means.*

Oh.

Yeah, so none of us like to think about that stuff with her. Who would? Of course I remembered Leah's panic that first month after she joined the pack—and I remembered cringing away from it just like everyone else. Because she couldn't be *pregnant*—not unless there was some really freaky religious immaculate crap going on. She hadn't been with anyone since Sam. And then, when the weeks dragged on and nothing turned into more nothing, she'd realized that her body wasn't following the normal patterns anymore. The horror—what *was* she now? Had her body changed because she'd become a werewolf? Or had she become a werewolf because her body was *wrong*? The only female werewolf in the history of forever. Was that because she wasn't as female as she should be?

None of us had wanted to deal with that breakdown. Obviously, it wasn't like we could *empathize.*

You know why Sam thinks we imprint, she thought, calmer now.

Sure. To carry on the line.

Right. To make a bunch of new little werewolves. Survival of the species, genetic override. You're drawn to the person who gives you the best chance to pass on the wolf gene.

I waited for her to tell me where she was going with this.

If I was any good for that, Sam would have been drawn to me.

Her pain was enough that I broke stride under it.

But I'm not. There's something wrong with me. I don't have the ability to pass on the gene, apparently, despite my stellar bloodlines. So I become a freak—the girlie-wolf—good for nothing else. I'm a genetic dead end and we both know it.

We do not, I argued with her. *That's just Sam's theory. Imprinting happens, but we don't know why. Billy thinks it's something else.*

I know, I know. He thinks you're imprinting to make stronger *wolves. Because you and Sam are such humongous monsters—bigger than our fathers. But either way, I'm still not a candidate. I'm . . . I'm menopausal. I'm twenty years old and I'm menopausal.*

Ugh. I *so* didn't want to have this conversation. *You don't know that, Leah. It's probably just the whole frozen-in-time thing.*

When you quit your wolf and start getting older again, I'm sure things will . . . er . . . pick right back up.

I might *think that*—except that no one's *imprinting on* me, *notwithstanding my impressive pedigree. You know*, she added thoughtfully, *if you weren't around, Seth would probably have the best claim to being Alpha—through his blood, at least. Of course, no one would ever consider me. . . .*

You really want *to imprint, or be imprinted on, or whichever?* I demanded. *What's wrong with going out and falling in love like a normal person, Leah? Imprinting is just another way of getting your choices taken away from you.*

Sam, Jared, Paul, Quil . . . they don't seem to mind.

None of them have a mind of their own.

You don't want to imprint?

Hell, no!

That's just because you're already in love with her. *That would go away, you know, if you imprinted. You wouldn't have to hurt over her anymore.*

Do you want to forget the way you feel about Sam?

She deliberated for a moment. *I think I do.*

I sighed. She was in a healthier place than I was.

But back to my original point, Jacob. I understand why your blond vampire is so cold—in the figurative sense. She's focused. She's got her eyes on the prize, right? Because you always want the very most what you can never, ever have.

You would *act like Rosalie? You* would *murder someone— because that's what she's doing, making sure no one interferes with Bella's death—you would do that to have a baby? Since when are you a breeder?*

I just want the options I don't have, Jacob. Maybe, if there was nothing wrong with me, I would never give it a thought.

You would kill for that? I demanded, not letting her escape my question.

That's not what she's doing. I think it's more like she's living vicariously. And . . . if Bella asked me to help her with this . . . She paused, considering. *Even though I don't think too much of her, I'd probably do the same as the bloodsucker.*

A loud snarl ripped through my teeth.

Because, if it was turned around, I'd want Bella to do that for me. And so would Rosalie. We'd both do it her way.

Ugh! You're as bad as they are!

That's the funny thing about knowing you can't have something. It makes you desperate.

And . . . that's my limit. Right there. This conversation is over.

Fine.

It wasn't enough that she'd agreed to stop. I wanted a stronger termination than that.

I was only about a mile from where I'd left my clothes, so I phased back to human and walked. I didn't think about our conversation. Not because there wasn't anything to think about, but because I couldn't stand it. I would *not* see it that way—but it was harder to keep from doing that when Leah had put the thoughts and emotions straight into my head.

Yeah, I wasn't running with her when this was finished. She could go be miserable in La Push. One little Alpha command before I left for good wasn't going to kill anybody.

It was real early when I got to the house. Bella was probably still asleep. I figured I'd poke my head in, see what was going on, give 'em the green light to go hunting, and then find a patch of grass soft enough to sleep on while human. I wasn't phasing back until Leah was asleep.

But there was a lot of low mumbling going on inside the house, so maybe Bella wasn't sleeping. And then I heard the machinery sound from upstairs again—the X-ray? Great. It looked like day four on the countdown was starting off with a bang.

Alice opened the door for me before I could walk in.

She nodded. "Hey, wolf."

"Hey, shortie. What's going on upstairs?" The big room was empty—all the murmurs were on the second floor.

She shrugged her pointy little shoulders. "Maybe another break." She tried to say the words casually, but I could see the flames in the very back of her eyes. Edward and I weren't the only ones who were burning over this. Alice loved Bella, too.

"Another rib?" I asked hoarsely.

"No. Pelvis this time."

Funny how it kept hitting me, like each new thing was a surprise. When was I going to stop being surprised? Each new disaster seemed kinda obvious in hindsight.

Alice was staring at my hands, watching them tremble.

Then we were listening to Rosalie's voice upstairs.

"See, I *told* you I didn't hear a crack. You need your ears checked, Edward."

There was no answer.

Alice made a face. "Edward's going to end up ripping Rose into small pieces, I think. I'm surprised she doesn't see that. Or maybe she thinks Emmett will be able to stop him."

"I'll take Emmett," I offered. "You can help Edward with the ripping part."

Alice half-smiled.

The procession came down the stairs then—Edward had Bella this time. She was gripping her cup of blood in both hands, and her face was white. I could see that, though he compensated for every tiny movement of his body to keep from jostling her, she was hurting.

"Jake," she whispered, and she smiled through the pain.

I stared at her, saying nothing.

Edward placed Bella carefully on her couch and sat on the floor by her head. I wondered briefly why they didn't leave her upstairs, and then decided at once that it must be Bella's idea. She'd want to act like things were normal, avoid the hospital setup. And he was humoring her. Naturally.

Carlisle came down slowly, the last one, his face creased with worry. It made him look old enough to be a doctor for once.

"Carlisle," I said. "We went halfway to Seattle. There's no sign of the pack. You're good to go."

"Thank you, Jacob. This is good timing. There's much that we need." His black eyes flickered to the cup that Bella was holding so tight.

"Honestly, I think you're safe to take more than three. I'm pretty positive that Sam is concentrating on La Push."

Carlisle nodded in agreement. It surprised me how willingly he took my advice. "If you think so. Alice, Esme, Jasper, and I will go. Then Alice can take Emmett and Rosa—"

"Not a chance," Rosalie hissed. "Emmett can go with you now."

"You should hunt," Carlisle said in a gentle voice.

His tone didn't soften hers. "I'll hunt when *he* does," she growled, jerking her head toward Edward and then flipping her hair back.

Carlisle sighed.

Jasper and Emmett were down the stairs in a flash, and Alice joined them by the glass back door in the same second. Esme flitted to Alice's side.

Carlisle put his hand on my arm. The icy touch did not feel good, but I didn't jerk away. I held still, half in surprise, and half because I didn't want to hurt his feelings.

"Thank you," he said again, and then he darted out the door with the other four. My eyes followed them as they flew across the lawn and then disappeared before I took another breath. Their needs must have been more urgent than I'd imagined.

There was no sound for a minute. I could feel someone glaring at me, and I knew who it would be. I'd been planning to take off and get some Z's, but the chance to ruin Rosalie's morning seemed too good to pass up.

So I sauntered over to the armchair next to the one Rosalie had and settled in, sprawling out so that my head was tilted toward Bella and my left foot was near Rosalie's face.

"Ew. Someone put the dog out," she murmured, wrinkling her nose.

"Have you heard this one, Psycho? How do a blonde's brain cells die?"

She didn't say anything.

"Well?" I asked. "Do you know the punch line or not?"

She looked pointedly at the TV and ignored me.

"Has she heard it?" I asked Edward.

There was no humor on his tense face—he didn't move his eyes from Bella. But he said, "No."

"Awesome. So you'll enjoy this, bloodsucker—a blonde's brain cells die *alone*."

Rosalie still didn't look at me. "I have killed a hundred times more often than you have, you disgusting beast. Don't forget that."

"Someday, Beauty Queen, you're going to get tired of just threatening me. I'm really looking forward to that."

"Enough, Jacob," Bella said.

I looked down, and she was scowling at me. It looked like yesterday's good mood was long gone.

Well, I didn't want to bug her. "You want me to take off?" I offered.

Before I could hope—or fear—that she'd finally gotten tired of me, she blinked, and her frown disappeared. She seemed totally shocked that I would come to that conclusion. "No! Of course not."

I sighed, and I heard Edward sigh very quietly, too. I knew he wished she'd get over me, too. Too bad he'd never ask her to do anything that might make her unhappy.

"You look tired," Bella commented.

"Dead beat," I admitted.

"*I'd* like to beat you dead," Rosalie muttered, too low for Bella to hear.

I just slumped deeper into the chair, getting comfortable. My bare foot dangled closer to Rosalie, and she stiffened. After a few minutes Bella asked Rosalie for a refill. I felt the wind as Rosalie blew upstairs to get her some more blood. It was really quiet. Might as well take a nap, I figured.

And then Edward said, "Did you say something?" in a puzzled tone. Strange. Because no one *had* said anything, and because Edward's hearing was as good as mine, and he should have known that.

He was staring at Bella, and she was staring back. They both looked confused.

"Me?" she asked after a second. "I didn't say anything."

He moved onto his knees, leaning forward over her, his expression suddenly intense in a whole different way. His black eyes focused on her face.

"What are you thinking about right now?"

She stared at him blankly. "Nothing. What's going on?"

"What were you thinking about a minute ago?" he asked.

"Just . . . Esme's island. And feathers."

Sounded like total gibberish to me, but then she blushed, and I figured I was better off not knowing.

"Say something else," he whispered.

"Like what? Edward, what's going on?"

His face changed again, and he did something that made my mouth fall open with a pop. I heard a gasp behind me, and I knew that Rosalie was back, and just as flabbergasted as I was.

Edward, very lightly, put both of his hands against her huge, round stomach.

"The f—" He swallowed. "It . . . the baby likes the sound of your voice."

There was one short beat of total silence. I could not move a muscle, even to blink. Then—

"Holy crow, you can hear him!" Bella shouted. In the next second, she winced.

Edward's hand moved to the top peak of her belly and gently rubbed the spot where it must have kicked her.

"Shh," he murmured. "You startled it . . . him."

Her eyes got all wide and full of wonder. She patted the side of her stomach. "Sorry, baby."

Edward was listening hard, his head tilted toward the bulge.

"What's he thinking now?" she demanded eagerly.

"It . . . he or she, is . . ." He paused and looked up into her eyes. His eyes were filled with a similar awe—only his were more careful and grudging. "He's *happy*," Edward said in an incredulous voice.

Her breath caught, and it was impossible not to see the fanatical gleam in her eyes. The adoration and the devotion. Big, fat tears overflowed her eyes and ran silently down her face and over her smiling lips.

As he stared at her, his face was not frightened or angry or burning or any of the other expressions he'd worn since their return. He was marveling with her.

"Of course you're happy, pretty baby, of course you are," she crooned, rubbing her stomach while the tears washed her cheeks. "How could you not be, all safe and warm and loved? I love you so much, little EJ, of course you're happy."

"What did you call him?" Edward asked curiously.

She blushed again. "I sort of named him. I didn't think you would want . . . well, you know."

"EJ?"

"Your father's name was Edward, too."

"Yes, it was. What—?" He paused and then said, "Hmm."

"What?"

"He likes my voice, too."

"Of course he does." Her tone was almost gloating now. "You have the most beautiful voice in the universe. Who wouldn't love it?"

"Do you have a backup plan?" Rosalie asked then, leaning over the back of the sofa with the same wondering, gloating look on her face that was on Bella's. "What if he's a she?"

Bella wiped the back of her hand under her wet eyes. "I kicked a few things around. Playing with Renée and Esme. I was thinking . . . Ruh-*nez*-may."

"Ruhnezmay?"

"R-e-n-e-s-m-e-e. Too weird?"

"No, I like it," Rosalie assured her. Their heads were close together, gold and mahogany. "It's beautiful. And one of a kind, so *that* fits."

"I still think he's an Edward."

Edward was staring off into space, his face blank as he listened.

"What?" Bella asked, her face just glowing away. "What's he thinking now?"

At first he didn't answer, and then—shocking all the rest of us again, three distinct and separate gasps—he laid his ear tenderly against her belly.

"He loves you," Edward whispered, sounding dazed. "He absolutely *adores* you."

In that moment, I knew that I was alone. All alone.

I wanted to kick myself when I realized how much I'd been counting on that loathsome vampire. How stupid—as if you could ever trust a leech! Of course he would betray me in the end.

I'd counted on him to be on my side. I'd counted on him to suffer more than I suffered. And, most of all, I'd counted on him to hate that revolting thing killing Bella more than I hated it.

I'd trusted him with that.

Yet now they were together, the two of them bent over the budding, invisible monster with their eyes lit up like a happy family.

And I was all alone with my hatred and the pain that was so bad it was like being tortured. Like being dragged slowly across a bed of razor blades. Pain so bad you'd take death with a smile just to get away from it.

The heat unlocked my frozen muscles, and I was on my feet.

All three of their heads snapped up, and I watched my pain ripple across Edward's face as he trespassed in my head again.

"Ahh," he choked.

I didn't know what I was doing; I stood there, trembling, ready to bolt for the very first escape that I could think of.

Moving like the strike of a snake, Edward darted to a small end table and ripped something from the drawer there. He tossed it at me, and I caught the object reflexively.

"Go, Jacob. Get away from here." He didn't say it harshly—he threw the words at me like they were a life preserver. He was helping me find the escape I was dying for.

The object in my hand was a set of car keys.

17. WHAT DO I LOOK LIKE? THE WIZARD OF OZ? YOU NEED A BRAIN? YOU NEED A HEART? GO AHEAD. TAKE MINE. TAKE EVERYTHING I HAVE.

I SORT OF HAD A PLAN AS I RAN TO THE CULLENS' GARAGE. The second part of it was totaling the bloodsucker's car on my way back.

So I was at a loss when I mashed the button on the keyless remote, and it was not his Volvo that beeped and flashed its lights for me. It was another car—a standout even in the long line of vehicles that were mostly all drool-worthy in their own ways.

Did he actually *mean* to give me the keys to an Aston Martin Vanquish, or was that an accident?

I didn't pause to think about it, or if this would change that second part of my plan. I just threw myself into the silky leather seat and cranked the engine while my knees were still crunched up under the steering wheel. The sound of the motor's purr might have made me moan another day, but right now it was all I could do to concentrate enough to put it in drive.

I found the seat release and shoved myself back as my foot rammed the pedal down. The car felt almost airborne as it leaped forward.

It only took seconds to race through the tight, winding drive. The car responded to me like my thoughts were steering rather than my hands. As I blew out of the green tunnel and onto the highway, I caught a fleeting glimpse of Leah's gray face peering uneasily through the ferns.

For half a second, I wondered what she'd think, and then I realized that I didn't care.

I turned south, because I had no patience today for ferries or traffic or anything else that meant I might have to lift my foot off the pedal.

In a sick way, it was my lucky day. If by lucky you meant taking a well-traveled highway at two hundred without so much as seeing one cop, even in the thirty-mile-an-hour speed-trap towns. What a letdown. A little chase action might have been nice, not to mention that the license plate info would bring the heat down on the leech. Sure, he'd buy his way out of it, but it might have been just a *little* inconvenient for him.

The only sign of surveillance I came across was just a hint of dark brown fur flitting through the woods, running parallel to me for a few miles on the south side of Forks. Quil, it looked like. He must have seen me, too, because he disappeared after a minute without raising an alarm.

Again, I almost wondered what his story would be before I remembered that I didn't care.

I raced around the long U-shaped highway, heading for the biggest city I could find. That was the first part of my plan.

It seemed to take forever, probably because I was still on the razor blades, but it actually didn't even take two hours before I was driving north into the undefined sprawl that was part Tacoma and part Seattle. I slowed down then, because I really wasn't trying to kill any innocent bystanders.

This was a stupid plan. It wasn't going to work. But, as I'd searched my head for any way at all to get away from the pain, what Leah'd said today had popped in there.

That would go away, you know, if you imprinted. You wouldn't have to hurt over her anymore.

Seemed like maybe getting your choices taken away from you wasn't the very worst thing in the world. Maybe feeling like *this* was the very worst thing in the world.

But I'd seen all the girls in La Push and up on the Makah rez and in Forks. I needed a wider hunting range.

So how do you look for a random soul mate in a crowd? Well, first, I needed a crowd. So I tooled around, looking for a likely spot. I passed a couple of malls, which probably would've been pretty good places to find girls my age, but I couldn't make myself stop. Did I *want* to imprint on some girl who hung out in a mall all day?

I kept going north, and it got more and more crowded. Eventually, I found a big park full of kids and families and skateboards and bikes and kites and picnics and the whole bit. I hadn't noticed till now—it was a nice day. Sun and all that. People were out celebrating the blue sky.

I parked across two handicapped spots—just begging for a ticket—and joined the crowd.

I walked around for what felt like hours. Long enough that the sun changed sides in the sky. I stared into the face of every girl who passed anywhere near me, making myself really look, noticing who was pretty and who had blue eyes and who looked good in braces and who had way too much makeup on. I tried to find something interesting about each face, so that I would know for sure that I'd really tried. Things like: This one had a really straight nose; that one should pull her hair out of her eyes; this one could do lipstick ads if the rest of her face was as perfect as her mouth. . . .

Sometimes they stared back. Sometimes they looked scared—like they were thinking, *Who is this big freak glaring at me?* Sometimes I thought they looked kind of interested, but maybe that was just my ego running wild.

Either way, nothing. Even when I met the eyes of the girl who was—no contest—the hottest girl in the park and probably in the city, and she stared right back with a speculation that *looked* like interest, I felt nothing. Just the same desperate drive to find a way out of the pain.

As time went on, I started noticing all the wrong things. Bella things. This one's hair was the same color. That one's eyes were sort of shaped the same. This one's cheekbones cut across her face in just the same way. That one had the same little crease between her eyes—which made me wonder what she was worrying about. . . .

That was when I gave up. Because it was beyond stupid to think that I had picked exactly the right place and time and I was going to simply walk into my soul mate just because I was so desperate to.

It wouldn't make sense to find her here, anyway. If Sam was right, the best place to find my genetic match would be in La Push. And, clearly, no one there fit the bill. If Billy was right, then who knew? What made for a stronger wolf?

I wandered back to the car and then slumped against the hood and played with the keys.

Maybe I was what Leah thought she was. Some kind of dead end that shouldn't be passed on to another generation. Or maybe it was just that my life was a big, cruel joke, and there was no escape from the punch line.

"Hey, you okay? Hello? You there, with the stolen car."

It took me a second to realize that the voice was talking to me, and then another second to decide to raise my head.

A familiar-looking girl was staring at me, her expression kind of anxious. I knew why I recognized her face—I'd already catalogued this one. Light red-gold hair, fair skin, a few gold-colored freckles sprinkled across her cheeks and nose, and eyes the color of cinnamon.

"If you're feeling that remorseful over boosting the car," she said, smiling so that a dimple popped out in her chin, "you could always turn yourself in."

"It's borrowed, not stolen," I snapped. My voice sounded horrible—like I'd been crying or something. Embarrassing.

"Sure, *that*'ll hold up in court."

I glowered. "You need something?"

"Not really. I was kidding about the car, you know. It's just that . . . you look really upset about something. Oh, hey, I'm Lizzie." She held out her hand.

I looked at it until she let it fall.

"Anyway . . . ," she said awkwardly, "I was just wondering

if I could help. Seemed like you were looking for someone before." She gestured toward the park and shrugged.

"Yeah."

She waited.

I sighed. "I don't need any help. She's not here."

"Oh. Sorry."

"Me, too," I muttered.

I looked at the girl again. Lizzie. She was pretty. Nice enough to try to help a grouchy stranger who must seem nuts. Why couldn't she be the one? Why did everything have to be so freaking complicated? Nice girl, pretty, and sort of funny. Why not?

"This is a beautiful car," she said. "It's really a shame they're not making them anymore. I mean, the Vantage's body styling is gorgeous, too, but there's just something about the Vanquish. . . ."

Nice girl *who knew cars*. Wow. I stared at her face harder, wishing I knew how to make it work. *C'mon, Jake—imprint already.*

"How's it drive?" she asked.

"Like you wouldn't believe," I told her.

She grinned her one-dimple smile, clearly pleased to have dragged a halfway civil response out of me, and I gave her a reluctant smile back.

But her smile did nothing about the sharp, cutting blades that raked up and down my body. No matter how much I wanted it to, my life was not going to come together like that.

I wasn't in that healthier place where Leah was headed. I wasn't going to be able to fall in love like a normal person. Not when I was bleeding over someone else. Maybe—if it was ten years from now and Bella's heart was long dead and I'd hauled myself through the whole grieving process and come out in one piece again—maybe then I could offer Lizzie a ride in a fast car and talk makes and models and get to know something about her and see if I liked her as a person. But that wasn't going to happen now.

Magic wasn't going to save me. I was just going to have to take the torture like a man. Suck it up.

Lizzie waited, maybe hoping I was going to offer her that ride. Or maybe not.

"I'd better get this car back to the guy I borrowed it from," I muttered.

She smiled again. "Glad to hear you're going straight."

"Yeah, you convinced me."

She watched me get in the car, still sort of concerned. I probably looked like someone who was about to drive off a cliff. Which maybe I would've, if that kind of move'd work for a werewolf. She waved once, her eyes trailing after the car.

At first, I drove more sanely on the way back. I wasn't in a rush. I didn't want to go where I was going. Back to that house, back to that forest. Back to the pain I'd run from. Back to being absolutely alone with it.

Okay, that was melodramatic. I wouldn't be *all* alone, but that was a bad thing. Leah and Seth would have to suffer with me. I was glad Seth wouldn't have to suffer long. Kid didn't deserve to have his peace of mind ruined. Leah didn't, either, but at least it was something she understood. Nothing new about pain for Leah.

I sighed big as I thought about what Leah wanted from me, because I knew now that she was going to get it. I was still pissed at her, but I couldn't ignore the fact that I could make her life easier. And—now that I knew her better—I thought she would probably do this for me, if our positions were reversed.

It would be interesting, at the very least, and strange, too, to have Leah as a companion—as a friend. We were going to get under each other's skin a lot, that was for sure. She wouldn't be one to let me wallow, but I thought that was a good thing. I'd probably need someone to kick my butt now and then. But when it came right down to it, she was really the only friend who had any chance of understanding what I was going through now.

I thought of the hunt this morning, and how close our minds had been for that one moment in time. It hadn't been a bad thing. Different. A little scary, a little awkward. But also nice in a weird way.

I didn't have to be all alone.

And I knew Leah was strong enough to face with me the months that were coming. Months and years. It made me tired to think about it. I felt like I was staring out across an ocean that I was going to have to swim from shore to shore before I could rest again.

So much time coming, and then so *little* time before it started. Before I was flung into that ocean. Three and a half more days, and here I was, wasting that little bit of time I had.

I started driving too fast again.

I saw Sam and Jared, one on either side of the road like sentinels, as I raced up the road toward Forks. They were well hidden in the thick branches, but I was expecting them, and I knew what to look for. I nodded as I blew past them, not bothering to wonder what they made of my day trip.

I nodded to Leah and Seth, too, as I cruised up the Cullens' driveway. It was starting to get dark, and the clouds were thick on this side of the sound, but I saw their eyes glitter in the glow of the headlights. I would explain to them later. There'd be plenty of time for that.

It was a surprise to find Edward waiting for me in the garage. I hadn't seen him away from Bella in days. I could tell from his face that nothing bad had happened to her. In fact, he looked more peaceful than before. My stomach tightened as I remembered where that peace came from.

It was too bad that—with all my brooding—I'd forgotten to wreck the car. Oh well. I probably wouldn't have been able to stand hurting *this* car, anyway. Maybe he'd guessed as much, and that's why he'd lent it to me in the first place.

"A few things, Jacob," he said as soon as I cut the engine.

I took a deep breath and held it for a minute. Then, slowly, I got out of the car and threw the keys to him.

"Thanks for the loan," I said sourly. Apparently, it would have to be repaid. "What do you want *now?*"

"Firstly . . . I know how averse you are to using your authority with your pack, but . . ."

I blinked, astonished that he would even dream of starting in on this one. "What?"

"If you can't or won't control Leah, then I—"

"Leah?" I interrupted, speaking through my teeth. "What happened?"

Edward's face was hard. "She came up to see why you'd left so abruptly. I tried to explain. I suppose it might not have come out right."

"What did she do?"

"She phased to her human form and—"

"Really?" I interrupted again, shocked this time. I couldn't process that. Leah letting her guard down right in the mouth of the enemy's lair?

"She wanted to . . . *speak* to Bella."

"To *Bella?*"

Edward got all hissy then. "I won't let Bella be upset like that again. I don't care how justified Leah thinks she is! I didn't hurt her—of course I wouldn't—but I'll throw her out of the house if it happens again. I'll launch her right across the river—"

"Hold *on*. What did she *say?*" None of this was making any sense.

Edward took a deep breath, composing himself. "Leah was unnecessarily harsh. I'm not going to pretend that I understand why Bella is unable to let go of you, but I do know that she does not behave this way to hurt you. She suffers a great deal over the pain she's inflicting on you, and on me, by asking you to stay. What Leah said was uncalled for. Bella's been crying—"

"Wait—Leah was yelling at Bella about *me?*"

He nodded one sharp nod. "You were quite vehemently championed."

Whoa. "I didn't ask her to do that."

"I know."

I rolled my eyes. Of course he knew. He knew everything.

But that was really something about Leah. Who would have believed it? Leah walking into the bloodsuckers' place *human* to complain about how *I* was being treated.

"I can't promise to control Leah," I told him. "I won't do that. But I'll talk to her, okay? And I don't think there'll be a repeat. Leah's not one to hold back, so she probably got it all off her chest today."

"I would say so."

"Anyway, I'll talk to Bella about it, too. She doesn't need to feel bad. This one's on me."

"I already told her that."

"Of course you did. Is she okay?"

"She's sleeping now. Rose is with her."

So the psycho was "Rose" now. He'd completely crossed over to the dark side.

He ignored that thought, continuing with a more complete answer to my question. "She's . . . better in some ways. Aside from Leah's tirade and the resulting guilt."

Better. Because Edward was hearing the monster and everything was all lovey-dovey now. Fantastic.

"It's a bit more than that," he murmured. "Now that I can make out the child's thoughts, it's apparent that he or she has remarkably developed mental facilities. He can understand us, to an extent."

My mouth fell open. "Are you *serious?*"

"Yes. He seems to have a vague sense of what hurts her now. He's trying to avoid that, as much as possible. He . . . *loves* her. Already."

I stared at Edward, feeling sort of like my eyes might pop out of their sockets. Underneath that disbelief, I could see right away that this was the critical factor. This was what had changed Edward—that the monster had convinced him of this *love*. He couldn't hate what loved Bella. It was probably why he couldn't hate me, either. There was a big difference, though. I wasn't killing her.

Edward went on, acting like he hadn't heard all that. "The progress, I believe, is more than we'd judged. When Carlisle returns—"

"They're not back?" I cut in sharply. I thought of Sam and Jared, watching the road. Would they get curious as to what was going on?

"Alice and Jasper are. Carlisle sent all the blood he was able to acquire, but it wasn't as much as he was hoping for—Bella will use up this supply in another day the way her appetite has grown. Carlisle stayed to try another source. I don't think that's necessary now, but he wants to be covered for any eventuality."

"Why isn't it necessary? If she needs more?"

I could tell he was watching and listening to my reaction carefully as he explained. "I'm trying to persuade Carlisle to deliver the baby as soon as he is back."

"*What?*"

"The child seems to be attempting to avoid rough movements, but it's difficult. He's become too big. It's madness to wait, when he's clearly developed beyond what Carlisle had guessed. Bella's too fragile to delay."

I kept getting my legs knocked out from under me. First, counting on Edward's hatred of the thing so much. Now, I'd realized that I thought of those four days as a sure thing. I'd banked on them.

The endless ocean of grief that waited stretched out before me.

I tried to catch my breath.

Edward waited. I stared at his face while I recovered, recognizing another change there.

"You think she's going to make it," I whispered.

"Yes. That was the other thing I wanted to talk to you about."

I couldn't say anything. After a minute, he went on.

"Yes," he said again. "Waiting, as we have been, for the child to be ready, that was insanely dangerous. At any moment it could have been too late. But if we're proactive about this, if we act quickly, I see no reason why it should not go well. Knowing the child's mind is unbelievably helpful. Thankfully, Bella and Rose agree with me. Now that I've convinced them it's safe for the child if we proceed, there's nothing to keep this from working."

"When will Carlisle be back?" I asked, still whispering. I hadn't got my breath back yet.

"By noon tomorrow."

My knees buckled. I had to grab the car to hold myself up. Edward reached out like he was offering support, but then he thought better of it and dropped his hands.

"I'm sorry," he whispered. "I am truly sorry for the pain this causes you, Jacob. Though you hate me, I must admit that I don't feel the same about you. I think of you as a . . . a brother in many ways. A comrade in arms, at the very least. I regret your suffering more than you realize. But Bella *is* going to survive"—when he said that his voice was fierce, even violent—"and I know that's what really matters to you."

He was probably right. It was hard to tell. My head was spinning.

"So I hate to do this now, while you're already dealing with too much, but, clearly, there is little time. I have to ask you for something—to beg, if I must."

"I don't have anything left," I choked out.

He lifted his hand again, as if to put it on my shoulder, but then let it drop like before and sighed.

"I know how much you have given," he said quietly. "But this is something you *do* have, and only you. I'm asking this of the true Alpha, Jacob. I'm asking this of Ephraim's heir."

I was way past being able to respond.

"I want your permission to deviate from what we agreed to in our treaty with Ephraim. I want you to grant us an exception. I want your permission to save her life. You know I'll do it anyway, but I don't want to break faith with you if there is any way to avoid it. We never intended to go back on our word, and we don't do it lightly now. I want your understanding, Jacob, because you know exactly why we do this. I want the alliance between our families to survive when this is over."

I tried to swallow. *Sam*, I thought. *It's Sam you want.*

"No. Sam's authority is assumed. It belongs to you. You'll never take it from him, but no one can rightfully agree to what I'm asking except for *you*."

It's not my decision.

"It is, Jacob, and you know it. Your word on this will condemn us or absolve us. Only you can give this to me."

I can't think. I don't know.

"We don't have much time." He glanced back toward the house.

No, there was no time. My few days had become a few hours.

I don't know. Let me think. Just give me a minute here, okay?

"Yes."

I started walking to the house, and he followed. Crazy how easy it was, walking through the dark with a vampire right beside me. It didn't feel unsafe, or even uncomfortable, really. It felt like walking next to anybody. Well, anybody who smelled bad.

There was a movement in the brush at the edge of the big lawn, and then a low whimper. Seth shrugged through the ferns and loped over to us.

"Hey, kid," I muttered.

He dipped his head, and I patted his shoulder.

"S'all cool," I lied. "I'll tell you about it later. Sorry to take off on you like that."

He grinned at me.

"Hey, tell your sister to back off now, okay? Enough."

Seth nodded once.

I shoved against his shoulder this time. "Get back to work. I'll spell you in a bit."

Seth leaned against me, shoving back, and then he galloped into the trees.

"He has one of the purest, sincerest, *kindest* minds I've ever heard," Edward murmured when he was out of sight. "You're lucky to have his thoughts to share."

"I know that," I grunted.

We started toward the house, and both of our heads snapped up when we heard the sound of someone sucking through a straw. Edward was in a hurry then. He darted up the porch stairs and was gone.

"Bella, love, I thought you were sleeping," I heard him say. "I'm sorry, I wouldn't have left."

"Don't worry. I just got so thirsty—it woke me up. It's a good thing Carlisle is bringing more. This kid is going to need it when he gets out of me."

"True. That's a good point."

"I wonder if he'll want anything else," she mused.

"I suppose we'll find out."

I walked through the door.

Alice said, "Finally," and Bella's eyes flashed to me. That infuriating, irresistible smile broke across her face for one second. Then it faltered, and her face fell. Her lips puckered, like she was trying not to cry.

I wanted to punch Leah right in her stupid mouth.

"Hey, Bells," I said quickly. "How ya doing?"

"I'm fine," she said.

"Big day today, huh? Lots of new stuff."

"You don't have to do that, Jacob."

"Don't know what you're talking about," I said, going to sit on the arm of the sofa by her head. Edward had the floor there already.

She gave me a reproachful look. "I'm *so* s—" she started to say.

I pinched her lips together between my thumb and finger.

"Jake," she mumbled, trying to pull my hand away. Her attempt was so weak it was hard to believe that she was really trying.

I shook my head. "You can talk when you're not being stupid."

"Fine, I won't say it," it sounded like she mumbled.

I pulled my hand away.

"Sorry!" she finished quickly, and then grinned.

I rolled my eyes and then smiled back at her.

When I stared into her eyes, I saw everything that I'd been looking for in the park.

Tomorrow, she'd be someone else. But hopefully alive, and that was what counted, right? She'd look at me with the same eyes, sort of. Smile with the same lips, almost. She'd still know me better than anyone who didn't have full access to the inside of my head.

Leah might be an interesting companion, maybe even a true friend—someone who would stand up for me. But she wasn't my *best* friend the way that Bella was. Aside from the impossible love I felt for Bella, there was also that other bond, and it ran bone deep.

Tomorrow, she'd be my enemy. Or she'd be my ally. And, apparently, that distinction was up to me.

I sighed.

Fine! I thought, giving up the very last thing I had to give. It made me feel hollow. *Go ahead. Save her. As Ephraim's heir, you have my permission, my word, that this will not violate the treaty. The others will just have to blame me. You were right— they can't deny that it's my right to agree to this.*

"Thank you." Edward's whisper was low enough that Bella didn't hear anything. But the words were so fervent that, from the corner of my eye, I saw the other vampires turning to stare.

"So," Bella asked, working to be casual. "How was your day?"

"Great. Went for a drive. Hung out in the park."

"Sounds nice."

"Sure, sure."

Suddenly, she made a face. "Rose?" she asked.

I heard Blondie chuckle. "Again?"

"I think I've drunk two gallons in the last hour," Bella explained.

Edward and I both got out of the way while Rosalie came to lift Bella from the couch and take her to the bathroom.

"Can I walk?" Bella asked. "My legs are so stiff."

"Are you sure?" Edward asked.

"Rose'll catch me if I trip over my feet. Which could happen pretty easily, since I can't see them."

Rosalie set Bella carefully on her feet, keeping her hands right at Bella's shoulders. Bella stretched her arms out in front of her, wincing a little.

"That feels good," she sighed. "Ugh, but I'm huge."

She really was. Her stomach was its own continent.

"One more day," she said, and patted her stomach.

I couldn't help the pain that shot through me in a sudden, stabbing burst, but I tried to keep it off my face. I could hide it for one more day, right?

"All righty, then. Whoops—oh, no!"

The cup Bella had left on the sofa tumbled to one side, the dark red blood spilling out onto the pale fabric.

Automatically, though three other hands beat her there, Bella bent over, reaching out to catch it.

There was the strangest, muffled ripping sound from the center of her body.

"Oh!" she gasped.

And then she went totally limp, slumping toward the floor. Rosalie caught her in the same instant, before she could fall. Edward was there, too, hands out, the mess on the sofa forgotten.

"Bella?" he asked, and then his eyes unfocused, and panic shot across his features.

A half second later, Bella screamed.

It was not just a scream, it was a blood-curdling shriek of agony. The horrifying sound cut off with a gurgle, and her eyes rolled back into her head. Her body twitched, arched in Rosalie's arms, and then Bella vomited a fountain of blood.

18. THERE ARE NO WORDS FOR THIS.

BELLA'S BODY, STREAMING WITH RED, STARTED TO TWITCH, jerking around in Rosalie's arms like she was being electrocuted. All the while, her face was blank—unconscious. It was the wild thrashing from inside the center of her body that moved her. As she convulsed, sharp snaps and cracks kept time with the spasms.

Rosalie and Edward were frozen for the shortest half second, and then they broke. Rosalie whipped Bella's body into her arms, and, shouting so fast it was hard to separate the individual words, she and Edward shot up the staircase to the second floor.

I sprinted after them.

"Morphine!" Edward yelled at Rosalie.

"Alice—get Carlisle on the phone!" Rosalie screeched.

The room I followed them to looked like an emergency ward set up in the middle of a library. The lights were brilliant and white. Bella was on a table under the glare, skin ghostly in the spotlight. Her body flopped, a fish on the sand. Rosalie pinned Bella down, yanking and ripping her clothes out of the way, while Edward stabbed a syringe into her arm.

How many times had I imagined her naked? Now I couldn't look. I was afraid to have these memories in my head.

"What's *happening*, Edward?"

"He's suffocating!"

"The placenta must have detached!"

Somewhere in this, Bella came around. She responded to their words with a shriek that clawed at my eardrums.

"Get him OUT!" she screamed. "He can't BREATHE! Do it NOW!"

I saw the red spots pop out when her scream broke the blood vessels in her eyes.

"The morphine—," Edward growled.

"NO! NOW—!" Another gush of blood choked off what she was shrieking. He held her head up, desperately trying to clear her mouth so that she could breathe again.

Alice darted into the room and clipped a little blue earpiece under Rosalie's hair. Then Alice backed away, her gold eyes wide and burning, while Rosalie hissed frantically into the phone.

In the bright light, Bella's skin seemed more purple and

black than it was white. Deep red was seeping beneath the skin over the huge, shuddering bulge of her stomach. Rosalie's hand came up with a scalpel.

"Let the morphine spread!" Edward shouted at her.

"There's no time," Rosalie hissed. "He's dying!"

Her hand came down on Bella's stomach, and vivid red spouted out from where she pierced the skin. It was like a bucket being turned over, a faucet twisted to full. Bella jerked, but didn't scream. She was still choking.

And then Rosalie lost her focus. I saw the expression on her face shift, saw her lips pull back from her teeth and her black eyes glint with thirst.

"No, Rose!" Edward roared, but his hands were trapped, trying to prop Bella upright so she could breathe.

I launched myself at Rosalie, jumping across the table without bothering to phase. As I hit her stone body, knocking her toward the door, I felt the scalpel in her hand stab deep into my left arm. My right palm smashed against her face, locking her jaw and blocking her airways.

I used my grip on Rosalie's face to swing her body out so that I could land a solid kick in her gut; it was like kicking concrete. She flew into the door frame, buckling one side of it. The little speaker in her ear crackled into pieces. Then Alice was there, yanking her by the throat to get her into the hall.

And I had to give it to Blondie—she didn't put up an ounce of fight. She *wanted* us to win. She let me trash her like that, to save Bella. Well, to save the thing.

I ripped the blade out of my arm.

"Alice, get her out of here!" Edward shouted. "Take her to Jasper and *keep* her there! Jacob, I need you!"

I didn't watch Alice finish the job. I wheeled back to the operating table, where Bella was turning blue, her eyes wide and staring.

"CPR?" Edward growled at me, fast and demanding.

"Yes!"

I judged his face swiftly, looking for any sign that he was going to react like Rosalie. There was nothing but single-minded ferocity.

"Get her breathing! I've got to get him out before—"

Another shattering crack inside her body, the loudest yet, so loud that we both froze in shock waiting for her answering shriek. Nothing. Her legs, which had been curled up in agony, now went limp, sprawling out in an unnatural way.

"Her spine," he choked in horror.

"Get it *out* of her!" I snarled, flinging the scalpel at him. "She won't feel anything now!"

And then I bent over her head. Her mouth looked clear, so I pressed mine to hers and blew a lungful of air into it. I felt her twitching body expand, so there was nothing blocking her throat.

Her lips tasted like blood.

I could hear her heart, thumping unevenly. *Keep it going,* I thought fiercely at her, blowing another gust of air into her body. *You promised. Keep your heart beating.*

I heard the soft, wet sound of the scalpel across her stomach. More blood dripping to the floor.

The next sound jolted through me, unexpected, terrifying. Like metal being shredded apart. The sound brought back the fight in the clearing so many months ago, the tearing sound of the newborns being ripped apart. I glanced over to see Edward's face pressed against the bulge. Vampire teeth—a surefire way to cut through vampire skin.

I shuddered as I blew more air into Bella.

She coughed back at me, her eyes blinking, rolling blindly.

"You stay with *me* now, Bella!" I yelled at her. "Do you hear me? Stay! You're not leaving me. Keep your heart beating!"

Her eyes wheeled, looking for me, or him, but seeing nothing.

I stared into them anyway, keeping my gaze locked there.

And then her body was suddenly still under my hands, though her breathing picked up roughly and her heart continued to thud. I realized the stillness meant that it was over. The internal beating was over. It must be out of her.

It was.

Edward whispered, "Renesmee."

So Bella'd been wrong. It wasn't the boy she'd imagined. No big surprise there. What *hadn't* she been wrong about?

I didn't look away from her red-spotted eyes, but I felt her hands lift weakly.

"Let me . . . ," she croaked in a broken whisper. "Give her to me."

I guess I should have known that he would always give her what she wanted, no matter how stupid her request might be. But I didn't dream he would listen to her now. So I didn't think to stop him.

Something warm touched my arm. That right there should have caught my attention. Nothing felt warm to me.

But I couldn't look away from Bella's face. She blinked and then stared, finally seeing something. She moaned out a strange, weak croon.

"Renes . . . mee. So . . . beautiful."

And then she gasped—gasped in pain.

By the time I looked, it was too late. Edward had snatched the warm, bloody thing out of her limp arms. My eyes flickered across her skin. It was red with blood—the blood that had flowed from her mouth, the blood smeared all over the creature, and fresh blood welling out of a tiny double-crescent bite mark just over her left breast.

"No, Renesmee," Edward murmured, like he was teaching the monster manners.

I didn't look at him or it. I watched only Bella as her eyes rolled back into her head.

With a last dull *ga-lump*, her heart faltered and went silent.

She missed maybe half of one beat, and then my hands were on her chest, doing compressions. I counted in my head, trying to keep the rhythm steady. One. Two. Three. Four.

Breaking away for a second, I blew another lungful of air into her.

I couldn't see anymore. My eyes were wet and blurry. But I was hyperaware of the sounds in the room. The unwilling *glug-glug* of her heart under my demanding hands, the pounding of my own heart, and another—a fluttering beat that was too fast, too light. I couldn't place it.

I forced more air down Bella's throat.

"What are you waiting for?" I choked out breathlessly, pumping her heart again. One. Two. Three. Four.

"Take the baby," Edward said urgently.

"Throw it out the window." One. Two. Three. Four.

"Give her to me," a low voice chimed from the doorway.

Edward and I snarled at the same time.

One. Two. Three. Four.

"I've got it under control," Rosalie promised. "Give me the baby, Edward. I'll take care of her until Bella . . ."

I breathed for Bella again while the exchange took place. The fluttering *thumpa-thumpa-thumpa* faded away with distance.

"Move your hands, Jacob."

I looked up from Bella's white eyes, still pumping her heart for her. Edward had a syringe in his hand—all silver, like it was made from steel.

"What's that?"

His stone hand knocked mine out of the way. There was a tiny crunch as his blow broke my little finger. In the same second, he shoved the needle straight into her heart.

"My venom," he answered as he pushed the plunger down.

I heard the jolt in her heart, like he'd shocked her with paddles.

"Keep it moving," he ordered. His voice was ice, was dead. Fierce and unthinking. Like he was a machine.

I ignored the healing ache in my finger and started pumping her heart again. It was harder, as if her blood was congealing there—thicker and slower. While I pushed the now-viscous blood through her arteries, I watched what he was doing.

It was like he was kissing her, brushing his lips at her throat, at her wrists, into the crease at the inside of her arm.

But I could hear the lush tearing of her skin as his teeth bit through, again and again, forcing venom into her system at as many points as possible. I saw his pale tongue sweep along the bleeding gashes, but before this could make me either sick or angry, I realized what he was doing. Where his tongue washed the venom over her skin, it sealed shut. Holding the poison and the blood inside her body.

I blew more air into her mouth, but there was nothing there. Just the lifeless rise of her chest in response. I kept pumping her heart, counting, while he worked manically over her, trying to put her back together. All the king's horses and all the king's men . . .

But there was nothing there, just me, just him.

Working over a corpse.

Because that's all that was left of the girl we both loved. This broken, bled-out, mangled corpse. We couldn't put Bella together again.

I knew it was too late. I knew she was dead. I knew it for sure because the pull was gone. I didn't feel any reason to be here beside her. *She* wasn't here anymore. So this body had no more draw for me. The senseless need to be near her had vanished.

Or maybe *moved* was the better word. It seemed like I felt the pull from the opposite direction now. From down the stairs, out the door. The longing to get away from here and never, ever come back.

"Go, then," he snapped, and he hit my hands out of the way again, taking my place this time. Three fingers broken, it felt like.

I straightened them numbly, not minding the throb of pain.

He pushed her dead heart faster than I had.

"She's not dead," he growled. "She's going to be fine."

I wasn't sure he was talking to me anymore.

Turning away, leaving him with his dead, I walked slowly to the door. So slowly. I couldn't make my feet move faster.

This was it, then. The ocean of pain. The other shore so far away across the boiling water that I couldn't imagine it, much less see it.

I felt empty again, now that I'd lost my purpose. Saving Bella had been my fight for so long now. And she wouldn't be saved. She'd willingly sacrificed herself to be torn apart by that monster's young, and so the fight was lost. It was all over.

I shuddered at the sound coming from behind me as I plodded down the stairs—the sound of a dead heart being forced to thud.

I wanted to somehow pour bleach inside my head and let it fry my brain. To burn away the images left from Bella's final minutes. I'd take the brain damage if I could get rid of that—the screaming, the bleeding, the unbearable crunching and snapping as the newborn monster tore through her from the inside out. . . .

I wanted to sprint away, to take the stairs ten at a time and race out the door, but my feet were heavy as iron and my body was more tired than it had ever been before. I shuffled down the stairs like a crippled old man.

I rested at the bottom step, gathering my strength to get out the door.

Rosalie was on the clean end of the white sofa, her back

to me, cooing and murmuring to the blanket-wrapped thing in her arms. She must have heard me pause, but she ignored me, caught up in her moment of stolen motherhood. Maybe she would be happy now. Rosalie had what she wanted, and Bella would never come to take the creature from her. I wondered if that's what the poisonous blonde had been hoping for all along.

She held something dark in her hands, and there was a greedy sucking sound coming from the tiny murderer she held.

The scent of blood in the air. Human blood. Rosalie was feeding it. Of course it would want blood. What else would you feed the kind of monster that would brutally mutilate its own mother? It might as well have been drinking Bella's blood. Maybe it was.

My strength came back to me as I listened to the sound of the little executioner feeding.

Strength and hate and heat—red heat washing through my head, burning but erasing nothing. The images in my head were fuel, building up the inferno but refusing to be consumed. I felt the tremors rock me from head to toe, and I did not try to stop them.

Rosalie was totally absorbed in the creature, paying no attention to me at all. She wouldn't be quick enough to stop me, distracted as she was.

Sam had been right. The thing was an aberration—its existence went against nature. A black, soulless demon. Something that had no right to be.

Something that had to be destroyed.

It seemed like the pull had not been leading to the door

after all. I could feel it now, encouraging me, tugging me forward. Pushing me to finish this, to cleanse the world of this abomination.

Rosalie would try to kill me when the creature was dead, and I would fight back. I wasn't sure if I would have time to finish her before the others came to help. Maybe, maybe not. I didn't much care either way.

I didn't care if the wolves, either set, avenged me or called the Cullens' justice fair. None of that mattered. All I cared about was my own justice. *My* revenge. The thing that had killed Bella would not live another minute longer.

If Bella'd survived, she would have hated me for this. She would have wanted to kill me personally.

But I didn't care. She didn't care what she had done to me—letting herself be slaughtered like an animal. Why should I take her feelings into account?

And then there was Edward. He must be too busy now—too far gone in his insane denial, trying to reanimate a corpse—to listen to my plans.

So I wouldn't get the chance to keep my promise to him, unless—and it was not a wager *I'd* put money on—I managed to win the fight against Rosalie, Jasper, and Alice, three on one. But even if I did win, I didn't think I had it in me to kill Edward.

Because I didn't have enough compassion for that. Why should I let him get away from what he'd done? Wouldn't it be more fair—more satisfying—to let him live with nothing, nothing at all?

It made me almost smile, as filled with hate as I was, to imagine it. No Bella. No killer spawn. And also missing as many members of his family as I was able to take down. Of course, he could probably put those back together, since I wouldn't be around to burn them. Unlike Bella, who would never be whole again.

I wondered if the creature could be put back together. I doubted it. It was part Bella, too—so it must have inherited some of her vulnerability. I could hear that in the tiny, thrumming beat of its heart.

Its heart was beating. Hers wasn't.

Only a second had passed as I made these easy decisions.

The trembling was getting tighter and faster. I coiled myself, preparing to spring at the blond vampire and rip the murderous thing from her arms with my teeth.

Rosalie cooed at the creature again, setting the empty metal bottle-thing aside and lifting the creature into the air to nuzzle her face against its cheek.

Perfect. The new position was perfect for my strike. I leaned forward and felt the heat begin to change me while the pull toward the killer grew—it was stronger than I'd ever felt it before, so strong it reminded me of an Alpha's command, like it would crush me if I didn't obey.

This time I *wanted* to obey.

The murderer stared past Rosalie's shoulder at me, its gaze more focused than any newborn creature's gaze should be.

Warm brown eyes, the color of milk chocolate—the exact same color that Bella's had been.

My shaking jerked to a stop; heat flooded through me, stronger than before, but it was a new kind of heat—not a burning.

It was a glowing.

Everything inside me came undone as I stared at the tiny porcelain face of the half-vampire, half-human baby. All the lines that held me to my life were sliced apart in swift cuts, like clipping the strings to a bunch of balloons. Everything that made me who I was—my love for the dead girl upstairs, my love for my father, my loyalty to my new pack, the love for my other brothers, my hatred for my enemies, my home, my name, my *self*—disconnected from me in that second— *snip, snip, snip*—and floated up into space.

I was not left drifting. A new string held me where I was.

Not one string, but a million. Not strings, but steel cables. A million steel cables all tying me to one thing—to the very center of the universe.

I could see that now—how the universe swirled around this one point. I'd never seen the symmetry of the universe before, but now it was plain.

The gravity of the earth no longer tied me to the place where I stood.

It was the baby girl in the blond vampire's arms that held me here now.

Renesmee.

From upstairs, there was a new sound. The only sound that could touch me in this endless instant.

A frantic pounding, a racing beat . . .

A changing heart.

BOOK THREE

❮❮ ❯❯

bella

CONTENTS

-+ +-

Personal affection is a luxury you can have only after all your enemies are eliminated. Until then, everyone you love is a hostage, sapping your courage and corrupting your judgment.

Orson Scott Card
Empire

PREFACE

NO LONGER JUST A NIGHTMARE, THE LINE OF BLACK
advanced on us through the icy mist stirred up by their
feet.

We're going to die, I thought in panic. I was desperate for
the precious one I guarded, but even to think of that was a
lapse in attention I could not afford.

They ghosted closer, their dark robes billowing slightly
with the movement. I saw their hands curl into bone-colored
claws. They drifted apart, angling to come at us from all
sides. We were outnumbered. It was over.

And then, like a burst of light from a flash, the whole
scene was different. Yet nothing changed—the Volturi still
stalked toward us, poised to kill. All that really changed was

how the picture looked to me. Suddenly, I was hungry for it. I *wanted* them to charge. The panic changed to bloodlust as I crouched forward, a smile on my face, and a growl ripped through my bared teeth.

19. BURNING

THE PAIN WAS BEWILDERING.

Exactly that—I was bewildered. I couldn't understand, couldn't make sense of what was happening.

My body tried to reject the pain, and I was sucked again and again into a blackness that cut out whole seconds or maybe even minutes of the agony, making it that much harder to keep up with reality.

I tried to separate them.

Non-reality was black, and it didn't hurt so much.

Reality was red, and it felt like I was being sawed in half, hit by a bus, punched by a prize fighter, trampled by bulls, and submerged in acid, all at the same time.

Reality was feeling my body twist and flip when I couldn't possibly move because of the pain.

Reality was knowing there was something so much more important than all this torture, and not being able to remember what it was.

Reality had come on so fast.

One moment, everything was as it should have been. Surrounded by people I loved. Smiles. Somehow, unlikely as it was, it seemed like I was about to get everything I'd been fighting for.

And then one tiny, inconsequential thing had gone wrong.

I'd watched as my cup tilted, dark blood spilling out and staining the perfect white, and I'd lurched toward the accident reflexively. I'd seen the other, faster hands, but my body had continued to reach, to stretch. . . .

Inside me, something had yanked the opposite direction.

Ripping. Breaking. Agony.

The darkness had taken over, and then washed away to a wave of torture. I couldn't breathe—I had drowned once before, and this was different; it was too hot in my throat.

Pieces of me shattering, snapping, slicing apart. . . .

More blackness.

Voices, this time, shouting, as the pain came back.

"The placenta must have detached!"

Something sharper than knives ripped through me—the words, making sense in spite of the other tortures. *Detached placenta*—I knew what that meant. It meant that my baby was dying inside me.

"Get him out!" I screamed to Edward. Why hadn't he done it yet? "He can't breathe! Do it now!"

"The morphine—"

He wanted to wait, to give me painkillers, while our baby was dying?!

"No! Now—," I choked, unable to finish.

Black spots covered the light in the room as a cold point of new pain stabbed icily into my stomach. It felt wrong— I struggled automatically to protect my womb, my baby, my little Edward Jacob, but I was weak. My lungs ached, oxygen burned away.

The pain faded away again, though I clung to it now. My baby, my baby, dying. . . .

How long had passed? Seconds or minutes? The pain was gone. Numb. I couldn't feel. I still couldn't see, either, but I could hear. There was air in my lungs again, scraping in rough bubbles up and down my throat.

"You stay with *me* now, Bella! Do you hear me? Stay! You're not leaving me. Keep your heart beating!"

Jacob? Jacob, still here, still trying to save me.

Of course, I wanted to tell him. Of course I would keep my heart beating. Hadn't I promised them both?

I tried to feel my heart, to find it, but I was so lost inside my own body. I couldn't feel the things I should, and nothing felt in the right place. I blinked and I found my eyes. I could see the light. Not what I was looking for, but better than nothing.

As my eyes struggled to adjust, Edward whispered, "Renesmee."

Renesmee?

Not the pale and perfect son of my imagination? I felt a moment of shock. And then a flood of warmth.

Renesmee.

I willed my lips to move, willed the bubbles of air to turn into whispers on my tongue. I forced my numb hands to reach.

"Let me . . . Give her to me."

The light danced, shattering off Edward's crystal hands. The sparkles were tinged with red, with the blood that covered his skin. And more red in his hands. Something small and struggling, dripping with blood. He touched the warm body to my weak arms, almost like I was holding her. Her wet skin was hot—as hot as Jacob's.

My eyes focused; suddenly everything was absolutely clear.

Renesmee did not cry, but she breathed in quick, startled pants. Her eyes were open, her expression so shocked it was almost funny. The little, perfectly round head was covered in a thick layer of matted, bloody curls. Her irises were a familiar—but astonishing—chocolate brown. Under the blood, her skin looked pale, a creamy ivory. All besides her cheeks, which flamed with color.

Her tiny face was so absolutely perfect that it stunned me. She was even more beautiful than her father. Unbelievable. Impossible.

"Renesmee," I whispered. "So . . . beautiful."

The impossible face suddenly smiled—a wide, deliberate smile. Behind the shell-pink lips was a full complement of snowy milk teeth.

She leaned her head down, against my chest, burrowing

against the warmth. Her skin was warm and silky, but it didn't give the way mine did.

Then there was pain again—just one warm slash of it. I gasped.

And she was gone. My angel-faced baby was nowhere. I couldn't see or feel her.

No! I wanted to shout. *Give her back to me!*

But the weakness was too much. My arms felt like empty rubber hoses for a moment, and then they felt like nothing at all. I couldn't feel them. I couldn't feel *me*.

The blackness rushed over my eyes more solidly than before. Like a thick blindfold, firm and fast. Covering not just my eyes but also my *self* with a crushing weight. It was exhausting to push against it. I knew it would be so much easier to give in. To let the blackness push me down, down, down to a place where there was no pain and no weariness and no worry and no fear.

If it had only been for myself, I wouldn't have been able to struggle very long. I was only human, with no more than human strength. I'd been trying to keep up with the supernatural for too long, like Jacob had said.

But this wasn't just about me.

If I did the easy thing now, let the black nothingness erase me, I would hurt them.

Edward. Edward. My life and his were twisted into a single strand. Cut one, and you cut both. If he were gone, I would not be able to live through that. If I were gone, he wouldn't live through it, either. And a world without Edward seemed completely pointless. Edward *had* to exist.

Jacob—who'd said goodbye to me over and over but kept

coming back when I needed him. Jacob, who I'd wounded so many times it was criminal. Would I hurt him again, the worst way yet? He'd stayed for me, despite everything. Now all he asked was that I stay for him.

But it was so dark here that I couldn't see either of their faces. Nothing seemed real. That made it hard not to give up.

I kept pushing against the black, though, almost a reflex. I wasn't trying to lift it. I was just resisting. Not allowing it to crush me completely. I wasn't Atlas, and the black felt as heavy as a planet; I couldn't shoulder it. All I could do was not be entirely obliterated.

It was sort of the pattern to my life—I'd never been strong enough to deal with the things outside my control, to attack the enemies or outrun them. To avoid the pain. Always human and weak, the only thing I'd ever been able to do was keep going. Endure. Survive.

It had been enough up to this point. It would have to be enough today. I would endure this until help came.

I knew Edward would be doing everything he could. He would not give up. Neither would I.

I held the blackness of nonexistence at bay by inches.

It wasn't enough, though—that determination. As the time ground on and on and the darkness gained by tiny eighths and sixteenths of my inches, I needed something more to draw strength from.

I couldn't pull even Edward's face into view. Not Jacob's, not Alice's or Rosalie's or Charlie's or Renée's or Carlisle's or Esme's . . . Nothing. It terrified me, and I wondered if it was too late.

I felt myself slipping—there was nothing to hold on to.

No! I had to survive this. Edward was depending on me. Jacob. Charlie Alice Rosalie Carlisle Renée Esme . . .

Renesmee.

And then, though I still couldn't see anything, suddenly I could *feel* something. Like phantom limbs, I imagined I could feel my arms again. And in them, something small and hard and very, very warm.

My baby. My little nudger.

I had done it. Against the odds, I *had* been strong enough to survive Renesmee, to hold on to her until she was strong enough to live without me.

That spot of heat in my phantom arms felt so real. I clutched it closer. It was exactly where my heart should be. Holding tight the warm memory of my daughter, I knew that I would be able to fight the darkness as long as I needed to.

The warmth beside my heart got more and more real, warmer and warmer. Hotter. The heat was so real it was hard to believe that I was imagining it.

Hotter.

Uncomfortable now. Too hot. Much, much too hot.

Like grabbing the wrong end of a curling iron—my automatic response was to drop the scorching thing in my arms. But there was nothing in my arms. My arms were not curled to my chest. My arms were dead things lying somewhere at my side. The heat was inside me.

The burning grew—rose and peaked and rose again until it surpassed anything I'd ever felt.

I felt the pulse behind the fire raging now in my chest and realized that I'd found my heart again, just in time to wish I never had. To wish that I'd embraced the blackness while I'd still had the chance. I wanted to raise my arms and claw my chest open and rip the heart from it—anything to get rid of this torture. But I couldn't feel my arms, couldn't move one vanished finger.

James, snapping my leg under his foot. That was nothing. That was a soft place to rest on a feather bed. I'd take that now, a hundred times. A hundred snaps. I'd take it and be grateful.

The baby, kicking my ribs apart, breaking her way through me piece by piece. That was nothing. That was floating in a pool of cool water. I'd take it a thousand times. Take it and be grateful.

The fire blazed hotter and I wanted to scream. To beg for someone to kill me now, before I lived one more second in this pain. But I couldn't move my lips. The weight was still there, pressing on me.

I realized it wasn't the darkness holding me down; it was my body. So heavy. Burying me in the flames that were chewing their way out from my heart now, spreading with impossible pain through my shoulders and stomach, scalding their way up my throat, licking at my face.

Why couldn't I move? Why couldn't I scream? This wasn't part of the stories.

My mind was unbearably clear—sharpened by the fierce pain—and I saw the answer almost as soon as I could form the questions.

The morphine.

It seemed like a million deaths ago that we'd discussed it—Edward, Carlisle, and I. Edward and Carlisle had hoped that enough painkillers would help fight the pain of the venom. Carlisle had tried with Emmett, but the venom had burned ahead of the medicine, sealing his veins. There hadn't been time for it to spread.

I'd kept my face smooth and nodded and thanked my rarely lucky stars that Edward could not read my mind.

Because I'd had morphine and venom together in my system before, and I knew the truth. I knew the numbness of the medicine was completely irrelevant while the venom seared through my veins. But there'd been no way I was going to mention that fact. Nothing that would make him more unwilling to change me.

I hadn't guessed that the morphine would have this effect—that it would pin me down and gag me. Hold me paralyzed while I burned.

I knew all the stories. I knew that Carlisle had kept quiet enough to avoid discovery while he burned. I knew that, according to Rosalie, it did no good to scream. And I'd hoped that maybe I could be like Carlisle. That I would believe Rosalie's words and keep my mouth shut. Because I knew that every scream that escaped my lips would torment Edward.

Now it seemed like a hideous joke that I was getting my wish fulfilled.

If I couldn't scream, *how could I tell them to kill me?*

All I wanted was to die. To never have been born. The whole of my existence did not outweigh this pain. Wasn't worth living through it for one more heartbeat.

Let me die, let me die, let me die.

And, for a never-ending space, that was all there was. Just the fiery torture, and my soundless shrieks, pleading for death to come. Nothing else, not even time. So that made it infinite, with no beginning and no end. One infinite moment of pain.

The only change came when suddenly, impossibly, my pain was doubled. The lower half of my body, deadened since before the morphine, was suddenly on fire, too. Some broken connection had been healed—knitted together by the scorching fingers of the flame.

The endless burn raged on.

It could have been seconds or days, weeks or years, but, eventually, time came to mean something again.

Three things happened together, grew from each other so that I didn't know which came first: time restarted, the morphine's weight faded, and I got stronger.

I could feel the control of my body come back to me in increments, and those increments were my first markers of the time passing. I knew it when I was able to twitch my toes and twist my fingers into fists. I knew it, but I did not act on it.

Though the fire did not decrease one tiny degree—in fact, I began to develop a new capacity for experiencing it, a new sensitivity to appreciate, separately, each blistering tongue of flame that licked through my veins—I discovered that I could think around it.

I could remember *why* I shouldn't scream. I could remember the reason why I'd committed to enduring this unendurable agony. I could remember that, though it felt impossible now, there was something that might be worth the torture.

This happened just in time for me to hold on when

the weights left my body. To anyone watching me, there would be no change. But for me, as I struggled to keep the screams and thrashing locked up inside my body, where they couldn't hurt anyone else, it felt like I'd gone from being *tied* to the stake as I burned, to *gripping* that stake to hold myself in the fire.

I had just enough strength to lie there unmoving while I was charred alive.

My hearing got clearer and clearer, and I could count the frantic, pounding beats of my heart to mark the time.

I could count the shallow breaths that gasped through my teeth.

I could count the low, even breaths that came from somewhere close beside me. These moved slowest, so I concentrated on them. They meant the most time passing. More even than a clock's pendulum, those breaths pulled me through the burning seconds toward the end.

I continued to get stronger, my thoughts clearer. When new noises came, I could listen.

There were light footsteps, the whisper of air stirred by an opening door. The footsteps got closer, and I felt pressure against the inside of my wrist. I couldn't feel the coolness of the fingers. The fire blistered away every memory of cool.

"Still no change?"

"None."

The lightest pressure, breath against my scorched skin.

"There's no scent of the morphine left."

"I know."

"Bella? Can you hear me?"

I knew, beyond all doubt, that if I unlocked my teeth I would lose it—I would shriek and screech and writhe and thrash. If I opened my eyes, if I so much as twitched a finger—any change at all would be the end of my control.

"Bella? Bella, love? Can you open your eyes? Can you squeeze my hand?"

Pressure on my fingers. It was harder not to answer this voice, but I stayed paralyzed. I knew that the pain in his voice now was nothing compared to what it *could* be. Right now he only *feared* that I was suffering.

"Maybe . . . Carlisle, maybe I was too late." His voice was muffled; it broke on the word *late.*

My resolve wavered for a second.

"Listen to her heart, Edward. It's stronger than even Emmett's was. I've never heard anything so *vital*. She'll be perfect."

Yes, I was right to keep quiet. Carlisle would reassure him. He didn't need to suffer with me.

"And her—her spine?"

"Her injuries weren't so much worse than Esme's. The venom will heal her as it did Esme."

"But she's so still. I *must* have done something wrong."

"Or something right, Edward. Son, you did everything I could have and more. I'm not sure I would have had the persistence, the faith it took to save her. Stop berating yourself. Bella is going to be fine."

A broken whisper. "She must be in agony."

"We don't know that. She had so much morphine in her system. We don't know the effect that will have on her experience."

Faint pressure inside the crease of my elbow. Another whisper. "Bella, I love you. Bella, I'm sorry."

I wanted so much to answer him, but I wouldn't make his pain worse. Not while I had the strength to hold myself still.

Through all this, the racking fire went right on burning me. But there was so much space in my head now. Room to ponder their conversation, room to remember what had happened, room to look ahead to the future, with still endless room left over to suffer in.

Also room to worry.

Where was my baby? Why wasn't she here? Why weren't they talking about her?

"No, I'm staying right here," Edward whispered, answering an unspoken thought. "They'll sort it out."

"An interesting situation," Carlisle responded. "And I'd thought I'd seen just about everything."

"I'll deal with it later. *We'll* deal with it." Something pressed softly to my blistering palm.

"I'm sure, between the five of us, we can keep it from turning into bloodshed."

Edward sighed. "I don't know which side to take. I'd love to flog them both. Well, later."

"I wonder what Bella will think—whose side she'll take," Carlisle mused.

One low, strained chuckle. "I'm sure she'll surprise me. She always does."

Carlisle's footsteps faded away again, and I was frustrated that there was no further explanation. Were they talking so mysteriously just to annoy me?

I went back to counting Edward's breaths to mark the time.

Ten thousand, nine hundred forty-three breaths later, a

different set of footsteps whispered into the room. Lighter. More . . . rhythmic.

Strange that I could distinguish the minute differences between footsteps that I'd never been able to hear at all before today.

"How much longer?" Edward asked.

"It won't be long now," Alice told him. "See how clear she's becoming? I can see her so much better." She sighed.

"Still feeling a little bitter?"

"Yes, thanks so much for bringing it up," she grumbled. "You would be mortified, too, if you realized that you were handcuffed by your own nature. I see vampires best, because I am one; I see humans okay, because I was one. But I can't see these odd half-breeds at all because they're nothing I've experienced. Bah!"

"Focus, Alice."

"Right. Bella's almost too easy to see now."

There was a long moment of silence, and then Edward sighed. It was a new sound, happier.

"She's really going to be fine," he breathed.

"Of course she is."

"You weren't so sanguine two days ago."

"I couldn't *see* right two days ago. But now that she's free of all the blind spots, it's a piece of cake."

"Could you concentrate for me? On the clock—give me an estimate."

Alice sighed. "So impatient. Fine. Give me a sec—"

Quiet breathing.

"Thank you, Alice." His voice was brighter.

How long? Couldn't they at least say it aloud for me? Was that too much to ask? How many more seconds would

I burn? Ten thousand? Twenty? Another day—eighty-six thousand, four hundred? More than that?

"She's going to be dazzling."

Edward growled quietly. "She always has been."

Alice snorted. "You know what I mean. *Look* at her."

Edward didn't answer, but Alice's words gave me hope that maybe I didn't resemble the charcoal briquette I felt like. It seemed as if I *must* be just a pile of charred bones by now. Every cell in my body had been razed to ash.

I heard Alice breeze out of the room. I heard the swish of the fabric she moved, rubbing against itself. I heard the quiet buzz of the light hanging from the ceiling. I heard the faint wind brushing against the outside of the house. I could hear *everything*.

Downstairs, someone was watching a ball game. The Mariners were winning by two runs.

"It's my *turn*," I heard Rosalie snap at someone, and there was a low snarl in response.

"Hey, now," Emmett cautioned.

Someone hissed.

I listened for more, but there was nothing but the game. Baseball was not interesting enough to distract me from the pain, so I listened to Edward's breathing again, counting the seconds.

Twenty-one thousand, nine hundred seventeen and a half seconds later, the pain changed.

On the good-news side of things, it started to fade from my fingertips and toes. Fading *slowly*, but at least it was doing something new. This had to be it. The pain was on its way out. . . .

And then the bad news. The fire in my throat wasn't the

same as before. I wasn't only on fire, but I was now parched, too. Dry as bone. So thirsty. Burning fire, and burning thirst . . .

Also bad news: The fire inside my heart got hotter.

How was that *possible?*

My heartbeat, already too fast, picked up—the fire drove its rhythm to a new frantic pace.

"Carlisle," Edward called. His voice was low but clear. I knew that Carlisle would hear it, if he were in or near the house.

The fire retreated from my palms, leaving them blissfully pain-free and cool. But it retreated to my heart, which blazed hot as the sun and beat at a furious new speed.

Carlisle entered the room, Alice at his side. Their footsteps were so distinct, I could even tell that Carlisle was on the right, and a foot ahead of Alice.

"Listen," Edward told them.

The loudest sound in the room was my frenzied heart, pounding to the rhythm of the fire.

"Ah," Carlisle said. "It's almost over."

My relief at his words was overshadowed by the excruciating pain in my heart.

My wrists were free, though, and my ankles. The fire was totally extinguished there.

"Soon," Alice agreed eagerly. "I'll get the others. Should I have Rosalie . . . ?"

"Yes—keep the baby away."

What? No. *No!* What did he mean, keep my baby away? What was he thinking?

My fingers twitched—the irritation breaking through my perfect façade. The room went silent besides the jackhammering of my heart as they all stopped breathing for a second in response.

A hand squeezed my wayward fingers. "Bella? Bella, love?"

Could I answer him without screaming? I considered that for a moment, and then the fire ripped hotter still through my chest, draining in from my elbows and knees. Better not to chance it.

"I'll bring them right up," Alice said, an urgent edge to her tone, and I heard the swish of wind as she darted away.

And then—*oh!*

My heart took off, beating like helicopter blades, the sound almost a single sustained note; it felt like it would grind through my ribs. The fire flared up in the center of my chest, sucking the last remnants of the flames from the rest of my body to fuel the most scorching blaze yet. The pain was enough to stun me, to break through my iron grip on the stake. My back arched, bowed as if the fire was dragging me upward by my heart.

I allowed no other piece of my body to break rank as my torso slumped back to the table.

It became a battle inside me—my sprinting heart racing against the attacking fire. Both were losing. The fire was doomed, having consumed everything that was combustible; my heart galloped toward its last beat.

The fire constricted, concentrating inside that one remaining human organ with a final, unbearable surge. The surge was answered by a deep, hollow-sounding thud. My heart stuttered twice, and then thudded quietly again just once more.

There was no sound. No breathing. Not even mine.

For a moment, the absence of pain was all I could comprehend.

And then I opened my eyes and gazed above me in wonder.

20. NEW

EVERYTHING WAS SO *CLEAR*.

Sharp. Defined.

The brilliant light overhead was still blinding-bright, and yet I could plainly see the glowing strands of the filaments inside the bulb. I could see each color of the rainbow in the white light, and, at the very edge of the spectrum, an eighth color I had no name for.

Behind the light, I could distinguish the individual grains in the dark wood ceiling above. In front of it, I could see the dust motes in the air, the sides the light touched, and the dark sides, distinct and separate. They spun like little planets, moving around each other in a celestial dance.

The dust was so beautiful that I inhaled in shock; the

air whistled down my throat, swirling the motes into a vortex. The action felt wrong. I considered, and realized the problem was that there was no relief tied to the action. I didn't need the air. My lungs weren't waiting for it. They reacted indifferently to the influx.

I did not need the air, but I *liked* it. In it, I could taste the room around me—taste the lovely dust motes, the mix of the stagnant air mingling with the flow of slightly cooler air from the open door. Taste a lush whiff of silk. Taste a faint hint of something warm and desirable, something that should be moist, but wasn't. . . . That smell made my throat burn dryly, a faint echo of the venom burn, though the scent was tainted by the bite of chlorine and ammonia. And most of all, I could taste an almost-honey-lilac-and-sun-flavored scent that was the strongest thing, the closest thing to me.

I heard the sound of the others, breathing again now that I did. Their breath mixed with the scent that was something just off honey and lilac and sunshine, bringing new flavors. Cinnamon, hyacinth, pear, seawater, rising bread, pine, vanilla, leather, apple, moss, lavender, chocolate. . . . I traded a dozen different comparisons in my mind, but none of them fit exactly. So sweet and pleasant.

The TV downstairs had been muted, and I heard someone—Rosalie?—shift her weight on the first floor.

I also heard a faint, thudding rhythm, with a voice shouting angrily to the beat. Rap music? I was mystified for a moment, and then the sound faded away like a car passing by with the windows rolled down.

With a start, I realized that this could be exactly right. Could I hear all the way to the freeway?

I didn't realize someone was holding my hand until whoever it was squeezed it lightly. Like it had before to hide the pain, my body locked down again in surprise. This was not a touch I expected. The skin was perfectly smooth, but it was the wrong temperature. Not cold.

After that first frozen second of shock, my body responded to the unfamiliar touch in a way that shocked me even more.

Air hissed up my throat, spitting through my clenched teeth with a low, menacing sound like a swarm of bees. Before the sound was out, my muscles bunched and arched, twisting away from the unknown. I flipped off my back in a spin so fast it should have turned the room into an incomprehensible blur—but it did not. I saw every dust mote, every splinter in the wood-paneled walls, every loose thread in microscopic detail as my eyes whirled past them.

So by the time I found myself crouched against the wall defensively—about a sixteenth of a second later—I already understood what had startled me, and that I had overreacted.

Oh. Of course. Edward wouldn't feel cold to me. We were the same temperature now.

I held my pose for an eighth of a second longer, adjusting to the scene before me.

Edward was leaning across the operating table that had been my pyre, his hand reached out toward me, his expression anxious.

Edward's face was the most important thing, but my peripheral vision catalogued everything else, just in case. Some instinct to defend had been triggered, and I automatically searched for any sign of danger.

My vampire family waited cautiously against the far wall by the door, Emmett and Jasper in the front. Like there *was* danger. My nostrils flared, searching for the threat. I could smell nothing out of place. That faint scent of something delicious—but marred by harsh chemicals—tickled my throat again, setting it to aching and burning.

Alice was peeking around Jasper's elbow with a huge grin on her face; the light sparkled off her teeth, another eight-color rainbow.

That grin reassured me and then put the pieces together. Jasper and Emmett were in the front to protect the others, as I had assumed. What I hadn't grasped immediately was that *I* was the danger.

All this was a sideline. The greater part of my senses and my mind were still focused on Edward's face.

I had never seen it before this second.

How many times had I stared at Edward and marveled over his beauty? How many hours—days, weeks—of my life had I spent dreaming about what I then deemed to be perfection? I thought I'd known his face better than my own. I'd thought this was the one sure physical thing in my whole world: the flawlessness of Edward's face.

I may as well have been blind.

For the first time, with the dimming shadows and limiting weakness of humanity taken off my eyes, I saw his face. I gasped and then struggled with my vocabulary, unable to find the right words. I needed better words.

At this point, the other part of my attention had ascertained that there was no danger here besides myself, and I automatically straightened out of my crouch; almost a whole second had passed since I'd been on the table.

I was momentarily preoccupied by the way my body moved. The instant I'd considered standing erect, I was already straight. There was no brief fragment of time in which the action occurred; change was instantaneous, almost as if there was no movement at all.

I continued to stare at Edward's face, motionless again.

He moved slowly around the table—each step taking nearly half a second, each step flowing sinuously like river water weaving over smooth stones—his hand still outstretched.

I watched the grace of his advance, absorbing it with my new eyes.

"Bella?" he asked in a low, calming tone, but the worry in his voice layered my name with tension.

I could not answer immediately, lost as I was in the velvet folds of his voice. It was the most perfect symphony, a symphony in one instrument, an instrument more profound than any created by man. . . .

"Bella, love? I'm sorry, I know it's disorienting. But you're all right. Everything is fine."

Everything? My mind spun out, spiraling back to my last human hour. Already, the memory seemed dim, like I was watching through a thick, dark veil—because my human eyes had been half blind. Everything had been so blurred.

When he said everything was fine, did that include Renesmee? Where was she? With Rosalie? I tried to remember her face—I knew that she had been beautiful—but it was irritating to try to see through the human memories. Her face was shrouded in darkness, so poorly lit. . . .

What about Jacob? Was *he* fine? Did my long-suffering

best friend hate me now? Had he gone back to Sam's pack? Seth and Leah, too?

Were the Cullens safe, or had my transformation ignited the war with the pack? Did Edward's blanket assurance cover all of that? Or was he just trying to calm me?

And Charlie? What would I tell him now? He must have called while I was burning. What had they told him? What did he think had happened to me?

As I deliberated for one small piece of a second over which question to ask first, Edward reached out tentatively and stroked his fingertips across my cheek. Smooth as satin, soft as a feather, and now exactly matched to the temperature of my skin.

His touch seemed to sweep beneath the surface of my skin, right through the bones of my face. The feeling was tingly, electric—it jolted through my bones, down my spine, and trembled in my stomach.

Wait, I thought as the trembling blossomed into a warmth, a yearning. Wasn't I supposed to lose this? Wasn't giving up this feeling a part of the bargain?

I was a newborn vampire. The dry, scorching ache in my throat gave proof to that. And I knew what being a newborn entailed. Human emotions and longings would come back to me later in some form, but I'd accepted that I would not feel them in the beginning. Only thirst. That was the deal, the price. I'd agreed to pay it.

But as Edward's hand curled to the shape of my face like satin-covered steel, desire raced through my dried-out veins, singing from my scalp to my toes.

He arched one perfect eyebrow, waiting for me to speak.

I threw my arms around him.

Again, it was like there was no movement. One moment I stood straight and still as a statue; in the same instant, he was in my arms.

Warm—or at least, that was my perception. With the sweet, delicious scent that I'd never been able to really take in with my dull human senses, but that was one hundred percent Edward. I pressed my face into his smooth chest.

And then he shifted his weight uncomfortably. Leaned away from my embrace. I stared up at his face, confused and frightened by the rejection.

"Um . . . carefully, Bella. Ow."

I yanked my arms away, folding them behind my back as soon as I understood.

I was too strong.

"Oops," I mouthed.

He smiled the kind of smile that would have stopped my heart if it were still beating.

"Don't panic, love," he said, lifting his hand to touch my lips, parted in horror. "You're just a bit stronger than I am for the moment."

My eyebrows pushed together. I'd known this, too, but it felt more surreal than any other part of this ultimately surreal moment. I was stronger than Edward. I'd made him say *ow*.

His hand stroked my cheek again, and I all but forgot my distress as another wave of desire rippled through my motionless body.

These emotions were so much stronger than I was used to that it was hard to stick to one train of thought despite the extra room in my head. Each new sensation overwhelmed me. I remembered Edward saying once—his voice in my head a weak shadow compared to the crystal, musical clarity I was hearing now—that his kind, *our* kind, were easily distracted. I could see why.

I made a concerted effort to focus. There was something I needed to say. The most important thing.

Very carefully, so carefully that the movement was actually discernible, I brought my right arm out from behind my back and raised my hand to touch his cheek. I refused to let myself be sidetracked by the pearly color of my hand or by the smooth silk of his skin or by the charge that zinged in my fingertips.

I stared into his eyes and heard my own voice for the first time.

"I love you," I said, but it sounded like singing. My voice rang and shimmered like a bell.

His answering smile dazzled me more than it ever had when I was human; I could really see it now.

"As I love you," he told me.

He took my face between his hands and leaned his face to mine—slow enough to remind me to be careful. He kissed me, soft as a whisper at first, and then suddenly stronger, fiercer. I tried to remember to be gentle with him, but it was hard work to remember anything in the onslaught of sensation, hard to hold on to any coherent thoughts.

It was like he'd never kissed me—like this was our first kiss. And, in truth, he'd never kissed me *this* way before.

It almost made me feel guilty. Surely I was in breach of the contract. I couldn't be allowed to have this, too.

Though I didn't need oxygen, my breathing sped, raced

as fast as it had when I was burning. This was a different kind of fire.

Someone cleared his throat. Emmett. I recognized the deep sound at once, joking and annoyed at the same time.

I'd forgotten we weren't alone. And then I realized that the way I was curved around Edward now was not exactly polite for company.

Embarrassed, I half-stepped away in another instantaneous movement.

Edward chuckled and stepped with me, keeping his arms tight around my waist. His face was glowing—like a white flame burned from behind his diamond skin.

I took an unnecessary breath to settle myself.

How different this kissing was! I read his expression as I compared the indistinct human memories to this clear, intense feeling. He looked . . . a little smug.

"You've been holding out on me," I accused in my singing voice, my eyes narrowing a tiny bit.

He laughed, radiant with relief that it was all over— the fear, the pain, the uncertainties, the waiting, all of it behind us now. "It was sort of necessary at the time," he reminded me. "Now it's your turn to not break *me*." He laughed again.

I frowned as I considered that, and then Edward was not the only one laughing.

Carlisle stepped around Emmett and walked toward me swiftly; his eyes were only slightly wary, but Jasper shadowed his footsteps. I'd never seen Carlisle's face before either, not really. I had an odd urge to blink—like I was staring at the sun.

"How do you feel, Bella?" Carlisle asked.

I considered that for a sixty-fourth of a second.

"Overwhelmed. There's so *much*. . . ." I trailed off, listening to the bell-tone of my voice again.

"Yes, it can be quite confusing."

I nodded one fast, jerky bob. "But I feel like me. Sort of. I didn't expect that."

Edward's arms squeezed lightly around my waist. "I told you so," he whispered.

"You are quite controlled," Carlisle mused. "More so than *I* expected, even with the time you had to prepare yourself mentally for this."

I thought about the wild mood swings, the difficulty concentrating, and whispered, "I'm not sure about that."

He nodded seriously, and then his jeweled eyes glittered with interest. "It seems like we did something right with the morphine this time. Tell me, what do you remember of the transformation process?"

I hesitated, intensely aware of Edward's breath brushing against my cheek, sending whispers of electricity through my skin.

"Everything was . . . very dim before. I remember the baby couldn't breathe. . . ."

I looked at Edward, momentarily frightened by the memory.

"Renesmee is healthy and well," he promised, a gleam I'd never seen before in his eyes. He said her name with an understated fervor. A reverence. The way devout people talked about their gods. "What do you remember after that?"

I focused on my poker face. I'd never been much of a liar.

"It's hard to remember. It was so dark before. And then . . .
I opened my eyes and I could see *everything*."

"Amazing," Carlisle breathed, his eyes alight.

Chagrin washed through me, and I waited for the heat
to burn in my cheeks and give me away. And then I remembered that I would never blush again. Maybe that
would protect Edward from the truth.

I'd have to find a way to tip off Carlisle, though. Someday.
If he ever needed to create another vampire. That possibility
seemed very unlikely, which made me feel better about
lying.

"I want you to think—to tell me everything you
remember," Carlisle pressed excitedly, and I couldn't help
the grimace that flashed across my face. I didn't want to have
to keep lying, because I might slip up. And I didn't want
to think about the burning. Unlike the human memories,
that part was perfectly clear and I found I could remember
it with far too much precision.

"Oh, I'm so sorry, Bella," Carlisle apologized immediately.
"Of course your thirst must be very uncomfortable. This
conversation can wait."

Until he'd mentioned it, the thirst actually wasn't un-
manageable. There was so much room in my head. A separate part of my brain was keeping tabs on the burn in my
throat, almost like a reflex. The way my old brain had
handled breathing and blinking.

But Carlisle's assumption brought the burn to the
forefront of my mind. Suddenly, the dry ache was all I could
think about, and the more I thought about it, the more
it hurt. My hand flew up to cup my throat, like I could
smother the flames from the outside. The skin of my neck

was strange beneath my fingers. So smooth it was somehow soft, though it was hard as stone, too.

Edward dropped his arms and took my other hand, tugging gently. "Let's hunt, Bella."

My eyes opened wider and the pain of the thirst receded, shock taking its place.

Me? Hunt? With Edward? But . . . *how?* I didn't know what to do.

He read the alarm in my expression and smiled encouragingly. "It's quite easy, love. Instinctual. Don't worry, I'll show you." When I didn't move, he grinned his crooked smile and raised his eyebrows. "I was under the impression that you'd always *wanted* to see me hunt."

I laughed in a short burst of humor (part of me listened in wonder to the pealing bell sound) as his words reminded me of cloudy human conversations. And then I took a whole second to run quickly through those first days with Edward—the true beginning of my life—in my head so that I would never forget them. I did not expect that it would be so uncomfortable to remember. Like trying to squint through muddy water. I knew from Rosalie's experience that if I thought of my human memories *enough*, I would not lose them over time. I did not want to forget one minute I'd spent with Edward, even now, when eternity stretched in front of us. I would have to make sure those human memories were cemented into my infallible vampire mind.

"Shall we?" Edward asked. He reached up to take the hand that was still at my neck. His fingers smoothed down the column of my throat. "I don't want you to be hurting," he added in a low murmur. Something I would not have been able to hear before.

"I'm fine," I said out of lingering human habit. "Wait. First."

There was so much. I'd never gotten to my questions. There were more important things than the ache.

It was Carlisle who spoke now. "Yes?"

"I want to see her. Renesmee."

It was oddly difficult to say her name. *My daughter*; these words were even harder to think. It all seemed so distant. I tried to remember how I had felt three days ago, and automatically, my hands pulled free of Edward's and dropped to my stomach.

Flat. Empty. I clutched at the pale silk that covered my skin, panicking again, while an insignificant part of my mind noted that Alice must have dressed me.

I knew there was nothing left inside me, and I faintly remembered the bloody removal scene, but the physical proof was still hard to process. All I knew was loving my little nudger *inside* of me. Outside of me, she seemed like something I must have imagined. A fading dream—a dream that was half nightmare.

While I wrestled with my confusion, I saw Edward and Carlisle exchange a guarded glance.

"What?" I demanded.

"Bella," Edward said soothingly. "That's not really a good idea. She's half human, love. Her heart beats, and blood runs in her veins. Until your thirst is positively under control . . . You don't want to put her in danger, do you?"

I frowned. Of course I must not want that.

Was I out of control? Confused, yes. Easily unfocused, yes. But dangerous? To her? My daughter?

I couldn't be positive that the answer was no. So I

would have to be patient. That sounded difficult. Because until I saw her again, she wouldn't be real. Just a fading dream . . . of a stranger . . .

"Where is she?" I listened hard, and then I could hear the beating heart on the floor below me. I could hear more than one person breathing—quietly, like they were listening, too. There was also a fluttering sound, a thrumming, that I couldn't place. . . .

And the sound of the heartbeat was so moist and appealing, that my mouth started watering.

So I would definitely have to learn how to hunt before I saw her. My stranger baby.

"Is Rosalie with her?"

"Yes," Edward answered in a clipped tone, and I could see that something he'd thought of upset him. I'd thought he and Rose were over their differences. Had the animosity erupted again? Before I could ask, he pulled my hands away from my flat stomach, tugging gently again.

"Wait," I protested again, trying to focus. "What about Jacob? And Charlie? Tell me everything that I missed. How long was I . . . unconscious?"

Edward didn't seem to notice my hesitation over the last word. Instead, he was exchanging another wary glance with Carlisle.

"What's wrong?" I whispered.

"Nothing is *wrong*," Carlisle told me, emphasizing the last word in a strange way. "Nothing has changed much, actually—you were only unaware for just over two days. It was very fast, as these things go. Edward did an excellent job. Quite innovative—the venom injection straight to your heart was his idea." He paused to smile proudly at his son and then sighed. "Jacob is still here, and Charlie still believes that you are sick. He thinks you're in Atlanta right now, undergoing tests at the CDC. We gave him a bad number, and he's frustrated. He's been speaking to Esme."

"I should call him . . . ," I murmured to myself, but, listening to my own voice, I understood the new difficulties. He wouldn't recognize this voice. It wouldn't reassure him. And then the earlier surprise intruded. "Hold on—Jacob is *still here?*"

Another glance between them.

"Bella," Edward said quickly. "There's much to discuss, but we should take care of you first. You have to be in pain. . . ."

When he pointed that out, I remembered the burn in my throat and swallowed convulsively. "But Jacob—"

"We have all the time in the world for explanations, love," he reminded me gently.

Of course. I could wait a little longer for the answer; it would be easier to listen when the fierce pain of the fiery thirst was no longer scattering my concentration. "Okay."

"Wait, wait, wait," Alice trilled from the doorway. She danced across the room, dreamily graceful. As with Edward and Carlisle, I felt some shock as I really looked at her face for the first time. So lovely. "You promised I could be there the first time! What if you two run past something reflective?"

"Alice—," Edward protested.

"It will only take a second!" And with that, Alice darted from the room.

Edward sighed.

"What is she talking about?"

But Alice was already back, carrying the huge, gilt-framed mirror from Rosalie's room, which was nearly twice as tall as she was, and several times as wide.

Jasper had been so still and silent that I'd taken no notice of him since he'd followed behind Carlisle. Now he moved again, to hover over Alice, his eyes locked on my expression. Because I was the danger here.

I knew he would be tasting the mood around me, too, and so he must have felt my jolt of shock as I studied his face, looking at it closely for the first time.

Through my sightless human eyes, the scars left from his former life with the newborn armies in the South had been mostly invisible. Only with a bright light to throw their slightly raised shapes into definition could I even make out their existence.

Now that I could see, the scars were Jasper's most dominant feature. It was hard to take my eyes off his ravaged neck and jaw—hard to believe that even a vampire could have survived so many sets of teeth ripping into his throat.

Instinctively, I tensed to defend myself. Any vampire who saw Jasper would have had the same reaction. The scars were like a lighted billboard. *Dangerous*, they screamed. How many vampires had tried to kill Jasper? Hundreds? Thousands? The same number that had died in the attempt.

Jasper both saw and felt my assessment, my caution, and he smiled wryly.

"Edward gave me grief for not getting you to a mirror before the wedding," Alice said, pulling my attention away from her frightening lover. "I'm not going to be chewed out again."

"Chewed out?" Edward asked skeptically, one eyebrow curving upward.

"Maybe I'm overstating things," she murmured absently as she turned the mirror to face me.

"And maybe this has solely to do with your own voyeuristic gratification," he countered.

Alice winked at him.

I was only aware of this exchange with the lesser part of my concentration. The greater part was riveted on the person in the mirror.

My first reaction was an unthinking pleasure. The alien creature in the glass was indisputably beautiful, every bit as beautiful as Alice or Esme. She was fluid even in stillness, and her flawless face was pale as the moon against the frame of her dark, heavy hair. Her limbs were smooth and strong, skin glistening subtly, luminous as a pearl.

My second reaction was horror.

Who *was* she? At first glance, I couldn't find my face anywhere in the smooth, perfect planes of her features.

And her eyes! Though I'd known to expect them, her eyes still sent a thrill of terror through me.

All the while I studied and reacted, her face was perfectly composed, a carving of a goddess, showing nothing of the turmoil roiling inside me. And then her full lips moved.

"The eyes?" I whispered, unwilling to say *my eyes*. "How long?

"They'll darken up in a few months," Edward said in a soft, comforting voice. "Animal blood dilutes the color more quickly than a diet of human blood. They'll turn amber first, then gold."

My eyes would blaze like vicious red flames for *months*?

"Months?" My voice was higher now, stressed. In the mirror, the perfect eyebrows lifted incredulously above her glowing crimson eyes—brighter than any I'd ever seen before.

Jasper took a step forward, alarmed by the intensity of my sudden anxiety. He knew young vampires only too well; did this emotion presage some misstep on my part?

No one answered my question. I looked away, to Edward and Alice. Both their eyes were slightly unfocused—reacting to Jasper's unease. Listening to its cause, looking ahead to the immediate future.

I took another deep, unnecessary breath.

"No, I'm fine," I promised them. My eyes flickered to the stranger in the mirror and back. "It's just . . . a lot to take in."

Jasper's brow furrowed, highlighting the two scars over his left eye.

"I don't know," Edward murmured.

The woman in the mirror frowned. "What question did I miss?"

Edward grinned. "Jasper wonders how you're doing it."

"Doing what?"

"Controlling your emotions, Bella," Jasper answered. "I've never seen a newborn do that—stop an emotion in its tracks that way. You were upset, but when you saw our concern, you reined it in, regained power over yourself. I was prepared to help, but you didn't need it."

"Is that wrong?" I asked. My body automatically froze as I waited for his verdict.

"No," he said, but his voice was unsure.

Edward stroked his hand down my arm, as if encouraging me to thaw. "It's very impressive, Bella, but we don't understand it. We don't know how long it can hold."

I considered that for a portion of a second. At any moment, would I snap? Turn into a monster?

I couldn't feel it coming on. . . . Maybe there was no way to anticipate such a thing.

"But what do you think?" Alice asked, a little impatient now, pointing to the mirror.

"I'm not sure," I hedged, not wanting to admit how frightened I really was.

I stared at the beautiful woman with the terrifying eyes, looking for pieces of me. There *was* something there in the shape of her lips—if you looked past the dizzying beauty, it was true that her upper lip was slightly out of balance, a bit too full to match the lower. Finding this familiar little flaw made me feel a tiny bit better. Maybe the rest of me was in there, too.

I raised my hand experimentally, and the woman in the mirror copied the movement, touching her face, too. Her crimson eyes watched me warily.

Edward sighed.

I turned away from her to look at him, raising one eyebrow.

"Disappointed?" I asked, my ringing voice impassive.

He laughed. "Yes," he admitted.

I felt the shock break through the composed mask on my face, followed instantly by the hurt.

Alice snarled. Jasper leaned forward again, waiting for me to snap.

But Edward ignored them and wrapped his arms tightly

around my newly frozen form, pressing his lips against my cheek. "I was rather hoping that I'd be able to hear your mind, now that it is more similar to my own," he murmured. "And here I am, as frustrated as ever, wondering what could possibly be going on inside your head."

I felt better at once.

"Oh well," I said lightly, relieved that my thoughts were still my own. "I guess my brain will never work right. At least I'm pretty."

It was becoming easier to joke with him as I adjusted, to think in straight lines. To be myself.

Edward growled in my ear. "Bella, you have *never* been merely pretty."

Then his face pulled away from mine, and he sighed. "All right, all right," he said to someone.

"What?" I asked.

"You're making Jasper more edgy by the second. He may relax a little when you've hunted."

I looked at Jasper's worried expression and nodded. I didn't want to snap here, if that was coming. Better to be surrounded by trees than family.

"Okay. Let's hunt," I agreed, a thrill of nerves and anticipation making my stomach quiver. I unwrapped Edward's arms from around me, keeping one of his hands, and turned my back on the strange and beautiful woman in the mirror.

21. FIRST HUNT

"THE WINDOW?" I ASKED, STARING TWO STORIES DOWN.

I'd never really been afraid of heights per se, but being able to see all the details with such clarity made the prospect less appealing. The angles of the rocks below were sharper than I would have imagined them.

Edward smiled. "It's the most convenient exit. If you're frightened, I can carry you."

"We have all eternity, and you're worried about the time it would take to walk to the back door?"

He frowned slightly. "Renesmee and Jacob are downstairs. . . ."

"Oh."

Right. I was the monster now. I had to keep away from scents that might trigger my wild side. From the people that I loved in particular. Even the ones I didn't really know yet.

"Is Renesmee . . . okay . . . with Jacob there?" I whispered. I realized belatedly that it must have been Jacob's heart I'd heard below. I listened hard again, but I could only hear the one steady pulse. "He doesn't like her much."

Edward's lips tightened in an odd way. "Trust me, she is perfectly safe. I know exactly what Jacob is thinking."

"Of course," I murmured, and looked at the ground again.

"Stalling?" he challenged.

"A little. I don't know how. . . ."

And I was very conscious of my family behind me, watching silently. Mostly silently. Emmett had already chuckled under his breath once. One mistake, and he'd be rolling on the floor. Then the jokes about the world's only clumsy vampire would start. . . .

Also, this dress—that Alice must have put me in sometime when I was too lost in the burning to notice— was not what I would have picked out for either jumping or hunting. Tightly fitted ice-blue silk? What did she think I would need it for? Was there a cocktail party later?

"Watch me," Edward said. And then, very casually, he stepped out of the tall, open window and fell.

I watched carefully, analyzing the angle at which he bent his knees to absorb the impact. The sound of his landing was very low—a muted thud that could have been a door softly closed, or a book gently laid on a table.

It didn't *look* hard.

Clenching my teeth as I concentrated, I tried to copy his casual step into empty air.

Ha! The ground seemed to move toward me so slowly that it was nothing at all to place my feet—what shoes had Alice put me in? Stilettos? She'd lost her mind—to place my silly shoes exactly right so that landing was no different than stepping one foot forward on a flat surface.

I absorbed the impact in the balls of my feet, not wanting to snap off the thin heels. My landing seemed just as quiet as his. I grinned at him.

"Right. Easy."

He smiled back. "Bella?"

"Yes?"

"That was quite graceful—even for a vampire."

I considered that for a moment, and then I beamed. If he'd just been saying that, then Emmett would have laughed. No one found his remark humorous, so it must have been true. It was the first time anyone had ever applied the word *graceful* to me in my entire life . . . or, well, existence anyway.

"*Thank* you," I told him.

And then I hooked the silver satin shoes off my feet one by one and lobbed them together back through the open window. A little too hard, maybe, but I heard someone catch them before they could damage the paneling.

Alice grumbled, "Her fashion sense hasn't improved as much as her balance."

Edward took my hand—I couldn't stop marveling at the smoothness, the comfortable temperature of his skin—and darted through the backyard to the edge of the river. I went along with him effortlessly.

Everything physical seemed very simple.

"Are we swimming?" I asked him when we stopped beside the water.

"And ruin your pretty dress? No. We're jumping."

I pursed my lips, considering. The river was about fifty yards wide here.

"You first," I said.

He touched my cheek, took two quick backward strides, and then ran back those two steps, launching himself from a flat stone firmly embedded in the riverbank. I studied the flash of movement as he arced over the water, finally turning a somersault just before he disappeared into the thick trees on the other side of the river.

"Show-off," I muttered, and heard his invisible laugh.

I backed up five paces, just in case, and took a deep breath.

Suddenly, I was anxious again. Not about falling or getting hurt—I was more worried about the forest getting hurt.

It had come on slowly, but I could feel it now—the raw, massive strength thrilling in my limbs. I was suddenly sure that if I wanted to tunnel *under* the river, to claw or beat my way straight through the bedrock, it wouldn't take me very long. The objects around me—the trees, the shrubs, the rocks . . . the house—had all begun to look very fragile.

Hoping very much that Esme was not particularly fond of any specific trees across the river, I began my first stride. And then stopped when the tight satin split six inches up my thigh. Alice!

Well, Alice always seemed to treat clothes as if they were disposable and meant for one-time usage, so she shouldn't mind this. I bent to carefully grasp the hem at the undamaged right seam between my fingers and, exerting the tiniest amount of pressure possible, I ripped the dress open to the top of my thigh. Then I fixed the other side to match.

Much better.

I could hear the muffled laughter in the house, and even the sound of someone gritting her teeth. The laughter came from upstairs and down, and I very easily recognized the much different, rough, throaty chuckle from the first floor.

So Jacob was watching, too? I couldn't imagine what he was thinking now, or what he was still doing here. I'd envisioned our reunion—if he could ever forgive me—taking place far in the future, when I was more stable, and time had healed the wounds I'd inflicted in his heart.

I didn't turn to look at him now, wary of my mood swings. It wouldn't be good to let any emotion take too strong a hold on my frame of mind. Jasper's fears had me on edge, too. I had to hunt before I dealt with anything else. I tried to forget everything else so I could *concentrate*.

"Bella?" Edward called from the woods, his voice moving closer. "Do you want to watch again?"

But I remembered everything perfectly, of course, and I didn't want to give Emmett a reason to find *more* humor in my education. This was physical—it should be instinctive. So I took a deep breath and ran for the river.

Unhindered by my skirt, it took only one long bound to reach the water's edge. Just an eighty-fourth of a second, and yet it was plenty of time—my eyes and my mind moved so quickly that one step was enough. It was simple to position my right foot just so against the flat stone and exert the adequate pressure to send my body wheeling up into the air. I was paying more attention to aim than force, and I erred on the amount of power necessary—but at least I didn't err on the side that would have gotten me wet. The fifty yard width was slightly *too* easy a distance. . . .

It was a strange, giddy, electrifying thing, but a short thing. An entire second had yet to pass, and I was across.

I was expecting the close-packed trees to be a problem, but they were surprisingly helpful. It was a simple matter to reach out with one sure hand as I fell back toward the earth again deep inside the forest and catch myself on a convenient branch; I swung lightly from the limb and landed on my toes, still fifteen feet from the ground on the wide bough of a Sitka spruce.

It was fabulous.

Over the sound of my peals of delighted laughter, I could hear Edward racing to find me. My jump had been twice as long as his. When he reached my tree, his eyes were wide. I leaped nimbly from the branch to his side, soundlessly landing again on the balls of my feet.

"Was that good?" I wondered, my breathing accelerated with excitement.

"Very good." He smiled approvingly, but his casual tone didn't match the surprised expression in his eyes.

"Can we do it again?"

"Focus, Bella—we're on a hunting trip."

"Oh, right." I nodded. "Hunting."

"Follow me . . . if you can." He grinned, his expression suddenly taunting, and broke into a run.

He was faster than me. I couldn't imagine how he moved his legs with such blinding speed, but it was beyond me.

However, I *was* stronger, and every stride of mine matched the length of three of his. And so I flew with him through the living green web, by his side, not following at all. As I ran, I couldn't help laughing quietly at the thrill of it; the laughter neither slowed me nor upset my focus.

I could finally understand why Edward never hit the trees when he ran—a question that had always been a mystery to me. It was a peculiar sensation, the balance between the speed and the clarity. For, while I rocketed over, under, and through the thick jade maze at a rate that should have reduced everything around me to a streaky green blur, I could plainly see each tiny leaf on all the small branches of every insignificant shrub that I passed.

The wind of my speed blew my hair and my torn dress out behind me, and, though I knew it shouldn't, it felt warm against my skin. Just as the rough forest floor shouldn't feel like velvet beneath my bare soles, and the limbs that whipped against my skin shouldn't feel like caressing feathers.

The forest was much more alive than I'd ever known— small creatures whose existence I'd never guessed at teemed in the leaves around me. They all grew silent after we passed, their breath quickening in fear. The animals had a much wiser reaction to our scent than humans seemed to. Certainly, it'd had the opposite effect on me.

I kept waiting to feel winded, but my breath came effortlessly. I waited for the burn to begin in my muscles, but my strength only seemed to increase as I grew accustomed to my stride. My leaping bounds stretched longer, and soon he was trying to keep up with me. I laughed again, exultant, when I heard him falling behind. My naked feet touched the ground so infrequently now it felt more like flying than running.

"Bella," he called dryly, his voice even, lazy. I could hear nothing else; he had stopped.

I briefly considered mutiny.

But, with a sigh, I whirled and skipped lightly to his side, some hundred yards back. I looked at him expectantly. He was smiling, with one eyebrow raised. He was so beautiful that I could only stare.

"Did you want to stay in the country?" he asked, amused. "Or were you planning to continue on to Canada this afternoon?"

"This is fine," I agreed, concentrating less on what he was saying and more on the mesmerizing way his lips moved when he spoke. It was hard not to become sidetracked with everything fresh in my strong new eyes. "What are we hunting?"

"Elk. I thought something easy for your first time . . ." He trailed off when my eyes narrowed at the word *easy*.

But I wasn't going to argue; I was too thirsty. As soon as I'd started to think about the dry burn in my throat, it was *all* I could think about. Definitely getting worse. My mouth felt like four o'clock on a June afternoon in Death Valley.

"Where?" I asked, scanning the trees impatiently. Now that I had given the thirst my attention, it seemed to taint every other thought in my head, leaking into the more pleasant thoughts of running and Edward's lips and kissing and . . . scorching thirst. I couldn't get away from it.

"Hold still for a minute," he said, putting his hands lightly on my shoulders. The urgency of my thirst receded momentarily at his touch.

"Now close your eyes," he murmured. When I obeyed, he raised his hands to my face, stroking my cheekbones. I felt my breathing speed and waited briefly again for the blush that wouldn't come.

"Listen," Edward instructed. "What do you hear?"

Everything, I could have said; his perfect voice, his breath, his lips brushing together as he spoke, the whisper of birds preening their feathers in the treetops, their fluttering heartbeats, the maple leaves scraping together, the faint clicking of ants following each other in a long line up the bark of the nearest tree. But I knew he meant something specific, so I let my ears range outward, seeking something different than the small hum of life that surrounded me. There was an open space near us—the wind had a different sound across the exposed grass—and a small creek, with a rocky bed. And there, near the noise of the water, was the splash of lapping tongues, the loud thudding of heavy hearts, pumping thick streams of blood. . . .

It felt like the sides of my throat had sucked closed.

"By the creek, to the northeast?" I asked, my eyes still shut.

"Yes." His tone was approving. "Now . . . wait for the breeze again and . . . what do you smell?"

Mostly him—his strange honey-lilac-and-sun perfume. But also the rich, earthy smell of rot and moss, the resin in the evergreens, the warm, almost nutty aroma of the small rodents cowering beneath the tree roots. And then, reaching out again, the clean smell of the water, which was surprisingly unappealing despite my thirst. I focused toward the water and found the scent that must have gone with the lapping noise and the pounding heart. Another warm smell, rich and tangy, stronger than the others. And yet nearly as unappealing as the brook. I wrinkled my nose.

He chuckled. "I know—it takes some getting used to."

"Three?" I guessed.

"Five. There are two more in the trees behind them."

"What do I do now?"

His voice sounded like he was smiling. "What do you feel like doing?"

I thought about that, my eyes still shut as I listened and breathed in the scent. Another bout of baking thirst intruded on my awareness, and suddenly the warm, tangy odor wasn't quite so objectionable. At least it would be something hot and wet in my desiccated mouth. My eyes snapped open.

"Don't think about it," he suggested as he lifted his hands off my face and took a step back. "Just follow your instincts."

I let myself drift with the scent, barely aware of my movement as I ghosted down the incline to the narrow meadow where the stream flowed. My body shifted forward automatically into a low crouch as I hesitated at the fern-fringed edge of the trees. I could see a big bull, two dozen antler points crowning his head, at the stream's edge, and the shadow-spotted shapes of the four others heading eastward into forest at a leisurely pace.

I centered myself around the scent of the male, the hot spot in his shaggy neck where the warmth pulsed strongest. Only thirty yards—two or three bounds—between us. I tensed myself for the first leap.

But as my muscles bunched in preparation, the wind shifted, blowing stronger now, and from the south. I didn't stop to think, hurtling out of the trees in a path perpendicular to my original plan, scaring the elk into the forest, racing after a new fragrance so attractive that there wasn't a choice. It was compulsory.

The scent ruled completely. I was single-minded as I traced it, aware only of the thirst and the smell that promised to quench it. The thirst got worse, so painful now that it confused all my other thoughts and began to remind me of the burn of venom in my veins.

There was only one thing that had any chance of penetrating my focus now, an instinct more powerful, more basic than the need to quench the fire—it was the instinct to protect myself from danger. Self-preservation.

I was suddenly alert to the fact that I was being followed. The pull of the irresistible scent warred with the impulse to turn and defend my hunt. A bubble of sound built in my chest, my lips pulled back of their own accord to expose my teeth in warning. My feet slowed, the need to protect my back struggling against the desire to quench my thirst.

And then I could hear my pursuer gaining, and defense won. As I spun, the rising sound ripped its way up my throat and out.

The feral snarl, coming from my own mouth, was so unexpected that it brought me up short. It unsettled me, and it cleared my head for a second—the thirst-driven haze receded, though the thirst burned on.

The wind shifted, blowing the smell of wet earth and coming rain across my face, further freeing me from the other scent's fiery grip—a scent so delicious it could only be human.

Edward hesitated a few feet away, his arms raised as if

to embrace me—or restrain me. His face was intent and cautious as I froze, horrified.

I realized that I had been about to attack him. With a hard jerk, I straightened out of my defensive crouch. I held my breath as I refocused, fearing the power of the fragrance swirling up from the south.

He could see reason return to my face, and he took a step toward me, lowering his arms.

"I have to get away from here," I spit through my teeth, using the breath I had.

Shock crossed his face. "*Can* you leave?"

I didn't have time to ask him what he meant by that. I knew the ability to think clearly would last only as long as I could stop myself from thinking of—

I burst into a run again, a flat-out sprint straight north, concentrating solely on the uncomfortable feeling of sensory deprivation that seemed to be my body's only response to the lack of air. My one goal was to run far enough away that the scent behind me would be completely lost. Impossible to find, even if I changed my mind . . .

Once again, I was aware of being followed, but I was sane this time. I fought the instinct to breathe—to use the flavors in the air to be sure it was Edward. I didn't have to fight long; though I was running faster than I ever had before, shooting like a comet through the straightest path I could find in the trees; Edward caught up with me after a short minute.

A new thought occurred to me, and I stopped dead, my feet planted. I was sure it must be safe here, but I held my breath just in case.

Edward blew past me, surprised by my sudden freeze.

He wheeled around and was at my side in a second. He put his hands on my shoulders and stared into my eyes, shock still the dominant emotion on his face.

"How did you do that?" he demanded.

"You let me beat you before, didn't you?" I demanded back, ignoring his question. And I'd thought I'd been doing so well!

When I opened my mouth, I could taste the air—it was unpolluted now, with no trace of the compelling perfume to torment my thirst. I took a cautious breath.

He shrugged and shook his head, refusing to be deflected. "Bella, how did you do it?"

"Run away? I held my breath."

"But how did you stop hunting?"

"When you came up behind me . . . I'm so sorry about that."

"Why are you apologizing to *me*? I'm the one who was horribly careless. I assumed no one would be so far from the trails, but I should have checked first. Such a stupid mistake! *You* have nothing to apologize for."

"But I growled at you!" I was still horrified that I was physically capable of such blasphemy.

"Of course you did. That's only natural. But I can't understand how you ran away."

"What else could I do?" I asked. His attitude confused me—what did he *want* to have happened? "It might have been someone I know!"

He startled me, suddenly bursting into a spasm of loud laughter, throwing his head back and letting the sound echo off the trees.

"Why are you laughing at me?"

He stopped at once, and I could see he was wary again.

Keep it under control, I thought to myself. I had to watch my temper. Just like I was a young werewolf rather than a vampire.

"I'm not laughing at you, Bella. I'm laughing because I am in shock. And I am in shock because I am completely amazed."

"Why?"

"You shouldn't be able to do any of this. You shouldn't be so . . . so rational. You shouldn't be able to stand here discussing this with me calmly and coolly. And, much more than any of that, you should *not* have been able to break off mid-hunt with the scent of human blood in the air. Even mature vampires have difficulty with that—we're always very careful of where we hunt so as not to put ourselves in the path of temptation. Bella, you're behaving like you're decades rather than days old."

"Oh." But I'd known it was going to be hard. That was why I'd been so on guard. I'd been expecting it to be difficult.

He put his hands on my face again, and his eyes were full of wonder. "What wouldn't I give to be able to see into your mind for just this one moment."

Such powerful emotions. I'd been prepared for the thirst part, but not this. I'd been so sure it wouldn't be the same when he touched me. Well, truthfully, it wasn't the same.

It was stronger.

I reached up to trace the planes of his face; my fingers lingered on his lips.

"I thought I wouldn't feel this way for a long time?" My

uncertainty made the words a question. "But I still *want* you."

He blinked in shock. "How can you even concentrate on that? Aren't you unbearably thirsty?"

Of course I was *now*, now that he'd brought it up again!

I tried to swallow and then sighed, closing my eyes like I had before to help me concentrate. I let my senses range out around me, tensed this time in case of another onslaught of the delicious taboo scent.

Edward dropped his hands, not even breathing while I listened farther and farther out into the web of green life, sifting through the scents and sounds for something not totally repellant to my thirst. There was a hint of something different, a faint trail to the east. . . .

My eyes flashed open, but my focus was still on sharper senses as I turned and darted silently eastward. The ground sloped steeply upward almost at once, and I ran in a hunting crouch, close to the ground, taking to the trees when that was easier. I sensed rather than heard Edward with me, flowing quietly through the woods, letting me lead.

The vegetation thinned as we climbed higher; the scent of pitch and resin grew more powerful, as did the trail I followed—it was a warm scent, sharper than the smell of the elk and more appealing. A few seconds more and I could hear the muted padding of immense feet, so much subtler than the crunch of hooves. The sound was up—in the branches rather than on the ground. Automatically I darted into the boughs as well, gaining the strategic higher position, halfway up a towering silver fir.

The soft thud of paws continued stealthily beneath me

now; the rich scent was very close. My eyes pinpointed the movement linked with the sound, and I saw the tawny hide of the great cat slinking along the wide branch of a spruce just down and to the left of my perch. He was big—easily four times my mass. His eyes were intent on the ground beneath; the cat hunted, too. I caught the smell of something smaller, bland next to the aroma of my prey, cowering in brush below the tree. The lion's tail twitched spasmodically as he prepared to spring.

With a light bound, I sailed through the air and landed on the lion's branch. He felt the shiver of the wood and whirled, shrieking surprise and defiance. He clawed the space between us, his eyes bright with fury. Half-crazed with thirst, I ignored the exposed fangs and the hooked claws and launched myself at him, knocking us both to the forest floor.

It wasn't much of a fight.

His raking claws could have been caressing fingers for all the impact they had on my skin. His teeth could find no purchase against my shoulder or my throat. His weight was nothing. My teeth unerringly sought his throat, and his instinctive resistance was pitifully feeble against my strength. My jaws locked easily over the precise point where the heat flow concentrated.

It was effortless as biting into butter. My teeth were steel razors; they cut through the fur and fat and sinews like they weren't there.

The flavor was wrong, but the blood was hot and wet and it soothed the ragged, itching thirst as I drank in an eager rush. The cat's struggles grew more and more feeble, and his screams choked off with a gurgle. The warmth of the blood radiated throughout my whole body, heating even my fingertips and toes.

The lion was finished before I was. The thirst flared again when he ran dry, and I shoved his carcass off my body in disgust. How could I still be thirsty after all that?

I wrenched myself erect in one quick move. Standing, I realized I was a bit of a mess. I wiped my face off on the back of my arm and tried to fix the dress. The claws that had been so ineffectual against my skin had had more success with the thin satin.

"Hmm," Edward said. I looked up to see him leaning casually against a tree trunk, watching me with a thoughtful look on his face.

"I guess I could have done that better." I was covered in dirt, my hair knotted, my dress bloodstained and hanging in tatters. Edward didn't come home from hunting trips looking like this.

"You did perfectly fine," he assured me. "It's just that . . . it was much more difficult for me to watch than it should have been."

I raised my eyebrows, confused.

"It goes against the grain," he explained, "letting you wrestle with lions. I was having an anxiety attack the whole time."

"Silly."

"I know. Old habits die hard. I like the improvements to your dress, though."

If I could have blushed, I would have. I changed the subject. "Why am I still thirsty?"

"Because you're young."

I sighed. "And I don't suppose there are any other mountain lions nearby."

"Plenty of deer, though."

I made a face. "They don't smell as good."

"Herbivores. The meat-eaters smell more like humans," he explained.

"Not that much like humans," I disagreed, trying not to remember.

"We could go back," he said solemnly, but there was a teasing light in his eye. "Whoever it was out there, if they were men, they probably wouldn't even mind death if you were the one delivering it." His gaze ran over my ravaged dress again. "In fact, they would think they were already dead and gone to heaven the moment they saw you."

I rolled my eyes and snorted. "Let's go hunt some stinking herbivores."

We found a large herd of mule deer as we ran back toward home. He hunted with me this time, now that I'd gotten the hang of it. I brought down a large buck, making nearly as much of a mess as I had with the lion. He'd finished with two before I was done with the first, not a hair ruffled, not a spot on his white shirt. We chased the scattered and terrified herd, but instead of feeding again, this time I watched carefully to see how he was able to hunt so neatly.

All the times that I had wished that Edward would not have to leave me behind when he hunted, I had secretly been just a little relieved. Because I was sure that seeing this would be frightening. Horrifying. That seeing him hunt would finally make him look like a vampire to me.

Of course, it was much different from this perspective, as a vampire myself. But I doubted that even my human eyes would have missed the beauty here.

It was a surprisingly sensual experience to observe Edward hunting. His smooth spring was like the sinuous strike of a snake; his hands were so sure, so strong, so completely inescapable; his full lips were perfect as they parted gracefully over his gleaming teeth. He was glorious. I felt a sudden jolt of both pride and desire. He was *mine*. Nothing could ever separate him from me now. I was too strong to be torn from his side.

He was very quick. He turned to me and gazed curiously at my gloating expression.

"No longer thirsty?" he asked.

I shrugged. "You distracted me. You're much better at it than I am."

"Centuries of practice." He smiled. His eyes were a disconcertingly lovely shade of honey gold now.

"Just one," I corrected him.

He laughed. "Are you done for today? Or did you want to continue?"

"Done, I think." I felt very full, sort of sloshy, even. I wasn't sure how much more liquid would fit into my body. But the burn in my throat was only muted. Then again, I'd known that thirst was just an inescapable part of this life.

And worth it.

I felt in control. Perhaps my sense of security was false, but I did feel pretty good about not killing anyone today. If I could resist totally human strangers, wouldn't I be able to handle the werewolf and a half-vampire child that I loved?

"I want to see Renesmee," I said. Now that my thirst

was tamed (if nothing close to erased), my earlier worries were hard to forget. I wanted to reconcile the stranger who was my daughter with the creature I'd loved three days ago. It was so odd, so wrong not to have her inside me still. Abruptly, I felt empty and uneasy.

He held out his hand to me. I took it, and his skin felt warmer than before. His cheek was faintly flushed, the shadows under his eyes all but vanished.

I was unable to resist stroking his face again. And again.

I sort of forgot that I was waiting for a response to my request as I stared into his shimmering gold eyes.

It was almost as hard as it had been to turn away from the scent of human blood, but I somehow kept the need to be careful firmly in my head as I stretched up on my toes and wrapped my arms around him. Gently.

He was not so hesitant in his movements; his arms locked around my waist and pulled me tight against his body. His lips crushed down on mine, but they felt soft. My lips no longer shaped themselves around his; they held their own.

Like before, it was as if the touch of his skin, his lips, his hands, was sinking right through my smooth, hard skin and into my new bones. To the very core of my body. I hadn't imagined that I could love him more than I had.

My old mind hadn't been capable of holding this much love. My old heart had not been strong enough to bear it.

Maybe this was the part of me that I'd brought forward to be intensified in my new life. Like Carlisle's compassion and Esme's devotion. I would probably never be able to do anything interesting or special like Edward, Alice, and

Jasper could do. Maybe I would just love Edward more than anyone in the history of the world had ever loved anyone else.

I could live with that.

I remembered parts of this—twisting my fingers in his hair, tracing the planes of his chest—but other parts were so new. He was new. It was an entirely different experience with Edward kissing me so fearlessly, so forcefully. I responded to his intensity, and then suddenly we were falling.

"Oops," I said, and he laughed underneath me. "I didn't mean to tackle you like that. Are you okay?"

He stroked my face. "Slightly better than *okay*." And then a perplexed expression crossed his face. "Renesmee?" he asked uncertainly, trying to ascertain what I wanted most in this moment. A very difficult question to answer, because I wanted so many things at the same time.

I could tell that he wasn't exactly averse to procrastinating our return trip, and it was hard to think about much besides his skin on mine—there really wasn't that much left of the dress. But my memory of Renesmee, before and after her birth, was becoming more and more dreamlike to me. More unlikely. All my memories of her were human memories; an aura of artificiality clung to them. Nothing seemed real that I hadn't seen with these eyes, touched with these hands.

Every minute, the reality of that little stranger slipped further away.

"Renesmee," I agreed, rueful, and I whipped back up onto my feet, pulling him with me.

22. PROMISED

THINKING OF RENESMEE BROUGHT HER TO THAT CENTER-stage place in my strange, new, and roomy but distractible mind. So many questions.

"Tell me about her," I insisted as he took my hand. Being linked barely slowed us.

"She's like nothing else in the world," he told me, and the sound of an almost religious devotion was there again in his voice.

I felt a sharp pang of jealousy over this stranger. He knew her and I did not. It wasn't fair.

"How much is she like you? How much like me? Or like I was, anyway."

"It seems a fairly even divide."

"She was warm-blooded," I remembered.

"Yes. She has a heartbeat, though it runs a little bit faster than a human's. Her temperature is a little bit hotter than usual, too. She sleeps."

"Really?"

"Quite well for a newborn. The only parents in the world who don't need sleep, and our child already sleeps through the night." He chuckled.

I liked the way he said *our child*. The words made her more real.

"She has exactly your color eyes—so that didn't get lost, after all." He smiled at me. "They're so beautiful."

"And the vampire parts?" I asked.

"Her skin seems about as impenetrable as ours. Not that anyone would dream of testing that."

I blinked at him, a little shocked.

"Of course no one would," he assured me again. "Her diet . . . well, she prefers to drink blood. Carlisle continues to try to persuade her to drink some baby formula, too, but she doesn't have much patience with it. Can't say that I blame her—nasty-smelling stuff, even for human food."

I gaped openly at him now. He made it sound like they were having conversations. "Persuade her?"

"She's intelligent, shockingly so, and progressing at an immense pace. Though she doesn't speak—yet—she communicates quite effectively."

"Doesn't. Speak. *Yet.*"

He slowed our pace further, letting me absorb this.

"What do you mean, she communicates effectively?" I demanded.

"I think it will be easier for you to . . . see for yourself. It's rather difficult to describe."

I considered that. I knew there was a lot that I needed to see for myself before it would be real. I wasn't sure how much more I was ready for, so I changed the subject.

"Why is Jacob still here?" I asked. "How can he stand it? Why should he?" My ringing voice trembled a little. "Why should he have to suffer more?"

"Jacob isn't suffering," he said in a strange new tone. "Though I might be willing to change his condition," Edward added through his teeth.

"Edward!" I hissed, yanking him to a stop (and feeling a little thrill of smugness that I was able to do it). "How can you say that? Jacob has given up *everything* to protect us! What I've put him through—!" I cringed at the dim memory of shame and guilt. It seemed odd now that I had needed him so much then. That sense of absence without him near had vanished; it must have been a human weakness.

"You'll see exactly how I can say that," Edward muttered. "I promised him that I would let him explain, but I doubt you'll see it much differently than I do. Of course, I'm often wrong about your thoughts, aren't I?" He pursed his lips and eyed me.

"Explain what?"

Edward shook his head. "I promised. Though I don't know if I really owe him anything at all anymore. . . ." His teeth ground together.

"Edward, I don't understand." Frustration and indignation took over my head.

He stroked my cheek and then smiled gently when

my face smoothed out in response, desire momentarily overruling annoyance. "It's harder than you make it look, I know. I remember."

"I don't like feeling confused."

"I know. And so let's get you home, so that you can see it all for yourself." His eyes ran over the remains of my dress as he spoke of going home, and he frowned. "Hmm." After a half second of thought, he unbuttoned his white shirt and held it out for me to put my arms through.

"That bad?"

He grinned.

I slipped my arms into his sleeves and then buttoned it swiftly over my ragged bodice. Of course, that left him without a shirt, and it was impossible not to find that distracting.

"I'll race you," I said, and then cautioned, "no throwing the game this time!"

He dropped my hand and grinned. "On your mark . . ."

Finding my way to my new home was simpler than walking down Charlie's street to my old one. Our scent left a clear and easy trail to follow, even running as fast as I could.

Edward had me beat till we hit the river. I took a chance and made my leap early, trying to use my extra strength to win.

"Ha!" I exulted when I heard my feet touch the grass first.

Listening for his landing, I heard something I did not expect. Something loud and much too close. A thudding heart.

Edward was beside me in the same second, his hands clamped down hard on the tops of my arms.

"Don't breathe," he cautioned me urgently.

I tried not to panic as I froze mid-breath. My eyes were the only things that moved, wheeling instinctively to find the source of the sound.

Jacob stood at the line where the forest touched the Cullens' lawn, his arms folded across his body, his jaw clenched tight. Invisible in the woods behind him, I heard now two larger hearts, and the faint crush of bracken under huge, pacing paws.

"Carefully, Jacob," Edward said. A snarl from the forest echoed the concern in his voice. "Maybe this isn't the best way—"

"You think it would be better to let her near the baby first?" Jacob interrupted. "It's safer to see how Bella does with me. I heal fast."

This was a test? To see if I could not kill Jacob before I tried to not kill Renesmee? I felt sick in the strangest way—it had nothing to do with my stomach, only my mind. Was this Edward's idea?

I glanced at his face anxiously; Edward seemed to deliberate for a moment, and then his expression twisted from concern into something else. He shrugged, and there was an undercurrent of hostility in his voice when he said, "It's your neck, I guess."

The growl from the forest was furious this time; Leah, I had no doubt.

What was with Edward? After all that we'd been through, shouldn't he have been able to feel some kindness for my best friend? I'd thought—maybe foolishly—that Edward was sort of Jacob's friend now, too. I must have misread them.

But what was Jacob doing? Why would he offer himself as a test to protect Renesmee?

It didn't make any sense to me. Even if our friendship had survived . . .

And as my eyes met Jacob's now, I thought that maybe it had. He still looked like my best friend. But he wasn't the one who had changed. What did I look like to him?

Then he smiled his familiar smile, the smile of a kindred spirit, and I was sure our friendship was intact. It was just like before, when we were hanging out in his homemade garage, just two friends killing time. Easy and *normal*. Again, I noticed that the strange need I'd felt for him before I'd changed was completely gone. He was just my friend, the way it was supposed to be.

It still made no sense what he was doing now, though. Was he really so selfless that he would try to protect me— with his own life—from doing something in an uncontrolled split second that I would regret in agony forever? That went way beyond simply tolerating what I had become, or miraculously managing to stay my friend. Jacob was one of the best people I knew, but this seemed like too much to accept from anyone.

His grin widened, and he shuddered slightly. "I gotta say it, Bells. You're a freak show."

I grinned back, falling easily into the old pattern. This was a side of him I understood.

Edward growled. "Watch yourself, mongrel."

The wind blew from behind me and I quickly filled my lungs with the safe air so I could speak. "No, he's right. The eyes are really something, aren't they?"

"Super-creepy. But it's not as bad as I thought it would be."

"Gee—thanks for the amazing compliment!"

He rolled his eyes. "You know what I mean. You still look like you—sort of. Maybe it's not the look so much as . . . you *are* Bella. I didn't think it would feel like you were still here." He smiled at me again without a trace of bitterness or resentment anywhere in his face. Then he chuckled and said, "Anyway, I guess I'll get used to the eyes soon enough."

"You will?" I asked, confused. It was wonderful that we were still friends, but it wasn't like we'd be spending much time together.

The strangest look crossed his face, erasing the smile. It was almost . . . guilty? Then his eyes shifted to Edward.

"Thanks," he said. "I didn't know if you'd be able to keep it from her, promise or not. Usually, you just give her everything she wants."

"Maybe I'm hoping she'll get irritated and rip your head off," Edward suggested.

Jacob snorted.

"What's going on? Are you two keeping secrets from me?" I demanded, incredulous.

"I'll explain later," Jacob said self-consciously—like he didn't really plan on it. Then he changed the subject. "First, let's get this show on the road." His grin was a challenge now as he started slowly forward.

There was a whine of protest behind him, and then Leah's gray body slid out of the trees behind him. The taller, sandy-colored Seth was right behind her.

"Cool it, guys," Jacob said. "Stay out of this."

I was glad they didn't listen to him but only followed after him a little more slowly.

The wind was still now; it wouldn't blow his scent away from me.

He got close enough that I could feel the heat of his body in the air between us. My throat burned in response.

"C'mon, Bells. Do your worst."

Leah hissed.

I didn't want to breathe. It wasn't right to take such dangerous advantage of Jacob, no matter if he was the one offering. But I couldn't get away from the logic. How else could I be sure that I wouldn't hurt Renesmee?

"I'm getting older here, Bella," Jacob taunted. "Okay, not technically, but you get the idea. Go on, take a whiff."

"Hold on to me," I said to Edward, cringing back into his chest.

His hands tightened on my arms.

I locked my muscles in place, hoping I could keep them frozen. I resolved that I would do at least as well as I had on the hunt. Worst-case scenario, I would stop breathing and run for it. Nervously, I took a tiny breath in through my nose, braced for anything.

It hurt a little, but my throat was already burning dully anyway. Jacob didn't smell that much more human than the mountain lion. There was an animal edge to his blood that instantly repelled. Though the loud, wet sound of his heart was appealing, the scent that went with it made my nose wrinkle. It was actually *easier* with the smell to temper my reaction to the sound and heat of his pulsing blood.

I took another breath and relaxed. "Huh. I can see what everyone's been going on about. You stink, Jacob."

Edward burst into laughter; his hands slipped from my shoulders to wrap around my waist. Seth barked a low chortle in harmony with Edward; he came a little closer while Leah retreated several paces. And then I was aware of another audience when I heard Emmett's low, distinct guffaw, muffled a little by the glass wall between us.

"Look who's talking," Jacob said, theatrically plugging his nose. His face didn't pucker at all while Edward embraced me, not even when Edward composed himself and whispered "I love you" in my ear. Jacob just kept grinning. This made me feel hopeful that things were going to be right between us, the way they hadn't been for so long now. Maybe now I could truly be his friend, since I disgusted him enough physically that he couldn't love me the same way as before. Maybe that was all that was needed.

"Okay, so I passed, right?" I said. "Now are you going to tell me what this big secret is?"

Jacob's expression became very nervous. "It's nothing you need to worry about this second. . . ."

I heard Emmett chuckle again—a sound of anticipation.

I would have pressed my point, but as I listened to Emmett, I heard other sounds, too. Seven people breathing. One set of lungs moving more rapidly than the others. Only one heart fluttering like a bird's wings, light and quick.

I was totally diverted. My daughter was just on the

other side of that thin wall of glass. I couldn't see her—the light bounced off the reflective windows like a mirror. I could only see myself, looking very strange—so white and still—compared to Jacob. Or, compared to Edward, looking exactly right.

"Renesmee," I whispered. Stress made me a statue again. Renesmee wasn't going to smell like an animal. Would I put her in danger?

"Come and see," Edward murmured. "I know you can handle this."

"You'll help me?" I whispered through motionless lips.

"Of course I will."

"And Emmett and Jasper—just in case?"

"We'll take care of you, Bella. Don't worry, we'll be ready. None of us would risk Renesmee. I think you'll be surprised at how entirely she's already wrapped us all around her little fingers. She'll be perfectly safe, no matter what."

My yearning to see her, to understand the worship in his voice, broke my frozen pose. I took a step forward.

And then Jacob was in my way, his face a mask of worry.

"Are you *sure*, bloodsucker?" he demanded of Edward, his voice almost pleading. I'd never heard him speak to Edward that way. "I don't like this. Maybe she should wait—"

"You had your test, Jacob."

It was Jacob's test?

"But—," Jacob began.

"But nothing," Edward said, suddenly exasperated. "Bella needs to see *our* daughter. Get out of her way."

Jacob shot me an odd, frantic look and then turned and nearly sprinted into the house ahead of us.

Edward growled.

I couldn't make sense of their confrontation, and I couldn't concentrate on it, either. I could only think about the blurred child in my memory and struggle against the haziness, trying to remember her face exactly.

"Shall we?" Edward said, his voice gentle again.

I nodded nervously.

He took my hand tightly in his and led the way into the house.

They waited for me in a smiling line that was both welcoming and defensive. Rosalie was several paces behind the rest of them, near the front door. She was alone until Jacob joined her and then stood in front of her, closer than was normal. There was no sense of comfort in that closeness; both of them seemed to cringe from the proximity.

Someone very small was leaning forward out of Rosalie's arms, peering around Jacob. Immediately, she had my absolute attention, my every thought, the way nothing else had owned them since the moment I'd opened my eyes.

"I was out just two days?" I gasped, disbelieving.

The stranger-child in Rosalie's arms had to be weeks, if not months, old. She was maybe twice the size of the baby in my dim memory, and she seemed to be supporting her own torso easily as she stretched toward me. Her shiny bronze-colored hair fell in ringlets past her shoulders. Her chocolate brown eyes examined me with an interest that was not at all childlike; it was adult, aware and intelligent. She raised one hand, reaching in my direction for a moment, and then reached back to touch Rosalie's throat.

If her face had not been astonishing in its beauty and

perfection, I wouldn't have believed it was the same child. My child.

But Edward *was* there in her features, and I was there in the color of her eyes and cheeks. Even Charlie had a place in her thick curls, though their color matched Edward's. She must be ours. Impossible, but still true.

Seeing this unanticipated little person did not make her more real, though. It only made her more fantastic.

Rosalie patted the hand against her neck and murmured, "Yes, that's her."

Renesmee's eyes stayed locked on mine. Then, as she had just seconds after her violent birth, she smiled at me. A brilliant flash of tiny, perfect white teeth.

Reeling inside, I took a hesitant step toward her.

Everyone moved very fast.

Emmett and Jasper were right in front of me, shoulder to shoulder, hands ready. Edward gripped me from behind, fingers tight again on the tops of my arms. Even Carlisle and Esme moved to get Emmett's and Jasper's flanks, while Rosalie backed to the door, her arms clutching at Renesmee. Jacob moved, too, keeping his protective stance in front of them.

Alice was the only one who held her place.

"Oh, give her some credit," she chided them. "She wasn't going to do anything. You'd want a closer look, too."

Alice was right. I was in control of myself. I'd been braced for anything—for a scent as impossibly insistent as the human smell in the woods. The temptation here was really not comparable. Renesmee's fragrance was perfectly balanced right on the line between the scent of the most beautiful perfume and the scent of the most delicious food. There was enough of the sweet vampire smell to keep the human part from being overwhelming.

I could handle it. I was sure.

"I'm okay," I promised, patting Edward's hand on my arm. Then I hesitated and added, "Keep close, though, just in case."

Jasper's eyes were tight, focused. I knew he was taking in my emotional climate, and I worked on settling into a steady calm. I felt Edward free my arms as he read Jasper's assessment. But, though Jasper was getting it firsthand, he didn't seem as certain.

When she heard my voice, the too-aware child struggled in Rosalie's arms, reaching toward me. Somehow, her expression managed to look impatient.

"Jazz, Em, let us through. Bella's got this."

"Edward, the risk——," Jasper said.

"Minimal. Listen, Jasper—on the hunt she caught the scent of some hikers who were in the wrong place at the wrong time. . . ."

I heard Carlisle suck in a shocked breath. Esme's face was suddenly full of concern mingled with compassion. Jasper's eyes widened, but he nodded just a tiny bit, as if Edward's words answered some question in his head. Jacob's mouth screwed up into a disgusted grimace. Emmett shrugged. Rosalie seemed even less concerned than Emmett as she tried to hold on to the struggling child in her arms.

Alice's expression told me that she was not fooled. Her narrowed eyes, focused with burning intensity on my borrowed shirt, seemed more worried about what I'd done to my dress than anything else.

"Edward!" Carlisle chastened. "How could you be so irresponsible?"

"I know, Carlisle, I know. I was just plain stupid. I should have taken the time to make sure we were in a safe zone before I set her loose."

"Edward," I mumbled, embarrassed by the way they stared at me. It was like they were trying to see a brighter red in my eyes.

"He's absolutely right to rebuke me, Bella," Edward said with a grin. "I made a huge mistake. The fact that you are stronger than anyone I've ever known doesn't change that."

Alice rolled her eyes. "Tasteful joke, Edward."

"I wasn't making a joke. I was explaining to Jasper why I know Bella can handle this. It's not my fault everyone jumped to conclusions."

"Wait," Jasper gasped. "She didn't hunt the humans?"

"She started to," Edward said, clearly enjoying himself. My teeth ground together. "She was entirely focused on the hunt."

"What happened?" Carlisle interjected. His eyes were suddenly bright, an amazed smile beginning to form on his face. It reminded me of before, when he'd wanted the details on my transformation experience. The thrill of new information.

Edward leaned toward him, animated. "She heard me behind her and reacted defensively. As soon as my pursuit broke into her concentration, she snapped right out of it. I've never seen anything to equal her. She realized at once what was happening, and then . . . *she held her breath and ran away.*"

"Whoa," Emmett murmured. "Seriously?"

"He's not telling it right," I muttered, more embarrassed than before. "He left out the part where I growled at him."

"Did ya get in a couple of good swipes?" Emmett asked eagerly.

"No! Of course not."

"No, not really? You really didn't attack him?"

"Emmett!" I protested.

"Aw, what a waste," Emmett groaned. "And here you're probably the one person who could take him—since he can't get in your head to cheat—and you had a perfect excuse, too." He sighed. "I've been *dying* to see how he'd do without that advantage."

I glared at him frostily. "I would never."

Jasper's frown caught my attention; he seemed even more disturbed than before.

Edward touched his fist lightly to Jasper's shoulder in a mock punch. "You see what I mean?"

"It's not natural," Jasper muttered.

"She could have turned on you—she's only hours old!" Esme scolded, putting her hand against her heart. "Oh, we should have gone with you."

I wasn't paying so much attention, now that Edward was past the punch line of his joke. I was staring at the gorgeous child by the door, who was still staring at me. Her little dimpled hands reached out toward me like she knew exactly who I was. Automatically, my hand lifted to mimic hers.

"Edward," I said, leaning around Jasper to see her better. "Please?"

Jasper's teeth were set; he didn't move.

"Jazz, this isn't anything you've seen before," Alice said quietly. "Trust me."

Their eyes met for a short second, and then Jasper nodded. He moved out of my way, but put one hand on my shoulder and moved with me as I walked slowly forward.

I thought about every step before I took it, analyzing my mood, the burn in my throat, the position of the others around me. How strong I felt versus how well they would be able to contain me. It was a slow procession.

And then the child in Rosalie's arms, struggling and reaching all this time while her expression got more and more irritated, let out a high, ringing wail. Everyone reacted as if—like me—they'd never heard her voice before.

They swarmed around her in a second, leaving me standing alone, frozen in place. The sound of Renesmee's cry pierced right through me, spearing me to the floor. My eyes pricked in the strangest way, like they wanted to tear.

It seemed like everyone had a hand on her, patting and soothing. Everyone but me.

"What's the matter? Is she hurt? What happened?"

It was Jacob's voice that was loudest, that raised anxiously above the others. I watched in shock as he reached for Renesmee, and then in utter horror as Rosalie surrendered her to him without a fight.

"No, she's fine," Rosalie reassured him.

Rosalie was reassuring Jacob?

Renesmee went to Jacob willingly enough, pushing her tiny hand against his cheek and then squirming around to stretch toward me again.

"See?" Rosalie told him. "She just wants Bella."

"She wants me?" I whispered.

Renesmee's eyes—my eyes—stared impatiently at me.

Edward darted back to my side. He put his hands lightly on my arms and urged me forward.

"She's been waiting for you for almost three days," he told me.

We were only a few feet away from her now. Bursts of heat seemed to tremble out from her to touch me.

Or maybe it was Jacob who was trembling. I saw his hands shaking as I got closer. And yet, despite his obvious anxiety, his face was more serene than I had seen it in a long time.

"Jake—I'm fine," I told him. It made me panicky to see Renesmee in his shaking hands, but I worked to keep myself in control.

He frowned at me, eyes tight, like he was just as panicky at the thought of Renesmee in my arms.

Renesmee whimpered eagerly and stretched, her little hands grasping into fists again and again.

Something in me clicked into place at that moment. The sound of her cry, the familiarity of her eyes, the way she seemed even more impatient than I did for this reunion—all of it wove together into the most natural of patterns as she clutched the air between us. Suddenly, she was absolutely real, and *of course* I knew her. It was perfectly ordinary that I should take that last easy step and reach for her, putting my hands exactly where they would fit best as I pulled her gently toward me.

Jacob let his long arms stretch so that I could cradle her, but he didn't let go. He shuddered a little when our skin touched. His skin, always so warm to me before, felt like an open flame to me now. It was almost the same temperature as Renesmee's. Perhaps one or two degrees difference.

Renesmee seemed oblivious to the coolness of my skin, or at least very used to it.

She looked up and smiled at me again, showing her square little teeth and two dimples. Then, very deliberately, she reached for my face.

The moment she did this, all the hands on me tightened, anticipating my reaction. I barely noticed.

I was gasping, stunned and frightened by the strange, alarming image that filled my mind. It *felt* like a very strong memory—I could still see through my eyes while I watched it in my head—but it was completely unfamiliar. I stared through it to Renesmee's expectant expression, trying to understand what was happening, struggling desperately to hold on to my calm.

Besides being shocking and unfamiliar, the image was also wrong somehow—I almost recognized my own face in it, my old face, but it was off, backward. I grasped quickly that I was seeing my face as others saw it, rather than flipped in a reflection.

My memory face was twisted, ravaged, covered in sweat and blood. Despite this, my expression in the vision became an adoring smile; my brown eyes glowed over their deep circles. The image enlarged, my face came closer to the unseen vantage point, and then abruptly vanished.

Renesmee's hand dropped from my cheek. She smiled wider, dimpling again.

It was totally silent in the room but for the heartbeats.

No one but Jacob and Renesmee was so much as breathing. The silence stretched on; it seemed like they were waiting for me to say something.

"What . . . was . . . *that*?" I managed to choke out.

"What did you see?" Rosalie asked curiously, leaning around Jacob, who seemed very much in the way and out of place at the moment. "What did she show you?"

"*She* showed me that?" I whispered.

"I told you it was hard to explain," Edward murmured in my ear. "But effective as means of communications go."

"What was it?" Jacob asked.

I blinked quickly several times. "Um. Me. I think. But I looked terrible."

"It was the only memory she had of you," Edward explained. It was obvious he'd seen what she was *showing* me as she thought of it. He was still cringing, his voice rough from reliving the memory. "She's letting you know that she's made the connection, that she knows who you are."

"But *how* did she do that?"

Renesmee seemed unconcerned with my boggling eyes. She was smiling slightly and pulling on a lock of my hair.

"How do I hear thoughts? How does Alice see the future?" Edward asked rhetorically, and then shrugged. "She's gifted."

"It's an interesting twist," Carlisle said to Edward. "Like she's doing the exact opposite of what you can."

"Interesting," Edward agreed. "I wonder. . . ."

I knew they were speculating away, but I didn't care. I was staring at the most beautiful face in the world. She was hot in my arms, reminding me of the moment when the blackness had almost won, when there was nothing in the world left to hold on to. Nothing strong enough to pull me through the crushing darkness. The moment when I'd thought of Renesmee and found something I would never let go of.

"I remember you, too," I told her quietly.

It seemed very natural to lean in and press my lips to her forehead. She smelled wonderful. The scent of her skin set my throat burning, but it was easy to ignore. It didn't strip the joy from the moment. Renesmee was real and I knew her. She was the same one I'd fought for from the beginning. My little nudger, the one who loved me from the inside, too. Half Edward, perfect and lovely. And half me—which, surprisingly, made her better rather than detracting.

I'd been right all along. She was worth the fight.

"She's fine," Alice murmured, probably to Jasper. I could feel them hovering, not trusting me.

"Haven't we experimented enough for one day?" Jacob asked, his voice a slightly higher pitch with stress. "Okay, Bella's doing great, but let's not push it."

I glared at him with real irritation. Jasper shuffled uneasily next to me. We were all crowded so close that every tiny movement seemed very big.

"What is your *problem*, Jacob?" I demanded. I tugged lightly against his hold on Renesmee, and he just stepped closer to me. He was pressed right up to me, Renesmee touching both of our chests.

Edward hissed at him. "Just because I understand, it doesn't mean I won't throw you out, Jacob. Bella's doing extraordinarily well. Don't ruin the moment for her."

"I'll help him toss you, dog," Rosalie promised, her voice seething. "I owe you a good kick in the gut." Obviously, there was no change in *that* relationship, unless it had gotten worse.

I glared at Jacob's anxious half-angry expression. His eyes were locked on Renesmee's face. With everyone pressed together, he had to be touching at least six different vampires at the moment, and it didn't even seem to bug him.

Would he really go through all this just to protect me from myself? What could have happened during my transformation—my alteration into something he hated—that would soften him so much toward the reason for its necessity?

I puzzled over it, watching him stare at my daughter. Staring at her like . . . like he was a blind man seeing the sun for the very first time.

"No!" I gasped.

Jasper's teeth came together and Edward's arms wrapped around my chest like constricting boas. Jacob had Renesmee out of my arms in the same second, and I did not try to hold on to her. Because I felt it coming—the snap that they'd all been waiting for.

"Rose," I said through my teeth, very slowly and precisely. "Take Renesmee."

Rosalie held her hands out, and Jacob handed my daughter to her at once. Both of them backed away from me.

"Edward, I don't want to hurt you, so please let go of me."

He hesitated.

"Go stand in front of Renesmee," I suggested.

He deliberated, and then let me go.

I leaned into my hunting crouch and took two slow steps forward toward Jacob.

"You didn't," I snarled at him.

He backed away, palms up, trying to reason with me. "You know it's not something I can control."

"You *stupid mutt*! How *could* you? *My baby!*"

He backed out the front door now as I stalked him, half-running backward down the stairs. "It wasn't my idea, Bella!"

"I've held her all of *one* time, and already you think you have some moronic wolfy claim to her? She's *mine*."

"I can share," he said pleadingly as he retreated across the lawn.

"Pay up," I heard Emmett say behind me. A small part of my brain wondered who had bet against this outcome. I didn't waste much attention on it. I was too furious.

"How dare you *imprint* on *my* baby? Have you lost your mind?"

"It was involuntary!" he insisted, backing into the trees.

Then he wasn't alone. The two huge wolves reappeared, flanking him on either side. Leah snapped at me.

A fearsome snarl ripped through my teeth back at her. The sound disturbed me, but not enough to stop my advance.

"Bella, would you try to listen for just a second? Please?" Jacob begged. "Leah, back off," he added.

Leah curled her lip at me and didn't move.

"Why should I listen?" I hissed. Fury reigned in my head. It clouded everything else out.

"Because you're the one who told me this. Do you remember? You said we belonged in each other's lives, right? That we were family. You said that was how you and I were supposed to be. So . . . now we are. It's what you wanted."

I glared ferociously. I did dimly remember those words. But my new quick brain was two steps ahead of his nonsense.

"You think you'll be part of my family as my *son-in-law*!" I screeched. My bell voice ripped through two octaves and still came out sounding like music.

Emmett laughed.

"Stop her, Edward," Esme murmured. "She'll be unhappy if she hurts him."

But I felt no pursuit behind me.

"No!" Jacob was insisting at the same time. "How can you even look at it that way? She's just a baby, for crying out loud!"

"That's my *point*!" I yelled.

"You know I don't think of her that way! Do you think Edward would have let me live this long if I did? All I want is for her to be safe and happy—is that so bad? So different from what you want?" He was shouting right back at me.

Beyond words, I shrieked a growl at him.

"Amazing, isn't she?" I heard Edward murmur.

"She hasn't gone for his throat even once," Carlisle agreed, sounding stunned.

"Fine, you win this one," Emmett said grudgingly.

"You're going to stay away from her," I hissed up at Jacob.

"I can't do that!"

Through my teeth: "*Try*. Starting *now*."

"It's not possible. Do you remember how much you wanted me around three days ago? How hard it was to be apart from each other? That's gone for you now, isn't it?"

I glared, not sure what he was implying.

"That was her," he told me. "From the very beginning. We had to be together, even then."

I remembered, and then I understood; a tiny part of me was relieved to have the madness explained. But that relief somehow only made me angrier. Was he expecting that to be enough for me? That one little clarification would make me okay with this?

"Run away while you still can," I threatened.

"C'mon, Bells! Nessie likes me, too," he insisted.

I froze. My breathing stopped. Behind me, I heard the lack of sound that was their anxious reaction.

"*What* . . . did you call her?"

Jacob took a step farther back, managing to look sheepish. "Well," he mumbled, "that name you came up with is kind of a mouthful and—"

"You nicknamed my daughter after the *Loch Ness Monster*?" I screeched.

And then I lunged for his throat.

23. MEMORIES

"I'M SO SORRY, SETH. I SHOULD HAVE BEEN CLOSER."

Edward was *still* apologizing, and I didn't think that was either fair or appropriate. After all, *Edward* hadn't completely and inexcusably lost control of his temper. *Edward* hadn't tried to rip Jacob's head off—Jacob, who wouldn't even phase to protect himself—and then accidentally broken Seth's shoulder and collarbone when he jumped in between. *Edward* hadn't almost killed his best friend.

Not that the best friend didn't have a few things to answer for, but, obviously, nothing Jacob had done could have mitigated my behavior.

So shouldn't *I* have been the one apologizing? I tried again.

"Seth, I—"

"Don't worry about it, Bella, I'm totally fine," Seth said at the same time that Edward said, "Bella, love, no one is judging you. You're doing so well."

They hadn't let me finish a sentence yet.

It only made it worse that Edward was having a difficult time keeping the smile off his face. I knew that Jacob didn't deserve my overreaction, but Edward seemed to find something satisfying in it. Maybe he was just wishing that he had the excuse of being a newborn so that he could do something physical about his irritation with Jacob, too.

I tried to erase the anger from my system entirely, but it was hard, knowing that Jacob was outside with Renesmee right now. Keeping her safe from me, the crazed newborn.

Carlisle secured another piece of the brace to Seth's arm, and Seth winced.

"Sorry, sorry!" I mumbled, knowing I'd never get a fully articulated apology out.

"Don't freak, Bella," Seth said, patting my knee with his good hand while Edward rubbed my arm from the other side.

Seth seemed to feel no aversion to having me sit beside him on the sofa as Carlisle treated him. "I'll be back to normal in half an hour," he continued, still patting my knee as if oblivious to the cold, hard texture of it. "Anyone would have done the same, what with Jake and Ness—" He broke off mid-word and changed the subject quickly. "I mean, at least you didn't bite me or anything. That would've sucked."

I buried my face in my hands and shuddered at the

thought, at the very real possibility. It could have happened so easily. And werewolves didn't react to vampire venom the same way humans did, they'd told me only now. It was poison to them.

"I'm a bad person."

"Of course you aren't. I should have—," Edward started.

"Stop that," I sighed. I didn't want him taking the blame for this the way he always took everything on himself.

"Lucky thing Ness—Renesmee's not venomous," Seth said after a second of awkward silence. "'Cause she bites Jake all the time."

My hands dropped. "She does?"

"Sure. Whenever he and Rose don't get dinner in her mouth fast enough. Rose thinks it's pretty hilarious."

I stared at him, shocked, and also feeling guilty, because I had to admit that this pleased me a teensy bit in a petulant way.

Of course, I already knew that Renesmee wasn't venomous. I was the first person she'd bitten. I didn't make this observation aloud, as I was feigning memory loss on those recent events.

"Well, Seth," Carlisle said, straightening up and stepping away from us. "I think that's as much as I can do. Try to not move for, oh, a few hours, I guess." Carlisle chuckled. "I wish treating humans were this instantaneously gratifying." He rested his hand for a moment on Seth's black hair. "Stay still," he ordered, and then he disappeared upstairs. I heard his office door close, and I wondered if they'd already removed the evidence of my time there.

"I can probably manage sitting still for a while," Seth

agreed after Carlisle was already gone, and then he yawned hugely. Carefully, making sure not to tweak his shoulder, Seth leaned his head against the sofa's back and closed his eyes. Seconds later, his mouth fell slack.

I frowned at his peaceful face for another minute. Like Jacob, Seth seemed to have the gift of falling asleep at will. Knowing I wouldn't be able to apologize again for a while, I got up; the motion didn't jostle the couch in the slightest. Everything physical was so easy. But the rest . . .

Edward followed me to the back windows and took my hand.

Leah was pacing along the river, stopping every now and then to look at the house. It was easy to tell when she was looking for her brother and when she was looking for me. She alternated between anxious glances and murderous glares.

I could hear Jacob and Rosalie outside on the front steps bickering quietly over whose turn it was to feed Renesmee. Their relationship was as antagonistic as ever; the only thing they agreed on now was that I should be kept away from my baby until I was one hundred percent recovered from my temper tantrum. Edward had disputed their verdict, but I'd let it go. I wanted to be sure, too. I was worried, though, that *my* one hundred percent sure and *their* one hundred percent sure might be very different things.

Other than their squabbling, Seth's slow breathing, and Leah's annoyed panting, it was very quiet. Emmett, Alice, and Esme were hunting. Jasper had stayed behind to watch me. He stood unobtrusively behind the newel post now, trying not to be obnoxious about it.

I took advantage of the calm to think of all the things

Edward and Seth had told me while Carlisle splinted Seth's arm. I'd missed a whole lot while I was burning, and this was the first real chance to catch up.

The main thing was the end of the feud with Sam's pack—which was why the others felt safe to come and go as they pleased again. The truce was stronger than ever. Or more binding, depending on your viewpoint, I imagined.

Binding, because the most absolute of all the pack's laws was that no wolf ever kill the object of another wolf's imprinting. The pain of such a thing would be intolerable for the whole pack. The fault, whether intended or accidental, could not be forgiven; the wolves involved would fight to the death—there was no other option. It had happened long ago, Seth told me, but only accidentally. No wolf would ever intentionally destroy a brother that way.

So Renesmee was untouchable because of the way Jacob now felt about her. I tried to concentrate on the relief of this fact rather than the chagrin, but it wasn't easy. My mind had enough room to feel both emotions intensely at the same time.

And Sam couldn't get mad about my transformation, either, because Jacob—speaking as the rightful Alpha—had allowed it. It rankled to realize over and over again how much I owed Jacob when I just wanted to be mad at him.

I deliberately redirected my thoughts in order to control my emotions. I considered another interesting phenomenon; though the silence between the separate packs continued, Jacob and Sam had discovered that Alphas could speak to each other while in their wolf form. It wasn't the same as before; they couldn't hear every thought the way they had prior to the split. It was more like speaking aloud, Seth had said. Sam could only hear the thoughts Jacob wanted to share, and vice versa. They found they could communicate over distance, too, now that they were talking to each other again.

They hadn't found all this out until Jacob had gone alone—over Seth's and Leah's objections—to explain to Sam about Renesmee; it was the only time he'd left Renesmee since first laying eyes on her.

Once Sam had understood how absolutely everything had changed, he'd come back with Jacob to talk to Carlisle. They'd spoken in human form (Edward had refused to leave my side to translate), and the treaty had been renewed. The friendly feeling of the relationship, however, might never be the same.

One big worry down.

But there was another that, though not as physically dangerous as an angry wolf pack, still seemed more urgent to me.

Charlie.

He'd spoken to Esme earlier this morning, but that hadn't kept him from calling again, twice, just a few minutes ago while Carlisle treated Seth. Carlisle and Edward had let the phone ring.

What would be the right thing to tell him? Were the Cullens right? Was telling him that I'd died the best, the kindest way? Would I be able to lie still in a coffin while he and my mother cried over me?

It didn't seem right to me. But putting Charlie or Renée in danger of the Volturi's obsession with secrecy was clearly out of the question.

There was still my idea—let Charlie see me, when

I was ready for that, and let him make his own wrong assumptions. Technically, the vampire rules would remain unbroken. Wouldn't it be better for Charlie if he knew that I was alive—sort of—and happy? Even if I was strange and different and probably frightening to him?

My eyes, in particular, were much too frightening right now. How long before my self-control and my eye color were ready for Charlie?

"What's the matter, Bella?" Jasper asked quietly, reading my growing tension. "No one is angry with you"—a low snarl from the riverside contradicted him, but he ignored it—"or even surprised, really. Well, I suppose we *are* surprised. Surprised that you were able to snap out of it so quickly. You did well. Better than anyone expects of you."

While he was speaking, the room became very calm. Seth's breathing slipped into a low snore. I felt more peaceful, but I didn't forget my anxieties.

"I was thinking about Charlie, actually."

Out front, the bickering cut off.

"Ah," Jasper murmured.

"We really have to leave, don't we?" I asked. "For a while, at the very least. Pretend we're in Atlanta or something."

I could feel Edward's gaze locked on my face, but I looked at Jasper. He was the one who answered me in a grave tone.

"Yes. It's the only way to protect your father."

I brooded for a moment. "I'm going to miss him so much. I'll miss everyone here."

Jacob, I thought, despite myself. Though that yearning was both vanished and defined—and I was vastly relieved that it was—he was still my friend. Someone who knew the real me and accepted her. Even as a monster.

I thought about what Jacob had said, pleading with me before I'd attacked him. *You said we belonged in each other's lives, right? That we were family. You said that was how you and I were supposed to be. So . . . now we are. It's what you wanted.*

But it didn't feel like how I'd wanted it. Not exactly. I remembered further back, to the fuzzy, weak memories of my human life. Back to the very hardest part to remember— the time without Edward, a time so dark I'd tried to bury it in my head. I couldn't get the words exactly right; I only remembered wishing that Jacob were my brother so that we could love each other without any confusion or pain. Family. But I'd never factored a daughter into the equation.

I remembered a little later—one of the many times that I'd told Jacob goodbye—wondering aloud who he would end up with, who would make his life right after what I'd done to it. I had said something about how whoever she was, she wouldn't be good enough for him.

I snorted, and Edward raised one eyebrow questioningly. I just shook my head at him.

But as much as I might miss my friend, I knew there was a bigger problem. Had Sam or Jared or Quil ever gone a whole day without seeing the objects of their fixations, Emily, Kim, and Claire? *Could* they? What would the separation from Renesmee do to Jacob? Would it cause him pain?

There was still enough petty ire in my system to make me glad, not for his pain, but for the idea of having Renesmee away from him. How was I supposed to deal with having her belong to Jacob when she only barely seemed to belong to me?

The sound of movement on the front porch interrupted my thoughts. I heard them get up, and then they were through the door. At exactly the same time, Carlisle came down the stairs with his hands full of odd things—a measuring tape, a scale. Jasper darted to my side. As if there was some signal I'd missed, even Leah sat down outside and stared through the window with an expression like she was expecting something that was both familiar and also totally uninteresting.

"Must be six," Edward said.

"So?" I asked, my eyes locked on Rosalie, Jacob, and Renesmee. They stood in the doorway, Renesmee in Rosalie's arms. Rose looked wary. Jacob looked troubled. Renesmee looked beautiful and impatient.

"Time to measure Ness—er, Renesmee," Carlisle explained.

"Oh. You do this every day?"

"Four times a day," Carlisle corrected absently as he motioned the others toward the couch. I thought I saw Renesmee sigh.

"Four times? Every day? *Why?*"

"She's still growing quickly," Edward murmured to me, his voice quiet and strained. He squeezed my hand, and his other arm wrapped securely around my waist, almost as if he needed the support.

I couldn't take my eyes off Renesmee to check his expression.

She looked perfect, absolutely healthy. Her skin glowed like backlit alabaster; the color in her cheeks was rose petals against it. There couldn't be anything wrong with such radiant beauty. Surely there could be nothing more dangerous in her life than her mother. Could there?

The difference between the child I'd given birth to and the one I'd met again an hour ago would have been obvious to anyone. The difference between Renesmee an hour ago and Renesmee now was subtler. Human eyes never would have detected it. But it was there.

Her body was slightly longer. Just a little bit slimmer. Her face wasn't quite as round; it was more oval by one minute degree. Her ringlets hung a sixteenth of an inch lower down her shoulders. She stretched out helpfully in Rosalie's arms while Carlisle ran the tape measure down the length of her and then used it to circle her head. He took no notes; perfect recall.

I was aware that Jacob's arms were crossed as tightly over his chest as Edward's arms were locked around me. His heavy brows were mashed together into one line over his deep-set eyes.

She had matured from a single cell to a normal-sized baby in the course of a few weeks. She looked well on her way to being a toddler just days after her birth. If this rate of growth held . . .

My vampire mind had no trouble with the math.

"What do we do?" I whispered, horrified.

Edward's arms tightened. He understood exactly what I was asking. "I don't know."

"It's slowing," Jacob muttered through his teeth.

"We'll need several more days of measurements to track the trend, Jacob. I can't make any promises."

"Yesterday she grew two inches. Today it's less."

"By a thirty-second of an inch, if my measurements are perfect," Carlisle said quietly.

"*Be* perfect, Doc," Jacob said, making the words almost threatening. Rosalie stiffened.

"You know I'll do my best," Carlisle assured him.

Jacob sighed. "Guess that's all I can ask."

I felt irritated again, like Jacob was stealing my lines—and delivering them all wrong.

Renesmee seemed irritated, too. She started to squirm and then reached her hand imperiously toward Rosalie. Rosalie leaned forward so that Renesmee could touch her face. After a second, Rose sighed.

"What does she want?" Jacob demanded, taking my line again.

"Bella, of course," Rosalie told him, and her words made my insides feel a little warmer. Then she looked at me. "How are you?"

"Worried," I admitted, and Edward squeezed me.

"We all are. But that's not what I meant."

"I'm in control," I promised. Thirstiness was way down the list right now. Besides, Renesmee smelled good in a very non-food way.

Jacob bit his lip but made no move to stop Rosalie as she offered Renesmee to me. Jasper and Edward hovered but allowed it. I could see how tense Rose was, and I wondered how the room felt to Jasper right now. Or was he focusing so hard on me that he couldn't feel the others?

Renesmee reached for me as I reached for her, a blinding smile lighting her face. She fit so easily in my arms, like they'd been shaped just for her. Immediately, she put her hot little hand against my cheek.

Though I was prepared, it still made me gasp to see the memory like a vision in my head. So bright and colorful but also completely transparent.

She was remembering me charging Jacob across the front lawn, remembering Seth leaping between us. She'd seen and heard it all with perfect clarity. It didn't look like *me*, this graceful predator leaping at her prey like an arrow arcing from a bow. It had to be someone else. That made me feel a very small bit less guilty as Jacob stood there defenselessly with his hands raised in front of him. His hands did not tremble.

Edward chuckled, watching Renesmee's thoughts with me. And then we both winced as we heard the crack of Seth's bones.

Renesmee smiled her brilliant smile, and her memory eyes did not leave Jacob through all the following mess. I tasted a new flavor to the memory—not exactly protective, more possessive—as she watched Jacob. I got the distinct impression that she was *glad* Seth had put himself in front of my spring. She didn't want Jacob hurt. He was *hers*.

"Oh, wonderful," I groaned. "Perfect."

"It's just because he tastes better than the rest of us," Edward assured me, voice stiff with his own annoyance.

"I told you she likes me, too," Jacob teased from across the room, his eyes on Renesmee. His joking was halfhearted; the tense angle of his eyebrows had not relaxed.

Renesmee patted my face impatiently, demanding my attention. Another memory: Rosalie pulling a brush gently through each of her curls. It felt nice.

Carlisle and his tape measure, knowing she had to stretch and be still. It was not interesting to her.

"It looks like she's going to give you a rundown of everything you missed," Edward commented in my ear.

My nose wrinkled as she dumped the next one on me. The smell coming from a strange metal cup—hard enough not to be bitten through easily—sent a flash burn through my throat. Ouch.

And then Renesmee was out of my arms, which were pinned behind my back. I didn't struggle with Jasper; I just looked at Edward's frightened face.

"What did I do?"

Edward looked at Jasper behind me, and then at me again.

"But she was remembering being thirsty," Edward muttered, his forehead pressing into lines. "She was remembering the taste of human blood."

Jasper's arms pulled mine tighter together. Part of my head noted that this wasn't particularly uncomfortable, let alone painful, as it would have been to a human. It was just annoying. I was sure I could break his hold, but I didn't fight it.

"Yes," I agreed. "And?"

Edward frowned at me for a second more, and then his expression loosened. He laughed once. "And nothing at all, it seems. The overreaction is mine this time. Jazz, let her go."

The binding hands disappeared. I reached out for Renesmee as soon as I was free. Edward handed her to me without hesitation.

"I can't understand," Jasper said. "I can't bear this."

I watched in surprise as Jasper strode out the back door. Leah moved to give him a wide margin of space as he paced to the river and then launched himself over it in one bound.

Renesmee touched my neck, repeating the scene of departure right back, like an instant replay. I could feel the question in her thought, an echo of mine.

I was already over the shock of her odd little gift. It seemed an entirely natural part of her, almost to be expected. Maybe now that I was part of the supernatural myself, I would never be a skeptic again.

But what was wrong with Jasper?

"He'll be back," Edward said, whether to me or Renesmee, I wasn't sure. "He just needs a moment alone to readjust his perspective on life." There was a grin threatening at the corners of his mouth.

Another human memory—Edward telling me that Jasper would feel better about himself if I "had a hard time adjusting" to being a vampire. This was in the context of a discussion about how many people I would kill my first newborn year.

"Is he mad at me?" I asked quietly.

Edward's eyes widened. "No. Why would he be?"

"What's the matter with him, then?"

"He's upset with himself, not you, Bella. He's worrying about . . . self-fulfilling prophecy, I suppose you could say."

"How so?" Carlisle asked before I could.

"He's wondering if the newborn madness is really as difficult as we've always thought, or if, with the right focus and attitude, anyone could do as well as Bella. Even now—perhaps he only has such difficulty because he believes it's natural and unavoidable. Maybe if he expected more of himself, he would rise to those expectations. You're making him question a lot of deep-rooted assumptions, Bella."

"But that's unfair," Carlisle said. "Everyone is different; everyone has their own challenges. Perhaps what Bella is doing goes beyond the natural. Maybe this is her gift, so to speak."

I froze with surprise. Renesmee felt the change, and touched me. She remembered the last second of time and wondered why.

"That's an interesting theory, and quite plausible," Edward said.

For a tiny space, I was disappointed. What? No magic visions, no formidable offensive abilities like, oh, shooting lightning bolts from my eyes or something? Nothing helpful or cool at all?

And then I realized what that might mean, if my "superpower" was no more than exceptional self-control.

For one thing, at least I had a gift. It could have been nothing.

But, much more than that, if Edward was right, then I could skip right over the part I'd feared the very most.

What if I didn't have to be a newborn? Not in the crazed killing-machine sense, anyway. What if I could fit right in with the Cullens from my first day? What if we didn't have to hide out somewhere remote for a year while I "grew up"? What if, like Carlisle, I never killed a single person? What if I could be a good vampire right away?

I could see Charlie.

I sighed as soon as reality filtered through hope. I couldn't see Charlie right away. The eyes, the voice, the perfected face. What could I possibly say to him; how could I even begin? I was furtively glad that I had some excuses for putting things off for a while; as much as I wanted to find some way to keep Charlie in my life, I was terrified of that first meeting. Seeing his eyes pop as he took in my new face, my new skin. Knowing that he was frightened. Wondering what dark explanation would form in his head.

I was chicken enough to wait for a year while my eyes cooled. And here I'd thought I would be so fearless when I was indestructible.

"Have you ever seen an equivalent to self-control as a talent?" Edward asked Carlisle. "Do you really think that's a gift, or just a product of all her preparation?"

Carlisle shrugged. "It's slightly similar to what Siobhan has always been able to do, though she wouldn't call it a gift."

"Siobhan, your friend in that Irish coven?" Rosalie asked. "I wasn't aware that she did anything special. I thought it was Maggie who was talented in that bunch."

"Yes, Siobhan thinks the same. But she has this way of deciding her goals and then almost . . . *willing* them into reality. She considers it good planning, but I've always wondered if it was something more. When she included Maggie, for instance. Liam was very territorial, but Siobhan wanted it to work out, and so it did."

Edward, Carlisle, and Rosalie settled into chairs as they continued with the discussion. Jacob sat next to Seth protectively, looking bored. From the way his eyelids drooped, I was sure he'd be unconscious momentarily.

I listened, but my attention was divided. Renesmee was

still telling me about her day. I held her by the window wall, my arms rocking her automatically as we stared into each other's eyes.

I realized that the others had no reason for sitting down. I was perfectly comfortable standing. It was just as restful as stretching out on a bed would be. I knew I would be able to stand like this for a week without moving and I would feel just as relaxed at the end of the seven days as I did at the beginning.

They must sit out of habit. Humans would notice someone standing for hours without ever shifting her weight to a different foot. Even now, I saw Rosalie brush her fingers against her hair and Carlisle cross his legs. Little motions to keep from being too still, too much a vampire. I would have to pay attention to what they did and start practicing.

I rolled my weight back to my left leg. It felt kind of silly.

Maybe they were just trying to give me a little alone time with my baby—as alone as was safe.

Renesmee told me about every minute happening of the day, and I got the feeling from the tenor of her little stories that she wanted me to know her every bit as much I wanted the same thing. It worried her that I had missed things— like the sparrows that had hopped closer and closer when Jacob had held her, both of them very still beside one of the big hemlocks; the birds wouldn't come close to Rosalie. Or the outrageously icky white stuff—baby formula—that Carlisle had put in her cup; it smelled like sour dirt. Or the song Edward had crooned to her that was so perfect Renesmee played it for me twice; I was surprised that I was in the background of that memory, perfectly motionless but looking fairly battered still. I shuddered, remembering that time from my own perspective. The hideous fire . . .

After almost an hour—the others were still deeply absorbed in their discussion, Seth and Jacob snoring in harmony on the couch—Renesmee's memory stories began to slow. They got slightly blurry around the edges and drifted out of focus before they came to their conclusions. I was about to interrupt Edward in a panic—was there something wrong with her?—when her eyelids fluttered and closed. She yawned, her plump pink lips stretching into a round O, and her eyes never reopened.

Her hand fell away from my face as she drifted to sleep—the backs of her eyelids were the pale lavender color of thin clouds before the sunrise. Careful not to disturb her, I lifted that hand back to my skin and held it there curiously. At first there was nothing, and then, after a few minutes, a flickering of colors like a handful of butterflies were scattering from her thoughts.

Mesmerized, I watched her dreams. There was no sense to it. Just colors and shapes and faces. I was pleased by how often my face—both of my faces, hideous human and glorious immortal—cropped up in her unconscious thoughts. More than Edward or Rosalie. I was neck and neck with Jacob; I tried not to let that get to me.

For the first time, I understood how Edward had been able to watch me sleep night after boring night, just to hear me talk in my sleep. I could watch Renesmee dream forever.

The change in Edward's tone caught my attention when he said, "Finally," and turned to gaze out the window. It was deep, purply night outside, but I could see just as far as before. Nothing was hidden in the darkness; everything had just changed colors.

Leah, still glowering, got up and slunk into the brush just as Alice came into view on the other side of the river. Alice swung back and forth from a branch like a trapeze artist, toes touching hands, before throwing her body into a graceful flat spin over the river. Esme made a more traditional leap, while Emmett charged right through the water, splashing water so far that splatters hit the back windows. To my surprise, Jasper followed after, his own efficient leap seeming understated, even subtle, after the others.

The huge grin stretching Alice's face was familiar in a dim, odd way. Everyone was suddenly smiling at me—Esme sweet, Emmett excited, Rosalie a little superior, Carlisle indulgent, and Edward expectant.

Alice skipped into the room ahead of everyone else, her hand stretched out in front of her and impatience making a nearly visible aura around her. In her palm was an everyday brass key with an oversized pink satin bow tied around it.

She held the key out for me, and I automatically gripped Renesmee more securely in my right arm so that I could open my left. Alice dropped the key into it.

"Happy birthday!" she squealed.

I rolled my eyes. "No one starts counting on the actual day of birth," I reminded her. "Your first birthday is at the year mark, Alice."

Her grin turned smug. "We're not celebrating your vampire birthday. Yet. It's September thirteenth, Bella. Happy nineteenth birthday!"

24. SURPRISE

"No. No way!" I shook my head fiercely and then shot a glance at the smug smile on my seventeen-year-old husband's face. "No, this doesn't count. I stopped aging three days ago. I am eighteen forever."

"Whatever," Alice said, dismissing my protest with a quick shrug. "We're celebrating anyway, so suck it up."

I sighed. There was rarely a point to arguing with Alice.

Her grin got impossibly wider as she read the acquiescence in my eyes.

"Are you ready to open your present?" Alice sang.

"Presents," Edward corrected, and he pulled another

key—this one longer and silver with a less gaudy blue bow—from his pocket.

I struggled to keep from rolling my eyes. I knew immediately what this key was to—the "after car." I wondered if I should feel excited. It seemed the vampire conversion hadn't given me any sudden interest in sports cars.

"Mine first," Alice said, and then stuck her tongue out, foreseeing his answer.

"Mine is closer."

"But look at how she's *dressed*." Alice's words were almost a moan. "It's been killing me all day. That is clearly the priority."

My eyebrows pulled together as I wondered how a key could get me into new clothes. Had she gotten me a whole trunkful?

"I know—I'll play you for it," Alice suggested. "Rock, paper, scissors."

Jasper chuckled and Edward sighed.

"Why don't you just tell me who wins?" Edward said wryly.

Alice beamed. "I do. Excellent."

"It's probably better that I wait for morning, anyway." Edward smiled crookedly at me and then nodded toward Jacob and Seth, who looked like they were crashed for the night; I wonder how long they'd stayed up this time. "I think it might be more fun if Jacob was awake for the big reveal, don't you agree? So that someone there is able to express the right level of enthusiasm?"

I grinned back. He knew me well.

"Yay," Alice sang. "Bella, give Ness—Renesmee to Rosalie."

"Where does she usually sleep?"

Alice shrugged. "In Rose's arms. Or Jacob's. Or Esme's. You get the picture. She has never been set down in her entire life. She's going to be the most spoiled half-vampire in existence."

Edward laughed while Rosalie took Renesmee expertly in her arms. "She is also the most *un*spoiled half-vampire in existence," Rosalie said. "The beauty of being one of a kind."

Rosalie grinned at me, and I was glad to see that the new comradeship between us was still there in her smile. I hadn't been entirely sure it would last after Renesmee's life was no longer tied to mine. But maybe we had fought together on the same side long enough that we would always be friends now. I'd finally made the same choice she would have if she'd been in my shoes. That seemed to have washed away her resentment for all my other choices.

Alice shoved the beribboned key in my hand, then grabbed my elbow and steered me toward the back door. "Let's go, let's go," she trilled.

"Is it outside?"

"Sort of," Alice said, pushing me forward.

"Enjoy your gift," Rosalie said. "It's from all of us. Esme especially."

"Aren't you coming, too?" I realized that no one had moved.

"We'll give you a chance to appreciate it alone," Rosalie said. "You can tell us about it . . . later."

Emmett guffawed. Something about his laugh made me feel like blushing, though I wasn't sure why.

I realized that lots of things about me—like truly hating

surprises, and not liking gifts in general much more—had not changed one bit. It was a relief and revelation to discover how much of my essential core traits had come with me into this new body.

I hadn't expected to be myself. I smiled widely.

Alice tugged my elbow, and I couldn't stop smiling as I followed her into the purple night. Only Edward came with us.

"There's the enthusiasm I'm looking for," Alice murmured approvingly. Then she dropped my arm, made two lithe bounds, and leaped over the river.

"C'mon, Bella," she called from the other side.

Edward jumped at the same time I did; it was every bit as fun as it had been this afternoon. Maybe a little bit more fun because the night changed everything into new, rich colors.

Alice took off with us on her heels, heading due north. It was easier to follow the sound of her feet whispering against the ground and the fresh path of her scent than it was to keep my eyes on her through the thick vegetation.

At no sign I could see, she whirled and dashed back to where I paused.

"Don't attack me," she warned, and sprang at me.

"What are you doing?" I demanded, squirming as she scrambled onto my back and wrapped her hands around my face. I felt the urge to throw her off, but I controlled it.

"Making sure you can't see."

"I could take care of that without the theatrics," Edward offered.

"You might let her cheat. Take her hand and lead her forward."

"Alice, I—"

"Don't bother, Bella. We're doing this my way."

I felt Edward's fingers weave through mine. "Just a few seconds more, Bella. Then she'll go annoy someone else." He pulled me forward. I kept up easily. I wasn't afraid of hitting a tree; the tree would be the only one getting hurt in that scenario.

"You might be a little more appreciative," Alice chided him. "This is as much for you as it is for her."

"True. Thank you again, Alice."

"Yeah, yeah. Okay." Alice's voice suddenly shot up with excitement. "Stop there. Turn her just a little to the right. Yes, like that. Okay. Are you ready?" she squeaked.

"I'm ready." There were new scents here, piquing my interest, increasing my curiosity. Scents that didn't belong in the deep woods. Honeysuckle. Smoke. Roses. Sawdust? Something metallic, too. The richness of deep earth, dug up and exposed. I leaned toward the mystery.

Alice hopped down from my back, releasing her grip on my eyes.

I stared into the violet dark. There, nestled into a small clearing in the forest, was a tiny stone cottage, lavender gray in the light of the stars.

It belonged here so absolutely that it seemed as if it must have grown from the rock, a natural formation. Honeysuckle climbed up one wall like a lattice, winding all the way up and over the thick wooden shingles. Late summer roses bloomed in a handkerchief-sized garden under the dark, deep-set windows. There was a little path of flat stones, amethyst in the night, that led up to the quaint arched wooden door.

I curled my hand around the key I held, shocked.

"What do you think?" Alice's voice was soft now; it fit with the perfect quiet of the storybook scene.

I opened my mouth but said nothing.

"Esme thought we might like a place of our own for a while, but she didn't want us too far away," Edward murmured. "And she loves any excuse to renovate. This little place has been crumbling away out here for at least a hundred years."

I continued staring, mouth gaping like a fish.

"Don't you like it?" Alice's face fell. "I mean, I'm sure we could fix it up differently, if you want. Emmett was all for adding a few thousand square feet, a second story, columns, and a tower, but Esme thought you would like it best the way it was meant to look." Her voice started to climb, to go faster. "If she was wrong, we can get back to work. It won't take long to—"

"Shh!" I managed.

She pressed her lips together and waited. It took me a few seconds to recover.

"You're giving me a house for my birthday?" I whispered.

"Us," Edward corrected. "And it's no more than a cottage. I think the word *house* implies more legroom."

"No knocking my house," I whispered to him.

Alice beamed. "You like it."

I shook my head.

"Love it?"

I nodded.

"I can't wait to tell Esme!"

"Why didn't she come?"

Alice's smile faded a little, twisted just off what it had been, like my question was hard to answer. "Oh, you know . . . they all remember how you are about presents. They didn't want to put you under too much pressure to like it."

"But of course I love it. How could I not?"

"They'll like that." She patted my arm. "Anyhoo, your closet is stocked. Use it wisely. And . . . I guess that's every-thing."

"Aren't you going to come inside?"

She strolled casually a few feet back. "Edward knows his way around. I'll stop by . . . later. Call me if you can't match your clothes right." She threw me a doubtful look and then smiled. "Jazz wants to hunt. See you."

She shot off into the trees like the most graceful bullet.

"That was weird," I said when the sound of her flight had vanished completely. "Am I really *that* bad? They didn't have to stay away. Now I feel guilty. I didn't even thank her right. We should go back, tell Esme—"

"Bella, don't be silly. No one thinks you're that un-reasonable."

"Then what—"

"Alone time is their other gift. Alice was trying to be subtle about it."

"Oh."

That was all it took to make the house disappear. We could have been anywhere. I didn't see the trees or the stones or the stars. It was just Edward.

"Let me show you what they've done," he said, pulling

my hand. Was he oblivious to the fact that an electric current was pulsing through my body like adrenaline-spiked blood?

Once again I felt oddly off balance, waiting for reactions my body wasn't capable of anymore. My heart should have been thundering like a steam engine about to hit us. Deafening. My cheeks should have been brilliant red.

For that matter, I ought to have been exhausted. This had been the longest day of my life.

I laughed out loud—just one quiet little laugh of shock—when I realized that this day would never end.

"Do I get to hear the joke?"

"It's not a very good one," I told him as he led the way to the little rounded door. "I was just thinking—today is the first and last day of forever. It's kind of hard to wrap my head around it. Even with all this extra room for wrapping." I laughed again.

He chuckled with me. He held his hand out toward the doorknob, waiting for me to do the honors. I stuck the key in the lock and turned it.

"You're such a natural at this, Bella; I forget how very strange this all must be for you. I wish I could *hear* it." He ducked down and yanked me up into his arms so fast that I didn't see it coming—and that was really something.

"Hey!"

"Thresholds are part of my job description," he reminded me. "But I'm curious. Tell me what you're thinking about right now."

He opened the door—it fell back with a barely audible creak—and stepped through into the little stone living room.

"Everything," I told him. "All at the same time, you know. Good things and things to worry about and things that are new. How I keep using too many superlatives in my head. Right now, I'm thinking that Esme is an artist. It's so perfect!"

The cottage room was something from a fairy tale. The floor was a crazy quilt of smooth, flat stones. The low ceiling had long exposed beams that someone as tall as Jacob would surely knock his head on. The walls were warm wood in some places, stone mosaics in others. The beehive fireplace in the corner held the remains of a slow flickering fire. It was driftwood burning there—the low flames were blue and green from the salt.

It was furnished in eclectic pieces, not one of them matching another, but harmonious just the same. One chair seemed vaguely medieval, while a low ottoman by the fire was more contemporary and the stocked book-shelf against the far window reminded me of movies set in Italy. Somehow each piece fit together with the others like a big three-dimensional puzzle. There were a few paintings on the walls that I recognized—some of my very favorites from the big house. Priceless originals, no doubt, but they seemed to belong here, too, like all the rest.

It was a place where anyone could believe magic existed. A place where you just expected Snow White to walk right in with her apple in hand, or a unicorn to stop and nibble at the rosebushes.

Edward had always thought that he belonged to the world of horror stories. Of course, I'd known he was dead wrong. It was obvious that he belonged *here*. In a fairy tale.

And now I was in the story with him.

I was about to take advantage of the fact that he hadn't gotten around to setting me back on my feet and that his wits-scramblingly beautiful face was only inches away when he said, "We're lucky Esme thought to add an extra room. No one was planning for Ness—Renesmee."

I frowned at him, my thoughts channeled down a less pleasant path.

"Not you, too," I complained.

"Sorry, love. I hear it in their thoughts all the time, you know. It's rubbing off on me."

I sighed. My baby, the sea serpent. Maybe there was no help for it. Well, *I* wasn't giving in.

"I'm sure you're dying to see the closet. Or, at least I'll *tell* Alice that you were, to make her feel good."

"Should I be afraid?"

"Terrified."

He carried me down a narrow stone hallway with tiny arches in the ceiling, like it was our own miniature castle.

"That will be Renesmee's room," he said, nodding to an empty room with a pale wooden floor. "They didn't have time to do much with it, what with the angry were-wolves. . . ."

I laughed quietly, amazed at how quickly everything had turned right when it had all had looked so nightmarish just a week ago.

Drat Jacob for making everything perfect *this* way.

"Here's our room. Esme tried to bring some of her island back here for us. She guessed that we would get attached."

The bed was huge and white, with clouds of gossamer floating down from the canopy to the floor. The pale wood floor matched the other room, and now I grasped that it was precisely the color of a pristine beach. The walls were that almost-white-blue of a brilliant sunny day, and the back wall had big glass doors that opened into a little hidden garden. Climbing roses and a small round pond, smooth as a mirror and edged with shiny stones. A tiny, calm ocean for us.

"Oh" was all I could say.

"I know," he whispered.

We stood there for a minute, remembering. Though the memories were human and clouded, they took over my mind completely.

He smiled a wide, gleaming smile and then laughed. "The closet is through those double doors. I should warn you—it's bigger than this room."

I didn't even glance at the doors. There was nothing else in the world but him again—his arms curled under me, his sweet breath on my face, his lips just inches from mine—and there was nothing that could distract me now, newborn vampire or not.

"We're going to tell Alice that I ran right to the clothes," I whispered, twisting my fingers into his hair and pulling my face closer to his. "We're going to tell her I spent hours in there playing dress-up. We're going to *lie*."

He caught up to my mood in an instant, or maybe he'd already been there, and he was just trying to let me fully appreciate my birthday present, like a gentleman. He pulled my face to his with a sudden fierceness, a low moan in his throat. The sound sent the electric current running through my body into a near-frenzy, like I couldn't get close enough to him fast enough.

I heard the fabric tearing under our hands, and I was glad *my* clothes, at least, were already destroyed. It was too late for his. It felt almost rude to ignore the pretty white bed, but we just weren't going to make it that far.

This second honeymoon wasn't like our first.

Our time on the island had been the epitome of my human life. The very best of it. I'd been so ready to string along my human time, just to hold on to what I had with him for a little while longer. Because the physical part wasn't going to be the same ever again.

I should have guessed, after a day like today, that it would be better.

I could really appreciate him now—could properly see every beautiful line of his perfect face, of his long, flawless body with my strong new eyes, every angle and every plane of him. I could taste his pure, vivid scent on my tongue and feel the unbelievable silkiness of his marble skin under my sensitive fingertips.

My skin was so sensitive under his hands, too.

He was all new, a different person as our bodies tangled gracefully into one on the sand-pale floor. No caution, no restraint. No fear—especially not that. We could love *together*—both active participants now. Finally equals.

Like our kisses before, every touch was more than I was used to. So much of himself he'd been holding back. Necessary at the time, but I couldn't believe how much I'd been missing.

I tried to keep in mind that I was stronger than he was, but it was hard to focus on anything with sensations so intense, pulling my attention to a million different places in my body every second; if I hurt him, he didn't complain.

A very, very small part of my head considered the interesting conundrum presented in this situation. I was never going to get tired, and neither was he. We didn't have to catch our breath or rest or eat or even use the bathroom; we had no more mundane human needs. He had the most beautiful, perfect body in the world and I had him all to myself, and it didn't feel like I was ever going to find a point where I would think, *Now I've had enough for one day.* I was always going to want more. And the day was never going to end. So, in such a situation, how did we ever *stop?*

It didn't bother me at all that I had no answer.

I sort of noticed when the sky began to lighten. The tiny ocean outside turned from black to gray, and a lark started to sing somewhere very close by—maybe she had a nest in the roses.

"Do you miss it?" I asked him when her song was done.

It wasn't the first time we'd spoken, but we weren't exactly keeping up a conversation, either.

"Miss what?" he murmured.

"All of it—the warmth, the soft skin, the tasty smell . . . I'm not losing anything at all, and I just wondered if it was a little bit sad for you that you were."

He laughed, low and gentle. "It would be hard to find someone *less* sad than I am now. Impossible, I'd venture. Not many people get every single thing they want, plus all the things they didn't think to ask for, in the same day."

"Are you avoiding the question?"

He pressed his hand against my face. "You *are* warm," he told me.

It was true, in a sense. To me, his hand was warm. It wasn't the same as touching Jacob's flame-hot skin, but it was more comfortable. More natural.

Then he pulled his fingers very slowly down my face, lightly tracing from my jaw to my throat and then all the way down to my waist. My eyes rolled back into my head a little.

"You *are* soft."

His fingers were like satin against my skin, so I could see what he meant.

"And as for the scent, well, I couldn't say I *missed* that. Do you remember the scent of those hikers on our hunt?"

"I've been trying very hard not to."

"Imagine kissing that."

My throat ripped into flames like pulling the cord on a hot-air balloon.

"Oh."

"Precisely. So the answer is no. I am purely full of joy, because I am missing *nothing*. No one has more than I do now."

I was about to inform him of the one exception to his statement, but my lips were suddenly very busy.

When the little pool turned pearl-colored with the sunrise, I thought of another question for him.

"How long does this go on? I mean, Carlisle and Esme, Em and Rose, Alice and Jasper—they don't spend all day locked in their rooms. They're out in public, fully clothed, all the time. Does this . . . *craving* ever let up?" I twisted myself closer into him—quite an accomplishment, actually—to make it clear what I was talking about.

"That's difficult to say. Everyone is different and, well, so far you're the very most different of all. The average young vampire is too obsessed with thirst to notice much else for a while. That doesn't seem to apply to you. With the average vampire, though, after that first year, other needs make themselves known. Neither thirst nor any other desire really ever *fades*. It's simply a matter of learning to balance them, learning to prioritize and manage. . . ."

"How long?"

He smiled, wrinkling his nose a little. "Rosalie and Emmett were the worst. It took a solid decade before I could stand to be within a five-mile radius of them. Even Carlisle and Esme had a difficult time stomaching it. They kicked the happy couple out eventually. Esme built them a house, too. It was grander than this one, but then, Esme knows what Rose likes, and she knows what you like."

"So, after ten years, then?" I was pretty sure that Rosalie and Emmett had nothing on us, but it might sound cocky if I went higher than a decade. "Everybody is normal again? Like they are now?"

Edward smiled again. "Well, I'm not sure what you mean by normal. You've seen my family going about life in a fairly human way, but you've been sleeping nights." He winked at me. "There's a tremendous amount of time left over when you don't have to sleep. It makes balancing your . . . interests quite easy. There's a reason why I'm the best musician in the family, why—besides Carlisle—I've read the most books, studied the most sciences, become fluent in the most languages. . . . Emmett would have you believe that I'm such a know-it-all because of the mind reading, but the truth is that I've just had a *lot* of free time."

We laughed together, and the motion of our laughter did interesting things to the way our bodies were connected, effectively ending that conversation.

25. FAVOR

It was only a little while later that Edward reminded me of my priorities.

It took him just one word.

"Renesmee . . ."

I sighed. She would be awake soon. It must be nearly seven in the morning. Would she be looking for me? Abruptly, something close to panic had my body freezing up. What would she look like today?

Edward felt the total distraction of my stress. "It's all right, love. Get dressed, and we'll be back to the house in two seconds."

I probably looked like a cartoon, the way I sprung up, then looked back at him—his diamond body faintly glinting in the diffuse light—then away to the west, where Renesmee waited, then back at him again, then back toward her, my head whipping from side to side a half dozen times in a second. Edward smiled, but didn't laugh; he was a strong man.

"It's all about balance, love. You're so good at all of this, I don't imagine it will take too long to put everything in perspective."

"And we have all night, right?"

He smiled wider. "Do you think I could bear to let you get dressed now if that weren't the case?"

That would have to be enough to get me through the daylight hours. I would balance this overwhelming, devastating desire so that I could be a good— It was hard to think the word. Though Renesmee was very real and vital in my life, it was still difficult to think of myself as a *mother.* I supposed anyone would feel the same, though, without nine months to get used to the idea. And with a child that changed by the hour.

The thought of Renesmee's speeding life had me stressed-out again in an instant. I didn't even pause at the ornately carved double doors to catch my breath before finding out what Alice had done. I just burst through, intent on wearing the first things I touched. I should have known it wouldn't be that easy.

"Which ones are mine?" I hissed. As promised, the room was bigger than our bedroom. It might have been bigger than the rest of the house put together, but I'd have to pace it off to be positive. I had a brief mental flash of Alice trying to persuade Esme to ignore classic proportions and allow this monstrosity. I wondered how Alice had won that one.

Everything was wrapped in garment bags, pristine and white, row after row after row.

"To the best of my knowledge, everything but this rack here"—he touched a bar that stretched along the half-wall to the left of the door—"is yours."

"All of this?"

He shrugged.

"Alice," we said together. He said her name like an explanation; I said it like an expletive.

"Fine," I muttered, and I pulled down the zipper on the closest bag. I growled under my breath when I saw the floor-length silk gown inside—baby pink.

Finding something normal to wear could take all day!

"Let me help," Edward offered. He sniffed carefully at the air and then followed some scent to the back of the long room. There was a built-in dresser there. He sniffed again, then opened a drawer. With a triumphant grin, he held out a pair of artfully faded blue jeans.

I flitted to his side. "How did you do that?"

"Denim has its own scent just like anything else. Now . . . stretch cotton?"

He followed his nose to a half-rack, unearthing a long-sleeved white t-shirt. He tossed it to me.

"Thanks," I said fervently. I inhaled each fabric, memorizing the scent for future searches through this madhouse. I remembered silk and satin; I would avoid those.

It only took him seconds to find his own clothes—if I hadn't seen him undressed, I would have sworn there was nothing more beautiful than Edward in his khakis and pale beige pullover—and then he took my hand. We darted through the hidden garden, leaped lightly over the stone wall, and hit the forest at a dead sprint. I pulled my hand free so that we could race back. He beat me this time.

Renesmee was awake; she was sitting up on the floor with Rose and Emmett hovering over her, playing with a little pile of twisted silverware. She had a mangled spoon in her right hand. As soon as she spied me through the glass, she chucked the spoon on the floor—where it left a divot in the wood—and pointed in my direction imperiously. Her audience laughed; Alice, Jasper, Esme, and Carlisle were sitting on the couch, watching her as if she were the most engrossing film.

I was through the door before their laughter had barely begun, bounding across the room and scooping her up from the floor in the same second. We smiled widely at each other.

She was different, but not so much. A little longer again, her proportions drifting from babyish to childlike. Her hair was longer by a quarter inch, the curls bouncing like springs with every movement. I'd let my imagination run wild on the trip back, and I'd imagined worse than this. Thanks to my overdone fears, these little changes were almost a relief. Even without Carlisle's measurements, I was sure the changes were slower than yesterday.

Renesmee patted my cheek. I winced. She was hungry again.

"How long has she been up?" I asked as Edward disappeared through the kitchen doorway. I was sure he was on his way to get her breakfast, having seen what she'd just thought as clearly as I had. I wondered if he would ever have noticed her little quirk, if he'd been the only one to know her. To him, it probably would have seemed like hearing anyone.

"Just a few minutes," Rose said. "We would have called you soon. She's been asking for you—*demanding* might be a better description. Esme sacrificed her second-best silver service to keep the little monster entertained." Rose smiled at Renesmee with so much gloating affection that the criticism was entirely weightless. "We didn't want to . . . er, bother you."

Rosalie bit her lip and looked away, trying not to laugh. I could feel Emmett's silent laughter behind me, sending vibrations through the foundations of the house.

I kept my chin high. "We'll get your room set up right away," I said to Renesmee. "You'll like the cottage. It's magic." I look up at Esme. "Thank you, Esme. So much. It's absolutely perfect."

Before Esme could respond, Emmett was laughing again—it wasn't silent this time.

"So it's still standing?" he managed to get out between his snickers. "I would've thought you two had knocked it to rubble by now. What were you doing last night? Discussing the national debt?" He howled with laughter.

I gritted my teeth and reminded myself of the negative consequences when I'd let my temper get away from me yesterday. Of course, Emmett wasn't as breakable as Seth. . . .

Thinking of Seth made me wonder. "Where're the wolves today?" I glanced out the window wall, but there had been no sign of Leah on the way in.

"Jacob took off this morning pretty early," Rosalie told

me, a little frown creasing her forehead. "Seth followed him out."

"What was he so upset about?" Edward asked as he came back into the room with Renesmee's cup. There must have been more in Rosalie's memory than I'd seen in her expression.

Without breathing, I handed Renesmee off to Rosalie. Super-self-control, maybe, but there was no way I was going to be able to feed her. Not yet.

"I don't know—or care," Rosalie grumbled, but she answered Edward's question more fully. "He was watching Nessie sleep, his mouth hanging open like the moron he is, and then he just jumped to his feet without any kind of trigger—that I noticed, anyway—and stormed out. *I* was glad to be rid of him. The more time he spends here, the less chance there is that we'll ever get the smell out."

"Rose," Esme chided gently.

Rosalie flipped her hair. "I suppose it doesn't matter. We won't be here that much longer."

"I still say we should go straight to New Hampshire and get things set up," Emmett said, obviously continuing an earlier conversation. "Bella's already registered at Dartmouth. Doesn't look like it will take her all that long to be able to handle school." He turned to look at me with a teasing grin. "I'm sure you'll ace your classes . . . apparently there's nothing interesting for you to do at night besides study."

Rosalie giggled.

Do not lose your temper, do not lose your temper, I chanted to myself. And then I was proud of myself for keeping my head.

So I was pretty surprised that Edward didn't.

He growled—an abrupt, shocking rasp of sound—and the blackest fury rolled across his expression like storm clouds.

Before any of us could respond, Alice was on her feet.

"What is he *doing*? What is that *dog* doing that has erased my schedule for the entire day? I can't see *anything*! No!" She shot me a tortured glance. "Look at you! You *need* me to show you how to use your closet."

For one second I was grateful for whatever Jacob was up to.

And then Edward's hands balled up into fists and he snarled, "He talked to Charlie. He thinks Charlie is following after him. Coming here. Today."

Alice said a word that sounded very odd in her trilling, ladylike voice, and then she blurred into motion, streaking out the back door.

"He told Charlie?" I gasped. "But—doesn't he understand? How could he do that?" Charlie *couldn't* know about me! About vampires! That would put him on a hit list that even the Cullens couldn't save him from. "No!"

Edward spoke through his teeth. "Jacob's on his way in now."

It must have started raining farther east. Jacob came through the door shaking his wet hair like a dog, flipping droplets on the carpet and the couch where they made little round gray spots on the white. His teeth glinted against his dark lips; his eyes were bright and excited. He walked with jerky movements, like he was all hyped-up about destroying my father's life.

"Hey, guys," he greeted us, grinning.

It was perfectly silent.

Leah and Seth slipped in behind him, in their human forms—for now; both of their hands were trembling with the tension in the room.

"Rose," I said, holding my arms out. Wordlessly, Rosalie handed me Renesmee. I pressed her close to my motionless heart, holding her like a talisman against rash behavior. I would keep her in my arms until I was sure my decision to kill Jacob was based entirely on rational judgment rather than fury.

She was very still, watching and listening. How much did she understand?

"Charlie'll be here soon," Jacob said to me casually. "Just a heads-up. I assume Alice is getting you sunglasses or something?"

"You assume *way* too much," I spit through my teeth. "What. Have. You. *Done?*"

Jacob's smile wavered, but he was still too wound up to answer seriously. "Blondie and Emmett woke me up this morning going on and on about you all moving cross-country. Like I could let you leave. Charlie was the biggest issue there, right? Well, problem solved."

"Do you even *realize* what you've done? The danger you've put him in?"

He snorted. "I didn't put him in danger. Except from you. But you've got some kind of supernatural self-control, right? Not as good as mind reading, if you ask me. Much less exciting."

Edward moved then, darting across the room to get in

Jacob's face. Though he was half a head shorter than Jacob, Jacob leaned away from his staggering anger as if Edward towered over him.

"That's just a *theory*, mongrel," he snarled. "You think we should test it out on *Charlie*? Did you consider the physical pain you're putting Bella through, even if she can resist? Or the emotional pain if she doesn't? I suppose what happens to Bella no longer concerns you!" He spit the last word.

Renesmee pressed her fingers anxiously to my cheek, anxiety coloring the replay in her head.

Edward's words finally cut through Jacob's strangely electric mood. His mouth dropped into a frown. "Bella will be in pain?"

"Like you've shoved a white-hot branding iron down her throat!"

I flinched, remembering the scent of pure human blood.

"I didn't know that," Jacob whispered.

"Then perhaps you should have asked first," Edward growled back through his teeth.

"You would have stopped me."

"You *should* have been stopped—"

"This isn't about me," I interrupted. I stood very still, keeping my hold on Renesmee and sanity. "This is about Charlie, Jacob. How could you put him in danger this way? Do you realize it's death or vampire life for him now, too?" My voice trembled with the tears my eyes could no longer shed.

Jacob was still troubled by Edward's accusations, but mine didn't seem to bother him. "Relax, Bella. I didn't tell him anything you weren't planning to tell him."

"But he's coming here!"

"Yeah, that's the idea. Wasn't the whole 'let him make the wrong assumptions' thing your plan? I think I provided a very nice red herring, if I do say so myself."

My fingers flexed away from Renesmee. I curled them back in securely. "Say it straight, Jacob. I don't have the patience for this."

"I didn't tell him anything about you, Bella. Not really. I told him about *me*. Well, *show* is probably a better verb."

"He phased in front of Charlie," Edward hissed.

I whispered, "You *what?*"

"He's brave. Brave as you are. Didn't pass out or throw up or anything. I gotta say, I was impressed. You should've seen his face when I started taking my clothes off, though. Priceless," Jacob chortled.

"You absolute *moron*! You could have given him a heart attack!"

"Charlie's fine. He's tough. If you'd give this just a minute, you'll see that I did you a favor here."

"You have half of that, Jacob." My voice was flat and steely. "You have thirty seconds to tell me every single word before I give Renesmee to Rosalie and rip your miserable head off. Seth won't be able to stop me this time."

"Jeez, Bells. You didn't used to be so melodramatic. Is that a vampire thing?"

"Twenty-six seconds."

Jacob rolled his eyes and flopped into the nearest chair. His little pack moved to stand on his flanks, not at all relaxed the way he seemed to be; Leah's eyes were on me, her teeth slightly bared.

"So I knocked on Charlie's door this morning and asked

him to come for a walk with me. He was confused, but when I told him it was about you and that you were back in town, he followed me out to the woods. I told him you weren't sick anymore, and that things were a little weird, but good. He was about to take off to see you, but I told him I had to show him something first. And then I phased." Jacob shrugged.

My teeth felt like a vise was pushing them together. "I want every word, you monster."

"Well, you said I only had thirty seconds—okay, okay." My expression must have convinced him that I wasn't in the mood for teasing. "Lemme see . . . I phased back and got dressed, and then after he started breathing again, I said something like, 'Charlie, you don't live in the world you thought you lived in. The good news is, nothing has changed—except that now you know. Life'll go on the same way it always has. You can go right back to pretending that you don't believe any of this.'

"It took him a minute to get his head together, and then he wanted to know what was really going on with you, with the whole rare-disease thing. I told him that you *had* been sick, but you were fine now—it was just that you'd had to change a little bit in the process of getting better. He wanted to know what I meant by 'change,' and I told him that you looked a lot more like Esme now than you looked like Renée."

Edward hissed while I stared in horror; this was headed in a dangerous direction.

"After a few minutes, he asked, real quietly, if you turned into an animal, too. And I said, 'She wishes she was that cool!'" Jacob chuckled.

Rosalie made a noise of disgust.

"I started to tell him more about werewolves, but I didn't even get the whole word out—Charlie cut me off and said he'd 'rather not know the specifics.' Then he asked if you'd known what you were getting yourself into when you married Edward, and I said, 'Sure, she's known all about this for years, since she first came to Forks.' He didn't like *that* very much. I let him rant till he got it out of his system. After he got calmed down, he just wanted two things. He wanted to see you, and I said it would be better if he gave me a head start to explain."

I inhaled deeply. "What was the other thing he wanted?"

Jacob smiled. "You'll like this. His main request is that he be told as little as possible about *all* of this. If it's not absolutely essential for him to know something, then keep it to yourself. Need to know, only."

I felt relief for the first time since Jacob had walked in. "I can handle that part."

"Other than that, he'd just like to pretend things are normal." Jacob's smile turned smug; he must suspect that I would be starting to feel the first faint stirrings of gratitude about now.

"What did you tell him about Renesmee?" I struggled to maintain the razor edge in my voice, fighting the reluctant appreciation. It was premature. There was still so much wrong with this situation. Even if Jacob's intervention had brought out a better reaction in Charlie than I'd ever hoped for . . .

"Oh yeah. So I told him that you and Edward had inherited a new little mouth to feed." He glanced at Edward.

"She's your orphaned ward—like Bruce Wayne and Dick Grayson." Jacob snorted. "I didn't think you'd mind me lying. That's all part of the game, right?" Edward didn't respond in any way, so Jacob went on. "Charlie was way past being shocked at this point, but he did ask if you were adopting her. 'Like a daughter? Like I'm sort of a grandfather?' were his exact words. I told him yes. 'Congrats, Gramps,' and all of that. He even smiled a little."

The stinging returned to my eyes, but not out of fear or anguish this time. Charlie was smiling at the idea of being a grandpa? Charlie would meet Renesmee?

"But she's changing so fast," I whispered.

"I told him that she was more special than all of us put together," Jacob said in a soft voice. He stood and walked right up to me, waving Leah and Seth off when they started to follow. Renesmee reached out to him, but I hugged her more tightly to me. "I told him, 'Trust me, you don't want to know about this. But if you can ignore all the strange parts, you're going to be amazed. She's the most wonderful person in the whole world.' And then I told him that if he could deal with that, you all would stick around for a while and he would have a chance to get to know her. But that if it was too much for him, you would leave. He said as long as no one forced too much information on him, he'd deal."

Jacob stared at me with half a smile, waiting.

"I'm not going to say thank you," I told him. "You're still putting Charlie at a huge risk."

"I *am* sorry about it hurting you. I didn't know it was like that. Bella, things are different with us now, but you'll always be my best friend, and I'll always love you. But I'll love you the right way now. There's finally a balance. We *both* have people we can't live without."

He smiled his very most Jacob-y smile. "Still friends?"

Try as hard as I could to resist, I had to smile back. Just a tiny smile.

He held out his hand: an offer.

I took a deep breath and shifted Renesmee's weight to one arm. I put my left hand in his—he didn't even flinch at the feel of my cool skin. "If I don't kill Charlie tonight, I'll consider forgiving you for this."

"*When* you don't kill Charlie tonight, you'll owe me huge."

I rolled my eyes.

He held out his other hand toward Renesmee, a request this time. "Can I?"

"I'm actually holding her so that my hands aren't free to kill you, Jacob. Maybe later."

He sighed but didn't push me on it. Wise of him.

Alice raced back through the door then, her hands full and her expression promising violence.

"You, you, and you," she snapped, glaring at the were-wolves. "If you must stay, get over in the corner and commit to being there for a while. I need to *see*. Bella, you'd better give him the baby, too. You'll need your arms free, any-way."

Jacob grinned in triumph.

Undiluted fear ripped through my stomach as the enormity of what I was about to do hit me. I was going to gamble on my iffy self-control with my pure human father as the guinea pig. Edward's earlier words crashed in my ears again.

*Did you consider the physical pain you're putting Bella through,
even if she can resist? Or the emotional pain if she doesn't?*

I couldn't imagine the pain of failure. My breathing
turned to gasps.

"Take her," I whispered, sliding Renesmee into Jacob's
arms.

He nodded, concern wrinkling his forehead. He gestured
to the others, and they all went to the far corner of the room.
Seth and Jake slouched on the floor at once, but Leah shook
her head and pursed her lips.

"Am I allowed to leave?" she griped. She looked uncomfortable in her human body, wearing the same dirty t-shirt
and cotton shorts she'd worn to shriek at me the other day,
her short hair sticking up in irregular tufts. Her hands were
still shaking.

"Of course," Jake said.

"Stay east so you don't cross Charlie's path," Alice
added.

Leah didn't look at Alice; she ducked out the back door
and stomped into the bushes to phase.

Edward was back at my side, stroking my face. "You can
do this. I know you can. I'll help you; we all will."

I met Edward's eyes with panic screaming from my face.
Was he strong enough to stop me if I made a wrong move?

"If I didn't believe you could handle it, we'd disappear
today. This very minute. But you can. And you'll be happier
if you can have Charlie in your life."

I tried to slow my breathing.

Alice held out her hand. There was a small white box on
her palm. "These will irritate your eyes—they won't hurt,
but they'll cloud your vision. It's annoying. They also won't

match your old color, but it's still better than bright red, right?"

She flipped the contact box into the air and I caught it.

"When did you—"

"Before you left on the honeymoon. I was prepared for several possible futures."

I nodded and opened the container. I'd never worn contacts before, but it couldn't be that hard. I took the little brown quarter-sphere and pressed it, concave side in, to my eye.

I blinked, and a film interrupted my sight. I could see through it, of course, but I could also see the texture of the thin screen. My eye kept focusing on the microscopic scratches and warped sections.

"I see what you mean," I murmured as I stuck the other one in. I tried to not blink this time. My eye automatically wanted to dislodge the obstruction.

"How do I look?"

Edward smiled. "Gorgeous. Of course—"

"Yes, yes, she always looks gorgeous," Alice finished his thought impatiently. "It's better than red, but that's the highest commendation I can give. Muddy brown. Your brown was much prettier. Keep in mind that those won't last forever—the venom in your eyes will dissolve them in a few hours. So if Charlie stays longer than that, you'll have to excuse yourself to replace them. Which is a good idea anyway, because humans need bathroom breaks." She shook her head. "Esme, give her a few pointers on acting human while I stock the powder room with contacts."

"How long do I have?"

"Charlie will be here in five minutes. Keep it simple."

Esme nodded once and came to take my hand. "The main thing is not to sit too still or move too fast," she told me.

"Sit down if he does," Emmett interjected. "Humans don't like to just stand there."

"Let your eyes wander every thirty seconds or so," Jasper added. "Humans don't stare at one thing for too long."

"Cross your legs for about five minutes, then switch to crossing your ankles for the next five," Rosalie said.

I nodded once at each suggestion. I'd noticed them doing some of these things yesterday. I thought I could mimic their actions.

"And blink at least three times a minute," Emmett said. He frowned, then darted to where the television remote sat on the end table. He flipped the TV on to a college football game and nodded to himself.

"Move your hands, too. Brush your hair back or pretend to scratch something," Jasper said.

"I said *Esme*," Alice complained as she returned. "You'll overwhelm her."

"No, I think I got it all," I said. "Sit, look around, blink, fidget."

"Right," Esme approved. She hugged my shoulders.

Jasper frowned. "You'll be holding your breath as much as possible, but you need to move your shoulders a little to make it *look* like you're breathing."

I inhaled once and then nodded again.

Edward hugged me on my free side. "You can do this," he repeated, murmuring the encouragement in my ear.

"Two minutes," Alice said. "Maybe you should start out

already on the couch. You've been sick, after all. That way he won't have to see you move right at first."

Alice pulled me to the sofa. I tried to move slowly, to make my limbs more clumsy. She rolled her eyes, so I must not have been doing a good job.

"Jacob, I need Renesmee," I said.

Jacob frowned, unmoving.

Alice shook her head. "Bella, that doesn't help me see."

"But I *need* her. She keeps me calm." The edge of panic in my voice was unmistakable.

"Fine," Alice groaned. "Hold her as still as you can and I'll *try* to see around her." She sighed wearily, like she'd been asked to work overtime on a holiday. Jacob sighed, too, but brought Renesmee to me, and then retreated quickly from Alice's glare.

Edward took a seat beside me and put his arms around Renesmee and me. He leaned forward and looked Renesmee very seriously in the eyes.

"Renesmee, someone special is coming to see you and your mother," he said in a solemn voice, as if he expected her to understand every word. Did she? She looked back at him with clear, grave eyes. "But he's not like us, or even like Jacob. We have to be very careful with him. You shouldn't tell him things the way you tell us."

Renesmee touched his face.

"Exactly," he said. "And he's going to make you thirsty. But you mustn't bite him. He won't heal like Jacob."

"Can she understand you?" I whispered.

"She understands. You'll be careful, won't you, Renesmee? You'll help us?"

Renesmee touched him again.

"No, I don't care if you bite Jacob. That's fine."

Jacob chuckled.

"Maybe you should leave, Jacob," Edward said coldly, glaring in his direction. Edward hadn't forgiven Jacob, because he knew that no matter what happened now, I was going to be hurting. But I'd take the burn happily if that were the worst thing I'd face tonight.

"I told Charlie I'd be here," Jacob said. "He needs the moral support."

"Moral support," Edward scoffed. "As far as Charlie knows, you're the most repulsive monster of us all."

"Repulsive?" Jake protested, and then he laughed quietly to himself.

I heard the tires turn off the highway onto the quiet, damp earth of the Cullens' drive, and my breathing spiked again. My heart ought to have been hammering. It made me anxious that my body didn't have the right reactions.

I concentrated on the steady thrumming of Renesmee's heart to calm myself. It worked pretty quickly.

"Well done, Bella," Jasper whispered in approval.

Edward tightened his arm over my shoulders.

"You're sure?" I asked him.

"Positive. You can do *anything*." He smiled and kissed me.

It wasn't precisely a peck on the lips, and my wild vampiric reactions took me off guard yet again. Edward's lips were like a shot of some addictive chemical straight into my nervous system. I was instantly craving more. It took all my concentration to remember the baby in my arms.

Jasper felt my mood change. "Er, Edward, you might

not want to distract her like that right now. She needs to be able to focus."

Edward pulled away. "Oops," he said.

I laughed. That had been *my* line from the very beginning, from the very first kiss.

"Later," I said, and anticipation curled my stomach into a ball.

"Focus, Bella," Jasper urged.

"Right." I pushed the trembly feelings away. Charlie, that was the main thing now. Keep Charlie safe today. We would have all night. . . .

"Bella."

"Sorry, Jasper."

Emmett laughed.

The sound of Charlie's cruiser got closer and closer. The second of levity passed, and everyone was still. I crossed my legs and practiced my blinks.

The car pulled in front of the house and idled for a few seconds. I wondered if Charlie was as nervous as I was. Then the engine cut off, and a door slammed. Three steps across the grass, and then eight echoing thuds against the wooden stairs. Four more echoing footsteps across the porch. Then silence. Charlie took two deep breaths.

Knock, knock, knock.

I inhaled for what might be the last time. Renesmee nestled deeper into my arms, hiding her face in my hair.

Carlisle answered the door. His stressed expression changed to one of welcome, like switching the channel on the TV.

"Hello, Charlie," he said, looking appropriately abashed.

After all, we were supposed to be in Atlanta at the Center for Disease Control. Charlie knew he'd been lied to.

"Carlisle," Charlie greeted him stiffly. "Where's Bella?"

"Right here, Dad."

Ugh! My voice was so wrong. Plus, I'd used up some of my air supply. I gulped in a quick refill, glad that Charlie's scent had not saturated the room yet.

Charlie's blank expression told me how off my voice was. His eyes zeroed in on me and widened.

I read the emotions as they scrolled across his face.

Shock. Disbelief. Pain. Loss. Fear. Anger. Suspicion. More pain.

I bit my lip. It felt funny. My new teeth were sharper against my granite skin than my human teeth had been against my soft human lips.

"Is that you, Bella?" he whispered.

"Yep." I winced at my wind-chime voice. "Hi, Dad."

He took a deep breath to steady himself.

"Hey, Charlie," Jacob greeted him from the corner. "How're things?"

Charlie glowered at Jacob once, shuddered at a memory, and then stared at me again.

Slowly, Charlie walked across the room until he was a few feet away from me. He darted an accusing glare at Edward, and then his eyes flickered back to me. The warmth of his body heat beat against me with each pulse of his heart.

"Bella?" he asked again.

I spoke in a lower voice, trying to keep the ring out of it. "It's really me."

His jaw locked.

"I'm sorry, Dad," I said.

"Are you okay?" he demanded.

"Really and truly great," I promised. "Healthy as a horse."

That was it for my oxygen.

"Jake told me this was . . . necessary. That you were dying." He said the words like he didn't believe them one bit.

I steeled myself, focused on Renesmee's warm weight, leaned into Edward for support, and took a deep breath.

Charlie's scent was a fistful of flames, punching straight down my throat. But it was so much more than pain. It was a hot stabbing of desire, too. Charlie smelled more delicious than anything I'd ever imagined. As appealing as the anonymous hikers had been on the hunt, Charlie was doubly tempting. And he was just a few feet away, leaking mouthwatering heat and moisture into the dry air.

But I wasn't hunting now. And this was my father.

Edward squeezed my shoulders sympathetically, and Jacob shot an apologetic glance at me across the room.

I tried to collect myself and ignore the pain and longing of the thirst. Charlie was waiting for my answer.

"Jacob was telling you the truth."

"That makes one of you," Charlie growled.

I hoped Charlie could see past the changes in my new face to read the remorse there.

Under my hair, Renesmee sniffed as Charlie's scent registered with her, too. I tightened my grip on her.

Charlie saw my anxious glance down and followed it. "Oh," he said, and all the anger fell off his face, leaving only shock behind. "This is her. The orphan Jacob said you're adopting."

"My niece," Edward lied smoothly. He must have decided

that the resemblance between Renesmee and him was too pronounced to be ignored. Best to claim they were related from the beginning.

"I thought you'd lost your family," Charlie said, accusation returning to his voice.

"I lost my parents. My older brother was adopted, like me. I never saw him after that. But the courts located me when he and his wife died in a car accident, leaving their only child without any other family."

Edward was so good at this. His voice was even, with just the right amount of innocence. I needed practice so that I could do that.

Renesmee peeked out from under my hair, sniffing again. She glanced shyly at Charlie from under her long lashes, then hid again.

"She's . . . she's, well, she's a beauty."

"Yes," Edward agreed.

"Kind of a big responsibility, though. You two are just getting started."

"What else could we do?" Edward brushed his fingers lightly over her cheek. I saw him touch her lips for just a moment—a reminder. "Would you have refused her?"

"Hmph. Well." He shook his head absently. "Jake says you call her Nessie?"

"No, we don't," I said, my voice too sharp and piercing. "Her name is Renesmee."

Charlie refocused on me. "How do you feel about this? Maybe Carlisle and Esme could—"

"She's mine," I interrupted. "I *want* her."

Charlie frowned. "You gonna make me a grandpa so young?"

Edward smiled. "Carlisle is a grandfather, too."

Charlie shot an incredulous glance at Carlisle, still standing by the front door; he looked like Zeus's younger, better-looking brother.

Charlie snorted and then laughed. "I guess that does sort of make me feel better." His eyes strayed back to Renesmee. "She sure is something to look at." His warm breath blew lightly across the space between us.

Renesmee leaned toward the smell, shaking off my hair and looking him full in the face for the first time. Charlie gasped.

I knew what he was seeing. My eyes—his eyes—copied exactly into her perfect face.

Charlie started hyperventilating. His lips trembled, and I could read the numbers he mouthed. He was counting backward, trying to fit nine months into one. Trying to put it together but not able to force the evidence right in front of him to make any sense.

Jacob got up and came over to pat Charlie on the back. He leaned in to whisper something in Charlie's ear; only Charlie didn't know we could all hear.

"Need to know, Charlie. It's okay. I promise."

Charlie swallowed and nodded. And then his eyes blazed as he took a step closer to Edward with his fists tightly clenched.

"I don't want to know everything, but I'm done with the lies!"

"I'm sorry," Edward said calmly, "but you need to know the public story more than you need to know the truth. If you're going to be part of this secret, the public story is the one that counts. It's to protect Bella and Renesmee as well as the rest of us. Can you go along with the lies for them?"

The room was full of statues. I crossed my ankles.

Charlie huffed once and then turned his glare on me. "You might've given me some warning, kid."

"Would it really have made this any easier?"

He frowned, and then he knelt on the floor in front of me. I could see the movement of the blood in his neck under his skin. I could feel the warm vibration of it.

So could Renesmee. She smiled and reached one pink palm out to him. I held her back. She pushed her other hand against my neck, thirst, curiosity, and Charlie's face in her thoughts. There was a subtle edge to the message that made me think that she'd understood Edward's words perfectly; she acknowledged thirst, but overrode it in the same thought.

"Whoa," Charlie gasped, his eyes on her perfect teeth. "How old is she?"

"Um . . ."

"Three months," Edward said, and then added slowly, "rather, she's the size of a three-month-old, more or less. She's younger in some ways, more mature in others."

Very deliberately, Renesmee waved at him.

Charlie blinked spastically.

Jacob elbowed him. "Told you she was special, didn't I?"

Charlie cringed away from the contact.

"Oh, c'mon, Charlie," Jacob groaned. "I'm the same person I've always been. Just pretend this afternoon didn't happen."

The reminder made Charlie's lips go white, but he

nodded once. "Just what *is* your part in all this, Jake?" he asked. "How much does Billy know? Why are you here?" He looked at Jacob's face, which was glowing as he stared at Renesmee.

"Well, I could tell you all about it—Billy knows absolutely everything—but it involves a lot of stuff about werewo—"

"Ungh!" Charlie protested, covering his ears. "Never mind."

Jacob grinned. "Everything's going to be great, Charlie. Just try to not believe anything you see."

My dad mumbled something unintelligible.

"Woo!" Emmett suddenly boomed in his deep bass. "Go Gators!"

Jacob and Charlie jumped. The rest of us froze.

Charlie recovered, then looked at Emmett over his shoulder. "Florida winning?"

"Just scored the first touchdown," Emmett confirmed. He shot a look in my direction, wagging his eyebrows like a villain in vaudeville. "'Bout time somebody scored around here."

I fought back a hiss. In front of Charlie? That was over the line.

But Charlie was beyond noticing innuendos. He took yet another deep breath, sucking the air in like he was trying to pull it down to his toes. I envied him. He lurched to his feet, stepped around Jacob, and half-fell into an open chair. "Well," he sighed, "I guess we should see if they can hold on to the lead."

26. SHINY

"I DON'T KNOW HOW MUCH WE SHOULD TELL RENÉE about this," Charlie said, hesitating with one foot out the door. He stretched, and then his stomach growled.

I nodded. "I know. I don't want to freak her out. Better to protect her. This stuff isn't for the fainthearted."

His lips twisted up to the side ruefully. "I would have tried to protect you, too, if I'd known how. But I guess you've never fit into the fainthearted category, have you?"

I smiled back, pulling a blazing breath in through my teeth.

Charlie patted his stomach absently. "I'll think of something. We've got time to discuss this, right?"

"Right," I promised him.

It had been a long day in some ways, and so short in others. Charlie was late for dinner—Sue Clearwater was cooking for him and Billy. *That* was going to be an awkward evening, but at least he'd be eating real food; I was glad someone was trying to keep him from starving due to his lack of cooking ability.

All day the tension had made the minutes pass slowly; Charlie had never relaxed the stiff set of his shoulders. But he'd been in no hurry to leave, either. He'd watched two whole games—thankfully so absorbed in his thoughts that he was totally oblivious to Emmett's suggestive jokes that got more pointed and less football-related with each aside— and the after-game commentaries, and then the news, not moving until Seth had reminded him of the time.

"You gonna stand Billy and my mom up, Charlie? C'mon. Bella and Nessie'll be here tomorrow. Let's get some grub, eh?"

It had been clear in Charlie's eyes that he hadn't trusted Seth's assessment, but he'd let Seth lead the way out. The doubt was still there as he paused now. The clouds were thinning, the rain gone. The sun might even make an appearance just in time to set.

"Jake says you guys were going to take off on me," he muttered to me now.

"I didn't want to do that if there was any way at all around it. That's why we're still here."

"He said you could stay for a while, but only if I'm tough enough, and if I can keep my mouth shut."

"Yes . . . but I can't promise that we'll never leave, Dad. It's pretty complicated. . . ."

"Need to know," he reminded me.

"Right."

"You'll visit, though, if you have to go?"

"I promise, Dad. Now that you know *just* enough, I think this can work. I'll keep as close as you want."

He chewed on his lip for half a second, then leaned slowly toward me with his arms cautiously extended. I shifted Renesmee—napping now—to my left arm, locked my teeth, held my breath, and wrapped my right arm very lightly around his warm, soft waist.

"Keep real close, Bells," he mumbled. "Real close."

"Love you, Dad," I whispered through my teeth.

He shivered and pulled away. I dropped my arm.

"Love you, too, kid. Whatever else has changed, that hasn't." He touched one finger to Renesmee's pink cheek. "She sure looks a lot like you."

I kept my expression casual, though I felt anything but. "More like Edward, I think." I hesitated, and then added, "She has your curls."

Charlie started, then snorted. "Huh. Guess she does. Huh. Grandpa." He shook his head doubtfully. "Do I ever get to hold her?"

I blinked in shock and then composed myself. After considering for a half second and judging Renesmee's appearance—she looked completely out—I decided that I might as well push my luck to the limit, since things were going so well today. . . .

"Here," I said, holding her out to him. He automatically made an awkward cradle with his arms, and I tucked Renesmee into it. His skin wasn't quite as hot as hers, but it made my throat tickle to feel the warmth flowing under the thin membrane. Where my white skin brushed him it left goose bumps. I wasn't sure if this was a reaction to my new temperature or totally psychological.

Charlie grunted quietly as he felt her weight. "She's . . . sturdy."

I frowned. She felt feather-light to me. Maybe my measure was off.

"Sturdy is good," Charlie said, seeing my expression. Then he muttered to himself, "She'll need to be tough, surrounded by all this craziness." He bounced his arms gently, swaying a little from side to side. "Prettiest baby I ever saw, including you, kid. Sorry, but it's true."

"I know it is."

"Pretty baby," he said again, but it was closer to a coo this time.

I could see it in his face—I could watch it growing there. Charlie was just as helpless against her magic as the rest of us. Two seconds in his arms, and already she owned him.

"Can I come back tomorrow?"

"Sure, Dad. Of course. We'll be here."

"You'd better be," he said sternly, but his face was soft, still gazing at Renesmee. "See you tomorrow, Nessie."

"Not you, too!"

"Huh?"

"Her name is *Renesmee*. Like Renée and Esme, put together. No variations." I struggled to calm myself without the deep breath this time. "Do you want to hear her middle name?"

"Sure."

"Carlie. With a C. Like Carlisle and Charlie put together."

Charlie's eye-creasing grin lit up his face, taking me off guard. "Thanks, Bells."

"Thank *you*, Dad. So much has changed so quickly. My head hasn't stopped spinning. If I didn't have you now, I don't know how I'd keep my grip on—on reality." I'd been about to say *my grip on who I was*. That was probably more than he needed.

Charlie's stomach growled.

"Go eat, Dad. We *will* be here." I remembered how it felt, that first uncomfortable immersion in fantasy—the sensation that everything would disappear in the light of the rising sun.

Charlie nodded and then reluctantly returned Renesmee to me. He glanced past me into the house; his eyes were a little wild for a minute as he stared around the big bright room. Everyone was still there, besides Jacob, who I could hear raiding the refrigerator in the kitchen; Alice was lounging on the bottom step of the staircase with Jasper's head in her lap; Carlisle had his head bent over a fat book in his lap; Esme was humming to herself, sketching on a notepad, while Rosalie and Emmett laid out the foundation for a monumental house of cards under the stairs; Edward had drifted to his piano and was playing very softly to himself. There was no evidence that the day was coming to a close, that it might be time to eat or shift activities in preparation for evening. Something intangible had changed in the atmosphere. The Cullens weren't trying as hard as they usually did—the human charade had slipped ever so slightly, enough for Charlie to feel the difference.

He shuddered, shook his head, and sighed. "See you

tomorrow, Bella." He frowned and then added, "I mean, it's not like you don't look . . . good. I'll get used to it."

"Thanks, Dad."

Charlie nodded and walked thoughtfully toward his car. I watched him drive away; it wasn't until I heard his tires hit the freeway that I realized I'd done it. I'd actually made it through the whole day without hurting Charlie. All by myself. I *must* have a superpower!

It seemed too good to be true. Could I really have both my new family and some of my old as well? And I'd thought that yesterday had been perfect.

"Wow," I whispered. I blinked and felt the third set of contact lenses disintegrate.

The sound of the piano cut off, and Edward's arms were around my waist, his chin resting on my shoulder.

"You took the word right out of my mouth."

"Edward, I did it!"

"You did. You were unbelievable. All that worrying over being a newborn, and then you skip it altogether." He laughed quietly.

"I'm not even sure she's really a vampire, let alone a newborn," Emmett called from under the stairs. "She's too *tame.*"

All the embarrassing comments he'd made in front of *my father* sounded in my ears again, and it was probably a good thing I was holding Renesmee. Unable to help my reaction entirely, I snarled under my breath.

"Oooo, scary," Emmett laughed.

I hissed, and Renesmee stirred in my arms. She blinked a few times, then looked around, her expression confused. She sniffed, then reached for my face.

"Charlie will be back tomorrow," I assured her.

"Excellent," Emmett said. Rosalie laughed with him this time.

"Not brilliant, Emmett," Edward said scornfully, holding out his hands to take Renesmee from me. He winked when I hesitated, and so, a little confused, I gave her to him.

"What do you mean?" Emmett demanded.

"It's a little dense, don't you think, to antagonize the strongest vampire in the house?"

Emmett threw his head back and snorted. *"Please!"*

"Bella," Edward murmured to me while Emmett listened closely, "do you remember a few months ago, I asked you to do me a favor once you were immortal?"

That rang a dim bell. I sifted through the blurry human conversations. After a moment, I remembered and I gasped, "Oh!"

Alice trilled a long, pealing laugh. Jacob poked his head around the corner, his mouth stuffed with food.

"What?" Emmett growled.

"Really?" I asked Edward.

"Trust me," he said.

I took a deep breath. "Emmett, how do you feel about a little bet?"

He was on his feet at once. "Awesome. Bring it."

I bit my lip for a second. He was just so *huge*.

"Unless you're too afraid . . . ?" Emmett suggested.

I squared my shoulders. "You. Me. Arm-wrestling. Dining room table. Now."

Emmett's grin stretched across his face.

"Er, Bella," Alice said quickly, "I think Esme is fairly fond of that table. It's an antique."

"Thanks," Esme mouthed at her.

"No problem," Emmett said with a gleaming smile. "Right this way, Bella."

I followed him out the back, toward the garage; I could hear all the others trailing behind. There was a largish granite boulder standing up out of a tumble of rocks near the river, obviously Emmett's goal. Though the big rock was a little rounded and irregular, it would do the job.

Emmett placed his elbow on the rock and waved me forward.

I was nervous again as I watched the thick muscles in Emmett's arm roll, but I kept my face smooth. Edward had promised I would be stronger than anyone for a while. He seemed very confident about this, and I *felt* strong. *That strong?* I wondered, looking at Emmett's biceps. I wasn't even two days old, though, and that ought to count for something. Unless nothing was normal about me. Maybe I wasn't as strong as a normal newborn. Maybe that's why control was so easy for me.

I tried to look unconcerned as I set my elbow against the stone.

"Okay, Emmett. I win, and you cannot say one more word about my sex life to anyone, not even Rose. No allusions, no innuendos—no nothing."

His eyes narrowed. "Deal. I win, and it's going to get a *lot* worse."

He heard my breath stop and grinned evilly. There was no hint of bluff in his eyes.

"You gonna back down so easy, little sister?" Emmett taunted. "Not much wild about *you*, is there? I bet that cottage doesn't have a scratch." He laughed. "Did Edward tell you how many houses Rose and I smashed?"

I gritted my teeth and grabbed his big hand. "One, two—"

"Three," he grunted, and shoved against my hand.

Nothing happened.

Oh, I could feel the force he was exerting. My new mind seemed pretty good at all kinds of calculations, and so I could tell that if he wasn't meeting any resistance, his hand would have pounded right through the rock without difficulty. The pressure increased, and I wondered randomly if a cement truck doing forty miles an hour down a sharp decline would have similar power. Fifty miles an hour? Sixty? Probably more.

It wasn't enough to move me. His hand shoved against mine with crushing force, but it wasn't unpleasant. It felt kind of good in a weird way. I'd been so very careful since the last time I woke up, trying so hard not to break things. It was a strange relief to use my muscles. To let the strength flow rather than struggling to restrain it.

Emmett grunted; his forehead creased and his whole body strained in one rigid line toward the obstacle of my unmoving hand. I let him sweat—figuratively—for a moment while I enjoyed the sensation of the crazy force running through my arm.

A few seconds, though, and I was a little bored with it. I flexed; Emmett lost an inch.

I laughed. Emmett snarled harshly through his teeth.

"Just keep your mouth shut," I reminded him, and then I smashed his hand into the boulder. A deafening crack echoed off the trees. The rock shuddered, and a piece—

about an eighth of the mass—broke off at an invisible fault line and crashed to the ground. It fell on Emmett's foot, and I snickered. I could hear Jacob's and Edward's muffled laughter.

Emmett kicked the rock fragment across the river. It sliced a young maple in half before thudding into the base of a big fir, which swayed and then fell into another tree.

"Rematch. Tomorrow."

"It's not going to wear off that fast," I told him. "Maybe you ought to give it a month."

Emmett growled, flashing his teeth. "Tomorrow."

"Hey, whatever makes you happy, big brother."

As he turned to stalk away, Emmett punched the granite, shattering off an avalanche of shards and powder. It was kind of neat, in a childish way.

Fascinated by the undeniable proof that I was stronger than the strongest vampire I'd ever known, I placed my hand, fingers spread wide, against the rock. Then I dug my fingers slowly into the stone, crushing rather than digging; the consistency reminded me of hard cheese. I ended up with a handful of gravel.

"Cool," I mumbled.

With a grin stretching my face, I whirled in a sudden circle and karate-chopped the rock with the side of my hand. The stone shrieked and groaned and—with a big poof of dust—split in two.

I started giggling.

I didn't pay much attention to the chuckles behind me while I punched and kicked the rest of the boulder into fragments. I was having too much fun, snickering away the whole time. It wasn't until I heard a new little giggle, a high-pitched peal of bells, that I turned away from my silly game.

"Did she just laugh?"

Everyone was staring at Renesmee with the same dumb-struck expression that must have been on my face.

"Yes," Edward said.

"Who *wasn't* laughing?" Jake muttered, rolling his eyes.

"Tell me you didn't let go a bit on your first run, dog," Edward teased, no antagonism in his voice at all.

"That's different," Jacob said, and I watched in surprise as he mock-punched Edward's shoulder. "Bella's supposed to be a grown-up. Married and a mom and all that. Shouldn't there be more dignity?"

Renesmee frowned, and touched Edward's face.

"What does she want?" I asked.

"Less dignity," Edward said with a grin. "She was having almost as much fun watching you enjoy yourself as I was."

"Am I funny?" I asked Renesmee, darting back and reaching for her at the same time that she reached for me. I took her out of Edward's arms and offered her the shard of rock in my hand. "You want to try?"

She smiled her glittering smile and took the stone in both hands. She squeezed, a little dent forming between her eyebrows as she concentrated.

There was a tiny grinding sound, and a bit of dust. She frowned, and held the chunk up to me.

"I'll get it," I said, pinching the stone into sand.

She clapped and laughed; the delicious sound of it made us all join in.

The sun suddenly burst through the clouds, shooting

long beams of ruby and gold across the ten of us, and I was immediately lost in the beauty of my skin in the light of the sunset. Dazed by it.

Renesmee stroked the smooth diamond-bright facets, then laid her arm next to mine. Her skin had just a faint luminosity, subtle and mysterious. Nothing that would keep her inside on a sunny day like my glowing sparkle. She touched my face, thinking of the difference and feeling disgruntled.

"You're the prettiest," I assured her.

"I'm not sure I can agree to that," Edward said, and when I turned to answer him, the sunlight on his face stunned me into silence.

Jacob had his hand in front of his face, pretending to shield his eyes from the glare. "Freaky Bella," he commented.

"What an amazing creature she is," Edward murmured, almost in agreement, as if Jacob's comment was meant as a compliment. He was both dazzling and dazzled.

It was a strange feeling—not surprising, I supposed, since everything felt strange now—this being a natural at something. As a human, I'd never been best at anything. I was okay at dealing with Renée, but probably lots of people could have done better; Phil seemed to be holding his own. I was a good student, but never the top of the class. Obviously, I could be counted out of anything athletic. Not artistic or musical, no particular talents to brag of. Nobody ever gave away a trophy for reading books. After eighteen years of mediocrity, I was pretty used to being average. I realized now that I'd long ago given up any aspirations of shining at anything. I just did the best with what I had, never quite fitting into my world.

So this was really different. I was amazing now—to them and to myself. It was like I had been born to be a vampire. The idea made me want to laugh, but it also made me want to sing. I had found my true place in the world, the place I fit, the place I shined.

27. TRAVEL PLANS

I TOOK MYTHOLOGY A LOT MORE SERIOUSLY SINCE I'D become a vampire.

Often, when I looked back over my first three months as an immortal, I imagined how the thread of my life might look in the Fates' loom—who knew but that it actually existed? I was sure my thread must have changed color; I thought it had probably started out as a nice beige, something supportive and non-confrontational, something that would look good in the background. Now it felt like it must be bright crimson, or maybe glistening gold.

The tapestry of family and friends that wove together around me was a beautiful, glowing thing, full of their bright, complementary colors.

I was surprised by some of the threads I got to include in my life. The werewolves, with their deep, woodsy colors, were not something I'd expected; Jacob, of course, and Seth, too. But my old friends Quil and Embry became part of the fabric as they joined Jacob's pack, and even Sam and Emily were cordial. The tensions between our families eased, mostly due to Renesmee. She was easy to love.

Sue and Leah Clearwater were interlaced into our life, too—two more I had not anticipated.

Sue seemed to have taken it on herself to smooth Charlie's transition into the world of make-believe. She came with him to the Cullens' most days, though she never seemed truly comfortable here the way her son and most of Jake's pack did. She did not speak often; she just hovered protectively near Charlie. She was always the first person he looked to when Renesmee did something disturbingly advanced—which was often. In answer, Sue would eye Seth meaningfully as if to say, *Yeah, tell me about it.*

Leah was even less comfortable than Sue and was the only part of our recently extended family who was openly hostile to the merger. However, she and Jacob had a new camaraderie that kept her close to us all. I asked him about it once—hesitantly; I didn't want to pry, but the relationship was so different from the way it used to be that it made me curious. He shrugged and told me it was a pack thing. She was his second-in-command now, his "beta," as I'd called it once long ago.

"I figured as long as I was going to do this Alpha thing for real," Jacob explained, "I'd better nail down the formalities."

The new responsibility made Leah feel the need to

check in with him often, and since he was always with Renesmee . . .

Leah was not happy to be near us, but she was the exception. Happiness was the main component in my life now, the dominant pattern in the tapestry. So much so that my relationship with Jasper was now much closer than I'd ever dreamed it would be.

At first I was really annoyed, though.

"Yeesh!" I complained to Edward one night after we'd put Renesmee in her wrought-iron crib. "If I haven't killed Charlie or Sue yet, it's probably not going to happen. I wish Jasper would stop hovering all the time!"

"No one doubts you, Bella, not in the slightest," he assured me. "You know how Jasper is—he can't resist a good emotional climate. You're so happy all the time, love, he gravitates toward you without thinking."

And then Edward hugged me tightly, because nothing pleased him more than my overwhelming ecstasy in this new life.

And I was euphoric the vast majority of the time. The days were not long enough for me to get my fill of adoring my daughter; the nights did not have enough hours to satisfy my need for Edward.

There was a flipside to the joy, though. If you turned the fabric of our lives over, I imagined the design on the backside would be woven in the bleak grays of doubt and fear.

Renesmee spoke her first word when she was exactly one week old. The word was *Momma,* which would have made my day, except that I was so frightened by her progress I could barely force my frozen face to smile back at her. It didn't help that she continued from her first word to her first sentence in the same breath. "Momma, where is Grandpa?" she'd asked in a clear, high soprano, only bothering to speak aloud because I was across the room from her. She'd already asked Rosalie, using her normal (or seriously abnormal, from another point of view) means of communication. Rosalie hadn't known the answer, so Renesmee had turned to me.

When she walked for the first time, fewer than three weeks later, it was similar. She'd simply stared at Alice for a long moment, watching intently as her aunt arranged bouquets in the vases scattered around the room, dancing back and forth across the floor with her arms full of flowers. Renesmee got to her feet, not in the least bit shaky, and crossed the floor almost as gracefully.

Jacob had burst into applause, because that was clearly the response Renesmee wanted. The way he was tied to her made his own reactions secondary; his first reflex was always to give Renesmee whatever she needed. But our eyes met, and I saw all the panic in mine echoed in his. I made my hands clap together, too, trying to hide my fear from her. Edward applauded quietly at my side, and we didn't need to speak our thoughts to know they were the same.

Edward and Carlisle threw themselves into research, looking for any answers, anything to expect. There was very little to be found, and none of it verifiable.

Alice and Rosalie usually began our day with a fashion show. Renesmee never wore the same clothes twice, partly because she outgrew her clothes almost immediately and partly because Alice and Rosalie were trying to create a baby album that appeared to span years rather than weeks.

They took thousands of pictures, documenting every phase of her accelerated childhood.

At three months, Renesmee could have been a big one-year-old, or a small two-year-old. She wasn't shaped exactly like a toddler; she was leaner and more graceful, her proportions were more even, like an adult's. Her bronze ringlets hung to her waist; I couldn't bear to cut them, even if Alice would have allowed it. Renesmee could speak with flawless grammar and articulation, but she rarely bothered, preferring to simply *show* people what she wanted. She could not only walk but run and dance. She could even read.

I'd been reading Tennyson to her one night, because the flow and rhythm of his poetry seemed restful. (I had to search constantly for new material; Renesmee didn't like repetition in her bedtime stories as other children supposedly did, and she had no patience for picture books.) She reached up to touch my cheek, the image in her mind one of us, only with *her* holding the book. I gave it to her, smiling.

"'There is sweet music here,'" she read without hesitation, "'that softer falls than petals from blown roses on the grass, or night-dews on still waters between walls of shadowy granite, in a gleaming pass—'"

My hand was robotic as I took the book back.

"If you read, how will you fall asleep?" I asked in a voice that had barely escaped shaking.

By Carlisle's calculations, the growth of her body was gradually slowing; her mind continued to race on ahead. Even if the rate of decrease held steady, she'd still be an adult in no more than four years.

Four years. And an old woman by fifteen.

Just fifteen years of life.

But she was so *healthy*. Vital, bright, glowing, and happy. Her conspicuous well-being made it easy for me to be happy with her in the moment and leave the future for tomorrow.

Carlisle and Edward discussed our options for the future from every angle in low voices that I tried not to hear. They never had these discussions when Jacob was around, because there *was* one sure way to halt aging, and that wasn't something Jacob was likely to be excited about. I wasn't. *Too dangerous!* my instincts screamed at me. Jacob and Renesmee seemed alike in so many ways, both half-and-half beings, two things at the same time. And all the werewolf lore insisted that vampire venom was a death sentence rather than a course to immortality. . . .

Carlisle and Edward had exhausted the research they could do from a distance, and now we were preparing to follow old legends at their source. We were going back to Brazil, starting there. The Ticunas had legends about children like Renesmee. . . . If other children like her had ever existed, perhaps some tale of the life span of half-mortal children still lingered. . . .

The only real question left was exactly when we would go.

I was the holdup. A small part of it was that I wanted to stay near Forks until after the holidays, for Charlie's sake. But more than that, there was a different journey that I knew had to come first—that was the clear priority. Also, it had to be a solo trip.

This was the only argument that Edward and I had gotten in since I'd become a vampire. The main point of contention was the "solo" part. But the facts were what they were, and my plan was the only one that made rational sense. I had to go see the Volturi, and I had to do it absolutely alone.

Even freed from old nightmares, from any dreams at all, it was impossible to forget the Volturi. Nor did they leave us without reminders.

Until the day that Aro's present showed up, I didn't know that Alice had sent a wedding announcement to the Volturi leaders; we'd been far away on Esme's island when she'd seen a vision of Volturi soldiers—Jane and Alec, the devastatingly powerful twins, among them. Caius was planning to send a hunting party to see if I was still human, against their edict (because I knew about the secret vampire world, I either must join it or be silenced . . . permanently). So Alice had mailed the announcement, seeing that this would delay them as they deciphered the meaning behind it. But they would come eventually. That was certain.

The present itself was not overtly threatening. Extravagant, yes, almost frightening in that very extravagance. The threat was in the parting line of Aro's congratulatory note, written in black ink on a square of heavy, plain white paper in Aro's own hand:

> ## I so look forward to seeing the new
> ## Mrs. Cullen in person.

The gift was presented in an ornately carved, ancient wooden box inlaid with gold and mother-of-pearl, ornamented with a rainbow of gemstones. Alice said the box itself was a priceless treasure, that it would have outshone just about any piece of jewelry besides the one inside it.

"I always wondered where the crown jewels disappeared to after John of England pawned them in the thirteenth century," Carlisle said. "I suppose it doesn't surprise me that the Volturi have their share."

The necklace was simple—gold woven into a thick rope of a chain, almost scaled, like a smooth snake that would curl close around the throat. One jewel hung suspended from the rope: a white diamond the size of a golf ball.

The unsubtle reminder in Aro's note interested me more than the jewel. The Volturi needed to see that I was immortal, that the Cullens had been obedient to the Volturi's orders, and they needed to see this *soon*. They could not be allowed near Forks. There was only one way to keep our life here safe.

"You're not going alone," Edward had insisted through his teeth, his hands clenching into fists.

"They won't hurt me," I'd said as soothingly as I could manage, forcing my voice to sound sure. "They have no reason to. I'm a vampire. Case closed."

"No. Absolutely no."

"Edward, it's the only way to protect her."

And he hadn't been able to argue with that. My logic was watertight.

Even in the short time I'd known Aro, I'd been able to see that he was a collector—and his most prized treasures were his *living* pieces. He coveted beauty, talent, and rarity in his immortal followers more than any jewel locked in his vaults. It was unfortunate enough that he'd begun to covet Alice's and Edward's abilities. I would give him no more reason to be jealous of Carlisle's family. Renesmee was beautiful and gifted and unique—she was one of a kind. He could not be allowed to see her, not even through someone's thoughts.

And I was the only one whose thoughts he could not hear. Of course I would go alone.

Alice did not see any trouble with my trip, but she was worried by the indistinct quality of her visions. She said they were sometimes similarly hazy when there were outside decisions that *might* conflict but that had not been solidly resolved. This uncertainty made Edward, already hesitant, extremely opposed to what I had to do. He wanted to come with me as far as my connection in London, but I wouldn't leave Renesmee without *both* her parents. Carlisle was coming instead. It made both Edward and me a little more relaxed, knowing that Carlisle would be only a few hours away from me.

Alice kept searching for the future, but the things she found were unrelated to what she was looking for. A new trend in the stock market; a possible visit of reconciliation from Irina, though her decision was not firm; a snowstorm that wouldn't hit for another six weeks; a call from Renée (I was practicing my "rough" voice, and getting better at it every day—to Renée's knowledge, I was still sick, but mending).

We bought the tickets for Italy the day after Renesmee turned three months. I planned for it to be a very short trip, so I hadn't told Charlie about it. Jacob knew, and he took Edward's view on things. However, today the argument was about Brazil. Jacob was determined to come with us.

The three of us, Jacob, Renesmee, and I, were hunting together. The diet of animal blood wasn't Renesmee's favorite thing—and that was why Jacob was allowed to come along.

Jacob had made it a contest between them, and that made her more willing than anything else.

Renesmee was quite clear on the whole good vs. bad as it applied to hunting humans; she just thought that donated blood made a nice compromise. Human food filled her and it seemed compatible with her system, but she reacted to all varieties of solid food with the same martyred endurance I had once given cauliflower and lima beans. Animal blood was better than *that*, at least. She had a competitive nature, and the challenge of beating Jacob made her excited to hunt.

"Jacob," I said, trying to reason with him again while Renesmee danced ahead of us into the long clearing, searching for a scent she liked. "You've got obligations here. Seth, Leah—"

He snorted. "I'm not my pack's nanny. They've all got responsibilities in La Push anyway."

"Sort of like you? Are you officially dropping out of high school, then? If you're going to keep up with Renesmee, you're going to have to study a lot harder."

"It's just a sabbatical. I'll get back to school when things . . . slow down."

I lost my concentration on my side of the disagreement when he said that, and we both automatically looked at Renesmee. She was staring at the snowflakes fluttering high above her head, melting before they could stick to the yellowed grass in the long arrowhead-shaped meadow that we were standing in. Her ruffled ivory dress was just a shade darker than the snow, and her reddish-brown curls managed to shimmer, though the sun was buried deeply behind the clouds.

As we watched, she crouched for an instant and then sprang fifteen feet up into the air. Her little hands closed around a flake, and she dropped lightly to her feet.

She turned to us with her shocking smile—truly, it wasn't something you could get used to—and opened her hands to show us the perfectly formed eight-pointed ice star in her palm before it melted.

"Pretty," Jacob called to her appreciatively. "But I think you're stalling, Nessie."

She bounded back to Jacob; he held his arms out at exactly the moment she leaped into them. They had the move perfectly synchronized. She did this when she had something to say. She still preferred not to speak aloud.

Renesmee touched his face, scowling adorably as we all listened to the sound of a small herd of elk moving farther into the wood.

"*Suuuure* you're not thirsty, Nessie," Jacob answered a little sarcastically, but more indulgently than anything else. "You're just afraid I'll catch the biggest one again!"

She flipped backward out of Jacob's arms, landing lightly on her feet, and rolled her eyes—she looked so much like Edward when she did that. Then she darted off toward the trees.

"Got it," Jacob said when I leaned as if to follow. He yanked his t-shirt off as he charged after her into the forest, already trembling. "It doesn't count if you cheat," he called to Renesmee.

I smiled at the leaves they left fluttering behind them, shaking my head. Jacob was more a child than Renesmee sometimes.

I paused, giving my hunters a few minutes' head start.

It would be beyond simple to track them, and Renesmee would love to surprise me with the size of her prey. I smiled again.

The narrow meadow was very still, very empty. The fluttering snow was thinning above me, almost gone. Alice had seen that it wouldn't stick for many weeks.

Usually Edward and I came together on these hunting trips. But Edward was with Carlisle today, planning the trip to Rio, talking behind Jacob's back. . . . I frowned. When I returned, I would take Jacob's side. He *should* come with us. He had as big a stake in this as any of us—his entire life was at stake, just like mine.

While my thoughts were lost in the near future, my eyes swept the mountainside routinely, searching for prey, searching for danger. I didn't think about it; the urge was an automatic thing.

Or perhaps there *was* a reason for my scanning, some tiny trigger that my razor-sharp senses had caught before I realized it consciously.

As my eyes flitted across the edge of a distant cliff, standing out starkly blue-gray against the green-black forest, a glint of silver—or was it gold?—gripped my attention.

My gaze zeroed in on the color that shouldn't have been there, so far away in the haze that an eagle wouldn't have been able to make it out. I stared.

She stared back.

That she was a vampire was obvious. Her skin was marble white, the texture a million times smoother than human skin. Even under the clouds, she glistened ever so slightly. If her skin had not given her away, her stillness would have. Only vampires and statues could be so perfectly motionless.

Her hair was pale, pale blond, almost silver. This was the gleam that had caught my eye. It hung straight as a ruler to a blunt edge at her chin, parted evenly down the center.

She was a stranger to me. I was absolutely certain I'd never seen her before, even as a human. None of the faces in my muddy memory were the same as this one. But I knew her at once from her dark golden eyes.

Irina had decided to come after all.

For one moment I stared at her, and she stared back. I wondered if she would guess immediately who I was as well. I half raised my hand, about to wave, but her lip twisted the tiniest bit, making her face suddenly hostile.

I heard Renesmee's cry of victory from the forest, heard Jacob's echoing howl, and saw Irina's face jerk reflexively to the sound when it echoed to her a few seconds later. Her gaze cut slightly to the right, and I knew what she was seeing. An enormous russet werewolf, perhaps the very one who had killed her Laurent. How long had she been watching us? Long enough to see our affectionate exchange before, I was sure.

Her face spasmed in pain.

Instinctually, I opened my hands in front of me in an apologetic gesture. She turned back to me, and her lip curled back over her teeth. Her jaw unlocked as she growled.

When the faint sound reached me, she had already turned and disappeared into the forest.

"Crap!" I groaned.

I sprinted into the forest after Renesmee and Jacob,

unwilling to have them out of my sight. I didn't know which direction Irina had taken, or exactly how furious she was right now. Vengeance was a common obsession for vampires, one that was not easy to suppress.

Running at full speed, it only took me two seconds to reach them.

"Mine is bigger," I heard Renesmee insist as I burst through the thick thornbushes to the small open space where they stood.

Jacob's ears flattened as he took in my expression; he crouched forward, baring his teeth—his muzzle was streaked with blood from his kill. His eyes raked the forest. I could hear the growl building in his throat.

Renesmee was every bit as alert as Jacob. Abandoning the dead stag at her feet, she leaped into my waiting arms, pressing her curious hands against my cheeks.

"I'm overreacting," I assured them quickly. "It's okay, I think. Hold on."

I pulled out my cell phone and hit the speed dial. Edward answered on the first ring. Jacob and Renesmee listened intently to my side as I filled Edward in.

"Come, bring Carlisle," I trilled so fast I wondered if Jacob could keep up. "I saw Irina, and she saw me, but then she saw Jacob and she got mad and ran away, I *think*. She hasn't shown up here—yet, anyway—but she looked pretty upset so maybe she will. If she doesn't, you and Carlisle have to go after her and talk to her. I feel so bad."

Jacob rumbled.

"We'll be there in half a minute," Edward assured me, and I could hear the whoosh of the wind his running made.

We darted back to the long meadow and then waited

silently as Jacob and I listened carefully for the sound of an approach we did not recognize.

When the sound came, though, it was very familiar. And then Edward was at my side, Carlisle a few seconds behind. I was surprised to hear the heavy pad of big paws following behind Carlisle. I supposed I shouldn't have been shocked. With Renesmee in even a hint of danger, of course Jacob would call in reinforcements.

"She was up on that ridge," I told them at once, pointing out the spot. If Irina was fleeing, she already had quite a head start. Would she stop and listen to Carlisle? Her expression before made me think not. "Maybe you should call Emmett and Jasper and have them come with you. She looked . . . really upset. She growled at me."

"What?" Edward said angrily.

Carlisle put a hand on his arm. "She's grieving. I'll go after her."

"I'm coming with you," Edward insisted.

They exchanged a long glance—perhaps Carlisle was measuring Edward's irritation with Irina against his helpfulness as a mind reader. Finally, Carlisle nodded, and they took off to find the trail without calling for Jasper or Emmett.

Jacob huffed impatiently and poked my back with his nose. He must want Renesmee back at the safety of the house, just in case. I agreed with him on that, and we hurried home with Seth and Leah running at our flanks.

Renesmee was complacent in my arms, one hand still resting on my face. Since the hunting trip had been aborted, she would just have to make do with donated blood. Her thoughts were a little smug.

28. THE FUTURE

CARLISLE AND EDWARD HAD NOT BEEN ABLE TO CATCH
up with Irina before her trail disappeared into the sound.
They'd swum to the other bank to see if her trail had picked
up in a straight line, but there was no trace of her for miles
in either direction on the eastern shore.

It was all my fault. She had come, as Alice had seen, to
make peace with the Cullens, only to be angered by my
camaraderie with Jacob. I wished I'd noticed her earlier,
before Jacob had phased. I wished we'd gone hunting
somewhere else.

There wasn't much to be done. Carlisle had called Tanya
with the disappointing news. Tanya and Kate hadn't seen

Irina since they'd decided to come to my wedding, and they were distraught that Irina had come so close and yet not returned home; it wasn't easy for them to lose their sister, however temporary the separation might be. I wondered if this brought back hard memories of losing their mother so many centuries ago.

Alice was able to catch a few glimpses of Irina's immediate future, nothing too concrete. She wasn't going back to Denali, as far as Alice could tell. The picture was hazy. All Alice could see was that Irina was visibly upset; she wandered in the snow-swathed wilderness—to the north? To the east?—with a devastated expression. She made no decisions for a new course beyond her directionless grieving.

Days passed and, though of course I forgot nothing, Irina and her pain moved to the back of my mind. There were more important things to think of now. I would leave for Italy in just a few days. When I got back, we'd all be off to South America.

Every detail had been gone over a hundred times already. We would start with the Ticunas, tracing their legends as well as we could at the source. Now that it was accepted that Jacob would come with us, he figured prominently in the plans—it was unlikely that the people who believed in vampires would speak to any of *us* about their stories. If we dead-ended with the Ticunas, there were many closely related tribes in the area to research. Carlisle had some old friends in the Amazon; if we could find them, they might have information for us, too. Or at least a suggestion as to where else we might go for answers. It was unlikely that the three Amazon vampires had anything to do with the legends of vampire hybrids themselves, as they were all female. There was no way to know how long our search would take.

I hadn't told Charlie about the longer trip yet, and I stewed about what to say to him while Edward and Carlisle's discussion went on. How to break the news to him just right?

I stared at Renesmee while I debated internally. She was curled up on the sofa now, her breathing slow with heavy sleep, her tangled curls splayed wildly around her face. Usually, Edward and I took her back to our cottage to put her to bed, but tonight we lingered with the family, he and Carlisle deep in their planning session.

Meanwhile, Emmett and Jasper were more excited about planning the hunting possibilities. The Amazon offered a change from our normal quarry. Jaguars and panthers, for example. Emmett had a whim to wrestle with an anaconda. Esme and Rosalie were planning what they would pack. Jacob was off with Sam's pack, setting things up for his own absence.

Alice moved slowly—for her—around the big room, unnecessarily tidying the already immaculate space, straightening Esme's perfectly hung garlands. She was re-centering Esme's vases on the console at the moment. I could see from the way her face fluctuated—aware, then blank, then aware again—that she was searching the future. I assumed she was trying to see through the blind spots that Jacob and Renesmee made in her visions as to what was waiting for us in South America until Jasper said, "Let it go, Alice; she's not our concern," and a cloud of serenity stole silently and invisibly through the room. Alice must have been worrying about Irina again.

She stuck her tongue out at Jasper and then lifted one crystal vase that was filled with white and red roses and turned toward the kitchen. There was just the barest hint of wilt to one of the white flowers, but Alice seemed intent on utter perfection as a distraction to her lack of vision tonight.

Staring at Renesmee again, I didn't see it when the vase slipped from Alice's fingers. I only heard the whoosh of the air whistling past the crystal, and my eyes flickered up in time to see the vase shatter into ten thousand diamond shards against the edge of the kitchen's marble floor.

We were perfectly still as the fragmented crystal bounced and skittered in every direction with an unmusical tinkling, all eyes on Alice's back.

My first illogical thought was that Alice was playing some joke on us. Because there was no way that Alice could have dropped the vase *by accident*. I could have darted across the room to catch the vase in plenty of time myself, if I hadn't assumed she would get it. And how would it fall through her fingers in the first place? Her perfectly sure fingers . . .

I had never seen a vampire drop anything by accident. Ever.

And then Alice was facing us, twisting in a move so fast it didn't exist.

Her eyes were halfway here and halfway locked on the future, wide, staring, filling her thin face till they seemed to overflow it. Looking into her eyes was like looking out of a grave from the inside; I was buried in the terror and despair and agony of her gaze.

I heard Edward gasp; it was a broken, half-choked sound.

"What?" Jasper growled, leaping to her side in a blurred rush of movement, crushing the broken crystal under his feet. He grabbed her shoulders and shook her sharply. She seemed to rattle silently in his hands. *"What, Alice?"*

Emmett moved into my peripheral vision, his teeth bared while his eyes darted toward the window, anticipating an attack.

There was only silence from Esme, Carlisle, and Rose, who were frozen just as I was.

Jasper shook Alice again. "What *is* it?"

"They're coming for us," Alice and Edward whispered together, perfectly synchronized. "All of them."

Silence.

For once, I was the quickest to understand—because something in their words triggered my own vision. It was only the distant memory of a dream—faint, transparent, indistinct as if I were peering through thick gauze. . . . In my head, I saw a line of black advancing on me, the ghost of my half-forgotten human nightmare. I could not see the glint of their ruby eyes in the shrouded image, or the shine of their sharp wet teeth, but I knew where the gleam should be. . . .

Stronger than the memory of the sight came the memory of the *feel*—the wrenching need to protect the precious thing behind me.

I wanted to snatch Renesmee up into my arms, to hide her behind my skin and hair, to make her invisible. But I couldn't even turn to look at her. I felt not like stone but ice. For the first time since I'd been reborn a vampire, I felt cold.

I barely heard the confirmation of my fears. I didn't need it. I already knew.

"The Volturi," Alice moaned.

"All of them," Edward groaned at the same time.

"Why?" Alice whispered to herself. "How?"

"When?" Edward whispered.

"Why?" Esme echoed.

"*When?*" Jasper repeated in a voice like splintering ice.

Alice's eyes didn't blink, but it was as if a veil covered them; they became perfectly blank. Only her mouth held on to her expression of horror.

"Not long," she and Edward said together. Then she spoke alone. "There's snow on the forest, snow on the town. Little more than a month."

"Why?" Carlisle was the one to ask this time.

Esme answered. "They must have a reason. Maybe to see . . ."

"This isn't about Bella," Alice said hollowly. "They're all coming—Aro, Caius, Marcus, every member of the guard, even the wives."

"The wives never leave the tower," Jasper contradicted her in a flat voice. "Never. Not during the southern rebellion. Not when the Romanians tried to overthrow them. Not even when they were hunting the immortal children. Never."

"They're coming now," Edward whispered.

"But *why?*" Carlisle said again. "We've done nothing! And if we had, what could we possibly do that would bring *this* down on us?"

"There are so many of us," Edward answered dully. "They must want to make sure that . . ." He didn't finish.

"That doesn't answer the crucial question! Why?"

I felt I knew the answer to Carlisle's question, and yet at the same time I didn't. Renesmee was the reason why, I was sure. Somehow I'd known from the very beginning that they would come for her. My subconscious had warned me before I'd known I was carrying her. It felt oddly expected now. As if I'd somehow always known that the Volturi would come to take my happiness from me.

But that still didn't answer the question.

"Go back, Alice," Jasper pleaded. "Look for the trigger. Search."

Alice shook her head slowly, her shoulders sagging. "It came out of nowhere, Jazz. I wasn't looking for them, or even for us. I was just looking for Irina. She wasn't where I expected her to be. . . ." Alice trailed off, her eyes drifting again. She stared at nothing for a long second.

And then her head jerked up, her eyes hard as flint. I heard Edward catch his breath.

"She decided to go to them," Alice said. "Irina decided to go to the Volturi. And then they will decide. . . . It's as if they're waiting for her. Like their decision was already made, and just waiting on her. . . ."

It was silent again as we digested this. What would Irina tell the Volturi that would result in Alice's appalling vision?

"Can we stop her?" Jasper asked.

"There's no way. She's almost there."

"What is she doing?" Carlisle was asking, but I wasn't paying attention to the discussion now. All my focus was on the picture that was painstakingly coming together in my head.

I pictured Irina poised on the cliff, watching. What had she seen? A vampire and a werewolf who were best friends. I'd been focused on that image, one that would obviously explain her reaction. But that was not all that she'd seen.

She'd also seen a child. An exquisitely beautiful child, showing off in the falling snow, clearly more than human . . .

Irina . . . the orphaned sisters . . . Carlisle had said that losing their mother to the Volturi's justice had made Tanya, Kate, and Irina purists when it came to the law.

Just half a minute ago, Jasper had said the words himself: *Not even when they were hunting the immortal children, . . .* The immortal children—the unmentionable bane, the appalling taboo . . .

With Irina's past, how could she apply any other reading to what she'd seen that day in the narrow field? She had not been close enough to hear Renesmee's heart, to feel the heat radiating from her body. Renesmee's rosy cheeks could have been a trick on our part for all she knew.

After all, the Cullens were in league with werewolves. From Irina's point of view, maybe this meant nothing was beyond us. . . .

Irina, wringing her hands in the snowy wilderness—not mourning Laurent, after all, but knowing it was her duty to turn the Cullens in, knowing what would happen to them if she did. Apparently her conscience had won out over the centuries of friendship.

And the Volturi's response to this kind of infraction was so automatic, it was already decided.

I turned and draped myself over Renesmee's sleeping

body, covering her with my hair, burying my face in her curls.

"Think of what she saw that afternoon," I said in a low voice, interrupting whatever Emmett was beginning to say. "To someone who'd lost a mother because of the immortal children, what would Renesmee look like?"

Everything was silent again as the others caught up to where I was already.

"An immortal child," Carlisle whispered.

I felt Edward kneel beside me, wrap his arms over us both.

"But she's wrong," I went on. "Renesmee isn't like those other children. They were frozen, but she grows so much every day. They were out of control, but she never hurts Charlie or Sue or even shows them things that would upset them. She *can* control herself. She's already smarter than most adults. There would be no reason. . . ."

I babbled on, waiting for someone to exhale with relief, waiting for the icy tension in the room to relax as they realized I was right. The room just seemed to get colder. Eventually my small voice trailed off into silence.

No one spoke for a long time.

Then Edward whispered into my hair. "It's not the kind of crime they hold a trial for, love," he said quietly. "Aro's seen Irina's *proof* in her thoughts. They come to destroy, not to be reasoned with."

"But they're wrong," I said stubbornly.

"They won't wait for us to show them that."

His voice was still quiet, gentle, velvet . . . and yet the pain and desolation in the sound was unavoidable. His voice was like Alice's eyes before—like the inside of a tomb.

"What can we do?" I demanded.

Renesmee was so warm and perfect in my arms, dreaming peacefully. I'd worried so much about Renesmee's speeding age—worried that she would only have little over a decade of life. . . . That terror seemed ironic now.

Little over a month . . .

Was this the limit, then? I'd had more happiness than most people ever experienced. Was there some natural law that demanded equal shares of happiness and misery in the world? Was my joy overthrowing the balance? Was four months all I could have?

It was Emmett who answered my rhetorical question.

"We fight," he said calmly.

"We can't win," Jasper growled. I could imagine how his face would look, how his body would curve protectively over Alice's.

"Well, we can't run. Not with Demetri around." Emmett made a disgusted noise, and I knew instinctively that he was not upset by the idea of the Volturi's tracker but by the idea of running away. "And I don't know that we *can't* win," he said. "There are a few options to consider. We don't have to fight alone."

My head snapped up at that. "We don't have to sentence the Quileutes to death, either, Emmett!"

"Chill, Bella." His expression was no different from when he was contemplating fighting anacondas. Even the threat of annihilation couldn't change Emmett's perspective, his ability to thrill to a challenge. "I didn't mean the pack. Be realistic, though—do you think Jacob or Sam is going to ignore an invasion? Even if it wasn't about Nessie? Not to mention that, thanks to Irina, Aro knows about our alliance with the pack now, too. But I was thinking of our other friends."

Carlisle echoed me in a whisper. "Other friends we don't have to sentence to death."

"Hey, we'll let them decide," Emmett said in a placating tone. "I'm not saying they have to fight with us." I could see the plan refining itself in his head as he spoke. "If they'd just stand beside us, just long enough to make the Volturi hesitate. Bella's right, after all. If we could force them to stop and listen. Though that might take away any reason for a fight. . . ."

There was a hint of a smile on Emmett's face now. I was surprised no one had hit him yet. I wanted to.

"Yes," Esme said eagerly. "That makes sense, Emmett. All we need is for the Volturi to pause for one moment. Just long enough to *listen.*"

"We'd need quite a show of witnesses," Rosalie said harshly, her voice brittle as glass.

Esme nodded in agreement, as if she hadn't heard the sarcasm in Rosalie's tone. "We can ask that much of our friends. Just to witness."

"We'd do it for them," Emmett said.

"We'll have to ask them just right," Alice murmured. I looked to see her eyes were a dark void again. "They'll have to be shown very carefully."

"Shown?" Jasper asked.

Alice and Edward both looked down at Renesmee. Then Alice's eyes glazed over.

"Tanya's family," she said. "Siobhan's coven. Amun's. Some of the nomads—Garrett and Mary for certain. Maybe Alistair."

"What about Peter and Charlotte?" Jasper asked half fearfully, as if he hoped the answer was no, and his old brother could be spared from the coming carnage.

"Maybe."

"The Amazons?" Carlisle asked. "Kachiri, Zafrina, and Senna?"

Alice seemed too deep into her vision to answer at first; finally she shuddered, and her eyes flickered back to the present. She met Carlisle's gaze for the tiniest part of a second, and then looked down.

"I can't see."

"What was that?" Edward asked, his whisper a demand. "That part in the jungle. Are we going to look for them?"

"I can't see," Alice repeated, not meeting his eyes. A flash of confusion crossed Edward's face. "We'll have to split up and hurry—before the snow sticks to the ground. We have to round up whomever we can and get them here to show them." She zoned again. "Ask Eleazar. There is more to this than just an immortal child."

The silence was ominous for another long moment while Alice was in her trance. She blinked slowly when it was over, her eyes peculiarly opaque despite the fact that she was clearly in the present.

"There is so much. We have to hurry," she whispered.

"Alice?" Edward asked. "That was too fast—I didn't understand. What was—?"

"I can't see!" she exploded back at him. "Jacob's almost here!"

Rosalie took a step toward the front door. "I'll deal with—"

"No, let him come," Alice said quickly, her voice straining

higher with each word. She grabbed Jasper's hand and began pulling him toward the back door. "I'll see better away from Nessie, too. I need to go. I need to really concentrate. I need to see everything I can. I have to go. Come on, Jasper, there's no time to waste!"

We all could hear Jacob on the stairs. Alice yanked, impatient, on Jasper's hand. He followed quickly, confusion in his eyes just like Edward's. They darted out the door into the silver night.

"Hurry!" she called back to us. "You have to find them all!"

"Find what?" Jacob asked, shutting the front door behind himself. "Where'd Alice go?"

No one answered; we all just stared.

Jacob shook the wet from his hair and pulled his arms through the sleeves of his t-shirt, his eyes on Renesmee. "Hey, Bells! I thought you guys would've gone home by now. . . ."

He looked up to me finally, blinked, and then stared. I watched his expression as the room's atmosphere finally touched him. He glanced down, eyes wide, at the wet spot on the floor, the scattered roses, the fragments of crystal. His fingers quivered.

"What?" he asked flatly. "What happened?"

I couldn't think where to begin. No one else found the words, either.

Jacob crossed the room in three long strides and dropped to his knees beside Renesmee and me. I could feel the heat shaking off his body as tremors rolled down his arms to his shaking hands.

"Is she okay?" he demanded, touching her forehead, tilting his head as he listened to her heart. "Don't mess with me, Bella, please!"

"Nothing's wrong with Renesmee," I choked out, the words breaking in strange places.

"Then who?"

"All of us, Jacob," I whispered. And it was there in my voice, too—the sound of the inside of a grave. "It's over. We've all been sentenced to die."

29. DEFECTION

W<small>E</small> <small>SAT THERE ALL NIGHT LONG, STATUES OF HORROR</small> and grief, and Alice never came back.

We were all at our limits—frenzied into absolute stillness. Carlisle had barely been able to move his lips to explain it all to Jacob. The retelling seemed to make it worse; even Emmett stood silent and still from then on.

It wasn't until the sun rose and I knew that Renesmee would soon be stirring under my hands that I wondered for the first time what could possibly be taking Alice so long. I'd hoped to know more before I was faced with my daughter's curiosity. To have some answers. Some tiny, tiny portion of hope so that I could smile and keep the truth from terrifying her, too.

My face felt permanently set into the fixed mask it had worn all night. I wasn't sure I had the ability to smile anymore.

Jacob was snoring in the corner, a mountain of fur on the floor, twitching anxiously in his sleep. Sam knew everything—the wolves were readying themselves for what was coming. Not that this preparation would do anything but get them killed with the rest of my family.

The sunlight broke through the back windows, sparkling on Edward's skin. My eyes had not moved from his since Alice's departure. We'd stared at each other all night, staring at what neither of us could live through losing: the other. I saw my reflection glimmer in his agonized eyes as the sun touched my own skin.

His eyebrows moved an infinitesimal bit, then his lips.

"Alice," he said.

The sound of his voice was like ice cracking as it melted. All of us fractured a little, softened a little. Moved again.

"She's been gone a long time," Rosalie murmured, surprised.

"Where could she be?" Emmett wondered, taking a step toward the door.

Esme put a hand on her arm. "We don't want to disturb . . ."

"She's never taken so long before," Edward said. New worry splintered the mask his face had become. His features were alive again, his eyes suddenly wide with fresh fear, extra panic. "Carlisle, you don't think—something preemptive? Would Alice have had time to see if they sent someone for her?"

Aro's translucent-skinned face filled my head. Aro, who

had seen into all the corners of Alice's mind, who knew everything she was capable of—

Emmett cussed loud enough that Jacob lurched to his feet with a growl. In the yard, his growl was echoed by his pack. My family was already a blur of action.

"Stay with Renesmee!" I all but shrieked at Jacob as I sprinted through the door.

I was still stronger than the rest of them, and I used that strength to push myself forward. I overtook Esme in a few bounds, and Rosalie in just a few strides more. I raced through the thick forest until I was right behind Edward and Carlisle.

"Would they have been able to surprise her?" Carlisle asked, his voice as even as if he were standing motionless rather than running at full speed.

"I don't see how," Edward answered. "But Aro knows her better than anyone else. Better than I do."

"Is this a trap?" Emmett called from behind us.

"Maybe," Edward said. "There's no scent but Alice and Jasper. Where were they going?"

Alice and Jasper's trail was curling into a wide arc; it stretched first east of the house, but headed north on the other side of the river, and then back west again after a few miles. We recrossed the river, all six jumping within a second of each other. Edward ran in the lead, his concentration total.

"Did you catch that scent?" Esme called ahead a few moments after we'd leaped the river for the second time. She was the farthest back, on the far left edge of our hunting party. She gestured to the southeast.

"Keep to the main trail—we're almost to the Quileute

border," Edward ordered tersely. "Stay together. See if they turned north or south."

I was not as familiar with the treaty line as the rest of them, but I could smell the hint of wolf in the breeze blowing from the east. Edward and Carlisle slowed a little out of habit, and I could see their heads sweep from side to side, waiting for the trail to turn.

Then the wolf smell was suddenly stronger, and Edward's head snapped up. He came to a sudden stop. The rest of us froze, too.

"Sam?" Edward asked in a flat voice. "What is this?"

Sam came through the trees a few hundred yards away, walking quickly toward us in his human form, flanked by two big wolves—Paul and Jared. It took Sam a while to reach us; his human pace made me impatient. I didn't want time to think about what was happening. I wanted to be in motion, to be doing something. I wanted to have my arms around Alice, to know beyond a doubt that she was safe.

I watched Edward's face go absolutely white as he read what Sam was thinking. Sam ignored him, looking straight at Carlisle as he stopped walking and began to speak.

"Right after midnight, Alice and Jasper came to this place and asked permission to cross our land to the ocean. I granted them that and escorted them to the coast myself. They went immediately into the water and did not return. As we journeyed, Alice told me it was of the utmost importance that I say nothing to Jacob about seeing her until I spoke to you. I was to wait here for you to come looking for her and then give you this note. She told me to obey her as if all our lives depended on it."

Sam's face was grim as he held out a folded sheet of paper, printed all over with small black text. It was a page out of a book; my sharp eyes read the printed words as Carlisle unfolded it to see the other side. The side facing me was the copyright page from *The Merchant of Venice*. A hint of my own scent blew off of it as Carlisle shook the paper flat. I realized it was a page torn from one of my books. I'd brought a few things from Charlie's house to the cottage; a few sets of normal clothes, all the letters from my mother, and my favorite books. My tattered collection of Shakespeare paperbacks had been on the bookshelf in the cottage's little living room yesterday morning. . . .

"Alice has decided to leave us," Carlisle whispered.

"What?" Rosalie cried.

Carlisle turned the page around so that we all could read.

Don't look for us. There isn't time to waste. Remember: Tanya, Siobhan, Amun, Alistair, all the nomads you can find. We'll seek out Peter and Charlotte on our way. We're so sorry that we have to leave you this way, with no goodbyes or explanations. It's the only way for us. We love you.

We stood frozen again, the silence total but for the sound of the wolves' heartbeats, their breathing. Their thoughts must have been loud, too. Edward was first to move again, speaking in response to what he heard in Sam's head.

"Yes, things are that dangerous."

"Enough that you would abandon your family?" Sam asked out loud, censure in his tone. It was clear that he had not read the note before giving it to Carlisle. He was upset now, looking as if he regretted listening to Alice.

Edward's expression was stiff—to Sam it probably looked angry or arrogant, but I could see the shape of pain in the hard planes of his face.

"We don't know what she saw," Edward said. "Alice is neither unfeeling nor a coward. She just has more information than we do."

"*We* would not—," Sam began.

"You are bound differently than we are," Edward snapped. "*We* each still have our free will."

Sam's chin jerked up, and his eyes looked suddenly flat black.

"But you should heed the warning," Edward went on. "This is not something you want to involve yourselves in. You can still avoid what Alice saw."

Sam smiled grimly. "*We* don't run away." Behind him, Paul snorted.

"Don't get your family slaughtered for pride," Carlisle interjected quietly.

Sam looked at Carlisle with a softer expression. "As Edward pointed out, we don't have the same kind of freedom that you have. Renesmee is as much a part of our family now as she is yours. Jacob cannot abandon her, and we cannot abandon him." His eyes flickered to Alice's note, and his lips pressed into a thin line.

"You don't know her," Edward said.

"Do you?" Sam asked bluntly.

Carlisle put a hand on Edward's shoulder. "We have much to do, son. Whatever Alice's decision, we would be foolish not to follow her advice now. Let's go home and get to work."

Edward nodded, his face still rigid with pain. Behind me, I could hear Esme's quiet, tearless sobs.

I didn't know how to cry in this body; I couldn't do anything but stare. There was no feeling yet. Everything seemed unreal, like I was dreaming again after all these months. Having a nightmare.

"Thank you, Sam," Carlisle said.

"I'm sorry," Sam answered. "We shouldn't have let her through."

"You did the right thing," Carlisle told him. "Alice is free to do what she will. I wouldn't deny her that liberty."

I'd always thought of the Cullens as a whole, an indivisible unit. Suddenly, I remembered that it had not always been so. Carlisle had created Edward, Esme, Rosalie and Emmett; Edward had created me. We were physically linked by blood and venom. I never thought of Alice and Jasper as separate—as adopted into the family. But in truth, Alice *had* adopted the Cullens. She had shown up with her unconnected past, bringing Jasper with his, and fit herself into the family that was already there. Both she and Jasper had known another life outside the Cullen family. Had she really chosen to lead another new life after she'd seen that life with the Cullens was over?

We were doomed, then, weren't we? There was no hope at all. Not one ray, one flicker that might have convinced Alice she had a chance at our side.

The bright morning air seemed thicker suddenly, blacker, as if physically darkened by my despair.

"*I'm* not going down without a fight," Emmett snarled low under his breath. "Alice told us what to do. Let's get it done."

The others nodded with determined expressions, and I realized that they were banking on whatever chance Alice had given us. That they were not going to give in to hopelessness and wait to die.

Yes, we all would fight. What else was there? And apparently we would involve others, because Alice had said so before she'd left us. How could we not follow Alice's last warning? The wolves, too, would fight with us for Renesmee.

We would fight, they would fight, and we all would die.

I didn't feel the same resolve the others seemed to feel. Alice knew the odds. She was giving us the only chance she could see, but the chance was too slim for her to bet on it.

I felt already beaten as I turned my back on Sam's critical face and followed Carlisle toward home.

We ran automatically now, not the same panicked hurry as before. As we neared the river, Esme's head lifted.

"There was that other trail. It was fresh."

She nodded forward, toward where she had called Edward's attention on the way here. While we were racing to *save* Alice . . .

"It has to be from earlier in the day. It was just Alice, without Jasper," Edward said lifelessly.

Esme's face puckered, and she nodded.

I drifted to the right, falling a little behind. I was sure

Edward was right, but at the same time . . . After all, how had Alice's note ended up on a page from my book?

"Bella?" Edward asked in an emotionless voice as I hesitated.

"I want to follow the trail," I told him, smelling the light scent of Alice that led away from her earlier flight path. I was new to this, but it smelled exactly the same to me, just minus the scent of Jasper.

Edward's golden eyes were empty. "It probably just leads back to the house."

"Then I'll meet you there."

At first I thought he would let me go alone, but then, as I moved a few steps away, his blank eyes flickered to life.

"I'll come with you," he said quietly. "We'll meet you at home, Carlisle."

Carlisle nodded, and the others left. I waited until they were out of sight, and then I looked at Edward questioningly.

"I couldn't let you walk away from me," he explained in a low voice. "It hurt just to imagine it."

I understood without more explanation than that. I thought of being divided from him now and realized I would have felt the same pain, no matter how short the separation.

There was so little time left to be together.

I held my hand out to him, and he took it.

"Let's hurry," he said. "Renesmee will be awake."

I nodded, and we were running again.

It was probably a silly thing, to waste the time away from Renesmee just for curiosity's sake. But the note bothered me. Alice could have carved the note into a boulder or tree trunk if she lacked writing utensils. She could have stolen a pad of Post-its from any of the houses by the highway. Why my book? When did she get it?

Sure enough, the trail led back to the cottage by a circuitous route that stayed far clear of the Cullens' house and the wolves in the nearby woods. Edward's brows tightened in confusion as it became obvious where the trail led.

He tried to reason it out. "She left Jasper to wait for her and came here?"

We were almost to the cottage now, and I felt uneasy. I was glad to have Edward's hand in mine, but I also felt as if I should be here alone. Tearing out the page and carrying it back to Jasper was such an odd thing for Alice to do. It felt like there was a message in her action—one I didn't understand at all. But it was my book, so the message *must* be for me. If it were something she wanted Edward to know, wouldn't she have pulled a page from one of his books . . . ?

"Give me just a minute," I said, pulling my hand free as we got to the door.

His forehead creased. "Bella?"

"Please? Thirty seconds."

I didn't wait for him to answer. I darted through the door, pulling it shut behind me. I went straight to the bookshelf. Alice's scent was fresh—less than a day old. A fire that I had not set burned low but hot in the fireplace. I yanked *The Merchant of Venice* off the shelf and flipped it open to the title page.

There, next to the feathered edge left by the torn page, under the words *The Merchant of Venice by William Shakespeare*, was a note.

Destroy this.

Below that was a name and an address in Seattle.

When Edward came through the door after only thirteen seconds rather than thirty, I was watching the book burn.

"What's going on, Bella?"

"She was here. She ripped a page out of my book to write her note on."

"Why?"

"I don't know why."

"Why are you burning it?"

"I—I—" I frowned, letting all my frustration and pain show on my face. I did not know what Alice was trying to tell me, only that she'd gone to great lengths to keep it from anyone but me. The one person whose mind Edward could not read. So she must want to keep him in the dark, and it was probably for a good reason. "It seemed appropriate."

"We don't know what she's doing," he said quietly.

I stared into the flames. I was the only person in the world who could lie to Edward. Was that what Alice wanted from me? Her last request?

"When we were on the plane to Italy," I whispered—this was not a lie, except perhaps in context—"on our way to rescue you . . . she lied to Jasper so that he wouldn't come after us. She knew that if he faced the Volturi, he would die. She was willing to die herself rather than put him in danger. Willing for me to die, too. Willing for you to die."

Edward didn't answer.

"She has her priorities," I said. It made my still heart

ache to realize that my explanation did not feel like a lie in any way.

"I don't believe it," Edward said. He didn't say it like he was arguing with me—he said it like he was arguing with himself. "Maybe it was just Jasper in danger. Her plan would work for the rest of us, but he'd be lost if he stayed. Maybe . . ."

"She could have told us that. Sent him away."

"But would Jasper have gone? Maybe she's lying to him again."

"Maybe," I pretended to agree. "We should go home. There's no time."

Edward took my hand, and we ran.

Alice's note did not make me hopeful. If there were any way to avoid the coming slaughter, Alice would have stayed. I couldn't see another possibility. So it was something else she was giving me. Not a way to escape. But what else would she think that I wanted? Maybe a way to salvage *something*? Was there anything I could still save?

Carlisle and the others had not been idle in our absence. We'd been separated from them for all of five minutes, and they were already prepared to leave. In the corner, Jacob was human again, with Renesmee on his lap, both of them watching us with wide eyes.

Rosalie had traded her silk wrap dress for a sturdy-looking pair of jeans, running shoes, and a button-down shirt made of the thick weave that backpackers used for long trips. Esme was dressed similarly. There was a globe on the coffee table, but they were done looking at it, just waiting for us.

The atmosphere was more positive now than before; it felt good to them to be in action. Their hopes were pinned on Alice's instructions.

I looked at the globe and wondered where we were headed first.

"We're to stay here?" Edward asked, looking at Carlisle. He didn't sound happy.

"Alice said that we would have to show people Renesmee, and we would have to be careful about it," Carlisle said. "We'll send whomever we can find back here to you—Edward, you'll be the best at fielding that particular minefield."

Edward gave one sharp nod, still not happy. "There's a lot of ground to cover."

"We're splitting up," Emmett answered. "Rose and I are hunting for nomads."

"You'll have your hands full here," Carlisle said. "Tanya's family will be here in the morning, and they have no idea why. First, you have to persuade them not to react the way Irina did. Second, you've got to find out what Alice meant about Eleazar. Then, after all that, will they stay to witness for us? It will start again as the others come—if we can persuade anyone to come in the first place." Carlisle sighed. "Your job may well be the hardest. We'll be back to help as soon as we can."

Carlisle put his hand on Edward's shoulder for a second and then kissed my forehead. Esme hugged us both, and Emmett punched us both on the arm. Rosalie forced a hard smile for Edward and me, blew a kiss to Renesmee, and then gave Jacob a parting grimace.

"Good luck," Edward told them.

"And to you," Carlisle said. "We'll all need it."

I watched them leave, wishing I could feel whatever hope bolstered them, and wishing I could be alone with the computer for just a few seconds. I had to figure out who this J. Jenks person was and why Alice had gone to such lengths to give his name to only me.

Renesmee twisted in Jacob's arms to touch his cheek.

"I don't know if Carlisle's friends will come. I hope so. Sounds like we're a little outnumbered right now," Jacob murmured to Renesmee.

So she knew. Renesmee already understood only too clearly what was going on. The whole imprinted-werewolf-gives-the-object-of-his-imprinting-whatever-she-wants thing was getting old pretty fast. Wasn't shielding her more important than answering her questions?

I looked carefully at her face. She did not look frightened, only anxious and very serious as she conversed with Jacob in her silent way.

"No, we can't help; we've got to stay here," he went on. "People are coming to see *you*, not the scenery."

Renesmee frowned at him.

"No, I don't have to go anywhere," he said to her. Then he looked at Edward, his face stunned by the realization that he might be wrong. "Do I?"

Edward hesitated.

"Spit it out," Jacob said, his voice raw with tension. He was right at his breaking point, just like the rest of us.

"The vampires who are coming to help us are not the same as we are," Edward said. "Tanya's family is the only one besides ours with a reverence for human life, and even they don't think much of werewolves. I think it might be safer—"

"I can take care of myself," Jacob interrupted.

"Safer for Renesmee," Edward continued, "if the choice to believe our story about her is not tainted by an association with werewolves."

"Some friends. They'd turn on you just because of who you hang out with now?"

"I think they would mostly be tolerant under normal circumstances. But you need to understand—accepting Nessie will not be a simple thing for any of them. Why make it even the slightest bit harder?"

Carlisle had explained the laws about immortal children to Jacob last night. "The immortal children were really that bad?" he asked.

"You can't imagine the depth of the scars they've left in the collective vampire psyche."

"Edward . . ." It was still odd to hear Jacob use Edward's name without bitterness.

"I know, Jake. I know how hard it is to be away from her. We'll play it by ear— see how they react to her. In any case, Nessie is going to have to be incognito off and on in the next few weeks. She'll need to stay at the cottage until the right moment for us to introduce her. As long as you keep a safe distance from the main house . . ."

"I can do that. Company in the morning, huh?"

"Yes. The closest of our friends. In this particular case, it's probably better if we get things out in the open as soon as possible. You can stay here. Tanya knows about you. She's even met Seth."

"Right."

"You should tell Sam what's going on. There might be strangers in the woods soon."

"Good point. Though I owe him some silence after last night."

"Listening to Alice is usually the right thing."

Jacob's teeth ground together, and I could see that he shared Sam's feelings about what Alice and Jasper had done.

While they were talking, I wandered toward the back windows, trying to look distracted and anxious. Not a difficult thing to do. I leaned my head against the wall that curved away from the living room toward the dining room, right next to one of the computer desks. I ran my fingers against the keys while staring into the forest, trying to make it look like an absentminded thing. Did vampires ever do things absentmindedly? I didn't think anyone was paying particular attention to me, but I didn't turn to make sure. The monitor glowed to life. I stroked my fingers across the keys again. Then I drummed them very quietly on the wooden desktop, just to make it seem random. Another stroke across the keys.

I scanned the screen in my peripheral vision.

No J. Jenks, but there was a Jason Jenks. A lawyer. I brushed the keyboard, trying to keep a rhythm, like the preoccupied stroking of a cat you'd all but forgotten on your lap. Jason Jenks had a fancy website for his firm, but the address on the homepage was wrong. In Seattle, but in a different zip code. I noted the phone number and then stroked the keyboard in rhythm. This time I searched the address, but nothing at all came up, as if the address didn't exist. I wanted to look at a map, but I decided I was pushing my luck. One more brush, to delete the history. . . .

I continued staring out the window and brushed the wood a few times. I heard light footsteps crossing the floor to me, and I turned with what I hoped was the same expression as before.

Renesmee reached for me, and I held my arms open. She launched herself into them, smelling strongly of werewolf, and nestled her head against my neck.

I didn't know if I could stand this. As much as I feared for my life, for Edward's, for the rest of my family's, it was not the same as the gut-wrenching terror I felt for my daughter. There had to be a way to save her, even if that was the only thing I could do.

Suddenly, I knew that this was all I wanted anymore. The rest I would bear if I had to, but not her life being forfeited. Not that.

She was the one thing I simply *had* to save.

Would Alice have known how I would feel?

Renesmee's hand touched my cheek lightly.

She showed me my own face, Edward's, Jacob's, Rosalie's, Esme's, Carlisle's, Alice's, Jasper's, flipping through all our family's faces faster and faster. Seth and Leah. Charlie, Sue, and Billy. Over and over again. Worrying, like the rest of us were. She was only worrying, though. Jake had kept the worst from her as far as I could tell. The part about how we had no hope, how we all were going to die in a month's time.

She settled on Alice's face, longing and confused. Where was Alice?

"I don't know," I whispered. "But she's Alice. She's doing the right thing, like always."

The right thing for Alice, anyway. I hated thinking of her that way, but how else could the situation be understood?

Renesmee sighed, and the longing intensified.

"I miss her, too."

I felt my face working, trying to find the expression that went with the grief inside. My eyes felt strange and dry; they blinked against the uncomfortable feeling. I bit my lip. When I took my next breath, the air hitched in my throat, like I was choking on it.

Renesmee pulled back to look at me, and I saw my face mirrored in her thoughts and in her eyes. I looked like Esme had this morning.

So this was what it felt like to cry.

Renesmee's eyes glistened wetly as she watched my face. She stroked my face, showing me nothing, just trying to soothe me.

I'd never thought to see the mother-daughter bond reversed between us, the way it had always been for Renée and me. But I hadn't had a very clear view of the future.

A tear welled up on the edge of Renesmee's eye. I wiped it away with a kiss. She touched her eye in amazement and then looked at the wetness on her fingertip.

"Don't cry," I told her. "It's going to be okay. You're going to be fine. I will find you a way through this."

If there was nothing else I could do, I would still save my Renesmee. I was more positive than ever that this was what Alice would give me. She would know. She would have left me a way.

30. IRRESISTIBLE

THERE WAS SO MUCH TO THINK ABOUT.

How was I going to find time alone to hunt down J. Jenks, and why did Alice want me to know about him?

If Alice's clue had nothing to do with Renesmee, what could I do to save my daughter?

How were Edward and I going to explain things to Tanya's family in the morning? What if they reacted like Irina? What if it turned into a fight?

I didn't know how to fight. How was I going to learn in just a month? Was there any chance at all that I could be taught fast enough that I might be a danger to any one member of the Volturi? Or was I doomed to be totally useless? Just another easily dispatched newborn?

So many answers I needed, but I did not get the chance to ask my questions.

Wanting some normality for Renesmee, I'd insisted on taking her home to our cottage at bedtime. Jacob was more comfortable in his wolf form at the moment; the stress was easier dealt with when he felt ready for a fight. I wished that I could feel the same, could feel ready. He ran in the woods, on guard again.

After she was deeply under, I put Renesmee in her bed and then went to the front room to ask my questions of Edward. The ones I was able to ask, at any rate; one of the most difficult of problems was the idea of trying to hide anything from him, even with the advantage of my silent thoughts.

He stood with his back to me, staring into the fire.

"Edward, I—"

He spun and was across the room in what seemed like no time at all, not even the smallest part of a second. I only had time to register the ferocious expression on his face before his lips were crushing against mine and his arms were locked around me like steel girders.

I didn't think of my questions again for the rest of that night. It didn't take long for me to grasp the reason for his mood, and even less time to feel exactly the same way.

I'd been planning on needing years just to somewhat organize the overwhelming passion I felt for him physically. And then centuries after that to enjoy it. If we had only a month left together . . . Well, I didn't see how I could stand to have this end. For the moment I couldn't help but be selfish. All I wanted was to love him as much as possible in the limited time given to me.

It was hard to pull myself away from him when the sun came up, but we had our job to do, a job that might be more difficult than all the rest of our family's searches put together. As soon as I let myself think of what was coming, I was all tension; it felt like my nerves were being stretched on a rack, thinner and thinner.

"I wish there was a way to get the information we need from Eleazar before we tell them about Nessie," Edward muttered as we hurriedly dressed in the huge closet that was more reminder of Alice than I wanted at the moment. "Just in case."

"But he wouldn't understand the question to answer it," I agreed. "Do you think they'll let us explain?"

"I don't know."

I pulled Renesmee, still sleeping, from her bed and held her close so that her curls were pressed against my face; her sweet scent, so close, overpowered every other smell.

I couldn't waste one second of time today. There were answers I needed, and wasn't sure how much time Edward and I would have alone today. If all went well with Tanya's family, hopefully we would have company for an extended period.

"Edward, will you teach me how to fight?" I asked him, tensed for his reaction, as he held the door for me.

It was what I expected. He froze, and then his eyes swept over me with a deep significance, like he was looking at me for the first or last time. His eyes lingered on our daughter sleeping in my arms.

"If it comes to a fight, there won't be much any of us can do," he hedged.

I kept my voice even. "Would you leave me unable to defend myself?"

He swallowed convulsively, and the door shuddered, hinges protesting, as his hand tightened. Then he nodded. "When you put it that way . . . I suppose we should get to work as soon as we can."

I nodded, too, and we started toward the big house. We didn't hurry.

I wondered what I could do that would have any hope of making a difference. I was a tiny bit special, in my own way—if having a supernaturally thick skull could really be considered special. Was there any use that I could put that toward?

"What would you say their biggest advantage is? Do they even have a weakness?"

Edward didn't have to ask to know I meant the Volturi.

"Alec and Jane are their greatest offense," he said emotionlessly, like we were talking of a basketball team. "Their defensive players rarely see any real action."

"Because Jane can burn you where you stand—mentally at least. What does Alec do? Didn't you once say he was even more dangerous than Jane?"

"Yes. In a way, he is the antidote to Jane. She makes you feel the worst pain imaginable. Alec, on the other hand, makes you feel nothing. Absolutely nothing. Sometimes, when the Volturi are feeling kind, they have Alec anesthetize someone before he is executed. If he has surrendered or pleased them in some other way."

"Anesthetic? But how is that more dangerous than Jane?"

"Because he cuts off your senses altogether. No pain, but also no sight or sound or smell. Total sensory deprivation. You are utterly alone in the blackness. You don't even feel it when they burn you."

I shivered. Was this the best we could hope for? To not see or feel death when it came?

"That would make him only equally as dangerous as Jane," Edward went on in the same detached voice, "in that they both can incapacitate you, make you into a helpless target. The difference between them is like the difference between Aro and me. Aro hears the mind of only one person at a time. Jane can only hurt the one object of her focus. I can hear everyone at the same time."

I felt cold as I saw where he was going. "And Alec can incapacitate us all at the same time?" I whispered.

"Yes," he said. "If he uses his gift against us, we will all stand blind and deaf until they get around to killing us—maybe they'll simply burn us without bothering to tear us apart first. Oh, we could try to fight, but we'll be more likely to hurt one another than we would be to hurt one of them."

We walked in silence for a few seconds.

An idea was shaping itself in my head. Not very promising, but better than nothing.

"Do you think Alec is a very good fighter?" I asked. "Aside from what he can do, I mean. If he had to fight without his gift. I wonder if he's ever even tried. . . ."

Edward glanced at me sharply. "What are you thinking?"

I looked straight ahead. "Well, he probably can't do that to me, can he? If what he does is like Aro and Jane and you.

Maybe . . . if he's never really had to defend himself . . . and I learned a few tricks—"

"He's been with the Volturi for centuries," Edward cut me off, his voice abruptly panicked. He was probably seeing the same image in his head that I was: the Cullens standing helpless, senseless pillars on the killing field—all but me. I'd be the only one who *could* fight. "Yes, you're surely immune to his power, but you are still a newborn, Bella. I can't make you that strong a fighter in a few weeks. I'm sure he's had training."

"Maybe, maybe not. It's the one thing I can do that no one else can. Even if I can just *distract* him for a while—"

Could I last long enough to give the others a chance?

"Please, Bella," Edward said through his teeth. "Let's not talk about this."

"Be reasonable."

"I will try to teach you what I can, but please don't make me think about you sacrificing yourself as a diversion—" He choked, and didn't finish.

I nodded. I would keep my plans to myself, then. First Alec and then, if I was miraculously lucky enough to win, Jane. If I could only even things out—remove the Volturi's overwhelming offensive advantage. Maybe then there was a chance. . . . My mind raced ahead. What if I *was* able to distract or even take them out? Honestly, why would either Jane or Alec ever have needed to learn battle skills? I couldn't imagine petulant little Jane surrendering her advantage, even to learn.

If I was able to kill them, what a difference that would make.

"I have to learn everything. As much as you can possibly cram into my head in the next month," I murmured.

He acted as if I hadn't spoken.

Who next, then? I might as well have my plans in order so that, if I did live past attacking Alec, there would be no hesitation in my strike. I tried to think of another situation where my thick skull would give me an advantage. I didn't know enough about what the others did. Obviously, fighters like the huge Felix were beyond me. I could only try to give Emmett his fair fight there. I didn't know much about the rest of the Volturi guard, besides Demetri. . . .

My face was perfectly smooth as I considered Demetri. Without a doubt, he would be a fighter. There was no other way he could have survived so long, always at the spear point of any attack. And he must always lead, because he was their tracker—the best tracker in the world, no doubt. If there had been one better, the Volturi would have traded up. Aro didn't surround himself with second best.

If Demetri didn't exist, then we *could* run. Whoever was left of us, in any case. My daughter, warm in my arms . . . Someone could run with her. Jacob or Rosalie, whoever was left.

And . . . if Demetri didn't exist, then Alice and Jasper could be safe forever. Is that what Alice had seen? That part of our family could continue? The two of them, at the very least.

Could I begrudge her that?

"Demetri . . . ," I said.

"Demetri is mine," Edward said in a hard, tight voice. I looked at him quickly and saw that his expression had turned violent.

"Why?" I whispered.

He didn't answer at first. We were to the river when he finally murmured, "For Alice. It's the only thanks I can give her now for the last fifty years."

So his thoughts were in line with mine.

I heard Jacob's heavy paws thudding against the frozen ground. In seconds, he was pacing beside me, his dark eyes focused on Renesmee.

I nodded to him once, then returned to my questions. There was so little time.

"Edward, why do you think Alice told us to ask Eleazar about the Volturi? Has he been in Italy recently or something? What could he know?"

"Eleazar knows everything when it comes to the Volturi. I forgot you didn't know. He used to be one of them."

I hissed involuntarily. Jacob growled beside me.

"What?" I demanded, in my head picturing the beautiful dark-haired man at our wedding wrapped in a long, ashy cloak.

Edward's face was softer now—he smiled a little. "Eleazar is a very gentle person. He wasn't entirely happy with the Volturi, but he respected the law and its need to be up-held. He felt he was working toward the greater good. He doesn't regret his time with them. But when he found Carmen, he found his place in this world. They are very similar people, both very compassionate for vampires." He smiled again. "They met Tanya and her sisters, and they never looked back. They are well suited to this lifestyle. If they'd never found Tanya, I imagine they would have eventually discovered a way to live without human blood on their own."

The pictures in my head were jarring. I couldn't make them match up. A compassionate Volturi soldier?

Edward glanced at Jacob and answered a silent question. "No, he wasn't one of their warriors, so to speak. He had a gift they found convenient."

Jacob must have asked the obvious follow-up question.

"He has an instinctive feel for the gifts of others—the extra abilities that some vampires have," Edward told him. "He could give Aro a general idea of what any given vampire was capable of just by being in proximity with him or her. This was helpful when the Volturi went into battle. He could warn them if someone in the opposing coven had a skill that might give them some trouble. That was rare; it takes quite a skill to even inconvenience the Volturi for a moment. More often, the warning would give Aro the chance to save someone who might be useful to him. Eleazar's gift works even with humans, to an extent. He has to really concentrate with humans, though, because the latent ability is so nebulous. Aro would have him test the people who wanted to join, to see if they had any potential. Aro was sorry to see him go."

"They let him go?" I asked. "Just like that?"

His smile was darker now, a little twisted. "The Volturi aren't supposed to be the villains, the way they seem to you. They are the foundation of our peace and civilization. Each member of the guard chooses to serve them. It's quite prestigious; they all are proud to be there, not forced to be there."

I scowled at the ground.

"They're only alleged to be heinous and evil by the criminals, Bella."

"We're not criminals."

Jacob huffed in agreement.

"They don't know that."

"Do you really think we can make them stop and listen?"

Edward hesitated just the tiniest moment and then shrugged. "If we find enough friends to stand beside us. Maybe."

If. I suddenly felt the urgency of what we had before us today. Edward and I both started to move faster, breaking into a run. Jacob caught up quickly.

"Tanya shouldn't be too much longer," Edward said. "We need to be ready."

How to be ready, though? We arranged and rearranged, thought and rethought. Renesmee in full view? Or hidden at first? Jacob in the room? Or outside? He'd told his pack to stay close but invisible. Should he do the same?

In the end, Renesmee, Jacob—in his human form again—and I waited around the corner from the front door in the dining room, sitting at the big polished table. Jacob let me hold Renesmee; he wanted space in case he had to phase quickly.

Though I was glad to have her in my arms, it made me feel useless. It reminded me that in a fight with mature vampires, I was no more than an easy target; I didn't need my hands free.

I tried to remember Tanya, Kate, Carmen, and Eleazar from the wedding. Their faces were murky in my ill-lit memories. I only knew they were beautiful, two blondes and two brunettes. I couldn't remember if there was any kindness in their eyes.

Edward leaned motionlessly against the back window wall, staring toward the front door. It didn't look like he was seeing the room in front of him.

We listened to the cars zooming past out on the freeway, none of them slowing.

Renesmee nestled into my neck, her hand against my cheek but no images in my head. She didn't have pictures for her feelings now.

"What if they don't like me?" she whispered, and all our eyes flashed to her face.

"Of course they'll—," Jacob started to say, but I silenced him with a look.

"They don't understand you, Renesmee, because they've never met anyone like you," I told her, not wanting to lie to her with promises that might not come true. "Getting them to understand is the problem."

She sighed, and in my head flashed pictures of all of us in one quick burst. Vampire, human, werewolf. She fit nowhere.

"You're special, that's not a bad thing."

She shook her head in disagreement. She thought of our strained faces and said, "This is my fault."

"No," Jacob, Edward, and I all said at exactly the same time, but before we could argue further, we heard the sound we'd been waiting for: the slowing of an engine on the freeway, the tires moving from pavement to soft dirt.

Edward darted around the corner to stand waiting by the door. Renesmee hid in my hair. Jacob and I stared at each other across the table, desperation on our faces.

The car moved quickly through the woods, faster than Charlie or Sue drove. We heard it pull into the meadow and stop by the front porch. Four doors opened and closed. They didn't speak as they approached the door. Edward opened it before they could knock.

"Edward!" a female voice enthused.

"Hello, Tanya. Kate, Eleazar, Carmen."

Three murmured hellos.

"Carlisle said he needed to talk to us right away," the first voice said, Tanya. I could hear that they all were still outside. I imagined Edward in the doorway, blocking their entrance. "What's the problem? Trouble with the werewolves?"

Jacob rolled his eyes.

"No," Edward said. "Our truce with the werewolves is stronger than ever."

A woman chuckled.

"Aren't you going to invite us in?" Tanya asked. And then she continued without waiting for an answer. "Where's Carlisle?"

"Carlisle had to leave."

There was a short silence.

"What's going on, Edward?" Tanya demanded.

"If you could give me the benefit of the doubt for just a few minutes," he answered. "I have something difficult to explain, and I'll need you to be open-minded until you understand."

"Is Carlisle all right?" a male voice asked anxiously. Eleazar.

"None of us is all right, Eleazar," Edward said, and then he patted something, maybe Eleazar's shoulder. "But physically, Carlisle is fine."

"Physically?" Tanya asked sharply. "What do you mean?"

"I mean that my entire family is in very grave danger. But before I explain, I ask for your promise. Listen to everything I say before you react. I am begging you to hear me out."

A longer silence greeted his request. Through the strained hush, Jacob and I stared wordlessly at each other. His russet lips paled.

"We're listening," Tanya finally said. "We will hear it all before we judge."

"Thank you, Tanya," Edward said fervently. "We wouldn't involve you in this if we had any other choice."

Edward moved. We heard four sets of footsteps walk through the doorway.

Someone sniffed. "I knew those werewolves were involved," Tanya muttered.

"Yes, and they're on our side. Again."

The reminder silenced Tanya.

"Where's your Bella?" one of the other female voices asked. "How is she?"

"She'll join us shortly. She's well, thank you. She's taken to immortality with amazing finesse."

"Tell us about the danger, Edward," Tanya said quietly. "We'll listen, and we'll be on your side, where we belong."

Edward took a deep breath. "I'd like you to witness for yourselves first. Listen—in the other room. What do you hear?"

It was quiet, and then there was movement.

"Just listen first, please," Edward said.

"A werewolf, I assume. I can hear his heart," Tanya said.

"What else?" Edward asked.

There was a pause.

"What is that thrumming?" Kate or Carmen asked. "Is that . . . some kind of a bird?"

"No, but remember what you're hearing. Now, what do you smell? Besides the werewolf."

"Is there a human here?" Eleazar whispered.

"No," Tanya disagreed. "It's not human . . . but . . . closer to human than the rest of the scents here. What is that, Edward? I don't think I've ever smelled that fragrance before."

"You most certainly have not, Tanya. Please, *please* remember that this is something entirely new to you. Throw away your preconceived notions."

"I promised you I would listen, Edward."

"All right, then. Bella? Bring out Renesmee, please."

My legs felt strangely numb, but I knew that feeling was all in my head. I forced myself not to hold back, not to move sluggishly, as I got to my feet and walked the few short feet to the corner. The heat from Jacob's body flamed close behind me as he shadowed my steps.

I took one step into the bigger room and then froze, unable to force myself farther forward. Renesmee took a deep breath and then peeped out from under my hair, her little shoulders tight, expecting a rebuff.

I thought I'd prepared myself for their reaction. For accusations, for shouting, for the motionlessness of deep stress.

Tanya skittered back four steps, her strawberry curls quivering, like a human confronted by a venomous snake. Kate jumped back all the way to the front door and braced herself against the wall there. A shocked hiss came from between her clenched teeth. Eleazar threw himself in front of Carmen in a protective crouch.

"Oh *please*," I heard Jacob complain under his breath.

Edward put his arm around Renesmee and me. "You promised to listen," he reminded them.

"Some things cannot be heard!" Tanya exclaimed. "How could you, Edward? Do you not know what this means?"

"We have to get out of here," Kate said anxiously, her hand on the doorknob.

"Edward . . ." Eleazar seemed beyond words.

"Wait," Edward said, his voice harder now. "Remember what you hear, what you smell. Renesmee is not what you think she is."

"There are no exceptions to this rule, Edward," Tanya snapped back.

"Tanya," Edward said sharply, "you can hear her heartbeat! Stop and think about what that means."

"Her heartbeat?" Carmen whispered, peering around Eleazar's shoulder.

"She's not a full vampire child," Edward answered, directing his attention toward Carmen's less hostile expression. "She is half-human."

The four vampires stared at him like he was speaking a language none of them knew.

"Hear me." Edward's voice shifted into a smooth velvet tone of persuasion. "Renesmee is one of a kind. I am her father. Not her creator—her biological father."

Tanya's head was shaking, just a tiny movement. She didn't seem aware of it.

"Edward, you can't expect us to—," Eleazar started to say.

"Tell me another explanation that fits, Eleazar. You can feel the warmth of her body in the air. Blood runs in her veins, Eleazar. You can smell it."

"How?" Kate breathed.

"Bella is her biological mother," Edward told her. "She conceived, carried, and gave birth to Renesmee while she was still human. It nearly killed her. I was hard-pressed to get enough venom into her heart to save her."

"I've never heard of such a thing," Eleazar said. His shoulders were still stiff, his expression cold.

"Physical relationships between vampires and humans are not common," Edward answered, a bit of dark humor in his tone now. "Human survivors of such trysts are even less common. Wouldn't you agree, cousins?"

Both Kate and Tanya scowled at him.

"Come now, Eleazar. Surely you can see the resemblance."

It was Carmen who responded to Edward's words. She stepped around Eleazar, ignoring his half-articulated warning, and walked carefully to stand right in front of me. She leaned down slightly, looking carefully into Renesmee's face.

"You seem to have your mother's eyes," she said in a low, calm voice, "but your father's face." And then, as if she could not help herself, she smiled at Renesmee.

Renesmee's answering smile was dazzling. She touched my face without looking away from Carmen. She imagined touching Carmen's face, wondering if that was okay.

"Do you mind if Renesmee tells you about it herself?" I asked Carmen. I was still too stressed to speak above a whisper. "She has a gift for explaining things."

Carmen was still smiling at Renesmee. "Do you speak, little one?"

"Yes," Renesmee answered in her trilling high soprano. All of Tanya's family flinched at the sound of her voice except for Carmen. "But I can show you more than I can tell you."

She placed her little dimpled hand on Carmen's cheek.

Carmen stiffened like an electric shock had run through her. Eleazar was at her side in an instant, his hands on her shoulders as if to yank her away.

"Wait," Carmen said breathlessly, her unblinking eyes locked on Renesmee's.

Renesmee "showed" Carmen her explanation for a long time. Edward's face was intent as he watched with Carmen, and I wished so much that I could hear what he heard, too. Jacob shifted his weight impatiently behind me, and I knew he was wishing the same.

"What's Nessie showing her?" he grumbled under his breath.

"Everything," Edward murmured.

Another minute passed, and Renesmee dropped her hand from Carmen's face. She smiled winningly at the stunned vampire.

"She really is your daughter, isn't she?" Carmen breathed, switching her wide topaz eyes to Edward's face. "Such a vivid gift! It could only have come from a very gifted father."

"Do you believe what she showed you?" Edward asked, his expression intense.

"Without a doubt," Carmen said simply.

Eleazar's face was rigid with distress. "Carmen!"

Carmen took his hands into her own and squeezed them. "Impossible as it seems, Edward has told you nothing but truth. Let the child show you."

Carmen nudged Eleazar closer to me and then nodded at Renesmee. "Show him, *mi querida.*"

Renesmee grinned, clearly delighted with Carmen's acceptance, and touched Eleazar lightly on the forehead.

"Ay caray!" he spit, and jerked away from her.

"What did she do to you?" Tanya demanded, coming closer warily. Kate crept forward, too.

"She's just trying to show you her side of the story," Carmen told him in a soothing voice.

Renesmee frowned impatiently. "Watch, please," she commanded Eleazar. She stretched her hand out to him and then left a few inches between her fingers and his face, waiting.

Eleazar eyed her suspiciously and then glanced at Carmen for help. She nodded encouragingly. Eleazar took a deep breath and then leaned closer until his forehead touched her hand again.

He shuddered when it began but held still this time, his eyes closed in concentration.

"Ahh," he sighed when his eyes reopened a few minutes later. "I see."

Renesmee smiled at him. He hesitated, then smiled a slightly unwilling smile in response.

"Eleazar?" Tanya asked.

"It's all true, Tanya. This is no immortal child. She's half-human. Come. See for yourself."

In silence, Tanya took her turn standing warily before me, and then Kate, both showing shock as that first image hit them with Renesmee's touch. But then, just like Carmen and Eleazar, they seemed completely won over as soon as it was done.

I shot a glance at Edward's smooth face, wondering if it could really be so easy. His golden eyes were clear, unshadowed. There was no deception in this, then.

"Thank you for listening," he said quietly.

"But there is the *grave danger* you warned us of," Tanya said. "Not directly from this child, I see, but surely from the Volturi, then. How did they find out about her? When are they coming?"

I was not surprised at her quick understanding. After all, what could possibly be a threat to a family as strong as mine? Only the Volturi.

"When Bella saw Irina that day in the mountains," Edward explained, "she had Renesmee with her."

Kate hissed, her eyes narrowing to slits. "*Irina* did this? To you? To Carlisle? *Irina?*"

"No," Tanya whispered. "Someone else . . ."

"Alice saw her go to them," Edward said. I wondered if the others noticed the way he winced just slightly when he spoke Alice's name.

"How could she do this thing?" Eleazar asked of no one.

"Imagine if you had seen Renesmee only from a distance. If you had not waited for our explanation."

Tanya's eyes tightened. "No matter what she thought . . . You are our family."

"There's nothing we can do about Irina's choice now. It's too late. Alice gave us a month."

Both Tanya's and Eleazar's heads cocked to one side. Kate's brow furrowed.

"So long?" Eleazar asked.

"They are all coming. That must take some preparation."

Eleazar gasped. "The entire guard?"

"Not just the guard," Edward said, his jaw straining tight. "Aro, Caius, Marcus. Even the wives."

Shock glazed over all their eyes.

"Impossible," Eleazar said blankly.

"I would have said the same two days ago," Edward said.

Eleazar scowled, and when he spoke it was nearly a growl. "But that doesn't make any sense. Why would they put themselves and the wives in danger?"

"It doesn't make sense from that angle. Alice said there was more to this than just punishment for what they think we've done. She thought you could help us."

"More than punishment? But what else is there?" Eleazar started pacing, stalking toward the door and back again as if he were alone here, his eyebrows furrowed as he stared at the floor.

"Where are the others, Edward? Carlisle and Alice and the rest?" Tanya asked.

Edward's hesitation was almost unnoticeable. He answered only part of her question. "Looking for friends who might help us."

Tanya leaned toward him, holding her hands out in front of her. "Edward, no matter how many friends you gather, we can't help you *win*. We can only die with you. You must know that. Of course, perhaps the four of us deserve that after what Irina has done now, after how we've failed you in the past—for her sake that time as well."

Edward shook his head quickly. "We're not asking you to fight and die with us, Tanya. You know Carlisle would never ask for that."

"Then what, Edward?"

"We're just looking for witnesses. If we can make them pause, just for a moment. If they would let us explain . . ." He touched Renesmee's cheek; she grabbed his hand and held it pressed against her skin. "It's difficult to doubt our story when you see it for yourself."

Tanya nodded slowly. "Do you think her past will matter to them so much?"

"Only as it foreshadows her future. The point of the restriction was to protect us from exposure, from the excesses of children who could not be tamed."

"I'm not dangerous at all," Renesmee interjected. I listened to her high, clear voice with new ears, imagining how she sounded to the others. "I never hurt Grandpa or Sue or Billy. I love humans. And wolf-people like my Jacob." She dropped Edward's hand to reach back and pat Jacob's arm.

Tanya and Kate exchanged a quick glance.

"If Irina had not come so soon," Edward mused, "we could have avoided all of this. Renesmee grows at an unprecedented rate. By the time the month is past, she'll have gained another half year of development."

"Well, that is something we can certainly witness," Carmen said in a decided tone. "We'll be able to promise that we've seen her mature ourselves. How could the Volturi ignore such evidence?"

Eleazar mumbled, "How, indeed?" but he did not look up, and he continued pacing as if he were paying no attention at all.

"Yes, we can witness for you," Tanya said. "Certainly that much. We will consider what more we might do."

"Tanya," Edward protested, hearing more in her thoughts

than there was in her words, "we don't expect you to fight with us."

"If the Volturi won't pause to listen to our witness, we cannot simply stand by," Tanya insisted. "Of course, I should only speak for myself."

Kate snorted. "Do you really doubt me so much, sister?"

Tanya smiled widely at her. "It *is* a suicide mission, after all."

Kate flashed a grin back and then shrugged nonchalantly. "I'm in."

"I, too, will do what I can to protect the child," Carmen agreed. Then, as if she couldn't resist, she held her arms out toward Renesmee. "May I hold you, *bebé linda*?"

Renesmee reached eagerly toward Carmen, delighted with her new friend. Carmen hugged her close, murmuring to her in Spanish.

It was like it had been with Charlie, and before that with all the Cullens. Renesmee was irresistible. What was it about her that drew everyone to her, that made them willing even to pledge their lives in her defense?

For a moment I thought that maybe what we were attempting might be possible. Maybe Renesmee could do the impossible and win over our enemies as she had our friends.

And then I remembered that Alice had left us, and my hope vanished as quickly as it had appeared.

31. TALENTED

"WHAT IS THE WEREWOLVES' PART IN THIS?" TANYA asked then, eyeing Jacob.

Jacob spoke before Edward could answer. "If the Volturi won't stop to listen about Nessie, I mean Renesmee," he corrected himself, remembering that Tanya would not understand his stupid nickname, "*we* will stop them."

"Very brave, child, but that would be impossible for more experienced fighters than you are."

"You don't know what we can do."

Tanya shrugged. "It is your own life, certainly, to spend as you choose."

Jacob's eyes flickered to Renesmee—still in Carmen's

arms with Kate hovering over them—and it was easy to read the longing in them.

"She is special, that little one," Tanya mused. "Hard to resist."

"A very talented family," Eleazar murmured as he paced. His tempo was increasing; he flashed from the door to Carmen and back again every second. "A mind reader for a father, a shield for a mother, and then whatever magic this extraordinary child has bewitched us with. I wonder if there is a name for what she does, or if it is the norm for a vampire hybrid. As if such a thing could ever be considered normal! A vampire hybrid, indeed!"

"Excuse me," Edward said in a stunned voice. He reached out and caught Eleazar's shoulder as he was about to turn again for the door. "What did you just call my wife?"

Eleazar looked at Edward curiously, his manic pacing forgotten for the moment. "A shield, I *think*. She's blocking me now, so I can't be sure."

I stared at Eleazar, my brows furrowing in confusion. Shield? What did he mean about my blocking him? I was standing right here beside him, not defensive in any way.

"A shield?" Edward repeated, bewildered.

"Come now, Edward! If I can't get a read on her, I doubt you can, either. Can you hear her thoughts right now?" Eleazar asked.

"No," Edward murmured. "But I've never been able to do that. Even when she was human."

"Never?" Eleazar blinked. "Interesting. That would indicate a rather powerful latent talent, if it was manifesting so clearly even before the transformation. I can't feel a way through her shield to get a sense of it at all. Yet she must be raw still—she's only a few months old." The look he gave Edward now was almost exasperated. "And apparently completely unaware of what she's doing. Totally unconscious. Ironic. Aro sent me all over the world searching for such anomalies, and you simply stumble across it by accident and don't even realize what you have." Eleazar shook his head in disbelief.

I frowned. "What are you talking about? How can I be a *shield*? What does that even mean?" All I could picture in my head was a ridiculous medieval suit of armor.

Eleazar leaned his head to one side as he examined me. "I suppose we were overly formal about it in the guard. In truth, categorizing talents is a subjective, haphazard business; every talent is unique, never exactly the same thing twice. But you, Bella, are fairly easy to classify. Talents that are purely defensive, that protect some aspect of the bearer, are always called *shields*. Have you ever tested your abilities? Blocked anyone besides me and your mate?"

It took me a few seconds, despite how quickly my new brain worked, to organize my answer.

"It only works with certain things," I told him. "My head is sort of . . . private. But it doesn't stop Jasper from being able to mess with my mood or Alice from seeing my future."

"Purely a mental defense." Eleazar nodded to himself. "Limited, but strong."

"Aro couldn't hear her," Edward interjected. "Though she was human when they met."

Eleazar's eyes widened.

"Jane tried to hurt me, but she couldn't," I said. "Edward

thinks Demetri can't find me, and that Alec can't bother me, either. Is that good?"

Eleazar, still gaping, nodded. "Quite."

"A shield!" Edward said, deep satisfaction saturating his tone. "I never thought of it that way. The only one I've ever met before was Renata, and what she did was so different."

Eleazar had recovered slightly. "Yes, no talent ever manifests in precisely the same way, because no one ever *thinks* in exactly the same way."

"Who's Renata? What does she do?" I asked. Renesmee was interested, too, leaning away from Carmen so that she could see around Kate.

"Renata is Aro's personal bodyguard," Eleazar told me. "A very practical kind of shield, and a very strong one."

I vaguely remembered a small crowd of vampires hovering close to Aro in his macabre tower, some male, some female. I couldn't remember the women's faces in the uncomfortable, terrifying memory. One must have been Renata.

"I wonder . . . ," Eleazar mused. "You see, Renata is a powerful shield against a physical attack. If someone approaches her—or Aro, as she is always close beside him in a hostile situation—they find themselves . . . diverted. There's a force around her that repels, though it's almost unnoticeable. You simply find yourself going a different direction than you planned, with a confused memory as to why you wanted to go that other way in the first place. She can project her shield several meters out from herself. She also protects Caius and Marcus, too, when they have a need, but Aro is her priority.

"What she does isn't actually physical, though. Like the vast majority of our gifts, it takes place inside the mind.

If she tried to keep *you* back, I wonder who would win?" He shook his head. "I've never heard of Aro's or Jane's gifts being thwarted."

"Momma, you're special," Renesmee told me without any surprise, like she was commenting on the color of my clothes.

I felt disoriented. Didn't I already know my gift? I had my super-self-control that had allowed me to skip right over the horrifying newborn year. Vampires only had one extra ability at most, right?

Or had Edward been correct in the beginning? Before Carlisle had suggested that my self-control could be something beyond the natural, Edward had thought my restraint was just a product of good preparation—*focus and attitude*, he'd declared.

Which one had been right? Was there *more* I could do? A name and a category for what I was?

"Can you project?" Kate asked interestedly.

"Project?" I asked.

"Push it out from yourself," Kate explained. "Shield someone besides yourself."

"I don't know. I've never tried. I didn't know I should do that."

"Oh, you might not be able to," Kate said quickly. "Heavens knows I've been working on it for centuries and the best I can do is run a current over my skin."

I stared at her, mystified.

"Kate's got an offensive skill," Edward said. "Sort of like Jane."

I flinched away from Kate automatically, and she laughed.

"I'm not sadistic about it," she assured me. "It's just something that comes in handy during a fight."

Kate's words were sinking in, beginning to make connections in my mind. *Shield someone besides yourself,* she'd said. As if there were some way for me to include another person in my strange, quirky silent head.

I remembered Edward cringing on the ancient stones of the Volturi castle turret. Though this was a human memory, it was sharper, more painful than most of the others—like it had been branded into the tissues of my brain.

What if I could stop that from happening ever again? What if I could protect him? Protect Renesmee? What if there was even the faintest glimmer of a possibility that I could shield them, too?

"You have to teach me what to do!" I insisted, unthinkingly grabbing Kate's arm. "You have to show me how!"

Kate winced at my grip. "Maybe—if you stop trying to crush my radius."

"Oops! Sorry!"

"You're shielding, all right," Kate said. "That move should have about shocked your arm off. You didn't feel anything just now?"

"That wasn't really necessary, Kate. She didn't mean any harm," Edward muttered under his breath. Neither of us paid attention to him.

"No, I didn't feel anything. Were you doing your electric-current thing?"

"I was. Hmm. I've never met anyone who couldn't feel it, immortal or otherwise."

"You said you project it? On your skin?"

Kate nodded. "It used to be just in my palms. Kind of like Aro."

"Or Renesmee," Edward interjected.

"But after a lot of practice, I can radiate the current all over my body. It's a good defense. Anyone who tries to touch me drops like a human that's been Tasered. It only downs him for a second, but that's long enough."

I was only half-listening to Kate, my thoughts racing around the idea that I might be able to protect my little family if I could just learn *fast* enough. I wished fervently that I might be good at this projecting thing, too, like I was somehow mysteriously good at all the other aspects of being a vampire. My human life had not prepared me for things that came naturally, and I couldn't make myself trust this aptitude to last.

It felt like I had never wanted anything so badly before this: to be able to protect what I loved.

Because I was so preoccupied, I didn't notice the silent exchange going on between Edward and Eleazar until it became a spoken conversation.

"Can you think of even one exception, though?" Edward asked.

I looked over to make sense of his comment and realized that everyone else was already staring at the two men. They were leaning toward each other intently, Edward's expression tight with suspicion, Eleazar's unhappy and reluctant.

"I don't want to think of them that way," Eleazar said through his teeth. I was surprised at the sudden change in the atmosphere.

"If you're right—," Eleazar began again.

Edward cut him off. "The thought was yours, not mine."

"If *I'm* right . . . I can't even grasp what that would mean. It would change everything about the world we've created. It would change the meaning of my life. What I have been a part of."

"Your intentions were always the best, Eleazar."

"Would that even matter? What have I done? How many lives . . ."

Tanya put her hand on Eleazar's shoulder in a comforting gesture. "What did we miss, my friend? I want to know so that I can argue with these thoughts. You've never done anything worth castigating yourself this way."

"Oh, haven't I?" Eleazar muttered. Then he shrugged out from under her hand and began his pacing again, faster even than before.

Tanya watched him for half a second and then focused on Edward. "Explain."

Edward nodded, his tense eyes following Eleazar as he spoke. "He was trying to understand why so many of the Volturi would come to punish us. It's not the way they do things. Certainly, we are the biggest mature coven they've dealt with, but in the past other covens have joined to protect themselves, and they never presented much of a challenge despite their numbers. We are more closely bonded, and that's a factor, but not a huge one.

"He was remembering other times that covens have been punished, for one thing or the other, and a pattern occurred to him. It was a pattern that the rest of the guard would never have noticed, since Eleazar was the one passing the pertinent intelligence privately to Aro. A pattern that only repeated every other century or so."

"What was this pattern?" Carmen asked, watching Eleazar as Edward was.

"Aro does not often personally attend a punishing expedition," Edward said. "But in the past, when Aro wanted something in particular, it was never long before evidence turned up proving that this coven or that coven had committed some unpardonable crime. The ancients would decide to go along to watch the guard administer justice. And then, once the coven was all but destroyed, Aro would grant a pardon to one member whose thoughts, he would claim, were particularly repentant. Always, it would turn out that this vampire had the gift Aro had admired. Always, this person was given a place with the guard. The gifted vampire was won over quickly, always so grateful for the honor. There were no exceptions."

"It must be a heady thing to be chosen," Kate suggested.

"Ha!" Eleazar snarled, still in motion.

"There is one among the guard," Edward said, explaining Eleazar's angry reaction. "Her name is Chelsea. She has influence over the emotional ties between people. She can both loosen and secure these ties. She could make someone feel bonded to the Volturi, to want to belong, to want to *please* them. . . ."

Eleazar came to an abrupt halt. "We all understood why Chelsea was important. In a fight, if we could separate allegiances between allied covens, we could defeat them that much more easily. If we could distance the innocent members of a coven emotionally from the guilty,

justice could be done without unnecessary brutality—
the guilty could be punished without interference, and the
innocent could be spared. Otherwise, it was impossible to
keep the coven from fighting as a whole. So Chelsea would
break the ties that bound them together. It seemed a great
kindness to me, evidence of Aro's mercy. I did suspect that
Chelsea kept our own band more tightly knit, but that, too,
was a good thing. It made us more effective. It helped us
coexist more easily."

This clarified old memories for me. It had not made
sense to me before how the guard obeyed their masters so
gladly, with almost lover-like devotion.

"How strong is her gift?" Tanya asked with an edge to
her voice. Her gaze quickly touched on each member of her
family.

Eleazar shrugged. "I was able to leave with Carmen."
And then he shook his head. "But anything weaker than
the bond between partners is in danger. In a normal coven,
at least. Those are weaker bonds than those in our family,
though. Abstaining from human blood makes us more
civilized—lets us form true bonds of love. I doubt she could
turn our allegiances, Tanya."

Tanya nodded, seeming reassured, while Eleazar continued with his analysis.

"I could only think that the reason Aro had decided
to come himself, to bring so many with him, is because
his goal is not punishment but acquisition," Eleazar said.
"He needs to be there to control the situation. But he needs
the entire guard for protection from such a large, gifted
coven. On the other hand, that leaves the other ancients
unprotected in Volterra. Too risky—someone might try to

take advantage. So they all come together. How else could he be sure to preserve the gifts that he wants? He must want them very badly," Eleazar mused.

Edward's voice was low as a breath. "From what I saw of his thoughts last spring, Aro's never wanted anything more than he wants Alice."

I felt my mouth fall open, remembering the nightmarish pictures I had imagined long ago: Edward and Alice in black cloaks with bloodred eyes, their faces cold and remote as they stood close as shadows, Aro's hands on theirs. . . . Had Alice seen this more recently? Had she seen Chelsea trying to strip away her love for us, to bind her to Aro and Caius and Marcus?

"Is that why Alice left?" I asked, my voice breaking on her name.

Edward put his hand against my cheek. "I think it must be. To keep Aro from gaining the thing he wants most of all. To keep her power out of his hands."

I heard Tanya and Kate murmuring in disturbed voices and remembered that they hadn't known about Alice.

"He wants you, too," I whispered.

Edward shrugged, his face suddenly a little too composed. "Not nearly as much. I can't really give him anything more than he already has. And of course that's dependant on his finding a way to force me to do his will. He knows me, and he knows how unlikely that is." He raised one eyebrow sardonically.

Eleazar frowned at Edward's nonchalance. "He also knows your weaknesses," Eleazar pointed out, and then he looked at me.

"It's nothing we need to discuss now," Edward said quickly.

Eleazar ignored the hint and continued. "He probably wants your mate, too, regardless. He must have been intrigued by a talent that could defy him in its human incarnation."

Edward was uncomfortable with this topic. I didn't like it, either. If Aro wanted me to do something—anything— all he had to do was threaten Edward and I would comply. And vice versa.

Was death the lesser concern? Was it really capture we should fear?

Edward changed the subject. "I think the Volturi were waiting for this—for some pretext. They couldn't know what form their excuse would come in, but the plan was already in place for when it did come. That's why Alice saw their decision before Irina triggered it. The decision was already made, just waiting for the pretense of a justification."

"If the Volturi are abusing the trust all immortals have placed in them . . . ," Carmen murmured.

"Does it matter?" Eleazar asked. "Who would believe it? And even if others could be convinced that the Volturi are exploiting their power, how would it make any difference? No one can stand against them."

"Though some of us are apparently insane enough to try," Kate muttered.

Edward shook his head. "You're only here to witness, Kate. Whatever Aro's goal, I don't think he's ready to tarnish the Volturi's reputation for it. If we can take away his argument against us, he'll be forced to leave us in peace."

"Of course," Tanya murmured.

No one looked convinced. For a few long minutes, nobody said anything.

Then I heard the sound of tires turning off the highway pavement onto the Cullens' dirt drive.

"Oh crap, Charlie," I muttered. "Maybe the Denalis could hang out upstairs until—"

"No," Edward said in a distant voice. His eyes were far away, staring blankly at the door. "It's not your father." His gaze focused on me. "Alice sent Peter and Charlotte, after all. Time to get ready for the next round."

32. COMPANY

THE CULLENS' ENORMOUS HOUSE WAS MORE CROWDED with guests than anyone would assume could possibly be comfortable. It only worked out because none of the visitors slept. Mealtimes were dicey, though. Our company co-operated as best they could. They gave Forks and La Push a wide berth, only hunting out of state; Edward was a gracious host, lending out his cars as needed without so much as a wince. The compromise made me very uncomfortable, though I tried to tell myself that they'd all be hunting somewhere in the world, regardless.

Jacob was even more upset. The werewolves existed to prevent the loss of human life, and here was rampant murder being condoned barely outside the packs' borders.

But under these circumstances, with Renesmee in acute danger, he kept his mouth shut and glared at the floor rather than the vampires.

I was amazed at the easy acceptance the visiting vampires had for Jacob; the problems Edward had anticipated had never materialized. Jacob seemed more or less invisible to them, not quite a person, but also not food, either. They treated him the way people who are not animal-lovers treat the pets of their friends.

Leah, Seth, Quil, and Embry were assigned to run with Sam for now, and Jacob would have happily joined them, except that he couldn't stand to be away from Renesmee, and Renesmee was busy fascinating the strange collection of Carlisle's friends.

We'd replayed the scene of Renesmee's introduction to the Denali coven a half dozen times. First for Peter and Charlotte, whom Alice and Jasper had sent our way without giving them any explanation at all; like most people who knew Alice, they trusted her instructions despite the lack of information. Alice had told them nothing about which direction she and Jasper were heading. She'd made no promise to ever see them again in the future.

Neither Peter nor Charlotte had ever seen an immortal child. Though they knew the rule, their negative reaction was not as powerful as the Denali vampires' had been at first. Curiosity had driven them to allow Renesmee's "explanation." And that was it. Now they were as committed to witnessing as Tanya's family.

Carlisle had sent friends from Ireland and Egypt.

The Irish clan arrived first, and they were surprisingly easy to convince. Siobhan—a woman of immense presence whose huge body was both beautiful and mesmerizing as it moved in smooth undulations—was the leader, but she and her hard-faced mate, Liam, were long used to trusting the judgment of their newest coven member. Little Maggie, with her bouncy red curls, was not physically imposing like the other two, but she had a gift for knowing when she was being lied to, and her verdicts were never contested. Maggie declared that Edward spoke the truth, and so Siobhan and Liam accepted our story absolutely before even touching Renesmee.

Amun and the other Egyptian vampires were another story. Even after two younger members of his coven, Benjamin and Tia, had been convinced by Renesmee's explanation, Amun refused to touch her and ordered his coven to leave. Benjamin—an oddly cheerful vampire who looked barely older than a boy and seemed both utterly confident and utterly careless at the same time—persuaded Amun to stay with a few subtle threats about disbanding their alliance. Amun stayed, but continued to refuse to touch Renesmee, and would not allow his mate, Kebi, to touch her, either. It seemed an unlikely grouping—though the Egyptians all looked so alike, with their midnight hair and olive-toned pallor, that they easily could have passed for a biological family. Amun was the senior member and the outspoken leader. Kebi never strayed farther away from Amun than his shadow, and I never heard her speak a single word. Tia, Benjamin's mate, was a quiet woman as well, though when she did speak there was great insight and gravity to everything she said. Still, it was Benjamin whom they all seemed to revolve around, as if he had some invisible magnetism the others depended upon for their balance. I saw Eleazar staring at the boy with wide eyes and assumed Benjamin had a talent that drew the others to him.

"It's not that," Edward told me when we were alone that night. "His gift is so singular that Amun is terrified of losing him. Much like we had planned to keep Renesmee from Aro's knowledge"—he sighed—"Amun has been keeping Benjamin from Aro's attention. Amun created Benjamin, knowing he would be special."

"What can he do?"

"Something Eleazar's never seen before. Something I've never heard of. Something that even your shield would do nothing against." He grinned his crooked smile at me. "He can actually influence the elements—earth, wind, water, and fire. True physical manipulation, no illusion of the mind. Benjamin's still experimenting with it, and Amun tries to mold him into a weapon. But you see how independent Benjamin is. He won't be used."

"You like him," I surmised from the tone of his voice.

"He has a very clear sense of right and wrong. I like his attitude."

Amun's attitude was something else, and he and Kebi kept to themselves, though Benjamin and Tia were well on their way to being fast friends with both the Denali and the Irish covens. We hoped that Carlisle's return would ease the remaining tension with Amun.

Emmett and Rose sent individuals—any nomad friends of Carlisle's that they could track down.

Garrett came first—a tall, rangy vampire with eager ruby eyes and long sandy hair he kept tied back with a leather thong—and it was apparent immediately that he was an adventurer. I imagined that we could have presented him with any challenge and he would have accepted, just to test himself. He fell in quickly with the Denali sisters, asking endless questions about their unusual lifestyle. I wondered if vegetarianism was another challenge he would try, just to see if he could do it.

Mary and Randall also came—friends already, though they did not travel together. They listened to Renesmee's story and stayed to witness like the others. Like the Denalis, they considered what they would do if the Volturi did not pause for explanations. All three of the nomads toyed with the idea of standing with us.

Of course, Jacob got more surly with each new addition. He kept his distance when he could, and when he couldn't he grumbled to Renesmee that someone was going to have to provide an index if anyone expected him to keep all the new bloodsuckers' names straight.*

Carlisle and Esme returned a week after they had gone, Emmett and Rosalie just a few days later, and all of us felt better when they were home. Carlisle brought one more friend home with him, though *friend* might have been the wrong term. Alistair was a misanthropic English vampire who counted Carlisle as his closest acquaintance, though he could hardly stand a visit more than once a century. Alistair very much preferred to wander alone, and Carlisle had called in a lot of favors to get him here. He shunned all company, and it was clear he didn't have any admirers in the gathered covens.

The brooding dark-haired vampire took Carlisle at his word about Renesmee's origins, refusing, like Amun, to

---

* *See page 756.*

touch her. Edward told Carlisle, Esme, and me that Alistair was afraid to be here, but more afraid of not knowing the outcome. He was deeply suspicious of all authority, and therefore naturally suspicious of the Volturi. What was happening now seemed to confirm all his fears.

"Of course, now they'll know I was here," we heard him grumble to himself in the attic—his preferred spot to sulk. "No way to keep it from Aro at this point. Centuries on the run, that's what this will mean. Everyone Carlisle's talked to in the last decade will be on their list. I can't believe I got myself sucked into this mess. What a fine way to treat your friends."

But if he was right about having to run from the Volturi, at least he had more hope of doing that than the rest of us. Alistair was a tracker, though not nearly as precise and efficient as Demetri. Alistair just felt an elusive pull toward whatever he was seeking. But that pull would be enough to tell him which direction to run—the opposite direction from Demetri.

And then another pair of unexpected friends arrived—unexpected, because neither Carlisle nor Rosalie had been able to contact the Amazons.

"Carlisle," the taller of the two very tall ferine women greeted him when they arrived. Both of them seemed as if they'd been stretched—long arms and legs, long fingers, long black braids, and long faces with long noses. They wore nothing but animal skins—hide vests and tight-fitting pants that laced on the sides with leather ties. It wasn't just their eccentric clothes that made them seem wild but everything about them, from their restless crimson eyes to their sudden, darting movements. I'd never met any vampires less civilized.

But Alice had sent them, and that was interesting news, to put it mildly. Why was Alice in South America? Just because she'd seen that no one else would be able to get in touch with the Amazons?

"Zafrina and Senna! But where's Kachiri?" Carlisle asked. "I've never seen you three apart."

"Alice told us we needed to separate," Zafrina answered in the rough, deep voice that matched her wild appearance. "It's uncomfortable to be away from each other, but Alice assured us that you needed us here, while she very much needed Kachiri somewhere else. That's all she would tell us, except that there was a great hurry . . . ?" Zafrina's statement trailed off into a question, and—with the tremor of nerves that never went away no matter how often I did this—I brought Renesmee out to meet them.

Despite their fierce appearance, they listened very calmly to our story, and then allowed Renesmee to prove the point. They were every bit as taken with Renesmee as any of the other vampires, but I couldn't help worrying as I watched their swift, jerky movements so close beside her. Senna was always near Zafrina, never speaking, but it wasn't the same as Amun and Kebi. Kebi's manner seemed obedient; Senna and Zafrina were more like two limbs of one organism— Zafrina just happened to be the mouthpiece.

The news about Alice was oddly comforting. Clearly, she was on some obscure mission of her own as she avoided whatever Aro had planned for her.

Edward was thrilled to have the Amazons with us,

because Zafrina was enormously talented; her gift could make a very dangerous offensive weapon. Not that Edward was asking for Zafrina to side with us in the battle, but if the Volturi did not pause when they saw our witnesses, perhaps they would pause for a different kind of scene.

"It's a very straightforward illusion," Edward explained when it turned out that I couldn't see anything, as usual. Zafrina was intrigued and amused by my immunity— something she'd never encountered before—and she hovered restlessly while Edward described what I was missing. Edward's eyes unfocused slightly as he continued. "She can make most people see whatever she wants them to see— see that, and nothing else. For example, right now I would appear to be alone in the middle of a rain forest. It's so clear I might possibly believe it, except for the fact that I can still feel you in my arms."

Zafrina's lips twitched into her hard version of a smile. A second later, Edward's eyes focused again, and he grinned back.

"Impressive," he said.

Renesmee was fascinated with the conversation, and she reached out fearlessly toward Zafrina.

"Can I see?" she asked.

"What would you like to see?" Zafrina asked.

"What you showed Daddy."

Zafrina nodded, and I watched anxiously as Renesmee's eyes stared blankly into space. A second later, Renesmee's dazzling smile lit up her face.

"More," she commanded.

After that, it was hard to keep Renesmee away from

Zafrina and her *pretty pictures.* I worried, because I was quite sure that Zafrina was able to create images that were not pretty at all. But through Renesmee's thoughts I could see Zafrina's visions for myself—they were as clear as any of Renesmee's own memories, like they were real—and thus judge for myself whether they were appropriate or not.

Though I didn't give her up easily, I had to admit it was a good thing Zafrina was keeping Renesmee entertained. I needed my hands. I had so much to learn, both physically and mentally, and the time was so short.

My first attempt at learning to fight did not go well.

Edward had me pinned in about two seconds. But instead of letting me wrestle my way free—which I absolutely could have—he'd leaped up and away from me. I knew immediately that something was wrong; he was still as stone, staring across the meadow we were practicing in.

"I'm sorry, Bella," he said.

"No, I'm fine," I said. "Let's go again."

"I can't."

"What do you mean, you can't? We just started."

He didn't answer.

"Look, I know I'm no good at this, but I can't get better if you don't help me."

He said nothing. Playfully, I sprang at him. He made no defense at all, and we both fell to the ground. He was motionless as I pressed my lips to his jugular.

"I win," I announced.

His eyes narrowed, but he said nothing.

"Edward? What's wrong? Why won't you teach me?"

A full minute passed before he spoke again.

"I just can't . . . bear it. Emmett and Rosalie know as much as I do. Tanya and Eleazar probably know more. Ask someone else."

"That's not fair! You're *good* at this. You helped Jasper before—you fought with him and all the others, too. Why not me? What did I do wrong?"

He sighed, exasperated. His eyes were dark, barely any gold to lighten the black.

"Looking at you that way, analyzing you as a target. Seeing all the ways I can kill you . . ." He flinched. "It just makes it too real for me. We don't have so much time that it will really make a difference who your teacher is. Anyone can teach you the fundamentals."

I scowled.

He touched my pouting lower lip and smiled. "Besides, it's unnecessary. The Volturi will stop. They will be made to understand."

"But if they don't! I *need* to learn this."

"Find another teacher."

That was not our last conversation on the subject, but I never swayed him an inch from his decision.

Emmett was more than willing to help, though his teaching felt to me a lot like revenge for all the lost arm-wrestling matches. If I could still bruise, I would have been purple from head to toe. Rose, Tanya, and Eleazar all were patient and supportive. Their lessons reminded me of Jasper's fighting instructions to the others last June, though those memories were fuzzy and indistinct. Some of the visitors found my education entertaining, and some even offered assistance. The nomad Garrett took a few turns—he was a surprisingly good teacher; he interacted so easily with others in general that I wondered how he'd never found a coven. I even fought once with Zafrina while Renesmee watched from Jacob's arms. I learned several tricks, but I never asked for her help again. In truth, though I liked Zafrina very much and I knew she wouldn't really hurt me, the wild woman scared me to death.

I learned many things from my teachers, but I had the sense that my knowledge was still impossibly basic. I had no idea how many seconds I would last against Alec and Jane. I only prayed that it would be long enough to help.

Every minute of the day that I wasn't with Renesmee or learning to fight, I was in the backyard working with Kate, trying to push my internal shield outside of my own brain to protect someone else. Edward encouraged me in this training. I knew he hoped I would find a way of contributing that satisfied me while also keeping me out of the line of fire.

It was just so hard. There was nothing to get a hold of, nothing solid to work with. I had only my raging desire to be of use, to be able to keep Edward, Renesmee, and as much of my family as possible safe with me. Over and over I tried to force the nebulous shield outside of myself, with only faint, sporadic success. It felt like I was wrestling to stretch an invisible rubber band—a band that would change from concrete tangibility into insubstantial smoke at any random moment.

Only Edward was willing to be our guinea pig—to receive shock after shock from Kate while I grappled incompetently with the insides of my head. We worked for hours at a time, and I felt like I should be covered in sweat from the exertion, but of course my perfect body didn't betray me that way. My weariness was all mental.

It killed me that it was Edward who had to suffer, my arms wrapped uselessly around him while he winced over and over from Kate's "low" setting. I tried as hard as I could to push my shield around us both; every now and then I would get it, and then it would slip away again.

I hated this practice, and I wished that Zafrina would help instead of Kate. Then all Edward would have to do was look at Zafrina's illusions until I could stop him from seeing them. But Kate insisted that I needed better motivation— by which she meant my hatred of watching Edward's pain. I was beginning to doubt her assertion from the first day we'd met—that she wasn't sadistic about the use of her gift. She seemed to be enjoying herself to me.

"Hey," Edward said cheerfully, trying to hide any evidence of distress in his voice. Anything to keep me from fighting practice. "That one barely stung. Good job, Bella."

I took a deep breath, trying to grasp exactly what I'd done right. I tested the elastic band, struggling to force it to remain solid as I stretched it away from me.

"Again, Kate," I grunted through my clenched teeth.

Kate pressed her palm to Edward's shoulder.

He sighed in relief. "Nothing that time."

She raised an eyebrow. "That wasn't low, either."

"Good," I huffed.

"Get ready," she told me, and reached out to Edward again.

This time he shuddered, and a low breath hissed between his teeth.

"Sorry! Sorry! Sorry!" I chanted, biting my lip. Why couldn't I get this right?

"You're doing an amazing job, Bella," Edward said, pulling me tight against him. "You've really only been working at this for a few days and you're already projecting sporadically. Kate, tell her how well she's doing."

Kate pursed her lips. "I don't know. She's obviously got tremendous ability, and we're only beginning to touch it. She can do better, I'm sure. She's just lacking incentive."

I stared at her in disbelief, my lips automatically curling back from my teeth. How could she think I lacked motivation with her shocking Edward right here in front of me?

I heard murmurs from the audience that had grown steadily as I practiced—only Eleazar, Carmen, and Tanya at first, but then Garrett had wandered over, then Benjamin and Tia, Siobhan and Maggie, and now even Alistair was peering down from a window on the third story. The spectators agreed with Edward; they thought I was already doing well.

"Kate . . . ," Edward said in a warning voice as some new course of action occurred to her, but she was already in motion. She darted along the curve of the river to where Zafrina, Senna, and Renesmee were walking slowly, Renesmee's hand in Zafrina's as they traded pictures back and forth. Jacob shadowed them from a few feet behind.

"Nessie," Kate said—the newcomers had quickly picked up the irritating nickname, "would you like to come help your mother?"

"No," I half-snarled.

Edward hugged me reassuringly. I shook him off just as Renesmee flitted across the yard to me, with Kate, Zafrina, and Senna right behind her.

"Absolutely not, Kate," I hissed.

Renesmee reached for me, and I opened my arms automatically. She curled into me, pressing her head into the hollow beneath my shoulder.

"But Momma, I *want* to help," she said in a determined voice. Her hand rested against my neck, reinforcing her desire with images of the two of us together, a team.

"No," I said, quickly backing away. Kate had taken a deliberate step in my direction, her hand stretched toward us.

"Stay away from us, Kate," I warned her.

"No." She began stalking forward. She smiled like a hunter cornering her prey.

I shifted Renesmee so that she was clinging to my back, still backing away at a pace that matched Kate's. Now my hands were free, and if Kate wanted to keep *her* hands attached to her wrists, she'd better keep her distance.

Kate probably didn't understand, never having known for herself the passion of a mother for her child. She must not have realized just how far past *too far* she'd already gone. I was so furious that my vision took on a strange reddish tint, and my tongue tasted like burning metal. The strength I usually worked to keep restrained flowed through my muscles, and I knew I could crush her into diamond-hard rubble if she pushed me to it.

The rage brought every aspect of my being into sharper focus. I could even feel the elasticity of my shield more exactly now—feel that it was not a band so much as a layer, a thin film that covered me from head to toe. With the anger rippling through my body, I had a better sense of it, a tighter hold on it. I stretched it around myself, out from myself, swaddling Renesmee completely inside it, just in case Kate got past my guard.

Kate took another calculated step forward, and a vicious snarl ripped up my throat and through my clenched teeth.

"Be careful, Kate," Edward cautioned.

Kate took another step, and then made a mistake even someone as inexpert as I could recognize. Just a short leap away from me, she looked away, turning her attention from me to Edward.

Renesmee was secure on my back; I coiled to spring.

"Can you hear anything from Nessie?" Kate asked him, her voice calm and easy.

Edward darted into the space between us, blocking my line to Kate.

"No, nothing at all," he answered. "Now give Bella some space to calm down, Kate. You shouldn't goad her like that. I know she doesn't seem her age, but she's only a few months old."

"We don't have time to do this gently, Edward. We're going to have to push her. We only have a few weeks, and she's got the potential to—"

"Back off for a minute, Kate."

Kate frowned but took Edward's warning more seriously than she'd taken mine.

Renesmee's hand was on my neck; she was remembering Kate's attack, showing me that no harm was meant, that Daddy was in on it. . . .

This did not pacify me. The spectrum of light I saw still seemed tainted with crimson. But I was in better control of myself, and I could see the wisdom of Kate's words. The anger helped me. I would learn faster under pressure.

That didn't mean I liked it.

"Kate," I growled. I rested my hand on the small of Edward's back. I could still feel my shield like a strong, flexible sheet around Renesmee and me. I pushed it farther, forcing it around Edward. There was no sign of a flaw in the stretchy fabric, no threat of a tear. I panted with the effort, and my words came out sounding breathless rather than furious. "Again," I said to Kate. "Edward only."

She rolled her eyes but flitted forward and pressed her palm to Edward's shoulder.

"Nothing," Edward said. I heard the smile in his voice.

"And now?" Kate asked.

"Still nothing."

"And now?" This time, there was the sound of strain in her voice.

"Nothing at all."

Kate grunted and stepped away.

"Can you see this?" Zafrina asked in her deep, wild voice, staring intently at the three of us. Her English was strangely accented, her words pulling up in unexpected places.

"I don't see anything I shouldn't," Edward said.

"And you, Renesmee?" Zafrina asked.

Renesmee smiled at Zafrina and shook her head.

My fury had almost entirely ebbed, and I clenched my teeth together, panting faster as I pushed out against the elastic shield; it felt like it was getting heavier the longer I held it. It pulled back, dragging inward.

"No one panic," Zafrina warned the little group watching me. "I want to see how far she can extend."

There was a shocked gasp from everyone there—Eleazar, Carmen, Tanya, Garrett, Benjamin, Tia, Siobhan, Maggie—everyone but Senna, who seemed prepared for whatever Zafrina was doing. The others' eyes were blank, their expressions anxious.

"Raise your hand when you get your sight back," Zafrina instructed. "Now, Bella. See how many you can shield."

My breath came out in a huff. Kate was the closest person to me besides Edward and Renesmee, but even she was about ten feet away. I locked my jaw and shoved, trying to heave the resisting, resilient safeguard farther from myself. Inch by inch I drove it toward Kate, fighting the reaction that fought back with every fraction that I gained. I only watched Kate's anxious expression while I worked, and I groaned quietly with relief when her eyes blinked and focused. She raised her hand.

"Fascinating!" Edward murmured under his breath. "It's like one-way glass. I can read everything they're thinking, but they can't reach me behind it. And I can hear Renesmee, though I couldn't when I was on the outside. I'll bet Kate could shock me now, because she's underneath the umbrella. I still can't hear you . . . hmmm. How does that work? I wonder if . . ."

He continued to mumble to himself, but I couldn't listen to the words. I ground my teeth together, struggling to force the shield out to Garrett, who was closest to Kate. His hand came up.

"Very good," Zafrina complimented me. "Now—"

But she'd spoken too soon; with a sharp gasp, I felt my shield recoil like a rubber band stretched too far, snapping back into its original shape. Renesmee, experiencing for the first time the blindness Zafrina had conjured for the others, trembled against my back. Wearily, I fought back against the elastic pull, forcing the shield to include her again.

"Can I have a minute?" I panted. Since I'd become a vampire, I hadn't felt the need to rest even once before this moment. It was unnerving to feel so drained and yet so strong at the same time.

"Of course," Zafrina said, and the spectators relaxed as she let them see again.

"Kate," Garrett called as the others murmured and drifted slightly away, disturbed by the moment of blindness; vampires were not used to feeling vulnerable. The tall, sandy-haired Garrett was the only non-gifted immortal who seemed drawn to my practice sessions. I wondered what the lure was for the adventurer.

"I wouldn't, Garrett," Edward cautioned.

Garrett continued toward Kate despite the warning, his lips pursed in speculation. "They say you can put a vampire flat on his back."

"Yes," she agreed. Then, with a sly smile, she wiggled her fingers playfully at him. "Curious?"

Garrett shrugged. "That's something I've never seen. Seems like it might be a bit of an exaggeration. . . ."

"Maybe," Kate said, her face suddenly serious. "Maybe it only works on the weak or the young. I'm not sure. You look strong, though. Perhaps you could withstand my gift." She stretched her hand out to him, palm up—a clear invitation. Her lips twitched, and I was pretty sure her grave expression was an attempt to hustle him.

Garrett grinned at the challenge. Very confidently, he touched her palm with his index finger.

And then, with a loud gasp, his knees buckled and he keeled over backward. His head hit a piece of granite with a sharp cracking noise. It was shocking to watch. My instincts recoiled against seeing an immortal incapacitated that way; it was profoundly wrong.

"I told you so," Edward muttered.

Garrett's eyelids trembled for a few seconds, and then his eyes opened wide. He stared up at the smirking Kate, and a wondering smile lit his face.

"Wow," he said.

"Did you enjoy that?" she asked skeptically.

"I'm not crazy," he laughed, shaking his head as he got slowly to his knees, "but that was sure something!"

"That's what I hear."

Edward rolled his eyes.

And then there was a low commotion from the front yard. I heard Carlisle speaking over a babble of surprised voices.

"Did Alice send you?" he asked someone, his voice unsure, slightly upset.

Another unexpected guest?

Edward darted into the house and most of the others imitated him. I followed more slowly, Renesmee still perched on my back. I would give Carlisle a moment. Let him warm up the new guest, prepare him or her or them for the idea of what was coming.

I pulled Renesmee into my arms as I walked cautiously around the house to enter through the kitchen door, listening to what I couldn't see.

"No one sent us," a deep whispery voice answered Carlisle's question. I was immediately reminded of the ancient voices of Aro and Caius, and I froze just inside the kitchen.

I knew the front room was crowded—almost everyone had gone in to see the newest visitors—but there was barely any noise. Shallow breathing, that was all.

Carlisle's voice was wary as he responded. "Then what brings you here now?"

"Word travels," a different voice answered, just as feathery as the first. "We heard hints that Volturi were moving against you. There were whispers that you would not stand alone. Obviously, the whispers were true. This is an impressive gathering."

"We are not challenging the Volturi," Carlisle answered in a strained tone. "There has been a misunderstanding, that is all. A very serious misunderstanding, to be sure, but one we're hoping to clear up. What you see are witnesses. We just need the Volturi to listen. We didn't—"

"We don't care what they say you did," the first voice interrupted. "And we don't care if you broke the law."

"No matter how egregiously," the second inserted.

"We've been waiting a millennium and a half for the Italian scum to be challenged," said the first. "If there is any chance they will fall, we will be here to see it."

"Or even to help defeat them," the second added. They spoke in a smooth tandem, their voices so similar that less sensitive ears would assume there was only one speaker. "If we think you have a chance of success."

"Bella?" Edward called to me in a hard voice. "Bring Renesmee here, please. Maybe we should test our Romanian visitors' claims."

It helped to know that probably half of the vampires

in the other room would come to Renesmee's defense if these Romanians were upset by her. I didn't like the sound of their voices, or the dark menace in their words. As I walked into the room, I could see that I was not alone in that assessment. Most of the motionless vampires glared with hostile eyes, and a few—Carmen, Tanya, Zafrina, and Senna—repositioned themselves subtly into defensive poses between the newcomers and Renesmee.

The vampires at the door were both slight and short, one dark-haired and the other with hair so ashy blond that it looked pale gray. They had the same powdery look to their skin as the Volturi, though I thought it was not so pronounced. I couldn't be sure about that, as I had never seen the Volturi except with human eyes; I could not make a perfect comparison. Their sharp, narrow eyes were dark burgundy, with no milky film. They wore very simple black clothes that could pass as modern but hinted at older designs.

The dark one grinned when I came into view. "Well, well, Carlisle. You *have* been naughty, haven't you?"

"She's not what you think, Stefan."

"And we don't care either way," the blonde responded. "As we said before."

"Then you're welcome to observe, Vladimir, but it is definitely not our plan to challenge the Volturi, as *we* said before."

"Then we'll just cross our fingers," Stefan began.

"And hope we get lucky," finished Vladimir.

In the end, we had pulled together seventeen witnesses—the Irish, Siobhan, Liam, and Maggie; the Egyptians,

Amun, Kebi, Benjamin, and Tia; the Amazons, Zafrina and Senna; the Romanians, Vladimir and Stefan; and the nomads, Charlotte and Peter, Garrett, Alistair, Mary, and Randall—to supplement our family of eleven. Tanya, Kate, Eleazar, and Carmen insisted on being counted as part of our family.

Aside from the Volturi, it was probably the largest friendly gathering of mature vampires in immortal history.

We all were beginning to be a little bit hopeful. Even I couldn't help it. Renesmee had won over so many in such a brief time. The Volturi only had to listen for just the tiniest second. . . .

The last two surviving Romanians—focused only on their bitter resentment of the ones who had overthrown their empire fifteen hundred years earlier—took everything in stride. They would not touch Renesmee, but they showed no aversion to her. They seemed mysteriously delighted by our alliance with the werewolves. They watched me practice my shield with Zafrina and Kate, watched Edward answer unspoken questions, watched Benjamin pull geysers of water from the river or sharp gusts of wind from the still air with just his mind, and their eyes glowed with their fierce hope that the Volturi had finally met their match.

We did not hope for the same things, but we all hoped.

33. FORGERY

"CHARLIE, WE'VE STILL GOT THAT STRICTLY NEED-TO-know company situation going. I know it's been more than a week since you saw Renesmee, but a visit is just not a good idea right now. How about I bring Renesmee over to see you?"

Charlie was quiet for so long that I wondered if he heard the strain beneath my façade.

But then he muttered, "Need to know, *ugh*," and I realized it was just his wariness of the supernatural that made him slow to respond.

"Okay, kid," Charlie said. "Can you bring her over this morning? Sue's bringing me lunch. She's just as horrified by my cooking as you were when you first showed up."

Charlie laughed and then sighed for the old days.

"This morning will be perfect." The sooner the better. I'd already put this off too long.

"Is Jake coming with you guys?"

Though Charlie didn't know anything about werewolf imprinting, no one could be oblivious to the attachment between Jacob and Renesmee.

"Probably." There was no way Jacob would voluntarily miss an afternoon with Renesmee sans bloodsuckers.

"Maybe I should invite Billy, too," Charlie mused. "But . . . hmm. Maybe another time."

I was only half paying attention to Charlie—enough to notice the strange reluctance in his voice when he spoke of Billy, but not enough to worry what *that* was about. Charlie and Billy were grown-ups; if there was something going on between them, they could figure it out for themselves. I had too many more important things to obsess over.

"See you in a few," I told him, and hung up.

This trip was about more than protecting my father from the twenty-seven oddly matched vampires—who all had sworn not to kill anyone in a three-hundred-mile radius, but still . . . Obviously, no human being should get anywhere near this group. This was the excuse I'd given Edward: I was taking Renesmee to Charlie so that he wouldn't decide to come here. It was a good reason for leaving the house, but not my real reason at all.

"Why can't we take your Ferrari?" Jacob complained when he met me in the garage. I was already in Edward's Volvo with Renesmee.

Edward had gotten around to revealing my *after* car; as he'd suspected, I had not been capable of showing the appropriate enthusiasm. Sure, it was pretty and fast, but I liked to *run*.

"Too conspicuous," I answered. "We could go on foot, but that would freak Charlie out."

Jacob grumbled but got into the front seat. Renesmee climbed from my lap to his.

"How are you?" I asked him as I pulled out of the garage.

"How do you think?" Jacob asked bitingly. "I'm sick of all these reeking bloodsuckers." He saw my expression and spoke before I could answer. "Yeah, I know, I know. They're the good guys, they're here to help, they're going to save us all. Etcetera, etcetera. Say what you want, I still think Dracula One and Dracula Two are creep-tacular."

I had to smile. The Romanians weren't my favorite guests, either. "I don't disagree with you there."

Renesmee shook her head but said nothing; unlike the rest of us, she found the Romanians strangely fascinating. She'd made the effort to speak to them aloud since they would not let her touch them. Her question was about their unusual skin and, though I was afraid they might be offended, I was kind of glad she'd asked. I was curious, too.

They hadn't seemed upset by her interest. Maybe a little rueful.

"We sat still for a very long time, child," Vladimir had answered, with Stefan nodding along but not continuing Vladimir's sentences as he often did. "Contemplating our own divinity. It was a sign of our power that everything came to us. Prey, diplomats, those seeking our favor. We sat on our thrones and thought ourselves gods. We didn't notice for a long time that we were changing—almost petrifying.

I suppose the Volturi did us one favor when they burned our castles. Stefan and I, at least, did not continue to petrify. Now the Volturi's eyes are filmed with dusty scum, but ours are bright. I imagine that will give us an advantage when we gouge theirs from their sockets."

I tried to keep Renesmee away from them after that.

"How long do we get to hang out with Charlie?" Jacob asked, interrupting my thoughts. He was visibly relaxing as we pulled away from the house and all its new inmates. It made me happy that I didn't really count as a vampire to him. I was still just Bella.

"For quite a while, actually."

The tone of my voice caught his attention.

"Is something going on here besides visiting your dad?"

"Jake, you know how you're pretty good at controlling your thoughts around Edward?"

He raised one thick black brow. "Yeah?"

I just nodded, cutting my eyes to Renesmee. She was looking out the window, and I couldn't tell how interested she was in our conversation, but I decided not to risk going any further.

Jacob waited for me to add something else, and then his lower lip pushed out while he thought about what little I'd said.

As we drove in silence, I squinted through the annoying contacts into the cold rain; it wasn't quite cold enough for snow. My eyes were not as ghoulish as they had been in the beginning—definitely closer to a dull reddish orange than to bright crimson. Soon they'd be amber enough for me to quit the contacts. I hoped the change wouldn't upset Charlie too much.

Jacob was still chewing over our truncated conversation when we got to Charlie's. We didn't talk as we walked at a quick human pace through the falling rain. My dad was waiting for us; he had the door open before I could knock.

"Hey, guys! It seems like it's been years! Look at you, Nessie! Come to Grampa! I swear you've grown half a foot. And you look skinny, Ness." He glared at me. "Aren't they feeding you up there?"

"It's just the growth spurt," I muttered. "Hey, Sue," I called over his shoulder. The smell of chicken, tomato, garlic, and cheese issued from the kitchen; it probably smelled good to everyone else. I could also smell fresh pine and packing dust.

Renesmee flashed her dimples. She never spoke in front of Charlie.

"Well, come on in out of the cold, kids. Where's my son-in-law?"

"Entertaining friends," Jacob said, and then snorted. "You're *so* lucky you're out of the loop, Charlie. That's all I'm going to say."

I punched Jacob lightly in the kidney while Charlie cringed.

"Ow," Jacob complained under his breath; well, I'd *thought* I'd punched lightly.

"Actually, Charlie, I have some errands to run."

Jacob shot a glance at me but said nothing.

"Behind on your Christmas shopping, Bells? You only have a few days, you know."

"Yeah, Christmas shopping," I said lamely. That explained the packing dust. Charlie must have put the old decorations up.

"Don't worry, Nessie," he whispered in her ear. "I got you covered if your mom drops the ball."

I rolled my eyes at him, but in truth, I hadn't thought about the holidays at all.

"Lunch's on the table," Sue called from the kitchen. "C'mon, guys."

"See you later, Dad," I said, and exchanged a quick look with Jacob. Even if he couldn't help but think about this near Edward, at least there wasn't much for him to share. He had no idea what I was up to.

Of course, I thought to myself as I got into the car, it wasn't like I had much idea, either.

The roads were slick and dark, but driving didn't intimidate me anymore. My reflexes were well up to the job, and I barely paid attention to the road. The problem was keeping my speed from attracting attention when I had company. I wanted to be done with today's mission, to have the mystery sorted out so that I could get back to the vital task of learning. Learning to protect some, learning to kill others.

I was getting better and better with my shield. Kate didn't feel the need to motivate me anymore—it wasn't hard to find reasons to feel angry, now that I knew that was the key—and so I mostly worked with Zafrina. She was pleased with my extension; I was able to cover almost a ten-foot area for more than a minute, though it exhausted me. This morning she'd been trying to find out if I could push the shield away from my mind altogether. I didn't see what the use of that would be, but Zafrina thought it would help strengthen me, like exercising muscles in the stomach and back rather than just the arms. Eventually, you could lift more weight when all the muscles were stronger.

I wasn't very good at it. I had only gotten one glimpse of the jungle river she was trying to show me.

But there were different ways to prepare for what was coming, and with only two weeks left, I worried that I might be neglecting the most important. Today I would rectify that oversight.

I'd memorized the appropriate maps, and I had no problem finding my way to the address that didn't exist online, the one for J. Jenks. My next step would be Jason Jenks at the other address, the one Alice had not given me.

To say that it wasn't a nice neighborhood would be an understatement. The most nondescript of all the Cullens' cars was still outrageous on this street. My old Chevy would have looked healthy here. During my human years, I would have locked the doors and driven away as fast as I dared. As it was, I was a little fascinated. I tried to imagine Alice in this place for any reason, and failed.

The buildings—all three stories, all narrow, all leaning slightly as if bowed by the pounding rain—were mostly old houses divided up into multiple apartments. It was hard to tell what color the peeling paint was supposed to be. Everything had faded to shades of gray. A few of the buildings had businesses on the first floor: a dirty bar with the windows painted black, a psychic's supply store with neon hands and tarot cards glowing fitfully on the door, a tattoo parlor, and a daycare with duct tape holding the broken front window together. There were no lamps on inside any of the rooms, though it was grim enough outside that the humans should have needed the light. I could hear the low mumbling of voices in the distance; it sounded like TV.

There were a few people about, two shuffling through the rain in opposite directions and one sitting on the shallow porch of a boarded-up cut-rate law office, reading a wet newspaper and whistling. The sound was much too cheerful for the setting.

I was so bemused by the carefree whistler, I didn't realize at first that the abandoned building was right where the address I was looking for should exist. There were no numbers on the dilapidated place, but the tattoo parlor beside it was just two numbers off.

I pulled up to the curb and idled for a second. I was getting into that dump one way or another, but how to do so without the whistler noticing me? I could park the next street over and come through the back. . . . There might be more witnesses on that side. Maybe the rooftops? Was it dark enough for that kind of thing?

"Hey, lady," the whistler called to me.

I rolled the passenger window down as if I couldn't hear him.

The man laid his paper aside, and his clothes surprised me, now that I could see them. Under his long ragged duster, he was a little too well dressed. There was no breeze to give me the scent, but the sheen on his dark red shirt looked like silk. His crinkly black hair was tangled and wild, but his dark skin was smooth and perfect, his teeth white and straight. A contradiction.

"Maybe you shouldn't park that car there, lady," he said. "It might not be here when you get back."

"Thanks for the warning," I said.

I shut off the engine and got out. Perhaps my whistling friend could give me the answers I needed faster than breaking and entering. I opened my big gray umbrella—not that I cared, really, about protecting the long cashmere sweaterdress I wore. It was what a human would do.

The man squinted through the rain at my face, and then his eyes widened. He swallowed, and I heard his heart accelerate as I approached.

"I'm looking for someone," I began.

"I'm someone," he offered with a smile. "What can I do for you, beautiful?"

"Are you J. Jenks?" I asked.

"Oh," he said, and his expression changed from anticipation to understanding. He got to his feet and examined me with narrowed eyes. "Why're you looking for J?"

"That's my business." Besides, I didn't have a clue. "Are you J?"

"No."

We faced each other for a long moment while his sharp eyes ran up and down the fitted pearl gray sheath I wore. His gaze finally made it to my face. "You don't look like the usual customer."

"I'm probably not the usual," I admitted. "But I do need to see him as soon as possible."

"I'm not sure what to do," he admitted.

"Why don't you tell me your name?"

He grinned. "Max."

"Nice to meet you, Max. Now, why don't you tell me what you do for *the usual*?"

His grin became a frown. "Well, J's usual clients don't

look a thing like you. Your kind doesn't bother with the downtown office. You just go straight up to his fancy office in the skyscraper."

I repeated the other address I had, making the list of numbers a question.

"Yeah, that's the place," he said, suspicious again. "How come you didn't go there?"

"This was the address I was given—by a very dependable source."

"If you were up to any good, you wouldn't be here."

I pursed my lips. I'd never been much good at bluffing, but Alice hadn't left me a lot of alternatives. "Maybe I'm not up to any good."

Max's face turned apologetic. "Look, lady—"

"Bella."

"Right. Bella. See, I need this job. J pays me pretty good to mostly just hang out here all day. I want to help you, I do, but—and of course I'm speaking hypothetically, right? Or off the record, or whatever works for you—but if I pass somebody through that could get him in trouble, I'm out of work. Do you see my problem?"

I thought for a minute, chewing on my lip. "You've never seen anyone like me here before? Well, *sort of* like me. My sister is a lot shorter than me, and she has dark spiky black hair."

"J knows your sister?"

"I think so."

Max pondered this for a moment. I smiled at him, and his breathing stuttered. "Tell you what I'll do. I'll give J a call and describe you to him. Let him make the decision."

What did J. Jenks know? Would my description mean something to him? That was a troubling thought.

"My last name is Cullen," I told Max, wondering if that was too much information. I was starting to get irritated with Alice. Did I really have to be quite this blind? She could have given me one or two more words. . . .

"Cullen, got it."

I watched as he dialed, easily picking out the number. Well, I could call J. Jenks myself if this didn't work.

"Hey J, it's Max. I know I'm never supposed to call you at this number except in an emergency. . . ."

Is there an emergency? I heard faintly from the other end.

"Well, not exactly. It's this girl who wants to see you. . . ."

I fail to see the emergency in that. Why didn't you follow normal procedure?

"I didn't follow normal procedure 'cause she don't look like any kind of normal—"

Is she a badge?!

"No—"

You can't be sure about that. Does she look like one of Kubarev's—?

"No—let me talk, okay? She says you know her sister or something."

Not likely. What does she look like?

"She looks like . . ." His eyes ran from my face to my shoes appreciatively. "Well, she looks like a freaking super-model, that's what she looks like." I smiled and he winked at me, then went on. "Rocking body, pale as a sheet, dark

brown hair almost to her waist, needs a good night's sleep—
any of this sounding familiar?"

*No, it doesn't. I'm not happy that you let your weakness for
pretty women interrupt—*

"Yeah, so I'm a sucker for the pretty ones, what's wrong
with that? I'm sorry I bothered you, man. Just forget it."

"Name," I whispered.

"Oh right. Wait," Max said. "She says her name is Bella
Cullen. That help?"

There was a beat of dead silence, and then the voice on
the other end was abruptly screaming, using a lot of words
you didn't often hear outside of truck stops. Max's whole
expression changed; all the joking vanished and his lips
went pale.

"Because you didn't ask!" Max yelled back, panicked.

There was another pause while J collected himself.

Beautiful and pale? J asked, a tiny bit calmer.

"I said that, didn't I?"

Beautiful and pale? What did this man know about
vampires? Was he one of us himself? I wasn't prepared for
that kind of confrontation. I gritted my teeth. What had
Alice gotten me into?

Max waited for a minute through another volley of
shouted insults and instructions and then glanced at me
with eyes that were almost frightened. "But you only meet
downtown clients on Thursdays—okay, okay! On it." He
slid his phone shut.

"He wants to see me?" I asked brightly.

Max glowered. "You could have told me you were a
priority client."

"I didn't know I was."

"I thought you might be a cop," he admitted. "I mean, you don't look like a cop. But you act kind of weird, beautiful."

I shrugged.

"Drug cartel?" he guessed.

"Who, me?" I asked.

"Yeah. Or your boyfriend or whatever."

"Nope, sorry. I'm not really a fan of drugs, and neither is my husband. *Just say no* and all that."

Max cussed under his breath. "Married. Can't catch a break."

I smiled.

"Mafia?"

"Nope."

"Diamond smuggling?"

"Please! Is that the kind of people you usually deal with, Max? Maybe you need a new job."

I had to admit, I was enjoying myself a little. I hadn't interacted with humans much besides Charlie and Sue. It was entertaining to watch him flounder. I was also pleased at how easy it was not to kill him.

"You've got to be involved in something big. *And* bad," he mused.

"It's not really like that."

"That's what they all say. But who else needs papers? Or can afford to pay J's prices for them, I should say. None of my business, anyway," he said, and then muttered the word *married* again.

He gave me an entirely new address with basic directions, and then watched me drive away with suspicious, regretful eyes.

At this point, I was ready for almost anything—some

kind of James Bond villain's high-tech lair seemed appropriate. So I thought Max must have given me the wrong address as a test. Or maybe the lair was subterranean, underneath this very commonplace strip mall nestled up against a wooded hill in a nice family neighborhood.

I pulled into an open spot and looked up at a tastefully subtle sign that read JASON SCOTT, ATTORNEY AT LAW.

The office inside was beige with celery green accents, inoffensive and unremarkable. There was no scent of vampire here, and that helped me relax. Nothing but unfamiliar human. A fish tank was set into the wall, and a blandly pretty blond receptionist sat behind the desk.

"Hello," she greeted me. "How can I help you?"

"I'm here to see Mr. Scott."

"Do you have an appointment?"

"Not exactly."

She smirked a little. "It could be a while, then. Why don't you have a seat while I—"

April! a man's demanding voice squawked from the phone on her desk. *I'm expecting a Ms. Cullen shortly.*

I smiled and pointed to myself.

Send her in immediately. Do you understand? I don't care what it's interrupting.

I could hear something else in his voice besides impatience. Stress. Nerves.

"She's just arrived," April said as soon as she could speak.

What? Send her in! What are you waiting for?

"Right away, Mr. Scott!" She got to her feet, fluttering her hands as she led the way down a short hallway, offering me coffee or tea or anything else I might have wanted.

"Here you are," she said as she ushered me through the door into a power office, complete with heavy wooden desk and vanity wall.

"Close the door behind you," a raspy tenor voice ordered.

I examined the man behind the desk while April made a hasty retreat. He was short and balding, probably around fifty-five, with a paunch. He wore a red silk tie with a blue-and-white-striped shirt, and his navy blazer hung over the back of his chair. He was also trembling, blanched to a sickly paste color, with sweat beading on his forehead; I imagined an ulcer churning away under the spare tire.

J recovered himself and rose unsteadily from his chair. He reached his hand across the desk.

"Ms. Cullen. What an absolute delight."

I crossed to him and shook his hand quickly once. He cringed slightly at my cold skin but did not seem particularly surprised by it.

"Mr. Jenks. Or do you prefer Scott?"

He winced again. "Whatever you wish, of course."

"How about you call me Bella, and I'll call you J?"

"Like old friends," he agreed, mopping a silk handkerchief across his forehead. He gestured for me to have a seat and took his own. "I must ask, am I finally meeting Mr. Jasper's lovely wife?"

I weighed that for a second. So this man knew Jasper, not Alice. Knew him, and seemed afraid of him, too. "His sister-in-law, actually."

He pursed his lips, as if he were grasping for meanings just as desperately as I was.

"I trust Mr. Jasper is in good health?" he asked carefully.

"I'm sure he is in excellent health. He's on an extended vacation at the moment."

This seemed to clear up some of J's confusion. He nodded to himself and templed his fingers. "Just so. You should have come to the main office. My assistants there would have put you straight through to me—no need to go through less hospitable channels."

I just nodded. I wasn't sure why Alice had given me the ghetto address.

"Ah, well, you're here now. What can I do for you?"

"Papers," I said, trying to make my voice sound like I knew what I was talking about.

"Certainly," J agreed at once. "Are we talking birth certificates, death certificates, drivers' licenses, passports, social security cards . . . ?"

I took a deep breath and smiled. I owed Max big time.

And then my smile faded. Alice had sent me here for a reason, and I was sure it was to protect Renesmee. Her last gift to me. The one thing she would know I needed.

The only reason Renesmee would need a forger was if she was running. And the only reason Renesmee would be running was if we had lost.

If Edward and I were running with her, she wouldn't need these documents right away. I was sure IDs were something Edward knew how to get his hands on or make himself, and I was sure he knew ways to escape without them. We could run with her for thousands of miles. We could swim with her across an ocean.

If we were around to save her.

And all the secrecy to keep this out of Edward's head. Because there was a good chance that everything he knew,

Aro would know. If we lost, Aro would certainly get the information he craved before he destroyed Edward.

It was as I had suspected. We couldn't win. But we must have a good shot at killing Demetri before we lost, giving Renesmee the chance to run.

My still heart felt like a boulder in my chest—a crushing weight. All my hope faded like fog in the sunshine. My eyes pricked.

Who would I put this on? Charlie? But he was so defenselessly human. And how would I get Renesmee to him? He was not going to be anywhere close to that fight. So that left one person. There really had never been anyone else.

I'd thought this through so quickly that J didn't notice my pause.

"Two birth certificates, two passports, one driver's license," I said in a low, strained tone.

If he noticed the change in my expression, he pretended otherwise.

"The names?"

"Jacob . . . Wolfe. And . . . Vanessa Wolfe." Nessie seemed like an okay nickname for Vanessa. Jacob would get a kick out of the Wolfe thing.

His pen scratched swiftly across a legal pad. "Middle names?"

"Just put something generic in."

"If you prefer. Ages?"

"Twenty-seven for the man, five for the girl." Jacob could pull it off. He was a beast. And at the rate Renesmee was growing, I'd better estimate high. He could be her stepfather. . . .

"I'll need pictures if you prefer finished documents," J said, interrupting my thoughts. "Mr. Jasper usually liked to finish them himself."

Well, that explained why J didn't know what Alice looked like.

"Hold on," I said.

This was luck. I had several family pictures shoved in my wallet, and the perfect one—Jacob holding Renesmee on the front porch steps—was only a month old. Alice had given it to me just a few days before . . . Oh. Maybe there wasn't that much luck involved after all. Alice knew I had this picture. Maybe she'd even had some dim flash that I would need it before she gave it to me.

"Here you go."

J examined the picture for a moment. "Your daughter is very like you."

I tensed. "She's more like her father."

"Who is not this man." He touched Jacob's face.

My eyes narrowed, and new sweat beads popped out on J's shiny head.

"No. That is a very close friend of the family."

"Forgive me," he mumbled, and the pen began scratching again. "How soon will you need the documents?"

"Can I get them in a week?"

"That's a rush order. It will cost twice as—but forgive me. I forgot with whom I was speaking."

Clearly, he knew Jasper.

"Just give me a number."

He seemed hesitant to say it aloud, though I was sure, having dealt with Jasper, he must have known that price wasn't really an object. Not even taking into consideration the bloated accounts that existed all over the world with the Cullens' various names on them, there was enough cash stashed all over the house to keep a small country afloat for a decade; it reminded me of the way there were always a hundred fishhooks in the back of any drawer at Charlie's house. I doubted anyone would even notice the small stack I'd removed in preparation for today.

J wrote the price down on the bottom of the legal pad.

I nodded calmly. I had more than that with me. I unclasped my bag again and counted out the right amount—I had it all paper-clipped into five-thousand-dollar increments, so it took no time at all.

"There."

"Ah, Bella, you don't really have to give me the entire sum now. It's customary for you to save half to ensure delivery."

I smiled wanly at the nervous man. "But I trust you, J. Besides, I'll give you a bonus—the same again when I get the documents."

"That's not necessary, I assure you."

"Don't worry about it." It wasn't like I could take it with me. "So I'll meet you here next week at the same time?"

He gave me a pained look. "Actually, I prefer to make such transactions in places unrelated to my various businesses."

"Of course. I'm sure I'm not doing this the way you expect."

"I'm used to having no expectations when it comes to the Cullen family." He grimaced and then quickly composed his face again. "Shall we meet at eight o'clock a week from tonight at The Pacifico? It's on Union Lake, and the food is exquisite."

"Perfect." Not that I would be joining him for dinner. He actually wouldn't like it much if I did.

I rose and shook his hand again. This time he didn't flinch. But he did seem to have some new worry on his mind. His mouth was pinched up, his back tense.

"Will you have trouble with that deadline?" I asked.

"What?" He looked up, taken off guard by my question. "The deadline? Oh, no. No worries at all. I will certainly have your documents done on time."

It would have been nice to have Edward here, so that I would know what J's real worries were. I sighed. Keeping secrets from Edward was bad enough; having to be away from him was almost too much.

"Then I'll see you in one week."

34. DECLARED

I HEARD THE MUSIC BEFORE I WAS OUT OF THE CAR. Edward hadn't touched his piano since the night Alice left. Now, as I shut the car door, I heard the song morph through a bridge and change into my lullaby. Edward was welcoming me home.

I moved slowly as I pulled Renesmee—fast asleep; we'd been gone all day—from the car. We'd left Jacob at Charlie's—he'd said he was going to catch a ride home with Sue. I wondered if he was trying to fill his head with enough trivia to crowd out the image of the way my face had looked when I'd walked through Charlie's door.

As I walked slowly to the Cullen house now, I recognized that the hope and uplift that seemed almost a visible aura around the big white house had been mine this morning, too. It felt alien to me now.

I wanted to cry again, hearing Edward play for me. But I pulled it together. I didn't want him to be suspicious. I would leave no clues in his mind for Aro if I could help it.

Edward turned his head and smiled when I came in the door, but kept playing.

"Welcome home," he said, as if this was just any normal day. As if there weren't twelve other vampires in the room involved in various pursuits, and a dozen more scattered around somewhere. "Did you have a good time with Charlie today?"

"Yes. Sorry I was gone so long. I stepped out to do a little Christmas shopping for Renesmee. I know it won't be much of an event, but . . ." I shrugged.

Edward's lips turned down. He quit playing and spun around on the bench so that his whole body was facing me. He put one hand on my waist and pulled me closer. "I hadn't thought much about it. If you *want* to make an event of it—"

"No," I interrupted him. I flinched internally at the idea of trying to fake more enthusiasm than the bare minimum. "I just didn't want to let it pass without giving her something."

"Do I get to see?"

"If you want. It's only a little thing."

Renesmee was completely unconscious, snoring delicately against my neck. I envied her. It would have been nice to escape reality, even for just a few hours.

Carefully, I fished the little velvet jewelry bag from my clutch without opening the purse enough for Edward to see the cash I was still carrying.

"It caught my eye from the window of an antique store while I was driving by."

I shook the little golden locket into his palm. It was round with a slender vine border carved around the outside edge of the circle. Edward popped the tiny catch and looked inside. There was space for a small picture and, on the opposite side, an inscription in French.

"Do you know what this says?" he asked in a different tone, more subdued than before.

"The shopkeeper told me it said something along the lines of *'more than my own life.'* Is that right?"

"Yes, he had it right."

He looked up at me, his topaz eyes probing. I met his gaze for a moment, then pretended to be distracted by the television.

"I hope she likes it," I muttered.

"Of course she will," he said lightly, casually, and I was sure in that second that he knew I was keeping something from him. I was also sure that he had no idea of the specifics.

"Let's take her home," he suggested, standing and putting his arm around my shoulders.

I hesitated.

"What?" he demanded.

"I wanted to practice with Emmett a little. . . ." I'd lost the whole day to my vital errand; it made me feel behind.

Emmett—on the sofa with Rose and holding the remote, of course—looked up and grinned in anticipation. "Excellent. The forest needs thinning."

Edward frowned at Emmett and then at me.

"There's plenty of time for that tomorrow," he said.

"Don't be ridiculous," I complained. "There's no such

thing as *plenty of time* anymore. That concept does not exist. I have a lot to learn and—"

He cut me off. "Tomorrow."

And his expression was such that not even Emmett argued.

I was surprised at how hard it was to go back to a routine that was, after all, brand new. But stripping away even that little bit of hope I'd been fostering made everything seem impossible.

I tried to focus on the positives. There was a good chance that my daughter was going to survive what was coming, and Jacob, too. If they had a future, then that was a kind of victory, wasn't it? Our little band must be going to hold their own if Jacob and Renesmee were going to have the opportunity to run in the first place. Yes, Alice's strategy only made sense if we were going to put up a really good fight. So, a kind of victory there, too, considering that the Volturi had never been seriously challenged in millennia.

It was not going to be the end of the world. Just the end of the Cullens. The end of Edward, the end of me.

I preferred it that way—the last part anyway. I would not live without Edward again; if he was leaving this world, then I would be right behind him.

I wondered idly now and then if there would be anything for us on the other side. I knew Edward didn't really believe so, but Carlisle did. I couldn't imagine it myself. On the other hand, I couldn't imagine Edward not existing somehow, somewhere. If we could be together in any place, then that was a happy ending.

And so the pattern of my days continued, just that much harder than before.

We went to see Charlie on Christmas Day, Edward, Renesmee, Jacob, and I. All of Jacob's pack were there, plus Sam, Emily, and Sue. It was a big help to have them there in Charlie's little rooms, their huge, warm bodies wedged into corners around his sparsely decorated tree—you could see exactly where he'd gotten bored and quit—and overflowing his furniture. You could always count on werewolves to be buzzed about a coming fight, no matter how suicidal. The electricity of their excitement provided a nice current that disguised my utter lack of spirit. Edward was, as always, a better actor than I was.

Renesmee wore the locket I'd given her at dawn, and in her jacket pocket was the MP3 player Edward had given her—a tiny thing that held five thousand songs, already filled with Edward's favorites. On her wrist was an intricately braided Quileute version of a promise ring. Edward had gritted his teeth over that one, but it didn't bother me.

Soon, so soon, I would be giving her to Jacob for safekeeping. How could I be bothered by any symbol of the commitment I was so relying on?

Edward had saved the day by ordering a gift for Charlie, too. It had shown up yesterday—priority overnight shipping—and Charlie spent all morning reading the thick instruction manual to his new fishing sonar system.

From the way the werewolves ate, Sue's lunch spread must have been good. I wondered how the gathering would have looked to an outsider. Did we play our parts well enough? Would a stranger have thought us a happy circle of friends, enjoying the holiday with casual cheer?

I think Edward and Jacob both were as relieved as I was when it was time to go. It felt odd to spend energy on the human façade when there were so many more important things to be doing. I had a hard time concentrating. At the same time, this was perhaps the last time I would see Charlie. Maybe it was a good thing that I was too numb to really register that.

I hadn't seen my mother since the wedding, but I found I could only be glad for the gradual distancing that had begun two years ago. She was too fragile for my world. I didn't want her to have any part of this. Charlie was stronger.

Maybe even strong enough for a goodbye now, but I wasn't.

It was very quiet in the car; outside, the rain was just a mist, hovering on the edge between liquid and ice. Renesmee sat on my lap, playing with her locket, opening and closing it. I watched her and imagined the things I would say to Jacob right now if I didn't have to keep my words out of Edward's head.

If it's ever safe again, take her to Charlie. Tell him the whole story someday. Tell him how much I loved him, how I couldn't bear to leave him even when my human life was over. Tell him he was the best father. Tell him to pass my love on to Renée, all my hopes that she will be happy and well. . . .

I would have to give Jacob the documents before it was too late. I would give him a note for Charlie, too. And a letter for Renesmee. Something for her to read when I couldn't tell her I loved her anymore.

There was nothing unusual about the outside of the Cullen house as we pulled into the meadow, but I could hear some kind of subtle uproar inside. Many low voices murmured and growled. It sounded intense, and it sounded like an argument. I could pick out Carlisle's voice and Amun's more often than the others.

Edward parked in front of the house rather than going around to the garage. We exchanged one wary glance before we got out of the car.

Jacob's stance changed; his face turned serious and careful. I guessed that he was in Alpha mode now. Obviously, something had happened, and he was going to get the information he and Sam would need.

"Alistair is gone," Edward murmured as we darted up the steps.

Inside the front room, the main confrontation was physically apparent. Lining the walls was a ring of spectators, every vampire who had joined us, except for Alistair and the three involved in the quarrel. Esme, Kebi, and Tia were the closest to the three vampires in the center; in the middle of the room, Amun was hissing at Carlisle and Benjamin.

Edward's jaw tightened and he moved quickly to Esme's side, towing me by the hand. I clutched Renesmee tightly to my chest.

"Amun, if you want to go, no one is forcing you to stay," Carlisle said calmly.

"You're stealing half my coven, Carlisle!" Amun shrieked, stabbing one finger at Benjamin. "Is that why you called me here? To *steal* from me?"

Carlisle sighed, and Benjamin rolled his eyes.

"Yes, Carlisle picked a fight with the Volturi, endangered his whole family, just to lure me here to my death," Benjamin said sarcastically. "Be reasonable, Amun. I'm committed to do the right thing here—I'm not joining any other coven.

You can do whatever you want, of course, as Carlisle has pointed out."

"This won't end well," Amun growled. "Alistair was the only sane one here. We should all be running."

"Think of who you're calling sane," Tia murmured in a quiet aside.

"We're all going to be slaughtered!"

"It's not going to come to a fight," Carlisle said in a firm voice.

"You say!"

"If it does, you can always switch sides, Amun. I'm sure the Volturi will appreciate your help."

Amun sneered at him. "Perhaps that *is* the answer."

Carlisle's answer was soft and sincere. "I wouldn't hold that against you, Amun. We have been friends for a long time, but I would never ask you to die for me."

Amun's voice was more controlled, too. "But you're taking my Benjamin down with you."

Carlisle put his hand on Amun's shoulder; Amun shook it off.

"I'll stay, Carlisle, but it might be to your detriment. I *will* join them if that's the road to survival. You're all fools to think that you can defy the Volturi." He scowled, then sighed, glanced at Renesmee and me, and added in an exasperated tone, "I will witness that the child has grown. That's nothing but the truth. Anyone would see that."

"That's all we've ever asked."

Amun grimaced, "But not all that you are getting, it seems." He turned on Benjamin. "I gave you life. You're wasting it."

Benjamin's face looked colder than I'd ever seen it; the

expression contrasted oddly with his boyish features. "It's a pity you couldn't replace my will with your own in the process; perhaps then you would have been satisfied with me."

Amun's eyes narrowed. He gestured abruptly to Kebi, and they stalked past us out the front door.

"He's not leaving," Edward said quietly to me, "but he'll be keeping his distance even more from now on. He wasn't bluffing when he spoke of joining the Volturi."

"Why did Alistair go?" I whispered.

"No one can be positive; he didn't leave a note. From his mutters, it's been clear that he thinks a fight is inevitable. Despite his demeanor, he actually does care too much for Carlisle to stand with the Volturi. I suppose he decided the danger was too much." Edward shrugged.

Though our conversation was clearly just between the two of us, of course everyone could hear it. Eleazar answered Edward's comment like it had been meant for all.

"From the sound of his mumblings, it was a bit more than that. We haven't spoken much of the Volturi agenda, but Alistair worried that no matter how decisively we can prove your innocence, the Volturi will not listen. He thinks they will find an excuse to achieve their goals here."

The vampires glanced uneasily at one another. The idea that the Volturi would manipulate their own sacrosanct law for gain was not a popular idea. Only the Romanians were composed, their small half-smiles ironic. They seemed amused at how the others wanted to think well of their ancient enemies.

Many low discussions began at the same time, but it was the Romanians I listened to. Maybe because the fair-haired Vladimir kept shooting glances in my direction.

"I do so hope Alistair was right about this," Stefan murmured to Vladimir. "No matter the outcome, word will spread. It's time our world saw the Volturi for what they've become. They'll never fall if everyone believes this nonsense about them protecting our way of life."

"At least when we ruled, we were honest about what we were," Vladimir replied.

Stefan nodded. "We never put on white hats and called ourselves saints."

"I'm thinking the time has come to fight," Vladimir said. "How can you imagine we'll ever find a better force to stand with? Another chance this good?"

"Nothing is impossible. Maybe someday—"

"We've been waiting for *fifteen hundred years*, Stefan. And they've only gotten stronger with the years." Vladimir paused and looked at me again. He showed no surprise when he saw that I was watching him, too. "If the Volturi win this conflict, they will leave with more power than they came with. With every conquest they add to their strengths. Think of what that newborn alone could give them"—he jerked his chin toward me—"and she is barely discovering her gifts. And the earth-mover." Vladimir nodded toward Benjamin, who stiffened. Almost everyone was eavesdropping on the Romanians now, like me. "With their witch twins they have no need of the illusionist or the fire touch." His eyes moved to Zafrina, then Kate.

Stefan looked at Edward. "Nor is the mind reader exactly necessary. But I see your point. Indeed, they will gain much if they win."

"More than we can afford to have them gain, wouldn't you agree?"

Stefan sighed. "I think I must agree. And that means . . . "

"That we must stand against them while there is still hope."

"If we can just cripple them, even, expose them . . ."

"Then, someday, others will finish the job."

"And our long vendetta will be repaid. At last."

They locked eyes for a moment and then murmured in unison. "It seems the only way."

"So we fight," Stefan said.

Though I could see that they were torn, self-preservation warring with revenge, the smile they exchanged was full of anticipation.

"We fight," Vladimir agreed.

I suppose it was a good thing; like Alistair, I was sure the battle was impossible to avoid. In that case, two more vampires fighting on our side could only help. But the Romanians' decision still made me shudder.

"We will fight, too," Tia said, her usually grave voice more solemn than ever. "We believe the Volturi will overstep their authority. We have no wish to belong to them." Her eyes lingered on her mate.

Benjamin grinned and threw an impish glance toward the Romanians. "Apparently, I'm a hot commodity. It appears I have to win the right to be free."

"This won't be the first time I've fought to keep myself from a king's rule," Garrett said in a teasing tone. He walked over and clapped Benjamin on the back. "Here's to freedom from oppression."

"We stand with Carlisle," Tanya said. "And we fight with him."

The Romanians' pronouncement seemed to have made the others feel the need to declare themselves as well.

"We have not decided," Peter said. He looked down at his tiny companion; Charlotte's lips were set in dissatisfaction. It looked like she'd made her decision. I wondered what it was.

"The same goes for me," Randall said.

"And me," Mary added.

"The packs will fight with the Cullens," Jacob said suddenly. "We're not afraid of vampires," he added with a smirk.

"Children," Peter muttered.

"Infants," Randall corrected.

Jacob grinned tauntingly.

"Well, I'm in, too," Maggie said, shrugging out from under Siobhan's restraining hand. "I know truth is on Carlisle's side. I can't ignore that."

Siobhan stared at the junior member of her coven with worried eyes. "Carlisle," she said as if they were alone, ignoring the suddenly formal feel of the gathering, the unexpected outburst of declarations, "I don't want this to come to a fight."

"Nor do I, Siobhan. You know that's the last thing I want." He half-smiled. "Perhaps you should concentrate on keeping it peaceful."

"You know that won't help," she said.

I remembered Rose and Carlisle's discussion of the Irish leader; Carlisle believed that Siobhan had some subtle but powerful gift to make things go her way—and yet Siobhan didn't believe it herself.

"It couldn't hurt," Carlisle said.

Siobhan rolled her eyes. "Shall I visualize the outcome I desire?" she asked sarcastically.

Carlisle was openly grinning now. "If you don't mind."

"Then there is no need for my coven to declare itself, is there?" she retorted. "Since there is no possibility of a fight." She put her hand back on Maggie's shoulder, pulling the girl closer to her. Siobhan's mate, Liam, stood silent and expressionless.

Almost everyone else in the room looked mystified by Carlisle and Siobhan's clearly joking exchange, but they didn't explain themselves.

That was the end of the dramatic speeches for the night. The group slowly dispersed, some off to hunt, some to while away the time with Carlisle's books or televisions or computers.

Edward, Renesmee, and I went to hunt. Jacob tagged along.

"Stupid leeches," he muttered to himself when we got outside. "Think they're so superior." He snorted.

"They'll be shocked when the *infants* save their superior lives, won't they?" Edward said.

Jake smiled and punched his shoulder. "Hell yeah, they will."

This wasn't our last hunting trip. We all would hunt again nearer to the time we expected the Volturi. As the deadline was not exact, we were planning to stay a few nights out in the big baseball clearing Alice had seen, just in case. All we knew was that they would come the day that the snow stuck to the ground. We didn't want the Volturi too close to town, and Demetri would lead them to wherever we were. I wondered who he would track in, and guessed that it would be Edward since he couldn't track me.

I thought about Demetri while I hunted, paying little attention to my prey or the drifting snowflakes that had finally appeared but were melting before they touched the rocky soil. Would Demetri realize that he couldn't track me? What would he make of that? What would Aro? Or was Edward wrong? There were those little exceptions to what I could withstand, those ways around my shield. Everything that was outside my mind was vulnerable—open to the things Jasper, Alice, and Benjamin could do. Maybe Demetri's talent worked a little differently, too.

And then I had a thought that brought me up short. The half-drained elk dropped from my hands to the stony ground. Snowflakes vaporized a few inches from the warm body with tiny sizzling sounds. I stared blankly at my bloody hands.

Edward saw my reaction and hurried to my side, leaving his own kill undrained.

"What's wrong?" he asked in a low voice, his eyes sweeping the forest around us, looking for whatever had triggered my behavior.

"Renesmee," I choked.

"She's just through those trees," he reassured me. "I can hear both her thoughts and Jacob's. She's fine."

"That's not what I meant," I said. "I was thinking about my shield—you really think it's worth something, that it will help somehow. I know the others are hoping that I'll be able to shield Zafrina and Benjamin, even if I can only keep it up for a few seconds at a time. What if that's a mistake? What if your trust in me is the reason that we fail?"

My voice was edging toward hysteria, though I had enough control to keep it low. I didn't want to upset Renesmee.

"Bella, what brought this on? Of course, it's wonderful that you can protect yourself, but you're not responsible for saving anyone. Don't distress yourself needlessly."

"But what if I can't protect anything?" I whispered in gasps. "This thing I do, it's faulty, it's erratic! There's no rhyme or reason to it. Maybe it will do nothing against Alec at all."

"Shh," he hushed me. "Don't panic. And don't worry about Alec. What he does is no different than what Jane or Zafrina does. It's just an illusion—he can't get inside your head any more than I can."

"But Renesmee does!" I hissed frantically through my teeth. "It seemed so natural, I never questioned it before. It's always been just part of who she is. But she puts her thoughts right into my head just like she does with everyone else. My shield has holes, Edward!"

I stared at him desperately, waiting for him to acknowledge my terrible revelation. His lips were pursed, as if he was trying to decide how to phrase something. His expression was perfectly relaxed.

"You thought of this a long time ago, didn't you?" I demanded, feeling like an idiot for my months of overlooking the obvious.

He nodded, a faint smile pulling up one corner of his mouth. "The first time she touched you."

I sighed at my own stupidity, but his calm had mellowed me some. "And this doesn't bother you? You don't see it as a problem?"

"I have two theories, one more likely than the other."

"Give me the least likely first."

"Well, she's your daughter," he pointed out. "Genetically half you. I used to tease you about how your mind was on a different frequency than the rest of óurs. Perhaps she runs on the same."

This didn't work for me. "But you hear her mind just fine. *Everyone* hears her mind. And what if Alec runs on a different frequency? What if—?"

He put a finger to my lips. "I've considered that. Which is why I think this next theory is much more likely."

I gritted my teeth and waited.

"Do you remember what Carlisle said to me about her, right after she showed you that first memory?"

Of course I remembered. "He said, 'It's an interesting twist. Like she's doing the exact opposite of what you can.'"

"Yes. And so I wondered. Maybe she took your talent and flipped it, too."

I considered that.

"You keep everyone out," he began.

"And no one keeps her out?" I finished hesitantly.

"That's my theory," he said. "And if she can get into your head, I doubt there's a shield on the planet who could keep her at bay. That will help. From what we've seen, no one can doubt the truth of her thoughts once they've allowed her to show them. And I think no one can keep her from showing them, if she gets close enough. If Aro allows her to explain. . . ."

I shuddered to think of Renesmee so close to Aro's greedy, milky eyes.

"Well," he said, rubbing my tight shoulders. "At least there's nothing that can stop him from seeing the truth."

"But is the truth enough to stop him?" I murmured.

For that, Edward had no answer.

35. DEADLINE

"HEADED OUT?" EDWARD ASKED, HIS TONE NONCHALANT. There was a sort of forced composure about his expression. He hugged Renesmee just a little bit tighter to his chest.

"Yes, a few last-minute things . . . ," I responded just as casually.

He smiled my favorite smile. "Hurry back to me."

"Always."

I took his Volvo again, wondering if he'd read the odometer after my last errand. How much had he pieced together? That I had a secret, absolutely. Would he have deduced the reason why I didn't confide in him? Did he guess that Aro might soon know everything he knew? I thought Edward could have come to that conclusion, which explained why he had demanded no reasons from me. I guessed he was trying not to speculate too much, trying to keep my behavior off his mind. Had he put this together with my odd performance the morning after Alice left, burning my book in the fire? I didn't know if he could have made that leap.

It was a dreary afternoon, already dark as dusk. I sped through the gloom, my eyes on the heavy clouds. Would it snow tonight? Enough to layer the ground and create the scene from Alice's vision? Edward estimated that we had about two more days. Then we would set ourselves in the clearing, drawing the Volturi to our chosen place.

As I headed through the darkening forest, I considered my last trip to Seattle. I thought I knew Alice's purpose in sending me to the dilapidated drop point where J. Jenks referred his shadier clients. If I'd gone to one of his other, more legitimate offices, would I have ever known what to ask for? If I'd met him as Jason Jenks or Jason Scott, legitimate lawyer, would I ever have unearthed J. Jenks, purveyor of illegal documents? I'd had to go the route that made it clear I was up to no good. That was my clue.

It was black when I pulled into the parking lot of the restaurant a few minutes early, ignoring the eager valets by the entrance. I popped in my contacts and then went to wait for J inside the restaurant. Though I was in a hurry to be done with this depressing necessity and back with my family, J seemed careful to keep himself untainted by his baser associations; I had a feeling a handoff in the dark parking lot would offend his sensibilities.

I gave the name *Jenks* at the podium, and the obsequious maître d' led me upstairs to a small private room with a fire crackling in a stone hearth. He took the calf-length ivory trench coat I'd worn to disguise the fact that I was wearing Alice's idea of appropriate attire, and gasped quietly at my oyster satin cocktail dress. I couldn't help being a little flattered; I still wasn't used to being beautiful to everyone rather than just Edward. The maître d' stuttered half-formed compliments as he backed unsteadily from the room.

I stood by the fire to wait, holding my fingers close to the flame to warm them a little before the inevitable handshake. Not that J wasn't obviously aware that there was something up with the Cullens, but it was still a good habit to practice.

For one half second, I wondered what it would feel like to put my hand in the fire. What it would feel like when I burned. . . .

J's entrance distracted my morbidity. The maître d' took his coat, too, and it was evident that I was not the only one who had dressed up for this meeting.

"I'm so sorry I'm late," J said as soon as we were alone.

"No, you're exactly on time."

He held out his hand, and as we shook I could feel that his fingers were still quite noticeably warmer than mine. It didn't seem to bother him.

"You look stunning, if I may be so bold, Mrs. Cullen."

"Thank you, J. Please, call me Bella."

"I must say, it's a different experience working with you than it is with Mr. Jasper. Much less . . . unsettling." He smiled hesitantly.

"Really? I've always found Jasper to have a very soothing presence."

His eyebrows pulled together. "Is that so?" he murmured politely while clearly still in disagreement. How odd. What had Jasper done to this man?

"Have you known Jasper long?"

He sighed, looking uncomfortable. "I've been working with Mr. Jasper for more than twenty years, and my old partner knew him for fifteen years before that. . . . He never changes." J cringed delicately.

"Yeah, Jasper's kind of funny that way."

J shook his head as if he could shake away the disturbing thoughts. "Won't you have a seat, Bella?"

"Actually, I'm in a bit of a hurry. I've got a long drive home." As I spoke, I took the thick white envelope with his bonus from my bag and handed it to him.

"Oh," he said, a little catch of disappointment in his voice. He tucked the envelope into an inside pocket of his jacket without bothering to check the amount. "I was hoping we could speak for just a moment."

"About?" I asked curiously.

"Well, let me get you your items first. I want to make sure you're satisfied."

He turned, placed his briefcase on the table, and popped the latches. He took out a legal-sized manila envelope.

Though I had no idea what I should be looking for, I opened the envelope and gave the contents a cursory glance. J had flipped Jacob's picture and changed the coloring so that it wasn't immediately evident that it was the same picture on both his passport and driver's license. Both looked perfectly sound to me, but that meant little. I glanced at the picture on Vanessa Wolfe's passport for a fraction of a second, and then looked away quickly, a lump rising in my throat.

"Thank you," I told him.

His eyes narrowed slightly, and I felt he was disappointed that my examination was not more thorough. "I can assure you every piece is perfect. All will pass the most rigorous scrutiny by experts."

"I'm sure they are. I truly appreciate what you've done for me, J."

"It's been my pleasure, Bella. In the future, feel free to come to me for anything the Cullen family needs." He didn't even hint at it really, but this sounded like an invitation for me to take over Jasper's place as liaison.

"There was something you wanted to discuss?"

"Er, yes. It's a bit delicate. . . ," He gestured to the stone hearth with a questioning expression. I sat on the edge of the stone, and he sat beside me. Sweat was dewing up on his forehead again, and he pulled a blue silk handkerchief from his pocket and began mopping.

"You are the sister of Mr. Jasper's wife? Or married to his brother?" he asked.

"Married to his brother," I clarified, wondering where this was leading.

"You would be Mr. Edward's bride, then?"

"Yes."

He smiled apologetically. "I've seen all the names many times, you see. My belated congratulations. It's nice that Mr. Edward has found such a lovely partner after all this time."

"Thank you very much."

He paused, dabbing at the sweat. "Over the years, you might imagine that I've developed a very healthy level of respect for Mr. Jasper and the entire family."

I nodded cautiously.

He took a deep breath and then exhaled without speaking.

"J, please just say whatever you need to."

He took another breath and then mumbled quickly, slurring the words together.

"If you could just assure me that you are not planning to kidnap the little girl from her father, I would sleep better tonight."

"Oh," I said, stunned. It took me a minute to understand the erroneous conclusion he'd drawn. "Oh no. It's nothing like that at all." I smiled weakly, trying to reassure him. "I'm simply preparing a safe place for her in case something were to happen to my husband and me."

His eyes narrowed. "Are you expecting something to happen?" He blushed, then apologized. "Not that it's any of my business."

I watched the red flush spread behind the delicate membrane of his skin and was glad—as I often was—that I was not the average newborn. J seemed a nice enough man, criminal behavior aside, and it would have been a shame to kill him.

"You never know." I sighed.

He frowned. "May I wish you the best of luck, then. And please don't be put out with me, my dear, but . . . if Mr. Jasper should come to me and ask what names I put on these documents . . ."

"Of course you should tell him immediately. I'd like nothing better than to have Mr. Jasper fully aware of our entire transaction."

My transparent sincerity seemed to ease a bit of his tension.

"Very good," he said. "And I can't prevail upon you to stay for dinner?"

"I'm sorry, J. I'm short on time at present."

"Then, again, my best wishes for your health and happiness. Anything at all the Cullen family needs, please don't hesitate to call on me, Bella."

"Thank you, J."

I left with my contraband, glancing back to see that J was staring after me, his expression a mixture of anxiety and regret.

The return trip took me less time. The night was black, and so I turned off my headlights and floored it. When I got back to the house, most of the cars, including Alice's Porsche and my Ferrari, were missing. The traditional vampires were going as far away as possible to satiate their thirst. I tried not to think of their hunting in the night, cringing at the mental picture of their victims.

Only Kate and Garrett were in the front room, arguing playfully about the nutritional value of animal blood. I inferred that Garrett had attempted a hunting trip vegetarian-style and found it difficult.

Edward must have taken Renesmee home to sleep. Jacob, no doubt, was in the woods close by the cottage. The rest of my family must have been hunting as well. Perhaps they were out with the other Denalis.

Which basically gave me the house to myself, and I was quick to take advantage.

I could smell that I was the first one to enter Alice and Jasper's room in a long while, maybe the first since the night they'd left us. I rooted silently through their huge closet until I found the right sort of bag. It must have been Alice's;

it was a small black leather backpack, the kind that was usually used as a purse, little enough that even Renesmee could carry it without looking out of place. Then I raided their petty cash, taking about twice the yearly income for the average American household. I guessed my theft would be less noticeable here than anywhere else in the house, since this room made everyone sad. The envelope with the fake passports and IDs went into the bag on top of the money. Then I sat on the edge of Alice and Jasper's bed and looked at the pitifully insignificant package that was all I could give my daughter and my best friend to help save their lives. I slumped against the bedpost, feeling helpless.

But what else could I do?

I sat there for several minutes with my head bowed before the inkling of a good idea came to me.

If . . .

If I was to assume that Jacob and Renesmee were going to escape, then that included the assumption that Demetri would be dead. That gave any survivors a little breathing room, Alice and Jasper included.

So why couldn't Alice and Jasper help Jacob and Renesmee? If they were reunited, Renesmee would have the best protection imaginable. There was no reason why this couldn't happen, except for the fact that Jake and Renesmee both were blind spots for Alice. How would she begin to look for them?

I deliberated for a moment, then left the room, crossing the hall to Carlisle and Esme's suite. As usual, Esme's desk was stacked with plans and blueprints, everything neatly laid out in tall piles. The desk had a slew of pigeonholes above the work surface; in one was a box of stationery. I took a fresh sheet of paper and a pen.

Then I stared at the blank ivory page for a full five minutes, concentrating on my decision. Alice might not be able to see Jacob or Renesmee, but she could see me. I visualized her seeing this moment, hoping desperately that she wasn't too busy to pay attention.

Slowly, deliberately, I wrote the words *RIO DE JANEIRO* in all caps across the page.

Rio seemed the best place to send them: It was far away from here, Alice and Jasper were already in South America at last report, and it wasn't like our old problems had ceased to exist just because we had worse problems now. There was still the mystery of Renesmee's future, the terror of her racing age. We'd been headed south anyway. Now it would be Jacob's, and hopefully Alice's, job to search for the legends.

I bowed my head again against a sudden urge to sob, clenching my teeth together. It was better that Renesmee go on without me. But I already missed her so much I could barely stand it.

I took a deep breath and put the note at the bottom of the duffel bag, where Jacob would find it soon enough.

I crossed my fingers that—since it was unlikely that his high school offered Portuguese—Jake had at least taken Spanish as his language elective.

There was nothing left now but waiting.

For two days, Edward and Carlisle stayed in the clearing where Alice had seen the Volturi arrive. It was the same killing field where Victoria's newborns had attacked last summer. I wondered if it felt repetitive to Carlisle, like déjà vu. For me, it would be all new. This time Edward and I would stand with our family.

We could only imagine that the Volturi would be tracking either Edward or Carlisle. I wondered if it would surprise them that their prey didn't run. Would that make them wary? I couldn't imagine the Volturi ever feeling a need for caution.

Though I was—hopefully—invisible to Demetri, I stayed with Edward. Of course. We only had a few hours left to be together.

Edward and I had not had a last grand scene of farewell, nor did I plan one. To speak the word was to make it final. It would be the same as typing the words *The End* on the last page of a manuscript. So we did not say our goodbyes, and we stayed very close to each other, always touching. Whatever end found us, it would not find us separated.

We set up a tent for Renesmee a few yards back into the protective forest, and then there was more déjà vu as we found ourselves camping in the cold again with Jacob. It was almost impossible to believe how much things had changed since last June. Seven months ago, our triangular relationship seemed impossible, three different kinds of heartbreak that could not be avoided. Now everything was in perfect balance. It seemed hideously ironic that the puzzle pieces would fit together just in time for all of them to be destroyed.

It started to snow again the night before New Year's Eve. This time, the tiny flakes did not dissolve into the stony ground of the clearing. While Renesmee and Jacob slept—

Jacob snoring so loudly I wondered how Renesmee didn't wake—the snow made first a thin icing over the earth, then built into thicker drifts. By the time the sun rose, the scene from Alice's vision was complete. Edward and I held hands as we stared across the glittering white field, and neither of us spoke.

Through the early morning, the others gathered, their eyes bearing mute evidence of their preparations—some light gold, some rich crimson. Soon after we all were together, we could hear the wolves moving in the woods. Jacob emerged from the tent, leaving Renesmee still sleeping, to join them.

Edward and Carlisle were arraying the others into a loose formation, our witnesses to the sides like galleries.

I watched from a distance, waiting by the tent for Renesmee to wake. When she did, I helped her dress in the clothes I'd carefully picked out two days before. Clothes that looked frilly and feminine but that were actually sturdy enough to not show any wear—even if a person wore them while riding a giant werewolf through a couple of states. Over her jacket I put on the black leather backpack with the documents, the money, the clue, and my love notes for her and Jacob, Charlie and Renée. She was strong enough that it was no burden to her.

Her eyes were huge as she read the agony on my face. But she had guessed enough not to ask me what I was doing.

"I love you," I told her. "More than anything."

"I love you, too, Momma," she answered. She touched the locket at her neck, which now held a tiny photo of her, Edward, and me. "We'll always be together."

"In our hearts we'll always be together," I corrected in

a whisper as quiet as a breath. "But when the time comes today, you have to leave me."

Her eyes widened, and she touched her hand to my cheek. The silent *no* was louder than if she'd shouted it.

I fought to swallow; my throat felt swollen. "Will you do it for me? Please?"

She pressed her fingers harder to my face. *Why?*

"I can't tell you," I whispered. "But you'll understand soon. I promise."

In my head, I saw Jacob's face.

I nodded, then pulled her fingers away. "Don't think of it," I breathed into her ear. "Don't tell Jacob until I tell you to run, okay?"

This she understood. She nodded, too.

I took from my pocket one last detail.

While packing Renesmee's things, an unexpected sparkle of color had caught my eye. A chance ray of sun through the skylight had hit the jewels on the ancient precious box stuffed high overhead on a shelf in an untouched corner. I considered it for a moment and then shrugged. After putting together Alice's clues, I couldn't hope that the coming confrontation would be resolved peacefully. But why not try to start things out as friendly as possible? I asked myself. What could it hurt? So I guess I must have had some hope left after all—blind, senseless hope—because I'd scaled the shelves and retrieved Aro's wedding present to me.

Now I fastened the thick gold rope around my neck and felt the weight of the enormous diamond nestle into the hollow of my throat.

"Pretty," Renesmee whispered. Then she wrapped her arms like a vise around my neck. I squeezed her against my chest. Interlocked this way, I carried her out of the tent and to the clearing.

Edward cocked one eyebrow as I approached, but otherwise did not remark on my accessory or Renesmee's. He just put his arms tight around us both for one long moment and then, with a deep sigh, let us go. I couldn't see a goodbye anywhere in his eyes. Maybe he had more hope for something after this life than he'd let on.

We took our place, Renesmee climbing agilely onto my back to leave my hands free. I stood a few feet behind the front line made up by Carlisle, Edward, Emmett, Rosalie, Tanya, Kate, and Eleazar. Close beside me were Benjamin and Zafrina; it was my job to protect them as long as I was able. They were our best offensive weapons. If the Volturi were the ones who could not see, even for a few moments, that would change everything.

Zafrina was rigid and fierce, with Senna almost a mirror image at her side. Benjamin sat on the ground, his palms pressed to the dirt, and muttered quietly about fault lines. Last night, he'd strewn piles of boulders in natural-looking, now snow-covered heaps all along the back of the meadow. They weren't enough to injure a vampire, but hopefully enough to distract one.

The witnesses clustered to our left and right, some nearer than others—those who had declared themselves were the closest. I noticed Siobhan rubbing her temples, her eyes closed in concentration; was she humoring Carlisle? Trying to visualize a diplomatic resolution?

In the woods behind us, the invisible wolves were still and ready; we could only hear their heavy panting, their beating hearts.

The clouds rolled in, diffusing the light so that it could have been morning or afternoon. Edward's eyes tightened as he scrutinized the view, and I was sure he was seeing this exact scene for the second time—the first time being Alice's vision. It would look just the same when the Volturi arrived. We only had minutes or seconds left now.

All our family and allies braced themselves.

From the forest, the huge russet Alpha wolf came forward to stand at my side; it must have been too hard for him to keep his distance from Renesmee when she was in such immediate danger.

Renesmee reached out to twine her fingers in the fur over his massive shoulder, and her body relaxed a little bit. She was calmer with Jacob close. I felt a tiny bit better, too. As long as Jacob was with Renesmee, she would be all right.

Without risking a glance behind, Edward reached back to me. I stretched my arm forward so that I could grip his hand. He squeezed my fingers.

Another minute ticked by, and I found myself straining to hear some sound of approach.

And then Edward stiffened and hissed low between his clenched teeth. His eyes focused on the forest due north of where we stood.

We stared where he did, and waited as the last seconds passed.

36. BLOODLUST

THEY CAME WITH PAGEANTRY, WITH A KIND OF BEAUTY.

They came in a rigid, formal formation. They moved together, but it was not a march; they flowed in perfect synchronicity from the trees—a dark, unbroken shape that seemed to hover a few inches above the white snow, so smooth was the advance.

The outer perimeter was gray; the color darkened with each line of bodies until the heart of the formation was deepest black. Every face was cowled, shadowed. The faint brushing sound of their feet was so regular it was like music, a complicated beat that never faltered.

At some sign I did not see—or perhaps there was no sign, only millennia of practice—the configuration folded outward. The motion was too stiff, too square to resemble the opening of a flower, though the color suggested that; it was the opening of a fan, graceful but very angular. The gray-cloaked figures spread to the flanks while the darker forms surged precisely forward in the center, each movement closely controlled.

Their progress was slow but deliberate, with no hurry, no tension, no anxiety. It was the pace of the invincible.

This was almost my old nightmare. The only thing lacking was the gloating desire I'd seen on the faces in my dream—the smiles of vindictive joy. Thus far, the Volturi were too disciplined to show any emotion at all. They also showed no surprise or dismay at the collection of vampires that waited for them here—a collection that looked suddenly disorganized and unprepared in comparison. They showed no surprise at the giant wolf that stood in our midst.

I couldn't help counting. There were thirty-two of them. Even if you did not count the two drifting, waifish black-cloaked figures in the very back, who I took to be the wives—their protected position suggesting that they would not be involved in the attack—we were still outnumbered. There were just nineteen of us who would fight, and then seven more to watch as we were destroyed. Even counting the ten wolves, they had us.

"The redcoats are coming, the redcoats are coming," Garrett muttered mysteriously to himself and then chuckled once. He slid one step closer to Kate.

"They did come," Vladimir whispered to Stefan.

"The wives," Stefan hissed back. "The entire guard. All of them together. It's well we didn't try Volterra."

And then, as if their numbers were not enough, while

the Volturi slowly and majestically advanced, more vampires began entering the clearing behind them.

The faces in this seemingly endless influx of vampires were the antithesis to the Volturi's expressionless discipline—they wore a kaleidoscope of emotions. At first there was the shock and even some anxiety as they saw the unexpected force awaiting them. But that concern passed quickly; they were secure in their overwhelming numbers, secure in their position behind the unstoppable Volturi force. Their features returned to the expression they'd worn before we'd surprised them.

It was easy enough to understand their mindset—the faces were that explicit. This was an angry mob, whipped to a frenzy and slavering for justice. I did not fully realize the vampire world's feeling toward the immortal children before I read these faces.

It was clear that this motley, disorganized horde—more than forty vampires altogether—was the Volturi's own kind of witness. When we were dead, they would spread the word that the criminals had been eradicated, that the Volturi had acted with nothing but impartiality. Most looked like they hoped for more than just an opportunity to witness—they wanted to help tear and burn.

We didn't have a prayer. Even if we could somehow neutralize the Volturi's advantages, they could still bury us in bodies. Even if we killed Demetri, Jacob would not be able to outrun this.

I could feel it as the same comprehension sunk in around me. Despair weighted the air, pushing me down with more pressure than before.

One vampire in the opposing force did not seem to

belong to either party; I recognized Irina as she hesitated in between the two companies, her expression unique among the others. Irina's horrified gaze was locked on Tanya's position in the front line. Edward snarled, a very low but fervent sound.

"Alistair was right," he murmured to Carlisle.

I watched Carlisle glance at Edward questioningly.

"Alistair was right?" Tanya whispered.

"They—Caius and Aro—come to destroy and acquire," Edward breathed almost silently back; only our side could hear. "They have many layers of strategy already in place. If Irina's accusation had somehow proven to be false, they were committed to find another reason to take offense. But they can see Renesmee now, so they are perfectly sanguine about their course. We could still attempt to defend against their other contrived charges, but first they have to stop, to hear the truth about Renesmee." Then, even lower. "Which they have no intention of doing."

Jacob gave a strange little huff.

And then, unexpectedly, two seconds later, the procession *did* halt. The low music of perfectly synchronized movements turned to silence. The flawless discipline remained unbroken; the Volturi froze into absolute stillness as one. They stood about a hundred yards away from us.

Behind me, to the sides, I heard the beating of large hearts, closer than before. I risked glances to the left and the right from the corners of my eyes to see what had stopped the Volturi advance.

The wolves had joined us.

On either side of our uneven line, the wolves branched out in long, bordering arms. I only spared a fraction of a second to note that there were more than ten wolves, to recognize the wolves I knew and the ones I'd never seen before. There were sixteen of them spaced evenly around us—seventeen total, counting Jacob. It was clear from their heights and oversized paws that the newcomers all were very, very young. I supposed I should have foreseen this. With so many vampires encamped in the neighborhood, a werewolf population explosion was inevitable.

More children dying. I wondered why Sam had allowed this, and then I realized he had no other choice. If any of the wolves stood with us, the Volturi would be sure to search out the rest. They had gambled their entire species on this stand.

And we were going to lose.

Abruptly, I was furious. Beyond furious, I was murderously enraged. My hopeless despair vanished entirely. A faint reddish glow highlighted the dark figures in front of me, and all I wanted in that moment was the chance to sink my teeth into them, to rip their limbs from their bodies and pile them for burning. I was so maddened I could have danced around the pyre where they roasted alive; I would have laughed while their ashes smoldered. My lips curved back automatically, and a low, fierce snarl tore up my throat from the pit of my stomach. I realized the corners of my mouth were turned up in a smile.

Beside me, Zafrina and Senna echoed my hushed growl. Edward squeezed the hand he still held, cautioning me.

The shadowed Volturi faces were still expressionless for the most part. Only two sets of eyes betrayed any emotion at all. In the very center, touching hands, Aro and Caius had paused to evaluate, and the entire guard had paused with them, waiting for the order to kill. The two did not look at each other, but it was obvious that they were communicating. Marcus, though touching Aro's other hand, did not seem part of the conversation. His expression was not as mindless as the guards', but it was nearly as blank. Like the one other time I'd seen him, he appeared to be utterly bored.

The bodies of the Volturi's witnesses leaned toward us, their eyes fixed furiously on Renesmee and me, but they stayed near the fringe of the forest, leaving a wide berth between themselves and the Volturi soldiers. Only Irina hovered close behind the Volturi, just a few paces away from the ancient females—both fair-haired with powdery skin and filmed eyes—and their two massive bodyguards.

There was a woman in one of the darker gray cloaks just behind Aro. I couldn't be sure, but it looked like she might actually be touching his back. Was this the other shield, Renata? I wondered, as Eleazar had, if she would be able to repel *me*.

But I would not waste my life trying to get to Caius or Aro. I had more vital targets.

I searched the line for them now and had no difficulty picking out the two petite, deep gray cloaks near the heart of the arrangement. Alec and Jane, easily the smallest members of the guard, stood just to Marcus's side, flanked by Demetri on the other. Their lovely faces were smooth, giving nothing away; they wore the darkest cloaks beside the pure black of the ancients. The witch twins, Vladimir had called them. Their powers were the cornerstone of the Volturi offensive. The jewels in Aro's collection.

My muscles flexed, and venom welled in my mouth.

Aro's and Caius's clouded red eyes flickered across our

line. I read disappointment in Aro's face as his gaze roved over our faces again and again, looking for one that was missing. Chagrin tightened his lips.

In that moment, I was nothing but grateful that Alice had run.

As the pause lengthened, I heard Edward's breath speed.

"Edward?" Carlisle asked, low and anxious.

"They're not sure how to proceed. They're weighing options, choosing key targets—me, of course, you, Eleazar, Tanya. Marcus is reading the strength of our ties to each other, looking for weak points. The Romanians' presence irritates them. They're worried about the faces they don't recognize—Zafrina and Senna in particular—and the wolves, naturally. They've never been outnumbered before. That's what stopped them."

"Outnumbered?" Tanya whispered incredulously.

"They don't count their witnesses," Edward breathed. "They are nonentities, meaningless to the guard. Aro just enjoys an audience."

"Should I speak?" Carlisle asked.

Edward hesitated, then nodded. "This is the only chance you'll get."

Carlisle squared his shoulders and paced several steps ahead of our defensive line. I hated to see him alone, unprotected.

He spread his arms, holding his palms up as if in greeting. "Aro, my old friend. It's been centuries."

The white clearing was dead silent for a long moment. I could feel the tension rolling off Edward as he listened to Aro's assessment of Carlisle's words. The strain mounted as the seconds ticked by.

And then Aro stepped forward out of the center of the Volturi formation. The shield, Renata, moved with him as if the tips of her fingers were sewn to his robe. For the first time, the Volturi ranks reacted. A muttered grumble rolled through the line, eyebrows lowered into scowls, lips curled back from teeth. A few of the guard leaned forward into a crouch.

Aro held one hand up toward them. "Peace."

He walked just a few paces more, then cocked his head to one side. His milky eyes glinted with curiosity.

"Fair words, Carlisle," he breathed in his thin, wispy voice. "They seem out of place, considering the army you've assembled to kill me, and to kill my dear ones."

Carlisle shook his head and stretched his right hand forward as if there were not still almost a hundred yards between them. "You have but to touch my hand to know that was never my intent."

Aro's shrewd eyes narrowed. "But how can your intent possibly matter, dear Carlisle, in the face of what you have done?" He frowned, and a shadow of sadness crossed his features—whether it was genuine or not, I could not tell.

"I have not committed the crime you are here to punish me for."

"Then step aside and let us punish those responsible. Truly, Carlisle, nothing would please me more than to preserve your life today."

"No one has broken the law, Aro. Let me explain." Again, Carlisle offered his hand.

Before Aro could answer, Caius drifted swiftly forward to Aro's side.

"So many pointless rules, so many unnecessary laws you

create for yourself, Carlisle," the white-haired ancient hissed. "How is it possible that you defend the breaking of one that truly matters?"

"The law is not broken. If you would listen—"

"We see the child, Carlisle," Caius snarled. "Do not treat us as fools."

"She is *not* an immortal. She is not a vampire. I can easily prove this with just a few moments—"

Caius cut him off. "If she is not one of the forbidden, then why have you massed a battalion to protect her?"

"Witnesses, Caius, just as you have brought." Carlisle gestured to the angry horde at the edge of the woods; some of them growled in response. "Any one of these friends can tell you the truth about the child. Or you could just look at her, Caius. See the flush of human blood in her cheeks."

"Artifice!" Caius snapped. "Where is the informer? Let her come forward!" He craned his neck around until he spotted Irina lingering behind the wives. "You! Come!"

Irina stared at him uncomprehendingly, her face like that of someone who has not entirely awakened from a hideous nightmare. Impatiently, Caius snapped his fingers. One of the wives' huge bodyguards moved to Irina's side and prodded her roughly in the back. Irina blinked twice and then walked slowly toward Caius in a daze. She stopped several yards short, her eyes still on her sisters.

Caius closed the distance between them and slapped her across the face.

It couldn't have hurt, but there was something terribly degrading about the action. It was like watching someone kick a dog. Tanya and Kate hissed in synchronization.

Irina's body went rigid and her eyes finally focused on

Caius. He pointed one clawed finger at Renesmee, where she clung to my back, her fingers still tangled in Jacob's fur. Caius turned entirely red in my furious view. A growl rumbled through Jacob's chest.

"This is the child you saw?" Caius demanded. "The one that was obviously more than human?"

Irina peered at us, examining Renesmee for the first time since entering the clearing. Her head tilted to the side, confusion crossed her features.

"Well?" Caius snarled.

"I . . . I'm not sure," she said, her tone perplexed.

Caius's hand twitched as if he wanted to slap her again. "What do you mean?" he said in a steely whisper.

"She's not the same, but I think it's the same child. What I mean is, she's changed. This child is bigger than the one I saw, but—"

Caius's furious gasp crackled through his suddenly bared teeth, and Irina broke off without finishing. Aro flitted to Caius's side and put a restraining hand on his shoulder.

"Be composed, brother. We have time to sort this out. No need to be hasty."

With a sullen expression, Caius turned his back on Irina.

"Now, sweetling," Aro said in a warm, sugary murmur. "Show me what you're trying to say." He held his hand out to the bewildered vampire.

Uncertainly, Irina took his hand. He held hers for only five seconds.

"You see, Caius?" he said. "It's a simple matter to get what we need."

Caius didn't answer him. From the corner of his eye,

Aro glanced once at his audience, his mob, and then turned back to Carlisle.

"And so we have a mystery on our hands, it seems. It would appear the child has grown. Yet Irina's first memory was clearly that of an immortal child. Curious."

"That's exactly what I'm trying to explain," Carlisle said, and from the change in his voice, I could guess at his relief. This was the pause we had pinned all our nebulous hopes on.

I felt no relief. I waited, almost numb with rage, for the layers of strategy Edward had promised.

Carlisle held out his hand again.

Aro hesitated for a moment. "I would rather have the explanation from someone more central to the story, my friend. Am I wrong to assume that this breach was not of your making?"

"There was no breach."

"Be that as it may, I *will* have every facet of the truth." Aro's feathery voice hardened. "And the best way to get that is to have the evidence directly from your talented son." He inclined his head in Edward's direction. "As the child clings to his newborn mate, I'm assuming Edward is involved."

Of course he wanted Edward. Once he could see into Edward's mind, he would know *all* our thoughts. Except mine.

Edward turned to quickly kiss my forehead and Renesmee's, not meeting my eyes. Then he strode across the snowy field, clapping Carlisle on the shoulder as he passed. I heard a low whimper from behind me—Esme's terror breaking through.

The red haze I saw around the Volturi army flamed

brighter than before. I could not bear to watch Edward cross the empty white space alone—but I also could not endure to have Renesmee one step closer to our adversaries. The opposing needs tore at me; I was frozen so tightly it felt like my bones might shatter from the pressure of it.

I saw Jane smile as Edward crossed the midpoint in the distance between us, when he was closer to them than he was to us.

That smug little smile did it. My fury peaked, higher even than the raging bloodlust I'd felt the moment the wolves had committed to this doomed fight. I could taste madness on my tongue—I felt it flow through me like a tidal wave of pure power. My muscles tightened, and I acted automatically. I threw my shield with all the force in my mind, flung it across the impossible expanse of the field—ten times my best distance—like a javelin. My breath rushed out in a huff with the exertion.

The shield blew out from me in a bubble of sheer energy, a mushroom cloud of liquid steel. It pulsed like a living thing—I could *feel* it, from the apex to the edges.

There was no recoil to the elastic fabric now; in that instant of raw force, I saw that the backlash I'd felt before was of my own making—I had been clinging to that invisible part of me in self-defense, subconsciously unwilling to let it go. Now I set it free, and my shield exploded a good fifty yards out from me effortlessly, taking only a fraction of my concentration. I could feel it flex like just another muscle, obedient to my will. I pushed it, shaped it to a long, pointed oval. Everything underneath the flexible iron shield was suddenly a part of me—I could feel the life force of everything it covered like points of bright heat, dazzling sparks of light surrounding me. I thrust the shield forward the length of the clearing, and exhaled in relief when I felt Edward's brilliant light within my protection. I held there, contracting this new muscle so that it closely surrounded Edward, a thin but unbreakable sheet between his body and our enemies.

Barely a second had passed. Edward was still walking to Aro. Everything had changed absolutely, but no one had noticed the explosion except for me. A startled laugh burst through my lips. I felt the others glancing at me and saw Jacob's big black eye roll down to stare at me like I'd lost my mind.

Edward stopped a few steps away from Aro, and I realized with some chagrin that though I certainly could, I *should* not prevent this exchange from happening. This was the point of all our preparations: getting Aro to hear our side of the story. It was almost physically painful to do it, but reluctantly I pulled my shield back and left Edward exposed again. The laughing mood had vanished. I focused totally on Edward, ready to shield him instantly if something went wrong.

Edward's chin came up arrogantly, and he held his hand out to Aro as if he were conferring a great honor. Aro seemed only delighted with his attitude, but his delight was not universal. Renata fluttered nervously in Aro's shadow. Caius's scowl was so deep it looked like his papery, translucent skin would crease permanently. Little Jane showed her teeth, and beside her Alec's eyes narrowed in concentration. I guessed that he was ready, like me, to act at a second's notice.

Aro closed the distance without pause—and really, what did he have to fear? The hulking shadows of the lighter gray cloaks—the brawny fighters like Felix—were but a few yards away. Jane and her burning gift could throw Edward on the ground, writhing in agony. Alec could blind and deafen him before he could take a step in Aro's direction. No one knew that I had the power to stop them, not even Edward.

With an untroubled smile, Aro took Edward's hand. His eyes snapped shut at once, and then his shoulders hunched under the onslaught of information.

Every secret thought, every strategy, every insight— everything Edward had heard in the minds around him during the last month—was now Aro's. And further back—every vision of Alice's, every quiet moment with our family, every picture in Renesmee's head, every kiss, every touch between Edward and me . . . All of that was Aro's now, too.

I hissed with frustration, and the shield roiled with my irritation, shifting its shape and contracting around our side.

"Easy, Bella," Zafrina whispered to me.

I clenched my teeth together.

Aro continued to concentrate on Edward's memories. Edward's head bowed, too, the muscles in his neck locking tight as he read back again everything that Aro took from him, and Aro's response to it all.

This two-way but unequal conversation continued long enough that even the guard grew uneasy. Low murmurs ran through the line until Caius barked a sharp order for silence. Jane was edging forward like she couldn't help herself, and Renata's face was rigid with distress. For a moment, I ex- amined this powerful shield that seemed so panicky and weak; though she was useful to Aro, I could tell she was no warrior. It was not her job to fight but to protect. There was no bloodlust in her. Raw as I was, I knew that if this were between her and me, I would obliterate her.

I refocused as Aro straightened, his eyes flashing open, their expression awed and wary. He did not release Edward's hand.

Edward's muscles loosened ever so slightly.

"You see?" Edward asked, his velvet voice calm.

"Yes, I see, indeed," Aro agreed, and amazingly, he sounded almost amused. "I doubt whether any two among gods or mortals have ever seen quite so clearly."

The disciplined faces of the guard showed the same disbelief I felt.

"You have given me much to ponder, young friend," Aro continued. "Much more than I expected." Still he did not release Edward's hand, and Edward's tense stance was that of one who listens.

Edward didn't answer.

"May I meet her?" Aro asked—almost pleaded—with sudden eager interest. "I never dreamed of the existence of such a thing in all my centuries. What an addition to our histories!"

"What is this about, Aro?" Caius snapped before Edward could answer. Just the question had me pulling Renesmee around into my arms, cradling her protectively against my chest.

"Something you've never dreamed of, my practical friend. Take a moment to ponder, for the justice we intended to deliver no longer applies."

Caius hissed in surprise at his words.

"Peace, brother," Aro cautioned soothingly.

This should have been good news—these were the words we'd been hoping for, the reprieve we'd never really thought possible. Aro had listened to the truth. Aro had admitted that the law had not been broken.

But my eyes were riveted on Edward, and I saw the muscles in his back tighten. I replayed in my head Aro's instruction for Caius to *ponder*, and heard the double meaning.

"Will you introduce me to your daughter?" Aro asked Edward again.

Caius was not the only one who hissed at this new revelation.

Edward nodded reluctantly. And yet, Renesmee had won over so many others. Aro always seemed the leader of the ancients. If he were on her side, could the others act against us?

Aro still gripped Edward's hand, and he now answered a question that the rest of us had not heard.

"I think a compromise on this one point is certainly acceptable, under the circumstance. We will meet in the middle."

Aro released his hand. Edward turned back toward us, and Aro joined him, throwing one arm casually over Edward's shoulder like they were the best of friends—all the while maintaining contact with Edward's skin. They began to cross the field back to our side.

The entire guard fell into step behind them. Aro raised a hand negligently without looking at them.

"Hold, my dear ones. Truly, they mean us no harm if we are peaceable."

The guard reacted to this more openly than before, with

snarls and hisses of protest, but held their position. Renata, clinging closer to Aro than ever, whimpered in anxiety.

"Master," she whispered.

"Don't fret, my love," he responded. "All is well."

"Perhaps you should bring a few members of your guard with us," Edward suggested. "It will make them more comfortable."

Aro nodded as if this was a wise observation he should have thought of himself. He snapped his fingers twice. "Felix, Demetri."

The two vampires were at his side instantaneously, looking precisely the same as the last time I'd met them. Both were tall and dark-haired, Demetri hard and lean as the blade of a sword, Felix hulking and menacing as an iron-spiked cudgel.

The five of them stopped in the middle of the snowy field.

"Bella," Edward called. "Bring Renesmee . . . and a few friends."

I took a deep breath. My body was tight with opposition. The idea of taking Renesmee into the center of the conflict . . . But I trusted Edward. He would know if Aro was planning any treachery at this point.

Aro had three protectors on his side of the summit, so I would bring two with me. It took me only a second to decide.

"Jacob? Emmett?" I asked quietly. Emmett, because he would be dying to go. Jacob, because he wouldn't be able to bear being left behind.

Both nodded. Emmett grinned.

I crossed the field with them flanking me. I heard another

rumble from the guard as they saw my choices—clearly, they did not trust the werewolf. Aro lifted his hand, waving away their protest again.

"Interesting company you keep," Demetri murmured to Edward.

Edward didn't respond, but a low growl slipped through Jacob's teeth.

We stopped a few yards from Aro. Edward ducked under Aro's arm and quickly joined us, taking my hand.

For a moment we faced each other in silence. Then Felix greeted me in a low aside.

"Hello again, Bella." He grinned cockily while still tracking Jacob's every twitch with his peripheral vision.

I smiled wryly at the mountainous vampire. "Hey, Felix."

Felix chuckled. "You look good. Immortality suits you."

"Thanks so much."

"You're welcome. It's too bad . . ."

He let his comment trail off into silence, but I didn't need Edward's gift to imagine the end. *It's too bad we're going to kill you in a sec.*

"Yes, too bad, isn't it?" I murmured.

Felix winked.

Aro paid no attention to our exchange. He leaned his head to one side, fascinated. "I hear her strange heart," he murmured with an almost musical lilt to his words. "I smell her strange scent." Then his hazy eyes shifted to me. "In truth, young Bella, immortality does become you most extraordinarily," he said. "It is as if you were designed for this life."

I nodded once in acknowledgment of his flattery.

"You liked my gift?" he asked, eyeing the pendant I wore.

"It's beautiful, and very, very generous of you. Thank you. I probably should have sent a note."

Aro laughed delightedly. "It's just a little something I had lying around. I thought it might complement your new face, and so it does."

I heard a little hiss from the center of the Volturi line. I glanced over Aro's shoulder.

Hmm. It seemed Jane wasn't happy about the fact that Aro had given me a present.

Aro cleared his throat to reclaim my attention. "May I greet your daughter, lovely Bella?" he asked sweetly.

This was what we'd hoped for, I reminded myself. Fighting the urge to take Renesmee and run for it, I walked two slow steps forward. My shield rippled out behind me like a cape, protecting the rest of my family while Renesmee was left exposed. It felt wrong, horrible.

Aro met us, his face beaming.

"But she's exquisite," he murmured. "So like you and Edward." And then louder, "Hello, Renesmee."

Renesmee looked at me quickly. I nodded.

"Hello, Aro," she answered formally in her high, ringing voice.

Aro's eyes were bemused.

"What is it?" Caius hissed from behind. He seemed infuriated by the need to ask.

"Half mortal, half immortal," Aro announced to him and the rest of the guard without turning his enthralled gaze from Renesmee. "Conceived so, and carried by this newborn while she was still human."

"Impossible," Caius scoffed.

"Do you think they've fooled me, then, brother?" Aro's expression was greatly amused, but Caius flinched. "Is the heartbeat you hear a trickery as well?"

Caius scowled, looking as chagrined as if Aro's gentle questions had been blows.

"Calmly and carefully, brother," Aro cautioned, still smiling at Renesmee. "I know well how you love your justice, but there is no justice in acting against this unique little one for her parentage. And so much to learn, so much to learn! I know you don't have my enthusiasm for collecting histories, but be tolerant with me, brother, as I add a chapter that stuns me with its improbability. We came expecting only justice and the sadness of false friends, but look what we have gained instead! A new, bright knowledge of ourselves, our possibilities."

He held out his hand to Renesmee in invitation. But this was not what she wanted. She leaned away from me, stretching upward, to touch her fingertips to Aro's face.

Aro did not react with shock as almost everyone else had reacted to this performance from Renesmee; he was as used to the flow of thought and memory from other minds as Edward was.

His smile widened, and he sighed in satisfaction. "Brilliant," he whispered.

Renesmee relaxed back into my arms, her little face very serious.

"Please?" she asked him.

His smile turned gentle. "Of course I have no desire to harm your loved ones, precious Renesmee."

Aro's voice was so comforting and affectionate, it took

me in for a second. And then I heard Edward's teeth grind together and, far behind us, Maggie's outraged hiss at the lie.

"I wonder," Aro said thoughtfully, seeming unaware of the reaction to his previous words. His eyes moved unexpectedly to Jacob, and instead of the disgust the other Volturi viewed the giant wolf with, Aro's eyes were filled with a longing that I did not comprehend.

"It doesn't work that way," Edward said, the careful neutrality gone from his suddenly harsh tone.

"Just an errant thought," Aro said, appraising Jacob openly, and then his eyes moved slowly across the two lines of werewolves behind us. Whatever Renesmee had shown him, it made the wolves suddenly interesting to him.

"They don't *belong* to us, Aro. They don't follow our commands that way. They're here because they want to be."

Jacob growled menacingly.

"They seem quite attached to you, though," Aro said. "And your young mate and your . . . family. *Loyal.*" His voice caressed the word softly.

"They're committed to protecting human life, Aro. That makes them able to coexist with us, but hardly with you. Unless you're rethinking your lifestyle."

Aro laughed merrily. "Just an errant thought," he repeated. "You well know how that is. We none of us can entirely control our subconscious desires."

Edward grimaced. "I do know how that is. And I also know the difference between that kind of thought and the kind with a purpose behind it. It could never work, Aro."

Jacob's vast head turned in Edward's direction, and a faint whine slipped from between his teeth.

"He's intrigued with the idea of . . . guard dogs," Edward murmured back.

There was one second of dead silence, and then the sound of the furious snarls ripping from the entire pack filled the giant clearing.

There was a sharp bark of command—from Sam, I guessed, though I didn't turn to look—and the complaint broke off into ominous quiet.

"I suppose that answers that question," Aro said, laughing again. *"This* lot has picked its side."

Edward hissed and leaned forward. I clutched at his arm, wondering what could be in Aro's thoughts that would make him react so violently, while Felix and Demetri slipped into crouches in synchronization. Aro waved them off again. They all returned to their former posture, Edward included.

"So much to discuss," Aro said, his tone suddenly that of an inundated businessman. "So much to decide. If you and your furry protector will excuse me, my dear Cullens, I must confer with my brothers."

37. CONTRIVANCES

Aro did not rejoin his anxious guard waiting on the north side of the clearing; instead, he waved them forward.

Edward started backing up immediately, pulling my arm and Emmett's. We hurried backward, keeping our eyes on the advancing threat. Jacob retreated slowest, the fur on his shoulders standing straight up as he bared his fangs at Aro. Renesmee grabbed the end of his tail as we retreated; she held it like a leash, forcing him to stay with us. We reached our family at the same time that the dark cloaks surrounded Aro again.

Now there were only fifty yards between them and us—a distance any of us could leap in just a fraction of a second.

Caius began arguing with Aro at once.

"How can you abide this infamy? Why do we stand here impotently in the face of such an outrageous crime, covered by such a ridiculous deception?" He held his arms rigidly at his sides, his hands curled into claws. I wondered why he did not just touch Aro to share his opinion. Were we seeing a division in their ranks already? Could we be that lucky?

"Because it's all true," Aro told him calmly. "Every word of it. See how many witnesses stand ready to give evidence that they have seen this miraculous child grow and mature in just the short time they've known her. That they have felt the warmth of the blood that pulses in her veins." Aro's gesture swept from Amun on one side across to Siobhan on the other.

Caius reacted oddly to Aro's soothing words, starting ever so slightly at the mention of *witnesses*. The anger drained from his features, replaced by a cold calculation. He glanced at the Volturi witnesses with an expression that looked vaguely . . . nervous.

I glanced at the angry mob, too, and saw immediately that the description no longer applied. The frenzy for action had turned to confusion. Whispered conversations seethed through the crowd as they tried to make sense of what had happened.

Caius was frowning, deep in thought. His speculative expression stoked the flames of my smoldering anger at the same time that it worried me. What if the guard acted again on some invisible signal, as they had in their march? Anxiously, I inspected my shield; it felt just as impenetrable as before. I flexed it now into a low, wide dome that arced over our company.

I could feel the sharp plumes of light where my family and friends stood—each one an individual flavor that I thought I would be able to recognize with practice. I already knew Edward's—his was the very brightest of them all. The extra empty space around the shining spots bothered me; there was no physical barrier to the shield, and if any of the talented Volturi got *under* it, it would protect no one but me. I felt my forehead crease as I pulled the elastic armor very carefully closer. Carlisle was the farthest forward; I sucked the shield back inch by inch, trying to wrap it as exactly to his body as I could.

My shield seemed to want to cooperate. It hugged his shape; when Carlisle shifted to the side to stand nearer to Tanya, the elastic stretched with him, drawn to his spark.

Fascinated, I tugged in more threads of the fabric, pulling it around each glimmering shape that was a friend or ally. The shield clung to them willingly, moving as they moved.

Only a second had passed; Caius was still deliberating.

"The werewolves," he murmured at last.

With sudden panic, I realized that most of the werewolves were unprotected. I was about to reach out to them when I realized that, strangely, I could still feel their sparks. Curious, I drew the shield tighter in, until Amun and Kebi—the farthest edge of our group—were outside with the wolves. Once they were on the other side, their lights vanished. They no longer existed to that new sense. But the wolves were still bright flames—or rather, half of them were. Hmm . . . I edged outward again, and as soon as Sam was under cover, all the wolves were brilliant sparks again.

Their minds must have been more interconnected than

I'd imagined. If the Alpha was inside my shield, the rest of their minds were every bit as protected as his.

"Ah, brother . . . ," Aro answered Caius's statement with a pained look.

"Will you defend that alliance, too, Aro?" Caius demanded. "The Children of the Moon have been our bitter enemies from the dawn of time. We have hunted them to near extinction in Europe and Asia. Yet Carlisle encourages a familiar relationship with this enormous infestation—no doubt in an attempt to overthrow us. The better to protect his warped lifestyle."

Edward cleared his throat loudly and Caius glared at him. Aro placed one thin, delicate hand over his own face as if he was embarrassed for the other ancient.

"Caius, it's the middle of the day," Edward pointed out. He gestured to Jacob. "These are not Children of the Moon, clearly. They bear no relation to your enemies on the other side of the world."

"You breed mutants here," Caius spit back at him.

Edward's jaw clenched and unclenched, then he answered evenly, "They aren't even werewolves. Aro can tell you all about it if you don't believe me."

Not werewolves? I shot a mystified look at Jacob. He lifted his huge shoulders and let them drop—a shrug. He didn't know what Edward was talking about, either.

"Dear Caius, I would have warned you not to press this point if you had told me your thoughts," Aro murmured. "Though the creatures think of themselves as werewolves, they are not. The more accurate name for them would be shape-shifters. The choice of a wolf form was purely chance. It could have been a bear or a hawk or a panther when the first change was made. These creatures truly have nothing to do with the Children of the Moon. They have merely inherited this skill from their fathers. It's genetic—they do not continue their species by infecting others the way true werewolves do."

Caius glared at Aro with irritation and something more—an accusation of betrayal, maybe.

"They know our secret," he said flatly.

Edward looked about to answer this accusation, but Aro spoke faster. "They are creatures of our supernatural world, brother. Perhaps even more dependant upon secrecy than we are; they can hardly expose us. Carefully, Caius. Specious allegations get us nowhere."

Caius took a deep breath and nodded. They exchanged a long, significant glance.

I thought I understood the instruction behind Aro's careful wording. False charges weren't helping convince the watching witnesses on either side; Aro was cautioning Caius to move on to the next strategy. I wondered if the reason behind the apparent strain between the two ancients—Caius's unwillingness to share his thoughts with a touch—was that Caius didn't care about the show as much as Aro did. If the coming slaughter was so much more essential to Caius than an untarnished reputation.

"I want to talk to the informant," Caius announced abruptly, and turned his glare on Irina.

Irina wasn't paying attention to Caius and Aro's conversation; her face was twisted in agony, her eyes locked on her sisters, lined up to die. It was clear on her face that she knew now her accusation had been totally false.

"Irina," Caius barked, unhappy to have to address her.

She looked up, startled and instantly afraid.

Caius snapped his fingers.

Hesitantly, she moved from the fringes of the Volturi formation to stand in front of Caius again.

"So you appear to have been quite mistaken in your allegations," Caius began.

Tanya and Kate leaned forward anxiously.

"I'm sorry," Irina whispered. "I should have made sure of what I was seeing. But I had no idea. . . ." She gestured helplessly in our direction.

"Dear Caius, could you expect her to have guessed in an instant something so strange and impossible?" Aro asked. "Any of us would have made the same assumption."

Caius flicked his fingers at Aro to silence him.

"We all know you made a mistake," he said brusquely. "I meant to speak of your motivations."

Irina waited nervously for him to continue, and then repeated, "My motivations?"

"Yes, for coming to spy on them in the first place."

Irina flinched at the word *spy*.

"You were unhappy with the Cullens, were you not?"

She turned her miserable eyes to Carlisle's face. "I was," she admitted.

"Because . . . ?" Caius prompted.

"Because the werewolves killed my friend," she whispered. "And the Cullens wouldn't stand aside to let me avenge him."

"The shape-shifters," Aro corrected quietly.

"So the Cullens sided with the *shape-shifters* against our own kind—against the friend of a friend, even," Caius summarized.

I heard Edward make a disgusted sound under his breath.

Caius was ticking down his list, looking for an accusation that would stick.

Irina's shoulders stiffened. "That's how I saw it."

Caius waited again and then prompted, "If you'd like to make a formal complaint against the shape-shifters—and the Cullens for supporting their actions—now would be the time." He smiled a tiny cruel smile, waiting for Irina to give him his next excuse.

Maybe Caius didn't understand real families—relationships based on love rather than just the love of power. Maybe he overestimated the potency of vengeance.

Irina's jaw jerked up, her shoulders squared.

"No, I have no complaint against the wolves, or the Cullens. You came here today to destroy an immortal child. No immortal child exists. This was my mistake, and I take full responsibility for it. But the Cullens are innocent, and you have no reason to still be here. I'm so sorry," she said to us, and then she turned her face toward the Volturi witnesses. "There was no crime. There's no valid reason for you to continue here."

Caius raised his hand as she spoke, and in it was a strange metal object, carved and ornate.

This was a signal. The response was so fast that we all stared in stunned disbelief while it happened. Before there was time to react, it was over.

Three of the Volturi soldiers leaped forward, and Irina was completely obscured by their gray cloaks. In the same instant, a horrible metallic screeching ripped through the clearing. Caius slithered into the center of the gray melee, and the shocking squealing sound exploded into a startling upward shower of sparks and tongues of flame. The soldiers leaped back from the sudden inferno, immediately retaking their places in the guard's perfectly straight line.

Caius stood alone beside the blazing remains of Irina, the metal object in his hand still throwing a thick jet of flame into the pyre.

With a small clicking sound, the fire shooting from Caius's hand disappeared. A gasp rippled through the mass of witnesses behind the Volturi.

We were too aghast to make any noise at all. It was one thing to know that death was coming with fierce, unstoppable speed; it was another thing to watch it happen.

Caius smiled coldly. "*Now* she has taken full responsibility for her actions."

His eyes flashed to our front line, touching swiftly on Tanya's and Kate's frozen forms.

In that second I understood that Caius had never underestimated the ties of a true family. *This* was the ploy. He had not wanted Irina's complaint; he had wanted her defiance. His excuse to destroy her, to ignite the violence that filled the air like a thick, combustible mist. He had thrown a match.

The strained peace of this summit already teetered more precariously than an elephant on a tightrope. Once the fight began, there would be no way to stop it. It would only escalate until one side was entirely extinct. Our side. Caius knew this.

So did Edward.

"Stop them!" Edward cried out, jumping to grab Tanya's arm as she lurched forward toward the smiling Caius with a maddened cry of pure rage. She couldn't shake Edward off before Carlisle had his arms locked around her waist.

"It's too late to help her," he reasoned urgently as she struggled. "Don't give him what he wants!"

Kate was harder to contain. Shrieking wordlessly like Tanya, she broke into the first stride of the attack that would end with everyone's death. Rosalie was closest to her, but before Rose could clinch her in a headlock, Kate shocked her so violently that Rose crumpled to the ground. Emmett caught Kate's arm and threw her down, then staggered back, his knees giving out. Kate rolled to her feet, and it looked like no one could stop her.

Garrett flung himself at her, knocking her to the ground again. He bound his arms around hers, locking his hands around his own wrists. I saw his body spasm as she shocked him. His eyes rolled back in his head, but his hold did not break.

"Zafrina," Edward shouted.

Kate's eyes went blank and her screams turned to moans. Tanya stopped struggling.

"Give me my sight back," Tanya hissed.

Desperately, but with all the delicacy I could manage, I pulled my shield even tighter against the sparks of my friends, peeling it back carefully from Kate while trying to keep it around Garrett, making it a thin skin between them.

And then Garrett was in command of himself again, holding Kate to the snow.

"If I let you up, will you knock me down again, Katie?" he whispered.

She snarled in response, still thrashing blindly.

"Listen to me, Tanya, Kate," Carlisle said in a low but intense whisper. "Vengeance doesn't help her now. Irina wouldn't want you to waste your lives this way. Think about what you're doing. If you attack them, we all die."

Tanya's shoulders hunched with grief, and she leaned into Carlisle for support. Kate was finally still. Carlisle and Garrett continued to console the sisters with words too urgent to sound like comfort.

And my attention returned to the weight of the stares that pressed down on our moment of chaos. From the corners of my eyes, I could see that Edward and everyone else besides Carlisle and Garrett were on their guard again as well.

The heaviest glare came from Caius, staring with enraged disbelief at Kate and Garrett in the snow. Aro was watching the same two, incredulity the strongest emotion on his face. He knew what Kate could do. He had felt her potency through Edward's memories.

Did he understand what was happening now—did he see that my shield had grown in strength and subtlety far beyond what Edward knew me to be capable of? Or did he think Garrett had learned his own form of immunity?

The Volturi guard no longer stood at disciplined attention—they were crouched forward, waiting to spring the counterstrike the moment we attacked.

Behind them, forty-three witnesses watched with very different expressions than the ones they'd worn entering the clearing. Confusion had turned to suspicion. The lightning-fast destruction of Irina had shaken them all. What had been her crime?

Without the immediate attack that Caius had counted on to distract from his rash act, the Volturi witnesses were left questioning exactly what was going on here. Aro glanced back swiftly while I watched, his face betraying him with one flash of vexation. His need for an audience had backfired badly.

I heard Stefan and Vladimir murmur to each other in quiet glee at Aro's discomfort.

Aro was obviously concerned with keeping his white hat, as the Romanians had put it. But I didn't believe that the Volturi would leave us in peace just to save their reputation. After they finished with us, surely they would slaughter their witnesses for that purpose. I felt a strange, sudden pity for the mass of the strangers the Volturi had brought to watch us die. Demetri would hunt them until they were extinct, too.

For Jacob and Renesmee, for Alice and Jasper, for Alistair, and for these strangers who had not known what today would cost them, Demetri had to die.

Aro touched Caius's shoulder lightly. "Irina has been punished for bearing false witness against this child." So that was to be their excuse. He went on. "Perhaps we should return to the matter at hand?"

Caius straightened, and his expression hardened into unreadability. He stared forward, seeing nothing. His face reminded me, oddly, of a person who'd just learned he'd been demoted.

Aro drifted forward, Renata, Felix, and Demetri automatically moving with him.

"Just to be thorough," he said, "I'd like to speak with a few of your witnesses. Procedure, you know." He waved a hand dismissively.

Two things happened at once. Caius's eyes focused on Aro, and the tiny cruel smile came back. And Edward hissed, his hands balling up in fists so tight it looked like the bones in his knuckles would split through his diamond-hard skin.

I was desperate to ask him what was going on, but Aro was close enough to hear even the quietest breath. I saw Carlisle glance anxiously at Edward's face, and then his own face hardened.

While Caius had blundered through useless accusations and injudicious attempts to trigger the fight, Aro must have been coming up with a more effective strategy.

Aro ghosted across the snow to the far western end of our line, stopping about ten yards from Amun and Kebi. The nearby wolves bristled angrily but held their positions.

"Ah, Amun, my southern neighbor!" Aro said warmly. "It has been so long since you've visited me."

Amun was motionless with anxiety, Kebi a statue at his side. "Time means little; I never notice its passing," Amun said through unmoving lips.

"So true," Aro agreed. "But maybe you had another reason to stay away?"

Amun said nothing.

"It can be terribly time-consuming to organize newcomers into a coven. I know that well! I'm grateful I have others to deal with the tedium. I'm glad your new additions have fit in so well. I would have loved to have been introduced. I'm sure you were meaning to come to see me soon."

"Of course," Amun said, his tone so emotionless that it was impossible to tell if there was any fear or sarcasm in his assent.

"Oh well, we're all together now! Isn't it lovely?"

Amun nodded, his face blank.

"But the reason for your presence here is not as pleasant, unfortunately. Carlisle called on you to witness?"

"Yes."

"And what did you witness for him?"

Amun spoke with the same cold lack of emotion. "I've observed the child in question. It was evident almost immediately that she was not an immortal child—"

"Perhaps we should define our terminology," Aro interrupted, "now that there seem to be new classifications. By immortal child, you mean of course a human child who had been bitten and thus transformed into a vampire."

"Yes, that's what I meant."

"What else did you observe about the child?"

"The same things that you surely saw in Edward's mind. That the child is his biologically. That she grows. That she learns."

"Yes, yes," Aro said, a hint of impatience in his otherwise amiable tone. "But specifically in your few weeks here, what did you see?"

Amun's brow furrowed. "That she grows . . . quickly."

Aro smiled. "And do you believe that she should be allowed to live?"

A hiss escaped my lips, and I was not alone. Half the vampires in our line echoed my protest. The sound was a low sizzle of fury hanging in the air. Across the meadow, a few of the Volturi witnesses made the same noise. Edward stepped back and wrapped a restraining hand around my wrist.

Aro did not turn to the noise, but Amun glanced around uneasily.

"I did not come to make judgments," he equivocated.

Aro laughed lightly. "Just your opinion."

Amun's chin lifted. "I see no danger in the child. She learns even more swiftly than she grows."

Aro nodded, considering. After a moment, he turned away.

"Aro?" Amun called.

Aro whirled back. "Yes, friend?"

"I gave my witness. I have no more business here. My mate and I would like to take our leave now."

Aro smiled warmly. "Of course. I'm so glad we were able to chat for a bit. And I'm sure we'll see each other again soon."

Amun's lips were a tight line as he inclined his head once, acknowledging the barely concealed threat. He touched Kebi's arm, and then the two of them ran quickly to the southern edge of the meadow and disappeared into the trees. I knew they wouldn't stop running for a very long time.

Aro was gliding back along the length of our line to the east, his guards hovering tensely. He stopped when he was in front of Siobhan's massive form.

"Hello, dear Siobhan. You are as lovely as ever."

Siobhan inclined her head, waiting.

"And you?" he asked. "Would you answer my questions the same way Amun has?"

"I would," Siobhan said. "But I would perhaps add a little more. Renesmee understands the limitations. She's no danger to humans—she blends in better than we do. She poses no threat of exposure."

"Can you think of none?" Aro asked soberly.

Edward growled, a low ripping sound deep in his throat.

Caius's cloudy crimson eyes brightened.

Renata reached out protectively toward her master.

And Garrett freed Kate to take a step forward, ignoring Kate's hand as she tried to caution him this time.

Siobhan answered slowly, "I don't think I follow you."

Aro drifted lightly back, casually, but toward the rest of his guard. Renata, Felix, and Demetri were closer than his shadow.

"There is no broken law," Aro said in a placating voice, but every one of us could hear that a qualification was coming. I fought back the rage that tried to claw its way up my throat and snarl out my defiance. I hurled the fury into my shield, thickening it, making sure everyone was protected.

"No broken law," Aro repeated. "However, does it follow then that there is no danger? No." He shook his head gently. "That is a separate issue."

The only response was the tightening of already stretched nerves, and Maggie, at the fringes of our band of fighters, shaking her head with slow anger.

Aro paced thoughtfully, looking as if he floated rather than touched the ground with his feet. I noticed every pass took him closer to the protection of his guard.

"She is unique . . . utterly, impossibly unique. Such a waste it would be, to destroy something so lovely. Especially when we could learn so much . . ." He sighed, as if unwilling to go on. "But there *is* danger, danger that cannot simply be ignored."

No one answered his assertion. It was dead silent as he continued in a monologue that sounded as if he spoke it for himself only.

"How ironic it is that as the humans advance, as their

faith in science grows and controls their world, the more free we are from discovery. Yet, as we become ever more uninhibited by their disbelief in the supernatural, they become strong enough in their technologies that, if they wished, they could actually pose a threat to us, even destroy some of us.

"For thousands and thousands of years, our secrecy has been more a matter of convenience, of ease, than of actual safety. This last raw, angry century has given birth to weapons of such power that they endanger even immortals. Now our status as mere myth in truth protects us from these weak creatures we hunt.

"This amazing child"—he lifted his hand palm down as if to rest it on Renesmee, though he was forty yards from her now, almost within the Volturi formation again—"if we could but know her potential—know with *absolute certainty* that she could always remain shrouded within the obscurity that protects us. But we know nothing of what she will become! Her own parents are plagued by fears of her future. We *cannot* know what she will grow to be." He paused, looking first at our witnesses, and then, meaningfully, at his own. His voice gave a good imitation of sounding torn by his words.

Still looking at his own witnesses, he spoke again. "Only the known is safe. Only the known is tolerable. The unknown is . . . a vulnerability."

Caius's smile widened viciously.

"You're reaching, Aro," Carlisle said in a bleak voice.

"Peace, friend." Aro smiled, his face as kind, his voice as gentle, as ever. "Let us not be hasty. Let us look at this from every side."

"May I offer a side to be considered?" Garrett petitioned in a level tone, taking another step forward.

"Nomad," Aro said, nodding in permission.

Garrett's chin lifted. His eyes focused on the huddled mass at the end of the meadow, and he spoke directly to the Volturi witnesses.

"I came here at Carlisle's request, as the others, to witness," he said. "That is certainly no longer necessary, with regard to the child. We all see what she is.

"I stayed to witness something else. You." He jabbed his finger toward the wary vampires. "Two of you I know—Makenna, Charles—and I can see that many of you others are also wanderers, roamers like myself. Answering to none. Think carefully on what I tell you now.

"These ancient ones did *not* come here for justice as they told you. We suspected as much, and now it has been proved. They came, misled, but with a valid excuse for their action. Witness now as they seek flimsy excuses to continue their true mission. Witness them struggle to find a justification for their true purpose—to destroy this family here." He gestured toward Carlisle and Tanya.

"The Volturi come to erase what they perceive as the competition. Perhaps, like me, you look at this clan's golden eyes and marvel. They are difficult to understand, it's true. But the ancient ones look and see something besides their strange choice. They see *power*.

"I have witnessed the bonds within this family—I say *family* and not *coven*. These strange golden-eyed ones deny their very natures. But in return have they found something worth even more, perhaps, than mere gratification of desire? I've made a little study of them in my time here, and it seems to me that intrinsic to this intense family binding—that which makes them possible at all—is the peaceful character of this life of sacrifice. There is no aggression here like we all saw in the large southern clans that grew and diminished so quickly in their wild feuds. There is no thought for domination. And Aro knows this better than I do."

I watched Aro's face as Garrett's words condemned him, waiting tensely for some response. But Aro's face was only politely amused, as if waiting for a tantrum-throwing child to realize that no one was paying attention to his histrionics.

"Carlisle assured us all, when he told us what was coming, that he did not call us here to fight. These witnesses"—Garrett pointed to Siobhan and Liam—"agreed to give evidence, to slow the Volturi advance with their presence so that Carlisle would get the chance to present his case.

"But some of us wondered"—his eyes flashed to Eleazar's face—"if Carlisle having truth on his side would be enough to stop the so-called justice. Are the Volturi here to protect the safety of our secrecy, or to protect their own power? Did they come to destroy an illegal creation, or a way of life? Could they be satisfied when the danger turned out to be no more than a misunderstanding? Or would they push the issue without the excuse of justice?

"We have the answer to all these questions. We heard it in Aro's lying words—we have one with a gift of knowing such things for certain—and we see it now in Caius's eager smile. Their guard is just a mindless weapon, a tool in their masters' quest for domination.

"So now there are more questions, questions that *you* must answer. Who rules you, nomads? Do you answer to someone's will besides your own? Are you free to choose your path, or will the Volturi decide how you will live?

"I came to witness. I stay to fight. The Volturi care nothing for the death of the child. They seek the death of our free will."

He turned, then, to face the ancients. "So come, I say! Let's hear no more lying rationalizations. Be honest in your intents as we will be honest in ours. We will defend our freedom. You will or will not attack it. Choose now, and let these witnesses see the true issue debated here."

Once more he looked to the Volturi witnesses, his eyes probing each face. The power of his words was evident in their expressions. "You might consider joining us. If you think the Volturi will let you live to tell *this* tale, you are mistaken. We may all be destroyed"—he shrugged— "but then again, maybe not. Perhaps we are on more equal footing than they know. Perhaps the Volturi have finally met their match. I promise you this, though—if we fall, so do you."

He ended his heated speech by stepping back to Kate's side and then sliding forward in a half-crouch, prepared for the onslaught.

Aro smiled. "A very pretty speech, my revolutionary friend."

Garrett remained poised for attack. "Revolutionary?" he growled. "Who am I revolting against, might I ask? Are you my king? Do you wish me to call you *master*, too, like your sycophantic guard?"

"Peace, Garrett," Aro said tolerantly. "I meant only to refer to your time of birth. Still a patriot, I see."

Garrett glared back furiously.

"Let us ask our witnesses," Aro suggested. "Let us hear their thoughts before we make our decision. Tell us, friends"—and he turned his back casually on us, moving a few yards toward his mass of nervous observers hovering even closer now to the edge of the forest—"what do you think of all this? I can assure you the child is not what we feared. Do we take the risk and let the child live? Do we put our world in jeopardy to preserve their family intact? Or does earnest Garrett have the right of it? Will you join them in a fight against our sudden quest for dominion?"

The witnesses met his gaze with careful faces. One, a small black-haired woman, looked briefly at the dark blond male at her side.

"Are those our only choices?" she asked suddenly, gaze flashing back to Aro. "Agree with you, or fight against you?"

"Of course not, most charming Makenna," Aro said, appearing horrified that anyone could come to that conclusion. "You may go in peace, of course, as Amun did, even if you disagree with the council's decision."

Makenna looked at her mate's face again, and he nodded minutely.

"We did not come here for a fight." She paused, exhaled, then said, "We came here to witness. And our witness is that this condemned family is innocent. Everything that Garrett claimed is the truth."

"Ah," Aro said sadly. "I'm sorry you see us in that way. But such is the nature of our work."

"It is not what I see, but what I feel," Makenna's maize-haired mate spoke in a high, nervous voice. He glanced at Garrett. "Garrett said they have ways of knowing lies. I, too, know when I am hearing the truth, and when I am not." With frightened eyes he moved closer to his mate, waiting for Aro's reaction.

"Do not fear us, friend Charles. No doubt the patriot truly believes what he says," Aro chuckled lightly, and Charles's eyes narrowed.

"That is our witness," Makenna said. "We're leaving now."

She and Charles backed away slowly, not turning before they were lost from view in the trees. One other stranger began to retreat the same way, then three more darted after him.

I evaluated the thirty-seven vampires that stayed. A few of them appeared just too confused to make the decision. But the majority of them seemed only too aware of the direction this confrontation had taken. I guessed that they were giving up a head start in favor of knowing exactly who would be chasing after them.

I was sure Aro saw the same thing I did. He turned away, walking back to his guard with a measured pace. He stopped in front of them and addressed them in a clear voice.

"We are outnumbered, dearest ones," he said. "We can expect no outside help. Should we leave this question undecided to save ourselves?"

"No, master," they whispered in unison.

"Is the protection of our world worth perhaps the loss of some of our number?"

"Yes," they breathed. "We are not afraid."

Aro smiled and turned to his black-clad companions.

"Brothers," Aro said somberly, "there is much to consider here."

"Let us counsel," Caius said eagerly.

"Let us counsel," Marcus repeated in an uninterested tone.

Aro turned his back to us again, facing the other ancients. They joined hands to form a black-shrouded triangle.

As soon as Aro's attention was engaged in the silent counsel, two more of their witnesses disappeared silently into the forest. I hoped, for their sakes, that they were fast.

This was it. Carefully, I loosened Renesmee's arms from my neck.

"You remember what I told you?"

Tears welled in her eyes, but she nodded. "I love you," she whispered.

Edward was watching us now, his topaz eyes wide. Jacob stared at us from the corner of his big dark eye.

"I love you, too," I said, and then I touched her locket. "More than my own life." I kissed her forehead.

Jacob whined uneasily.

I stretched up on my toes and whispered into his ear. "Wait until they're totally distracted, then run with her. Get as far from this place as you possibly can. When you've gone as far as you can on foot, she has what you need to get you in the air."

Edward's and Jacob's faces were almost identical masks of horror, despite the fact that one of them was an animal.

Renesmee reached for Edward, and he took her in his arms. They hugged each other tightly.

"This is what you kept from me?" he whispered over her head.

"From Aro," I breathed.

"Alice?"

I nodded.

His face twisted with understanding and pain. Had that been the expression on my face when I'd finally put together Alice's clues?

Jacob was growling quietly, a low rasp that was as even and unbroken as a purr. His hackles were stiff and his teeth exposed.

Edward kissed Renesmee's forehead and both her cheeks, then he lifted her to Jacob's shoulder. She scrambled agilely onto his back, pulling herself into place with handfuls of his fur, and fit herself easily into the dip between his massive shoulder blades.

Jacob turned to me, his expressive eyes full of agony, the rumbling growl still grating through his chest.

"You're the only one we could ever trust her with," I murmured to him. "If you didn't love her so much, I could never bear this. I know you can protect her, Jacob."

He whined again, and dipped his head to butt it against my shoulder.

"I know," I whispered. "I love you, too, Jake. You'll always be my best man."

A tear the size of a baseball rolled into the russet fur beneath his eye.

Edward leaned his head against the same shoulder where he'd placed Renesmee. "Goodbye, Jacob, my brother . . . my son."

The others were not oblivious to the farewell scene. Their eyes were locked on the silent black triangle, but I could tell they were listening.

"Is there no hope, then?" Carlisle whispered. There was no fear in his voice. Just determination and acceptance.

"There is absolutely hope," I murmured back. *It could be true,* I told myself. "I only know my own fate."

Edward took my hand. He knew that he was included. When I said *my fate*, there was no question that I meant the two of us. We were just halves of the whole.

Esme's breath was ragged behind me. She moved past us, touching our faces as she passed, to stand beside Carlisle and hold his hand.

Suddenly, we were surrounded by murmured goodbyes and I love you's.

"If we live through this," Garrett whispered to Kate, "I'll follow you anywhere, woman."

"Now he tells me," she muttered.

Rosalie and Emmett kissed quickly but passionately.

Tia caressed Benjamin's face. He smiled back cheerfully, catching her hand and holding it against his cheek.

I didn't see all the expressions of love and pain. I was distracted by a sudden fluttering pressure against the outside of my shield. I couldn't tell where it came from, but it felt like it was directed at the edges of our group, Siobhan and Liam particularly. The pressure did no damage, and then it was gone.

There was no change in the silent, still forms of the counseling ancients. But perhaps there was some signal I'd missed.

"Get ready," I whispered to the others. "It's starting."

38. POWER

"Chelsea is trying to break our bindings," Edward whispered. "But she can't find them. She can't feel us here. . . ." His eyes cut to me. "Are you doing that?"

I smiled grimly at him. "I am *all* over this."

Edward lurched away from me suddenly, his hand reaching out toward Carlisle. At the same time, I felt a much sharper jab against the shield where it wrapped protectively around Carlisle's light. It wasn't painful, but it wasn't pleasant, either.

"Carlisle? Are you all right?" Edward gasped frantically.

"Yes. Why?"

"Jane," Edward answered.

The moment that he said her name, a dozen pointed attacks hit in a second, stabbing all over the elastic shield, aimed at twelve different bright spots. I flexed, making sure the shield was undamaged. It didn't seem like Jane had been able to pierce it. I glanced around quickly; everyone was fine.

"Incredible," Edward said.

"Why aren't they waiting for the decision?" Tanya hissed.

"Normal procedure," Edward answered brusquely. "They usually incapacitate those on trial so they can't escape."

I looked across at Jane, who was staring at our group with furious disbelief. I was pretty sure that, besides me, she'd never seen anyone remain standing through her fiery assault.

It probably wasn't very mature. But I figured it would take Aro about half a second to guess—if he hadn't already—that my shield was more powerful than Edward had known; I already had a big target on my forehead and there was really no point in trying to keep the extent of what I could do a secret. So I grinned a huge, smug smile right at Jane.

Her eyes narrowed, and I felt another stab of pressure, this time directed at me.

I pulled my lips wider, showing my teeth.

Jane let out a high-pitched scream of a snarl. Everyone jumped, even the disciplined guard. Everyone but the ancients, who didn't so much as look up from their conference. Her twin caught her arm as she crouched to spring.

The Romanians started chuckling with dark anticipation.

"I told you this was our time," Vladimir said to Stefan.

"Just look at the witch's face," Stefan chortled.

Alec patted his sister's shoulder soothingly, then tucked her under his arm. He turned his face to us, perfectly smooth, completely angelic.

I waited for some pressure, some sign of his attack, but I felt nothing. He continued to stare in our direction, his pretty face composed. Was he attacking? Was he getting through my shield? Was I the only one who could still see him? I clutched at Edward's hand.

"Are you okay?" I choked out.

"Yes," he whispered.

"Is Alec trying?"

Edward nodded. "His gift is slower than Jane's. It creeps. It will touch us in a few seconds."

I saw it then, when I had a clue of what to look for.

A strange clear haze was oozing across the snow, nearly invisible against the white. It reminded me of a mirage—a slight warping of the view, a hint of a shimmer. I pushed my shield out from Carlisle and the rest of the front line, afraid to have the slinking mist too close when it hit. What if it stole right through my intangible protection? Should we run?

A low rumbling murmured through the ground under our feet, and a gust of wind blew the snow into sudden flurries between our position and the Volturi's. Benjamin had seen the creeping threat, too, and now he tried to blow the mist away from us. The snow made it easy to see where he threw the wind, but the mist didn't react in any way. It was like air blowing harmlessly through a shadow; the shadow was immune.

The triangular formation of the ancients finally broke apart when, with a racking groan, a deep, narrow fissure opened in a long zigzag across the middle of the clearing. The earth rocked under my feet for a moment. The drifts of snow plummeted into the hole, but the mist skipped right across it, as untouched by gravity as it had been by wind.

Aro and Caius watched the opening earth with wide eyes. Marcus looked in the same direction without emotion.

They didn't speak; they waited, too, as the mist approached us. The wind shrieked louder but didn't change the course of the mist. Jane was smiling now.

And then the mist hit a wall.

I could taste it as soon as it touched my shield—it had a dense, sweet, cloying flavor. It made me remember dimly the numbness of Novocain on my tongue.

The mist curled upward, seeking a breach, a weakness. It found none. The fingers of searching haze twisted upward and around, trying to find a way in, and in the process illustrating the astonishing size of the protective screen.

There were gasps on both sides of Benjamin's gorge.

"Well done, Bella!" Benjamin cheered in a low voice.

My smile returned.

I could see Alec's narrowed eyes, doubt on his face for the first time as his mist swirled harmlessly around the edges of my shield.

And then I knew that I could do this. Obviously, I would be the number-one priority, the first one to die, but as long as I held, we were on more than equal footing with the Volturi. We still had Benjamin and Zafrina; they had no supernatural help at all. As long as I held.

"I'm going to have to concentrate," I whispered to

Edward. "When it comes to hand to hand, it's going to be harder to keep the shield around the right people."

"I'll keep them off you."

"No. You *have* to get to Demetri. Zafrina will keep them away from me."

Zafrina nodded solemnly. "No one will touch this young one," she promised Edward.

"I'd go after Jane and Alec myself, but I can do more good here."

"Jane's mine," Kate hissed. "She needs a taste of her own medicine."

"And Alec owes me many lives, but I will settle for his," Vladimir growled from the other side. "He's mine."

"I just want Caius," Tanya said evenly.

The others started divvying up opponents, too, but they were quickly interrupted.

Aro, staring calmly at Alec's ineffective mist, finally spoke.

"Before we vote," he began.

I shook my head angrily. I was tired of this charade. The bloodlust was igniting in me again, and I was sorry that I would help the others more by standing still. I *wanted* to fight.

"Let me remind you," Aro continued, "whatever the council's decision, there need be no violence here."

Edward snarled out a dark laugh.

Aro stared at him sadly. "It will be a regrettable waste to our kind to lose any of you. But you especially, young Edward, and your newborn mate. The Volturi would be glad to welcome many of you into our ranks. Bella, Benjamin, Zafrina, Kate. There are many choices before you. Consider them."

Chelsea's attempt to sway us fluttered impotently against my shield. Aro's gaze swept across our hard eyes, looking for any indication of hesitation. From his expression, he found none.

I knew he was desperate to keep Edward and me, to imprison us the way he had hoped to enslave Alice. But this fight was too big. He would not win if I lived. I was fiercely glad to be so powerful that I left him no way *not* to kill me.

"Let us vote, then," he said with apparent reluctance.

Caius spoke with eager haste. "The child is an unknown quantity. There is no reason to allow such a risk to exist. It must be destroyed, along with all who protect it." He smiled in expectation.

I fought back a shriek of defiance to answer his cruel smirk.

Marcus lifted his uncaring eyes, seeming to look through us as he voted.

"I see no immediate danger. The child is safe enough for now. We can always reevaluate later. Let us leave in peace." His voice was even fainter than his brothers' feathery sighs.

None of the guard relaxed their ready positions at his disagreeing words. Caius's anticipatory grin did not falter. It was as if Marcus hadn't spoken at all.

"I must make the deciding vote, it seems," Aro mused.

Suddenly, Edward stiffened at my side. "Yes!" he hissed.

I risked a glance at him. His face glowed with an expression of triumph that I didn't understand—it was the expression an angel of destruction might wear while the world burned. Beautiful and terrifying.

There was a low reaction from the guard, an uneasy murmur.

"Aro?" Edward called, nearly shouted, undisguised victory in his voice.

Aro hesitated for a second, assessing this new mood warily before he answered. "Yes, Edward? You have something further . . . ?"

"Perhaps," Edward said pleasantly, controlling his unexplained excitement. "First, if I could clarify one point?"

"Certainly," Aro said, raising his eyebrows, nothing now but polite interest in his tone. My teeth ground together; Aro was never more dangerous than when he was gracious.

"The danger you foresee from my daughter— this stems entirely from our inability to guess how she will develop? That is the crux of the matter?"

"Yes, friend Edward," Aro agreed. "If we could but be positive . . . be *sure* that, as she grows, she will be able to stay concealed from the human world—not endanger the safety of our obscurity . . ." He trailed off, shrugging.

"So, if we could only know for sure," Edward suggested, "exactly what she will become . . . then there would be no need for a council at all?"

"If there was some way to be *absolutely* sure," Aro agreed, his feathery voice slightly more shrill. He couldn't see where Edward was leading him. Neither could I. "Then, yes, there would be no question to debate."

"And we would part in peace, good friends once again?" Edward asked with a hint of irony.

Even more shrill. "Of course, my young friend. Nothing would please me more."

Edward chuckled exultantly. "Then I do have something more to offer."

Aro's eyes narrowed. "She is absolutely unique. Her future can only be guessed at."

"Not absolutely unique," Edward disagreed. "Rare, certainly, but not one of a kind."

I fought the shock, the sudden hope springing to life, as it threatened to distract me. The sickly-looking mist still swirled around the edges of my shield. And, as I struggled to focus, I felt again the sharp, stabbing pressure against my protective hold.

"Aro, would you ask Jane to stop attacking my wife?" Edward asked courteously. "We are still discussing evidence."

Aro raised one hand. "Peace, dear ones. Let us hear him out."

The pressure disappeared. Jane bared her teeth at me; I couldn't help grinning back at her.

"Why don't you join us, Alice?" Edward called loudly.

"Alice," Esme whispered in shock.

Alice!

Alice, Alice, Alice!

"Alice!" "Alice!" other voices murmured around me.

"Alice," Aro breathed.

Relief and violent joy surged through me. It took all my will to keep the shield where it was. Alec's mist still tested, seeking a weakness—Jane would see if I left any holes.

And then I heard them running through the forest, flying, closing the distance as quickly as they could with no slowing effort at silence.

Both sides were motionless in expectation. The Volturi witnesses scowled in fresh confusion.

Then Alice danced into the clearing from the southwest, and I felt like the bliss of seeing her face again might knock me off my feet. Jasper was only inches behind her, his sharp eyes fierce. Close after them ran three strangers; the first was a tall, muscular female with wild dark hair—obviously Kachiri. She had the same elongated limbs and features as the other Amazons, even more pronounced in her case.

The next was a small olive-toned female vampire with a long braid of black hair bobbing against her back. Her deep burgundy eyes flitted nervously around the confrontation before her.

And the last was a young man . . . not quite as fast nor quite as fluid in his run. His skin was an impossible rich, dark brown. His wary eyes flashed across the gathering, and they were the color of warm teak. His hair was black and braided, too, like the woman's, though not as long. He was beautiful.

As he neared us, a new sound sent shock waves through the watching crowd—the sound of another heartbeat, accelerated with exertion.

Alice leaped lightly over the edges of the dissipating mist that lapped at my shield and came to a sinuous stop at Edward's side. I reached out to touch her arm, and so did Edward, Esme, Carlisle. There wasn't time for any other welcome. Jasper and the others followed her through the shield.

All the guard watched, speculation in their eyes, as the latecomers crossed the invisible border without difficulty. The brawny ones, Felix and the others like him, focused their suddenly hopeful eyes on me. They had not been sure of what my shield repelled, but it was clear now that it would not stop a physical attack. As soon as Aro gave the order, the blitz would ensue, me the only object. I wondered how many Zafrina would be able to blind, and how much that would slow them. Long enough for Kate and Vladimir to take Jane and Alec out of the equation? That was all I could ask for.

Edward, despite his absorption in the coup he was directing, stiffened furiously in response to their thoughts. He controlled himself and spoke to Aro again.

"Alice has been searching for her own witnesses these last weeks," he said to the ancient. "And she does not come back empty-handed. Alice, why don't you introduce the witnesses you've brought?"

Caius snarled. "The time for witnesses is past! Cast your vote, Aro!"

Aro raised one finger to silence his brother, his eyes glued to Alice's face.

Alice stepped forward lightly and introduced the strangers. "This is Huilen and her nephew, Nahuel."

Hearing her voice . . . it was like she'd never left.

Caius's eyes tightened as Alice named the relationship between the newcomers. The Volturi witnesses hissed amongst themselves. The vampire world was changing, and everyone could feel it.

"Speak, Huilen," Aro commanded. "Give us the witness you were brought to bear."

The slight woman looked to Alice nervously. Alice nodded in encouragement, and Kachiri put her long hand on the little vampire's shoulder.

"I am Huilen," the woman announced in clear but strangely accented English. As she continued, it was apparent she had prepared herself to tell this story, that she had practiced. It flowed like a well-known nursery rhyme. "A century and a half ago, I lived with my people, the Mapuche. My sister was Pire. Our parents named her after the snow on the mountains because of her fair skin. And she was very beautiful—too beautiful. She came to me one day in secret and told me of the angel that found her in the woods, that visited her by night. I warned her." Huilen shook her head mournfully. "As if the bruises on her skin were not warning enough. I knew it was the Libishomen of our legends, but she would not listen. She was bewitched.

"She told me when she was sure her dark angel's child was growing inside her. I didn't try to discourage her from her plan to run away—I knew even our father and mother would agree that the child must be destroyed, Pire with it. I went with her into the deepest parts of the forest. She searched for her demon angel but found nothing. I cared for her, hunted for her when her strength failed. She ate the animals raw, drinking their blood. I needed no more confirmation of what she carried in her womb. I hoped to save her life before I killed the monster.

"But she loved the child inside her. She called him Nahuel, after the jungle cat, when he grew strong and broke her bones—and loved him still.

"I could not save her. The child ripped his way free of her, and she died quickly, begging all the while that I would care for her Nahuel. Her dying wish—and I agreed.

"He bit me, though, when I tried to lift him from her

body. I crawled away into the jungle to die. I didn't get far—the pain was too much. But he found me; the newborn child struggled through the underbrush to my side and waited for me. When the pain ended, he was curled against my side, sleeping.

"I cared for him until he was able to hunt for himself. We hunted the villages around our forest, staying to ourselves. We have never come so far from our home, but Nahuel wished to see the child here."

Huilen bowed her head when she was finished and moved back so she was partially hidden behind Kachiri.

Aro's lips were pursed. He stared at the dark-skinned youth.

"Nahuel, you are one hundred and fifty years old?" he questioned.

"Give or take a decade," he answered in a clear, beautifully warm voice. His accent was barely noticeable. "We don't keep track."

"And you reached maturity at what age?"

"About seven years after my birth, more or less, I was full grown."

"You have not changed since then?"

Nahuel shrugged. "Not that I've noticed."

I felt a shudder tremble through Jacob's body. I didn't want to think about this yet. I would wait till the danger was past and I could concentrate.

"And your diet?" Aro pressed, seeming interested in spite of himself.

"Mostly blood, but some human food, too. I can survive on either."

"You were able to create an immortal?" As Aro gestured to Huilen, his voice was abruptly intense. I refocused on my shield; perhaps he was seeking a new excuse.

"Yes, but none of the rest can."

A shocked murmur ran through all three groups.

Aro's eyebrows shot up. "The rest?"

"My sisters." Nahuel shrugged again.

Aro stared wildly for a moment before composing his face.

"Perhaps you would tell us the rest of your story, for there seems to be more."

Nahuel frowned.

"My father came looking for me a few years after my mother's death." His handsome face distorted slightly. "He was pleased to find me." Nahuel's tone suggested the feeling was not mutual. "He had two daughters, but no sons. He expected me to join him, as my sisters had.

"He was surprised I was not alone. My sisters are not venomous, but whether that's due to gender or a random chance . . . who knows? I already had my family with Huilen, and I was not *interested*"—he twisted the word— "in making a change. I see him from time to time. I have a new sister; she reached maturity about ten years back."

"Your father's name?" Caius asked through gritted teeth.

"Joham," Nahuel answered. "He considers himself a scientist. He thinks he's creating a new super-race." He made no attempt to disguise the disgust in his tone.

Caius looked at me. "Your daughter, is she venomous?" he demanded harshly.

"No," I responded. Nahuel's head snapped up at Aro's question, and his teak eyes turned to bore into my face.

Caius looked to Aro for confirmation, but Aro was absorbed in his own thoughts. He pursed his lips and stared at Carlisle, and then Edward, and at last his eyes rested on me.

Caius growled. "We take care of the aberration here, and then follow it south," he urged Aro.

Aro stared into my eyes for a long, tense moment. I had no idea what he was searching for, or what he found, but after he had measured me for that moment, something in his face changed, a faint shift in the set of his mouth and eyes, and I knew that Aro had made his decision.

"Brother," he said softly to Caius. "There appears to be no danger. This is an unusual development, but I see no threat. These half-vampire children are much like us, it appears."

"Is that your vote?" Caius demanded.

"It is."

Caius scowled. "And this Joham? This immortal so fond of experimentation?"

"Perhaps we *should* speak with him," Aro agreed.

"Stop Joham if you will," Nahuel said flatly. "But leave my sisters be. They are innocent."

Aro nodded, his expression solemn. And then he turned back to his guard with a warm smile.

"Dear ones," he called. "We do not fight today."

The guard nodded in unison and straightened out of their ready positions. The mist dissipated swiftly, but I held my shield in place. Maybe this was *another* trick.

I analyzed their expressions as Aro turned back to us. His face was as benign as ever, but unlike before, I sensed a strange blankness behind the façade. As if his scheming was over. Caius was clearly incensed, but his rage was turned inward now; he was resigned. Marcus looked . . . bored; there really was no other word for it. The guard was impassive and disciplined again; there were no individuals among them, just the whole. They were in formation, ready to depart. The Volturi witnesses were still wary; one after another, they departed, scattering into the woods. As their numbers dwindled, the remaining sped up. Soon they were all gone.

Aro held his hands out to us, almost apologetic. Behind him, the larger part of the guard, along with Caius, Marcus, and the silent, mysterious wives, were already drifting quickly away, their formation precise once again. Only the three that seemed to be his personal guardians lingered with him.

"I'm so glad this could be resolved without violence," he said sweetly. "My friend, Carlisle—how pleased I am to call you friend again! I hope there are no hard feelings. I know you understand the strict burden that our duty places on our shoulders."

"Leave in peace, Aro," Carlisle said stiffly. "Please remember that we still have our anonymity to protect here, and keep your guard from hunting in this region."

"Of course, Carlisle," Aro assured him. "I am sorry to earn your disapproval, my dear friend. Perhaps, in time, you will forgive me."

"Perhaps, in time, if you prove a friend to us again."

Aro bowed his head, the picture of remorse, and drifted backward for a moment before he turned around. We watched in silence as the last four Volturi disappeared into the trees.

It was very quiet. I did not drop my shield.

"Is it really over?" I whispered to Edward.

His smile was huge. "Yes. They've given up. Like all bullies, they're cowards underneath the swagger." He chuckled.

Alice laughed with him. "Seriously, people. They're not coming back. Everybody can relax now."

There was another beat of silence.

"Of all the rotten luck," Stefan muttered.

And then it hit.

Cheers erupted. Deafening howls filled the clearing. Maggie pounded Siobhan on the back. Rosalie and Emmett kissed again—longer and more ardently than before. Benjamin and Tia were locked in each other's arms, as were Carmen and Eleazar. Esme held Alice and Jasper in a tight embrace. Carlisle was warmly thanking the South American newcomers who had saved us all. Kachiri stood very close to Zafrina and Senna, their fingertips interlocked. Garrett picked Kate up off the ground and swung her around in a circle.

Stefan spit on the snow. Vladimir ground his teeth together with a sour expression.

And I half-climbed the giant russet wolf to rip my daughter off his back and then crushed her to my chest. Edward's arms were around us in the same second.

"Nessie, Nessie, Nessie," I crooned.

Jacob laughed his big, barky laugh and poked the back of my head with his nose.

"Shut up," I mumbled.

"I get to stay with you?" Nessie demanded.

"Forever," I promised her.

We had forever. And Nessie was going to be fine and healthy and strong. Like the half-human Nahuel, in a hundred and fifty years she would still be young. And we would all be together.

Happiness expanded like an explosion inside me—so extreme, so violent that I wasn't sure I'd survive it.

"Forever," Edward echoed in my ear.

I couldn't speak anymore. I lifted my head and kissed him with a passion that might possibly set the forest on fire.

I wouldn't have noticed.

39. THE HAPPILY EVER
AFTER

"So it was a combination of things there at the end, but what it really boiled down to was . . . Bella," Edward was explaining. Our family and our two remaining guests sat in the Cullens' great room while the forest turned black outside the tall windows.

Vladimir and Stefan had vanished before we'd stopped celebrating. They were extremely disappointed in the way things had turned out, but Edward said that they'd enjoyed the Volturi's cowardice almost enough to make up for their frustration.

Benjamin and Tia were quick to follow after Amun and Kebi, anxious to let them know the outcome of the conflict; I was sure we would see them again—Benjamin and Tia, at least. None of the nomads lingered. Peter and Charlotte had a short conversation with Jasper, and then they were gone, too.

The reunited Amazons had been anxious to return home as well—they had a difficult time being away from their beloved rain forest—though they were more reluctant to leave than some of the others.

"You must bring the child to see me," Zafrina had insisted. "Promise me, young one."

Nessie had pressed her hand to my neck, pleading as well.

"Of course, Zafrina," I'd agreed.

"We shall be great friends, my Nessie," the wild woman had declared before leaving with her sisters.

The Irish coven continued the exodus.

"Well done, Siobhan," Carlisle complimented her as they said goodbye.

"Ah, the power of wishful thinking," she answered sarcastically, rolling her eyes. And then she was serious. "Of course, this isn't over. The Volturi won't forgive what happened here."

Edward was the one to answer that. "They've been seriously shaken; their confidence is shattered. But, yes, I'm sure they'll recover from the blow someday. And then . . ." His eyes tightened. "I imagine they'll try to pick us off separately."

"Alice will warn us when they intend to strike," Siobhan said in a sure voice. "And we'll gather again. Perhaps the time will come when our world is ready to be free of the Volturi altogether."

"That time may come," Carlisle replied. "If it does, we'll stand together."

"Yes, my friend, we will," Siobhan agreed. "And how can

we fail, when *I* will it otherwise?" She let out a great peal of laughter.

"Exactly," Carlisle said. He and Siobhan embraced, and then he shook Liam's hand. "Try to find Alistair and tell him what happened. I'd hate to think of him hiding under a rock for the next decade."

Siobhan laughed again. Maggie hugged both Nessie and me, and then the Irish coven was gone.

The Denalis were the last to leave, Garrett with them—as he would be from now on, I was fairly sure. The atmosphere of celebration was too much for Tanya and Kate. They needed time to grieve for their lost sister.

Huilen and Nahuel were the ones who stayed, though I had expected those last two to go back with the Amazons. Carlisle was deep in fascinated conversation with Huilen; Nahuel sat close beside her, listening while Edward told the rest of us the story of the conflict as only he knew it.

"Alice gave Aro the excuse he needed to get out of the fight. If he hadn't been so terrified of Bella, he probably would have gone ahead with their original plan."

"Terrified?" I said skeptically. "Of *me?*"

He smiled at me with a look I didn't entirely recognize— it was tender, but also awed and even exasperated. "When will you ever see yourself clearly?" he said softly. Then he spoke louder, to the others as well as to me. "The Volturi haven't fought a fair fight in about twenty-five hundred years. And they've never, never fought one where they were at a disadvantage. Especially since they gained Jane and Alec, they've only been involved with unopposed slaughterings.

"You should have seen how we looked to them! Usually, Alec cuts off all sense and feeling from their victims while they go through the charade of a counsel. That way, no one can run when the verdict is given. But there we stood, ready, waiting, outnumbering them, with gifts of our own while their gifts were rendered useless by Bella. Aro knew that with Zafrina on our side, they would be the blind ones when the battle commenced. I'm sure our numbers would have been pretty severely decimated, but *they* were sure that theirs would be, too. There was even a good possibility that they would lose. They've never dealt with that possibility before. They didn't deal with it well today."

"Hard to feel confident when you're surrounded by horse-sized wolves," Emmett laughed, poking Jacob's arm.

Jacob flashed a grin at him.

"It was the wolves that stopped them in the first place," I said.

"Sure was," Jacob agreed.

"Absolutely," Edward agreed. "That was another sight they've never seen. The true Children of the Moon rarely move in packs, and they are never much in control of themselves. Sixteen enormous regimented wolves was a surprise they weren't prepared for. Caius is actually terrified of werewolves. He almost lost a fight with one a few thousand years ago and never got over it."

"So there are *real* werewolves?" I asked. "With the full moon and silver bullets and all that?"

Jacob snorted. "*Real.* Does that make me imaginary?"

"You know what I mean."

"Full moon, yes," Edward said. "Silver bullets, no—that was just another one of those myths to make humans feel like they had a sporting chance. There aren't very many of them left. Caius has had them hunted into near extinction."

"And you never mentioned this because . . . ?"

"It never came up."

I rolled my eyes, and Alice laughed, leaning forward—she was tucked under Edward's other arm—to wink at me.

I glared back.

I loved her insanely, of course. But now that I'd had a chance to realize that she was really home, that her defection was only a ruse because Edward had to believe that she'd abandoned us, I was beginning to feel pretty irritated with her. Alice had some explaining to do.

Alice sighed. "Just get it off your chest, Bella."

"How could you do that to me, Alice?"

"It was necessary."

"Necessary!" I exploded. "You had me totally convinced that we were all going to die! I've been a wreck for weeks."

"It might have gone that way," she said calmly. "In which case you needed to be prepared to save Nessie."

Instinctively, I held Nessie—asleep now on my lap—tighter in my arms.

"But you knew there were other ways, too," I accused. "You knew there was hope. Did it ever occur to you that you could have told me everything? I know Edward had to think we were at a dead end for Aro's sake, but you could have told *me*."

She looked at me speculatively for a moment. "I don't think so," she said. "You're just not that good an actress."

"This was about my *acting skills*?"

"Oh, take it down an octave, Bella. Do you have any idea how *complicated* this was to set up? I couldn't even be sure that someone like Nahuel existed—all I knew was that I would be looking for something I couldn't see! Try to imagine searching for a blind spot—not the easiest thing I've ever done. Plus we had to send back the key witnesses, like we weren't in enough of a hurry. And then keeping my eyes open all the time in case you decided to throw me any more instructions. At some point you're going to have to tell me what exactly is in Rio. Before any of *that*, I had to try to see every trick the Volturi might come in with and give you what few clues I could so you would be ready for their strategy, and I only had just a few hours to trace out all the possibilities. Most of all, I had to make sure you'd all believe that I was ditching out on you, because Aro had to be positive that you had nothing left up your sleeves or he never would have committed to an out the way he did. And if you think I didn't feel like a schmuck—"

"Okay, okay!" I interrupted. "Sorry! I know it was rough for you, too. It's just that . . . well, I missed you like crazy, Alice. Don't do that to me again."

Alice's trilling laugh rang through the room, and we all smiled to hear that music once more. "I missed you, too, Bella. So forgive me, and try to be satisfied with being the superhero of the day."

Everyone else laughed now, and I ducked my face into Nessie's hair, embarrassed.

Edward went back to analyzing every shift of intention and control that had happened in the meadow today, declaring that it was my shield that had made the Volturi run away with their tails between their legs. The way everyone looked at me made me uncomfortable. Even Edward. It was like I had grown a hundred feet during the course of the morning. I tried to ignore the impressed looks, mostly keeping my eyes on Nessie's sleeping face and Jacob's unchanged expression. I would always be just Bella to him, and that was a relief.

The hardest stare to ignore was also the most confusing one.

It wasn't like this half-human, half-vampire Nahuel was used to thinking of me in a certain way. For all he knew, I went around routing attacking vampires every day and the scene in the meadow had been nothing unusual at all. But the boy never took his eyes off me. Or maybe he was looking at Nessie. That made me uncomfortable, too.

He couldn't be oblivious to the fact that Nessie was the only female of his kind that wasn't his half-sister.

I didn't think this idea had occurred to Jacob yet. I kind of hoped it wouldn't soon. I'd had enough fighting to last me for a while.

Eventually, the others ran out of questions for Edward, and the discussion dissolved into a bunch of smaller conversations.

I felt oddly tired. Not sleepy, of course, but just like the day had been long enough. I wanted some peace, some normality. I wanted Nessie in her own bed; I wanted the walls of my own little home around me.

I looked at Edward and felt for a moment like I could read *his* mind. I could see he felt exactly the same way. Ready for some peace.

"Should we take Nessie . . ."

"That's probably a good idea," he agreed quickly. "I'm sure she didn't sleep soundly last night, what with all the snoring."

He grinned at Jacob.

Jacob rolled his eyes and then yawned. "It's been a while

since I slept in a bed. I bet my dad would get a kick out of having me under his roof again."

I touched his cheek. "Thank you, Jacob."

"Anytime, Bella. But you already know that."

He got up, stretched, kissed the top of Nessie's head, and then the top of mine. Finally, he punched Edward's shoulder. "See you guys tomorrow. I guess things are going to be kind of boring now, aren't they?"

"I fervently hope so," Edward said.

We got up when he was gone; I shifted my weight carefully so that Nessie was never jostled. I was deeply grateful to see her getting a sound sleep. So much weight had been on her tiny shoulders. It was time she got to be a child again—protected and secure. A few more years of childhood.

The idea of peace and security reminded me of someone who didn't have those feelings all the time.

"Oh, Jasper?" I asked as we turned for the door.

Jasper was sandwiched tight in between Alice and Esme, somehow seeming more central to the family picture than usual. "Yes, Bella?"

"I'm curious—why is J. Jenks scared stiff by just the sound of your name?"

Jasper chuckled. "It's just been my experience that some kinds of working relationships are better motivated by fear than by monetary gain."

I frowned, promising myself that I would take over that working relationship from now on and spare J the heart attack that was surely on the way.

We were kissed and hugged and wished a good night to our family. The only off note was Nahuel again, who looked intently after us, as if he wished he could follow.

Once we were across the river, we walked barely faster than human speed, in no hurry, holding hands. I was sick of being under a deadline, and I just wanted to take my time. Edward must have felt the same.

"I have to say, I'm thoroughly impressed with Jacob right now," Edward told me.

"The wolves make quite an impact, don't they?"

"That's not what I mean. Not once today did he think about the fact that, according to Nahuel, Nessie will be fully matured in just six and a half years."

I considered that for a minute. "He doesn't see her that way. He's not in a hurry for her to grow up. He just wants her to be happy."

"I know. Like I said, impressive. It goes against the grain to say so, but she could do worse."

I frowned. "I'm not going to think about that for approximately six and a half more years."

Edward laughed and then sighed. "Of course, it looks like he'll have some competition to worry about when the time comes."

My frown deepened. "I noticed. I'm grateful to Nahuel for today, but all the staring was a little weird. I don't care if she is the only half-vampire he's not related to."

"Oh, he wasn't staring at her—he was staring at you."

That's what it had seemed like . . . but that didn't make any sense. "Why would he do that?"

"Because you're alive," he said quietly.

"You lost me."

"All his life," he explained, "—and he's fifty years older than I am—"

"Decrepit," I interjected.

He ignored me. "He's always thought of himself as an evil creation, a murderer by nature. His sisters all killed their mothers as well, but they thought nothing of it. Joham raised them to think of the humans as animals, while they were gods. But Nahuel was taught by Huilen, and Huilen loved her sister more than anyone else. It shaped his whole perspective. And, in some ways, he truly hated himself."

"That's so sad," I murmured.

"And then he saw the three of us—and realized for the first time that just because he is half immortal, it doesn't mean he is inherently evil. He looks at me and sees . . . what his father should have been."

"You *are* fairly ideal in every way," I agreed.

He snorted and then was serious again. "He looks at you and sees the life his mother should have had."

"Poor Nahuel," I murmured, and then sighed because I knew I would never be able to think badly of him after this, no matter how uncomfortable his stare made me.

"Don't be sad for him. He's happy now. Today, he's finally begun to forgive himself."

I smiled for Nahuel's happiness and then thought that today belonged to happiness. Though Irina's sacrifice was a dark shadow against the white light, keeping the moment from perfection, the joy was impossible to deny. The life I'd fought for was safe again. My family was reunited. My daughter had a beautiful future stretching out endlessly in front of her. Tomorrow I would go see my father; he would see that the fear in my eyes had been replaced with joy, and he would be happy, too. Suddenly, I was sure that I wouldn't find him there alone. I hadn't been as observant as I might have been in the last few weeks, but in this moment it was like I'd known all along. Sue would be with Charlie—the werewolves' mom with the vampire's dad—and he wouldn't be alone anymore. I smiled widely at this new insight.

But most significant in this tidal wave of happiness was the surest fact of all: I was with Edward. Forever.

Not that I'd want to repeat the last several weeks, but I had to admit they'd made me appreciate what I had more than ever.

The cottage was a place of perfect peace in the silver-blue night. We carried Nessie to her bed and gently tucked her in. She smiled as she slept.

I took Aro's gift from around my neck and tossed it lightly into the corner of her room. She could play with it if she wished; she liked sparkly things.

Edward and I walked slowly to our room, swinging our arms between us.

"A night for celebrations," he murmured, and he put his hand under my chin to lift my lips to his.

"Wait," I hesitated, pulling away.

He looked at me in confusion. As a general rule, I didn't pull away. Okay, it was more than a general rule. This was a first.

"I want to try something," I informed him, smiling slightly at his bewildered expression.

I put my hands on both sides of his face and closed my eyes in concentration.

I hadn't done very well with this when Zafrina had tried to teach me before, but I knew my shield better now. I understood the part that fought against separation from me, the automatic instinct to preserve self above all else.

It still wasn't anywhere near as easy as shielding other

people along with myself. I felt the elastic recoil again as my shield fought to protect me. I had to strain to push it entirely away from me; it took all of my focus.

"Bella!" Edward whispered in shock.

I knew it was working then, so I concentrated even harder, dredging up the specific memories I'd saved for this moment, letting them flood my mind, and hopefully his as well.

Some of the memories were not clear—dim human memories, seen through weak eyes and heard through weak ears: the first time I'd seen his face . . . the way it felt when he'd held me in the meadow . . . the sound of his voice through the darkness of my faltering consciousness when he'd saved me from James . . . his face as he waited under a canopy of flowers to marry me . . . every precious moment from the island . . . his cold hands touching our baby through my skin . . .

And the sharp memories, perfectly recalled: his face when I'd opened my eyes to my new life, to the endless dawn of immortality . . . that first kiss . . . that first night . . .

His lips, suddenly fierce against mine, broke my concentration.

With a gasp, I lost my grip on the struggling weight I was holding away from myself. It snapped back like stressed elastic, protecting my thoughts once again.

"Oops, lost it!" I sighed.

"I *heard* you," he breathed. "How? How did you do that?"

"Zafrina's idea. We practiced with it a few times."

He was dazed. He blinked twice and shook his head.

"Now you know," I said lightly, and shrugged. "No one's ever loved anyone as much as I love you."

"You're almost right." He smiled, his eyes still a little wider than usual. "I know of just one exception."

"Liar."

He started to kiss me again, but then stopped abruptly.

"Can you do it again?" he wondered.

I grimaced. "It's very difficult."

He waited, his expression eager.

"I can't keep it up if I'm even the slightest bit distracted," I warned him.

"I'll be good," he promised.

I pursed my lips, my eyes narrowing. Then I smiled.

I pressed my hands to his face again, hefted the shield right out of my mind, and then started in where I'd left off—with the crystal-clear memory of the first night of my new life . . . lingering on the details.

I laughed breathlessly when his urgent kiss interrupted my efforts again.

"Damn it," he growled, kissing hungrily down the edge of my jaw.

"We have plenty of time to work on it," I reminded him.

"Forever and forever and forever," he murmured.

"That sounds exactly right to me."

And then we continued blissfully into this small but perfect piece of our forever.

the end

VAMPIRE INDEX

Alphabetically by coven

≫ ≪

* vampire possesses a quantifiable supernatural talent
– bonded pair (oldest listed first)
~~struck~~ deceased before beginning of this novel

THE AMAZON COVEN
Kachiri
Senna
Zafrina*

THE DENALI COVEN
Eleazar* – Carmen
Irina – ~~Laurent~~
Kate*
~~Sasha~~
Tanya
~~Vasilii~~

THE EGYPTIAN COVEN
Amun – Kebi
Benjamin* – Tia

THE IRISH COVEN
Maggie*
Siobhan* – Liam

THE OLYMPIC COVEN
Carlisle – Esme
Edward* – Bella*
Jasper* – Alice*
Renesmee*
Rosalie – Emmett

THE ROMANIAN COVEN
Stefan
Vladimir

THE VOLTURI COVEN
Aro* – Sulpicia
Caius – Athenodora
Marcus* – ~~Didyme~~*

THE VOLTURI GUARD (PARTIAL)
Alec*
Chelsea* – Afton*
Corin*
Demetri*
Felix
Heidi*
Jane*
Renata*
Santiago

THE AMERICAN NOMADS (PARTIAL)
Garrett
~~James~~* – ~~Victoria~~*
Mary
Peter – Charlotte
Randall

THE EUROPEAN NOMADS (PARTIAL)
Alistair*
Charles* – Makenna

Acknowledgments

-<- ->-

As always, an ocean of thanks to:

My awesome family, for all their incomparable love and support.

My talented and hawt publicist, Elizabeth Eulberg,
for creating STEPHENIE MEYER out of the raw clay
that was once just a mousy Steph.

The whole team at Little, Brown Books for Young Readers
for five years of enthusiasm, faith, support, and incredibly hard work.

All the amazing site creators and administrators in the Twilight Saga
online fandom; you people astound me with your coolness.

My brilliant, beautiful fans, with your unparalleled good taste in books,
music, and movies, for continuing to love me more than I deserve.

The bookstores who have made this series a hit
with their recommendations; all authors are indebted to you
for your love of and passion for literature.

The many bands and musicians that keep me motivated;
did I mention Muse already? I did? Too bad.
Muse, Muse, Muse . . .

New gratitude to:

The best band-that-never-was: Nic and the Jens, featuring Shelly C.
(Nicole Driggs, Jennifer Hancock, Jennifer Longman, and Shelly
Colvin). Thanks for taking me under your collective wing, guys.
I would be a shut-in without you.

My long-distance pals and fonts of sanity,
Cool Meghan Hibbett and Kimberly "Shazzer" Suchy.

My peer support, Shannon Hale, for understanding *everything,*
and for feeding my love of zombie humor.

Makenna Jewell Lewis for the use of her name, and her mother,
Heather, for her support of the Arizona Ballet.

The new guys on my "writing inspiration" playlist:
Interpol, Motion City Soundtrack, and Spoon.

PRAISE FOR THE JANE TENNISON SERIES:

'La Plante excels in her ability to pick out details that give her portrayal of life in a police station a rare ring of authenticity'
Sunday Telegraph

'It may be apprentice Tennison, b... ...ge La Plante'
The Indep...

'Fast-paced, tense and a gre... ...s of the detective chief inspector will be de... ...ad how it all started'
...n

'Enthralling ... ... from the creator of hit TV dram... ...ries *Prime Suspect*'
Heat

'A rollicking period piece'
Mail On Sunday

'This is Lynda La Plante at her best. It is a read-in-one sitting and a must-read for all fans'
Woman's Way

'A rite-of-passage novel with an absorbingly twisty plot'
Guardian

'The pace is breathless and the plot is satisfyingly full of twists and turns'
Independent On Sunday

'La Plante recounts how Tennison the doe-eyed optimist turns into the steely-eyed pragmatist loved by her fans'
The Irish Times

'A fascinating insight into how Mirren's mature Tennison developed'
Irish Independent

'A terrific, gutsy back story for the heroine of TV's *Prime Suspect*'
Woman & Home

Lynda La Plante

HIDDEN KILLERS

SIMON &
SCHUSTER

London · New York · Sydney · Toronto · New Delhi

A CBS COMPANY

First published in Great Britain by Simon & Schuster UK Ltd, 2016
A CBS COMPANY

This paperback published 2017

1 3 5 7 9 10 8 6 4 2

Simon & Schuster UK Ltd
1st Floor
Gray's Inn Road
London WC1X 8HB

Simon & Schuster Australia, Sydney
Simon & Schuster India, New Delhi

www.simonandschuster.co.uk
www.simonandschuster.com.au
www.simonandschuster.co.in

A CIP catalogue record for this book
is available from the British Library

Paperback ISBN: 978-1-4711-4056-3
Export Paperback ISBN: 978-1-4711-6303-6
eBook ISBN: 978-1-4711-4057-0
Audio ISBN: 978-1-4711-5999-2

Typeset in the UK by M Rules
Printed and bound by CPI Group (UK) Ltd, Croydon, CR0 4YY

MIX
Paper from
responsible sources
FSC® C020471

To my many loyal readers. Your support through e-mail and social media has been a constant encouragement to me, and makes all the hard work worthwhile.

ACKNOWLEDGEMENTS

I would like to thank Stephen Ross and Dan Ross at Ross Bennet Smith for their continuing support, advice and lasting friendship. At one time we enjoyed owning racehorses together but this last year has contained more hurdles than I could ever have anticipated, and Stephen and Dan have successfully guided me over them.

My thanks also to Robin Hilton and James Sully at Sheridans for their outstanding legal and professional advice during some very challenging negotiations.

I am very fortunate to have Simon & Schuster as my publishing company, with constant support and friendship from Suzanne Baboneau and Ian Chapman. I am extremely grateful not only for their friendship over many years, but also for their dedicated professionalism. I have had tremendous support from all the team at S&S, including Emma Capron, Mattie Whitehead, Celine Kelly, Tamsin Shelton, Ian Allen, and Jane Pizzey.

My thanks also to Louise Davies for her editorial advice and guidance. Sometimes it is hard to accept structural amendments to something you have created, but for me the changes have always proved to be worthwhile.

My thanks also to the UK sales, marketing and PR departments: Gill Richardson, Dominic Brendon, Rumana Haider, Laura Hough, Sally Wilks, Sara-Jade Virtue, Richard Hawton, Dawn Burnett, Rich Vlietstra, Jessica Jackson; and finally, Matthew Johnson who has designed the brilliant book jacket. Everyone at S&S Australia and Jonathan Ball in South Africa.

As well as the incredible support from Simon & Schuster, I have Nigel Stoneman working beside me. Nigel runs La Plante Global and is a consummate professional and a joy to work with. He not only handles all the exciting projects we have coming in the future, but manages the ongoing publicity events, TV appearances and other interviews. He makes sure I get from A to B without mishap – which is not always an easy task!

I would also like to thank Tory Macdonald, my Personal Assistant, who is still helping me to take the stress out of my life. Her organisational skills continue to be quite extraordinary.

My thanks go to the Metropolitan Women Police Association, particularly Beverley Edwards, Eileen Turnbull, Siobhan Elam, Gina Negus, Janice Gammon, Wendy Rowe, Monica Tett, Valierie Lowe and Kathi Broad.

Last, but by no means least, my sincere thanks to Callum (Cass) Sutherland. As Cass was stationed at Hackney Police Station during the 1970s, all of the police procedure I have used is very accurate. His ideas and his own memories of that period are a constant source of inspiration throughout the Tennison series. I would also like to thank his wife, Anne Sutherland, who was stationed alongside him and who has provided me with the details of what life was like for a very young female probationary officer attached to the Met.

HIDDEN KILLERS

PROLOGUE

For WPC Jane Tennison the months following the bank explosion, which caused the tragic deaths of DCI Len Bradfield and WPC Kathleen Morgan, were a difficult and painfully sad time. The truth was the incident deeply affected everyone in the Met, but most notably at Hackney Police Station, where many officers found their colleagues' deaths hard to deal with and all too raw to discuss. The imposing four-storey redbrick-and-white-stone building had numerous stone-flagged corridors and winding staircases. The cells were located in the cold and dingy basement, and there were small cramped offices on the ground and first floors. The whole place needed redecorating and the station was long overdue for a refurbishment. But no changes had been made since the abortive bank raid involving the death of two loved and respected officers. It wasn't as if it had never happened or would ever be forgotten; it was just rarely, if ever, spoken about. However, the likes of Sergeant Harris ensured the daily routine and hard graft continued, and a new DCI gave the detectives a strength and determination to continue working at the station.

DS Spencer Gibbs was placed on sick leave to recover from the burn injuries to his hands. Several detectives had tried to get in contact with him, even leaving messages at his home address, but to no avail. It seemed he didn't want any visitors and it soon became common knowledge, through the new DCI, that DS Gibbs had asked for a transfer to another station. Sadly, the whole incident left the young DC Mike Hudson, who was also injured in the explosion, too traumatized to return to work, and after attending the funerals of his colleagues he handed in his warrant card and resigned from the Met.

Despite her emotional and professional involvement in the devastating events, Jane was now even more determined to complete her probation and be confirmed as a fully-fledged police constable. As the weeks and months passed, she made admirable progress, not only in the classroom at her continuation training exams, but also on the streets where she made a number of good arrests. By anyone's standards, it was an impressive array of both male and female suspects, for various offences such as shoplifting, criminal damage, drunk and disorderly and handling stolen goods. Most notably there were two occasions, after a call over the radio, when Jane was first on the scene and had caught the burglars red-handed.

It was towards the end of her probation, in the last week of August 1974, when Jane spent a week on compulsory attachment with the Traffic Division. Although it was a great adrenalin rush racing around London at high speed with blue lights and sirens, to a variety of personal injury and vehicle accidents, being a Traffic officer was not a future she had any desire to pursue in the Met. She was crossing off the days in her pocket diary, longing for Monday, 9th September, which marked her final two weeks of probation and a plain-clothes attachment to Hackney CID.

Jane had already contemplated directly approaching DCS Metcalf who, shortly after the bank explosion, had given her his word that if she continued performing well as a probationer he would give her a 'personal recommendation' should she desire to become a detective. His promise had been made well over a year ago now, and although she had seen Metcalf numerous times at the station, he had never raised the subject. Jane decided that it would be best to show a keen interest during her CID attachment and perform well, then she would be in a better position to approach him.

CHAPTER ONE

On Wednesday, 4th September, Jane was on the 2 p.m. late shift parade as Sergeant Harris inspected and posted the C Relief uniform officers to their beats and panda car duties for the shift. As Jane was about to be given her posting Detective Inspector Nicholas Moran entered the room and, as was the norm, everyone stood to attention for a senior officer. Harris had a look of disapproval on his face as he didn't like his parades interrupted, least of all by the CID. Moran nodded his approval at the officers' show of respect then gestured for everyone to sit down as he turned to Harris.

'Please finish posting your officers to their duties, Sergeant Harris, then I'd like to address them regarding some indecent assaults that have occurred on the ground in the last few weeks.'

'I've finished, so you can address them now. But if you could make it brief I'd be obliged as *my* officers need to get out on patrol,' Harris said, in a pompous manner.

'Thank you,' Moran replied with a skewed smile that conveyed his displeasure at Harris's attitude.

DI Moran was an experienced and well-respected

detective, having worked on the Clubs and Vice Unit at Scotland Yard prior to his recent promotion and transfer to Hackney CID. He was in his mid-thirties, with blond hair that was neat, tidy and collar length. He wore a dark navy blue suit and white shirt with a button-down collar, blue tie and black Cuban-heeled ankle boots that made him look taller that his actual five feet ten inches. Jane had seen him on a few previous occasions but being a probationary WPC she had not come into direct contact with him; the word around the station was that he was on the fast track and going places.

Moran told the officers that over the last few weeks a number of young women had been indecently assaulted after dark, in both the Victoria Park and London Fields areas of Hackney, and he strongly suspected the same man was responsible for all the attacks. He explained that the majority of the assaulted women had been prostitutes, probably because they were easy targets who would be least likely to report an assault. However, the last two victims were not prostitutes and the fear was that the suspect was becoming less discriminating about whom he attacked. As Moran spoke, all the officers present, apart from Harris, wrote down the information in their force-issue pocket books.

'The suspect is about five feet eight inches tall, with a deep-voiced London accent. He wore all-black clothing, which consisted of a waist length bomber-style jacket, black roll-neck jumper and trousers.' Moran paused to let the officers write down the details.

'What about his colour and facial description?' Harris

6

asked, in a manner that implied Moran was lacking in his information on the suspect.

'Don't know, Sergeant Harris,' Moran said, and deliberately paused while Harris sat back with a smug grin. He then continued: 'Sadly none of the victims would recognize the assailant again as he had his face covered during each attack.'

Harris kept quiet as Moran went on to say that he and some of his detectives would be carrying out undercover surveillance, with a decoy, at London Fields for the next few nights. He wanted two officers patrolling Victoria Park just after dark and the station panda cars should, if possible, make a sweep round the park at least every half-hour. This, Moran informed them, was a deliberate ploy to entice the suspect over to London Fields where there would be no uniform presence. Harris made an entry in the parade book, which was on the desk in front of him, and informed PC Jackson and PC Oliver that they would now be patrolling Victoria Park for the shift.

'However, should the officers patrolling Victoria Park see anyone acting suspiciously, or matching the partial description of the suspect, they have my permission to stop and question the person about their movements. If you're not happy with any explanation or answers they give, arrest them and phone the CID office. One of my detectives will be manning a radio and they will be on a different frequency to you. Are there any questions?'

Harris promptly closed the parade book and stood up. 'Right, you all know your postings so book out your radios and vehicles, then get out on patrol ... and no cups of tea beforehand.'

Jane raised her hand, attracting Moran's attention. 'Yes, officer?'

'Sorry, sir ... it wasn't about your case or the suspect. It's just that Sergeant Harris hasn't posted me to a beat yet. I could cover Victoria Park as well, Sergeant, or relieve the officers for their refs break?' Jane asked, hoping that she might get the chance to stop and arrest the suspect in Victoria Park.

The frown on Harris's face said it all. Jane was well accustomed to his condescending, chauvinistic attitude.

'I've done the patrol postings ... you're in comms on the radio and VDU, Tennison.'

DI Moran gestured to Jane. 'Ah, yes, you're Jane Tennison? I'd like to have a chat with you about bringing your CID attachment forward to—'

Harris interrupted. 'She needs to be on comms to relieve the early turn officer.'

'And I need a female officer to act as a decoy tonight, Sergeant Harris ... unless you fancy putting on a wig, skirt and high heels yourself,' Moran said, in a tone that sounded as if he was being serious.

Harris ushered everyone out of the parade room, then slammed the door and turned to Moran.

'May I have a word, sir?' Harris said, indignantly. He walked a few steps away from Jane, followed by Moran.

Jane couldn't believe that even now, with only a few days of her probation left to serve, Harris still acted like a petulant child when it came to female officers' career opportunities. She also knew he was not a fan of the CID and often stated that young detectives didn't have much brawn or brains and depended on experienced uniform men like himself to get them out of trouble. Although Harris pretended to whisper to Moran it was obvious he wanted her to hear every word.

'You do realize that Tennison is still a probationer and inexperienced, and when it comes to the ways of the CID she may not be up to scratch, evidentially, if you make an arrest?'

'If you are suggesting my detectives would encourage a uniform officer to fabricate evidence then I very much resent your remark, Harris. Rest assured, her well-being will be paramount throughout the surveillance operation.'

Moran looked at his watch before continuing. 'You'd better get a move on ... the early turn duty sergeant will be waiting for you to relieve him.'

Harris gritted his teeth as he left the parade room. Moran gestured for Jane to sit down. He pulled over a chair for himself, using the back of it as an arm rest and swinging his legs either side. Although she didn't know Moran, judging by his cheeky smile and snazzy suit, Jane had formed an early impression that he reckoned himself as a bit of a charmer. Moran pulled a pack of Players from his pocket, took two cigarettes out, put the pack back in his pocket, and offered one to Jane, who declined. He tucked the spare cigarette behind his ear and lit the other with a Zippo lighter. For a fraction of a second Jane remembered DCI Bradfield using a similar lighter. But the moment passed as Moran flicked his Zippo closed, inhaled on the cigarette and blew out a ring of smoke.

'You obviously heard what I said to Sergeant Harris?'

Jane nodded. 'Yes, sir, and I'd really like to work with you on your operation.'

'A WDC from Dalston nick was going to act as the decoy tonight, but she went sick an hour ago and I need someone to replace her. A couple of the lads in the office recommended you as a bit of a looker, with a good arrest record,' he said, in a serious voice.

'Thank you, sir,' she replied, slightly embarrassed.

'There are obviously risks involved, but I can assure you that we will be watching you discreetly from an observation van. There will also be further backup nearby. But the choice is yours ... if you don't want to be a decoy, I totally understand and you'll still be welcome on your two-week CID attachment.'

'I'd be honoured to be a decoy, and I know your detectives will watch my back.'

Moran sat upright and slapped his hands on the back of the chair.

'That's great, darlin' ... and whether or not we arrest the pervert you can add the next three weekdays with us as additional to your CID attachment.'

'Thank you, sir, I won't let you down.'

'I'm sure you won't, but first you'll need to get the right clobber together.'

'OK,' she said, wondering what he was going to say next.

'You'll need to tart yourself up a bit ... You've got to look sexy ... sort out your hair and makeup, maybe get a long wig or something and look like you're up for a good time ... You all right with that?'

Jane nodded and Moran asked if she had any 'scanty'

clothing to wear for the job. When Jane replied that she didn't Moran pulled out a leather wallet from his suit jacket and handed Jane two ten pound notes.

'Here's a score. Use it, but get receipts so I can claim the dosh back as expenses for the decoy operation.'

Moran looked at his watch and stood up. 'Right, it'll be dark by eight p.m. so you go get yourself sorted and be back here for a half-seven briefing in the CID office.'

Jane nodded and Moran used his foot to shove the chair back against the wall before leaving the room. Jane sat for a few moments trying to think what clothes she had that might be suitable, but nothing came instantly to mind. This was a big opportunity and she didn't want to blow it. Looking at the money Moran had given her Jane wondered if she'd find anything suitable at Chelsea Girl or British Home Stores, but she doubted it. And Carnaby Street clothes would be too expensive.

She was relieved that she had nearly five hours to get ready. But first she had to inform the miserable Sergeant Harris that she was now officially on her CID attachment. She headed out of the briefing room and down the stone-flagged corridor with its peeling green paint and fading notices. Eventually she tracked him down in the snooker room and explained that DI Moran had said she needed to buy the appropriate clothes for her undercover assignment.

'No doubt you'll have the "appropriate" clothing at the section house, Tennison, so I won't be authorizing any cash for you to buy anything.'

He wafted his cue for her to leave, then bent down over the snooker table to line up for a shot on the black ball. Jane walked to the door then smiled as she turned back to Harris, who was just about to take his shot.

'That's fine, Sarge ... DI Moran gave me a score.' Harris pushed his cue forward and his hand slipped, causing the tip to scrape into the green baize, almost tearing it.

'Whoops!' she said, closing the door quickly behind her.

Jane took her uniform jacket and hat from her locker and left the station to get the 253 bus to Ede House, her home now for almost two years. Ten minutes later she was hurrying up the stairs to her room. She took off her uniform skirt and hung it in the wardrobe. Pushing the coat hangers apart one by one she looked through her clothes, even though she knew she didn't really have any that fitted the term 'scanty'. She thought about the money DI Moran had given her, but felt bad about spending it on something tacky that she would never wear again. In desperation Jane pulled on a pair of jeans, a white T-shirt and short jacket, but looking in the wardrobe mirror she realized she would definitely need to buy some suitable clothes.

There was one person she knew who used to wear boob tubes, hot pants, miniskirts and long boots on a night out to the disco. Jane laughed, remembering how her sister Pam would sneak out of the family flat with her outfit in a shoulder bag, so that her disapproving parents wouldn't see. She would then nip to a friend's house to change before going out to places like the Empire Ballroom in Leicester Square. One time Pam had arrived home after midnight and as she let herself into the dark hall she had fallen over on her high wedge boots, and their mother, hearing the commotion, had hurried from her bedroom.

'Do you know what time it is?' she had said so loudly that Jane had come out of her room. Pam had very obviously been drinking as she swung the bag with her clothes that she intended changing back into and had to prop herself up against the wall.

'I am only late cos I have been sick, I had a prawn cocktail at Norma's.'

Mrs Tennison had shaken her head, and told Jane to get her sister some Bisodol for her upset stomach, and, looking ashamed, she had returned to her bedroom.

'How much have you had to drink?' Jane had demanded as she had helped her sister to the bathroom and taken off her coat.

'Just a few Babychams, s'nothin', but I stayed on dancing and didn't get time to change back into ...' She hadn't finished as she had started to retch and Jane had to help her to the toilet. As Pam had bent over Jane couldn't believe that she was wearing a miniskirt so short she could see her knickers, and even more shocking, was that Pam was not wearing a bra under her silky frilly blouse.

'You are not wearing your brassiere,' Jane said in a harsh whisper.

'Oh for goodness sake, get with it, I haven't worn one for ages, nobody wears them now.'

'Well, I do,' Jane said, taking from the medical cabinet the pink Bisodol bottle and holding it out just as Pam was violently sick.

Jane took a bus towards her parents' home in Maida Vale, stopping off at Pam's salon, which was only a short distance from the family flat.

Pam was surprised to see her and Jane briefly explained that she was going on an undercover operation and needed to change her appearance. Pam made her wait until she had finished her client's tint, and then said she only had twenty minutes before she would have to comb the tint through as the other hairdresser wasn't in until later.

In the small back annexe of the salon there was a bag full of wigs. Pam explained that when they were training junior stylists the wigs were pinned to a head stand and would be cut or coloured. There were short bobs, long straggly blondes, and frizzy permed wigs, none in very good condition. Jane tried some of them on but they looked so false, until she put on a curly dark chestnut-coloured wig.

'Can I borrow this one, Pam?'

'Yes, but you'll have to return it ... that's real hair. What else do you need?'

'Do you have any makeup here?'

'Yes, cos sometimes I'm in so early I don't have time to do my face. I've also got a lot of samples as I do the makeup for the hair models when I'm doing one of the stylist events.'

Pam tipped out from a cardboard box an array of foundations and lipsticks, eyebrow pencils, liquid eyeliner and false eyelashes. Jane checked herself in a mirror, still unsure about the wig.

'If you wait around I can do your makeup for you and

comb out the wig and put some carmen rollers in it. You could do with a trim as well.'

'No, I have to go, but another time. I really appreciate this.'

Jane eventually left with the wig and some of Pam's spare makeup in a paper carrier bag. Pam had rather enjoyed helping and showing her how she could change her appearance, demonstrating how to stick on the false eyelashes. The sisters hadn't even discussed how long it had been since they had seen each other, or how things were going with Pam's new husband, Tony. A sixteen-year-old junior was sweeping up and washing around the basins; she couldn't help overhearing Pam and Jane's conversation. As soon as Jane left she asked Pam what it was all about. Pam tapped the side of her nose conspiratorially.

'Can't say, Cheryl, but my sister's a police officer, going undercover.'

She turned away and returned to her client who glanced at her watch, indicating that she had been waiting too long.

'Right, let me just comb this through for you, that extra ten minutes will give a better overall colour.'

If Pam had been surprised to see Jane, Mrs Tennison was even more so. She immediately thought something terrible had happened, and it took a while for Jane to calm her down and explain that she was only there for a quick visit as she fibbed that there was a patrol car waiting, and she just wanted to give her mum a hug and a kiss. Mr Tennison was out playing bowls, which was fortunate, as it meant that Jane could see her mother, get what she needed and leave. Her bedroom was always just as she had left it, and it made her feel quite emotional. Everything was neat and orderly, although that soon changed as Jane rummaged through her wardrobe and overhead cupboards.

'Why don't you tell me what you're looking for, dear, and maybe I can help you find it?'

'It was just a costume I had years ago, when we did a school play ... and some things I had for a Halloween party,' Jane said, standing on a stool and rifling through an assortment of her clothes in the cupboard.

'They might be in Pam's old bedroom ... I put lots of things in there for the Salvation Army. There's some of her clothes she doesn't want in there as well. Daddy and I were going to drop them off but haven't got round to it yet. Do you want me to look for anything special? Is it for a party?'

'Yes, it's for one of the officers that's leaving ... but don't worry, Mum, I'll go and have a look.'

Jane stepped down from the stool. There was no way she was going to tell her mother exactly why she needed to find the costumes.

Jane could not believe how many plastic bags were stacked in Pam's old bedroom. Mrs Tennison started opening one after another.

'Is it fancy dress, dear? Here's that pair of thigh length boots Pam wore as Dick Whittington ... they cost a lot of money because she bought them from Biba ... they're not real patent leather, and fit up over the knee.'

Jane and her mother sorted through old clothes, most of which were Pam's and were things she wouldn't be

seen dead in now that she was a qualified hairdresser
and ran the local salon. Jane selected the clothes she
wanted and put them into an empty plastic bag. She
hugged her mother and left her refolding and packing
up the discarded items. Mrs Tennison wanted her to stay
for an early dinner but Jane was eager to get back to the
section house and try everything on.

'I have to go, Mum, but thanks for all your help.'

'Well, I hope it's a fun party, dear ... Daddy and I
will get all these other things to the Salvation Army ...
not that I think any of their people would want to wear
some of Pam's clothes. She used to worry me so much ...
all those flared trousers and skimpy tops.'

'Bye, Mum.'

Jane stuffed the wig and makeup into the same bag as
the clothes and left her mother still packing everything
else away.

By the time she returned to the section house it was
almost 6 p.m. On her bed she laid out a miniskirt, a
sequined stretch boob tube, a maroon padded bra, a
pair of fishnet tights and the awful fake patent leather
boots. She had also taken a frilly blouse, some blue
plastic hooped earrings and an array of bangles and
beads. Jane brushed the dark auburn wig to get some
of the tangles out, then pinned back her own hair and
pulled the wig on. It hung down to her shoulders and,
looking at herself in the mirror, she couldn't believe
how different it made her appear. She put on the frilly
blouse and then discarded it for a red boob tube, pulling it down to put on the padded bra and eventually
showing a lot of cleavage. She smiled, thinking how her

mother would have had a heart attack if she could see what she looked like.

After Jane had pulled on the fishnet tights and zipped up the leather miniskirt, she had to stand on a chair to see herself in the sink mirror. She decided against the miniskirt and tried on a pair of dark green velvet hot pants instead. Climbing back onto the chair to check the outfit, she had a déjà vu moment. When she had first started her probation at Hackney, there had been the wretchedly sad investigation into the murder of a young prostitute called Julie Ann Collins. It was strange for Jane to recall how she had reacted when she had first seen the Polaroid crime scene photographs of the murdered girl. The seventeen-year-old Julie Ann, a heroin addict, had been wearing boots and hot pants when her body had been discovered.

The memory triggered a sudden wave of sadness as images of Kath and DCI Bradfield sprung back into her mind. Jane had to clench her hands into fists to fight back unexpected tears. She didn't want to remember them, not now, not when she was about to begin undercover work. It could jeopardise her chances of gaining a much longed-for place in the CID. She became angry with herself for being emotional, and as she had done so often before, she refused to let herself cry. It felt as if someone was squeezing her heart and she had to force herself to take slow, deep breaths until the pressure subsided. She had told no one about these 'attacks', which were now less frequent, and she was certain she was capable of controlling them.

Jane stepped down from the chair and took out all

of Pam's makeup, spreading it out on her small writing desk: the pale pink lipstick, the rouge and pots of eye shadows, and sticks of pan makeup. Pam had been quite a rebellious teenager, and Jane couldn't help smiling at how different they were. Perhaps it was just as well that Pam had started work in the salon straight from school and had met her husband and married so young, or she might have ended up going off the rails. Sisters they may be, but they had very little in common. Since Pam had got married and Jane had moved into the section house, they rarely saw each other.

It took Jane several attempts, using a small magnifying mirror, to stick on the false eyelashes. She had never worn them before, and found the tiny tube of glue very fiddly. She used one of the darker sticks of pan to cover her face and work into her neck as Pam had shown her. There was no makeup brush, so she had to apply the rouge with a tissue. Jane chose a blue eye shadow and then wet the mascara from the tap at her washbasin and applied two thick coats, being careful not to unstick the eyelashes. She spent a long time checking her reflection and then lastly put on the pale pink lipstick.

It was nearly 7 p.m. and Jane realized she'd better get a move on as she didn't want to be late for the briefing in the CID office. She began to feel almost satisfied with her appearance until she realized that it was going to be quite cold as she would be out late, so she tied the blouse she had discarded in a knot around her waist. She realized it wouldn't be warm enough but she reckoned the adrenalin rush of working undercover would keep her from feeling the cold. Finally, she clipped on the big hoop earrings and pulled the cheap bracelets onto her wrists. She rather hesitantly looked at her police issue shoulder bag, but knowing she wouldn't be using it, she picked up the plastic makeup bag that belonged to Pam and popped her warrant card inside. It had a floral print and a zip and she could use it as her purse.

Jane practised walking up and down the length of her small room. The boots made it difficult as the plastic kept rubbing her knees, and she had to constantly pull up the flap at the top. They were platform and had a stacked wedge heel, making it very hard to walk properly and mimic a confident 'hooker's stride', swinging her hips and turning her head as if looking for punters.

Jane continued to increase her confidence by practising her new role on the bus journey from the section house back to the station. To begin with, she was very nervous and self-conscious, wondering if anyone would recognize her or try to approach her. In recent months she had arrested several Toms for soliciting and she remembered how they gave a 'cold shoulder' steely eyed look when questioned. For her journey to work Jane had taken off the earrings and bracelets and was wearing her black raincoat over her disguise. She went into the station via the back entrance in case anyone saw her walking in by the front counter. As she walked along the corridor to the locker room two uniform officers stopped to question her.

'Oi, what d'you think you're doin' on police premises, luv?'

'The same as you, luv ... it's me, WPC Tennison ... want to see my ID?'

One of them muttered 'Fuckin' Ada', as they both moved off sharply down the corridor. The fact that they had not recognized her gave Jane a boost.

While storing her coat in her locker Jane had another moment of déjà vu. It was over something completely unconnected, but after being confident about controlling her emotions, this came on so strongly she had to brace herself. Jane had forgotten to spray on any perfume, and she had a visualization of Kath and her heavy French scent, which all the men used to tease her about. Kath had once sprayed Jane with it to get rid of the smell of Dettol from the first post-mortem she had attended.

Her recollection was suddenly interrupted by a loud knock on the locker room door, and DI Moran's voice.

'Two rather stunned uniform lads just said they'd seen you in the corridor ... all right if I come in and have a look?'

'Yes, sir,' Jane said, brushing herself down and shaking her head so the wig would look better.

'My God, you look the part ... especially the sequined boob tube, which is very revealing,' he said, his eyes transfixed on her, adding, 'This is for you.' He tossed her a pale blue waist length rabbit fur coat. 'It'll be pretty cold out there so you'll need something to keep you warm that goes with the rest of the gear. It's evidence in a handling case, but for now it's yours.' Jane gratefully put on the cheap rabbit fur jacket, which reeked of patchouli oil.

'I'll just check my makeup and then I'll be up for the briefing, sir.'

'Your makeup's fine. I'd like to get out on the plot,

so I'll brief you in the obo van. Get the duty sergeant to book you out with us ... the obo van is in the yard.'

Jane clipped on the earrings and went to the front office where Sergeant Rodgers was sitting at the duty desk. She liked Sergeant Rodgers. Unlike Harris he had a sense of humour and didn't bark out orders. He nearly fell off his seat when he saw Jane, but she was quick to identify herself to him and reassure him that she was not a trespasser in the station.

'Bloody hell, you look lovely, Tennison. Harris said you were getting dressed up for a UC job, but I never imagined you looking anything like this.'

Jane smiled, but realized he wasn't joking as he stared at her in admiration.

'Fancy me, do you, Sarge?'

'I dunno how you done it ... you look like a movie star. Pity I got a wife, three kids and a cross-breed Alsatian at home. Listen, good luck tonight, be careful and don't go sticking your neck out. You'll have plenty of backup out there, so use it.'

'Thanks, Sarge. Can you book me out with the CID, please?'

Rodgers nodded and watched as Jane sashayed off down the corridor before booking her out in the station duty book. He noted that WPC 517 Tennison had left the station at 7.45 p.m. to work with CID on an attachment. Closing the duty book he tapped it with his hand and sighed. He knew how young Tennison was, and doubted that she had any concept of what she might have to face. Looking like a tough street-wise Tom could get her into a nasty situation.

CHAPTER TWO

Jane felt nervous in the obo van as they made their way over to London Fields. DI Moran gave her a small concealed radio, which he placed in the pocket of the blue rabbit fur coat. He had already made a small hole in the pocket for the earpiece and a small hand-held mic. He ran the wire for the speaker down the inside of the left sleeve of the jacket and the earpiece to the middle of her neck, up into the wig and into her left ear. Moran explained that it worked the same as a normal police radio and all she had to do was hold the mic in her left hand and press the small transmitter button whenever she wanted to communicate with him.

'Here, take this just in case you need to use it,' he said, as he produced a truncheon from his inside jacket pocket and handed it to her. 'Self-preservation always comes first so you hit 'em where it hurts most, as hard as you can if anything happens. OK?'

Jane nodded as she held the truncheon in her hand. 'Where am I going to put it? It's too big for my coat pocket and I don't fancy trying to squeeze it down the back of this boob tube or these hot pants.'

Moran laughed and pulled a rubber band out of his pocket. 'Up your right sleeve, and use the band to hold it in place.' He helped her with the truncheon and instructed her to make a radio test call to him once she was dropped off.

'You still up for this?' he asked, in a serious tone.

'Yes, sir. If I'm honest, I'm just a bit nervous.'

'That's to be expected ... but I've got plain clothes backup cars nearby, covering both sides of the Fields. The uniform officers are aware of what's going on should we need them as well. DC Ashton is driving the obo van and we will be the nearest to you at all times. I'll be running the show ... my call sign will be Gold, yours is Silver and the rest of the troops, should we need them, will be Bronze.'

Jane gave a small nod of recognition to Ashton, a pale freckle-faced twenty-eight-year-old who had recently married. Like many of the CID officers, he had also been on Bradfield's team.

Moran smiled at Jane reassuringly. 'Not many Toms are working the patch after what's been happening, but with less foot traffic we can tail you more easily.'

Arriving at London Fields' west side entrance Moran told Jane to follow the path past the outdoor Lido and hang around there for a while, 'as if touting for business'. They would park up in a suitable vantage point to watch her, and after ten to fifteen minutes she was to follow the central path through the park to the south entrance at Lansdowne Drive, then turn back on herself and walk through the park to the north entrance at Richmond Road. Moran said that if nothing had happened within the next hour or so she could jump back in the obo van to have a hot coffee, before repeating the route through the Fields.

From the front of the obo van DC Ashton called out that it was all clear. Moran checked the rear, then opened the back door to let Jane out, telling her that rather than looking for punters she should let them come to her.

The cold outside air mixed with Jane's nerves and she felt a shudder down her spine as she started to walk towards the Lido. She raised her left hand to her mouth and pressed the transmitter button on the mic.

'Gold to Silver receiving, over,' she said, without at first realizing her nervous error.

'You're Silver, and yes, Gold is receiving ... Over.'

Jane could have kicked herself and responded, 'Silver received.'

Moran was joined in the obo van by the young and relatively inexperienced Detective Constable Brian Edwards. Edwards was a rawboned six-footer with thick dark curly hair, and usually looked as if he had just fallen out of bed. Tonight, however, both men were dressed in dark polo-neck sweaters and black trousers. Moran wore a black leather jacket and Edwards a black bomber jacket. It was too dark to use the spy holes and they had a better view looking out of the rear window, which had a reflective foil-like sheet on it so no one could see in.

London Fields was virtually desolate. There was hardly anyone about and nobody who could be described as acting in a suspicious manner. Jane kept on walking. By now she was feeling very tired and cold when over the radio came Moran's voice.

'Gold to Silver, white male, late sixties coming towards you, approach with caution.'

Jane tensed as he moved closer, she took a deep breath, and felt the adrenalin rush of nerves. She could smell the alcohol as the man weaved and tottered towards her.

'Which way to the Cat and Mutton, my darling one?' he slurred.

In the obo van Moran became alert and told Edwards to stand by.

'I'm sorry, mate, I dunno,' Jane said in a dreadful attempt at a cockney accent as she passed him.

'False alarm,' Moran muttered. 'He's pissed out of his head. I'm beginning to think this is a waste of everyone's time.'

He opened a can of beer and lit a cigarette while Edwards had a cup of coffee from his flask and ate his sandwich.

It was now just after 10 p.m. and Jane made her way along the tarmac path, past the Lido yet again. She was struggling to walk in the thigh length boots that were by now really hurting her feet and had given her a blister on her right heel. But she had to keep up appearances, even though she was continually having to adjust her hot pants as they rode up her thighs. The cold night air penetrated through the frilly cheesecloth shirt that was tied tightly round her waist.

Jane couldn't believe that she hadn't even come across a 'legitimate prostitute' having sex up against a tree, or a park bench, as she had seen before when out on uniform patrol. But she realized that the fact that there were no prostitutes about was actually in her favour. It meant she avoided any angry confrontations with local Toms questioning what a new girl was doing on their patch. Jane knew that an uptight prostitute, or worse still a drunk prostitute, could be a real handful to deal with.

She carried on walking along the path, the pain from the blister getting worse, when she was suddenly aware of someone approaching quickly behind her. She gripped the radio mic in her hand, ready to press the talk button if she needed to. She could hear the sound of deep breathing and panting coming nearer. Jane's heart was pounding as she turned her head slightly, to look over her left shoulder, and saw the figure of a man in a hooded black tracksuit within inches of her. She had a sudden urge to scream but controlled herself as he jogged on past her.

Jane felt an incredible sense of relief as she looked to her left along Martello Street, on the east side of London Fields. In the distance, she could see the obo van moving slowly with its lights out. She was really glad she hadn't jumped the gun and radioed in for assistance, and taking a deep breath she walked on. The fact that neither Moran nor Edwards had radioed her about the jogger made her wonder how visible she was to them.

Jane's heart was still beating faster than usual. As she passed under a large tree she was startled by some conkers falling from the branches of the chestnut tree above her. Relieved, Jane smiled, but then she heard a much heavier thud behind her. Before she could turn around a black leather-gloved hand was clamped over her mouth while the other hand grabbed her round the chest, pinning her left arm to her side. The sudden attack caused the mic in her left hand to fall loose from the sleeve of the rabbit fur jacket, and dangle like a kid's glove on a string.

Jane's assailant groped and squeezed at her right breast with his left hand and started to drag her backwards towards the covered entrance of the Lido. Jane struggled to break free and desperately tried to look over her shoulder towards where she had last seen the obo van. She attempted to scream, but the leather-gloved hand tightened around her mouth. A man's voice whispered harshly in her ear.

'I've got a knife ... so keep your mouth shut, you fucking thieving whore ... or I'll cut your throat wide open this time.'

Jane nodded vigorously to indicate that she understood, and the leather-gloved hand relaxed its pressure slightly. Jane then realized that he couldn't be holding a knife as there was one hand over her mouth and the other was groping her breast. Her instinct took over and she opened her mouth wide and bit down as hard as she could on the gloved hand. As the assailant released his grip Jane screamed loudly and spun around quickly to confront her attacker. The man had a stocking over his head, making him unrecognizable, and he was wearing a black roll-neck sweater and black trousers. Jane understood exactly what he was intending to do to her when she saw his erect penis sticking out of his unzipped trousers.

In an instant Jane kicked her attacker hard in the groin. She pulled the truncheon free from inside her sleeve and hit him on the side of the head with all her strength, knocking him to the ground. The force of the impact against his skull made her lose her grip on the truncheon, causing it to fly out of her hand and onto the grass a few feet away.

Enraged, the assailant was growling and moving slowly. Like a bear about to make its final move on its prey he gradually stood up, the growling getting louder and louder as spittle foamed through the stocking mask. Jane managed to retrieve the radio mic, and pressing the transmitter screamed, 'Urgent Assistance!' and yelled at the top of her voice that she was a police officer. The attacker, as if confused by the revelation, froze momentarily before turning to run. Jane lunged at him, grabbing his right shoulder from behind. In his desperate effort to escape, the assailant elbowed her in the mouth causing her lip to split and bleed. He started to run, and although Jane was determined to give chase she knew she'd never be able to catch him in the boots she was wearing.

Suddenly she saw DI Moran and DC Edwards running at speed towards the assailant and together they tackled him hard from behind, knocking him heavily to the ground. As he tried to get up Moran pulled his head back by his hair and smashed his face down onto the pathway, causing his nose to split and bleed profusely. The two detectives then pinned him to the ground, pulled his hands behind his back and DC Edwards handcuffed him.

Jane felt a mixture of fear and relief as she heard the two-tone sirens of the police cars making their way to the Fields. Moran spoke into his portable radio.

'All units from Gold, stand down. Suspect has been arrested and WPC Tennison is safe and well. We only require a uniform van for the prisoner to be taken to Golf Hotel.'

'You were supposed to be covering my back! Where the hell were you?' Jane shouted.

Moran calmed her down, explaining that their view from the obo van had become partially blocked as Jane had passed between some large trees.

'It wasn't until we heard you scream that we realized something was wrong. I mean, where on earth did he come from? It's as if he appeared from nowhere.'

Jane's hand was trembling as she pointed to the chestnut tree. 'Up there ... he must have been up there, and jumped down. He grabbed me from behind, covered my mouth with his hand and said he'd cut my throat if I screamed. I couldn't get to the radio transmitter or shout for help until I bit him and he let me go.'

The attacker now started shouting that he'd done nothing wrong, earning him a well-aimed kick in the side of his ribs from DI Moran. He pulled the stocking up off his head revealing a man in his early thirties, clean shaven and with neatly cut hair.

Moran looked at Jane as he put the stocking in a plastic bag. 'He's your arrest, Tennison, so go ahead and caution him.'

Jane licked at her split lip, tasting the blood as she spoke. 'I'm arresting you for an indecent and serious

assault on a police officer. You do not have to say anything unless you wish to do so, but what you say may be
given in evidence.'

'I've done fuck all! That bitch suddenly attacked me
and started screaming ... Look at my head!'

Moran gave him another kick in the ribs to silence
him. He pulled the attacker up from the floor and
noticed with disgust that the man's now flaccid penis
was hanging out of his trousers. He glanced at Jane
who glared straight back at him. By now her fear had
been replaced by the buzz of adrenalin from making an
arrest.

'Don't look at me – I'm not putting that thing back in
his trousers!'

Moran laughed, surprised by her ability to make a
joke after what she had been subjected to. DC Edwards
roughly zipped up the assailant's fly, and hauled him
away screeching in agony.

The prisoner was placed in the back of the police van,
flanked by two officers and with DC Edwards sitting
opposite him. DI Moran drove Jane back to the station
in the obo van, and asked her to go over everything that
happened and what her assailant had said.

She was still energized as she repeated how she had
been attacked from behind and how he had threatened
to cut her throat.

'I bit down on his hand as hard as I could so he
released his hold.'

'Good girl ... sorry you had to go through that, but
you did well. Are you all right?'

'Yes, sir.'

Her heart was beating rapidly and she suddenly felt unable to stop shaking. Taking a few deep breaths she managed to calm herself down, forcing back the feelings of fear. In some ways she was more concerned that DI Moran might notice she had been panic stricken.

He had noticed and gave her a sidelong glance. As he concentrated on the road ahead he spoke quietly.

'You know, at some stage in our careers we've all had the guts kicked out of us. I don't mean literally of course ... but once you've had to face that fear and been able to deal with it, the next time isn't nearly as bad. It's not just the adrenalin rush that helps you get through something like tonight, but the satisfaction that you caught the bastard.'

Jane had not expected Moran to be so understanding. She smiled bravely and even attempted to make a joke.

'You been dressed up as a Tom to make an arrest, have you, sir?'

He chuckled, shaking his head.

'I never put a bad guy away that didn't deserve it, that's all you've got to know about me, Tennison.'

Back at the station Jane asked to be excused so she could sort out her split lip. Moran nodded, instructing DC Edwards to find the duty officer. Jane went to the ladies', then after washing her hands she inspected her cut lip in the mirror. It wasn't as swollen as she thought it would be, but she knew it would take at least a week or so before it healed. That meant not visiting her parents for a while. She put on some makeup and lipstick to conceal the cut, and thought about what Moran had said to her. She was more confident that she had handled the situation well under extreme pressure, but there had been a moment when she had really feared for her life. When the stocking had been removed from her attacker's head she had been surprised to see that he was actually quite a good-looking man, and not the ugly, vicious person she had envisaged.

Jane thought about taking off her wig, but decided against it as it made her feel even more like an undercover officer working with the CID.

As she stared at herself in the mirror above the cracked washbasin, it triggered another memory. She was in the washroom standing by Kath Morgan as she was getting ready to go on her first plain-clothed assignment; she had been so excited and eager to catch a burglar robbing old-age pensioners. Kath had been such a feisty woman, not afraid of anyone or anything, and regaled everyone by describing how she had brought the scrote burglar down with a rugby tackle. She had been laughing in the incident room as she told everyone how she had grabbed him by his hair and discovered that he was in fact wearing a Marc Bolan-style wig. She missed Kath – Jane was the only woman at Hackney, apart from clerical staff. As she left the washroom she noticed that there was a laminated 'LADIES TOILET' sign on the door. Smiling, she remembered the notice that Kath had handwritten and pinned to the door, which some of the male officers had then adorned with phallic cartoon drawings. A proper sign would have pleased Kath.

Jane headed down the corridor towards the small B Relief tea kitchen that officers used when the canteen was closed. She had a key to the cupboard for the tea bags and tins of instant coffee, which was kept locked as the contents were always disappearing. Her head ached and she was hunting for a bottle of aspirin when DC Edwards hurried towards her.

'You'd better get back to the charge room ... I've got to go and find Sergeant Harris ... he was supposed to be there ages ago. The guv is getting so fed up he wants to shove a snooker cue up his backside if he doesn't appear soon.'

'That's where you'll find him, he's usually in there having a game. If you like I can go and find him?'

'No ... no ... it's fine, I'll do it. A couple of uniforms are with the prisoner and he's handcuffed, so he's not going anywhere. But DI Moran has gone walkabout as well.'

Edwards ran his fingers through his mop of unruly hair. His arms seemed too long, even for his size. He had always had a dishevelled appearance. Sergeant Harris had complained about his untidiness on several occasions and Jane had even overheard him asking Edwards why his trousers never had a crease in them. The following day poor Edwards had turned up for work with the burnt imprint of an iron on his flared trousers.

Jane continued along the corridor into the B kitchen annexe. Unlocking the cupboard she pulled out a bottle of aspirin and filled a glass of water from the tap.

Edwards banged on the door.

'OK, I tracked him down ... see you in the charge room. Hey ... I couldn't have a couple of those aspirin, could I? I've got a terrible headache.'

Jane handed him a glass of water and watched as he tipped four aspirin into his palm. She noticed that his hand was shaking.

'Are you all right, Brian?'

Edwards swallowed all four tablets in one mouthful and gulped down the rest of the water.

'Yeah, I'm fine ... It's just that DI Moran makes me nervous. You know it wasn't my fault that bastard got you tonight. He clipped me one ... I'm sorry you were put through that, Jane.'

She gave him a friendly pat on the shoulder as he left and said she would see him in the charge room. She poured a fresh glass of water and took two aspirin, sipping the remains of the water before she rinsed the glass under the hot water and left it on the draining board.

Jane had been alone for a few minutes with the handcuffed prisoner when Sergeant Harris walked in, clearly irritated at being dragged away from his game of snooker.

'Where's Moran? I thought he was in charge of things?'

'He just went out to look for you.'

'Well, he obviously didn't look hard enough, did he?' Harris replied sarcastically, sitting behind the charge desk. He took out a large custody sheet from the drawer, clipped it to a board, and removed a pen from his top pocket, as DC Edwards walked in.

'Right, who's the arresting officer and what are the facts?'

At that moment Harris took a second look at Jane, causing him to shake his head in disbelief.

'What on earth do you think you look like, Tennison?'
Jane gave him a cheeky grin. 'A prostitute on the
game, Sarge. I thought you'd know that . . .'

Edwards laughed but Harris was not amused. DI
Moran walked into the room just as Harris chastised
Jane for what he felt was as an impudent comment.

'Don't get funny with me, Tennison . . . I've got your
final probationer's report to do in the next couple of
weeks.' He turned to Moran. 'Ah, good, you've decided
to join us . . .'

'As it happens, Harris, I needed a leak, which is a
much more pleasurable experience than talking to you.
Now, can we get on with booking the prisoner in?'

Harris grunted but he knew he was pushing his
luck with Moran who, although much younger than
him, was senior in rank. Harris asked for the facts of
the arrest and Moran asked Jane to recount what had
happened.

'I was working on attachment with the CID as a
decoy in London Fields this evening—'

'I already know that, Tennison. I don't need chapter
and verse, just get to the nitty gritty, please.'

Harris's mockery was making her feel nervous.
'Unseen by me the suspect jumped out of a tree, grabbed
me from behind, covered my mouth and fondled my
breasts—'

Harris interrupted, while writing on the charge sheet.
'So he's been arrested for indecent assault, I take it?'

Moran didn't relish getting into a slanging match
with Harris, least of all in front of a prisoner. From
his pocket he pulled the plastic bag containing the

stocking mask and threw it down onto the desk.

'I think you should know that this scrote wore that mask. It would have scared the shit out of most women, but not WPC Tennison. He elbowed her in the face.while trying to escape, and also had this knife in his pocket when I searched him at the scene.'

Moran took the flick knife from his pocket, which was also in a plastic bag, and placed it on the table next to the stocking.

Jane was confused. She had not seen Moran find the knife, and DC Edwards hadn't mentioned it. She glanced towards Edwards with a questioning look, but he was staring at the knife.

'I didn't let Tennison see this at the scene as she was obviously shocked by what happened to her. The attacker threatened to "cut her throat" if she screamed. Suffice to say, Sergeant Harris, he wasn't trying to drag her to London Fields Lido for a midnight swim! He is also suspected of a number of other sexual assaults and a recent rape.'

Jane knew that a teenage girl had been raped about two weeks ago on Hackney's ground, but she had no idea that the indecent assault suspect was believed to be responsible for it. The handcuffed prisoner, who was standing to one side listening, reacted angrily for the first time since he'd been brought into the station.

'This is bullshit! I never had a knife on me! That officer already searched me before he left the room for a piss ... This is a fit up!'

The expression on Harris's face was one of pure contempt as he glared at the prisoner before turning to Jane.

'Did he say he had a knife, and did he cause that cut to your lip?'

Jane nodded. Harris stared at the prisoner harder. 'What have you got to say for yourself?'

The prisoner took a deep breath as they all waited to hear his reply.

'I was walking through the park minding my own business when she asked me if I wanted sex … I told her I wasn't interested, then she started attacking me. She kicked me in the bollocks then hit me round the head with a truncheon—'

Harris interrupted. 'In nearly thirty years' service I've heard every lie and excuse in the book from sick perverts like you. For your information WPCs aren't issued with truncheons.'

'Well, she had one in her hand! And those two bastards smashed up my face and used me for football practice! I swear before God, I am telling the truth … I've been set up!'

Harris told him to shut up and looked at Jane. 'Did you have a truncheon, Tennison?'

Jane was now becoming worried about the fact she'd used a truncheon on a suspect and glanced towards DI Moran for support. He raised his hand slightly to calm her.

'I loaned WPC Tennison my truncheon, knowing that she was acting as a decoy in an area where other women had been attacked. It was for her own protection,' Moran said quietly.

Harris hesitated, then turned with a cynical smile towards the suspect.

'... Which was good thinking as this pervert not only assaulted her but he was carrying a knife.'

Harris glanced towards Jane. 'I take it that, being in fear of your life, you used the truncheon within the law to protect yourself?'

Jane realized he was asking a leading question and hastily agreed that was the case.

'Yes, Sergeant, and then—'

Harris interrupted, leading her again. 'You would have aimed for his shoulder, as per the Police Instruction Book, but this was literally a matter of life and death so you realized you had to incapacitate the suspect and hit him on the head as hard as you could, being a female.'

Jane smiled. 'Yes, Sergeant, that's exactly what happened. And before I hit him on the head I kicked him in the groin and—'

Harris cut her off. 'As is standard procedure, I need to inspect the truncheon that was used.'

Moran had picked up the truncheon and now pulled it out from his inside jacket pocket. He was about to hand it over but Harris just glanced at it.

'Looks fine to me ... no blood on it. I take it the rib and facial injuries to the prisoner occurred when he slipped and fell trying to escape, correct?'

Moran and Edwards spoke in unison.

'That's correct.'

The prisoner, now extremely agitated, tried to interrupt, but Harris pointed a finger at him, making it clear he had better keep his mouth shut. He then asked the prisoner for his name, date of birth and address. The prisoner replied that he was John Allard, born 20th February 1941, living at 33 Hall Road, East Ham.

Harris was still recording the prisoner's property on the arrest sheet as DI Moran checked his height against the measuring stick. He told the prisoner to remove his clothing, which he bagged up for forensics, and gave him a prisoner issue boiler suit to wear. As the prisoner undressed, both Harris and Moran noticed how athletic and muscular he was.

'Do a bit of weight training, do you?' Harris asked, and the prisoner replied that he liked to keep fit and work out.

Moran cynically replied, 'Yeah, but obviously not enough to escape from a female police officer! I think you're lying because you've been nicked before and are probably wanted. I'll call you Allard for now, but we'll take your fingerprints so we can get them up to the Yard tonight to be checked against criminal records, then no doubt we'll find out who you really are.'

'Allard' became increasingly sullen and demanded to speak to a solicitor. Harris refused him a phone call unless he gave his real details, but he insisted he had, so Harris denied the call on the grounds that it might interfere with the course of the investigation.

Harris stood up. 'You three go and write up your arrest notes. I'll take the pervert's prints and we'll also have a little chat as to why he shouldn't hit police officers ... especially female officers.'

Harris grabbed the prisoner by the scruff of his neck and literally lifted him off his feet, hauled him towards the fingerprint room and slammed him up against the wall while he opened the door. As Allard cried out, Harris looked over his shoulder at Jane. 'The results of the probationer's final exams are in envelopes on the duty desk.'

Jane hurried to the duty desk and, finding the envelope with her name on it, tucked it into her pocket and joined Moran and Edwards in the CID office.

Moran handed her a CID pocket book and said that while she was on attachment any arrests, interview notes, etc., were to be recorded in it. Jane felt honoured to be given the book. 'Thank you, sir,' she said.

'You're welcome. It would be best if you write the notes, then myself and Edwards can agree and countersign them from the point where we tackled the suspect. Edwards, help Jane, will you? I'll write up the notes from our perspective in the obo van.' He pointed to the kettle in the corner and asked Jane to make him a coffee, then left the room.

As Jane wrote up the arrest notes Edwards said he'd make the coffee. She took the results envelope out of her pocket, placed it on the table and stared at it. When Edwards asked why she wasn't opening it she replied that it wasn't because she thought she had failed, it was more that she was worried about getting a good mark. She decided she would open it when she got back to the section house later.

Edwards snatched the envelope from the table and Jane tried to grab it back, but he held it up high out of her reach. As soon as she backed off slightly he quickly opened the envelope, pulled out the paper inside and unfolded it.

'Bloody hell! You passed with flying colours ... ninety-four per cent! You little swot – you'll be a sergeant before we know it!'

Despite being annoyed by Edwards's antics, Jane was thrilled with the result. 'I've only just about completed my two years' probation, so I don't have enough service to sit the sergeant's exam.'

'Anyone with two years' service can apply to sit the exam, but you'll need the recommendation of a senior officer to do it.'

'I'm not really interested in uniform promotion at the moment, though. First and foremost I'd like to become a detective.'

'Well, your good work tonight will help, that's for sure,' Edwards replied, as Moran returned.

'You two should be getting on with your notes, not yapping. When you've finished bring them to me in my office, Tennison, and I'll check them.'

With Edwards's assistance it didn't take Jane long to write up the notes on her arrest. Edwards pointed out that although Harris had 'led' her through why she used the truncheon it was best, in accordance with the Met instruction book, that she say she aimed for the suspect's elbow, but he suddenly ducked and she unintentionally hit his head.

'Also, don't write anything about the kicks to his ribs or how he got the cut to his face, or the nosebleed. He fell while trying to escape, OK?'

Jane felt a sudden chill. It was as if she was back sitting at home with DCI Bradfield when he had asked her to tell a similar lie after DS Gibbs had assaulted the black drug dealer, Terrence O'Duncie, during the Julie Ann Collins murder investigation.

'You all right, Jane, you look a bit pale?'

'Yes, fine. I know the score about the injuries ... I've been down that road before. You know, I didn't actually see a knife in the suspect's hand?'

'He told you he had one, so what's the problem?'

'Did you see DI Moran find that knife?'

Edwards frowned.

'No ... but if he said he found it in the suspect's pocket then that's good enough for me. Hang on, are you suggesting he might have planted evidence?'

Jane could tell he was upset by her insinuation. 'No, not at all. If he did actually have a knife on him then I am even more worked up about what could have happened to me. I didn't realize he was suspected of the rape as well ... I thought it was just indecent assaults.'

'There is no strong evidence. The victim had been out celebrating her seventeenth birthday and was attacked from behind on her way home. She didn't see his face, but she did see a flick knife, and the suspect even said he had a knife and told her not to scream. DI Moran's been dealing with it and he wanted to see how the prisoner would react when told he was a suspect ... It certainly got him fired up, so you never know, Moran might be right.'

'Why didn't he mention that he suspected the same person to me before the operation?'

'He told me not to mention it to you as he didn't want to make you worried about being a decoy. In hindsight, after what happened tonight, maybe he should have told you ... But as I said he's got no evidence the same man committed the rape. It's just an assumption based on some similarities to the indecent assaults.'

Jane didn't reply. She read through her notes again and then went to Moran's office and handed him the pocket book to read. She watched with interest and observed that he had a habit of nodding as he was reading. She hoped it was a sign that he was agreeing with her notes.

He smiled and looked up at her. 'Good explanation for the use of a truncheon, but a defence lawyer will accuse you of intentionally aiming for the head. The bit where the suspect said "I've got a knife ... so keep your mouth shut, you fucking thieving whore" – is that, and the rest of what he said, word for word?'

'Yes, as far as I can recall, sir.'

Moran had a look of contempt in his eyes, but not for Jane. 'Nasty piece of work, isn't he? These notes are good, Tennison. Brief, yet concise and covering the relevant points about his attempted escape. You can elaborate further about the operation and how scared you were in your statement ... but do that tomorrow, as I'm sure you'll want to get off for some shut-eye soon.'

'Not really, I still feel wide awake.'

'That's the adrenalin still pumping after making such a good arrest,' he said, as he countersigned the arrest notes and handed the pocket book back to Jane.

'You'll need to get Harris to sign them as well, as he's the duty sergeant and he booked in the prisoner. Oh, and the rabbit fur jacket ... can you leave it on the chair there? It's evidence in a case, so I need to put it back in the property store.'

Jane removed the jacket. 'Thanks for letting me use it, sir, it kept me warm.' She placed it on the chair and left the room.

As she went downstairs to the front office she was surprised to see Sergeant Harris at the duty desk, though he was reading *The Sun* while drinking coffee and puffing away on a pipe. Jane asked him if he would sign her notes and handed him the pocket book.

'Oh, CID notebook now, is it? Uniform IRB not good enough for you now?' he said in a jovial manner that made Jane apprehensive, as it was unusual for him. 'Has DI Moran checked and countersigned these?'

'Yes, Sarge, and DC Edwards helped me write them.'

'Well, no doubt everything is tight as a duck's arse when it comes to the evidence of arrest.' He flicked briefly through the pages, stopping longer to read and take in the bit where Jane was initially attacked and threatened. He looked her in the eye and spoke softly.

'How are you feeling? D'you need to take a couple of days' leave?'

'No thanks, I'm fine, Sarge. Especially now Allard, or whoever he may be, is in a cell and going nowhere.'

'Well, that's mainly down to you, young lady. If you hadn't smacked him one he'd probably have got away before the cavalry turned up. So, what was your final exam result?'

'It was good, Sarge ... I got ninety-four per cent.'

'Congratulations.'

'Thank you, Sarge. Is it right you can sit the sergeant's exam after your probationary period is over?' she asked, because she thought that DC Edwards was wrong.

Harris cocked his head to one side, then gave her a cynical grin.

'Yes, if authorized by the Divisional Commander, who would of course seek the advice and wisdom of an experienced sergeant like me ... But even if by some miracle you were allowed to sit the exam, and passed, you can't be made sergeant until you have five years' service. Now, even though you have nearly finished your probation you will still be under my supervision and I will be responsible for your Annual Qualification Reports. I think you could say that your future regarding any promotion is in my hands.'

In the last year and a half Jane had learned not to let his demeaning attitude annoy her, as that was what he wanted. She wasn't the only person he belittled, it was just his nature. She smiled, refusing to be rattled by his attitude. 'I'm not really interested in promotion yet. I'd like to become a detective constable first.'

'Listen, Tennison, although your arrest tonight is commendable I doubt you would make the grade yet as you need more uniform experience. Being a decoy for one night is very different from being a detective and investigating major crime.'

Jane looked him in the eye. 'Will you be putting that in my final report?'

'I need to be frank with you. In my honest opinion, as your reporting sergeant, I feel you might be better suited to something like mounted branch or maybe even being a "black rat",' Harris said, referring to what many officers called the Traffic police.

Harris handed Jane the fingerprints he'd taken from the suspect and told her to give them to DI Moran. They would need to be passed on to C3 Fingerprint Bureau at the Yard for comparison to prints on record, especially those wanted for crime and outstanding marks at crime scenes, particularly sex crimes.

'D'you intend wearing that wig and looking like a Tom all night? Go and get cleaned up,' Harris said, and dismissed her with a wave of his hand.

Jane went to the ladies' locker room and removed the heavy makeup before returning to the CID office. She had been to DI Moran's office with the prints but he wasn't there. Edwards looked up from his paperwork.

'Moran went downstairs to put the rabbit fur jacket back in the property store, and release another prisoner he had in on suspicion of dishonest handling, then he was going home.'

Jane held up the set of fingerprints. 'Harris said I was to give him these prints so—'

DC Edwards interrupted and explained that Moran had already instructed the night duty SOCO to take the suspect's fingerprints to the Yard. Jane asked if he and DI Moran would be interviewing the suspect in the morning. Edwards replied that Moran had suggested she could sit in on the interview for experience, and he was to take the suspect's clothes and other evidence to the forensic lab. He explained that they might find fibres from the other victims' clothing on them, or vice versa. Jane said it would be a fantastic result if they found anything that linked him to the rape. Edwards said he hoped so too as there was no real evidence to charge him with the rape unless he admitted it.

'I doubt he'll ever do that ... seems he's going to fight this case all the way, and the only thing we've got on him so far is the attack on me.'

'Well, even if it is, Jane, there's no way out for him. Judges detest people who assault police officers so he'll get a long stretch for that alone.'

Edwards yawned and said he was going to get some sleep on the armchair in the snooker room, and go straight to the forensics lab first thing in the morning. He suggested to Jane that she should go and get some kip too, as Moran wanted to start interviewing the prisoner at 10 a.m. about the other assaults he was suspected of committing. Jane asked him what time she should come in. Edwards said Moran was an early bird and would probably be in at 8 a.m. to prep for the interview, so Jane said she would be in at 7.30 a.m. As she thanked Edwards for coming to her rescue he asked if she was OK, as it had been a tough night.

'I was pretty shaken up at the time, but I'm fine now.'

'Listen, you did a good job. I'd have been shitting myself if I were in your shoes ... even more so if he'd pulled the knife to my throat.'

Jane joked, 'He technically had two offensive weapons ...'

Edwards looked puzzled.

'The knife ... and his erect penis!'

Edwards laughed.

'You'd make a good detective, Jane ... Go on, bugger

off and get some kip. Don't walk back or you might get arrested as a Tom! Get the night shift to drop you off at the section house.'

Jane suddenly realized that she'd forgotten to tell Harris that DI Moran had said she could start her CID attachment as from now. She wished Moran was still there to tell Harris himself. She considered just not telling him, but knew that would probably annoy him even more. She headed back to the desk to find Harris.

Harris frowned at her. 'When I said get cleaned up, I meant the clothes as well . . . your attire is totally inappropriate in the station and far too revealing.'

Jane turned to leave. She was feeling really tired and certainly not in the mood for any of his caustic remarks.

'Hang on, hang on, Tennison . . . what did you want?'

'It was about my CID attachment, but it doesn't matter now.'

'DI Moran spoke with me while I released his other prisoner. I agreed with him about your extended attachment, even though it will leave me one short on late shift for the rest of the week. That was a good arrest and you'll learn a lot assisting Moran with the interview. I don't always see eye to eye with him, but he's a good and respected detective by all accounts. But for Chrissakes don't come in wearing all that ridiculous gear . . . and pull that glittering boob tube thingy up over your tits.'

'Thanks, Sarge.' Jane smiled, deliberately over-accentuating the action of adjusting her boob tube.

As Edwards had advised, Jane got a ride back to the section house. Once in her bedroom she removed her wig, revealing her own hair plastered to her head. Her eyes stung as she pulled off the false eyelashes. Her split lip was now very swollen on one side, and a vivid dark bruise had spread onto her cheek. She took a long shower, relishing the hot water as there was nobody else using the communal bathroom. She washed her hair and, returning to her room, gently applied some antiseptic cream to the cut on her lip. She was totally exhausted. Looking at her shocking reflection she said to herself, 'My God, I look as though I've just done two rounds in a boxing ring.'

She hesitated as she recalled Moran's rough treatment of the prisoner, and the way he had controlled the whole situation, including her. He was so different from Bradfield, the only other DCI she'd worked with, who had been a gentle giant. Moran behaved like a street fighter and Jane was unsure if she was impressed by that or not.

It was 2 a.m. by the time she actually got into bed, and she'd have to get up in four hours. Lying curled on her side she found it hard to stop her brain churning over the events of the night.

She went over and over in her mind the sort of questions they might ask the suspect. She realized he would probably deny everything, but knew he would go down for a few years for the attack on her. Despite her bruised face and swollen lip, she had to admit that she had enjoyed the evening's events. The rush of adrenalin made up for the fear of being attacked and she'd liked being part of the team. Now, more than ever, Jane was determined to join the CID.

CHAPTER THREE

Feeling nauseous from lack of sleep Jane went to the canteen and got a strong black coffee and a bacon sandwich, which she carried to the CID office. The office was empty, so she sat at DC Edwards's desk and ate her breakfast.

'That looks good.' Glancing up, she saw a dapper-looking DI Moran coming out of his office.

'Oh sorry, sir, I didn't mean to be late on parade.'

'You're not ... I'm early. And we don't have parades in the CID, just nine to five and two to ten shifts, and a rotation of one DS and a DC on a week's night shift. We've had some good news ... Fingerprint Bureau got a match for the prisoner ... he's not John Allard, he's Peter Allard, with one previous conviction for ABH in his late teens, in a pub fight. The address on his arrest sheet from back then is just up the road, in Stoke Newington. But his name isn't shown on the current Voters' Register.'

'That's good that you got him identified, sir. Maybe he'll tell us where he lives now?'

'I doubt it, there might be evidence at his address that he doesn't want us to find. So that's why I want you to visit the last known address for Peter Allard to see if the current owners knew anything about him, or where he moved to.' Moran handed her a bit of paper with Allard's details and his last known address.

'Will that be before or after the interview, sir?'

'Before. If we get something positive then we can use it to put him under pressure. In the meantime, I've got a meeting with DCS Metcalf about Allard's arrest.'

Jane didn't want to ask Moran if he was going to tell Metcalf that she had been the arresting officer. She hoped he would as it would help when it came to asking him about joining the CID.

Moran handed Jane the log book and keys for one of the CID cars. 'I haven't been given the five-week basic driving course yet, so I'm not authorized to drive police vehicles,' she said.

'OK, well, go and see if you can get a lift in a panda car, or go by bus.'

Jane hurriedly finished her coffee and went to the comms room to book out a radio and ask about getting a lift to Stoke Newington. There were only two panda cars on patrol, and they were both dealing with incidents, so she caught the bus to Stoke Newington High Street and walked the rest of the way to Kynaston Road, a quiet street lined with terraced houses built after the war. After repeatedly knocking on the door of number 23 and getting no answer, Jane felt it had been a wasted journey. She posted a note through the letterbox for the occupier, giving a phone number, and asking them to contact her at Hackney CID regarding a previous occupant of the premises. Before leaving she decided to see if any of the neighbours were in. An elderly lady answered the door of one of the small terraced houses and, after she had seen her warrant card, invited Jane in.

The narrow hall was lined with cat litter trays. The carpet looked as if it hadn't been vacuumed for years, and was thick with balls of cat fur. Mrs Walker introduced herself and asked Jane if she liked cats. There was little Jane could say. The pungent smell of moggies was overpowering in the hall, but in the living room it was almost suffocating. There were felines perched on every possible surface, even the piano keys.

Jane took out her notebook and perched perilously on the arm of a cat-clawed sofa. Mrs Walker was standing next to a small, tiled fireplace. On the mantelpiece was an array of cheaply framed photographs of cats.

'Thank you for letting me in, Mrs Walker. I just have a few questions – nothing serious.'

'That's OK, dear, you ask away, and call me Eadie.'

'Did you know the Allard family, Mrs Walker?'

'Eadie ... Yes, I knew them very well. There was John and Hilda and their children Peter and Cherrie. The daughter had something wrong with her. I used to babysit when they were nippers.'

'Do the family still live there?'

'No, they moved out at least twelve, or more, years ago. The parents divorced and sold up ... I don't know where they went, or where the children moved to.'

'Mrs Wal ... I mean Eadie, do you know what job Peter did?'

'Oh, he was about eighteen when they left. He was

very nice and bought me some flowers when he came
to say goodbye. He was such a lovely handsome boy.
I was so surprised when he got in a bit of bother for
punching a lad in a pub, but his mum and dad said it
was in self-defence. He used to do all kinds of different
jobs, anything so he could pay his way really. I remember laughing when he was a nipper as I'd ask what he
wanted to be when he grew up and he said that he
wanted to be a cabbie, like his dad. He loved going out
with his dad in the taxi. I think the divorce upset him . . .
but that's life for ya, innit?'

'Thank you . . . you've been very helpful.'

'That's all right, love. You get to my age an' yer glad
of a bit of company. Is Peter in some kind of trouble?'

'No, we just need to trace him about something.
Thank you for your time.'

Jane left the house and, turning left at the end of the
street, called into Stoke Newington Police Station, which
was a ten-minute walk away, unaware that the back
of her jacket and skirt were covered in cat hairs. She
showed her warrant card to a PC at the front counter
and asked if she could use a phone to make an urgent
call regarding an investigation she was carrying out for
DI Moran of Hackney CID. The officer showed her the
way to the PCs' writing room and said she could use the
phone in there. Jane called the Public Carriage Office at
Penton Street, Islington and asked if they had a licensed
cab driver under the name of Peter Allard. The lady at
the cab office replied that she was very busy, but would
do her best to look in their card index within the next
hour. Jane gave her the phone number of the comms

room at Hackney and asked her to leave the details with them.

Jane then spoke to Hackney and explained that she was expecting an important call from the Public Carriage Office and asked if they could radio the result straight through to her when it came. Satisfied that she'd covered all bases, she thanked the PC at the front counter and caught the bus back to Hackney, but rather than going straight to the station she decided to return to the scene where she had been attacked, as she wanted to have a proper look at it in daylight.

It was hard to get a clear view from the spot where Allard pounced on her, because of the trees. But from what she could see there were no black cabs parked up in London Fields' east or west side. Jane decided to walk down Martello Street, following the path of the main railway line above it, as it had quiet side roads that ran underneath the arches.

As she turned left into Lamb Lane Jane noticed a black cab parked up by the junction with Mentmore Terrace. She stopped to take a closer look and jotted down the licence number on the rear of the cab. As she was doing so a man dressed in greasy overalls, carrying a ratchet spanner, approached her.

'Is there a problem?'

'No, I'm just checking something . . . is this your cab?'

'Why do you want to know?' he asked, with an inquisitive stare.

Jane had totally forgotten she was in plain clothes and quickly took her warrant card out to show the man.

'I'm a mechanic at the garage. This cab is one we're

repairing,' he explained politely, pointing to the large dent and scratches above the rear offside wheel arch.

It transpired that around the corner in Mentmore Terrace, out of Jane's view, there was a cab repair garage with a number of taxis parked up that were booked in for mechanical or bodywork repairs. Wondering if any of the parked up cabs weren't there to be repaired Jane asked if the mechanic had a record of which cabs he was working on. The mechanic led her into the office and handed her a list attached to a clipboard. The list had the black cab licence numbers of all the vehicles that were being booked in at the garage. He explained that the licence plate was on the rear boot, below the index plate. Jane didn't want to tell him that she already knew this, and began checking the cabs in the road until she discovered one that was not on the list.

With a mounting sense of excitement, Jane radioed through to the station. The information she was waiting for had been received but the comms operator had been busy and had forgotten to contact her. According to records at the PCO a Peter Allard was a registered cab driver and his licence number was 7614, with an address in Walthamstow. Jane told the comms officer that the licence number matched a cab she was looking at and that the owner, Peter Allard, was currently in custody at Hackney.

'Allard had a car key on him which was put in the prisoner's property locker in the charge room. Can you get the key booked out and brought down to me so I can see if it fits the cab, and inform DI Moran? Over.'

'I'll get DI Moran's approval first. He may want to

send a class one driver down with the key to bring the suspect vehicle to the station yard.'

Jane waited anxiously, pacing the pavement next to the parked cab, but it wasn't long before the reply came that DI Moran wanted the vehicle brought to the station for examination by a SOCO. The comms officer told her that as soon as the area car driver had finished the call he was on he'd collect Allard's car key and be with her as quickly as he could.

Jane kept checking her watch every five minutes. Nearly half an hour had passed and she was anxious to get back to the station, fearing that DI Moran may start interviewing Peter Allard with another detective. Eventually an officer arrived. The key fitted and he drove the cab to Hackney while Jane was driven back to the station in a patrol car. She hurried to the CID office and brought Moran up to speed with the latest developments.

'Bloody good work, Tennison. Job well done ... but I should have been informed about the developments as soon as you spoke with the Allards' old neighbour.' He paused. 'I'm not sure if you realize, but you've got cat hairs all over the back of your suit ...'

'Sorry, sir.' Jane brushed self-consciously at the fluff covering her skirt.

Having just returned from the lab DC Edwards joined them and reported that Paul Lawrence, the lab liaison sergeant, would let Moran know as soon as they got any positive results.

'He's the best lab sergeant in the force. Brilliant eye for detail, so we're lucky to have him working on this for us,' Moran said as he walked out.

Jane nodded in agreement. 'DCI Bradfield said the same thing about him.' The recollection of Bradfield filled her with momentary pain.

Edwards sensed her reaction and patted Jane's shoulder gently, which she acknowledged with a small smile.

'It's been hard to adjust to working alongside someone like Moran ... he's very different. He doesn't play rugby ... we all used to be in the police rugby team and have a few jars afterwards, and a laugh. Have you seen Spencer Gibbs at all?'

Jane shook her head.

'No, I haven't.'

'For the first few months after it happened the station was so quiet ... Nobody wanted to talk about it. Gibbs used to be singing in the showers all the time, and playing with his rock band ... I've phoned him a few times, and written to him, but I've had nothing back.'

'I remember you emulating him, the way you used to slap the suspects around.'

'Yeah ... yeah ... Gibbs was a bit of a naughty boy, but he was a good cop. It's not the done thing now. I leave that to the boss.'

Moran walked back in.

'Leave what to the boss, Edwards?'

'Er, to get the forensic results from DS Lawrence, sir.'

'Bollocks to that. You two, get SOCO and go over that cab with a fine tooth comb. While you're doing that I'm going to type up a search warrant for the suspect's address, and I want you, Edwards, to take it to the magistrate for approval and signature.'

'Sorry, guv . . . Do you want me to do the cab over, or go to the magistrate?'

'For Chrissakes, Brian, get on and do both of them!'

The cab at the station yard was as clean as a whistle inside, but they found a fresh shirt and jeans in a plastic bag on the back seat. Underneath the driver's seat was a cabbie's cash bag with money in it, and in the glove compartment was a wallet containing money and a photograph of two young children with a pretty, dark-haired oriental woman. There was also a set of house keys and a cab driver's green neck tag, with a licence number on it that matched the one they had been given by the PCO for Peter Allard. Jane and Edwards left the SOCO to take fibre tapings from the driver's seat, although he said that he didn't hold out much hope as the vehicle had obviously been carefully cleaned.

On their return to the station they updated Moran and showed him what they had recovered from the cab. Moran suspected that Allard had probably been using the cab as a cover to travel to and from the scenes of his attacks, on the basis that police officers rarely, if ever, stop black cabs. He decided that he wanted to interview Allard before they visited his home address, which they now knew was 45 Grove Road, Walthamstow. Jane asked Moran if he thought the suspect would keep silent as he knew none of the victims could identify him because he wore a stocking mask.

'Admittedly with the others there is only circumstantial evidence due to the similarity in the attacks . . . but now I've got some leverage on him.'

'What leverage, sir?' Jane asked.

'You'll find out during the interview, darlin' ... so let's get cracking.'

Jane and DC Edwards went down the stone-flagged corridor to the basement level where the cells were situated. The duty officer unlocked Allard's cell. Allard seemed very depressed and was unable to make eye contact, especially with Jane. As he held his wrists out to the duty officer to be handcuffed he turned and, for the first time, looked directly at Jane. He spoke softly.

'I am so sorry for what I did ... I feel very ashamed ...'

Surprised, Jane nodded. Edwards led Allard out of his cell, along the corridor and up the narrow concrete steps to DI Moran's office on the first floor.

Moran got straight to the point and asked Allard if he was responsible for the recent spate of indecent assaults in London Fields and Victoria Park. Allard remained head bowed and flatly denied involvement in any assaults of any kind, even the one on 'her', he stated, pointing to Jane. He claimed that he heard the detectives saying at the time that they didn't see what had happened between him and the woman because their view was blocked by the trees.

Jane couldn't believe what she was hearing. Allard had just apologized to her, and now here he was shamefacedly denying it to Moran. She watched, incredulous, as he insisted that Jane was lying.

Allard stated that the male detectives believed her lie, and that they had planted a knife on him. Moran sat back and stared into Allard's dark, angry eyes.

'Come on, we both know you're lying, John. Oh sorry, forgive me ... I mean Peter ... It is Peter Allard I'm speaking to, isn't it?'

The use of his proper name caused a visible nervous twitch in Allard's face. Moran leaned across the table.

'Bet you're wondering what else we know about you, Peter?'

Allard shook his head and stupidly denied that was his name. Moran laughed.

'Peter, you're digging a bigger hole for yourself – your prints have been matched to a set held at the Yard from your previous arrest for ABH during a pub fight. You hit a young woman, didn't you?'

Allard once again demanded a phone call. Moran casually remarked that he wasn't allowed to call anyone until he admitted his true identity and told them where he lived. Then he could call whoever he liked. Allard looked worried as Moran pulled the green licence tag from his pocket and started to swing it like a pendulum in front of Allard.

'We found this in a black cab that was parked up by London Fields, which is currently being forensically examined in our yard. This tag, and the licence number on the cab, are both registered to you.'

Allard hung his head. Moran pressed on.

'WPC Tennison here, who you state is a liar, did a little digging ... she even went to your old home address and spoke to a neighbour who remembered you, as well as your dad, who was also a cab driver. WPC Tennison checked with the Public Carriage Office and obtained your home address in Walthamstow. Take a look at this photograph, Peter ... nice-looking woman and two kids ... look at it. Chinese, is she?'

Allard pressed back in his chair.

'What ... you married to a slitty eyed chinky woman, are you?'

Allard was now shaking. 'I'm not married, I don't have kids, and my name is *John.*'

Moran slapped the desk hard with the flat of his hand. 'Start telling the truth ... the more you lie, the worse it gets. There's no way out for the attack on WPC Tennison – you'll be going to prison.'

Allard said nothing. Moran swung around in his chair, then rocked back and forth for a moment before continuing.

'You gave a false name because you needed time to think about what you were going to tell your chinky girlfriend. In fact, the reason you asked to make a phone call, before we found out who you really were, was not to contact a solicitor but to call your chinky woman with a fabricated story.'

'She's not Chinese ...! She's Filipino!'

'Ahhhh, Filipino eh? Are these two kids yours?'

'Yes ... And her name is Marie. I want to tell her the truth before you bastards lie about me to her. She'll know I've been fitted up!'

'Fitted up? Look what you did to WPC Tennison's face!' Moran exclaimed, pointing to Jane.

She stared towards Allard as he lowered his head. His fists were clenched and Jane could feel the animosity and rage in him as he fought to maintain control.

'At last we get the revelation that Marie is your wife, and you are obviously Peter Allard? Well, for me it's all a bit late in the day ... you've taken the piss, Peter. So, when we execute our search warrant at your home WPC Tennison will be telling your wife that you are a pervert, and that you attacked her and split her lip. Then there's all the other defenceless women whose lives are in a mess because of what you did to them.'

Allard started to open and close his tight balled fists and tilted his head sideways to look towards Jane. He stared at her, his eyes shifting as if unable to recognize her as the woman he had assaulted.

'You can deny everything at the Old Bailey if you want, but no jury in the world will believe you over us. If you're found guilty you will go down for a long time, but for how long is in your hands. Admitting all the indecent assault offences will be a plus for you in the judge's eyes, and I'll even put in a good word about how you helped us before he sentences you.'

'I keep telling you, I've got nothing to admit to—'

Moran pushed the picture of Marie and the children closer to Allard.

'Take a good look at your children, because you won't be seeing them for a long time ... probably not even after you're eventually released. Not once your wife sees you for the pervert that you really are. But, if you admit all your crimes I may not have to tell her every sickening detail about what you did. I might even let her visit you in the cells ...'

There was a long pause. Moran glanced towards Jane who was making copious notes. He picked up the photograph and tapped the desk with the edge of it, waiting. Eventually Allard sighed and slowly looked up.

'This is the God's honest truth. I used my dad's first name cos he'd passed away and had never been in any trouble. The ABH on the woman in the pub was years ago, and I only pushed her but she fell and cut her head on a table. Marie doesn't know about it, and I didn't want her to be hurt by the police lies about the ABH, like my parents were. I never did anything wrong ... I've been stitched up, and you can't make me admit to something that I haven't done.'

'Tell me what a cab driver was doing up a tree in London Fields in the middle of the night?'

Allard pointed to Jane. 'She made that up ... you even said yourself that she didn't see me. I felt ill, so I parked my cab and went for a walk. She approached me and asked if I wanted sex. She started screaming and then you lot turned up and kicked the shit out of me, for nothing.'

'Fine, you keep on lying ... but your clothing and the stocking mask have gone to forensics and will be checked to see if any of the fibres on them match those recovered from the clothing of the other indecent assault victims ... and the young girl who was raped.'

'I want to make a phone call, I want to speak with a solicitor!' Allard's voice was raw and edgy.

Annoyed that Allard wouldn't break, Moran ordered him to be taken back down to the cells. Two uniform officers came to escort him, and as he walked out he turned and stared at Jane.

'Why are you doing this to me? Why are you lying?' Allard had a pitiful expression on his face, as his dark eyes held hers for a moment, then he turned away as he was escorted out of Moran's office. Jane asked if she really was going to be the one to tell Allard's wife what happened. Moran sighed and said that if Allard had confessed she would have been, but as he hadn't been broken yet, Moran would tell Allard's wife and when she had a meltdown Jane could talk to her while they searched the house. He also remarked that he wouldn't be surprised if the wife had been knocked about and, as so often happens in domestic violence cases, she was probably too scared to report it and was in self-denial.

Jane wondered why, during the interview, Moran never asked Allard any direct questions about the rape of the teenage girl. She approached the question from a more discreet angle.

'If you'll be questioning Allard in more detail about the rape, sir, could I sit in again?'

'We'll see. I was hoping he'd confess to the indecent assaults, then I could use the similar facts in each case to press him further about the rape, and maybe even charge him with it. Though it would be a bit of a wing and a prayer if it got to trial.'

Moran instructed Jane to type up the report of the interview, after which she was to accompany him and Edwards on the search of Allard's home.

CHAPTER FOUR

Jane struck the typewriter keys angrily as she typed up her report recording Allard's refusal to admit his assault against her. Her stomach rumbled as she hadn't had time for lunch, and the lack of sleep the previous night was catching up with her, but as she detailed Allard's accusation that she was the one lying, she didn't feel so tired any more. Instead she couldn't wait to go on the search to his house and prove he was guilty of the crimes he wouldn't admit. Jane stood up and was just rolling the report out of the typewriter when DI Moran and DC Edwards stopped by the incident room. Moran gestured to her.

'Get your coat, Tennison, we've got a search warrant for Allard's house. That's the good news. The bad news is that it's quite a trek to bloody Walthamstow.'

Before Jane could reply Moran and Edwards had continued down the corridor. Jane looked longingly at the sandwich and cup of coffee on her desk. She was ravenous, so she grabbed the sandwich in one hand, and her hat and coat in the other. As Harris passed the doorway, he looked in.

'You'd better not think about eating that in the patrol car, Tennison ...'

Jane sighed and hurriedly took a few large bites of her sandwich before putting the remainder of it back on the plate on her desk, and rushing out to the yard to join Moran and Edwards.

The Allards' home in Walthamstow was a privately owned, three-bedroom semi-detached house. It had a rather neglected front garden, which appeared to be the norm in that street. Moran parked the car and got out, followed by Jane, Edwards and the SOCO. Moran banged on the front door, which was answered by a petite, attractive Asian woman.

'I'm DI Moran, are you Marie Allard?'

'Yes, I am.' The woman looked frightened. 'Oh my God! Has something happened to Peter? He not come home and I been worried sick ...'

Moran interrupted, saying that her husband had been arrested and that he had a warrant to search the premises. He handed her a copy of the warrant as he pushed the door open and walked in, followed by the three others.

The inside of the premises was well kept, with the usual children's toys scattered about. The hall had parquet flooring, with a floral printed runner that continued up the stairs. The bannisters were painted white and large framed pictures of the Allard children hung on the white walls. The children, aged eight and five, were out in the garden playing with an older woman. Marie pointed to the living room and asked them to go in. Moran went first, followed by Jane. Edwards and the SOCO remained in the hall. The room had a distinct oriental influence, with bamboo furniture, various fake potted plants, and a print of Vladimir Tretchikoff's 'Chinese Girl'. There was a pale green rug, and on the windowsill in the corner was a gaudy statue of the Virgin Mary standing next to a cheap vase containing a velvet rose. Moran asked Marie to sit down.

He didn't waste time and explained that her husband had been arrested for a number of sexual assaults and rape. Marie couldn't believe what she was hearing, shaking her head in disbelief.

'Do you understand English, Mrs Allard? You're Filipino, aren't you?'

Marie looked affronted at Moran's questions and replied curtly.

'Yes, course I understand you ... I already spoken to you. I just in shock. My husband is gentle man and never hurt me or my children.'

Moran pointed to Jane and told Marie that her 'gentle' husband had attacked and molested WPC Tennison, threatened to cut her throat with a knife and punched her in the face. Marie looked shocked. She couldn't believe what she was hearing and kept repeating, 'No ... you wrong, you wrong ... it not true.' Moran continued and told her that if he hadn't been stopped he would have raped WPC Tennison as, it was suspected, he had done on a previous occasion to a teenage girl.

Marie was shaking uncontrollably. Her dark curly hair had a low fringe and she kept touching her forehead and tugging at a stray curl. She looked at Jane, her eyes welling up with tears, as if wanting her to say it wasn't true.

Jane was surprised by Moran's directness towards Marie. It was as if he'd had enough of being messed around by Peter Allard and was determined to get to the truth, by whatever means necessary.

Jane touched her cut lip and spoke softly. 'It is true, Mrs Allard. He did this to me, and he had a knife in his possession. I believed at the time that he would have raped me, but for my colleagues' intervention.'

Marie was clearly in a state of shock and started to cry. At that moment the children rushed in, stopping when they saw their mother. Marie tried to smile and assured them that she was fine and had just had a bit of bad news.

'I'm sorry, children, come here.' Hilda Allard followed the children into the room. Seeing Marie's distress she, like her daughter-in-law, immediately thought something had happened to her son, Peter. Moran was as blunt with her as he had been with Marie. He explained that he would need to search the house, including the children's bedroom, and it would be best if their gran took them out for a walk. Hilda flatly refused and insisted that she wanted to be with her daughter-in-law. She was quite overweight with tight permed grey hair and big raw hands. Marie was struggling to control her emotions, but took a deep breath and turned to her mother-in-law.

'It OK, Hilda, I be OK ... Maybe it best if you take children to your place, and I call you later.'

Hilda was hesitant but eventually agreed. After

removing her apron and collecting her handbag she left the house with the children. Moran waited until the front door closed behind them before asking Marie, in a softer tone than before, if her husband had ever abused her. Marie shook her head, her wide dark eyes blinking rapidly.

'No! Never! We been married for ten years ...'

Moran sat beside Marie and kept his voice quiet. 'Is it all right if I call you Marie?' She nodded and he continued.

'Women who are abused, or frightened of their husbands, are often in denial and say nothing because of fear of further violence. Your husband committed a violent sexual assault last night, and similarly other assaults he is suspected of, as well as a rape. These were all committed late in the evening, between ten and midnight. Were you never concerned about what Peter was doing out late at night?'

'He drive a cab and always work evening shifts, some time until early hours. Then he can be with the children in the day. I only worried this morning when he not come home.'

Moran glanced at Jane and, turning back to Marie, asked if she had a normal, healthy, sexual relationship with her husband. Marie looked offended and shook her head.

'My sex life not to do with you.'

Moran shrugged his shoulders. 'Well, it can't have been that great if he had to go out and attack other women.'

Marie became tight lipped and continued to tug at

her hair, winding the strands through her fingers in an almost obsessive manner. Moran got up from the sofa, walked over to Jane and stood with his back to Marie. Leaning forward, in a hushed voice, he said to her, 'I think she's hiding something . . . I want you to stay with her and see if you can get her to open up. I'll go and search upstairs with Edwards and the SOCO.'

'Yes, sir.'

She felt that Moran had been a bit harsh on Marie as she may have been totally unaware of what her husband was like outside his home life. It seemed unlikely to Jane, by the state Marie was in, that she would deliberately portray a loving family façade to protect her husband. When the others had left the room Jane sat down beside her, saying softly that the news must be an awful shock for her and asking if she would like a cup of tea or coffee. Marie shook her head, and without looking at Jane asked if her husband really had attacked her.

Jane hesitated before answering.

'Yes, he did . . . but my split lip happened while he was trying to escape, so it may have been accidental . . .'

'I can't believe it! He never been violent towards me . . . never in all our time together. We've known each other since we were teenagers.'

'So are you saying that your husband has never hit you?'

'Never! I keep telling you, he is very gentle, kind, man. And he take care of us, here in our nice house.'

'Do you own this house?'

'No, we rent it. We been here five years. Before that we had very nice house in Maidstone.'

'I'm so sorry but I need to ask you some embarrassing questions about your sex life.'

Marie began to frantically twist the curl on her forehead between her fingers. Without looking at Jane she asked if their discussion was confidential and just between the two of them.

'Yes, Marie, it is completely confidential.'

Jane felt bad knowing that she would later have to report whatever Marie told her to DI Moran.

Marie took a deep breath, stopped nervously twisting her hair and looked at Jane.

'He always been gentle in bed, and even though we not have sex recently, he never been pushy or forced himself on me. He would never do that ... he always very thoughtful, even now when ...' She stopped and Jane sensed she was holding back about something.

'What did you mean when you said you hadn't had sex recently?' Jane asked gently.

Marie continued, saying that it had been about six months. She had an ovarian cyst, which made sex very painful, and she was waiting for an operation on the NHS.

Jane sympathized.

'I am so sorry, Marie. I had an aunt with the same problem, and I remember she said it was extremely painful. So if you couldn't have sexual intercourse in the normal way, did you try any other methods?'

Marie blushed and bowed her head, deeply embarrassed as she continued explaining that although they couldn't have full sex she regularly pleasured her husband with masturbation and oral sex.

'He want me to try anal sex but it hurt too much, so he stopped and he never ask again. You see what I mean about him being kind and gentle?'

'And you were never suspicious when he was out late at night?'

'No, never. He sometimes call me three or four times to make sure I am OK.'

'Thank you for your honesty, Marie.'

Marie seemed relieved to have discussed such personal matters, and was calmer now. 'Please, tell me what my husband has done? I can't believe it.'

'I'm afraid I can't go into the details of the investigation.'

'Please ... I need to know, to try and make sense ... Why you here? Why you searching my home?'

'All I can tell you, Marie, is that your husband is adamant he didn't commit any indecent assaults or rape ... but he did attack me.'

Marie looked perplexed. 'If he didn't do them, then why he attack you?'

'I don't know ... only he can answer that. You need to ask him yourself, Marie. They might let you speak to him if you visit the station later. Here's my contact information at the station – please call me if you have any questions or want to tell me anything else.'

Jane scribbled her details onto a clean page in her notebook, which she then tore out and gave to Marie.

As Marie put the folded note into her pocket DI Moran walked back into the room. 'We've searched yours and the children's bedrooms, but why is the third bedroom locked?'

'My husband uses it as a gym, he didn't want the children going there and hurting themselves on the equipment.'

'Do you have the key?'

'I don't know where he keeps it.'

'Isn't that a bit strange? That your husband wouldn't tell you where the key was?'

'I don't know, not really.' Marie shrugged.

Moran looked at her hard, then left the room to go back upstairs.

Jane noticed that Marie had become very tense, her hands clenched at her side. Suddenly there was a loud crashing sound from upstairs as the officers kicked open the locked door. Marie was on her feet in an instant, running up the stairs and shouting at them to stop ruining her house. Jane followed to try to calm her down. The bedroom door had partially come away from its hinges and the lock lay on the floor among splinters of wood. Inside the small room was a five-foot-high thick wooden pole with bits of rounded twelve-inch wooden handles sticking out of it. Two rectangular leather bags of sand were screwed into the wall and hanging above them was a collection of martial arts swords, and two wooden sticks connected at one end by a short chain. On another wall were pictures of Bruce Lee and other martial arts posters from the film *Enter the Dragon*.

DC Edwards was looking around the room.

'What the fuck is all this?' He pointed to the wooden figure in the middle of the room.

The SOCO grinned. 'That's a Wing Chun dummy, for

practising martial arts. Some of the indentation marks on it are from a knife. The wooden things on a chain are nunchucks, and the sand bags are for karate punching.'

Moran and Edwards looked at each other, bemused.

'You into all this martial arts crap then?' Moran asked.

The SOCO shrugged. 'Not really ... I just like watching martial arts films. If your man uses this sort of gear a lot, then his hands and feet are lethal weapons.'

Moran looked at Marie who was hovering in the doorway.

'Does he spend much time in here?'

She nodded, saying that her husband practised martial arts and used the equipment regularly.

'He a keep fit fanatic, and he not even drink.'

Moran looked inside the wardrobe. There was a small travel suitcase on a shelf. He pulled it down and found that it was locked. He turned to Marie.

'I don't suppose you know where the key to this is either?'

Before she could answer he grabbed one of the large knives from the wall and cut the material on top of the case open, ripping it back to expose the contents.

Inside the travel case were a number of pornographic magazines, together with a clear plastic bag containing a quantity of pills. Concealed in the middle of the magazines were two folding pocket knives. Moran hadn't seen this type of knife before, and looked at Edwards while he held them up. The SOCO interjected.

'They're called balisongs, guv, originating from the Philippines and used in martial arts. I'd guess the pills are steroids of some sort. They're not illegal, though, a lot of body builders use them and—'

Moran interrupted him. 'Yes, I know what steroids are, thank you ... they also affect a man's sex drive and make them violent. All makes sense as far as our suspect is concerned.'

Edwards picked up one of the magazines and flicked through it, hastily dropping it back in the case.

'Ugh, some of the pages are stuck together!'

Moran had seen enough and instructed the SOCO to bag up the weapons and suitcase with its contents as evidence. He looked at Jane and, not caring that Marie was still within earshot, asked about their discussion about her sex life. Marie looked forlornly at Jane, hoping that she wouldn't reveal details about the private conversation they'd had. Moran had put Jane on the spot, and she hesitated, looking at Marie as he became impatient for an answer.

'Come on, out with it!'

Jane tapped Moran's elbow.

'Sir, could I possibly have a word with you in private?'

'What?'

'Marie is incredibly shy, but she has admitted that they have been unable to have sexual intercourse for some time.'

Moran looked quizzically at Jane.

'For Chrissakes, Tennison! She's going to be cross-examined in court if she gives evidence for the defence. If she can't tell me about it, you tell me.'

Jane looked at Marie regretfully, sad that she was having to breach her confidence so openly.

She went on to tell Moran about Marie's ovarian cyst, how she pleasured her husband, and that he'd asked her for anal sex. Moran gestured towards one of the hard-core magazines entitled *Anal Pleasures* and, holding it up sarcastically, said that it was obvious where her husband got that idea from. An embarrassed and tearful Marie looked at Jane with disgust, saying that if they'd finished searching they could get out of her house. By now Moran had really lost his patience and held up more of the magazines in front of her.

'You see the sort of filth that your husband likes to look at and wank over, Mrs Allard ... just because you can't satisfy him? He takes these pills and gets so worked up he prowls the streets in a mask then molests and rapes defenceless young women. I find it hard to believe you didn't suspect something was wrong.'

Marie began sobbing and demanded that they get out of the house.

'I not want you here any more ... You bad people ... You been in my children's bedroom.'

In the car Moran was jubilant at what they had uncovered. Although circumstantial, the porn maga-zines and the steroid pills were all good enough evidence to show Allard's state of mind and propensity to commit sexual assaults. Jane was quiet and Moran asked her what the problem was.

'I'm sorry but I just felt for Mrs Allard. In effect she is an innocent victim. I mean, maybe at one time her husband was a good man.'

'Grow up! That's utter bollocks! There have probably been more sexual assaults carried out by him in and around London that we don't know about. Indecent assault wasn't enough for him so he went on to rape, and if we hadn't caught him when we did there would have been more rapes and probably a murder committed by him as well. Mrs Allard's state of mind is not your problem. Her husband brought this on himself and if she at any point suspected something was amiss she should have told someone. Like that tough-looking mother-in-law ... judging by the size of her hands I wouldn't be surprised if she could give someone a walloping.'

It was nearly 4 p.m. when they returned to the station.

'You both head up to the canteen and get something to eat while you write up your notes. I'll join you after I've booked in the property we seized from Allard's house,' DI Moran instructed DC Edwards and Jane.

Sergeant Harris was at his desk in the front office and on seeing Moran he mentioned, 'Allard has been asking to speak with a solicitor.'

'I want to do a further interview first, before getting a solicitor involved,' Moran replied as they walked together through to the charge room.

'But now we know Allard's identity and address he should legally be allowed to consult with a solicitor,' Harris pushed.

'I know the rules, Sergeant Harris, but with the evidence I found at Allard's house, and what his wife told us, I reckon I can get him to confess to all the indecent assaults ... and the rape. A solicitor is just going to tell him to say nothing.'

'I'll stick my neck out if you think you can get him

to roll over. I'll mark up on his sheet that he hasn't requested a solicitor. He's allowed one phone call so let me tell him that after the search of his house his wife was in a hell of a state and he should phone her. You never know, it might work in your favour and get him to finally tell the truth.'

Moran was on a high so he told Harris to go ahead, as after what he'd said to Allard's wife she probably thought her precious husband was now the scum of the earth. He also hoped that her emotional distress would make Allard feel at his lowest ebb, and that would make it easier to break him during an interview.

Moran put the small travelling case down on the charge room table, opened it up and showed Harris the pornographic magazines, balisong knives and the tablets. Harris picked up a magazine and flicked through it, pausing here and there to take a good look. Moran asked Harris if he'd mind listing the property as he wanted to get some food in his stomach before the second interview with Allard. Harris nodded and asked how Tennison was. Moran shrugged.

'She needs to toughen up a bit.'

Surprised by Moran's comment Harris remarked, 'Jane must have thought she was going to be raped, though.'

'No, not about that ... she was terrific last night. But her attitude with Mrs Allard ... she was a bit soft and kind of pussy-footed around with the woman. I think she needs to be tougher in those kind of situations and not get emotionally involved.'

'You know Tennison has expressed an interest in

joining the CID, but I don't think she's ready for it yet. What do you think?' Harris asked.

'In some ways I agree. She's obviously not afraid of the rough end of the job, but investigative-wise she's got a lot to learn yet, which could make her a liability in certain situations.'

Harris didn't need to say anything. He knew what Moran meant by 'certain situations' and finding missing evidence if and when necessary. Moran went up to the canteen, leaving Harris checking over the items from the suitcase. It was quite a lengthy process as he was spending time studying the porno magazines, and paying even more attention to the fitness and body building magazines.

DS Lawrence had called from the lab to say that they had found fibres from the suspect's clothes on two of the indecent assault victims, but nothing, as yet, connecting him to the rape. Moran, accompanied by Jane, got ready to re-interview Allard. Harris informed them that Allard had phoned his wife and had spoken with her for at least ten minutes, and appeared to be quite distressed both during and after the call. Harris had tried to listen in but it was difficult as he was booking in a noisy drunk who kept singing 'Underneath the Arches' at the top of his voice. However, Harris said that he thought Allard may have confessed to his wife, and most surprisingly he hadn't asked for a solicitor after the call.

Moran booked out the property seized from the martial arts room for the interview. A clearly subdued Allard was brought up from the cells and taken to Moran's office.

Moran opened the interview by getting right to the point. 'Have you changed your mind and decided to finally tell the truth and admit these assaults?'

'Why were you so horrible to my wife?'

'You've no one but yourself to blame for this situation. If you had admitted the offences before we went to your house then things may have been different,' Moran calmly responded.

The suitcase was then placed on the desk in front of Allard.

'Do the porn magazines and the two martial arts knives belong to you?'

'Yeah. I like to keep fit by training at Wing Chun. I use the balisong knives and nunchucks on the wooden dummy I have in the spare room.'

Moran glanced at Jane as she made notes.

'Thing is, Peter, that doesn't explain the hardcore porn magazines,' Moran said in an amiable way, which surprised Jane after his approach and attitude in the first interview and at the house during the search.

'I bought them from a sex shop in Soho.'

'For masturbating?'

Allard looked embarrassed and said nothing.

'OK, Peter, I understand that you're embarrassed, but I'll take that as a "yes". What can you tell me about these pills ... are they steroids?'

Allard nodded.

'Tell me, did you feel an even greater sexual urge when you took them, as opposed to looking at the porn?'

'I took them because they helped me train longer and

harder, and gave me greater muscle definition, all right? It's not illegal to buy them.'

'Maybe not, but we know about the problems with your sex life at home. Listen, Peter, I can understand how frustrated you must have felt ... all pent up and in need of sex ... it must have really pissed you off not getting sex from your wife?'

Allard tightened his lips, clenched his teeth and took a deep breath.

'None of this is her fault, none of it. She didn't know what I was doing and just thought I was out working nights in the cab.'

'Did you tell her what you'd done when you called her on the phone earlier?'

Allard slowly lowered his head, then replied that his wife had told him to tell the truth.

Moran nodded. 'She's right, Peter, because it will be better for you in the long run. So take your time and go slowly ... WPC Tennison will be writing down your confessions.'

Allard kept his head lowered, eyes to the ground, as he explained that he had tried to cope with his wife being unable to have full sex with him. He even appeared to be embarrassed when he said that they had found ways round it.

Moran tapped the desk. 'I know – she told us she'd give you a hand or a blow job instead ... but I'm more interested in the women you forced yourself on.'

Jane saw Allard tighten his hands into fists. He appeared sickened at the way Moran had spoken about his wife, and Jane watched with interest as Allard took deep breaths to calm himself down, breathing in through his nose and holding it before releasing it through his mouth with a slight hissing sound.

'OK ... it started because I wanted to stop the feeling of anger ... my frustration ... understand? I paid prostitutes for sex in the back of the cab. Anyway, one night this tart ripped me off by snatching my money bag and running off. You know, I honest to God despised myself for what I was doing, but this slag angered me so much. I mean, she got away with a whole day's takings, and I'd done two runs to Heathrow Airport. So I decided I'd take what I wanted from prostitutes without paying, as they would be unlikely to tell the police. I would park my cab near known prostitute haunts, dress up in dark clothes and watch them. When one walked away from a group, or her pimp, I reckoned she was probably going home and I would follow. I'd put on the stocking mask, grab them from behind and feel their breasts and vagina while I touched my penis.'

'It turned you on and you masturbated.'

Allard nodded and Moran looked over at Jane to see if she was keeping up with taking down the details. She continued writing for a moment before giving him a small nod to continue. Moran leaned back in his chair. He spoke in a very matter-of-fact tone.

'Well, Peter, seems you underestimated two prostitutes who came forward to report you. And two of your other victims were not on the game, they were just young women innocently walking home after an enjoyable night out or, as in the case of your arrest, a WPC acting as a decoy. You following me, Peter? Because, apart from WPC Tennison, you have destroyed those women's lives and they're now afraid to leave their homes.'

Allard looked shocked and tried to explain that from the way they were dressed he thought that they were all prostitutes.

'Well, you were wrong. So how about you start helping me out by giving me full details of your attacks? That means I need you to describe the victims and where and when the attacks occurred.'

Allard started talking. It transpired that there had been two other attacks the police didn't even know about. Moran tapped the desk with his pencil as if mulling over everything he had just heard.

'OK, I notice that you haven't admitted exactly what you did to these women.'

Allard shook his head. He took another long deep breath before he said quietly that he felt ashamed and found the details difficult to talk about.

Moran leaned closer to Allard. 'OK, Peter, I can understand you have feelings of guilt, who wouldn't, but see how much better you feel after telling the truth about what you did?'

Allard nodded.

'And I can also understand that it must be even harder for you to admit to rape. I took a statement from the young victim ... it was harrowing, even for me, so don't make her relive the whole thing in court. Tell me the truth ... tell me exactly what happened, in your own words.'

Allard looked Moran in the eye then slowly turned

to face Jane. For the first time she noticed that without that flare of anger in his face, Allard was exceptionally good-looking. His thick hair was well cut, he had high cheekbones with wide apart, deep set, dark brown eyes, and when he lowered them in a submissive manner he had long, thick eyelashes.

'I have never raped anyone and I am so sorry for what I did to you ... I honestly never meant to hurt you. I was just trying to get away ... please believe me. I am truly sorry.'

Jane jumped as Moran suddenly banged the flat of his hand down on the desk.

'You scared the shit out of her! If she hadn't resisted and we weren't there you would have raped her, wouldn't you?'

Allard looked shocked.

'No ... No! I swear before God, I never raped any of the women! That was never on my mind. I only touched them and masturbated.'

'Indecent assault wasn't enough for you ... you wanted more. You needed full sex to satisfy your urges and the only way you'd get that is by raping a young girl.'

'No ... No, you're wrong, I—'

'Then why did you have a flick knife on you? The exact same type of knife that the teenage rape victim described seeing?'

Allard began twisting uncomfortably in the chair.

'Please! ... I didn't commit any rapes! You *know* I wasn't carrying a knife. I've never carried a knife, not even in my cab.' He nodded towards Jane. 'I only told her and the others I was carrying one so they wouldn't scream!'

Moran accused him of being a liar. But Allard was adamant, claiming that he only ever committed the indecent assaults and he would plead guilty to those in court.

'You think we're stupid? You're only admitting the assaults as the lesser of two evils ... Right? *Right?*'

Allard looked pleadingly at Jane.

'Honest, I wasn't carrying a knife ... I was never going to rape you ... I've never raped anyone!'

'Bullshit! You couldn't have consensual sex with your wife, anal or otherwise, so the only way you could eventually satisfy your needs was to commit a rape.'

Allard refused to answer. Moran accused him again. Allard still said nothing.

'You think I don't know steroids make a man sexually violent, and that you're remaining silent because of your guilt about committing rape? She was seventeen the same day you raped her, and she's now so traumatized she won't leave her home.'

Allard said nothing as he sat up straight. Moran paused, looked him in the eye and nodded, as if he'd just realized something.

'You also don't want to admit to the rape because of your wife. You think she'll accept the indecent assaults because they are in some way her fault, but raping a teenage girl, she won't accept that. Well, even if you don't confess, believe me, I will make sure she comes to realize it was you and sees you for the animal that you really are.'

Allard looked helplessly at Jane.

'Why don't you tell him the truth? I might have said I had a knife, but I didn't ... that was only to frighten you. I thought you were someone else. Why are you lying? You know I've been set up with the flick knife, because he wants to charge me with a rape I didn't commit.'

Jane didn't know whether to believe Allard or not. There was something about his desperate pleas that made her feel uneasy about the whole situation. Moran picked up his desk phone, called the duty desk and asked for a uniform PC to be sent up to his office. He then told Allard that they would conclude the interview for now as he had further enquiries to make. Jane partially held up the pen in her hand as she had a question she wanted to ask. Irritated, Moran repeated that the interview was over.

Feeling frustrated, Jane went to the CID office, where DC Edwards was sitting at his desk writing.

'Where is everyone?' she asked.

'They're in the pub celebrating one of the detectives' birthdays. As soon as I've finished these notes on the search of Allard's house I'm joining them, if you want to come?'

'DI Moran is with DCS Metcalf and he wants you to prepare the charges against Allard for all the indecent assaults.'

Edwards looked annoyed and mumbled something about having enough bloody work to do already and missing out on the booze-up.

'I have to do the CRO 74, but could give you a hand as well if you need it?'

'I have to go downstairs and get some blank charge sheets and the Guide to the Wording of Police Charges for an indecent assault and assault on a police officer,' Edwards said as he walked towards the door.

Jane shouted across the room, 'Moran said the list of the victims' names was on his desk.'

Edwards raised his hand to acknowledge he'd heard her as he left the room.

Jane thought she'd be helpful and get the list from Moran's office. She looked on his desk and to one side in a plastic desk tray she saw the list on top of a thick file. She picked up the list and noticed the file underneath had 'DI Moran' and 'Indecent Assaults' written on it. She was curious, picked up the file, placed it on the desk in front of her, sat down and started to flick through the victims' statements. It quickly struck Jane that not one of the six victims mentioned actually seeing a knife, but in all of the cases the suspect had worn a stocking mask and said 'I've got a knife so don't scream!' Jane remembered Allard saying something similar, but couldn't quite recall his exact words.

She was about to replace the file when she saw another file with Moran's name on it marked 'Lamb Lane Rape' in the plastic desk tray. She knew that Lamb Lane was only a stone's throw away from London Fields where she was attacked and, opening the file, she took out the victim's statement and started to read the salient points. The suspect had grabbed the victim from behind and held a flick knife to her throat and said, 'If you scream or struggle I'll cut your neck.' Again she believed this was similar to what had been said to her by Allard. Jane read on. The rape victim stated that when the man had been on top of her and had penetrated her she noticed he had bad body odour and that his breath smelt of alcohol. Jane recalled Marie saying that her husband didn't drink and she also remembered the sweet smell of aftershave when Allard had grabbed her from behind. However, what really struck Jane was that in the rape victim's statement the assailant was wearing a black balaclava with eye holes, not a stocking pulled down over his face.

She heard someone in the CID office and quickly put the rape statement back. She picked up both files from the desk to put them back in the tray, but in her haste she dropped them.

'What are you doing?'

She looked up and saw DC Edwards staring at her. 'I, er, was trying to find the list of victims and just picked up some files when I heard your voice ... It startled me and I dropped them.'

Edwards helped her pick up the statements, which she put back in the case files. He noticed DI Moran's name on the Indecent Assaults file and asked Jane if she'd been lumbered with writing the report. Jane nervously shook her head, saying that she was just interested in reading the victims' statements. Edwards sensed from her tone and demeanour that something was wrong, even more so when he noticed that she'd also dropped the rape file.

'Did you ask Moran if you could look through these files?'

Jane knew it wasn't worth lying. 'No, but I didn't really know much about any of the cases so I was just having a quick read of the statements.'

'Listen, Jane, one thing you don't do is go snooping through a senior officer's files. If Moran found out, you'd never get in the CID, in fact you wouldn't even be allowed to cross the threshold into the main office again!'

'Are you going to tell him?' Jane asked, looking worried.

Edwards hesitated at first, then reassured Jane that she could trust him to keep quiet, but he sensed something else was making her nervous and asked her what it was.

Jane explained that no one had seen a knife in any of the indecent assaults, and in every attack the suspect wore a stocking mask, but in the rape he wore a balaclava. She was about to continue when Edwards interrupted.

'So what? It's a form of mask, just like the stocking Allard wore. Moran is way more experienced than the two of us, and if he thinks all the attacks and the rape are linked then he has good reason. He can't just ignore Allard as a possible suspect, can he?'

'No, I appreciate that, but the attacker in the rape held a knife to the victim's throat and said "If you scream or struggle I'll cut your neck—"'

Again Edwards interrupted. 'Yeah, exactly like Allard said to you, Jane. So let's just agree to differ and get on with what DI Moran told us to do.'

'It's not what he said to me ... and there are other glaring differences between last night's assault on me and the rape.'

Edwards looked at her. She had her CID pocket book in her hand.

'Allard said to me, and this is word for word . . .' Jane looked at her pocket book. '"I've got a knife . . . so keep your mouth shut, you fucking thieving whore, or I'll cut your throat wide open this time", but he didn't even hold a knife to my throat.'

'For Chrissakes, Jane, apart from a word or two it's the same . . . so just drop it.'

'The rape victim also said her attacker smelt of BO. Allard was so close to me that I could smell his aftershave.'

'So? He could have been sweating like a pig after stuffing himself with steroids, for all we know.'

Again she referred to her pocket book. 'Allard said in the interview, "I paid prostitutes for sex in the back of the cab. Anyway, one night this tart ripped me off by snatching my money bag and running off."'

'It's called motive, Jane, he's telling you why he committed his crimes. No, I'm wrong . . . he's actually trying to blame prostitutes for the fact he became a pervert. He also attacked women who weren't prostitutes!'

Edwards was losing his patience.

'But he thought they were . . . just like he did with me. In fact, I think it's possible he thought I was the same prostitute who stole money from him, that's why he said "thieving whore". It was personal . . . maybe he wasn't going to rape me, maybe he was going to drag me behind the Lido so he could beat me up.'

'Oh, and that makes it all right, does it? That means Allard's not so bad after all?'

Jane persisted. 'I'm not saying that . . .'

'Then what are you saying?'

Jane took a deep breath and sighed. 'I think Moran planted a knife on Allard because he was already convinced the person committing the indecent assaults and the rape were one and the same ... And I don't know what to do about it.'

'Now you really are losing it, Jane, accusing a DI of planting evidence.'

She looked at Edwards and could tell he had doubts. 'So you're saying that senior officers aren't dishonest?'

'Come on, Jane, what would the point be in the guvnor planting a knife? It doesn't take the case much further as there's no other evidence that Allard committed the rape. He isn't even charging him with the rape, so where's your fit-up theory then?'

Jane looked confused. 'He isn't?'

'Well, he only said to prepare the charges for the indecent assaults and the one on you, didn't he?'

'Well, he might charge him later.'

'Why? He knows that if he did the Solicitors' Department will read through the statements and see the inconsistences between the indecent assaults and the rape.'

'I don't understand.'

'Jane, there's no way they would run a trial with no positive identification and only the knife as evidence. So take my advice and let it drop.'

'But it's not right ...'

'If you say anything to DI Moran, or anyone else for that matter, then you can forget ever making detective.'

'Are you being serious?'

'Yes, I am. You'll become persona non grata ... no

one will ever trust you, or work with you. Look at the way we all had to cover for Bradfield's screw-up – even you.'

'My God, Brian! Bradfield died! What we're discussing here is whether someone planted evidence, or not.'

'Someone? Someone ...? Nick Moran can be an arsehole, but he's got a number of Commissioners' commendations and is well respected. Apart from anything else I'll get dragged into something that might get blown out of all proportion. I've only been a DC for three years and I'm not prepared to screw up my career.'

'I understand your predicament, and under the circumstances I'll let it rest.' She walked out, unable to discuss it further as Edwards obviously didn't want to continue.

As Jane walked along the corridor towards the ladies' locker room DCS Metcalf was heading towards her wearing a smart suit and tie. Jane saluted and said, 'All correct, sir,' which was the normal address to senior officers. Metcalf smiled and informed her that 'All correct' is fine to a detective and that the salute was for senior officers in uniform.

'It's just force of habit,' Jane replied.

'DI Moran has been updating me on your arrest of Allard and how well you coped under extreme pressure. I'm impressed, congratulations on an excellent job.'

'Thank you,' said Jane. 'Could I possibly have a word about my future career and becoming a detective?'

Metcalf looked at his watch. 'I saw the result of your final probationer's exam – your marks were excellent and top of the class. As it happens, after speaking with

DI Moran I was going to have a chat with you about your future, but I have an appointment to go to right now. What shift are you on tomorrow?'

'I'm on my CID attachment and not sure whether I'll be on a late or early shift.'

'I see. I'm out all afternoon and won't be coming back to the station.'

'I could come in early? In my own time if necessary?'

Metcalf agreed. 'See me in my office at ten a.m.'

Feeling exhilarated by his compliments, Jane went into the ladies' and then returned to the CID office. DC Edwards was at his desk writing up the charges. He raised his finger and pointed to DI Moran's office and mouthed, 'He's in there.' She quickly grabbed a CRO 74 from the file cabinet and after putting some carbon paper between the sheets placed it in a typewriter. She opened her pocket book and started to fill out all of Allard's details and circumstances of arrest to be placed on criminal records at Scotland Yard.

'Has one of you two been going through my files? The statements are out of order.'

Jane looked up and saw a stern-faced Moran standing in his office doorway holding up the Indecent Assaults file. She looked at Edwards and knew that she had to tell him it was her, but she was so nervous she couldn't instantly think of a valid reason. As she turned back to Moran, Edwards suddenly spoke up.

'Sorry, sir, I was looking through the file and dropped it by mistake. I didn't realize I'd put things back in the wrong order.'

'What were you looking through them for?'

'I couldn't read one of the victims' names on your list and I just wanted to double-check it against the statement for the charge sheet.'

'Well, next time ask me ... I don't like people rummaging around on my desk.'

'Sorry, sir, it won't happen again,' Edwards said.

Jane mouthed 'Thank you' to Edwards as Sergeant Harris walked in.

'Allard's wife has rung to ask if she can visit him,' Harris announced.

Moran shrugged. 'She can, but not until tomorrow morning as we have to formally charge, fingerprint and photograph him this evening.'

'OK, I'll ring her back and inform her.'

Having completed the criminal records form Jane was tired and decided to go back to the section house rather than go for a drink. It was only a ten-minute bus ride and she always stood on the footplate ready to hop off at her stop. As the bus travelled down the road she noticed a tall, statuesque girl pushing a pram with a toddler in it. The girl was dusky skinned, and had long dark hair that hid most of her face. What caught Jane's interest was that she was wearing a pale blue rabbit fur coat, identical to the one she had worn as a decoy. She shuddered as she recalled what had happened to her at the hands of Peter Allard. It really sunk home that she could have been seriously assaulted, to the point of Grievous Bodily Harm, if it hadn't been for Moran and Edwards.

CHAPTER FIVE

Jane walked into Hackney Police Station at 9.30 a.m., just as Marie Allard was coming out from reception. Jane realized that she must have visited her husband. Marie looked awful, as if she was in a world of her own. Jane called out her name but Marie carried on walking until Jane caught up with her.

'Marie, how are you doing?'

Marie suddenly broke down in tears. 'I was prepared to stand by him for what he done, even though it was bad and wrong, but I could never forgive him for rape.'

'I understand. But although your husband initially lied about the assaults, he has always denied the rape and he isn't being charged with it.'

Marie stepped back angrily. 'What you talking about ... he admitting it.'

Jane was shocked, instantly feeling that she had been stupid to have believed Allard's lies and doubt Moran's integrity.

'I'm so sorry ... you must feel as if your world has been torn apart. Did he confess to you just now, during your visit?'

'No, I not seen him. He was taken to the Magistrates' Court before I got there.'

Jane was confused. 'How do you know he confessed?'

Marie was in floods of tears. 'That detective inspector who came to the house, he saw me just now in the station. He say Peter been charged with the rape and indecent assaults and he be remanded in custody at the court to stand trial.'

Jane was now even more shocked. 'He confessed to DI Moran?'

'Yes, in an interview last night. I not believe it at first, but Moran show me Peter's signed confession and I see his signature.'

Jane didn't know what to say to Marie. She had genuinely believed that Peter Allard was innocent of the rape, but to hear that he had made a signed confession made her feel naïve and foolish for what she had said to DC Edwards about Moran planting the knife.

Jane told Marie that she had to go to work, and hurried into the station. She went straight to the CID office to speak with DI Moran. There were a few detectives at their own desks, but Moran's office was empty. Jane went over to Edwards's desk and spoke to him in a low voice.

'Where's Moran?'

'He's gone to the Magistrates' Court with Allard, to object to bail.'

Flustered, Jane took a deep breath.

'Is it true that Allard signed a confession?'

Edwards nodded. He had a raging headache as he'd drunk too much at the birthday bash the previous evening.

'I can't believe Allard signed a confession . . . were you present?'

Edwards could see some of the other detectives looking at them both.

'Not here, Jane,' he whispered. 'I'll meet you downstairs in five minutes.'

Jane waited impatiently for him in the locker room, tidying herself up in preparation for her meeting with Metcalf. She looked at her watch. There was only ten minutes left before she was due to be in his office.

DC Edwards walked in and shut the door.

'I'm sorry for what I said yesterday, Brian, but I really thought Allard was telling the truth about not being involved in the rape. What did he say? I mean, why did he suddenly confess?'

'I don't know – I wasn't present at the confession as I'd already gone to the pub.'

'Did Moran say anything to you at the pub?'

'He didn't come to the pub, but he was all cock-a-hoop about it first thing this morning. He said he'd charged Allard with the indecent assaults and was fingerprinting him when he suddenly broke down and made a signed confession. Moran couldn't believe it himself.'

There was something about his tone of voice that didn't sit right with Jane.

'So, Moran was alone in the fingerprint room with Allard when he confessed?'

Edwards nodded.

'Should Moran have had someone else present when he wrote down the actual confession?'

'There's no fixed rule about needing two people

present, it's just advisable to counter any allegations of it being false,' Edwards explained.

Jane hesitated before she spoke. 'You're not convinced about the confession, are you? Do you think we should take it further ... speak with Metcalf maybe? I'm seeing him in a minute about joining the department—'

Edwards was quick to interject.

'No, I don't ... definitely not. If you raise any queries regarding Allard being fitted up by DI Moran, the first thing you'll be asked for is proof ... and the fact is you don't have any. It's his word against yours, and you won't win.'

'Come on, Brian, you know DI Moran obviously decided Allard was guilty of the rape as soon as we arrested him. When Allard lied about what happened with me Moran decided his course of action and planted the knife. The more Allard lied, the more it played into his hands ... he'll probably claim that Allard's emotional stress with his wife made him break down and confess—'

'For Chrissakes, Jane, wake up and get real! You've got more to lose than gain here. Why ruin your career for a piece of shit like Allard? He split your lip, he terrified the life out of you and other helpless women whose lives he's ruined, not to mention not giving a damn about his wife's feelings. He'll get a long stretch, whatever happens ... and to be frank he'll get what he deserves.'

Jane shook her head. 'For a crime he may not have committed ...'

'Listen to me, Jane, neither of us knows the truth, but if he's signed a confession he's screwed. We both know he

lied at the start about his arrest and who he really was ...
Allard did himself no favours, so you and I don't owe
him anything. Lemme tell you, there have been plenty
of people like the guv who look upon a fit-up as what is
called "noble cause justice". You might think they have
a warped sense of loyalty to the job in bending the rules
and making up confessions or fabricating evidence if they
are convinced someone is guilty. I don't ... I really don't,
because if the ends justify the means, that's a success. If
you want to be part of CID you'd better get used to it and
learn to turn a blind eye fast.'

Jane took a deep breath and looked at him in disbelief
as he turned to leave.

'Wait a minute ... I can't believe what you're saying!
That's not justice, it's corruption, whatever way you
look at it.'

Edwards ran his fingers through his hair and sighed
as his cheeks flushed.

'That's the big dilemma, Jane. But with no proof
there's no case ... so there's nothing you can say, no
matter how bad you feel about it. You need to learn
quickly who the bent cops are and try to avoid working
with them. If they try to get you involved in something
dodgy, just say no and walk away. But don't ever say
anything to anyone else because everyone will think
you're a grass and ostracize you.'

Jane shook her head. 'I'd be hated because I told the
truth about a dishonest police officer? That can't be
right.'

Edwards sighed; his head was really throbbing now.
'No one said it was right, Jane, it's just the way it is.

It's how you define the word "corrupt", and in my eyes Moran isn't corrupt. He doesn't take backhanders or steal from drug dealers.'

'Really? Well, do you think Moran might have assaulted or threatened Allard to get him to sign a false confession? Is that what you define as "noble"?'

'For Chrissakes, Jane, no way ... He might have come off second best in the fingerprint room, or in a cell alone, with a bloke like Allard who has karate skills and is a martial arts expert.'

'There's no need to be sarcastic, Brian ... Whatever you say, I don't believe Allard would have knowingly signed a false confession if he was innocent.'

He was losing his patience. 'It's Moran's word against Allard's, and we can't be sure of the truth either way. I'm on your side, Jane, but I'm not stupid enough to shout about it. So let's just forget we ever had this conversation, OK? After what you did the other night you've already got one foot in the door of the department ... don't fuck it all up now. Go and see Metcalf and reap the rewards, and we'll do the lab form for the steroids when you've finished.'

Edwards walked out of the locker room. Jane waited a few moments as the implications of their discussion sank in. This was some learning curve. She looked in the mirror and put some foundation over the bruise above her cut lip, powdered her swollen cheek then headed out of the locker room for her meeting with Metcalf.

Jane knocked on the door. 'Ah, Jane.' Metcalf invited her in, gesturing to her to sit down. 'I hear you've had good news and that Allard has admitted the rape?'

'Yes, sir,' Jane replied against her will.

'Excellent. When this case appears at the Old Bailey the judge will no doubt commend you. You'll also be put forward for a Commissioner's Commendation for your part in the arrest of a very dangerous man.'

Jane sat bolt upright on the hard-backed chair. 'I'm sure that the trial will be very interesting. Do you think Allard will actually plead guilty?'

Metcalf laughed. 'Given he has confessed his crimes and signed a statement to that effect, he'd be mad to go for a not guilty claim and risk a much longer sentence.' He smiled coldly. 'Anyway, let's talk about your future, Tennison . . . Tell me, where do you see yourself in three or five years' time?'

'I'd like to think I'd be a detective, sir.'

He gave her an icy stare. 'Are you sure that's what you want? It may not be the best career path for you at this time.'

Jane was taken aback by Metcalf's attitude. He had promised he would recommend her for the CID after DCI Bradfield's death.

'Excuse me, sir, can I ask if DI Moran or Sergeant Harris have said anything to you about me joining the CID?'

'No . . . why do you ask? Is there a problem between you and them?'

Jane blushed. 'No, sir. I had told them I'd like to join the department and I just wondered if they had spoken to you favourably, or otherwise, about me.'

'Detective Moran said you did a good job on the Allard arrest, and Sergeant Harris has never mentioned you ... but I try to avoid conversations with him as he usually has something to moan about.'

He gave a short bark.

'Could I ask why you think the CID may be the wrong career path for me?'

Metcalf formed a church steeple with his fingers, and leaned his elbows on the desk.

'I'm not saying that being a detective isn't right, but it may not be the right choice in the long term. There is always the possibility of a more rewarding opportunity.'

'What would that opportunity be, sir?'

'Well, if you sit the sergeant's promotion exam and got a mark in the nineties you would automatically be considered for the Special Course.'

'I see ... but Sergeant Harris has already said he wouldn't recommend me to sit the exam yet.'

Metcalf glanced away, staring at a small stain high on the wall behind her.

'Well, Jane, I would recommend you for accelerated promotion, whereby you could be a uniform sergeant within three years and an inspector within five.'

Jane paused for thought. She then said quietly, 'It's very tempting to have a go at accelerated promotion, but I think first I'd like to make detective, work in the CID and maybe sit the exam later.'

'But you could still apply for the CID even if you pass the promotion exam,' Metcalf pointed out. 'You might find it worth studying to sit the exam in January next year, then apply for the CID once you've passed.'

Again Jane took time to think about it. 'Could I

become a detective and then sit the exam after a year or two in the CID?' she asked politely.

She could tell that Metcalf was now becoming a trifle impatient as he drummed his fingertips on the edge of the desk.

'If you pass the exam, as a detective, you would be required to work in uniform for one year before you could return as a detective sergeant.'

Jane bit down on her bottom lip. One side of her mouth was still scarred where Allard had struck her but she kept tight control and audaciously reminded Metcalf of their previous conversation after Bradfield's death. Metcalf's cheeks turned pink. It was hard to determine if it was from anger, or whether he had forgotten that conversation.

Eventually he said very quietly, 'I'm a man of my word and if that's what you want then I'll recommend you for the next CID interview board in about a month's time. But I'm only able to recommend you, and passing the board is entirely down to how you perform on the day in front of the panel.' Metcalf peered at her and his tone became brisk. 'Do your homework and brush up on CID procedure.' He stood up to signal that their meeting was over and Jane saluted him.

'I wish you'd stop doing that, Tennison ... a handshake will suffice.'

'Thank you very much, sir, I will remember that.'

Standing ramrod straight she walked out, very pleased with herself, and reckoned she had handled the meeting well.

Jane went straight to the property store to book out

the steroids recovered from Allard's address. PC Doig, the property officer, was a pleasant, rotund old soul who originated from Glasgow. He had a strong Scottish accent that, even after twenty-five years in London, was often hard to understand. He was badly injured after being hit by a car in the line of duty and had spent the last four years assigned to desk duties in the 'dungeon', as officers referred to the basement property store.

'Hello, wee Jane, how ye doin'? I heard you pulled a real belter the other night, arrestin' that rotten bastard Allard for rape. That's a nasty cut he gave your lip.'

'Thanks, Dougal, but it wasn't just me who made the arrest.'

'You're a canny lass that's fer sure. Now, what're you aboot?'

'The bag of tablets in the Allard case, please.'

'Aye, did ye see them magazines he had? I could na believe the dirty pictures in 'em when I had a wee gander.' He walked off down the aisle of high shelving to look for the property.

Jane tried not to laugh at his remark about the magazines, as he'd obviously had a good 'gander'.

'Right, here ye are. I need yer ta sign in the book here. Are they going ta the lab?'

'Yes,' Jane said.

PC Doig put the bag of tablets down on the desk and opened up the property book. He pulled a pen out of his pocket and handed it to Jane, asking her to fill out each section with the date, property exhibit number, case name and description of the property. The page was nearly full and as she filled out each section she couldn't help but notice the entries above the one she was making. The dates went back three days and she was surprised that nowhere among the entries for withdrawal or deposit was there a blue rabbit fur coat. Moran's name was there but only relating to the deposit of the Allard property. She flicked back a few pages to double-check, but still found no entry for the coat. Jane distinctly remembered Moran saying the fur coat was evidence in a 'handling' case and asking her to leave it on a chair in his office as he needed to put it back in the property store.

'The fur coat I used for the decoy operation . . . I was just wondering if it was returned to the store, as it was evidence in a case?'

'What fur coat? I've nay had any fur coats in here. If I did, believe me I'd be wearin' it . . . it's that damn cold doon here.'

'It was blue rabbit fur, and waist length.'

'Nope, d'nay what yer talkin' aboot, Janey . . . If it was ta do with an overnight prisoner then it may never have got doon here, and could ha been locked in the charge room cabinet.'

The word 'prisoner' sparked a memory in Jane's mind. It was DC Edwards telling her that Moran had gone downstairs to put the fur jacket back in the property store, and release a prisoner he had in on suspicion of dishonest handling. Then Sergeant Harris had told her that DI Moran released his other prisoner the same night she arrested Allard.

She filled out the rest of the details about the steroids in the property book. Why had Moran lied to her about the rabbit fur coat? It just didn't make sense ... unless there was something he wanted to hide. She thanked PC Doig for his help.

Jane went straight to the charge room to look through the prisoner arrest and release records for the twenty-four-hour period before and after Allard's arrest. She was thankful there was no one there, other than a cleaner. She went over to the bookshelf, removed the 'Prisoner' book and sat down at the charge room desk to look through it. It didn't take long. Early in the morning on the day of the decoy operation, DI Moran had arrested a Mary Kelly, aged twenty-nine, unemployed, and of no fixed abode. Jane's eyes opened wide when she read that Kelly was arrested on suspicion of handling stolen goods and Moran had released her, without charge, in the early hours of the morning ... after Peter Allard was arrested. The 'Prisoner' book didn't say what the 'stolen goods' were, but Jane knew it would be recorded on Mary Kelly's arrest sheet, which would be kept in date order in a large binder, along with all the prisoners kept in custody at Hackney. As she was about to replace the 'Prisoner' book the charge room door opened and Sergeant Harris appeared.

'What are you up to, Tennison?'

She'd already prepared an answer in anticipation that someone might walk in on her, and pointed to the bag of steroids on the table.

'I've got to fill out a lab form regarding those tablets and I needed the time we booked Allard in. I forgot to put it in my notes and couldn't remember,' she said and then stood up, replaced the 'Prisoner' book on the shelf and quickly left the room before Harris could say anything. She was annoyed that she was unable to see what property was logged against Mary Kelly's arrest record, but was almost certain it had to be the blue rabbit fur coat. She'd try to sneak back later to have a look, but the more Jane uncovered the more she felt something was seriously wrong.

She thought about the woman she had seen on the way back to the section house the previous evening. The tall, dusky skinned, statuesque girl who was wearing a pale blue rabbit fur coat. Jane wondered if she was Mary Kelly, but the reality was it could have just been a coincidence and she didn't get a good look at the woman's face so she doubted she would recognize her again. Jane also knew that as Mary Kelly was released without charge no fingerprints or photograph would have been taken, but she might have a criminal record for previous offences. An idea occurred to her and she decided to seek out PC Donaldson.

PC Donaldson, the station collator, was one of the oldest and longest-serving officers at Hackney. He was overweight with ruddy cheeks and a thatch of white hair. He was perched on a stool in front of his desk reading a newspaper, his chipped mug of coffee beside him. There were other chairs in the room but he found them uncomfortable because of his bad back and preferred the stool as it kept him more upright. The room was crammed with filing cabinets, large and small, containing files and card indexes on every known criminal and persons of interest in Hackney. The basement room had strip lights and only one window, which was so high up it was dirty and cobwebbed, and had obviously never been opened.

'Morning, Tennison,' he said with a warm smile.

Jane had become very fond of Donaldson. He was always pleasant and helpful and she stood smiling as she watched his wide bum splay over the edges of the stool. His police issue trousers hung a few inches above his ankles and revealed his thick crepe-soled black polished shoes.

'I just wanted to check out someone's name with you.'

Donaldson eased himself down from his stool. 'No problem ... the name is?'

'Mary Kelly.'

'I know that name ...'

Jane looked pleased. 'Do you? What do you know about her?'

Donaldson paused as he looked through the female index cards under the name 'Kelly'. He turned to Jane.

'That's strange, there's no Mary Kelly in here ...'

'If someone is arrested, but not charged, their details and reason for arrest should still be filled out on a form and submitted to you?'

'Yes, but sometimes officers forget or can't be bothered.'

Jane became worried. Could Moran have deliberately failed to submit, or have even destroyed, Mary Kelly's collator's card?

Donaldson suddenly clicked his fingers. 'Got it! Mary Jane Kelly, she was his last victim.'

Jane looked excited. 'Whose last victim? Did someone assault Mary?'

Donaldson looked at her as if she was a bit dim. 'No, Mary Jane Kelly was Jack the Ripper's last victim . . . that's why the name was familiar. I've read every book on that crime and watched an old movie about him . . . still shockin' all these years later. She was a prostitute addicted to rot-gut gin . . .'

Jane felt deflated, but suddenly thought of a long shot on the back of what Donaldson had said. 'Do you keep records of women arrested for prostitution?'

Donaldson smiled. 'Yes I do, but there's so many . . . and they use and share a multitude of different names. Some of them could fill a phone book! It's hard to remember who's who, so I put together a photograph album of them all.'

He went to a cabinet and took out a large photo album filled with pages of various women, of all ages and skin colours. 'As you can see, each one is numbered and I have a corresponding index card or file for each number. I keep the main index card under the name they gave when first arrested and charged.'

Jane sighed. She'd only seen the woman in the rabbit fur coat briefly, and from a side-on view. Nevertheless, nothing ventured, nothing gained. She sat at the spare table and started to flick through the pages, each of which had nine photographs. Donaldson sat back up on his stool and continued to read his newspaper.

Although Jane was frustrated and growing impatient she took her time. After ten minutes she was halfway through the album without seeing anyone she even remotely recognized. It didn't help that all the pictures were black and white and taken from chest height. It was another five minutes before a picture caught her attention. It wasn't the dusky faced girl herself, but the coat she was wearing. Jane was almost certain it was the same fur coat she had been given to wear as a decoy, and if it was she wanted to know why and who it belonged to.

'This one here, number three hundred and twenty-six ... I think this might be her.'

Donaldson leaned over his desk to a small notebook that had 'TOMS' written on the front of it. He licked his finger and started to turn over the pages.

'Ah ha, here it is ... Janet Brown! You ever seen her? She's the dizzy blonde who does impressions on *Who Do You Do*. She's really good, and very funny.'

Jane was lost. She didn't have a clue why Donaldson suddenly wanted to talk about TV impressionists. He went over to one of the female index filing trays, pulled it open and after a second or two pulled out an envelope containing some index cards. He placed it on the table in front of Jane and removed the cards.

'Number three hundred and twenty-six is Janet Brown, but not the impressionist ... First arrest for soliciting eight years ago, CRO number D72/261.' He flicked the card over. 'Aliases Lily, Sugar Susie, Jane, Angie ... to name but a few.' He stopped reading out the list of aliases and ran his finger down the page.

'Looks like she's never used the name Mary Kelly before, and come to think of it I can't recall a Tom who has. I remember seeing the Ripper crime scene pictures of Mary Kelly in the Black Museum at the Yard ... her body was horribly mutilated.'

Jane felt ill at ease. The more she found out about Moran's involvement in the arrest of the so-called Mary Kelly, the more suspicious she became. She had nothing concrete to go on, but she was determined to dig deeper. Donaldson picked up Brown's mug shot and tapped it.

'This may not be the girl you're looking for ... as I said, many of them share and use the same names. The best way to confirm someone's identity is through their fingerprints, as they can be matched to the first sets ever taken on their CRO file at the Yard.'

Jane already knew about fingerprints. It was as if Donaldson had forgotten that she had nearly two years' service, but she didn't want to offend him so just thanked him for the information. She was eager to read Janet Brown's cards and concentrated on what was in front of her.

Janet was five feet eight inches tall and weighed 125 pounds. To Jane this indicated she must be a slender woman. Her date of birth was 20th February 1945, making her twenty-nine. Jane looked at the scrap of paper she had made notes on about Mary Kelly's arrest. The date of birth was the same. The most recent mug shot of Janet was five months old, having been sent over from West End Central Police Station after she was arrested by a local PC for prostitution in Soho. The picture surprised Jane because she was exceptionally beautiful, with dark skin, dark hair, wide almond shaped eyes, a small neat nose and wide dark lips, which were probably accentuated with lipstick. There was a sullenness to her expression, and the hand that held up the card had long painted nails.

Janet's last arrest, in 1972, was for loitering for prostitution in London Fields. It then dawned on her that DC Edwards had said DI Moran used to be on the Clubs and Vice Unit. She looked up at Donaldson.

'Is Clubs and Vice based at Scotland Yard?'

'No, they work out of West End Central. Why?'

'Nothing, I just wondered if they might know of Janet Brown.' But the truth was she was wondering if there was a connection between Moran and Janet Brown from his time with Clubs and Vice.

Jane sighed. Everything seemed to be going from bad to worse. She noticed that Janet had never served a prison sentence, which she thought was strange due to the number of arrests she had had for soliciting. Jane questioned Donaldson about it, and he shrugged.

'Could be a soft magistrate, or it's possible she's a snout for someone on the Vice Squad and trades details of pimps and johns to avoid prison. If she appeared in court and a good word is put in by the Vice officer she'd probably just get a fine. Paying it off just means turning a few more tricks in one night.'

'Sounds like a vicious circle,' Jane remarked.

Donaldson put his arm on her shoulder. 'Will you keep your eye on the shop for me while I nip up to the canteen for a couple of sausage rolls and a coffee?'

Jane nodded and gave Donaldson a warm smile. No sooner had he left the room than he popped his head back round the door.

'Do you want anything?'

'No, thank you.'

He smiled and jokingly said, 'And no sneaking any of

my index cards out the room . . . you know it's against the rules.'

Jane grabbed the memo pad from Donaldson's desk and started to make shorthand notes from Janet Brown's cards. One of the cards gave some details of her background. It stated that she was born in King's Cross, her mother was English and father an American GI. She had lived in America for part of her life, then returned to London after her mother had died. Jane wished the card had more details about Janet Brown's life, but she knew that it was normal for only a brief family history to be recorded on a CRO file. What was of interest was the fact that Janet Brown gave her address, when last arrested in Soho, as 86 Graham Road, Hackney.

Having recorded as much as she could on the memo pad Jane ripped off the pages she'd written on, folded them up and put them in her handbag. She gathered up the cards to put them back in the envelope and on opening it saw a copy of an Incident Report Book, which was used by uniform officers, and had been filled out by PC 489 Grant, who was based at Hackney, but on a different relief to Jane. The IRB was about a 'Serious Assault' on 23 August 1974. She also recalled having read the teenager's statement saying that her rape had occurred on the 23rd, but had not been reported until two days later when she had an emotional breakdown in front of her mother. To Jane it seemed obvious that the same man may have attacked Janet Brown and the teenager. She couldn't understand how, or why, DI Moran had missed the connection. Jane opened the IRB and started to read it.

*On 23.8.74 I was night duty patrol covering 5
beat. Just after midnight I received a radio call
about a drunk woman outside the basement flat
of 58 Navarino Road. I attended the scene and
the woman had a severely bruised face and what
appeared to be a knife wound to her neck and
chest. She was semi-conscious and did not smell
of alcohol. I also noticed that her clothes were
in disarray and there was a handbag on the floor
next to her. She was wearing a blue fur coat,
white top, miniskirt and long boots.*

*I asked her what happened but she was
incoherent and in a state of shock. I called
an ambulance and accompanied her to the
Homerton Hospital. She said nothing during
the journey. I looked in the handbag to try and
identify the woman and found a letter addressed
to Miss J. Brown of 86 Graham Road.*

*At the hospital she was treated immediately in
the casualty area and sedated, thus I was unable
to get any information from her. I contacted the
Night Duty CID and informed them of a possible
GBH/Rape, and that the attending doctor said
no one would be able to speak to her until the
following morning.*

*CID said they would make an entry in their
Night Duty Occurrence Book for the DI to see
in the morning, and also asked me to make out
a crime report sheet on my return to the station.
(Major Crime 1324 refers.)*

I left the hospital and returned to Hackney

where I checked the collator's index cards and found a record for a Janet Brown, who from the mug shot was the same woman I escorted to the hospital.

Lifting the mug shot up Jane found two more black and white photographs. One looked as if it had been taken around the same time as the mug shot, but the other photograph was more recent and shocked her. Janet had severe bruises around her eyes and one of them was bulging like a ping pong ball. Her lips were swollen and split. It was very obvious that she had suffered a severe beating. Checking over the dates and times of the various arrests for soliciting there was a brief mention of the assault stating that J. Brown had come into the station to report it, but had later withdrawn the complaint and refused to press charges. She was unable to give a description of the assailant.

Listed on the crime sheet was a memo from DI Moran stating that the victim refused to substantiate the allegation and had said the injuries were as a result of a fall. 'No crime' was then underlined.

Jane couldn't believe what she'd just read. She was now convinced that Janet Brown, Mary Kelly and J. Brown were the same woman. Moran must be hiding something, not just from her, but from everyone else in the station. Navarino Road, where the woman was found, was just a stone's throw from the north end of London Fields.

Jane was now certain she had been wearing Janet Brown's rabbit fur coat on the night she was assaulted. She could find no mention of whether or not she was an informer. Even if she was, all informants were usually registered under a false name and a record kept under lock and key in a cabinet by the DCI.

Donaldson returned and Jane handed him the index cards.

'She took a severe beating.'

'Yep, I noticed that ... But you know these girls risk that happening. A lot of them are out soliciting to pay for their drugs. You arrest them, and in the worst cases they do time in Holloway Prison, but then they get out and go straight back to work. They have these scum pimps who they pay for so-called protection, but a lot of the time it's those creeps who knock them around.'

'Do you think Janet has a pimp?'

'I don't know, sweetheart, maybe ... Some of them work out of flats over in Mayfair. That's where the top brass work nowadays. They get customers from the Dorchester Hotel, and some of them even have the cheek to dress up fancy and go into the bars.'

'Do you think Janet could work in Mayfair?'

He shook his head and said he doubted it as she was a darkie. Jane was eager to leave and thanked Donaldson again. As she opened the door she turned back.

'You know, I think you're one of the best officers here in Hackney ... You're always so helpful, and I really appreciate it.'

'Well, thank you, Tennison ... nice to know I'm appreciated. But I just do my job. I'll be retired soon. I loved being a copper out on the beat ... gets lonely down here. After I got wounded I reckoned I'd be back in civvies, but luckily I was allocated this position.'

'Wounded?'

'Yep, got shot by one of the Krays' gang . . . big shoot-out.'

Jane looked horrified and Donaldson laughed.

'Na, not really . . . tripped over a drainpipe and broke me hip!'

Later that day, before she was officially on duty, Jane came across DI Moran in the CID office, his Cuban-heeled boots up on the desk, leaning back in his chair and looking at the topless model on page three of *The Sun*. He was wearing a rather snazzy suit and a colourful tie. DC Edwards was typing at his desk and looked over at her. He almost gave her a warning glance, as he nodded his head towards Moran. Jane knew that Allard had been taken into the Magistrates' Court and bail had been denied but she still asked, rather tentatively, 'How did it go this morning? Good news about the confession, sir . . .'

'Yeah, yeah . . . I was about to go off duty last night when I was told Allard wanted to speak to me. Next thing I knew he started pouring his heart out about the rape and admitted that he wore a balaclava because his wife said something about some tights of hers going missing.'

He stood up, tossing the newspaper to one side.

Jane nodded. Although Moran sounded perfectly plausible she was still dubious and asked what Allard had done with the balaclava. Moran didn't flinch.

'He said he threw it in a rubbish bin after the rape.'

He glanced at his watch.

'Listen, I'm busy and can't stop and chat all day . . .

Allard is not the only case I have to deal with. But thanks for all your help and for making the arrest. By the way, Allard also signed the notes you took during the interview after the search and you'll need to counter-sign them sometime ... you'll find them on my desk.'

Jane smiled as he hurried past her, and she went into his office to look over his desk. There were numerous files so she had to search through everything to find the notes. Just as she was beginning to sift through them, Sergeant Harris barged into the main room.

'Good, you're here ... take over the front desk, Tennison. I've got a drunk down in the cells who's creating havoc. You know Allard was remanded in custody and his defence solicitor has requested an "old style" committal, which'll be heard next week. Have you signed the notes from DI Moran?'

'I haven't finished working on them yet.'

'I just need you to sign what's there.'

Jane came out of Moran's office. She leaned on a desk and flicked quickly through the documents until she saw the note slip requesting her signature. She signed it and passed it over to Harris. He took it and jerked his head for her to get to the front desk.

Jane hurried out as Harris organized the papers and Moran walked back in with a cup of coffee.

'You get her to sign them?'

'Yeah, here you go.'

Harris handed them to Moran, and left. There was a tense atmosphere in the room as Edwards glanced over, not missing anything that had just taken place, but he quickly returned to typing.

'You got a problem, Brian?'

'No, guv.'

'Good, because we don't have one and we are going to get that piece of karate shit put away for a long stretch.'

'I hope Jane will be able to handle being questioned in court . . . It'll be her first time and some of these barristers are lethal.'

Moran walked into his office, kicking the door open wider with his foot.

'Do me a favour . . . he's going to plead guilty for a string of assaults as well as the rape. We have his confession, so she might not even be called to the witness box.'

Edwards said nothing as Moran's door slammed shut. He hoped it would run that smoothly. He jerked his tie loose and his collar button came off and rolled onto the floor. He knew that if Tennison was called to give evidence he would be too, and just the thought of it brought him out in a sweat.

CHAPTER SIX

A week later, Jane paced nervously up and down the police officers' waiting room at Old Street Magistrates' Court, going over her notes on the arrest and interviews of Peter Allard. She had given evidence at the Magistrates' Court during her probation, but they had only been minor offences for shoplifting, criminal damage and drunk and disorderly where her evidence was straightforward and the defence solicitor asked only a few questions in cross-examination. Giving evidence at Crown Court was a different matter.

On his first appearance at court earlier in the week Allard was granted legal aid and represented by the duty solicitor. He offered a plea of guilty to the indecent assault charges and assault on a police officer. However, when he was told about his client's initial denial concerning the rape charge and the alleged confession, Allard's solicitor had requested an old-style committal on the rape alone. On hearing the evidence the magistrate would decide if the case should be committed to the Old Bailey for trial by jury.

DC Edwards sat quietly, biting his fingernails, while

121

DI Moran read *The Sun* and drank tea from a polystyrene cup.

'It's not as if you're gripping the rail at the big house, so bloody well sit down and stop worrying, Tennison,' Moran said sternly, then, licking his finger, flicked over to page three as usual and commented on the breasts of Jilly Johnson.

Jane sat down next to DC Edwards and spoke quietly. 'What's he mean by gripping the rail?'

'Giving evidence at the Old Bailey under a hostile defence barrister,' DC Edwards replied.

'Allard's got a barrister representing him today, hasn't he?' Jane asked apprehensively.

'Yes, a QC, and by all accounts he's a bit of an ogre who likes to attack police officers in the witness box.'

DI Moran closed his newspaper and threw it down on the table next to him.

'Would you two shut up! The magistrate will have read your statements and you'll be cross-examined by Allard's counsel, that's all ... it's no big deal.' He looked at Edwards. 'What are you doing? Trying to put the fear of God in her? Allard made the confession to me, so I'm the one who'll get all the flack, not you!'

'I was just trying to prepare her, sir.'

'Oh shut up, Edwards.'

Moran looked at Jane.

'You'll be fine ... Just stay calm and answer yes or no, three bags full, sir ... all right?'

At that moment the door to the waiting room opened and the court usher stuck her head round the door.

'Right, your case is under way in Court One.'

Jane jumped up, brushed her uniform down and headed towards the door.

'Where are you going?' the usher asked.

'To sit in court,' Jane replied, somewhat confused by the question.

'I'm sorry but DI Moran is on first. You have to wait in here and not discuss the case with your colleague. I will come and get you when it's your turn to give evidence.'

Moran sighed as he stood up.

'She's fairly new to all this. You can sit in after you've given your evidence, Tennison, but not while another officer is giving evidence – otherwise you'd know the questions that were put to me and the answers I gave, which kind of goes against the course of justice.'

That's rich coming from you, Jane thought to herself, as Moran left the room.

After the usher closed the door Edwards looked at Jane with a worried expression.

'Moran wants me to say I saw him search Allard at the scene of the arrest. He's adamant he had the flick knife on him—'

Jane shook her head as she interrupted Edwards. 'But we both know you didn't see him search Allard, and neither of us saw the knife until Moran produced it out of thin air in the charge room.'

'Yeah, but if the confession wasn't genuine then why would Allard even sign it? Allard could just be trying to muddy the waters and Moran could be telling the truth. Maybe we're wrong.'

'Who are you trying to convince, me or yourself? I

agree it's strange that Allard should sign a confession if it was false, but for all we know Moran could have threatened him about his wife and kids, or tricked him somehow ... who knows? There's no way I'm fabricating evidence and saying that I saw Allard searched at the scene, and neither should you. Like Moran just said, he's the one who will take the flack ... besides it's his career on the line, not ours, if he's lying.'

'You're right, Jane, and at the end of the day the magistrate will decide if there is enough evidence to commit for trial.'

'Which is unlikely when you look at the facts of the rape compared to the indecent assaults. I took another look at the rape victim's statement and the way he smelt of body odour and ...'

Edwards stood up and moved towards the door.

'Where are you going?'

'I need the loo again,' Edwards said, as he hurried out of the room. Jane shouted after him to get her a coffee then continued reading over her notes. She was now feeling more nervous than before after everything he had just said.

When Edwards returned fifteen minutes later he looked pale, almost as if he'd been sick. Jane suspected he had, though she didn't ask. She stood up and moved towards the door.

'You need a pee as well?'

'No, I asked you to get me a coffee. Do you want one?'

'Sorry, I forgot. I'd better not have one in case I'm called next.'

Jane went into the cell area of the court and asked the custody sergeant if she could get a coffee. He smiled and told her to help herself, but to leave five pence in the small metal tin next to the kettle. She took her time as she didn't want to get into a deliberation about the case with DC Edwards, so she had a quick chat with a PC whom she recognized from the section house. As she returned to the officers' waiting room with her coffee she crossed the entrance hall of the courts and saw Marie Allard coming out of Court One in floods of tears.

'Are you all right, Marie?' Jane asked, as she approached her out of concern.

Marie slowly looked up at Jane with a mixture of contempt and loathing in her eyes.

'You all in this pack of lies together, aren't you? You don't care about the truth. My husband admitted the indecent assaults, but he never confessed to rape, did he?'

Jane felt apprehensive. She didn't really know what to say, but she was upset by the state Marie was in.

'I don't know, Marie ... I wasn't present when DI Moran took the confession.'

'I just sat in there and listened to him lie. Peter deserve whatever he get for assaulting those poor women, but not to go to prison for years for something he not do.'

'It may not come to that, Marie. The magistrate could decide there's not enough evidence to send your husband for trial.'

'And if he go to trial, what happen then? Will you stand up for him and tell truth?'

Jane didn't know what to say and regretted ever approaching Marie Allard. The courtroom door opened and the usher looked surprised to see Jane.

'What do you think you're doing, officer?' she asked.

'I was just asking Mrs Allard if she was all right, as she looked very upset.'

'Well, you should not be speaking to the defendant's wife – it is totally inappropriate. Now please return to the officers' waiting room and tell DC Edwards he has been called to give evidence.'

Jane felt distressed that she had made such a stupid error. She had been genuinely concerned about Marie Allard, but resigned herself that what was done was done and there was nothing untoward in her approach. As she entered the waiting room she told DC Edwards that he'd been called. Jane looked at him.

'Brian, there's something you need to know.'

'What? What's happened? Tell me quickly, before I go in there.'

'I just got told off for speaking with Marie Allard ... she was in an awful state.'

'You what? How could you be so stupid? She might get called by the defence as a witness.'

'I don't think so. She was sitting in court listening to Moran give his evidence so she can't be a witness.'

'Of course she can – the magistrate may have allowed her to sit in as she could be giving evidence on her husband's character.'

'But I thought—'

'Well, you thought wrong. For Christ's sake, what did you say to her?' Edwards began to ask, as the waiting room door opened and the usher stood there with a frown.

'I hope you two are not discussing the case, especially not Officer Tennison's inappropriate conversation with Mrs Allard?'

'No,' Edwards replied, as he sheepishly left the room.

Jane spent the next half-hour worrying about what she may now be asked and what to say when she was called. A part of her considered that maybe it would be some form of justice if her actions caused the rape case against Allard to be thrown out, but it could also be the end of any ambitions she had of ever joining the CID. It was over half an hour later before the usher came and collected Jane. As she walked into the court she could see Peter Allard looking forlorn in the dock, as did his wife who was now sitting in the public area. DI Moran and DC Edwards were seated in the corner of the room. Edwards looked nervous and avoided eye contact with Jane, whereas Moran had a smug grin on his face as if the case was going his way. As Jane entered the witness box the usher handed her a Bible and a card with the oath written on it. Jane raised the Bible in her right hand, looked over at Moran and read the oath.

'I swear by Almighty God that the evidence I shall give shall be the truth, the whole truth and nothing but the truth. Jane Tennison WPC 517 attached to Hackney Police Station.'

Allard's barrister stood up. 'I am Anthony Nichols QC and represent Mr Allard. May I say, officer, you read the oath with some conviction.'

'Thank you, sir,' Jane replied, glad that he had appreciated it in the manner she intended.

'May I ask, though, why you directed it towards DI Moran and not the magistrate as is normal practice when an officer takes the oath?'

Realizing her mistake Jane looked at the magistrate. 'Sorry, sir, it was remiss of me.'

The magistrate smiled. 'That's all right, officer. Please continue, Mr Nichols.'

'Well, let's hope it was a faux pas, officer, as opposed to an inference towards the truthfulness of evidence that we have heard from DI Moran today.'

Nichols was in his late forties, with fading red hair carefully combed over to hide its thinning. He wore a pinstripe suit and blue cotton shirt with a white collar.

'My client wishes to express his deep regret about the indecent assault, not only on you but the other women, and that cutting your lip with his elbow during the arrest had not in any way been deliberate. However, he pleads guilty to that offence as, although it had been reckless behaviour, it nevertheless constituted an assault on a police officer.'

Jane said nothing in reply to the barrister's remarks. Nichols flicked over a page in his notes, which were laid out on the table in front of him.

'My only question to you about the arrest of Mr Allard is whether or not at any time he had possession of a knife?'

'He said he'd got a knife.'

'Yes, but did you *see* one, officer?'

'Sorry, no . . . not until I was at the station.'

'Did you physically search him at the station?'

'No, DI Moran did.'

'And you saw him find the flick knife on Mr Allard at this point?'

'No, I was in the police surgeon's room treating my cut lip.'

'Where was DC Edwards at this time?'

'I assume he was in the charge room with DI Moran.'

'Well, you assume wrong. According to the evidence he just gave he was in fact looking for the duty sergeant to come and book the prisoner in.'

'I wasn't aware of that.'

'Were you aware that DI Moran searched Mr Allard at the time of his arrest and allegedly found the flick knife in his possession?'

'No, I only knew when DI Moran produced the knife from his own pocket in the charge room that he said he found it on the defendant.'

Nichols was about to continue when the magistrate interrupted.

'Is there any point in pursuing this line of questioning? DC Edwards has told you he saw DI Moran search the defendant at the scene and put something in his own pocket, but being dark he could not say what it was. It's reasonable to assume it was the flick knife. DI Moran has stated that, because WPC Tennison was in such a distressed state having just been savagely attacked by your client, he decided it was best not to mention, or show her, the knife, until they had returned to the station.'

'It is relevant, sir, because I believe that DI Moran left

the charge room on the pretext of needing the toilet so he could get the flick knife to plant on Mr Allard in his first step towards falsely implicating him in the rape.'

'Well, DC Edwards has said that he never saw DI Moran leave the charge room, and although he went to get the custody sergeant he was certain the DI would never leave a prisoner alone, particularly for such serious offences.'

'Well, my client is adamant that DI Moran left the room briefly and I would argue that DC Edwards is lying.'

The magistrate frowned.

'And the officers argue that your client is lying, Mr Nichols, but it is a matter for me to decide who is telling the truth or not. So please move on with your questioning of WPC Tennison.'

Jane couldn't believe what she had just heard and now understood why Edwards had avoided eye contact with her, and Moran had looked so smug when she entered the courtroom. She was nervously anticipating Mr Nichols asking if she thought Edwards was lying and Moran had planted the knife but was surprised when, as advised by the magistrate, he changed his line of questioning.

Nichols flicked over to another page of his notes and spoke in a begrudging tone.

'Moving on as requested. Now, WPC Tennison, you were present during two interviews that DI Moran conducted with Mr Allard?'

'Yes.'

'And would you accept that in the first interview he

lied in essence because he was worried about what his wife would think of him?'

'Yes, and I think that was why he gave us false details about who he really was.'

'And in the second interview he admitted his crimes. Apart from the rape, that is?'

'Yes, that is correct.'

'And you contemporaneously recorded the interviews on the correct forms.'

'Yes, I did.'

'Did you ask Mr Allard to read and sign the interview notes?'

'After the first interview DI Moran asked him to and he did, but after the second interview I didn't personally because—'

'A confession to a number of indecent assaults and a denial to a violent rape, yet you didn't follow one of the basic principles of the Judges' Rules concerning the interrogation of a suspect?'

'I had to take Allard back down to the cells and he was asking to make a phone call and to contact a solicitor—'

'A solicitor he never got, yet was entitled to speak with under the Judges' Rules. Tell me, WPC Tennison, do you even know what the Judges' Rules are?'

'Yes, we had to learn them at training school—'

'Well, they obviously didn't sink in where you're concerned, did they?'

Jane felt embarrassed and flustered. Although her experience in court was limited she knew Nichols was playing mind games with her.

'It was remiss of me not to, and at the time I should have said something, but DI Moran was in charge of the case and didn't mention the signing of the notes until later.'

'When did you sign the notes of the second interview?'

'The following morning.'

'And when did DI Moran and my client sign them?'

'I don't know, but as I recall their signatures were already on each page when I signed them.'

'Were you present when the alleged confession was made to, and recorded by, DI Moran?'

'No.'

'Have you taken part in a conspiracy with your colleagues to frame an innocent man with a crime he did not commit?'

'No, I have not,' Jane replied strongly, resenting his accusation.

'Do you think DI Moran has fabricated evidence and been supported in his lies by DC Edwards?'

Jane had no choice but to pause and think how she should best answer the question. She now knew that Brian Edwards had lied to the court, yet in some ways she sympathized with him and realized it was probably down to the fear of being ostracized by his colleagues. As for Moran, she knew deep down he had lied and looking up she could see the expression on his face. It was then that Jane wanted to shout out at the top of her voice 'Moran is a liar', but she couldn't do it. She couldn't ruin her own career on a gut feeling with no evidence.

'I'm surprised the question is something you have to think about, officer, as the answer should be a simple yes or no,' Nichols said with arrogance, pushing her for a reply.

'Sorry, I was upset by your insinuation that I or my colleagues were in any way dishonest. So the answer to your question is *no*.'

'Do you know Marie Allard?'

'Yes.'

'And have spoken with her on three occasions, I believe?'

The magistrate stopped taking notes and looked up at Mr Nichols.

'According to the papers I have read, WPC Tennison only met Marie Allard when she went to search the house.'

Nichols now informed the magistrate that on the morning of Peter Allard's first court appearance Jane spoke briefly with Marie outside the police station and then again at court this morning. The magistrate looked perturbed and asked Jane what the conversation was about. Before Jane could answer, Nichols informed him that Mrs Allard said WPC Tennison innocently asked how she was, and after expressing her concerns about the evidence against Mr Allard, WPC Tennison had said that the magistrate might decide there was not enough evidence to send the rape charge for trial.

The magistrate gave Jane a stern look before continuing. 'And what makes you think that, officer?'

Again, Nichols added fuel to the fire with a haughty smile. 'Exactly what I was wondering, sir, and may I also add that at the meeting outside the station WPC Tennison seemed surprised and somewhat shocked when Mrs Allard informed her that her husband had allegedly confessed to DI Moran.'

Jane looked crestfallen. She knew Nichols had belittled her and her evidence, yet in other ways she knew she'd dug a hole for herself. Now she wished it would open further and swallow her up so she could get away from what was becoming an intimidating and uncomfortable experience. Jane knew that, after her earlier answer about DI Moran and DC Edwards, she had to avoid intimating they had lied, even if it meant dropping herself further in the mire. She took a deep breath before continuing.

'I read all the indecent assault victims' statements and compared them with my own experience at the hands of the defendant. It seems to me that his actions, accent and words used differed from those carried out in the rape. The flick knife was actually seen and physically used in the rape and the assailant wore a balaclava, as opposed to a stocking mask like the defendant did when arrested by me.'

Mr Nichols nodded. 'Very astute, officer, and apart from the false confession, an argument I was going to put forward as to why there is not a prima facie case or evidence to commit Mr Allard to the Old Bailey for trial.'

The magistrate did not look best pleased with either Jane or Mr Nichols. Jane could sense that no matter what Mr Nichols said, or even if she herself had stated that she believed Moran had fabricated the evidence, there was no way the case was not going to be committed for trial.

The magistrate removed his glasses and put them down on the desk.

'I have read the police report, as well as all the victims' statements, the defendant's interviews and his confession. At first Allard lied about the attack on WPC Tennison, then he lied about who he was and where he lived, facts he has since admitted. Once faced with insurmountable evidence, and the knowledge that his wife knew of his crimes regarding the indecent assaults, he capitulated and admitted his guilt. But he still denied the more serious crime of rape. It seems to me that there is always the possibility that his guilt eventually weighed so heavy that he did indeed confess to the rape. I see no reason why he would sign a false confession. However, that said, it is for a jury to determine guilt or innocence and from the evidence I have heard and reviewed so far the rape charge will be committed to the Old Bailey for trial.'

Nichols did not look pleased and asked if he could bring one further thing to the magistrate's attention.

'If you must, Mr Nichols, but I fail to see what you can add to change my mind.'

Nichols now asked the usher to hand Jane a photocopy of the original second interview and said he wanted her to look at the bottom of each page and confirm that she had signed each and every page. As Jane flicked through the document the magistrate asked Nichols what the purpose of the exercise was, as the defendant was not challenging anything asked or said in either of the interviews contemporaneously recorded by WPC Tennison. Nichols asked him to bear with him for a couple more minutes.

As Jane looked through the interview she noticed that there were two pages that did not bear her signature. She was about to flick back when Nichols spoke.

'Is there a problem, officer?'

Jane looked glum as she put the notes down on the witness box. 'I don't appear to have signed two pages of the interview, yet DI Moran and Mr Allard have. It may have been an error on my behalf.'

'Oh, don't worry about that. I don't suspect you of anything untoward. We all make mistakes when we are in a rush and not concentrating. Do you have a pen?'

'Yes,' Jane replied, wondering what was going on in Nichols's mind.

'I know the interview is a photocopy of the original, but would you mind quickly signing the two pages for my benefit, just so everything is tickety-boo for my file?'

Jane got out her pen, flicked through to the pages that were unsigned, duly wrote her name and number and held out the papers to the usher to return to Mr Nichols.

'Please double-check the pages you just signed.'

Jane was puzzled. 'I know I just signed them and you saw me do it, so why?'

'Read the two pages you just inadvertently signed,' Nichols said pointedly.

Jane now turned to the two pages, put the others to one side and couldn't believe what she started to read. It was the alleged confession made by Peter Allard written by DI Moran.

Nichols picked up on her expression of amazement.

'You see how easy it is to be tricked into signing something when you are confused and flustered, as was Peter Allard when DI Moran asked him to sign what he believed was the record of the second interview. Like DI Moran did, I simply slipped the confession into the middle of the bundle and you, in all innocence, signed the confession as if you were guilty of a crime you never committed.'

Jane felt awful but now realized that Nichols was probably right and DI Moran had indeed tricked Peter Allard into signing the false confession by slipping it into the bundle and then removing it before she signed the record of the interview. She looked up at Moran but he didn't bat an eyelid, and Mr Nichols, having made his point to the magistrate, sat down.

The magistrate didn't look impressed and cleared his throat.

'You have made your point by using WPC Tennison as a scapegoat, Mr Nichols. However, I am still of the opinion that the charge of rape will be committed to the Old Bailey for trial. I also accept that your client has pleaded to the indecent assaults and assault on a police officer, for which I can sentence him today. In my opinion, the penalties of imprisonment in this court are inadequate with regard to the seriousness of the offences. Therefore, I will commit him for sentencing in custody at the higher court by the presiding judge on completion of the rape trial.'

Peter Allard jumped up in the dock, pleaded his innocence and shouted that he had been tricked by DI Moran. The magistrate told him to sit down and be quiet, but he wouldn't desist and now Marie Allard joined in by shouting that the officers were all liars. It became so unruly that the magistrate ordered Allard to be taken to the cells and his wife removed from the courtroom. When this was done the magistrate stood up, said the case was over and that all parties could leave, then he left the room by his personal side entrance.

As Jane stepped out of the witness box she looked at Moran and Edwards with disgust and let them leave the room before her.

Jane picked up her police hat from the waiting room. There was no sign of Moran or Edwards. She stepped into the street and was relieved to see that Marie Allard wasn't there. As she stood at the bus stop an unmarked CID car pulled up and Moran leaned out of the passenger window.

'You want a lift back to the station?'

'No, I'll make my own way.'

'Please yourself,' he replied in a dour tone. 'You did all right in there, Allard's barrister thought he was bloody Perry Mason.' Moran waved his arm for DC Edwards to drive off.

Marie was making the children's breakfast of cereal and scrambled eggs on toast. The kettle was on and the toast was under the grill. She had already called them twice and could hear them running noisily from room to room. The 'nice house' was in complete disarray, with cupboards and drawers open everywhere.

'Breakfast! Come to the table NOW!' she shouted, as she went out of the kitchen into the hall. Her son ran out from the sitting room, followed by her daughter. The little girl had a red velvet rose clipped into her hair. It was the treasured rose from the vase next to the statue of the Virgin Mary.

Marie snatched it from the child's hair, screeching, 'You know never to touch that ... you very, very naughty girl, and you get punished.'

'Punished like Susie Luna,' her son said gleefully.

Marie was shocked and looked so frightened that he felt guilty.

'Sorry, Mama ...'

'Sit down at the table. Do as I say right *now*, both of you.'

Marie went into the sitting room. She crossed herself and kissed her crucifix, and tried to calm herself down. How did her son know that name? What made him say it? The fear gripped her again. She was about to replace the rose in the vase next to the Virgin Mary, but instead she tore it to shreds, stuffing the frail leaves and velvet petals into her apron pocket.

Marie went back into the kitchen to finish preparing the children's breakfast. They sat very quietly watching her as she frantically whisked the eggs in a bowl, spilling some on the counter. The toast was now burning under the grill, and the kettle was whistling loudly. Then the phone started ringing shrilly in the hall, making her physically jump. She turned the kettle off and grabbed the toast from under the grill, almost throwing it onto the table.

'You put on butter,' she said to the children. The phone carried on ringing as Marie hurried to answer it.

'Hello?'

She heard nothing but silence. Puzzled, Marie asked again, 'Hello? Hello – who is this?'

Irritated by the silence, she was about to hang up when a voice crooning the words of a familiar Rolling Stones song began to come through the phone. Marie froze as the voice got louder and louder.

'Who is this?' Marie asked again. But the voice didn't stop, now almost screaming the words to 'Angie' down the line.

'What you want?' Marie was crying now, shaking, her hand gripping the phone, unable to put it down.

The singing stopped abruptly and a hoarse voice answered.

'Five hundred pounds in used notes. If you report this call, I got the evidence to put your husband away for rape. I'll call again in two days.'

Marie heard the line go dead. The receiver felt like a heavy weight in her hand as she slowly replaced it. She stood rooted with fear in the hallway. She didn't know what to do.

CHAPTER SEVEN

Jane looked out of the window; the leaves were falling now and the warmth of September had long gone and an autumn chill was in the air. She was sitting nervously in a small ante-room at Scotland Yard, wearing full uniform. While a PA was working busily at a nearby desk, Jane took a final look at some small note cards she had written. A male uniform officer came out of the interview room in a state of distress. Pulling off his clip-on police tie he kicked at a chair, and Jane, now even more nervous, got up to go in, but the PA told her to wait and said that she would be called when they were ready.

Over the PA's intercom Jane heard a gruff male voice asking for WPC Tennison to be sent in. She stood up and smoothed out her uniform, picking off some fluff from her jacket. She took a deep breath and entered the room.

Three men, a Commander, a Detective Chief Superintendent and a DCI, sat behind a long table. Jane was invited to take a seat opposite them and the Commander, who was sitting between the two other officers, flipped open a file with her name on it. 'WPC

Tennison, we know your name, would you be kind enough to tell us who will be interviewing you today?'

Jane looked puzzled as there were no name cards. However, she'd done her research and knew the three senior officers' names. She looked at each of them as she gave their names.

'You'd be surprised how many people don't do their homework and get it wrong, like the last officer.'

Next the Commander asked why she thought she should be made detective. Jane swallowed. 'During my time in uniform I feel I have proved myself capable through hard work and tenacity.'

The DCI asked, 'Have you any registered informants?'

'No, sir, I reacted on anonymous information. I did some research before obtaining a search warrant which resulted in the discovery of a quantity of stolen goods.'

She was then asked what the goods were and sheepishly replied they were clothes from Woolworths, but it was an organized gang of women shoplifters who were selling the goods on a market stall.

'Hardly the crime of the century,' said the DCI. 'Well, I expected to hear something a bit more interesting and worthy of someone who wants to become a Met detective.'

'I recently acted as a decoy and subsequently arrested a man who was wanted for a series of indecent assaults on women, as well as a rape.'

'Did he indecently assault you?' the Commander asked.

'Yes,' Jane replied, blushing and wondering if they already knew about the case.

'What exactly did he do?' the Superintendent asked. It felt as if he was revelling in Jane's obvious embarrassment.

'He touched me, sir . . .'

He smirked. 'How did he touch you? Was it a quick squeeze or a full-on grope?'

'He grabbed me from behind, and he groped my breast. Then he tried to drag me to a darkened area by the Lido. When I attempted to break away from him he hit me in the mouth with his elbow, splitting my lip. I thought he was going to rape me, sir.'

The Commander looked at her file and then glanced up at her, tapping the page with his finger.

'It states here that the suspect alleged that in actual fact you assaulted him?'

Jane was tight-lipped as she informed them that the suspect attacked her first and that she had defended herself.

The Commander turned over another page, again tapping it with his forefinger.

'According to this report it says that you hit him across the head with a truncheon, also delivering a well-aimed kick to his groin?'

One of the other two men sitting at the table winced, saying that he didn't know women carried truncheons. Jane was becoming very tense.

'I borrowed one from a colleague and had it tucked up my coat sleeve.'

They smiled.

'Forward thinking and good planning – well done. No doubt he deserved a good whack across the head.'

The Detective Chief Superintendent asked, 'Has he been convicted?'

'The magistrate committed him for sentencing in custody at the higher court on completion of the rape trial.'

He turned to another page, and whispered to his colleagues.

The DCI picked up the report, and took over the questioning. He remarked that Jane had previously been interviewed by A10 department over an allegation that a DS Gibbs had assaulted a drug dealer and had stolen his money.

Jane was very defensive, but maintained her control, as she explained, 'The drug dealer withdrew the allegation and DS Gibbs has been reinstated to duty.'

The Commander pointed out that this didn't mean it hadn't happened. He took the report back and flicked to yet another page. It seemed like an age before he looked up again.

'You were interviewed by A10 a second time over a botched bank raid, during which an explosion occurred and a DCI Bradfield and WPC Morgan were both killed?'

Jane became very subdued. 'I was the officer who initiated the investigation when I recognized the main suspect's voice from an audio tape.' It was very difficult to ascertain what all three men were thinking. They whispered to one another, and passed the reports back and forth, reading and turning pages.

The Commander then quoted from DCS Metcalf's report, which said that Jane had stuck to her guns about the suspect and although the investigation had ended in tragedy she was above reproach and had acted in a professional manner at all times. He was recommending her for the rank of detective. She felt the blood rushing to her cheeks. Metcalf had done as he had promised after all. The Commander added, 'The final decision, however, rests with us. Please wait outside.'

Jane stood up, gave a slight nod, and walked out. As she closed the door behind her, her legs felt like jelly. She sat back down in the chair outside the interview room.

The PA looked up. 'You're the final candidate, how did it go?' she asked sympathetically.

Jane frowned. 'Not too well.'

'Well, don't look so worried. There's another board for detective in a year's time.'

Jane sank back in her seat, convinced she had failed. The intercom buzzed and she was called back into the interview room again. She stood in front of the panel trying to hide the shake in her legs.

The Commander spoke. 'It has been a tough decision and we are not all in agreement. The CID in London only has a handful of women within their ranks and you have been recommended by DCS Metcalf, a highly respected and astute senior officer. However, you're still young in service compared to so many of the other candidates, and there are only a limited number of vacancies to be filled . . .' He paused before asking Jane for her warrant card, which she handed to him. He took it, smiled, and handed her back a new one. When she looked at it she saw the words 'Detective Constable Tennison'.

The panel congratulated her and told her that as

from Monday she would be posted to Bow Street Police Station CID. She was to report there at 10 a.m. to meet her new DCI. Jane's legs still felt very wobbly as she left, this time not with trepidation but with sheer excitement. She was so happy that she wanted to shout the news out to the world, and dance down the wide staircase.

After her interview, lightheaded with relief, she'd headed to Oxford Street and decided to treat herself to some clothes before going to see her parents to tell them the good news. That Friday evening Jane stood at the familiar front door, still wearing her uniform under a new raincoat. She had a bag of new clothes in one hand and a bottle of champagne in the other. She didn't use her key as she wanted to give her parents a surprise. She couldn't wait to tell them the good news. Mrs Tennison opened the front door and, seeing the bottle of champagne, she clapped her hands before Jane could say a word.

'Oh! Pam didn't tell me she'd spoken to you!'

Jane was confused.

'About what?' she asked, as she dropped the shopping bags in the hallway and took off her raincoat.

Her mother rushed into the living room to announce that Jane had arrived with a bottle of champagne. Jane followed her mother into the room, holding her new warrant card in one hand and the champagne bottle in the other.

'I'm really excited about this! ... Look at my new—'

Pam grabbed the bottle, grinning, as Mrs Tennison said, 'So are we! It's such wonderful news, isn't it?'

'How did you know?' Jane asked.

'Pam told us, of course! We're absolutely thrilled! I'll get some champagne glasses so we can all celebrate.'

'How did she know I'd passed the interview board?' Jane asked, somewhat confused. There was a stunned silence in the room.

'I'll be starting at the famous Bow Street Police Station on Monday.'

'Oh ... we thought you'd come to celebrate Pam's wonderful news.'

'What news?' Jane asked.

'She's pregnant, so you'll soon be an auntie.'

Mrs Tennison went into the kitchen and opened the cupboards looking for champagne glasses. Almost as if it was an afterthought she asked, 'Will you still be in uniform at Bow Street?'

Jane patiently explained that she was now a member of the plain-clothed CID and that she'd been made detective. She proudly held up her new warrant card. Mrs Tennison glanced at it and then handed it back.

'I think it's safer in uniform, dear, after what happened to those detectives in the bank explosion.'

Pam now joined them.

'I would think that central London isn't a very safe place, what with that bank explosion. And now you're really going to have to take care of yourself as you'll have responsibilities as an auntie. If you agree we both want to have you as Godmother.'

Mrs Tennison very obviously didn't want to talk about Jane's work and told her father to get a tray for the glasses and open the bottle of champagne so that they could celebrate Pam's pregnancy.

Jane felt totally deflated. It was as if her news was trivial in comparison. She tried to put on a brave face, smiling and then toasting Pam with her champagne. Mrs Tennison asked Jane if she would be moving back home.

'Not at present.'

'How will you get to and from Bow Street?'

Jane said that she hadn't had time to look at the best route yet. Mr Tennison opened a drawer in the kitchen and took out an *A – Z*.

'Right, always best to be prepared ... let's have a look. You can get the Central Line to Holborn, then change onto the Piccadilly Line for one stop to Covent Garden, then walk through Covent Garden to Bow Street.'

It was unbelievable. Suddenly everyone was concentrating on the route for her to get to her new job.

Mrs Tennison was quick to point out that the Bakerloo Line from Maida Vale was just down the road and went directly to Charing Cross. Bow Street was only a short walk from there. So Jane should move back home.

Mr Tennison changed the subject. Pam, who always liked being in the spotlight and had just snatched it from Jane with her news about being pregnant, began asking everyone to list the names they all liked best for either a boy or a girl. Jane sipped the rather tepid champagne and glanced at her father. He raised his glass to her.

'Congratulations, my darling ... You must be very proud, as am I. You're going to be Detective Jane Tennison ... good girl, shows they must think a lot of you.'

'Thank you, Daddy, I am very proud.'

'I know, if Pam has a girl let's call her Jane!'

'Oh no!' Pam objected. 'Plain Jane? No. I think she should be called Tiffany.'

'You don't want to call a baby girl after a lampshade!' Jane's mother said, horrified.

'A Tiffany shade, Mother, is of great value.'

As usual Jane saw her sister dominating the conversation and stealing her limelight. 'What about Victoria?' She might as well add her own two pennies worth, she thought, smiling as she sipped her champagne.

CHAPTER EIGHT

Jane looked around at the flushed faces of her colleagues. They were squashed into the saloon bar of the Warburton Arms, which was full of people celebrating the weekend. She'd just finished her last shift at Hackney before starting at Bow Street on Monday and was heading out of the station door when Harris accosted her. 'Didn't think we'd let you leave without saying goodbye, did you, love?' Blushing, Jane had been escorted to the pub across the road and now all the team were there. They had passed an envelope around to fund an open bar, with Ron the landlord monitoring the cash flow. He had provided sandwiches, sausage rolls and packets of crisps on the counter, alongside bottles of red and white wine. Everyone congratulated Jane and wished her well, especially DI Moran who had obviously been drinking more than his fair share. His tie was pulled loose under his open shirt collar, and he had one arm around DC Edwards's shoulders, who was also looking rather drunk.

'Well, you're going to be up against it at Bow Street, Tennison ... everything is on high alert after the bomb in Guildford today. You better be careful in the West End too, with it being close to Covent Garden Market, where you get a lot of dross, and drop-ins from any of the Met officers going to the courts. Who's the DCI there?'

Jane shrugged her shoulders. 'I'm not sure, sir.'

'Well, it's always good to have a change of scenery, but it depends on who's the guv, you know ... You can get a lot of flack. If you want my advice, and you can take it or leave it, but ...'

He used two fingers to point to his eyes, and then directed them to Jane's.

'Keep your eyes open, listen and learn, and above all ... remember ...' Moran seemed to lose track of what he was saying, as Edwards propped him up.

'Just remember ... keep your nose clean, right, Brian?'

'Yes, guv.'

Jane had drunk more of Ron's lukewarm white wine than usual. Sergeant Harris was also getting into the swing of it and insisted on passing Jane a drink and taking over the conversation. He clinked her glass so hard it almost shattered.

'Congratulashuns!' he slurred, downing his entire glass and placing it back on the bar. 'So you'll be stationed at Bow Street ... Here's something I bet you didn't know ... Sherlock Holmes wrote about the station in his story "The Man with the Harelip" ... no, that's not right ... it was "The Man with the *Twisted* Lip" ... I don't usually come to these dos but I felt on this occasion I should as, I have to admit, I'm proud of you, Tennison ... You've handled yourself very well under extreme circumshtances ... Have another drink ...'

'No, thank you, I'm fine.' Jane held up her still half full glass.

'Yes, you are fine, but you know, we've all been marked ... every one of us ... doesn't matter how long ago, it's inside ... and you come in here like always and you see youngsters like you moving on, but they're like ghosts ... You keep expecting to see Kath Morgan with her G and T putting money in the juke box, and Len Bradfield over at the billiard table slapping a fiver down ... he was a bloody useless player.'

Harris picked up another glass of wine.

'Sorry ... don't want to put a dampener on things ... like I said, it was some time ago now, and I don't usually make an appearance at these leaving drinks ... They're mostly just an excuse for everyone to get pissed ... have you got a drink?'

'I'm all right, Sarge. I'm glad to have this opportunity to thank you for all your help while I've been here.'

He cocked his head to one side, then he suddenly leaned forward and gave her a dry kiss on her cheek.

'Maybe I know more than you ever realized ... you handled yourself well, considering how close you were to Bradfield.'

Jane flushed and was suddenly eager to leave, not wanting to discuss her relationship.

Harris said quietly, 'We all have secrets, some best kept that way. I have one that I've never let be known.'

Jane couldn't help herself. 'You, Sergeant?'

'Yes, but you keep this to yourself. I'm part of a

ballroom formation team, and we've got a good chance of being in the finals at Blackpool ... Old Time waltz is my speciality.'

Jane was completely taken aback as he gave her a sweeping gesture with his arm and stumbled backwards, bumping into Edwards. Moran suddenly stepped in beside Jane and reached for a glass of wine. He had a lit cigarette in his mouth and leaned closer to her, keeping his voice low.

'We'll get a few more drinks down him and if the right music's on the juke box he dances, and we all have a good laugh! He never remembers in the morning ... when he's had too much to drink he always gives away his ballroom dancing secret.'

Moran gave Jane a lopsided smile but his expression was serious.

'Everyone has secrets, don't they, Jane?'

Jane was uneasy, not about the increasingly drunk Harris, but about the way in which Moran had looked at her when he had said 'everyone has secrets'. Did they all know about her relationship with Bradfield, her secret? Did they make derogatory remarks about it and gossip about her being a one-night stand after he had sent her off the case? Jane was blushing profusely and just wanted to leave.

'So, we're going to have a snooker game and get down to some serious drinking ... are you up for it?' Moran asked.

'Actually, I think I should just go back to the section house and get a good night's sleep.'

Jane turned to put her glass on the bar and thank

Ron. The envelope funds had now all been spent, and the plates of food were empty. Pints of beer were being lined up and numerous officers from the station were crowding the bar.

'I'll walk you over there. It's late, and this is a dodgy area at night.'

Moran held her elbow and guided her through the crowds. As they reached the pub's double doors Jane insisted that she was more than capable of walking back by herself. Moran pushed one door open and leaned in towards her.

'I just want to straighten something out. You seemed a bit tense after the court hearing . . . is anything bothering you? If it is, just spit it out so we can clear the air. Do you have a problem, Tennison?' Moran cocked his head to one side, exhaling a lungful of cigarette smoke.

Jane hesitated, then shook her head. She didn't feel that this was either the time or place to discuss her reservations, and Moran was too close for comfort. He appeared to have sobered up and his deep, piercing eyes were making her feel nervous.

'No, sir . . . no problem.'

'Good. I have masses of cases coming in, but we'll be seeing each other when the Allard trial kicks off. In the meantime I'll give your thanks to everyone.'

She gave him a small smile, doubting whether anyone would have actually missed her leaving the pub. The festive atmosphere inside had become rather raucous.

'Goodbye then, Tennison, and good luck . . . Detective Constable . . .'

'Thank you, sir.'

Jane walked down the pavement to cross over the road to the section house. When she turned back to the pub Moran was still watching her. He tossed his cigarette butt onto the ground and stamped it out with the heel of his Cuban boot. Perhaps he was aware of her infatuation with Bradfield, and maybe even knew that she had slept with him. But it didn't really matter now, she was moving on and away from Hackney.

CHAPTER NINE

Jane had spent Sunday tidying her room, changing the bed linen and generally preparing for her new job at Bow Street. She had meant to allow herself plenty of time on Monday morning but her alarm didn't go off. She dressed hurriedly, glad that she had taken the time to lay out her new suit and blouse the previous night, and was on her way within fifteen minutes.

Remembering her father's instructions, she took the Underground to Covent Garden, which was just a short walk from Bow Street. She passed the Royal Opera House, with its beautiful white pillars and marble steps, having picked up her pace to cut across from the big fruit and vegetable market. The wonderful heady scent from the huge array of flower stalls was enough to lift anyone's senses, but Jane was just intent on reaching Bow Street Station as quickly as possible as delays on the Underground meant she was running late.

As she waited to cross the busy road she looked at the station building. It didn't remind her of Hackney, but it was of the same era – the heavy station doors with the iron blue lamp above them. No wonder Conan Doyle

156

used it in his story – it looked like a very intimidating Victorian building.

Jane hurried in through the main entrance. Inside it was a similar layout to her old station. There was the reception desk with the wooden counter, and a flap that could be lifted to allow officers to pass in and out, and very worn red leather chairs lined one wall.

The desk sergeant was terse and suggested that, as she was late, she should go directly to be introduced to her DCI and wouldn't have time to be shown around. He didn't introduce himself, or give her the chance to ask if she could use the ladies' cloakroom to tidy herself up. Instead he banged up the counter flap and gestured for her to follow him. He strode ahead through the annexe room, and then along a stone tiled corridor. Jane struggled to keep up as she desperately tried to tuck stray strands of hair back into place and make herself present-able. She was still carrying her raincoat and shoulder bag as they climbed a small flight of stone stairs onto the first-floor landing. Numerous offices led off the corridor and she could hear the sound of telephones ringing and the officers manning the comms room radioing out to the patrol cars. She might be in the glamorous West End now but the inside of a police station remained the same wherever you were. The familiarity was reassuring and Jane was comforted by the faded, yellowing walls and the vast array of posters. They reached the DCI's office and the duty sergeant turned to face her. Jane asked if he could just give her a moment to tidy her hair but he seemed totally uninterested. He held out his hand for her raincoat as he knocked on the DCI's door.

'I don't usually do this ... show you to his office. But you're late and ... There's a WDC Jane Tennison to see you, sir.'

Jane glanced at the plaque on the door: 'DCI P SHEPHERD'.

'Come in.' The voice was quiet and authoritative.

Jane entered the DCI's office. She was surprised to find that Shepherd was a diminutive and unassuming man. He was about five foot eight with a very pallid complexion and an unlined, boyish face. He had thick wavy hair that was parted to one side, with short side-burns, giving him an even more youthful appearance. His desk and walls were adorned with pictures of his wife and teenaged kids, with not one police photo, badge or crest. Before he could say a word there was another knock on the door and the sergeant ushered in DI Spencer Gibbs.

Shepherd introduced the two of them to one another. Jane was surprised that Gibbs barely reacted as he explained to the DCI that they already knew each other from Hackney. She was shocked by his gaunt appearance and slightly offended by his refusal to look at her. They both drew up chairs to sit in front of Shepherd's desk.

'Jane, I am sure you know that after a long period of sick leave, followed by light duties at NSY, Gibbs was recently promoted to DI and sent here to Bow Street. I am obviously aware that you must have both had a very emotional period after the explosion that killed DCI Len Bradfield and WPC Kath Morgan. However, I feel sure that, although the experience will have left an indelible scar, it was more than eighteen months ago. Time is a great healer and I trust that you can now both concentrate on your future here at Bow Street and that working together will not be a problem.'

Jane noticed Gibbs tense up at the mention of the explosion, and saw him grip the side of the chair seat with both hands. It was still very raw for them both and Jane, unlike Gibbs, had remained at Hackney where the two of them had been based at the time of the incident. In many ways she agreed with what Shepherd had said about time being a great healer, but she knew instinctively that perhaps she had coped far better than Gibbs.

After a brief talk about what DCI Shepherd expected, and how he encouraged his officers to be a team and always share information, he asked DI Gibbs to show Jane to the CID office and introduce her to the CID clerk, Edith, who would allocate her a desk. Jane and Gibbs both replaced their chairs, shook the DCI's hand and left his office.

As soon as the door closed behind them Gibbs gave Jane a sidelong glance, gesturing for her to follow him. He was even thinner than she remembered and his hair still stood up like a wire brush. He was wearing a smart suit with a thin tie, a fashionable small-collared shirt, with the cuffs a bit short over his skinny wrists and long tapering fingers. He was also wearing rather smart shoes with tassels and moved like a dancer as if he was about to spin round to face her on his heels.

'How's your rock band?'

'We broke up.' He changed the subject. 'You look very smart and ready for business.'

'Thank you ... you look very dapper yourself.'

'Dapper?'

'I like your shoes.'

He looked down at his feet, and then back up at her.

'I ordered this suit from Mannie Charles ... d'you remember him?'

'Not really.'

'He was the tailor who was selling all the hooky suits to the CID. We all ordered them, and found out later they were nicked from Horne Brothers' warehouse and the labels were switched. We'd all got them made to measure and paid up front ... he delivered them after ...'

Gibbs turned away, pulling at the knot in his tie.

'Kath Morgan had one made, and the guv ... he'd wanted this flashy lining, with six buttons on the breast ... old Sergeant Harris took it cos he was the only man as tall as Len. I didn't know what to do with it, and Harris said, you know the way he was, "I'll have that", and it was still in the plastic wrapping. Anyway, I reckon when he saw the striped silk lining he knew he'd never wear it ...'

Gibbs turned on his heels before Jane could reply. She followed him as he headed down the corridor and a few uniform officers passed them. Jane asked him how he was, but he ignored her. She continued speaking.

'I understand how you must feel about Bradfield and Kath ... I think everyone has found it really difficult.'

Gibbs came to an abrupt stop and spun to face her.

'No, you don't know how I feel ... It just threw me a bit to see you. I've got to go. The ladies' locker room is straight ahead and the CID room, DCI's and DI's rooms are all on this floor. See you later.'

Gibbs strode off, then paused to turn back.

'The duty sergeant, Eric Fuller, is a bit of a pompous prat and just like old Sergeant Harris – but a foot shorter!'

Jane found her way to the ladies' locker room. She was surprised at the number of lockers that had been allocated. There were obviously more female staff members than there had been at Hackney Station. She took the key from locker 12, placed her handbag inside, and hung her jacket on the relevant hook. She then quickly tidied up her hair and made her way to the CID office.

The door was halfway along the corridor, and the room itself was far larger than the cramped and dated office at Hackney. Not that this office had any modern equipment, but it was much lighter and the desks were newer. She remembered the embarrassing incidents when she had snagged her stockings on the wooden desks at Hackney, and hoped she wouldn't be doing the same in this office.

The two clerical women on the far side of the room were busily typing reports. The matriarch of the office was a very solid, stout woman with small round spectacles and had her grey hair in a tight bun. She rose to her feet, removed her spectacles and in a very loud voice asked, 'Are you WDC Jane Tennison?'

'Yes,' Jane replied nervously.

'I am Edith Pickard, a former policewoman. I never liked being thrown in at the deep end with integration ... I preferred the specialist role in the women's force, which

I've now worked in for many years. I was very disillusioned as I was only ever given a day's warning that I was to be assigned to full shift duties with the men.'

Jane was puzzled at to why Edith needed to tell her all of this.

'I am very pleased to meet you.' Jane extended her hand.

Edith gripped her hand and shook it vigorously.

'I've allocated you a desk at the back. You'll be the only WDC here at Bow Street. We have twelve male detectives and two detective sergeants.'

Jane made her way towards the empty desk, which had a rather dilapidated-looking office chair with one wheel missing. There was a wilting pot plant on the desk.

Edith patted the sleeve of her mauve jumper.

'I've always had a tinge of regret that I left the force, and I have to admit that I am a tad jealous that such a young girl has been assigned to us ... But I'm sure we will get along very well. The two ladies on the far side are Gillian Thomas and Irene Marsden, both diligent and hard-working clerks. With a DCI like Shepherd we all have to keep on our toes. Right, let me explain the functioning of the office and the shifts. The CID duty book is kept in that drawer, and the crime book in that drawer.'

Jane looked up as a figure appeared in the doorway. Edith glanced over.

'Good morning, sir. I was just introducing young Jane Tennison here to the workings of our office, and how you like to keep it very ship-shape.'

DCI Shepherd gave her a wan smile.

'I don't know what I would do without your more than capable hands, Edith.'

Shepherd turned to Jane and asked if she had seen DI Gibbs as he was not in his office or in the canteen. Jane recalled Gibbs's abrupt departure and suspected he'd left the station but she didn't want to get him into trouble. 'Sorry, sir, he said he needed to go.'

Shepherd put his hands on his hips.

'Bugger it ... Edith, are there any other detectives about? I've had uniform officers calling in a suspicious death at a flat in Aldwych.'

'I'm so sorry, sir, but we have two court sessions today and the other officers are dealing with investigations.'

Shepherd was clearly irritated by everyone's absence, and was annoyed that he would have to attend himself when he was so busy with paperwork and reports. He looked at Jane.

'Tennison, leave a message on Gibbs's desk telling him to be at the scene as soon as he returns.'

He walked briskly out of the office. Edith handed Jane her official notebook and two sharpened pencils.

Jane said softly, 'I wish he'd asked me to attend ...'

'Good heavens, it's only your first day! You've got a lot to learn ... he's not going to entrust you with a sus death yet.'

Just as Jane was wondering if she should have asked DCI Shepherd whether she could accompany him, he popped his head back into the room and said, 'You haven't got time to chat, Tennison ... Grab your coat and get a move on!'

Edith pursed her lips. Obviously she had been mistaken and this new WDC knew how to get ahead. It hadn't been like that in her day, not that she would ever think of returning to uniform. She'd had enough; and it was only a suspicious death, so hardly anything to get excited about.

It was a short walk from Bow Street Station to the flat in Aldwych. Shepherd walked briskly, with Jane keeping up beside him, as he spoke about his wife and children, and how in his book 'family always comes first'. Jane nodded, getting an impression of her new DCI as a family man – a hard thing to be in the police force, what with the long, irregular hours and the frequent after-hours get-togethers in the pub.

They arrived at a four-storey building split into flats. The PC at the front door stated that a Barry Dawson, aged twenty-six, had returned home from work earlier that morning to find his wife Shirley, twenty-three, dead in the bath while his baby daughter was sleeping in the playpen.

'Where is he now?' Shepherd asked impatiently.

'Mr Dawson is in a highly distressed state, sir. Both he and the child are currently with the next-door neighbour in the basement flat. The police doctor arrived to pronounce "life extinct" and is already upstairs. He requested the attendance of the laboratory liaison sergeant but he was busy dealing with another scene, sir, so we've been waiting for backup. There's also a dog, sir, in a cage. We haven't let it out as we're not sure what to do with it – he's a bit nasty.'

DCI Shepherd looked at his watch and told the PC that he would like to speak with Mr Dawson, but first he wanted to view the scene and talk to the doctor. As they stood outside the flat DCI said, 'Tennison, don't touch or disturb anything.'

He put his hands in his coat pockets and lifted them up towards Jane, somewhat reminiscent of a flasher, demonstrating his method of allaying the urge to touch anything at the crime scene. Jane took a pair of thin leather driving gloves out of her handbag and put them on.

They proceeded together up to the top floor, passing a payphone mounted on the wall. On the top-floor landing there was a collapsible Maclaren pushchair leaning up against the wall. The front door was open and they went inside into the narrow hallway. There was a double bedroom to the left, a single box room beside it, a bathroom on the right, and a living room, kitchen and dining area ahead. No lights were on apart from inside the bathroom. Shepherd tapped on the open bathroom door and walked in, followed by Jane. The doctor, dictated by procedure, was crouching down by the bath feeling for a pulse on the victim's left hand. She was motionless and face up in the bath, her eyes wide open, as if frozen in time and staring into space. Her long, thick dark hair floated around her head in the scarlet blood-stained water. The tap end of the bath had a blood smear down it. A dressing gown was on the floor next to the bath. DCI Shepherd introduced Jane to Dr Henry, who gave her a noncommittal glance as she took out her notebook.

Dr Henry lifted the victim's head out of the water, then let her head go, and it sank slowly down into the water. Suddenly a few bubbles escaped from her mouth and nose. Jane gasped.

'She's breathing!'

Dr Henry laughed and explained that the bubbles were just some trapped air in the chest, which had been released by him moving her. It was difficult for Jane to take everything in. The small bathroom was full of various shampoos, medications and creams, numerous baby lotions and a bucket of dirty nappies. There was a towel rack holding some grubby towels, and the lino floor was stained and marked as if it had been laid many years ago. The washbasin was cracked with a dirty rim around it, and on the edge of it stood a plastic cup containing toothbrushes and a tube of toothpaste.

'Right, your victim – she may have had an underlying heart condition that caused her to fall, but doubtful at her young age. From the injury to the forehead it looks like she slipped in the bath and fell forward and may have knocked herself out and subsequently drowned. The wound is not that deep and there is a blood smear on the main tap but she could have bled freely from it. The water is cold so most likely she was originally taking a bath sometime in the early morning.'

'So nothing suspicious?' DCI asked, as he looked at his watch.

'Not that I can see,' the doctor replied, and started to fill out a form, adding that the water on the floor had probably come from the splash overflow when she slipped and banged her head.

Leaving the doctor to complete his forms, Jane and DCI Shepherd moved out of the bathroom and went towards the bedroom. Shepherd glanced into the room from the doorway. The curtains were closed, the bed unmade and the room smelt musty. It was very scruffy and untidy. There was a baby's cot near the bed with filthy sheets, and piles of dirty clothes were strewn around the floor. Shepherd could see nothing untoward. Nor was there anything in the second small box room. It looked as if the occupants were starting to redecorate, but it was full of odd bits and pieces of furniture.

They moved on to the living room, which contained a baby's playpen scattered with toys, and a high chair with a full bowl of food, a spoon and a baby's bottle of milk that looked untouched. A three-bar electric fire was burning bright orange and nearby was a laden clothes horse. Beside it stood an ironing board with an unplugged iron and a blouse draped over it, ready to be pressed.

Through an archway Jane noticed an old dark velvet sofa and a worn armchair. Off to one side was the kitchen area with a sink and a draining board stacked with dirty pans and crockery. Old-fashioned cupboards lined the wall around the cooker and fridge, and the floor had a threadbare carpet with large gaps showing the floorboards beneath. Behind the sofa was a dog in a small cage which began leaping up and down, snarling and growling as Jane approached. Jane froze as it leaped towards her, trying to get through the bars. The DCI pointed out that the sofa was covered in white dog hairs so it was obvious that the dog must have usually been free to roam around the flat.

'Don't let it out – that's a bull terrier. We'll have to get the owner to come in and sort it out ... they can sometimes be very aggressive.'

Shepherd looked at his watch again.

'We're just treating this as a non-suspicious accidental death.'

'Should I get the uniform PC to radio the station and see if a lab liaison sergeant is now available, sir?'

DCI Shepherd glanced at her as if she was stupid.

'What for? There's no forced entry, no signs of a disturbance ... totally non-suspicious. And you heard the Doc say that it's accidental?'

Jane hesitated.

'Yes, I know, sir ... Should I get a photographer to the scene?'

Shepherd ignored her. He was obviously eager to leave and went to the open front door shouting down to the PC to radio the station and ask them to see if a SOCO was now available to take some snaps of the body.

'Snaps?' Jane thought, appalled. She felt that his manner was incredibly uncaring and insensitive, considering that the victim's husband might be able to hear him shouting.

Shepherd turned back to Jane and told her he would return to the station and call the coroner's officer to let him know about the death.

'The coroner's officer will arrange for undertakers to attend and remove the body to Westminster mortuary. Tennison, you take a statement from the husband. It doesn't have to be here and now, but we'll need it for the coroner's report.'

He turned and walked out before Jane could ask any further questions, leaving her unsure about exactly what to do next.

She returned to the bathroom and the doctor handed her his scene examination report. Jane noticed a rolled up bath slip mat by the washbasin, next to a child's potty, and remarked to Dr Henry how tragic it was that they had a slip mat and hadn't used it. He was as eager to leave as Shepherd, and pointed out that the mat was probably for the child. Jane hovered as he closed his medical case, and tentatively asked what she should do.

'The coroner's officer will sort everything and advise you accordingly. Now, I have to dash, my dear – I've got a prisoner to examine at West End Central.'

It was a very eerie feeling for Jane to be alone with the dead body in the bath. She still couldn't get over the young woman's eyes, curious as to why they were open, staring at her as if crying out for help in the last moments of death as she drowned. The dog was still barking in its cage and Jane was relieved when DI Gibbs walked into the bathroom, despite him smelling like a brewery.

He held up the note she had left and anxiously asked what she had told the DCI.

'That you'd had to go out.'

'OK, thanks ... So what's going on here?'

Jane told him what Dr Henry had said and that the DCI had gone back to the station, instructing her to treat the death as non-suspicious and complete a report for the coroner.

Gibbs moved past Jane and crouched down to examine the dead woman.

'I'll bet any money on it that the DCI has no intention of going back to the station. He got the PC downstairs to radio in and inform the coroner's officer of the details. He finds excuses to slip away so he can get home to his wife and kids. He doesn't socialize or drink much either. His nickname is "Timex" because he's always looking at his watch!'

Jane smiled, glad of him being with her. Gibbs sat back on his heels and took a closer look at the victim's face.

'I hate it when they have their eyes open like this ... freaks me out. Did the Doc say how long she'd been dead?'

'No, all he said was that she must have got into the bath early this morning as the water's cold. She slipped forward, I think, and hit her forehead and he said she might have knocked herself out and then fallen back into the water.'

'So what's he saying ...? She steps into the bath, slips forward, smacks her forehead against the middle tap? Funny ... I would think that if she fell forward she would be face down in the bath. Unless she was standing up when she fell and hit her head, then recoiled backwards?'

Gibbs dipped his fingers into the water, then reached up to the towel rail to dry them.

'Ughhh, these are soaking wet ... that's odd ... Did the husband say he used them to mop up the water at all?'

'I haven't spoken to him yet. The wound might have

bled so she was still alive when she fell in the bath,' Jane said, gesturing with her hand towards the body.

Gibbs sighed and looked around the dirty bathroom. The PC from downstairs appeared, and shouted towards them from the open front door. The dog started barking hysterically again.

'There's still no photographer available. The coroner's officer has been informed and undertakers should be here in about an hour. I'm supposed to be off duty at three p.m. and the station has radioed asking if they want another PC to relieve me here at the premises.'

Gibbs walked out of the bathroom. 'I'll authorize you four hours of overtime, even if you only end up doing two.'

'Thank you very much, sir. The neighbour has contacted Dawson's mother and she's on her way over from Rotherhithe in a cab.'

Gibbs turned to Jane. 'The victim's husband is a Barry Dawson. His wife's name is Shirley,' she told him, glancing at her notebook.

'OK, well, I should be getting back to the station.'

'I'm unsure what to do at the scene, Spence. I mean, do I just stay here and wait for someone to come and help me?'

'Draw a sketch plan of the bathroom scene in your notebook. As we can't get hold of a photographer, take as much detail as you think they'll need.'

The dog started barking again and Gibbs went into the sitting room. She saw him bending down to the cage and shouted for him not to open it. The dog went berserk again, hurling his body at the cage bars.

'Do you think I should call the dog section to take it to Battersea?' Jane asked.

'No, Dawson can take the vicious thing with him to his mother's, it can't stay here. We don't know if it's been fed or how long it's been caged up.'

He walked back into the living room and stood with his arms folded. He glanced around the room, and then crossed over to some shelves where there was a stereo system alongside a ringed record holder. He thumbed through the albums and pulled one out.

'Jim Morrison ... The Doors ... Well, at least he's got good taste in music, which is more than can be said for the state of this dump ... This was Bradfield's favourite band.'

Jane watched as he carefully replaced the album into the record holder and quickly changed the subject.

'Do you want to speak to the victim's husband?' Jane asked.

'No I don't, unless he wants to say something. If so, it's your job and you need to gain experience in dealing with these kinds of situation.'

'I'd be grateful if you came with me, Spence.' Jane didn't want to make a mistake on her first case.

Gibbs cocked his head to one side and grinned.

'OK, where is he?'

'With Mr Cook, the next-door neighbour.'

Jane and Gibbs left the same officer manning the front door of the house and went next door. The neighbour, a retired bus driver, lived in the basement with his invalid wife. When Gibbs knocked Jane could hear a baby crying. Mr Arnold Cook opened the door. He had so far been very accommodating but from the expression on his face he was now clearly eager for everyone to leave.

'My wife is very frail and I need to get her lunch. They're in the front room, and the baby has done nothing but cry. Barry is distressed ... such a terrible thing.'

'Thank you very much, sir. I'm Detective Inspector Gibbs and this is WDC Tennison. If we could just have a few words with Mr Dawson I'm sure we can be out of your way quickly.'

Mr Cook led them to the sitting room doorway. His wife was in a wheelchair in the hall by their open kitchen door.

'Are they still here, Arnold? I can hear the baby crying ... have you given them a cup of tea?'

'Yes, love, now you go back into the kitchen.'

'You'll have to push me ... I can't turn this chair.'

Mr Cook waved his hands for Gibbs and Jane to go into the sitting room as he tended to his wife.

Barry Dawson had long, mousy blond hair tied in a ponytail, with blue eyes that were set wide apart. He had a very fit physique and was rocking his baby daughter in his arms. The little girl was clearly distressed, and was red faced from crying. She kept calling out 'Mama' between screams and was probably also hungry. Jane gave the baby a sympathetic smile.

Dawson paced up and down trying to soothe her, then stopped by a tea tray with a plate of biscuits. He picked one up and gave it to the little girl who eagerly grasped it in her tiny hand and started sucking at it.

As the baby was now placated, Gibbs and Jane introduced themselves and gave their condolences.

'I believe you found your wife, Mr Dawson, is that right?'

Dawson gritted his teeth and looked as though he was about to break down, but took several deep breaths to calm himself.

'Sorry ... I'm so sorry. She needs changing, and my wife ... Oh God! I can't believe this has happened ...'

'It's all right, sir ... it can't be easy for you. We'll try and get this over with as quickly as possible. When you found her, was she lying back in the bath, not face down?'

'When I opened the door she was lying there in the bath, facing upwards ... And dear God, her eyes were wide open ...' he sobbed.

It took a short while longer before he was able to compose himself enough to give them a clear statement of what had happened. As he did so the little girl fell asleep in his arms and Jane began to take some cursory notes in her pocket book.

Barry Dawson stated that he was a porter at St Thomas' Hospital. He had been on an early shift and said that when he had left their flat in the morning his wife hadn't been feeling well, and had recently been complaining of headaches and dizzy spells. Barry had tried phoning the communal phone in their building a number of times in the morning to see how she was, but there had been no answer. He said that he usually always called at around 10 a.m. to check that she had taken the dog out for a walk. Desperately worried about her and the child, Barry had asked his boss to let him leave at around 11 a.m and on returning home he had found his wife's body in the bath. In a state of shock, and not knowing what to do, he had run to his neighbour, Mr Cook, who had dialled 999.

Jane held up her pencil.

'Excuse me, Mr Dawson ... Could I just verify the timings? You called home at 10 a.m., but there was no reply?'

'He just said that, Tennison,' Gibbs interjected.

At that moment the doorbell rang and on answering it Mr Cook returned to say that a Mrs Dawson was at the front door.

'Oh thank God, it's my mum ... MUM!'

Mr Cook stepped back from the sitting room door as Rita Dawson hurried into the room. She was very over weight, and only five foot two, with badly dyed red hair. She was wearing a floral midi skirt with open sandals and white socks.

'Oh Jesus, God ... I can't believe this ...'

There was an outburst of grief between them. The child started crying and Mrs Dawson took her from her son's arms.

'Oh you poor little soul ... she's sopping wet, Barry! Have you fed her? She must be hungry.'

Rita calmed and soothed the child, who stopped crying when she was given another biscuit to suck on. Rita asked what had happened as Barry slumped into the winged-back chair, holding his head in his hands.

'Dear God, Ma ... I found Shirley ... She was in the bath ... I kept on ringing her and when I got no answer I came home from work.' He broke down in tears again.

Jane explained what the police doctor had said and also advised them that she needed to get a statement from Barry. He was becoming more and more upset, repeating over and over that he shouldn't have gone to work knowing she wasn't well.

'What are you talking about? What's going on? ... I don't understand what you're talking about,' Rita said.

'It's my fault, Mum ... it's all my fault ...' Barry replied.

Jane quietly explained that there had been a tragic accident and that it wasn't Mr Dawson's fault.

'But I will need to take a full statement from you, Mr Dawson,' Jane explained.

'Do I have to do it now?'

Jane was sympathetic and said that he didn't have to do it straight away, but then Gibbs stood up.

'It would be helpful if you could do it now, sir, so that we have all the facts written down.'

'Listen, I think poor Barry has been through enough at the moment and needs to be with his daughter. They should both come home with me,' Mrs Dawson said, suddenly protective of her son and grandchild.

Gibbs glanced at Jane and shrugged, saying that tomorrow or the next day would do.

'I need to get some clothes ... but I can't face going into the flat again,' Barry replied.

Rita comforted him. 'I'll stay with you, darlin', but I've got to get some of my granddaughter's possessions too ... She needs nappies, pyjamas, and some of her toys, her bottles ... I need her pushchair ...'

Gibbs, by now becoming rather frazzled, instructed Jane to accompany them to the flat and mentioned his concerns about the dog.

'What's the matter with the dog? He's not got out, has he? Is he lost?' Mrs Dawson said.

Jane quickly replied, 'No, he's in the flat. It's just that he was getting very agitated, growling and snapping at us in his cage.'

'Well, it's no wonder with all the comings and goings ... It's not in his nature to be vicious, he's usually a softie, even with strangers. He's probably hungry and wondering what's going on as he's been locked in his cage all day.'

Something about Mrs Dawson's reply jarred with Jane, then she realized that Mrs Dawson seemed more concerned about the dog and had hardly reacted to the fact that her daughter-in-law had been found dead in the bath.

By the time they had been let out of the basement by Mr Cook and had returned to the Dawsons' flat the little girl was screaming again. Mrs Dawson tried to calm her, jiggling her up and down in her arms. Jane found the noise wearing, making it hard for her to think.

They headed up the stairs, with Barry lagging behind. Mrs Dawson displayed a toughness about her as she firmly told her son that whatever he was feeling he had to help get everything sorted to take over to her place. They all went into the flat and Gibbs quickly closed the bathroom door. Mrs Dawson fetched a large, scruffy suitcase and collected her granddaughter's belongings. She instructed Barry to pick up some dog food and gather whatever clothes he needed.

Jane and Gibbs stood to one side.

'She's a tough broad, isn't she?' he said quietly.

Jane nodded. 'Yes ... But I think right now they're both in shock. They're sort of acting on automatic pilot.'

Gibbs ran his hands through his hair. 'Yeah, tell me about it ...'

Mrs Dawson picked up feeding bottles and nappies, and threw a few baby toys into the suitcase. She did everything while the little girl was balanced on her hip. Barry handed a few of his own personal items to his mother to add into the open case on the bed. He crossed over to the dog's cage. The dog had not barked once since they had returned and was now cowering in the cage, shaking. Jane noticed that in Barry's presence he seemed completely submissive, his tail between his legs. 'See, I told you he's a softie,' Mrs Dawson said, sticking a rather dirty dummy into the child's mouth.

'Go and shut the case, love, and ask them to get us a ride home. I'll start going down with the pushchair.'

Barry clipped a lead onto the dog's collar and went into the bedroom to get the suitcase.

Jane offered to help but Mrs Dawson shook her head and then looked slowly around the flat.

'You know, she was a shockingly lazy girl ... young, you see, never done housework, and to be honest I've not really taken it all in, but she was a good mother ... God knows how it happened.'

'She may have fallen while she was getting into the bath, and hit her head.'

'Terrible thing is I was supposed to come by early this morning. I had a problem with my washing machine and had to wait in for an engineer to fix it. Shocking to think that if I'd been here I would've found her.'

'Do you have a set of house keys, Mrs Dawson?'

'Yes, but I was going to babysit ... I often come by and help out when I'm not workin'. I take Heidi to the local playground and walk the dog.'

Barry closed the suitcase and, with the dog following on the lead, he went out of the bedroom and handed Jane his wife's key to lock the door behind them. Jane asked him if he could come into the station the following afternoon to make a statement. Mrs Dawson was still by the open front door.

'Have you told them at work yet, Barry? You'd better, because you're in no fit state to go in.'

Barry replied that he hadn't told them yet, and had only come home because he was worried when Shirley hadn't answered the phone. He seemed to be in a daze, standing with the suitcase in one hand and the cowering dog on the lead in the other. Gibbs told them he could take them over to Rotherhithe, but told Barry that he needed to make sure the dog was kept on a lead in the back of the car.

As they headed down the stairs Gibbs turned to Jane.

'Listen, I'm going to go straight home after I've dropped them off.'

'What? ... Am I going to be left here on my own then?'

'You'll be all right. Just call it a day once the body's been taken to the mortuary by the undertakers. I'll see you in the morning and we can go over what you should put in your report for the coroner.'

Jane stood uncertainly in the doorway for a while, then decided she would make a few enquiries with the other tenants. She went outside to find the uniform officer who was still standing patiently in the street by the main entrance to the building, which was one of a substantial row of Victorian houses divided into large high-ceilinged flats.

'Look, I'm going to see the tenants, but call me if the undertakers arrive, OK?'

'Will do,' said the PC, hoping he wouldn't have to wait much longer. Now he'd had the promise of overtime regardless, he was keen to head back to the station.

Jane knocked on the door of the ground-floor flat but, as she'd expected, there was no reply. She had already been told that the couple left for work early and she just wanted to make sure. She was about to walk up to the first-floor flat when Mr Cook appeared at the front door.

'Is everything all right?'

Jane nodded and he stepped further inside the hall.

'The people in that flat won't be back until after six.'

'Do you know their names?'

'Yes, Mr and Mrs Johnson. But I only know them to say hello to ... nice couple ... they work in the City.'

'Do you know who lives in the first-floor flat?'

'Nobody, it's empty. You'd have to contact the landlord. I think he's going to do it up because the previous tenants moved out a good few weeks ago. Same as the basement, it's empty and full of old furniture.'

'Thank you very much. Do you know how long Mr and Mrs Dawson have lived in the top flat?'

'Why, do you think something's not quite right?' he asked.

'No ... obviously there has been a tragic incident, but I need some family background details to give to the Coroner's Office.'

Mr Cook explained that they had moved in about a year ago and seemed a nice couple. He said that he got on quite well with them, but they didn't really socialize as such.

'My wife is wheelchair bound and I'm her main carer. I'm always very busy, so I don't really know them all that well.'

'When was the last time you saw her?'

'My wife?'

'No, Mr Cook, Shirley Dawson.'

'Well, not today, obviously. To be honest I can't remember if I saw her yesterday, but she did walk the dog regularly. Then today Barry banged on our door in a dreadful state, rambling incoherently that something had happened to his wife. I told him to stay at my place while I went up to their flat, and when I opened the bathroom door I saw Shirley in the bath. I was going to check for a pulse on her neck, but when I put my hand in the bath I could feel that the water was cold and it was obvious she was dead. So I thought it best not to touch her. I found little Heidi sleeping in the playpen in the living room.'

'So their daughter was in the flat?'

'Yes, I picked Heidi up and took her downstairs so that I could call the police. Barry was in a terrible state and he said that he had tried to call his wife. It was a regular thing he did, you know. Like I said, she would walk the dog of a morning. Barry works at St Thomas' and Shirley stayed at home to mind the child, so when I got back to my place I called 999 ...'

Jane continued making notes, then hesitated. She found it strange that Barry hadn't dialled 999 himself, or picked up his daughter before going to Mr Cook's flat. She also underlined the note she had made that Mr Cook said he opened the bathroom door.

'The bathroom door was closed when you went into the flat, Mr Cook?'

'Yes.'

'Thank you very much, you have been very helpful. Do you recall the landlord's name?'

'No, he's not my landlord. All I know is that he's a nasty piece of work, and a real cheapskate. He owns the head lease and charges heavy money for doin' maintenance work ... but as you can see it's not that clean on the stairs and landings, and the gutters are all in bad shape.'

'Thank you, Mr Cook.'

Jane went back upstairs to the Dawsons' flat and half closed the front door behind her. She checked her watch and wondered how long she would have to wait for the undertakers. She thought about making herself a cup of tea but didn't think she should, and the filthy sink full of dirty cups was not very appealing. She looked around the room and opened her notebook to write about the state of the flat. She flicked back and forth, looking at what she had written when questioning Mr Cook. Something else struck her as being unusual. The high chair tray had a bowl of cereal and a bottle of milk that looked untouched on it, but when Mr Cook had entered the Dawsons' flat to check on Shirley he said he found the baby asleep in the playpen. Jane wondered if Shirley had run a bath for herself, prepared the child's breakfast and then at some point later decided to have a bath, leaving Heidi in her playpen.

As Jane sat on the edge of the dog-haired sofa she noticed a camera partly hidden behind a cushion. It was a little Kodak 126 Instamatic. The reel had twenty-four photos but only five had been used. She hesitated, then decided that rather than making detailed notes and drawings of the flat she would use the camera to record the scene. She felt certain that Barry Dawson wouldn't mind her using it.

Jane started in the bathroom. She lifted up the dressing gown left beside the bath, and hung it on the back of the bathroom door. Under it was a pair of panties and a bra. She placed them on the same hook as the dressing gown. Using the camera she then took two photographs of the deceased. She felt queasy looking at the dead woman's eyes wide open, and backed out of the bathroom deciding to use up the rest of the film on the other rooms.

The PC from downstairs appeared and asked how much longer she was going to be. Jane explained that she was waiting for the undertakers and when they arrived he could go.

'I'm sorry, you've been here a long time. I don't know your name?'

'Arthur Miller, Detective.'

Jane smiled. 'Very auspicious name, if you have literary ambitions.'

He shook his head, obviously not having a clue what she was talking about.

'Runs in my family. Father was Alfred, my grandfather was Albert – all of us are AM. Used to get some laughs just using our initials, and my sister was called Pamela, PM.' He chuckled, then hitched up his trousers.

'Truth is I need to use a bathroom ... I've been on duty since ten this morning.'

'I don't think you can use this bathroom, but I'm sure Mr Cook in the basement flat next door will oblige as he's been very helpful.'

'Thanks ... If I go there now, I'll come straight back.'

'Yes, that's fine.'

PC Miller left Jane finishing the reel of photographs, but there was still no sign of the undertakers. She was about to go and use the communal payphone to check back with the station when Miller returned and said he was now back on duty at the front door. He stood staring at her as Jane remained by the open bathroom door, then sighed and joined her, looking into the bathroom.

'How do you intend to get the body out of the bath?'

'Well, I don't ... The undertakers will do that.'

'No they won't, because that's not their job, if you don't mind me saying so. It's your role and you have to bag and tag as you're dealing with the scene. The undertakers will take the body to the mortuary, but in all my years I know they won't move a body. They really are "more'n my job's worths". But far be it from me to tell you what you should do.'

Miller turned to walk off. Jane was so unsure of herself that she touched his arm as he went.

'Please don't go . . . I mean, I really don't know what I should do. I've never been in this situation before.'

'Well, I can send out for a body sheet, and bring it up to you. But I'd say that first up you should pull the plug out of the bath.'

'Right, yes. I'll do that. How long will you be before you bring up a body sheet? Or could I just use one of the sheets from the flat?'

'No, you'd better wait. It's got to be plastic. I'll radio in for one to be brought over. Would you like a cup of tea?'

'I'd love one . . . but I don't think we should use the kitchen, besides which it's not very clean.'

'Mr Cook's bringing me one over. Nice chap, letting me use their toilet. His wife's crippled, you know, and he's her main carer.'

'Yes, I know. I would really love a cup of tea.'

She heard him thudding back down the stairs and went into the bathroom. She looked at the bath and noticed that the plug chain was broken and not connected to the overflow waste pipe. There were no blood stains anywhere around the lip of the bath, only the still visible smear on the tap. She had no choice other than to remove her jacket, take off her leather gloves, roll up her sleeve and stick her hand in the cold blood-stained water to pull out the plug. The victim's legs were either side of her hand and she closed her eyes as she felt for the chain and gave it a jerk. The stained water gurgled and then began to seep down the plug hole.

Jane was sitting on a chair in the living room writing up her notes when Miller came back. He was carrying a large white plastic sheet under one arm and two cups of tea.

'Thank you so much.' She took the tea and sipped. It was very sweet, very strong and not particularly warm but she drank it all before placing it down on the coffee table. Miller waited, then helped her unfold the wide plastic sheet, which was the size of a small double bed.

'Right, let's have a look at her and work out the best way to get her out.'

They stood side by side at the bath tub. The body was wrinkled from being in the water for so long, her long wet thick hair dripping around her shoulders.

'Well, good thing is she looks a bit underweight. First, lift her hands above her head and I'll get her feet. On the count of three we'll lift her body up and over the bath rim and onto the sheet.'

Jane asked Miller if he'd got any rubber gloves. He shook his head. It didn't seem to bother him but it made Jane feel very queasy.

'I'm going to the kitchen to see if there are any washing-up gloves to wear.'

Miller shrugged and waited, his hands on his hips. Jane returned, saying that she couldn't find any.

'Right, we've got no choice. On the count of three . . . one . . . two . . . lift her arms up, and three.'

Jane used her bare hands to lift the body. The arms were slippery and cold and on the first attempt Jane lost her grip and toppled forward. Miller was holding on to Shirley's feet and ankles.

'A dead body is always heavier than you think, even when it's a petite female. Right, let's go again. One . . . two . . . three, lift.'

They managed to lift the body onto the sheet.

'Now put her arms at the side of her body, wrap the sheet over and twist and tape the ends, so you end up with what looks like a big Christmas cracker.'

Miller left Jane to finish wrapping up the ends as he went back on duty. Jane waited impatiently for the undertakers to arrive.

Several hours later, feeling tired and emotionally drained, Jane left the mortuary having booked in the body and been told to prepare a report for the coroner. As she left through the rear yard, she saw DS Paul Lawrence, the lab liaison sergeant, outside smoking with a cup of tea. She didn't approach him immediately, wanting a few moments to prepare herself as her heart beat rapidly. She had this reaction almost every time she saw him, since he had been the one to tell her that neither Kath nor Bradfield had survived the explosion.

Lawrence glanced up and saw her. He took in the strained look on her face.

'Hi there ... Are you coping all right?'

'I'm fine, thank you. Please don't give me the spaniel eyes.'

'Sorry?'

'I've moved on, Paul, and I really don't want to talk about what happened,' she said sharply.

'Um, spaniels have brown eyes ... mine are blue. I was told you got a thrashing from some bastard when you were acting as a decoy?'

'Oh, sorry ... yes. I'm sort of recovered from that. I thought you were referring to what happened at Hackney.'

'I doubt if any of us will ever be able to fully recover from that nightmare. You know what Sergeant Harris always says? "They were marked", and you either come through to the other side of it, or you lose it.' Seeing her stricken face he changed the subject.

'I heard you were at the scene of an accidental death as well? Never pleasant ... I think I'm due to do a forensic search at the victim's flat. I've been dealing with a PM from a homosexual murder in Knightsbridge. I'm getting sick and tired of being shuffled from one station to the next, and spending hours in the lab. What are you doing here?'

'I brought the body in with the undertakers. PC May, who was on duty, was really rather unpleasant and abrupt ... He told me that I needed to type up a sudden death report. I also need to get a reel of film developed at Boots, with photos of the scene on it.'

Lawrence looked puzzled and asked why she was taking scene pictures to the chemists and not the lab. Jane explained that there had been no photographer available at the death scene, so she'd used a camera she found at the flat. Lawrence laughed.

'Listen, when I'm finished at the mortuary I'll be walking back over Lambeth Bridge to the Met lab so I'll take the film to the photographic branch for development.'

'Oh, thank you.' Jane handed him the roll of film.

'I'll contact you at Bow Street when they're ready.'

'I'm sorry if I sounded rude earlier. I didn't mean to. I've been on this case all day and I'm exhausted. Do you think I could make out the report first thing in the morning? DS Gibbs said he would walk me through it, but he's gone off duty.'

Lawrence shrugged. He finished his tea, dropped his cigarette end into the dregs and threw the polystyrene cup into the bin.

'Look out for Gibbs. He took Bradfield's death badly ... Had a bit of a meltdown. His attachment at Bow Street, and working under DCI Shepherd, will be very different for him. Shepherd's a "go by the rules" and "get off home" time watcher. He won't tolerate Gibbs's old ways.'

Jane smiled and nodded, as Lawrence patted her arm.

'Good to see you, Jane. As you were on the non-suspicious death and I've just been called back to do a forensic search, I presume that it's conclusive?'

'Well, I'm not too sure exactly what the next step is. Her husband, Barry Dawson, mentioned that she had been very anxious and had been feeling unwell.'

'Did you find any medication at the flat?'

'No, I didn't.'

'Well, you should maybe check that out. If you like I can be over there tomorrow, when I have some free time.'

'I'd appreciate that, thank you.'

As he walked off Jane felt relieved that Lawrence would be at the flat the next day. Right now she just wanted to get back to her room at the section house and have a long bath. She needed to cleanse herself from the grime and the terrible smells in the Dawsons' flat, as well as the experience of having to lift the body out of the bath. She looked at the bloody water stains on the cuffs of her shirt and shuddered. She thought of the body and changed her mind – she'd have a shower instead.

*

Marie Allard had just put her children to bed and was making herself an omelette and a cup of tea when the phone rang. Her heart started racing every time the phone rang at this hour. She knew it would not be her mother-in-law and, as she had arranged with her husband that he would call from prison mid-morning, after the children had been taken to school, she knew it couldn't be him either.

Marie went into the hall towards the ringing phone. She slowly picked up the receiver and took deep breaths as she heard the coins drop and knew who the caller was.

'Hello?' she said, nervously.

It was the same horrible sing-song voice again, coming through the receiver quietly at first. Marie began to shake as the voice got louder.

'Angie, Angie . . .'

'Leave me alone! I paid you . . . I did what you asked . . . just leave me alone!'

'Can't do that. I want another five hundred. Unless you want him to be put away for rape. Same procedure . . . get off the bus, put the envelope into the rubbish bin and get on the next bus. Need it by Tuesday . . . you got the time to get the money.'

Marie was in tears as the caller hung up. She replaced the receiver, then ran into the kitchen as she remembered she had left the pan with the butter on the gas ring ready to cook her omelette. It was burnt and smoking and she hurled it into the sink. She couldn't eat anything now, and felt the bile come up from her stomach as she retched. Since Peter's arrest she had lost a lot of weight, and she had been unable to sleep. She knew deep down that she had to tell someone what was going on but she was scared. She was even afraid to mention it to Peter when he called. He always sounded so depressed and often broke down weeping because he missed the children. He constantly told her how much he loved her, and how sorry he was for all the distress he was putting her through. He protested that he was innocent and had been fitted up by the police. He also told her repeatedly that she must not blame herself, and her inability to be intimate, for his behaviour. It did, stupidly, make her feel that it was her fault. As they only ever had a few minutes for each call she hadn't told him about this 'Angie' person and the blackmail, but she knew she would have to soon as she couldn't cope any more. The constant questioning in her mind never stopped. She did blame herself and the guilt was consuming her.

Her mother-in-law had succeeded in finding a driver to rent Peter's cab and give her a cut of his takings, so there was some money coming in. But paying off this 'Angie' was eating into their savings. Sitting in her immaculate kitchen, filled with the smell of burnt butter, Marie didn't even have the energy to wash the pan. She closed her eyes, telling herself over and over that she should go to the police. She had to tell someone, but what if this 'Angie' did have evidence to prove Peter had committed a rape? She doubted that she would be able to cope or face the consequences.

Marie went upstairs, checked that the children were sleeping and then undressed and cleaned her teeth.

She hadn't washed her hair or worn makeup for days. She crawled into bed and curled up into a ball. But she couldn't sleep as all she could hear playing over and over in her mind was that raucous voice screaming, 'Angie, Angie, Angie, Angie...'

CHAPTER TEN

Jane arrived at Bow Street, refreshed and on time but feeling slightly nervous. She had to write up a coroner's report, which she had never done before, and she was worried she would make a mistake. On entering the building she found Gibbs coming out of his office carrying a cup of coffee. He was very obviously in need of a shave and a clean shirt, and Jane was unsure whether he had come into work early, or if he had in fact been there all night. Gibbs beamed at her.

'Morning, Tennison! I see you have replaced the official uniform with something a little more glamorous ... the navy suit and crisp white shirt suit you well.'

'Thank you. I've got to do a coroner's report and I could really do with a bit of guidance.'

He made a point of looking at his watch.

'... if you have the time?' Jane added.

'For you, WDC Tennison, I always have time.'

Jane couldn't tell if Gibbs was being serious or sarcastic. However, he took her through exactly what was required. They recorded the date the body was found,

Monday, 7th October, and that it had been reported by the victim's husband, Barry Dawson. They also recorded the doctor's notes and as she typed up the report Gibbs sat on the edge of her desk, making sure everything had been done properly.

'You've got to make two copies: one for the coroner and one for records. Then get it over there ASAP as they'll want to do the PM at the mortuary. Although as far as I can make out it's all done and dusted.'

Edith marched in, looking as though she was in a foul temper.

Gibbs opened his arms wide and grinned at her.

'Good God, Edith, you grow more lovely every day!'

'And you look as if you've had another night on the tiles. Go and have a shave before DCI Shepherd sees you looking like that.'

Gibbs laughed and walked out.

Edith thumped her briefcase down on the desk, opened it up and took out her sandwiches and flask.

'Is everything all right, Edith?' Jane asked.

'No, it is not. I've had problems with my mother. The carer was late ... She's such a dope of a girl, but Mother can't be left on her own as she has dementia. It's very difficult making sure she doesn't wander off. I have had to put child gates at the top of the stairs as she's very adept at sneaking out of the house, often only in her nightdress. One time she was stark naked!'

'That sounds very stressful. Has she been suffering for a long time?'

Edith muttered, 'Too long.'

Jane handed Edith the copies of her report and folded

the top sheet into an envelope to take it over to the Coroner's Office.

'I'm just going up to the canteen for breakfast – can I get you a cup of tea, Edith?'

'No, thank you, I bring my own,' said Edith, indicating the Thermos. 'I like to get everything sorted before the others get here.'

Jane nodded then she hurried out, losing her bearings slightly before heading up the stone stairs to the third floor. As it was still early she didn't have to queue, so she picked up a tray and got a plate of scrambled eggs with bacon and toast, and a cup of coffee. As she turned to make her way towards the rows of Formica-topped tables she saw Gibbs sitting at the far side, finishing his breakfast.

'Do you mind if I join you, Spence?' she asked, and he shrugged.

Jane sat down opposite him and noticed that most of his eggs and bacon were untouched as he lit a cigarette and pushed the plate away.

'I just spoke to DS Lawrence ... he said he wasn't too happy about some of the photographs from the Dawsons' flat. He said he was going over there, and asked if you could leave the keys with the duty sergeant so that he can collect them,' Spence said, putting the lighter back in his pocket.

'I don't mind going over there to meet him.'

'Fine, but when you've finished with him go and find out when they're doing the PM on Dawson's wife.'

'Are you going to take a statement from him?' Jane asked.

'If you want to do it, go ahead. We might as well get the case closed, and move on to something else.'

Jane started to eat her scrambled eggs and felt the table shaking from Gibbs's foot constantly twitching beneath it. He looked around the canteen, then back at Jane as she pushed her unfinished plate aside. The toast was soggy and the eggs were overdone.

'Shall I also check out St Thomas' Hospital, where Barry Dawson works?'

'Why?' Gibbs snapped.

She shrugged. 'It's just that he said he left work because his wife didn't answer the phone and he was concerned, so he came home ...'

'Well, I doubt you'll need to go there if it's a non-sus death. Any reason to think he was lying?'

'There were a few things at his flat that didn't quite add up. For example, the little girl's high chair had her drinking bottle and bowl of cereal on it, untouched. Yet the neighbour who found Mrs Dawson said the baby was sleeping in her playpen.'

Gibbs leaned on his elbows. 'So?'

'Well, if Barry Dawson found his wife in the bath when he got home, why didn't he call 999 instead of going to a neighbour? And why didn't he pick up his daughter?'

'Come on ... He finds his wife dead in the bath, freaks out and runs next door. The guy was totally emotionally drained, and if his daughter was asleep why wake her up? Listen, Jane, if you don't mind me saying so, don't start digging around trying to find something untoward. The Doc confirmed accidental non-suspicious death.'

Gibbs pushed his chair back.

'I'm going to get a shave ... beady-eyed Edith doesn't miss a trick. A word of warning about her: you start nosing around about a case that's not your business – that's out of order. She's known as "Cop Out" because she left the force to be chained to a typewriter. And she's all over DCI Shepherd like a rash.'

Jane didn't reply as he walked out of the canteen. He was obviously impatient to get on to another case. She finished her coffee and carried her dirty dishes to the counter, tipping her cutlery into the tub of soapy water.

At the Coroner's Office she was told that, as yet, no PM had been organized for that morning. Jane decided she would go to the mother-in-law's address in Rotherhithe to get a statement from Barry Dawson as she needed details regarding the time he had returned home and found his wife.

She also wanted to ask a few more personal questions regarding his relationship with Shirley, to see if there was anything that gave further indication of exactly how the 'accident' had occurred. Something didn't feel quite right, whatever Spencer said.

Jane gave the details of her whereabouts to the duty sergeant, then caught a bus. It was almost ten o'clock when she arrived at 15 Allcott Road. It was a rather run-down area with council houses that had small, mostly paved, front gardens strewn with bicycles, and motor-bikes parked up alongside the rubbish bins. Number 15 had a chipped blue door with an empty milk crate standing next to the doormat.

Jane rang the bell and waited. There was the sound

of a dog barking loudly, which Jane presumed was the one taken from the Dawsons' flat. Rita opened the front door, still wearing a dressing gown and slippers, and holding the dog back by its collar. She pursed her lips in irritation on seeing Jane.

'I've only just fed Heidi ... She's been crabby all night long and has had me up and down. But come on in and I'll get Barry down ... he's still in bed. Down, Buster, good dog.'

Mrs Dawson restrained the dog as Jane nervously followed her inside into an immaculate, lino-covered hallway with flowery wallpaper. Mrs Dawson gestured towards a door leading into a lounge.

'Go on in, and he'll be with you. I'll put Buster out in the back yard. Do you want a cup of anything?'

'No, thank you.'

'What's your name, dear, I've forgotten?'

'I'm WDC Jane Tennison.'

Mrs Dawson nodded and closed the door. The room was spotless, with a large, overstuffed sofa and chairs and a coffee table in front of a big fake coal electric fire. On the mantelpiece were numerous photographs of the little girl, Heidi, and a few wedding pictures of Barry and Shirley. Jane sat on the comfortable easy chair and opened her notebook, waiting for Barry. She heard Mrs Dawson calling him, and the dog started barking again. Then there was the sound of someone hurrying down the stairs.

'Did you call the hospital? I don't want you losing your job.'

'Yes, I've called them. Can I have a cup of tea, Mum?'

'I'll bring one in for you. I'm not going into the school today so I'll give Heidi a bath.'

'Thanks, Mum.'

Jane turned to the door as Barry walked in. He was wearing a clean pressed denim shirt and jeans with loafer shoes but no socks. It was obvious that he had just bathed as his wet hair was combed back from his face and he smelt of some kind of lemon soap. Jane stood up and Barry shook her hand.

'Sorry to keep you waiting . . . I didn't get much sleep. I don't know what I would do without Mum.'

Jane sat back down and Barry stood for a moment, deciding where he should sit, then went over and sat in the centre of the sofa.

'I heard your mother saying she wasn't going into school – is she a teacher?'

'No, she's a cleaner at the local primary school, and does the kids' lunches as well. She's always worked, even when my dad was alive. He passed away a few years ago. He was a hard grafter and ran a small garage repair yard, and Mum sold it on to his partner. She could have moved out from here but all her friends are local, and if it wasn't for her we'd never have been able to get the deposit for our flat. She also helps out with the mortgage.'

'Oh, so you own the top-floor flat?'

'Yes. The one below us was rented, then the landlord got rid of the tenants and now he's doing it up to sell it. The couple on the ground floor also own theirs.'

'What about the basement?'

'That's just full of junk and I think he's going to do

that up as well. He owns the head lease of the property and he's supposed to keep the communal areas painted and carpeted but hasn't done anything since we moved in despite charging us maintenance. The roof has problems as well, but he's a typical shark landlord.'

Jane made a few notes, more interested in putting Barry at his ease as he constantly kept looking over at the photographs, then turned back to face her.

'My mum only works part time, doing the lunches, and she can probably take Heidi with her. I don't know what I'd do without her ... She's going to see about a local nursery school that takes them at Heidi's age. Shirley was going to start looking into it ...' Barry turned away, close to tears.

'This shouldn't take too long, Mr Dawson. I just need to have a clear time frame of exactly what happened yesterday. I'm sorry if it distresses you, but if you could give me the details of when exactly you left for work ...'

'Six o'clock in the morning. I was on early shift. We do alternate two weeks, of days and then nights.'

Jane jotted in her notebook, while Barry continued. 'I was quite busy up to around my break time, then I went into the canteen for breakfast.'

'What time was that?'

'Oh, it'd be about seven thirty. Then at ten o'clock I went to use the payphone in the casualty department. It was a regular thing I did ... call home to see if Shirley was OK. Usually she would be waiting with Buster and Heidi to go out for a walk. Anyway, I rang, but got no reply. I remember I had to ask one of the other porters for some change, so it might have been a bit after ten when I called. As I got no answer I stood around a while, then I started to get worried.'

'Why was that?'

'Well, she hadn't answered and the night before she'd not been feeling very well. She used to get these sort of anxiety feelings, which was why I always made sure I called her. I started to get worried. I'm not sure how many times I tried the number. You see, she was still in bed when I left for work, and so I really got concerned.'

Jane waited. Barry clasped and unclasped his hands, then gave a long sigh.

'I left the hospital and got the bus home. I'm not sure of the exact time but I let myself in and called out to her, but got no reply. Heidi was in her playpen fast asleep, so I went into the bedroom and then ...' He bowed his head as his eyes filled with tears.

'I went into the bathroom and I found her ...' he sniffed, trying to control himself. 'I'm sorry, but I still can't really take it all in. It all seems like a blur, you know ... running next door and getting the old bloke to go and see Shirley ... He went over and the next minute he's got Heidi and he's calling 999.'

'Why didn't you call the police yourself?'

'I don't know ... I don't know ... it was seeing her in the bath ... Oh God! If only I'd come home earlier, you know, not waited, because she really wasn't herself the night before. Maybe I shouldn't have gone into work ... I just keep on asking myself these questions, over and over ... what if ... what if ...?'

'Did Shirley suffer from depression?'

He looked up and gave a small shrug. 'Not really, it was just that she would get very anxious.'

'Was she on any medication?'

'No, just took something from over the counter at Boots.'

'Did she see a doctor about her anxiety?'

'No. We have a local GP, but I don't think she'd been to see him recently.'

The door opened and Mrs Dawson walked in carrying a mug of tea and a tea towel. She crossed over to a small coffee table and lifted it up to put it beside her son. Then she picked up a magazine to place down on the polished surface and put down his mug.

'Are you all right, son?'

Barry's face crumpled and he stood up, saying that he needed to go to the bathroom.

'Excuse me,' he said to Jane and left the room.

'He's taken it very badly ... done nothing but cry. I mean, for all her faults he loved Shirley. He was a good husband and dotes on Heidi.'

Mrs Dawson picked up one of the wedding photographs and, with almost a compulsive need to clean, wiped the glass and frame.

'She was lovely looking, but oh dear ... shocking at keeping the flat clean. I was always going over there to give it a good hoover and dust. I've even taken home bags of washing for Heidi and Barry. I was there one time and she was ironing his best shirt. I told her that wasn't the best way to iron, that you should always start on the sleeves, then the two sides and lastly the back. Then use a spray starch for the cuffs and the collar.

Shirley says to me that it was a waste of time as who sees all of the shirt when you wear a jacket. Lazy she was, but he didn't mind. Not even when it was more takeaway than anything cooked.'

'So did this create friction between you and your daughter-in-law?'

'Oh no, she was a lovely girl ... just not used to looking after the flat. To be honest, Barry was always about to do some redecorating, but working such long hours he never really got around to it. Shirley never had a mother to teach her anythin' domestic ... well, she obviously had one but she was placed in foster care when she was Heidi's age ... she was shoved from pillar to post until she was in her teens ... that's how they met.'

'I'm sorry ... how did they meet?'

'One of my best friends, Norma, is a foster carer. God knows how many kids she's looked after in her lifetime. She's a bit too old to take on any more kids now ... But she brought Shirley around here a few times, and they got on well, and the next thing he's got engaged to her.'

Jane remained silent as Mrs Dawson picked up one framed photograph after another, dusted it and replaced it in exactly the same position. She then turned to look towards the door and moved closer, lowering her voice.

'You know, one time there was a bit of a rumour that Heidi wasn't his – Shirley was a few weeks gone when they married, you see – but he wouldn't have it. Worships that little girl, and she's got his blond hair and blue eyes. Shirley was ... well, we never really knew anything about her background, but she was not all white.'

203

'So was there someone else Shirley was seeing?'

'Now listen to me ... don't go adding two and two and making it five. It was just a rumour. Shirley was engaged to Barry at eighteen and there was never anybody else since they were married. She might have been a bit jealous and that made her anxious, but Barry never messed around. He loved her and I've been out of line saying anything against her. The way I like to keep everything spick and span was the way his dad used to like it. He always said he could eat his dinner off my kitchen floor.'

Barry walked in and she immediately straightened up.

'What you been saying, Mum?'

'Nothing ... I was just saying how your dad liked the house immaculate. He'd come in from work and straight into the bath for a scrub up, because being a mechanic he wore greasy overalls and had filthy hands.'

'I don't think this is the time to go into that, Mum. He's been gone a long time and you know how grateful I am, and always will be, for what he did for me and Shirley.'

Mrs Dawson realized she had said too much and gestured to his mug of tea.

'Don't let that go cold, Barry.'

Jane watched as he ushered his mother out of the room, closing the door behind her.

'She's always had a few things against Shirley, me marrying her for one. She reckoned she was too young, but she paid for the wedding, her frock and everything. Shirley had no family and had been in foster care for most of her life, but I never wanted anyone else.'

Jane watched him as he stared at his wedding photographs. He was close to tears, and Jane stood up, closed her notebook and picked up her handbag.

'I'll type this up and then you'll be asked to sign the handwritten copy. I have to inform you that you will be required to make a formal identification at the mortuary.'

'What? I don't understand . . .'

'I'm afraid it's necessary. Maybe you could ask your mother to accompany you? Or she could make the identification herself?'

'But I've already seen her. I really don't want to do this . . . I can't . . . I mean, I don't want to have to see her again!'

'I can make a call from here and order a car to take you to the mortuary. Or if you agree I can make an appointment for later this afternoon, and meet you there? May I use the telephone to arrange it?'

Jane was shown into the hall and used the telephone on a small table to call the Coroner's Office.

She was relieved when Barry agreed to make his own way to the mortuary and said he could be there at two o'clock. He was obviously distressed but said that he needed his mother to stay at home to look after Heidi. As he went upstairs to get ready, Mrs Dawson came into the hall.

'Let me show you out, dear. He's taken this very badly . . . I keep on thinking that if I hadn't had trouble with my washing machine, I'd have been there, and I would have found her instead of poor Barry.'

'Yes, you said you were going to babysit . . .?'

'That's right . . . but my washing machine went on the

blink so I had to wait for the engineer. Shirley had a hair appointment so I was going to their flat to look after Heidi. She used to get her hair straightened, because it was so curly. I was relieved, I can tell you, when Heidi was born and had Barry's blond hair. It's impossible to get a comb through those curls ... I know because some of the kids at the school need a special type of Afro comb.'

Jane tried to steer her back onto the subject.

'I'm sorry, Mrs Dawson, I'm just trying to piece together the time frame. So, you were going to go to your son's flat on the morning that Shirley was found in the bath?'

'Yes ... I did try to call her, you know, to let her know I wouldn't be coming, but she didn't answer the phone.'

'What time was that, Mrs Dawson?'

Rita hesitated, then shrugged.

'Well, it would've been early ... like a quarter to nine ... but like I said, the phone rang and rang. Maybe she didn't hear it because she was running a bath ... but I wasn't that worried.'

'Why not?'

'Well, if I didn't turn up she would've taken Heidi to the salon with her ... to Pearls and Curls, over in Brick Lane by the market.'

'Did Barry know you were going to be at the flat?'

'Yes – like I said, I often go over there to give Shirley a hand—'

She suddenly stopped and took a sharp intake of breath.

'Oh God! ... I can't believe she's never going to be there again!'

After comforting her Jane thanked Rita and went to the front door to leave. As the door closed behind her she took out her notebook and jotted down some notes, including the name of the hair salon. Something didn't quite add up.

Jane went back to the station to type up the statement ready for Barry to sign when they met at the mortuary. Edith was in the incident room and told Jane that DS Lawrence had called and wanted to speak to her regarding some photographs. There were a number of detectives working in the room at the various desks. The two clerks were busy as there had been a spate of break-ins and a complaint from market holders about being threatened.

Edith was carrying an overflowing ashtray across to the waste bin. Pulling a face in disgust she emptied out the cigarette butts into the bin.

'The DCI wanted to see you as well. There's been a pickpocket incident on a female tourist in Soho – the perp is slashing handbag straps with a razor. DCI wants you to go to the Marquee Club on Wardour Street to interview the manager about it.'

Sighing, Jane checked her watch and grabbed her coat.

Jane was sitting on a bar stool taking notes from a young barman with a Newcastle accent. The night-club was being vacuumed and the dingy bar was filled with dirty glasses and bags of empty beer bottles being removed to the bins.

'So are you aware of anyone inside the club being robbed?'

'No, but I only work on certain days of the week ... I mostly do clearing up in the mornings, and different staff come in for night work.'

'Do you know what time they will be coming on duty?'

'No, you'll have to ask the manager as he lists the staff. But he's not here right now.'

Jane took down what few details she could report and left the club, walking back down Wardour Street. She passed a seedy strip club called 'Dolls House', with a heavy-set bouncer standing outside, his arms folded across his huge chest. There were afternoon and lunch-time shows advertised outside: 'Live Girls, Live Dancers, Live Girls, Live Dancers', flashed the neon signs. Loud music was thudding from the narrow entrance that was concealed with cheap plastic curtains.

As Jane stepped off the pavement into the road to avoid the bouncer, a woman came out of the club. Jane stopped and stared. The woman was wearing the same, or similar, blue rabbit fur coat that Jane had worn when she had acted as a decoy. She looked at the woman's face, certain it was the same woman she had seen in the photographs, the woman who had been pushing the baby stroller. But before Jane could even contemplate approaching her the woman hailed a taxi and climbed inside, passing within feet of Jane.

'Tarra, Angie!' the bouncer yelled. Jane was confused for a moment, then she recalled the list of aliases on the charge sheet and knew it had to be Janet Brown, aka Angie, who had been held at Hackney Station. She watched the taxi disappear then walked back to the strip club as the bouncer ushered in the nervous punters. There were various sexy photographs of the strippers in provocative poses displayed in a cracked glass cabinet.

Jane looked over the photographs and noticed a semi-nude shot of the woman. The bouncer swished through the plastic curtains and confronted her.

'Live girls, you want to see live girls, darlin'?'

Jane turned away abruptly and could hear him laughing.

'Takes all sorts, love! ... Live girls, dancing jig jiggy.'

Jane caught the bus back and finished her half-eaten sandwich. She had so many things to think about. Having to show Barry Dawson the body of his wife, detail the so-called bag snatcher, and yet uppermost in her mind was the woman called Angie. There was something that kept on niggling her about her arrest. The photographs of her beaten face, and why Jane had been asked to wear her coat the night she had been assaulted. Lastly she thought about the forthcoming trial of Peter Allard. There was no confirmed date but she knew it would be announced soon and she wasn't looking forward to it.

Jane sighed. 'Why do you care?' she muttered to herself. After what he had subjected her to, she felt angry with herself for wasting time thinking about him. She had loathed being grilled by his defence counsel and she knew the interrogation was likely to be worse at the trial. But what really worried her was the fact she was certain Moran had planted the knife and lied about the confession. She wondered if Moran had also lied about

Janet Brown, or Angie; and why he had her rabbit fur coat?

Jane opened her notebook and jotted down a reminder to contact old Donaldson from Hackney Collator's Office. She knew he would have the home address of Janet Brown because she remembered seeing it on the charge sheet. She couldn't recall it offhand but just for her own peace of mind she wanted to have an off-the-record meeting with the woman in the blue rabbit fur coat.

CHAPTER ELEVEN

The prison visiting room was jam-packed, and the noise was deafening. Uniformed prison officers patrolled between the small tables allocated for the visitors. As most of the prisoners were on remand, they allowed children to accompany the visitors.

Marie Allard sat anxiously opposite her husband. She had made an effort with her appearance and had washed her hair and put on some makeup, but she still looked gaunt and unwell. Peter was also bothered by the din. He was clearly very tense and kept on twisting his head, complaining that his neck hurt and they wouldn't give him anything for the pain.

'They took away what I brought in at reception ... your mum has sent in a package,' Marie said, unsure how to broach the subject of the blackmail.

Wanting to put it off as long as possible, she discussed the kids and Peter was adamant that they should not be brought in to see him. After what felt like an interminably long time he leaned forward and looked directly into her eyes.

'Are you all right?'

'I'm OK. Your mum is handling rent from taxi and we also getting a cut of the fares.'

'I know that, she told me that when she came in. And you've got our savings if there's any major funds you need for the house. The mortgage is being paid direct from the account. You're not sick, are you?'

'No, no ... but I need to tell you something ...' She was close to tears. 'I not know what to do ...'

'Do about what?'

Marie took a deep breath. 'I got a phone call ... I not know if it man or woman ... they sing words, at first quiet then shouting. I don't know what to do ... they scream out someone's name ...'

'What?'

'On the phone. I get scared to pick up the phone again in case it them. You know someone called Andy?'

'Who?'

'It's maybe a woman ... strange accent ... like some kind of song, over and over ... then in horrid voice saying she know something about you.'

Peter straightened up in the chair.

'I dunno anyone called Andy. Are you sure you heard it right?'

'Maybe Andy, or Angie ... I don't know.'

'Angie? Was it Angie?'

'Yes, maybe ... you know a woman with that name?'

Peter clenched his fist and shook his head as Marie took out a handkerchief and blew her nose.

'She say she got evidence against you for that rape charge and that she could have you put away for long time.'

'What? Are you crazy? You know I was fitted up by the cops! I never signed that confession, it was a lie! I swear before God I am telling you the truth, Marie.'

'She want more money . . .'

'What?'

'I said she want more money. Please don't shout at me! I paid her five hundred so she not go to police.'

'Christ Almighty! You already paid her? Are you out of your mind? Just repeat exactly what this bitch is saying to you, because this is blackmail! You know that, don't you? It's bloody blackmail!'

'I know what it is, Peter, but she keep saying she has evidence that she can prove you done the rape. I very worried . . . I paid her first time, but she call me again and want another five hundred.'

Peter held his head in his hands. He knew who it could be, but he wasn't about to tell Marie. He looked over at the officers, then turned back to his wife.

'Go from the beginning, Marie, because I'm not quite understanding what this is all about.'

Bit by bit Marie told him everything. She recounted how she had been instructed to take the money wrapped in a newspaper and put it into a bin by the 73 bus stop on Park Lane. She was crying when she said that she had done exactly as she had been asked, then took the next bus that came so she never saw who collected the money.

Peter kept on rubbing at his neck, then running his hands through his hair. He was sweating and obviously very agitated. Seeing his wife crying and being unable to calm her made it worse.

'Should I go to police?' Marie looked at her husband. He was still in good shape despite his complaints about the food being pigswill.

'Listen, I would lay money that it's that bent fucking officer who stitched me up. I don't know anyone called Angie, I swear on my kids' lives I don't ... I mean, five hundred quid is a hell of a lot of money ... it's more'n a month's takings for God's sake, and it's blackmail ... it's bloody blackmail!'

'She want me to do same as I did before, on Tuesday. Tell me what to do, Peter. I not know what to do.'

He took a deep breath.

'Right, my worries are that if this bitch is trying it on then you need to contact the cops. But then part of me is freaking out because I am innocent, Marie, and I'm banged up in here until I can prove it at the trial. I didn't rape anyone, and that woman is lying because there is no evidence against me. But if she's workin' with that bent DI Moran they could screw me over ... so maybe try and find out who she is, and do what she wants.'

'You mean pay her again? But I should go to police?'

'Listen to me, OK? Yeah, go to the police but, and listen good, if you find a connection with this bitch and it's to Moran then the case against me will be slung out of court, understand me? You need to find out if there is a connection, sweetheart, that's all I'm saying.'

'I not know, Peter, I so nervous about doing it again ...'

'You're going to have to do it, Marie. If you do I can get that false confession thrown out. This is what you do – make it look like you get back on the bus. You have to find out who she is, because it's all a pack of lies.'

'I not understand. You mean, I leave money like before, but not get on bus? Please don't lie to me, Peter ... if you know who she is then why would she say these things?'

Peter became increasingly agitated as Marie started crying again. He leaned closer and patted the table with the flat of his hand.

'Money ... that's obvious, isn't it? But we need to find out exactly what they're trying on.'

Marie wouldn't meet his eyes, refusing to look up.

'Look at me ... we can get through this. We've talked about what I did, Marie, you know why I did those stupid assaults. I mean, it was me being frustrated because we couldn't have sex. I'm disgusted at myself and you know I love you more than anything else in the world. I love my kids and I want to make it up to you. I never raped anyone ... it was just me grabbing their tits, feeling them up. It was dumb and stupid and I am so ashamed because of how it's turned out. I want to get out of here. My defence lawyer is really positive the case against me will be thrown out, and after the time spent in here I'll be released straight away.'

Marie nodded, but she was still frightened and unable to look at him.

'So what you want me to do?'

'Pay her ... find out who the hell she is, because it's all bullshit. I'm innocent and I'm scared they're trying it all on and using you. There's no evidence connecting me to that rape, because I didn't do it!'

'What if it has to do with Susie Luna?'

Allard sighed deeply and leaned back, shaking his head.
'Don't even think of that ... it was over a long time
ago. This is what is important, and I'm depending on
you. Don't you dare tell Mum about this blackmailing
bitch. I don't want her worried. You know what she's
like, so just keep this between us until we know if this
bent detective is behind it.'

The clanging bell rang loudly to indicate that visiting
time was over. Marie agreed to drop the money again
and said goodbye, watching as her husband was led
away. She tried to smile when he glanced back at her
but when she left the prison her head was throbbing so
much she thought she was going to faint. She felt sick
and couldn't stop herself from breaking down in tears.
By the time she got home she was shaking. She had only
just taken her coat off when the phone rang. Her hand
shook even more as she picked it up.

'Hello, Marie? It's me.' It was her mother-in-law. 'I
rang earlier to find out how Peter was. Did you take the
food parcel in?'

'Yes, Hilda, I did.'

'Are you all right? You sound very down, dear.'

'That prison always give me big headache. Peter was
OK ... he still waiting for the date of trial.'

'Taking their bloody time. Listen, I was goin' to pop
over as I have some cash for you from the bloke using
Peter's taxi. It's not a lot but he pays the rent regular into
the account.'

'Can you pick up kids from school?'

'All right, love, I can do that. So I'll come by later
then, all right?'

'Thank you, Hilda.'

Marie replaced the receiver and sat down on the stairs, her head in her hands. She started crying because deep down she had thought Peter would tell her to report the blackmail to the police. She was trying to accept his reason for her not doing so, that it was the police officer who lied about his confession. She had to force herself to trust her husband but she couldn't silence the nagging doubt that he'd known who Angie was.

Eventually Marie went into the kitchen to prepare the children's tea. She made an effort to clean up the kitchen, set the table and had made boiled eggs with toasted soldiers ready, when the front door opened.

'We're home, love!' Mrs Allard called from the hall-way. She took off the children's coats and hung them up on the hooks along with all the other outdoor clothes.

'Tea's on table. No need to get them changed, they can do it later.'

'OK, go on in, the pair of you.'

Hilda hung up her own coat as Marie ushered the children into the kitchen. They sat down obediently as she poured two glasses of milk and told them they could have ice-cream after their eggs. Hilda walked in and gave a cursory glance at the table.

'Shall I take their heads off for you? Then you can dip the soldiers in. I always like eggs for breakfast, but never mind. Just tap the top of the egg – you don't want to eat bits of shell now, do you?'

Marie said quietly that they could do that themselves and she would go and run them a bath.

She sat on the edge of the bath, making sure the water

was not too hot and poured in some Matey bubble bath to make it smell nice, watching as the bath filled with bubbles. She took two towels from the airing cupboard and rested them on the heated towel rail. She could hear Hilda downstairs organizing the children while they finished their tea. Eventually they went into their bedroom and took off their school clothes, putting on their dressing gowns in preparation for their bath.

Marie let Hilda take over in the bathroom and collected clothing to put in the washing machine, having already laid out clean shirts and underwear for the following morning.

Returning to the kitchen she saw the dirty dishes piled up on the draining board, and by the time she had washed and cleaned up the mess left on the table, she could hear the shouts and yells from upstairs. They wanted to watch TV but Marie didn't want them coming down so she went to the stairs and called up.

'Do your homework, then I'll read story.'

It was a while before Hilda joined her in the kitchen, carrying in her handbag.

'What's all that wood hammered across Peter's games room for?'

'Police damaged door, and I not want the children going in there. He has knives in there, and he always keep it locked.'

'Bloody disgusting. Did the coppers take anything away?'

'Yes.'

'Fitting him up they are ... I dunno how, but we'll get through this, Marie. The kids're washed and clean and playing, but it's earlier than usual. Maybe let them come down and see a bit of TV before bedtime?'

'I still got headache. After you go I read to them. You want cup of tea?'

'I'll do it, love.'

'I already made a pot, yes or no?'

'Yes, I'll have a cuppa while we go over the accounts. The bloke that's renting out Peter's taxi is paying in weekly with a cut of his takings and I'm putting it into your joint bank account. But I want you to see how much you can depend on coming in.'

Hilda opened her bag, took out a small notebook and an envelope of cash.

'If you give it to me I can put it in the account myself.'

'Whatever ... it's just what Peter told me to do as I know exactly how much we should be getting in. Not that I don't trust the bloke but I've asked that he details all the fares. He's getting a good price to rent the taxi and he's using our Peter's ID, which is not exactly legal as all taxi drivers are supposed to have done their knowledge tests.'

'I know, I know ...' Marie put down a mug of tea in front of Hilda and opened a packet of biscuits.

'Are you all right?' Hilda asked, spooning in sugar and stirring her tea.

Marie sat down opposite her mother-in-law.

'I mean, if there is anything you don't understand you should tell me because being Filipino I'm sometimes not sure if you do.'

'I been here since I was thirteen years old ... of course I understand and I very capable of doing our accounts.'

'No need to get snappy with me, dear. Don't think I don't understand the strain you must be going through, but so am I and I've got Cherrie, who's a constant worry. She's not to be told . . . she wouldn't understand anyway but she keeps on asking when Peter's coming round. He's such a good son, and takes such good care of Cherrie. He always has done, ever since we knew she wasn't right. But it's a heavy weight on my shoulders because I have to take her back and forth to the mental care home. I always think she was the reason their dad left, and going through the divorce was a terrible time.'

Marie sighed. She had heard the story so many times before, but she didn't have the strength to interrupt so she just sat there nodding

'I never thought I'd get through it, but after he died we had the taxi and he'd only just started paying it off. So it was virtually new for Peter to take over and he made it a good business, working all hours. He's a good provider, and I know if anything, God forbid, was ever to happen to me he'd take over caring for Cherrie. He's a good man.'

'Shall I count money?' Marie said, unable to listen to her mother-in-law's repetitive conversation.

'You've got to be positive, Marie. I can see you're not looking your best. Have they given you a date for the operation?'

Marie was counting out the bank notes from the envelope.

'Not yet.'

Hilda drained her mug of tea and placed it carefully back down on the table.

'He told me all about it. I'm not laying any blame on you, love, but my son is a handsome man and you know what they say – if they're not getting it at home they'll stray, that's what this is all about. I know Peter. He was always one for the ladies and when he was a teenager they were all after him. He could have had his pick, I can tell you.'

Marie glanced up as she made a note of the amount on the back of the envelope. She knew her mother-in-law had never approved of her or, for that matter, really liked her. It had been difficult to handle. Even when her children were born Hilda made disparaging remarks about them looking oriental. Eventually she had grown to admire their silky dark hair, as Peter had similar colouring. Now she never admitted ever saying anything untoward, but Marie had heard Peter giving his mother a severe talking to, even threatening that if she didn't appreciate his love for Marie then she would not be allowed to see her grandchildren.

'One hundred and twenty pounds.' Marie tucked the money into the envelope.

'And you got all his savings to pay out for the mortgage. And you know if you ever do get short, which I doubt, I've got a few quid and also the benefits for Cherrie.'

Marie could not even think about telling Hilda about the phone calls, and just wanted her to leave.

'Did you give Peter the food parcel?'

'I told you, yes.'

'I'll visit him tomorrow. And you said there's still no news about the date for the trial?'

'No.'

'It's disgusting. He's innocent and it's breaking my heart because I know my son. I hope you keep a positive attitude. I think you should take the kids in to see him as it's tearing him up being away from them.'

'I not want to do that.'

'Why not?'

Marie picked up her mug and rinsed it in the sink.

'I not think they should see him in prison.'

'Remand, Marie, he's not in prison, he's on remand.'

'It's still prison. I already get sick when I take them to school and pick them up because the other mothers stare at me. It's been in the newspapers, Hilda ... they too young to understand why their dad is away. I not taking them to those awful visiting sections.'

'Listen to me, your husband is a good father and a good son. If any of those bitches say anything, or give you nasty looks, you tell 'em to piss off and mind their own business. If you don't stand up for him like I'm doing, how do you think he will feel?'

Marie gave up. She didn't have the energy to argue, and, thankfully, Hilda looked at her watch as she had to collect Cherrie.

'I have to go. I can come by again tomorrow.'

Marie followed Hilda into the hall as she got her coat. She opened the front door and stood patiently waiting.

'Call me tomorrow and I can be here to make their tea.'

'I call you.'

Hilda hesitated then leaned close and gave a dry kiss to Marie's cheek.

'Put the money in the bank.'

'Yes, I will.'

'Tarra, love.'

Marie closed the front door and slipped the key chain on. She looked over to the stairs where her children were standing side by side on the top step.

'When's Daddy coming home?'

Marie went up the stairs and took her son Kim by the hand. 'You have to be a big boy because you are eight years old and Mummy needs you to be very well behaved.'

Leann, Marie's little girl, put her arms around her mother's neck. 'I am a very good girl and I always look after you, Mummy.'

Marie kissed her. 'Yes, sweetheart.'

'I'm five years old.'

'You're my big girl.'

'So when is Daddy coming home?' Kim repeated.

Marie answered abruptly, 'I don't know ... I don't know. And please don't ask me again.'

'Has he been naughty?'

Marie's eyes filled with tears. 'Yes, and you know when you are naughty you have to be punished.'

CHAPTER TWELVE

An old Victorian archway covered the rather majestic entrance into the stone cobbled yard of the mortuary, where the mortuary vans and ambulances were parked. The reception area was housed in a modern extension, and was accessed through two large glass doors. Inside, the floor was covered with blue linoleum and there was a small reception desk, which was invariably empty as they were always short-staffed and there was never an employee to work behind it.

A row of straight-backed chairs lined one wall and the overhead lights gave the reception area a yellowish hue. Although the reception was some distance from the rooms used for post-mortems and the chill section where the bodies were kept, a faint smell of Dettol permeated the area. The smell became much stronger along the corridors.

Jane had arrived five minutes late and Barry Dawson was already in the reception sitting on one of the hard-backed chairs. He was obviously nervous and as soon as she passed through the double glassed entry door, he rose to his feet. Jane gave him a friendly smile of encouragement. Having now been to the mortuary on numerous occasions she was familiar with the routine, but she had never previously handled a viewing alone.

'I just have to check if there is an assistant mortician available.'

'Do I wait here?'

'Yes please, Mr Dawson. Have a seat and I will come straight out.'

Barry sat back down, hunching his shoulders. One knee jerked as he kept his eyes on the door through which Jane had entered. It took longer than she had said as there was no assistant around, but eventually it was organized and the numbered drawer 312 listed and checked as holding the body of Shirley Dawson. Jane opened the door and gestured for Barry to join her. He hurried towards her and Jane again gave him a nod of encouragement as she let him pass her before closing the door behind them.

Barry was standing ramrod straight as Jane explained quietly that he just had to confirm his wife's identity. They would usually have taken the body into the small chapel next to the mortuary, but due to staff shortages they would have to see Shirley in the chill room. The assistant slid open drawer 312. The body was covered with a white shroud, which was slowly eased back. Shirley's eyes were closed, her hair had been combed neatly away from her face and, apart from the stitched wound in the centre of her forehead, it was as if she was sleeping. Barry looked down. He ran his fingers on his right hand over his lips, swallowed and Jane could hear his sharp intake of breath.

'Is this your wife, Shirley Dawson?' Jane asked quietly.

'Yes ... yes, it's Shirley.'

Jane gave a small nod to the assistant who covered Shirley's face and slid back the drawer. Barry remained standing and she had to gently take his arm and guide him out of the room. Back in the reception area he started to cry.

'They will be doing a post-mortem this afternoon, Mr Dawson, and—'

'I need to go to the flat to get things for Heidi. Can I go back there?' She was surprised by his question.

'I'll contact you as soon as we have clearance.'

He nodded and wiped the tears on his face with the back of his hand. He was obviously deeply distressed.

'Would you like me to get you a taxi?'

'No ... no, I need to get some fresh air, walk for a while. I can't quite cope at the moment.'

Barry left and she saw him hurrying down the road, only then remembering that she should have told him about using the camera she had found in his flat. She was disinclined to hurry after him so instead she turned in the opposite direction to make her way to the Dawsons' flat to meet up with DS Lawrence.

Jane had become more resilient since her initiation in the morgue with DCI Bradfield. She had been at the identification of the murder victim Julie Ann Collins. Nevertheless, it could not be described as easy and she completely understood why Barry Dawson had been so distraught. By the time she got to the Dawsons' flat it was almost four o'clock. She buzzed the entry bell for the top flat. The lock clicked back loudly as she entered the hall and made her way up the stairs. The front door to the flat was wide open and as she stepped through the entrance there was the flash of a camera.

'Hi . . . it's only me,' she said, as Lawrence turned and smiled.

He had long, thick blond hair with a centre parting. It often fell forward so he had a habit of continually running his fingers through his hair to keep it off his face. Lawrence was always well dressed, but was rather old-fashioned in comparison to many of the Met police. He wore cord trousers and cotton shirts, with a tweed jacket that had leather elbow pads. He often had a woollen tie drawn down to the second button of his shirt. Jane had also noticed that his brown brogues were always rather scuffed, but despite his traditional appearance he had a very youthful manner.

'I expected you earlier . . . I had to get the keys from the duty sergeant as Gibbs said they would be left there for me. I've been taking some decent photographs. I picked up the ones you took with the Kodak but they're not that clear.' He indicated a brown envelope left on the small coffee table as he packed his camera away.

'I've done a good check over the place, and if it's OK with you I'll be getting back to the station.'

Jane was sifting through the photographs. As Lawrence had pointed out, they weren't good quality.

'This one I took of the dressing gown on the bathroom floor,' she said, holding up the photo.

'What about it?'

'Well, it's just odd . . . if you were taking a bath and wearing the dressing gown, that would come off first, then the underwear. But the knickers and bra were folded underneath it.'

Lawrence glanced at the photo. 'Well, it's on a hook in the bathroom now.'

'Yes, I did that.'

He cocked his head to one side. 'Shouldn't do that . . . I mean, not that I think there's anything suspicious. Maybe that's just the way she undressed.'

Lawrence stood beside her as she thumbed through the rest of the photographs until she reached one with a woman turning towards the camera.

'Is that the victim?' he asked, and Jane shook her head.

'No, I don't know who she is. There were a few photographs already on the roll of film . . . same woman again . . . and another one.'

Lawrence leaned closer as she fanned out the three photographs. They all seemed to have been taken as if the woman was unaware of being photographed.

'Maybe a friend? But it's odd that the woman is never looking into the camera and seems unaware she's being photographed. Mind you, I've seen a lot stranger . . . and some pornographic ones that beggar belief . . .'

'Did you really mean it when you said you were becoming fed up with working as a forensic liaison?'

'Yes. We're always strapped for finances and there's a lot of new scientific experiments coming on board. I'm finding it more and more frustrating because I spend most of my life checking fingerprints or, like today, looking over a crime scene that basically isn't one. I've applied to work with CID but the reality is forensic sections are deemed more important, and probably they are. It's just frustrating because I'd like to become more involved in the investigations instead of being stuck in a lab twenty-four-hours a day.'

Surprised at his outburst, Jane asked, 'But what you do is becoming more and more vital to investigations, isn't it?'

'Yes, I know … but try telling that to DI Moran … even DCI Shepherd isn't that encouraging. You know, the only person who really drew me in, and encouraged me, was Len Bradfield. After what happened to him I sort of allowed myself to get buried in the lab. Part of that was because of the guilt, and I still feel it.'

'Guilt?'

'Yes. I had the chance to stop him going ahead with the operation. I knew early on that he was taking risks, but he persuaded me … he even had me on the team. I've never felt such adrenalin … Facing the outcome has been hard because I keep on thinking that if I had intervened he might still be alive.'

Lawrence smiled sadly, running his fingers through his hair as Jane replied.

'But you can't blame yourself, Paul. If you do, then how do you think I feel? If I hadn't recognized that voice on the tape, if I hadn't identified the bank robber and his family, the operation would never have taken place.'

He touched her shoulder. 'Do you really believe that?'

'Yes. I don't dwell on it, I can't … but it took me a long time to get over the awful feeling of guilt.' Jane thought about the way her heart would suddenly beat rapidly, and her breath quicken. How reminders, even seeing Lawrence today, brought back the feeling of helplessness and panic that she'd had to teach herself to control.

'You are very young, and were just a probationary officer then. I think both Spence and I carry the responsibility within us because of our positions ... it rears up when you least expect it. All I really want to do now is get onto an investigation and prove myself capable of handling it.'

There was a moment of embarrassed silence, as if he felt he had disclosed too much of himself, and he gave another sad smile.

'Sorry ... didn't mean to lay that on you, Jane. Can you lock up and organize getting the key back to Mr Dawson?'

'Yes, of course.'

Lawrence left as Jane put the photographs and negatives into her bag. She felt depressed, but at the same time pleased that he had confided in her as she had always liked him. Now even more so. She checked the time and realized she would soon be off duty, so might as well return to the section house. As she locked the front door and headed down the stairs the door of the flat below opened and a thick-set, swarthy man wearing a fawn donkey jacket gestured towards her.

'Are you anything to do with the flat above? Only I need to check something out in their bathroom.'

Jane introduced herself and explained that there had been a tragic incident and that Mrs Dawson had been found dead.

'What?'

'Mrs Dawson had an accident and—'

'Is their bath water running?'

She found it extraordinary that he showed no reaction whatsoever and said sharply that she was certain the bath water was turned off.

'Well, it might be turned off now but you come and take a look at this. I don't have a key to the Dawsons' flat because they own the place but I might need to put in a claim for water damage.'

Jane followed the objectionable man into the flat, which was stripped down to the floorboards with ladders and tins of paint lined up in the entrance hall.

'I'm having the place refurbished and redecorated but this is really bad damage.'

'I'm sorry, I didn't get your name?'

'Eric de Silva. I own this place, plus the head lease of the entire property. Come on through here.'

Jane dutifully followed him into the bathroom, which was directly below the Dawsons' bathroom.

He pointed up to the ceiling. 'Look at that. This was only painted a week ago.'

The ceiling was wet and a pinkish water mark covered one side of the wall. He then pointed at the floor.

'See, it's dripped down the wall onto the floor. That's water damage. Their mains water tap needs to be turned off in case this is from their water tank as it's directly above this bathroom.'

Jane agreed but refused to hand over the keys to him. She couldn't wait to get away from him and returned upstairs saying she would double-check that all the taps were turned off.

The bath taps were off, and the kitchen taps likewise. She located the water tank and mains tap in the airing cupboard and made sure these were also turned off. Returning to the bathroom she stood in the doorway. Something didn't make sense. The water marks in the flat below were obviously recent, and when she checked the water level rim still obvious in the bath it was in no way reaching the waste pipe or top of the bath. The pinkish colour of the water down in the flat below could be caused by the blood from Shirley's head wound. But when her body was found there was no way the bath had overflowed. Jane had pulled out the plug so she knew exactly what level the water had been.

Bending down she could see that part of the board surrounding the bath was quite loose, and when she gave it a hard tug a section moved back easily. Jane jerked and pulled again and this time the old cheap surround came away. Leaning it against her legs she could see that there were pools of water still beneath the bath. The corking was sodden and wet. She propped the board back and decided that she needed to speak with De Silva again. She hurried down the stairs but the flat door was locked and there was no answer when she knocked. She went back upstairs to get her handbag and was about to leave when she saw the tea mug left on a side table. It had been brought in for her by the duty officer, from the next-door neighbour, when she was first there. She picked up the mug to return it, locking the door behind her.

Jane headed down to the basement flat and rang the doorbell. Mr Cook opened the door. Jane explained she was returning the mug.

'Who is it?'

'It's the policewoman, love. Come on in, the wife's on sentry duty.' He laughed, opening the door wider and gesturing with his hand for Jane to follow him.

'I really have to get back to the station.'

'Be nice if you gave her an update on what happened next door.'

'Yes of course, you were very helpful, Mr Cook,' Jane said, as she went into their sitting room. His wife was in her wheelchair positioned by their basement window. This was the room where Barry had been with the baby and his mother-in-law.

Mrs Cook wheeled herself round to be able to face Jane, and indicated for her to sit on the sofa.

'Make us a cuppa, will you love?'

Her husband nodded and walked out. Jane perched on the edge of the sofa and gave Mrs Cook a few details about the incident, and explained that they were waiting for a post-mortem report but it appears to have been a tragic accident.

'Shockin' . . . I had spent ages in the kitchen cos poor Barry was in here in a terrible state. Then he had the baby with him howlin' . . . give me a headache. Mind you, it was more action than I seen for years. That poor girl, drownin' like that.'

'Did you know her well?'

'No, just to give a wave. I sit by the window . . . not that I can see that much, bein' in the basement. But I always saw her with the dog of a morning. Sometimes she'd bend down and give me a smile.'

'She went out regularly in the morning, didn't she?'

233

'Yes, always about ten o'clockish, baby in the push-chair ... pretty little thing ... tragic now, havin' no mother. But he's a good lad.'

'How well did you know Barry?'

'Not well. He's come in a few times, but they were just a young couple. He always said if we ever needed him he'd be over, but my husband takes care of everything.'

Mr Cook walked in with a tea tray and a packet of ginger biscuits.

'I really can't stay, but thank you.' Jane half rose, wanting to leave.

'Did you tell her about the door?'

Mrs Cook waved her hand. 'No, I hadn't got around to it. Being in the basement we can hear it, you know, if any of the tenants next door buzz their door open. What they do is ring the bell for who they're seein' and they can buzz the front door open from their flat.'

Jane had used it and Lawrence had opened the door for her. Mr Cook came back in with a teapot.

'I don't know if she did go in but I heard the buzz. What time did I say it was?'

Jane was becoming impatient and looked at Mr Cook.

'She's talking about the morning, you know, when Barry found the poor girl.'

'That's right ... I was sitting here having my morning cup of tea, in me dressing gown. I can tell if there's any post for us or if the paper boy's delivered, but it was about eight, was it?'

Mr Cook poured the tea, and held up the milk jug. Jane smiled, thanking him.

'So, at eight o'clock ...'

'Yes, or maybe a bit earlier. First, there was the woman, up and down, up and down ... you can hear quite clearly down here ... you know, footsteps on the pavement outside, click, click, click ...'

'I'm sorry, I don't quite follow. You saw a woman outside?'

'That's right. She went back and forth, and then I heard the clunk from next door ... you know, like I said, as if someone had let her in.'

'Can you describe this woman?'

'No, love. Look for yourself, I can only see the feet and up to the knees.'

'You are sure it was a woman?'

'Yes, dear ... men don't go wearin' high-heeled black patent leather shoes now, do they?'

Jane smiled but the shoes caught her interest. 'Was there anything else you noticed about the shoes? Were they unusual in any way?'

'Expensive I'd say, pointed at the front and with very high heels ... maybe four or five inches.'

'Thank you, Mrs Cook, you've been very helpful. Just to make sure I've got it right ... you saw this woman pacing up and down, then you heard the buzzer from next door, and it was around eight o'clock on the morning that Shirley was found ...'

'Yes, dear, that's right ... I don't know if it means anything.'

Jane smiled politely and thanked the couple again for their hospitality. As it was already after 6 p.m. she didn't return to the station but went back to the section house.

In her room she spent time compiling her notes before getting an early night. As she reflected on her findings, the Cooks' information about the mystery caller and the water-stained ceiling, she knew it wouldn't make her popular but tomorrow morning she would discuss her concerns with DCI Shepherd.

CHAPTER THIRTEEN

Jane was eager to share her thoughts with DI Gibbs but he wasn't in his office, or in the canteen, so she took her coffee and toast back to the incident room. She had just sat down at her desk to type up her report when Paul Lawrence walked in carrying notes for Edith to pass on about another case he was working on.

'Can I have a quick word, Paul?' Jane asked.

He looked at his watch, then smiled. 'Sure, but make it fast as I've got a date with some blood tests.'

Jane gave him a brief rundown about the water marks in the flat below the Dawsons', and then told him about the neighbour hearing the door release buzzer allowing someone to enter. She also explained that the owners of the ground-floor flat had left for work, and the middle flat was empty, so she believed it was possibly Shirley who let the woman in. As she was describing the black patent leather stiletto shoes seen by Mrs Cook from the basement window, DCI Shepherd walked in and interrupted.

'I just spoke with PC May at the mortuary. Pathologist agreed with me and Doc Henry. He concluded that the

237

Shirley Dawson case was accidental death by drowning. There was water in her lungs and stomach, and the injury to her head was consistent with a fall in the bath.'

Lawrence looked at the DCI. 'It might not be that straightforward, sir. Tennison has raised a couple of things that she thinks are out of place. I'd like to visit the scene with her.'

'What things?'

'Just some inconsistencies. Tennison was at the victim's flat yesterday and there appears to be water damage to the flat below the Dawsons'—'

The DCI interrupted. 'Well, obviously the bath water splashed about and overflowed after she'd slipped and cut her head open.'

'There's also the possibility the victim may have had a female visitor that morning,' Jane said.

'How do you know that?' the DCI asked, looking annoyed.

'I spoke with a neighbour, sir, Mrs Cook. She saw a woman who she believes rang the doorbell at the flats, and then she heard the buzzer for the door latch go ... I believe the woman was let in by Shirley Dawson—'

'Hang on, Tennison, just stop right there. The neighbour saw a woman yet only "believes" she rang the doorbell and went in ... What nonsense is that?'

Jane explained the circumstances of Mrs Cook being in a wheelchair, and being able to see people's feet from her basement flat.

'They were very expensive-looking patent leather shoes, with pointed toes and a high stiletto heel, and ...'

The DCI raised his eyes to the ceiling and shook his

head. Even Lawrence looked at Jane rather surprised by what she'd just said, though he didn't doubt it was true.

Shepherd smiled at Jane and quietly said, 'So our new WDC wants to challenge my opinion, the police doctor's opinion and the wisdom of a pathologist in favour of a woman in a wheelchair who saw a pair of patent leather shoes?'

'Well, I do question it, sir ...'

'Do you really, Tennison? It's been classified as non-suspicious and PC May has informed the coroner of that fact. Now, get out there and start investigating that pickpocket with the razor before he does some real harm to anyone who tries to stop him.'

Jane wanted to add that she also wasn't happy with Barry Dawson's behaviour, but Lawrence looked at her and surreptitiously shook his head for her to keep quiet.

'Who was the pathologist that carried out the examination, sir?' Lawrence asked.

DCI Shepherd looked at him sternly, but Lawrence was quick to give his reason for the question.

'Tennison will need his name for her report.'

'That new chap, who's just come down from Leeds ...'

'Dr Forrest,' Lawrence said. The DCI nodded and then left the room. Jane sighed and lifted up her hands.

'Honestly, it's as if I am not allowed to have an opinion!'

'Forrest's an old boy who's self-opinionated and lazy. Rumour has it he screwed up a few jobs in Leeds by misdiagnosis and only applied for the job down here cos he was under pressure to hang up his medical bag and retire.'

'Could we get someone else to look at Shirley Dawson's body?'

'I doubt it ... besides, it's not protocol. Prof Martin is head of the Pathology department. He and Forrest are drinking buddies. You'll need something more to persuade the coroner to give the go-ahead for a second PM.'

'Will you help me, Paul? I just have a feeling something is wrong, but I don't know enough about forensics and dead bodies ...'

Lawrence shook his head.

'But why not? You told me yesterday that you wanted to have a more central role in investigation – this could be your opportunity. Please, Paul, I have such a strong gut feeling about this.'

'Gut feelings are not a bad thing, as you already know from when you recognized the bank raider's voice. But you need to find hard evidence to prove them. I'm in the lab all morning, but after lunch let's meet at the Dawsons' flat and we'll go over it inch by inch together. If we find anything solid to go on I'll approach another pathologist I know for advice and an off-the-record second opinion. In the meantime, why don't you make some enquiries about Barry Dawson at the hospital? See if his statement about what time he left the hospital and returned home matches with his work records.'

Jane nodded. 'Thank you, I'll call you.'

Lawrence left Jane alone in the CID room. She was halfway through reading the autopsy report when Edith arrived for work. She was in a very tetchy mood again as her mother was continuing to be difficult.

Not wanting to be drawn into a long discussion about

what Edith's mother had got up to in the night, Jane left the autopsy report on her desk to finish later and said, 'Edith, I'm going over to St Thomas' Hospital to check a few details out.'

Edith rolled some fresh paper into her typewriter.

'On whose authority? I've got you down for making further enquiries about this bag slasher ... is DI Gibbs going with you?'

'No, he's not in yet.'

Edith looked at her watch. 'That man is skating on thin ice. He is supposed to be working on the bag slasher case. Well, go along to St Thomas' and I'll tell Gibbs when he deigns to come in.'

'It's still very early,' Jane said, hoping she hadn't got DI Gibbs in trouble.

'Early birds, my dear, catch the worms. Right, let me go over this autopsy report and hopefully that's one case sorted.'

Jane was at St Thomas' Hospital by eight thirty. She went straight to the porters' rest room in the basement. It was a very untidy, smelly room with old wing-backed chairs, worn carpet and overflowing bins. There were food plates from the canteen left on a low table, with full ashtrays and old newspapers littered around. The off duty night porter was resting in one of the moth-eaten chairs, as the morning shift came on ready to work.

Jane was able to check that Barry Dawson was on duty and had arrived on time that day as usual. However, nobody could recall seeing him after he clocked on at six forty-five and it was suggested that Jane go up to one of the wards on the second floor as the porter, a Mario

Goncalves, was handling patients scheduled for theatre and he had been on duty the same morning.

Jane made her way towards the nurses' bay to ask if Mario Goncalves was available to have a quick chat. The nurses were drinking tea and one was at an open cabinet selecting medication to put into rows of small containers with name tags. Jane introduced herself. They were very pleasant and offered her a cup of tea, explaining that Mario was taking a patient to the X-ray unit but was expected back any moment. Jane declined the offer of tea and stood beside the small horseshoe desk. On one wall there was a large cork noticeboard with time schedules, postcards and patients' room numbers pinned to it. There were also menus, a diet sheet listing special needs, and numerous photographs of nurses' outings and birthday parties, plus a few thank-you cards.

Jane checked her watch. She had to constantly step aside as one nurse after another came into the bay or left. She glanced back at the cork board for something to do, and one photograph caught her attention. It looked as if it was some kind of celebration party, and she recognized one of the girls in the photo as the nurse selecting the medications. But there was a redhead standing behind her and Jane moved closer for a better look.

'Excuse me?' Jane looked at the nurse who was locking up the medication cupboard.

'In this photograph ... who is that red-headed girl standing behind you?'

'That's Katrina. It was a drinks do for the new Sister.'

'Does Katrina work here?'

'She did, but she left about eight or nine days ago. She wasn't happy and didn't get along with us. There was a bit of a situation.'

'Could I ask you what it was?'

The nurse wheeled her trolley out from the bay. 'Not entirely sure ... not my business really. Can you excuse me?'

Jane had to step aside, and turned to one of the other nurses. 'Why did Katrina leave?'

There were hooded looks between her and her colleagues. Jane explained that she was making enquiries regarding a police investigation and would be grateful if they could answer her question. A plump nurse stepped forward and introduced herself as the Ward Sister.

'Her name is Katrina Harcourt. Basically she was not up to a very professional standard as she had been working with some agency before she came here. In fact, she wasn't here for that long ... no more than eight or nine months.'

Jane opened her bag and took out the envelope of photographs she had developed from the reel of film. She selected the black and white photograph of the woman caught on camera.

'This is her, isn't it?'

'Yes, she had really auburn hair. Very pretty ... but like I said, we all have a job to do here and she wasn't very well liked.'

'Do you have an address for her?'

The nurse was becoming rather irritated by Jane as the phone kept on ringing and they were preparing to go on the wards. They were able to give Jane the last address they had for Katrina, which was the nurses' accommodation close to the hospital, then Mario appeared with a wheelchair. He was very affable and good-looking, and stacked the wheelchair into the annexe before he joined her in the corridor. They sat on some hard-backed chairs as Jane introduced herself and asked him about the morning of Shirley's death.

Mario said that everyone was very sad for Barry as he had not, as yet, returned to work but had called in explaining his reasons.

Mario was able to confirm that Barry had eaten breakfast as usual in the canteen that day. Then he recalled that later that morning he had been in the A&E corridor when Barry had asked him for some change to use the payphone.

'It was about ten thirty. He had been calling for some time and asked me for change as he said he couldn't get through. He was very agitated.'

'Did he say why?'

'Yeah, he said he was trying to call his wife, but wasn't getting any reply. So he had called his mother, but he was very concerned. I gave him some change, but I had an emergency to attend so I didn't see him again.'

'Did you know a nurse called Katrina Harcourt?'

Mario appeared evasive, and shrugged his shoulders.

'Yeah, she worked here on Ward C . . . but I wouldn't say I knew her.'

'Did Barry know her?'

'Like I just said, she used to work here so we all get to know each other. She left under a bit of a cloud, but that's all I know.'

Jane thanked Mario, then went up to the canteen to double-check if any of the serving ladies recalled seeing Barry having breakfast that morning. It was rather a pointless enquiry as they all remembered seeing Barry at breakfast every day if he was on the morning shift, as he was a regular, but none of them could confirm categorically seeing him that particular day.

The row of houses was quite run-down and they were mostly divided up into bedsits. Gassiot House, the address she had been given, was at the end of the row. Jane rang the bell for number 12. She was about to turn away when the front door was opened by a woman carrying a mop and bucket.

'Do you know if anyone is in number twelve?' Jane said as she showed her ID.

'I don't, love. I just clean the landings and hallways, but not the rooms.'

'Do you mind if I go and check.'

'No, go ahead – it's on the second landing.'

Jane moved up the wide staircase. The threadbare carpet had bald patches and the wide polished oak bannister rail was obviously from a more affluent period when the property was perhaps privately owned. It appeared that every room had now been made into bedsits. There were bathrooms on each floor and the ceiling was cracked and peeling in places.

Number 12 was at the end of the corridor. Jane knocked, waited, then tried again. There was no response. She was about to try one more time when the door opened.

'Yeah?'

'I'm so sorry to disturb you—'

'Listen, I've not had time to clear up ... you're early.' The girl was wearing flannelette pyjamas and had tousled hair, with a sleeping mask around her neck. She swung the door open and gestured for Jane to come in.

'I'm on nights ... this is really inconvenient.'

Jane stepped into the shambolic room, which had the curtains drawn shut and two single beds on either side. The unmade bed had sheets and blankets piled up on it, with cardboard boxes on the floor beside it. Hanging on the back of the door was a nurse's uniform and cape.

'I would like to introduce myself, as I think you may be confused.' Jane took out her warrant card and held it up. 'I am Detective Constable Jane Tennison. I'm making enquiries about Katrina Harcourt.'

'What?'

'I'm sorry, what is your name?'

'Brenda March. I thought you were here to take up the other bed. Katrina doesn't live here any more, and she's cleaned out all her stuff.'

Brenda sat on her bed and switched on a bedside lamp. The untidy room was quite large, with a chest of drawers covered in makeup and perfume bottles. There was a huge free-standing wardrobe with the doors open and a jumble of clothes spilling out, and a dirty laundry bag dumped beside it. On a side table was an electric kettle with bottles of milk, tins of coffee and tea bags, and packets of biscuits. Chipped mugs were lined up alongside a saucer with used teaspoons.

'I am sorry to inconvenience you but I just need to ask a few questions about Katrina.'

'As I said, she doesn't live here any more and there's another nurse moving in today. I am going to tidy up, but she left her side in a mess. I didn't get in until after my shift and I'm really knackered. Katrina paid up until the end of the week, so I've had the place to myself.'

Jane glanced further around the room. There was a washbasin with dirty towels on a rail, and a broken mirror above it.

'How well did you know Katrina?'

Brenda shrugged and got up to open the cheap curtains.

'Well, she slept here, but I wouldn't say I knew her that well. We were often on different shifts so she'd be sleeping when I was working. But she was OK. What's this about?'

'I'm just making enquiries and would like to talk to her. Do you have a forwarding address for her?'

'No, she left in quite a hurry. Said she didn't get on with the new Ward Sister and was fed up, so she packed her stuff. In fact, I wasn't here. I think she has parents in Brighton.'

'Do you know Barry Dawson?'

'Yes, he's a porter at the hospital. I was told that his wife had died ... is that what this is about?'

'Did Katrina know him?'

'I suppose so. I mean, it's a big hospital but you do eventually get to know most of the staff.'

'What can you tell me about Katrina?'

'Like I just said, I didn't really know her. I mean, we

weren't friends. Sometimes we'd have a drink in the pub after work with everyone. She was very attractive, very stylish, but she was quite edgy cos she knew the other nurses didn't really get along with her. They didn't reckon she pulled her weight and wasn't as professional because she had mostly worked in care homes before. She didn't take to all the rules and regulations you have to adhere to when you're in a hospital like St Thomas'. Apparently she was often late and complained a lot.'

'Did she have a boyfriend?'

Brenda frowned. 'I think she had someone, but I dunno who. She was quite secretive about whoever it was. You know, if it was a doctor the gossip goes round like wildfire. Everyone always thinks that nurses go after the doctors. She used to get all dressed up and she had some nice clothes.'

'So you think she was having an affair with someone from the hospital?'

'Well, I did think it might be a doctor or one of the surgeons, but I never saw her with any of them outside the hospital. Whoever it was gave her a necklace ... oh yes, and a nice ring ... she showed me the ring, it was a garnet but not that extravagant.'

'So when she showed you the ring what did she say?'

Brenda sighed. 'She didn't actually show it to me ... it was on her bedside table and being a bit nosey when I was here I took a look at it. There was a card with a heart on it as well. Look, I don't know what all this is really about. She was very unpleasant when I asked her if it was an engagement ring, because I was obviously letting her know I'd seen it. She had a temper on her and was telling me to mind my own business. I just let her rant on at me because I had been nosey. She sort of apologized for being so nasty to me and then she told me that the reason she was so upset was because of a previous engagement she had and whoever it was broke her heart.'

'To someone from the hospital?'

'No, she said it was a while ago. She was preparing her wedding, had a designer dress, bridesmaids and everything arranged by her parents and he must have dumped her ... she became very upset and said she didn't want to talk about it any more because she had virtually had a nervous breakdown about it.'

'Did she mention to you who it was? Maybe gave you his name?'

'No, just that he was a doctor and that he had hurt her deeply. And he cost her family so much money as they couldn't get the deposit back from the venue they'd booked for the reception.'

'That must have been awful for her.'

'I suppose it was, and that was why she was so secretive about who she was seeing. She did tell me something else ...' Brenda chuckled.

'What else?'

'Well, she said that she took a pair of scissors and cut her wedding dress to shreds. It was a bit freaky because she started to laugh, you know, as if it was funny ... but obviously it wasn't. Anyway, it was shortly after that that she left and we never discussed it again.'

Jane smiled and thanked Brenda, apologizing for waking her. She was unsure just what she had gained from the interview; however, she did now know that

Barry Dawson's statement about when he had left the hospital was confirmed by Mario Goncalves.

On the bus back to the station Jane went over her notes and jotted down the timing of Katrina leaving the hospital and bedsit. This would have been a week before Shirley Dawson drowned. She was uncertain about the connection, it just made her wonder why there were three photographs of Katrina Harcourt on the roll of film from the Dawsons' camera.

Jane used a payphone to call DS Lawrence at the lab. She agreed to meet up with him at the station so they could walk to the Dawsons' flat. It was almost midday when they set off and Jane gave Lawrence the details about her visit to the hospital and her questioning of Brenda March. He listened attentively and then asked if Jane could be on the wrong track, as from what he had gathered Barry appeared to be very distressed about his wife's death.

'Yes, he was . . . but I have a suspicion that perhaps he could be the man having an affair with Katrina. There is also the possibility that it was Katrina who had been outside their flat on the morning Shirley died.'

'All this from the photographs we developed?'

'Yes, it was Katrina. Even though the photos were black and white I recognized her from a photograph at the hospital. She has red hair.'

'Well, Mrs Cook only saw a woman's feet so that's going to be hard to prove. Also we can't be one hundred percent certain she went into the Dawsons' flat. We also don't have her fingerprints on record, so that can't help us.'

Climbing up the stairs to the flat, they discovered the

front door was ajar. Lawrence indicated to Jane to be silent as he moved in front of her and entered the hall. They could see no one, but the sound of hammering drew them towards the bathroom.

Barry Dawson was on his knees hammering the bath panel into place. He had a bag of tools with screwdrivers and heavier hammers beside him. Lawrence knocked on the door and Barry turned round in shock.

'Mr Dawson, I am Detective Sergeant Lawrence and you already know WDC Tennison. Can you explain exactly what you are doing here?'

Barry stood up, his face flushed. 'I was repairing the bath panel, putting it back into place. I have every right to be here ... it's my flat and I need more clothes for myself and Heidi. Perhaps you could tell me what *you* are doing here?'

'OK, Mr Dawson, you can get what you need but then you must leave. We'll contact you as soon as you are allowed access. We're just having a once-over to be totally satisfied. I am a forensic officer and I have been asked by the coroner to examine the flat.'

'I haven't finished.'

'Just leave it as it is, Mr Dawson. WDC Tennison will accompany you to get the items you need.'

Barry didn't take long. He used an old holdall, taking clothes for his daughter and a few items for himself, and said that he would be returning to work the following day. Jane watched him silently, and when he was ready to leave she walked him to the front door.

'One more thing, Mr Dawson. I have to apologize as I used your camera while I was here, to photograph the bathroom.' Jane gestured to the small Kodak camera she had left on the coffee table.

'That's not mine. I've never seen it before.'

'Oh, well, we'll reimburse you for the reel of film I used. There were some photographs that had already been taken on it.'

Jane went to her bag and took out the envelope containing the images. She selected the three black and white photographs of Katrina and handed them to him. She watched closely as he glanced at them, but he showed no reaction and appeared to be unperturbed.

'I don't know who this is. I don't want them.'

He tore up the photographs, tossed them onto the table next to the camera and left the flat carrying the holdall. Lawrence came out from the bathroom.

'Well, it's still sodden beneath the bath, and the tide mark is clearly shown. I used the screwdriver Mr Dawson was using – come and have a look.'

Lawrence leaned over the bath and indicated with the screwdriver that the waste pipe was blocked. He felt it wasn't a recent blockage but was a build-up of hairs and thick soap that had congealed.

'No water could have leaked down below this way – it had to have come from the bath being overfilled.'

'I know the water level was not high because I pulled the plug out, and as you can see from the blood-stained rim it was nowhere near overflowing.'

'Might have happened when she fell backwards and the level rose.'

She watched as he tested the small residue of blood still on the central tap, and then looked around.

'No other blood drops. This is the only congealed blood at the scene, so it's likely that when she hit her head, she subsequently fell backwards and slid under the water, drowning.'

'Was she standing up when she hit her head?'

He frowned, then shrugged. Jane watched as he took samples of the blockage and then photographed the bath.

'Barry said he didn't own the camera and when he was shown the photographs of Katrina he denied knowing her, and then tore them up.'

'Well, that's interesting ... but you still have the negatives?'

'Yes.'

'OK ... now, get into the bath. I need you to show me something.'

'What?'

He laughed. 'Just want to test something. I remember when we first met, at the autopsy of that murdered girl, and old Professor Martin asked you to get on the floor as he wanted to demonstrate how he thought the victim had been beaten. He asked you to put up your arm as if protecting your body from the blows ...'

'Don't remind me! I was so embarrassed because I thought he wanted me to lie on the floor. I smelt of Dettol for days afterwards, it was all over my uniform.'

Lawrence smiled at the memory.

'Right, step into the bath. There was no mat, right, so take off your shoes and in you get.'

He held her hand as she stepped into the bath.

'Now, we are presuming the water was turned off

and the bath was filled. So, did she step in and find that it was boiling hot, leaned towards the taps, slipped and cracked her head? Just try it.'

In her stocking feet Jane leaned towards the central tap. She pretended to hit her head, and then leaned back.

'It would be more likely that she would end up forward, on her knees?'

He nodded, then took Jane's hand to help her out.

'But if she really cracked her head hard she could have lost her balance and been unconscious, falling back into the water,' he said.

Jane put on her shoes and followed him out of the bathroom.

'OK, let me have a good look over the place and take some more photographs.'

Jane was fascinated by how carefully Lawrence moved around the flat. The high chair was still in place and the food remained on the tray. He examined the playpen, then stood at the ironing board. Near to that was a clothes horse with a few items ready to be ironed, with a water spray and some starch in a basket.

The iron was on its side, not placed into the section at the end of the board. Lawrence examined the iron very closely, running his finger along the rim. He took close-up pictures of the iron and Jane smiled as he had a habit of muttering to himself. The iron had been recently cleaned. He looked around to see if there was a rag or something that had been used to wipe it because it had a faint smell of Dettol. He then replaced the iron and checked the flex, bending down to the socket on the wall beside it.

'This is interesting ... it looks to me as if the plug was wrenched out of the socket because the wires are not only frayed, which could be a result of frequent use, but two of the wires are disconnected so the iron would not be usable. And it could give you an electric shock if you tried to use it.'

He stood up with his hands on his hips.

'OK, I don't like this. Blouse on the ironing board ready to be pressed ... baby's food on the high chair tray ... next-door neighbour hears the front door buzzer after she has seen a woman pacing up and down outside the basement ...'

'That was at eight o'clock,' Jane said.

'Right. But we know Barry was calling the payphone on the landing at the hospital trying to reach Shirley at ten or ten thirty, but received no answer. He leaves the hospital and arrives home at eleven to find his wife dead in the bath.'

'One more thing,' Jane added. 'His mother said she was going to be here at the flat but didn't turn up because she was waiting for an engineer. Barry said he made a call to his mother so he would know she was not here with Shirley as arranged. A witness said he appeared to be very anxious and subsequently left the hospital. But surely if he also knew his wife was going to have a hair appointment why was he so anxious that she didn't answer the phone?'

Lawrence checked his watch.

'OK, I am going to pull in a favour and see if I can get a more experienced pathologist to get over to the mortuary and check Shirley's body. I'm going to have to move fast before it's released for burial because I need to know whether her head injury is in fact totally consistent with the fall in the bath.'

Jane could feel the tension mounting.

'I keep thinking about Barry's reaction to the camera. He said he didn't know Katrina, but he had to know her from the hospital.'

Lawrence replied, 'Maybe he didn't own the camera. What if it belonged to Shirley? Taking a long shot, what if she had used it to take the photographs of Katrina as she had found out Barry was having an affair with her?'

'Brenda said she had a mystery boyfriend from the hospital,' Jane interjected.

'So, what we have is a possible motive ...' Lawrence continued. 'A love affair, right? She confronted Barry and they had an argument. On the other hand, it could all be inconclusive.'

'I honestly don't think he killed her,' Jane said, biting her lip.

'Or perhaps they were in it together,' Lawrence continued. 'You need to trace this Katrina and find out if she was involved with Barry. Dig up whatever you can on her, but until we have more we keep this just between ourselves and don't inform DCI Shepherd. We need to prove that this was not accidental death, but murder.'

'I'll go back to the station,' Jane said, collecting her bag.

Lawrence grinned. 'Well, I'm going to have do a bit of schmoozing to get old Professor Martin on board. He may be a pain in the arse but he's top notch ... when he's sober.'

Jane laughed. She had met 'old Prof Martin' numerous times since she had first met Lawrence. She had learned that alongside his drinking and cigar smoking, his jovial and loud bellowing voice was often a cover as he was a very knowledgeable and dedicated man.

Lawrence held open the front door for her as they left.

'We might be in luck. I doubt the coroner will release the body for the undertakers' embalming before the funeral on Monday ... let's hope not.'

They split up outside the Dawsons' flat and Jane walked the few yards to pass the basement next door. She was going to continue but paused and bent down, looking through the railings. Mrs Cook was sitting in her wheelchair knitting, but she looked up as if she had heard her footsteps. Jane gave a small wave and Mrs Cook smiled and waved back. Jane was satisfied that Mrs Cook was possibly right about the high-heeled footsteps. She was beginning to feel very confident that this was going to be her first murder case with the new station.

CHAPTER FOURTEEN

Jane completed her notes on the enquiries at St Thomas' Hospital and what she and Lawrence had determined from their visit to the Dawsons' flat. It was five-thirty and, after checking any messages and details that had been listed for her to oversee, she had nothing left to do. There was a report file disclosing that there had been further bag snatches in Wardour Street and one report from the Marquee Club that there had been a theft of a woman's handbag, but there was no point going now, better to wait until later as she might catch the manager. She had a few words with the duty sergeant before leaving, then decided that to fill the time she'd do a catch-up at Hackney to see if there had been any developments or if a trial date had been set for Peter Allard.

It felt strange returning to her old stamping ground. DI Moran ran the CID at Hackney very differently to the way DCI Bradfield had done and the atmosphere felt a little strained, even more so when she entered the CID office. DC Brian Edwards was wearing an overcoat and had cotton wool stuck in one ear, with a streaming nose. He looked up when Jane knocked on the door.

'Hi there,' Jane said.

Edwards sneezed loudly.

'Stay well away from me – I'm contaminated. I've had this bloody cold for two days. As you can see, everyone has scarpered out of the office.'

'Why don't you go home?'

'The guv's asked me to do all this checking into old cases, and wants to see if I can get a result before Allard's trial.'

'So we haven't got a date yet?'

'Nope ... But it can't be far off. I've found out that five years ago Allard used to rent a property in Maidstone, worked as a bus driver, then returned to London after his father died and took over his taxi.'

'What's this got to do with his trial?' Jane asked.

Edwards became hesitant, blowing his nose. 'Moran's concerned that there might be questions about the confession ... He reckons the pattern of Allard's assaults, and the attack on you, means that there could have been more in his past.'

'Have you found anything that might be connected?'

'Give me a break – have you any idea how many sexual assaults take place in these areas ... Hackney, Peckham, Walthamstow? I haven't even started on Maidstone yet because that'll be a different force. And you know how protective forces are about their own information.'

Edwards sneezed loudly again.

'Bless you!' Jane said. 'Is DI Moran in his office?'

'No. He went out to buy a christening present for DC Ashton's new baby.'

Surprised by Moran's enthusiasm for gift buying, Jane thanked Edwards and went out of the CID office, heading down to the Collator's Office in the basement. On the way she popped into the ladies' locker room, giving an affectionate tap to the 'LADIES ONLY' sign on the door. Kath's legacy was still intact. As she came out five minutes later she bumped straight into DI Moran, who was carrying an enormous donkey-shaped piñata.

'Good evening, Tennison. I can only presume you're here for the celebration drinks for DC Ashton's baby girl?'

'No, sir. Actually I just came in to see if we had a trial date for Peter Allard.'

'No, we haven't. Those wankers at the court are taking their bloody time, as usual. The boys will be surprised to see you.'

'If you don't mind me saying so, sir, I don't think a donkey piñata is a particularly appropriate present for a newborn baby?'

Moran chuckled loudly.

'No ... no, Tennison. We fill it with shillings wrapped in pound notes, and we all take turns in hitting it with a truncheon, but not too hard ... then hopefully it will be Ashton who smashes it open and collects the loot.'

'That's a very innovative idea, sir. Whoever thought of that?' Jane replied, clearly thinking that it wasn't innovative at all.

Moran beamed in response. 'I did! And for the baby I've got this ...'

He delved into his coat pocket and pulled out a small pink teddy bear.

'So, are you coming over to the Warburton to have a drink with us?' he asked.

'Thank you, sir.'

As Moran walked away with the huge piñata tucked under his arm he turned back to Jane.

'I'll let you have the first crack at the donkey!'

Jane watched Moran as he went down the corridor, looking rather ridiculous. She had just had the perfect opportunity to discuss with him her concerns about the blue rabbit fur coat, and couldn't really understand why she hadn't done so. But if she spoke to the collator it would probably iron out her queries.

Donaldson was getting ready to go home and seemed surprised to see her.

'How is it at Bow Street?'

'Fine. Rather quiet actually. I was dropping in to see if a trial date had been set for Peter Allard.'

Donaldson shrugged and Jane hesitated before asking him if she could take a look at Janet Brown's file and record sheet. He looked at his watch and seemed ill at ease.

'It's nothing important, just for personal reasons.'

She watched him go to a filing cabinet and waited as he sifted through the drawer and then slowly closed it.

'Not here.'

'I don't understand.'

Donaldson picked up his coat from a hook behind the door, and folded it over his arm.

'I didn't think files were allowed to be removed from the Collator's Office,' Jane said, as Donaldson picked up an old battered briefcase left beside his desk.

'I can't help you, but sometimes one of the detectives might come in. Now, I need to lock up and get home.'

Jane sensed he was being evasive and was certain he was lying, but she didn't want to question him any further as he was getting impatient for her to leave. She had always found Donaldson to be very helpful in the past and she was disappointed.

She had a light supper in the canteen upstairs and could see the ostracized Brian Edwards sitting in a corner by himself, sneezing loudly. He looked terrible and everyone else was clearly avoiding him. On the next table the young DC Ashton joined a few other officers. He was carrying a tray with shepherd's pie and a syrup sponge and custard, and was surprised to see her.

'Have you been assigned back here again?'

'No, I just couldn't resist the food. I hear congratulations are in order, and that you're a father now.'

'Yeah, it was a bit of a surprise – not exactly a shotgun wedding, but sooner than we'd planned. Are you coming over to the Warburton later? Moran's organized it.'

'Yes, looking forward to it.'

After applying some lipstick and tidying herself up in the ladies' locker room, Jane made her way over to the Warburton Arms.

The usual array of sausage rolls, cheese and ham sandwiches and obligatory packets of crisps were being laid out on the bar counter by Ron. DC Donaldson was unloading beer from two crates, and placing the bottles beside the food. Jane wondered if this was the reason he had been in such a hurry to leave the Collator's Office.

She was still confused as to why the file on Janet Brown was missing. Jane crossed over to Donaldson as he poured a beer for himself.

'All these beers are on the house, and we've got three bottles of white and three red ... what's your fancy, Jane?'

'I'll have a glass of white, please.'

'Well, go and get the bottle opened, and ask Ron for some ice.'

At that moment the double doors to the pub banged open. Moran led the team in, still holding the donkey piñata. He shouted at Ron.

'Ron, we need to get this thing hung up!'

Ron looked at him in total bewilderment.

'What the hell is that?'

'It's a piñata. It's full of cash and we're going to take it in turns to hit it with a truncheon, and whoever smashes it open gets the contents!'

'Well, you're not hanging that pissatto, or whatever it is, in the main bar. You can take it into the snooker room and hang it up from one of the lights in there. But if anyone damages the table or the lights, you'll be paying for it.'

The celebration for Ashton's baby was beginning to spiral out of control. Everyone was eager to attack the piñata, but Moran was refusing to allow a truncheon near it until they had consumed all the drinks he had provided. He kept on repeating, to one officer after another, 'Don't bloody hit it hard ... this is for Ashton. He's broke, and he needs to get all the cash inside.'

At one point he even put his arm around Jane and

repeated his warning to her. 'I know you can throw a good whack with a truncheon because of Allard. But just tap it.'

Jane smiled. 'Yes, sir, I'll just tap it.'

'Good. I asked Spence to come over as he knew DC Ashton before he got hitched – poor sod – said he was on an assignment at the Marquee Club. Haw haw! If his band are playing they'll empty the place.'

At that point there was a very loud cheer as the team were impatient for the 'smash and grab'. By this time DC Ashton, who had obviously had more than his fair share of free drinks, was wearing a white hat with a bobble on top. Hanging around his neck was a huge sugared dummy that one of the other officers had bought from the market fair.

'Quiet, everybody!' Moran yelled. 'As everyone knows, we've all chipped in for the amazing contents of our donkey. And the first person to attempt to smash it open is DC Donaldson.'

Yet again Moran, now clearly inebriated, whispered loudly, 'Don't hit it too hard!'

This encouraged everyone to cheer, in unison, 'Tap, tap, tap ... Tap, tap, tap ...'

As each officer used their truncheons one after the other, Moran encouraged Jane to use his truncheon to attempt to break it open. Jane was terrified that she might hit it too hard.

As she raised Moran's truncheon DC Edwards yelled, 'Go on, Tennison, hit it like you hit that rapist!'

Jane had a momentary flashback of how she had struck Peter Allard and almost unintentionally she drew her right hand back and walloped the donkey, which by now had a very bedraggled leg and tail. She had meant to aim for the head, but accidentally hit the belly. There was a massive 'Whoooaaa' as a large split appeared. Jane was mortified that the contents were about to come spilling out, as Moran yelled, 'Give the truncheon to the new Daddy!'

Jane quickly passed the truncheon to Ashton. There was a loud cheer of encouragement as he took a full swing and hit the target dead centre. The donkey burst open, and instead of the usual array of sweets out fell all the cash contributed by his colleagues.

Jane felt quite emotional as she watched the young detective, almost in tears, as he realized how much everyone had given to support him.

It was now coming up to ten o'clock and the party was beginning to wind down. Jane thought she would take the opportunity to go to the Marquee Club as so far she had only been able to question a member of staff in the daytime. Moran noticed that she was getting ready to leave.

'Are you off now, Jane? You got me quite worried there, when you took that swing at the donkey. I thought you were going to bust it wide open!'

Jane couldn't work Moran out. One moment he seemed so affable and obviously well liked, and was clearly a very generous man. But there was just something else that she couldn't quite put her finger on, and she wasn't sure that she could entirely trust him. As she turned away Moran took her elbow and leaned in close.

'I hear you were asking Donaldson about a missing file? Take my advice, Tennison – don't meddle, or ever question anything I've done ... I'll always get to hear about it. Trust me, we're going to put Allard away for a long time.'

Jane was about to think of something to say, but he turned away, the opportunity gone. She saw him go to Donaldson and say something in his ear; both of them turned to look at Jane as she left the pub. Jane took a bus to Regent Street and walked along Oxford Street, looking into the lit-up windows of all the big stores. She wasn't that interested in fashion and crossed over Oxford Street towards Wardour Street. There were groups of young teenagers standing smoking outside the Marquee Club. There were posters for music groups pinned up outside, and the big crowds had not yet arrived to see the main band playing that evening.

Jane showed her warrant card to gain entrance and walked down the stairs into the club and bar area. It was busier than she had anticipated and there was a band tuning up on the small stage. She felt and looked out of place and was beginning to think she shouldn't have even considered being there on her own. She was relieved to see DI Spencer Gibbs sitting on a stool at the bar. He looked very dishevelled and was wearing tight leather trousers and a stained T-shirt under a dirty denim jacket.

'Hey there.'

Jane moved closer and was shocked when he turned towards her and appeared to be very drunk.

'I was just going to do a bit of a catch-up and ask about the report—'

She didn't have the chance to finish as he lurched forward off his stool and made a grab for her arm.

'Let's go ...' he slurred, and gripped her elbow tightly, manoeuvring her roughly through a group of drinkers. Jane didn't argue as Gibbs was really pushing her forward and up the stairs, his hand deep into her back as they passed lines of clubbers coming down the stairs. When they got outside she turned on him.

'There was no need to do that.'

Gibbs straightened up, took hold of her arm again and hurried her along the street.

'What's the matter with you?' she said, dragging her arm free.

'I'll tell you what's the matter with me, Tennison ... I'm down there acting as a piss artist and you come in sticking out like a sore thumb with copper written all over you.'

'What?'

'I'm doing undercover, trying to track down the bastard that uses a razor to cut the straps of women's handbags. He should have had a go at yours ... it's a police issue shoulder bag! What the hell were you doing, and who told you to work the club tonight?'

'I meant to get a new bag,' she replied sheepishly, not mentioning that she had showed her warrant card to get in.

'Terrific.'

'I'm sorry, I just saw that there had been further reports ...'

'Christ,' he muttered, and then looked up and down the road.

'You want a coffee? I can't go back in for a while now.'

Jane nodded and they headed back into Oxford Street, then left into Poland Street and left again into D'Arblay Street to a small cappuccino bar. It was rather seedy with a shelf counter and high stools, and Jane sat with her back to a wall, unseen from the wide window onto the street. Gibbs bought two cappuccinos and joined her. He opened three packs of brown sugar, heaping them onto the froth in his cup, then used a spoon to stir it before tapping it against the saucer.

'We reckon whoever is nicking all the gear might move up a notch and use his razor on one of the chicks' faces, as reports are coming in that the attacks are getting nastier. He's probably a junkie needing money fast cos he's now working the clubs as well as out on the street, but he's an amateur. We got professional pickpockets around here, some work in gangs – like the South Americans.'

Jane sipped the frothy coffee, and apologized again.

'Listen, I won't say anything about this tonight, Jane, but you need to sharpen up and get into line. You're in CID now and you don't go batting solo. Do you think I would stay in a club on my own? I've got two other guys outside bloody backing me up.'

'I'm sorry. I was just at a loose end. I went over to Hackney to see if there was any update on the rape case but they are still waiting for a trial date.'

'What rape case?'

'It's just an old case, pretty straightforward.'

Gibbs lit a cigarette, and inhaled deeply. He gave a brief glance around, took out a hip flask, unscrewed the cap and tipped a measure into his half-full cup.

'Can I tell you something?' Jane asked quietly.

'Sure.'

'I don't know if you know this, but I was used as a decoy. And, well, I've just got this feeling that something's not quite adding up and I'm not sure what to do about it. I wore a blue rabbit fur coat that belonged to a prostitute called Janet Brown.'

Jane continued telling him about seeing Janet Brown's file in the Collator's Office, and that it had subsequently disappeared. She went on to describe how she had seen her exit one of the strip clubs the last time she had been in Wardour Street, but she didn't get the opportunity to talk to her. Gibbs didn't look at her as she explained about her concerns regarding the knife and the signed confession Peter Allard had made, and how tough it had been in court.

'I don't know if he did the rape he is accused of.'

Gibbs turned and looked at her, shaking his head. 'Wait ... wait, I'm trying to follow you, darlin', but you get attacked and smacked in the mouth by this guy, who has admitted the sexual assaults?'

'Yes, but not the rape.'

'Did he also admit to the assault on you?'

'Eventually, yes he did, and when it happened he said that he was holding a knife to my throat, and I managed to kick him off me. Then DI Moran and DC Edwards arrested him. He swore that he didn't mean to attack me and I got his elbow in my mouth, which caused my lip to split and bleed. But he maintained that it was only because he was trying to escape arrest.'

Gibbs gave a sarcastic laugh.

'I didn't see the knife, and then DI Moran produced it as evidence, and next the signed confession.'

'What the hell is your problem, Jane?'

'It's just that a few things don't add up . . . I mean, do you think Moran would plant evidence?'

'What?'

'For the rape?'

Gibbs leaned back. 'Do you give a shit? Or, more to the point, do you care?'

'Yes I do, because the rape will be a far longer sentence and if he is innocent—'

'Innocent? Christ, Jane, are you out of your mind? What the hell are you doing wasting time even contemplating whether there was any kind of subversive activity? Did he or didn't he have a knife – it's just bullshitting and I hope the bastard goes away for as long as possible. I would say that is Moran's only interest. He's a good cop, and a tough one who worked Clubs and Vice for years. Moran's sticking his neck out as he said he found the knife and didn't involve any other officers. And if you don't mind me saying so, you've only just got your foot into the CID, so mind your business.'

Jane looked away as Gibbs took out his hip flask again and emptied the contents into the remainder of his coffee.

'I hear you've been seeing a lot of Paul Lawrence. What's he doing?'

'Well, he was very supportive when I queried the non-suspicious death.'

'Oh, you queried it, did you? Well, aren't you just a busy know-all? Let me give you another word of warning – don't go behind DCI Shepherd's back either. He has a mean streak: although he might appear to be a quiet, affable type, he's got a steel core and he goes by the book. If you start encouraging Paul Lawrence to work outside his forensic duties—'

Jane interrupted. 'I haven't done that!'

'That's not what I've heard. You've got him working on this non-sus death as a possible murder because of evidence you are digging up. Let me tell you, you dig up anything and you give it to the team ... that includes me.'

'I just haven't discussed certain things because Paul said we needed further evidence ...'

'We? We needed further evidence? Listen to yourself! And what's Paul Lawrence "Forensic Detective" investigating on your say so?'

'It's not my "say so". He just agreed with me.'

'Jesus Christ, Jane! Haven't you listened to anything I've been telling you? You have to stop this and not drag Paul into something that could get him into deep trouble.'

'Well, for your information I am not "dragging" him anywhere. Maybe you don't know as much about him as you think you do. In reality he is fed up with forensic science and spending most of his time in a laboratory checking out fingerprints and toxicology reports. He's told me he wants to become a more integral part of the CID.'

'Did he also tell you about how he's been coping?'

Jane looked confused. 'I don't understand.'

'Lawrence almost had a nervous breakdown, although I don't know if you can ever really have an "almost" breakdown ... Unlike me, he stayed on at Hackney after Bradfield and Kath died. I got out, and I got help. Lawrence didn't. So let me tell you, behind that floppy hair of his and his tweed suit, Mr Affability has been tormenting himself—'

Jane interrupted him, becoming very defensive. 'He's talked about that to me, that he's apportioned some of the blame to himself about what happened. I think every one of us has felt guilty in some way.'

'Guilty? I don't feel guilty. I was having the best time of my life. I've never known such an adrenalin buzz ... there's nothing like catching blaggers red-handed, and this wasn't for a couple of Rolex watches, this was big time. So I've never felt any guilt. I had the horror. I heard Len say to Kath what a great moment it was. I saw the way she looked up at him ... she was so proud, and he was as steady as a rock. Then ... boom ... they were gone. I had their blood and brains splattered all over me. I'm not guilty, Jane, I'm damaged.'

Gibbs stopped himself, knocked back his coffee, his legs jumping again. He stood up. 'OK, I'm out of here. I'm going back to the club to do the job I've been ordered to do. Why don't you get off home?'

Jane gave a rueful smile and thanked him for the coffee. 'I'll finish my drink first, Spence.' She watched him leave from the window of the café. He didn't look back at her but headed along the street towards Wardour

Street. She wasn't bothered about finishing the cold cappuccino, she just didn't want to walk with him. She waited until he was out of sight then left the café, and walked down Wardour Street in the opposite direction to Gibbs towards Shaftesbury Avenue.

As she walked south she passed numerous lowlife and bouncers standing outside seedy strip clubs with thudding music. The street was filling up with clubbers, mainly groups of young guys drinking from beer cans and laughing loudly. Jane kept to the edge of the pavement and only glanced towards the club she had seen Janet Brown leave. The same muscle-bound thuggish bouncer was bellowing out 'Live girls', but after her dressing down from Gibbs Jane had no intention of even attempting to see if Janet Brown was working there.

Blinking arrows pointed to a side turning leading to Berwick Street, and opposite were two strip clubs. It was déjà vu because hurrying out from one of them was Janet Brown, wearing the rabbit fur coat. Jane had to wait for the traffic to move before she could cross the road and hurry towards her. She saw her with a young boy who was getting out of a taxi. Janet handed the boy something and then to Jane's disappointment got into the taxi before she even got close. The boy was still standing outside the dirty plastic strip curtains at the open doorway to 'Sexy Slave Dancers'.

He was wearing filthy jeans, worn plimsolls and an oversized man's jacket, and he had short dirty red hair surrounding a grimy face. The closer Jane got to him it became clear he was even younger than she had thought.

'Excuse me, can I talk to you for a second?'

'What-d-ya-want?' he said through gapped teeth.

'I need to talk to the woman I just saw you with, in the blue fur coat.'

'She gone to work.' He turned as if to walk away.

'Is it a club?'

He glared at Jane. 'What you want to know fer?'

'Please ... I really need to talk to her.'

'You're fuckin' filth, aintcha? Well, piss off.'

He did a duck to pass Jane and she caught his sleeve. 'Just a minute ...'

He was too fast and was off, heading in the direction of Berwick Street. During the day this was filled with market stalls, but at night there were numerous sleazy strip clubs, doors opening up for the rooms above and the call girls were out in force. Jane followed and was able to see the boy entering one of the small stores selling girlie magazines. A sign was stuck to the dirty window, saying 'ADULT LITERATURE'. Inside were racks of glossy porn magazines with just a counter, shelves and a till. On one shelf there were what purported to be 8mm Disney films, but in reality the boxes contained hardcore porn imported from Amsterdam.

There was a red light bulb making the dingy shopfront glow with a reddish tinge. A woman was stacking books and shoving them into piles beneath the counter. She had bleached blonde hair and two glittering slides either side of her head. Her face was plastered with thick makeup and outlines over the edge of her lips in a bright orange red. As Jane walked in the woman stuck out her chest. She wore a tight knitted sweater with crochet flowers.

'Yes, love? If you're after the Lesbian section it's on the shelf behind you.'

She smelt of powerful, sickly sweet perfume. Jane showed her warrant card, which didn't seem to faze the woman at all.

'Listen, we paid out this week, darlin', so don't try it on with me. I got a lot of work to do and I am not interested in havin' the female touch, if you know what I mean.'

'I just wanted to ask that young boy something. I'm not here for any other reason.'

'I don't know him ... never saw anyone comin' in.' She lit a cigarette.

'I just saw him walk in,' Jane said firmly.

'Well, maybe he just walked out the back way. I dunno ... I'm busy, love, doing the inventory.'

'What's through there?'

'Just a back room for the storage. But, lovey, if you want to start snoopin' around in here you'll need a warrant. Like I said, we paid up.'

Two girls walked in and passed directly behind Jane, entering the door she had seen the red-haired boy go through. The blonde woman ignored Jane as she continued checking over paperbacks and stacking them below the counter.

'I would just like to talk to the boy, please.'

Unseen by Jane, the blonde pressed a bell beneath the counter. Next minute banging into the small shop via the same door came a pot-bellied man wearing a black suede fringed cowboy jacket, with a silver cowboy buckle over his expansive waist and baggy green cords.

'What's goin' on?' he said angrily.

'She just walked in, Stevie. Shows me her warrant card and wants to go out back to talk to Ginger.'

'What the fuck do you want, darlin', because we already have an arrangement and we don't like Old Bill standing in full view of the effin' winder.'

'I just want to have a few words with the boy I saw coming in here. I am not here for any other reason. This lady here denied seeing him when I saw him walking in.'

'What you want with Ginger?'

'I don't think that is any of your business. Now, if he is here please could I talk to him?'

Jane was losing patience but at the same time becoming very unnerved by Stevie's attitude.

'He works for the girls and would have gone out the back way. Now, you just piss off, all right?'

'I'm sorry but he looked about twelve years old ... What exactly do you mean that he works here?'

Stevie hitched up his trousers and gestured to the blonde to leave.

'He's just earnin' a few quid, darlin' ... the strippers don't like leavin' their gear unattended in the clubs' dressin' rooms when they're on the stage, so they pay him and he makes sure nothin' gets nicked.'

Jane was shocked but stood her ground.

'I really don't want to come back. I just want to have a few words with him here, or outside your shop. It's about someone I need to contact.'

Two more girls walked in and it was obvious by the

way they were dressed they were on the game. They smiled at Stevie and went into the back room. Stevie hesitated, then followed them.

He bellowed, 'Oi Ginger, come outta there ... now, before you get me angry.'

The same ginger-haired boy slunk out and Stevie gripped him by his neck, pushing him towards Jane.

'I dunno what you been up to but this copper wants to talk to you. Now get outta here wiv her, and if it's thievin' I'll have ya knocked to hell an' back.'

The boy was not afraid of the muscle head man, instead he shrugged him away and looked at Jane.

'What you want?'

'Get the hell outta the shop ... go on, move it!' Stevie jerked his thumb towards the door.

Jane went outside with the boy, who didn't seem at all bothered by her presence. He leaned against a wall near the shop entrance.

'I don't want to get you into trouble, Ginger, but I saw you getting out of a taxi, then a woman wearing a blue rabbit fur coat got inside.'

'I don't remember.'

'I saw you not ten minutes ago. Now, I need to know where she was going.'

'No fuckin' idea ... She works the clubs, that's all I know. She taxi hops, goin' to any amount of strip clubs round here, or maybe goin' home.'

'Do you know her address?'

'No.'

'What's her name?'

'You pick one ... they all use different ones. I think

it's Janine, but don't quote me. That's show business, ain't it.'

'How old are you?'

'Twenty-one.'

Jane sighed and tried another tack. 'Look, you are only young and shouldn't even be out here at this hour, never mind working the clubs as Stevie told me.'

'Yeah, well, I got a sick mother wiv lung cancer and no dad ... I gotta earn a crust for me sisters. All I do is just look out for their belongings and they give us a few coppers.'

'I don't want to report you to the social services, Ginger, so please tell me where you think I might be able to contact that woman.'

'She might have gone over to the nightclub in Swallow Street. I swear by Almighty God that's all I know ...! Give us a break, darlin', I don't want Stevie and the old lady givin' me a hard time.'

Jane sighed and shook her head.

'All right, thank you.'

He gave her a cheeky, gap-toothed smile. 'Any time, sweetheart ... take it easy.'

Jane walked off, contemplated heading over to Swallow Street, which was a narrow lane off Piccadilly Circus leading into Regent Street. But remembering Gibbs's warning about working alone, she caught the late bus back to the section house.

Over the last few days, Jane had been inundated with a number of petty crimes connected to the major upheaval with the proposed move of the Covent Garden market.

As she had the entire weekend off, she decided that she would see her parents. She was looking forward to the safe normality of her home after her week in the murky world of strip clubs and prostitution.

Jane had made thorough notes about her encounter in the adult bookshop, which she was sure was also a brothel, and would check everything out the following Monday. It had been such a revelation being in that seedy part of London, and she was concerned about the references to CID being paid off to turn a blind eye.

When Jane arrived at the flat it was, unusually, her father who answered the door and ushered her in, indicating for her to be quiet.

'What's wrong, Dad?'

Mr Tennison shut the door. 'Your mother's in with Pam ... it's not good news ... she's very distressed. When she got here she was crying her eyes out.'

'What's happened?'

Mrs Tennison came out into the corridor.

'Jane ... I didn't expect you. You never called, did you?'

'No, Mum. I've got the day off. Is everything all right?'

'No ... Did you tell her, Daddy?'

'No, she's only just arrived.'

'Mum, what's happened?'

Mrs Tennison gestured for Jane to follow her into the lounge.

'Pam has had a miscarriage. She started feeling poorly and then had terrible stomach cramps. She went into the toilet and ...'

'Has she been to the hospital?'

'Yes. Tony took her to the emergency ward at St Mary's but they confirmed it. Nothing they could do. Are you going to stay for lunch?'

'Yes, if it's not too much trouble?'

'No, I'm doing a pork roast. You go on into our bedroom and talk to Pam.'

Pam was lying down with a wet flannel folded on her forehead. Jane sat beside her.

'I am so sorry, Pam ... Mum's just told me.'

Pam slowly removed the face cloth. Her face was puffy and she was red eyed from crying.

'It happened when I went to the toilet ... such terrible pains, and then ...'

'Did they tell you why it happened?'

'No, Tony said it was because of being on my feet all day at the salon, but this very nice doctor said that pregnant women can work up to eight and a half months so it wasn't because of me working. But I won't go back just yet.'

'No, you should just rest.'

'I started getting all the baby things. I didn't choose pink or blue because we didn't know if it was a boy or a girl,' Pam said as she began to cry.

Mrs Tennison walked in carrying a mug of tea for Jane.

'Here you are, Jane dear. Would you like another cup before lunch, Pam?'

'Yes please, Mum.'

Mrs Tennison walked out and closed the door silently behind her.

'It won't be the end, Pam ... I'm sure you'll get pregnant again.'

'I know, I know ... that's what the doctors said. But it won't be for a while, because I have to give my body time to heal.'

'Yes, I know, the body is very resilient.'

'I know that. I'm on my feet all day. You have no idea how long it takes to do a perm. And I've wondered if it is the smell of doing a perm that's caused the miscarriage. It's very pungent, you know.

'I had this client who was really very objectionable. Complained that the rubber of the rollers smelt. I said to her, "Well, if you think they smell bad, you should go to another salon." Well, she didn't like that. And then as she was leaving she wanted to book in a second appointment. I said to her, "I might not be here in three months' time." Because that's how long you have to wait before you can do a perm again. Well, she got very upset and apologized to me for being rude. And then I said, "I'm pregnant, that's why I won't be here."' Pam's face crumpled.

Jane patted her hand. 'Don't upset yourself.'

'Well, I am upset. I'm not pregnant, am I?'

It was a difficult couple of hours before they eventually left the bedroom and went to have lunch. Mrs Tennison had set the small table in the living room, as she liked to keep the dining room for formal occasions. The pork had already been carved and there were roast potatoes, carrots, spinach and gravy.

'Have you got any apple sauce, Mother?' Pam asked.

Mrs Tennison jumped up.

'Of course, darling, of course we have ... it's apple and mint jelly, is that all right, Pam?'

'I'd prefer just apple sauce, but never mind ...'

Jane noticed that, as distraught as her sister was, Pam still managed to pile the food onto her plate.

Mrs Tennison said that she'd made an apple pie, but she was out of custard so they were going to have it with Wall's ice-cream slices instead.

Jane reached over and patted her mother's hand.

'That sounds lovely, Mum.'

Mrs Tennison smiled.

'So, let's talk about something different ... Jane, why don't you tell us what you've been doing this week? We haven't seen you since you started your new job. Are there any other female officers working at the station?'

'I am actually the only female detective ... but I do have a wonderful mentor, Edith, who runs the main office.' Jane exaggerated to reassure her mother. 'She used to be a policewoman so she knows all the ropes, and she has a lot to deal with because her mother sadly suffers from dementia.'

Pam pushed her empty plate to one side, and leaned her elbows on the table.

'Well, that's worrying, having the only other police-woman suffering from dementia.'

'No, Pam, Edith doesn't have dementia – her mother does. Sometimes she escapes from the house, and once poor Edith found her wandering naked in the street!'

The doorbell prevented her having to continue her description of Edith. Mrs Tennison started clearing the lunch plates as Pam's husband, Tony, came into the living room.

282

'Would you like some apple pie and ice-cream, Tony?' Mrs Tennison asked him.

'That would be lovely, thank you.'

Tony pulled up a chair to sit beside Pam.

'How are you feeling, my darling?'

Pam picked up her napkin and used it as a handkerchief, blowing her nose.

'It comes over me in waves, Tony, the grief ... I'm finding it very hard to deal with. One minute I was wondering what maternity dress to put on, and the next I was on the toilet ...'

Tony patted her hand.

'I know, darling, it's terrible, just terrible, but we have to be strong.'

Jane looked at her rather overweight brother-in-law as he too started to weep.

'I am so sorry, Tony ... it's very sad, and we all feel deeply for your loss.'

'Could I just have the apple pie without the ice-cream, please?' Tony asked, as Mrs Tennison placed the apple pie on the table.

By the time they both left Jane just wanted to go back to the section house and really didn't feel in the mood to discuss her work. It wasn't until she was about to leave that her father asked if everything was all right at Bow Street.

'Everything's fine, Dad. I really like being in plain clothes with the CID.'

'Anything interesting?'

'Not really ... I'm just a fledgling detective so I'm not assigned to anything important.' She gently placed her hand to touch his lips, whispering, 'I'm all right, Daddy.'

Jane didn't mention being used as a decoy, the fact that she had been assaulted, or that she was now working on her first possible murder inquiry. She never even broached the subject of the strip clubs or young Ginger working with the strippers. It wasn't that she didn't want to, but her life was so different to Pam's and she understood that they had lost their first grandchild and that was all they were really interested in for the moment.

After Jane had left the Tennison flat, her father had made a pot of tea for her mother and they had sat down beside each other on the sofa.

'I thought she looked well,' Mr Tennison said.

'She didn't, poor girl ... but it's hardly surprising. Mind you, she's still young so they've got many more years to keep trying.'

'I meant Jane ...'

'Oh, yes ... I was going to say to her that she should call more often and not just turn up without letting us know. It was lucky I was doing a pork roast so we had plenty of food.'

Mr Tennison stood up, saying that he would start on the washing up.

'Thank you, dear. I noticed Jane didn't offer to help ... but that's her, never very domestic really, was she?'

Mr Tennison turned on the hot water and began to scrape off the grease from the baking tray. He looked over the array of pans and dirty dishes as his wife sat cupping her hands round her tea. He squirted in the washing-up liquid and used the plastic bowl to soak the dishes. It took him almost half an hour, balancing the plates on the draining board before moving on to scrub the baking trays he had left to soak. Mrs Tennison was still sitting staring into space, her tea cup empty, when he went in to take it from her.

'Are you all right, darling?'

Mrs Tennison seemed to be miles away and was almost startled when he took the cup from her hands.

'I had a scare, do you remember, with Michael? I went to bed for two weeks, and didn't dare put my feet on the ground in case I had a miscarriage. But it was all right, and then I had Jane and then Pam so I'm sure she'll get pregnant again. But she should give up work at the salon ... she spends too many hours standing.'

Mr Tennison patted her head gently, knowing what she was really thinking about. Their first-born son, Michael, was only two when he had drowned in the neighbour's pond. They had both buried their grief tightly beneath the surface, but when it rose the pain was excruciating. He returned to the sink to dry the plates as he recalled Jane running towards him, her arms outstretched with Michael's small worn teddy bear in one hand.

Mr Tennison was ashamed about what had happened. After Michael's tragic drowning he had hidden his son's favourite toy in his desk drawer. Jane had somehow found it, even though he had given strict instructions that the room he used as a home office was out of bounds, as it was 'where Daddy worked'. He had wrapped the small teddy bear in tissue paper and tucked it into the bottom drawer of his desk, along with a silver napkin ring and one of Michael's small slippers. Jane had always been inquisitive and had discovered his secret mementos. She had gleefully run towards her father to share her discovery with him, and he had slapped her very hard and had scolded her for being so naughty and going into his office.

The young Jane had been shocked as she had never been physically reprimanded so severely. Mr Tennison recalled the way her blue eyes had glared at him, as she recoiled. In a very grown-up manner she had said, 'I didn't mean to upset you, but you shouldn't be nasty to me. I thought you would like to hold Michael's teddy bear and I was just happy that I found him.'

Mr Tennison had been left speechless, and had been unable for some time to go to her and apologize. He had tried to explain why he had reacted in such an awful way but Jane had just walked away from him. As young as she was it had been a considerable time before she forgave him. When she did she simply climbed up onto his knee one night and put her hand gently over his lips.

'It's all right, Daddy.'

That had been the way she had said goodbye to him at the door earlier, her blue eyes holding his and touching his lips as she had done all those years ago as a child. Mr Tennison wondered if everything was all right with her work. He felt guilty that neither he nor his wife had asked how her new job was going.

Mrs Tennison remained sitting by herself as he finished the dishes, drying them all and placing them back into the cupboards. He wiped all the kitchen surfaces.

'All ship-shape, dear,' he said brightly, and she turned and smiled.

'Thank you, dear.'

CHAPTER FIFTEEN

Marie sat on the end seat of the lower deck of the number 73 bus. She'd been lucky to get a seat, as the bus was packed full of Saturday shoppers. She had the thick envelope containing the money on her lap, wrapped inside an old newspaper. When the bus stopped by The Grosvenor House Hotel in Park Lane she got off and watched as the bus drew away, just as she had done previously. As she had been instructed, Marie placed the parcel of money into the litter bin attached to the bus stop. She had to dig it in among dirty cartons and used bus tickets before she was able to make sure it wasn't too visible. She then got onto the next bus as soon as it drew up.

Marie remained on the foot stand, holding on to the bar, as the bus moved slowly down Park Lane. A few moments later her heart was pounding as she jumped from the moving bus. She had to gasp for breath as she hurried back towards the litter bin where she had left the money. Marie moved along the pavement close to the buildings in the hope she would not be seen, but she could clearly see the 73 bus stop and the litter bin. She kept on edging closer, just as Peter had instructed her to do, in the hope of catching the woman red-handed and being able to confront her.

A scruffy red-haired boy was running towards Marie. He then stopped and with his back to her rummaged in the bin. Marie watched as he took out the wrapped envelope and tossed the newspaper covering aside, running back up Park Lane towards Marble Arch. Marie hurried after him and saw him turn into Green Street, then he disappeared from her sight for a moment.

As she rounded the corner Marie could see the boy up ahead, approaching a taxi with its engine ticking over and the passenger door open. The boy dived inside and the door slammed shut as the taxi moved off. Marie closed her eyes, wanting to weep with frustration as she reluctantly turned back towards Park Lane.

Inside the taxi Janet Brown hugged the envelope close to her chest and held a ten pound note up between her fingers.

'Good work, Ginger ... here you go, as promised.'

He reached out to take it, but Janet held it away from him.

'You gotta keep your mouth shut about this and not tell a soul. If you do, I'll find out and you'll get a whippin'.'

'I won't tell no one.'

'OK ... You get this tenner for now. There'll be more for you to do but you got to keep your mouth shut.'

She dangled the note in front of him and Ginger snatched it, kissing it with glee.

'I luv ya! Can yer drop me off at Carnaby Street? Gonna get a new pair o' shoes.'

It was a short cab ride from Green Street to North Audley Street, then round the top of Grosvenor Square onto Brook Street. The taxi crossed Regent Street onto Great Marlborough Street, where Ginger got out. Janet watched him run past the big posh store Liberty, heading towards Carnaby Street. She had another look inside the envelope, then leaned back and smiled.

'Easy money.'

She started humming to herself. 'Angie, Angie . . .'

It was early on Sunday morning at the mortuary and DS Lawrence and Professor Martin's qualified assistant, who had been working alongside him on numerous cases, were walking into the mortuary. Angus McLean knew how to deal with the garrulous pathologist. He admired him and had learned a vast amount while working with him. Angus also knew that he was earmarked to take over when the old boy retired, which would be in the not too distant future. Angus was rake thin with horn-rimmed glasses. He had come from working-class roots but his sharp intellect and diligence had brought him to Martin's attention. He had been very hesitant about agreeing to meet with Lawrence and was worried that Professor Martin would not approve.

DS Lawrence had been equally reluctant to ask for the favour, but repeatedly said that he just wanted a second opinion and told Angus that he was not required to do anything unethical. They were given access to the chill section at the mortuary by an assistant mortician, whom Lawrence reassured by saying that he was welcome to remain with them as it was just going to be a quick appraisal of the non-suspicious death notice. The body had not yet been released for burial, so there was nothing untoward about the visit.

Angus looked at Lawrence.

'OK, let me take a look at her.'

Jane stripped her bed and put fresh sheets on, leaving the used ones in the laundry bag for the cleaners to collect the following day. She then went to the laundry room and did her washing and ironing. Back in her room she hung up her pressed shirt and put her clean underwear in the drawer, gave her shoes a quick polish, and then made her way out to pick up a newspaper.

She was surprised to see DS Lawrence entering the building. He hurried towards her and asked if he could have a few words as he needed to give her an update. They went into the quiet room and although the TV set was on the room was empty.

'I've just come from the mortuary, and want to talk a few things over with you. First you need to understand that when you have a non-suspicious death it is not unusual that a detailed PM is not required. It's not exactly cutting corners, but it's not as in-depth as for a suspicious murder.'

'Yes, you discussed this before.'

'Right, but if there had been a very detailed PM it would entail the removal of the scalp and the face being lifted, to check the frontal wound.

'I am not inferring that there was anything incorrect about the report. But if the assumption was that the blow to her forehead from the taps was not that heavy

or deep but enough to maybe render the victim unconscious, I would have taken steps to ensure there was no
other head wound.'

'How do you mean?'

'She had very thick hair. There was a considerable
amount of blood in the bath water, which makes it
obvious that she was alive in the water as she continued
bleeding. Her hair was still wet when her body was
brought into the mortuary and dried by the time the PM
took place.'

'Are you saying that there could have been another
wound?'

'Possibly. But this would only have been discovered
if the victim's head was shaved. Again, I am not saying
that the PM was fast-tracked, as this is often the case
when you have a coroner's report stating that it was a
non-suspicious death.'

Jane cocked her head to one side. 'It would be interesting to find out, but we don't have much time as the
family have been given clearance for the burial. Do you
think you have enough evidence to get a second PM
done?'

Lawrence ran his hands through his hair.

'No, we don't have enough evidence ... Also I don't
want to get my friend in any trouble as his information
was off the record and Professor Martin probably won't
be happy. If anyone could prove another PM should be
done it would be the old boy himself.'

'So what do you suggest we do?'

Lawrence was becoming increasingly concerned. 'Our
problem is this: if we believe Barry Dawson was involved

then we would have to prove that he did have time to get out of the hospital, kill his wife and then return to work to make the phone calls to give himself an alibi.'

Jane could feel Lawrence's hesitancy, and was unsure what to say to him. He continued.

'Also, we have to consider the possibility that someone else killed Shirley Dawson, and if so who and for what reason?'

'Well, maybe it could have been the woman who visited her? Or, if she was having an affair, could there be another suspect? I mean, if we believe that Shirley buzzed someone in, it's likely that she knew them.'

'Yes, but if it was Barry he would have had his own front door key.'

Jane sighed. They were getting nowhere and had nothing to support their possible motives. Lawrence stood up and Jane sensed what was coming.

'I have to tread very carefully, Jane ... if I am wrong, if we both are, then this could really get us into deep water. I think we should just call it quits because I am not prepared to jeopardize my career and be put back in uniform.'

'Is Dawson back at work at the hospital?' Jane asked.

Lawrence shrugged. Using the page on which he had sketched Shirley's head to demonstrate the wounds he jotted down his phone number and address.

'I don't know. Why don't you sleep on it? If you think of anything then call me, but I'm not going any further with this. I'm sorry ...'

Jane smiled, hiding her disappointment. 'Yes, maybe you're right.'

They walked out together and she headed up the stairs to her room.

She sat on her bed and stared at the sketch and was about to toss it into the waste bin. She had been so excited as she had been the one to instigate the possibility that Shirley Dawson was a murder victim. She knew DS Lawrence had been of the same opinion but he had now decided against trying to prove it. The small sketch had no face but if she closed her eyes she could see Shirley, her eyes wide open, her hair floating in the bloody bath water. Jane recalled what it had felt like to lift her lifeless body out of the bath and wrap her in the plastic sheet.

She had made up her mind. Even if Paul Lawrence wanted to walk away, she could not. It was not a question of proving that she was right but of wanting justice for Shirley Dawson.

It took over an hour for her to get to St Thomas' Hospital and she went directly to the porters' rest room. She was told that, due to his recent absence from the wards, Barry Dawson was on a weekend shift and was working in the A&E department. Jane made her way to A&E and eventually spotted Barry Dawson pushing an empty wheelchair from a curtained booth.

'Mr Dawson . . .'

Barry turned, surprised to see her. Jane walked beside him and asked if they could talk privately. Barry hesitated before checking the time and saying that he would be on a tea break in ten minutes and could join her in the small coffee bar attached to the department.

It was a good fifteen minutes before he showed up. The coffee bar was closed and the shutters were pulled down to the counter. Barry sat down in a chair opposite her and apologized for keeping her waiting, explaining that it had taken a while to get a patient up to a ward.

Jane had her notebook open and thanked him for agreeing to see her, explaining that she simply wanted to double-check a few things with him. She discussed his alibi and how he had called home to talk to Shirley as he had been concerned about her.

'That's right. As I told you, she had said that she wasn't feeling well. We had this arrangement that I called her at the same time every morning when I was on early shift. When she didn't answer I was worried, so I called my mother because she was going over to the flat to look after Heidi. But my mother said she had to wait in for an engineer to fix her washing machine. So I tried Shirley again, but still got no answer. That's when I decided to go home.'

Jane nodded and jotted down what he had said.

'So, did you need permission to leave the hospital?'

'By rights, yes ... but I had a break coming up so I just left.'

'So what time exactly did you get to your flat?'

'About eleven to eleven thirty. Then I found her in the bath and went to the neighbours to call for help.'

'Why didn't you use the payphone on the landing at your flat?'

'I was in a terrible state ... I wasn't thinking straight.'

'Can you describe exactly what happened after your visit to the neighbour?'

'I've told you all this ... I don't understand why you're asking me to tell you all over again.'

'Just to make sure the report is correct and that your statement can be verified, Mr Dawson.'

'I went next door. Mr Cook said he would go up and see Shirley and he brought Heidi back as she was crying, although when I left she had been sleeping in her play-pen. We called the police and an ambulance, and then my mother came ...'

'When you went home and found Shirley in the bath, did you touch her? Move her at all? Even feel her pulse to see if she was alive?'

'No ... no ... I knew she was dead. I didn't need to touch her, I knew it. I work here, so I know the signs. I was in complete shock.'

Jane closed her notebook.

'Thank you. That all seems to tally up. And there was no one else in your flat, is that correct?'

He leaned back in his seat.

'No, I let myself in and the bathroom door was open. I called out for Shirley and then went in and found her.'

Jane put the lid on her pen. Having watched numerous interrogations by now, she gave the appearance of being satisfied with Barry's statements. He pushed his chair back, presuming the meeting was over.

'Just one more thing, Mr Dawson ... I showed you the photographs of this woman.'

Jane slid the pictures of the woman whom Barry had previously denied knowing towards him. He had ripped them up but was unaware that Jane had the negatives and had made copies, which were now being laid down, facing towards him, on the table.

'We now know that these are photographs of Katrina Harcourt.'

Barry turned away; his knee was jerking.

'We are also aware that Katrina worked here at St Thomas'. It's therefore a bit confusing for us to find photographs of her on a reel of film taken from a camera that was in your flat. You also denied that the camera belonged to you. So can you explain why you have three photographs of Katrina Harcourt?'

Barry was becoming agitated.

'If you didn't take these photographs, and say that the camera didn't belong to you, could it have been your wife's? Is it possible that she took the pictures?'

He shrugged.

'If you look at the photographs, Mr Dawson, they appear to have been taken when Miss Harcourt was not aware of being photographed. Would Shirley have any reason to want to take pictures of Katrina?'

'I don't know.'

'Mr Dawson, I think you need to start being honest with me. I've spoken to Brenda, who shared a room with Katrina, and she said that Katrina was having an affair with someone. It was quite a heated relationship and had been going on for some time.'

He turned away and sighed. 'All right ... I'm sorry, I was sort of freaked out. The truth is ... I was seeing her.'

'Did Shirley find out?'

'No ... no, she did not. I had finished with Katrina ...

it was just a stupid fling, and I regretted it. I told Katrina I didn't want to see her again and then she left the hospital.'

'Just a fling? But you bought her a ring, didn't you?' Jane was flying by her shirt tail because she had no proof that Barry had purchased a ring, let alone given it to Katrina, but she recalled what Brenda, Katrina's flatmate, had said and decided to see if she could get a reaction from him.

'You know, Barry, I am really trying to piece this all together, but some of it just doesn't make sense. You deny that you own the camera, and at first you refused to admit that you identified Katrina in the photographs.'

'Yes ... yes, I did.'

'Why did you lie about it?'

'I was just trying to cover up the fact that maybe Shirley had found out after all ... But I swear to God, she never said anything to me. Now I'll never be able to explain because she's dead ...'

'So Barry, you now admit that you were having an affair with Katrina? To me it sounds like more than just a fling, because you bought her a ring, didn't you?'

'OK, yes, I did ... but it was to sort of finish the situation, you know, say it was over and that I loved my wife and didn't want to lose her or Heidi.'

'I see. And Katrina just accepted the end of the affair, did she?'

'Yes. She decided to leave the hospital and get a job elsewhere.'

'Mr Dawson, I don't want to sound rude ... I've not only seen these photographs of Katrina, but I've also seen a photograph of her in the nurses' bay. She's a very attractive woman. According to Brenda, the girl she shared a room with, she always dressed very beautifully, was rather sophisticated, and I am sure would not like the description of your relationship being "just a fling".'

'Yes, she was very beautiful, and classy with it, and I have to admit that to begin with I was amazed that she would even be interested in someone like me. Then I found out that she put herself about a bit ... I wasn't the only one.'

'Can you give me the name of anyone else at the hospital that she was seeing?' Jane asked.

'No, I can't! She had her own private life that was nothing to do with me. To be honest I had wanted to end it much sooner, but she could get aggressive and told me that I would be very sorry if I broke up with her, and that there would be serious consequences. All the lies I've told were to cover up my shame about betraying Shirley ... I was petrified that Katrina was going to report me to the hospital. I was never serious about us – as I just said, it was a stupid affair. She put it about and there were plenty of others having sex with her.'

'And you're certain Shirley didn't find out? I mean, if this camera doesn't belong to you and was found in your flat, the photographs must have been taken by Shirley. Was she going to confront you?'

'No! I told you, she didn't know ... But maybe she had found out and that's why she was so anxious lately ...'

'I see. So when you say Shirley wasn't feeling well when you left for work, was it perhaps because, as you've just suggested, she was very anxious because she had found out? And that was why you were so worried when she didn't answer the phone for your usual call?'

'Yes ... yes, I admit that now ... that's why I was so concerned.'

'I don't quite understand this, Barry. You knew that your mother was going to babysit Heidi that day because Shirley had a hair appointment in the morning?'

Barry was sweating and was clearly feeling very uncomfortable.

'Yes, but my mother wasn't answering the phone there either. So then I called my mother at her house, and she told me that she hadn't been able to babysit because there was something wrong with her washing machine.'

'So, on previous occasions when Shirley had a hair appointment did she ever take Heidi with her? Your mother wasn't concerned when she tried to contact Shirley and didn't get an answer – she presumed that your wife had taken your daughter with her to the hair salon.'

Barry was visibly flustered.

'Listen, you're making this stuff up. I'm not going to answer any more of your questions.'

He pushed his chair back so hard that it toppled over. He picked it up, slamming it back down, then leaned towards Jane.

'You've got no right.'

Barry walked away, his hands clenched into fists. Jane picked up the photographs and slipped them back into her notebook. If she had any suspicions before that Barry Dawson had played some part in the death of his wife, she was now even more concerned. It was imperative for her to find Katrina Harcourt.

Jane didn't feel it was necessary to talk to Brenda again, but as she turned the corner in the corridor she bumped straight into her and decided it was too good an opportunity to miss. Brenda didn't recognize her, and Jane had to repeat her name and show her warrant card.

'I'm so sorry. I've been on duty since the crack of dawn. The Ward Sister is off at her son's wedding, and we're down two nurses ... it's been chaos here.'

'I'm sorry to ask this of you, Brenda, but it is a police matter. I wonder if you could possibly retrieve Katrina Harcourt's records for me?'

Brenda sighed. 'Well, you're in luck – I've got the Ward Sister's keys. Whether or not they'll still have Katrina's records on file is another story, but I'll have a look.'

Jane waited patiently outside the small office for ten minutes until Brenda reappeared.

'Sorry I've taken so long, but I had to go through drawer after drawer in the filing cabinets ... I can't let you take this away, but you can have a look at it here.' Brenda handed Jane Katrina's file.

'If you want my opinion, either she falsified her CV, or the high demand for nurses enabled her to continue working via an agency. If you read that report she was totally ill-equipped to be on any hospital rota for supply nursing staff.'

'Thank you very much for this, Brenda.'

'I'll go and get a cup of tea while you read it, then I'll have to put it back in the filing cabinet. Here, hide it in this newspaper and don't tell anybody you've seen it.'

*

After calling DS Lawrence, Jane left the hospital and hailed a taxi to take her to his home address. She was surprised to discover that he lived in a small, out of the way mews near the Baker Street gates into Regent's Park. Number 17 Sussex Mews was tucked into a cobbled side turning in a row of well-kept houses with adjoining garages. Jane rang the bell and waited. After a moment Lawrence opened the door and gestured for her to follow him in through a small comfortable lounge. The furnishings were rather old-fashioned, with numerous antiques and framed paintings.

'Help yourself,' he said, pointing to an open bottle of Chablis on a small table.

Jane folded her coat over a chair, and poured herself a small glass of wine. She had not anticipated that DS Lawrence would be living in such an affluent area, and took a good look around as she sipped her drink.

'Before you feel the need to ask, this place belongs to a relative. There's a demolition order for it to be pulled down within the next couple of years, to build a university college. Right, you can fill me in while I put the pasta on – I presume you're hungry?'

'Yes, I am. I didn't have any lunch. Thank you.'

Jane followed him into a very small kitchen annexe. As Lawrence prepared a pan of boiling water for the spaghetti, and opened a jar of Bolognese sauce, Jane gave him the details of her meeting with Barry Dawson. While she was speaking, he had taken out cutlery and napkins, and she had followed him back to the sitting room where he pulled out the leaf of a table leaning against the wall. He drew up two chairs, then returned to the kitchen to put the pasta into one pan and the sauce in to another.

'Katrina Harcourt was fired, she didn't leave of her own accord. She was late for duty three times and she was on the geriatric ward and never answered the patients' calls. She left poor old ladies desperate for bed pans ... Apparently it was the second time they had caught her being abusive to elderly patients. I took a look at her CV – she's registered with various different nursing agencies, but had mostly been working in care homes.'

Lawrence pulled out a chair for Jane and heaped far too much spaghetti and sauce into her bowl, but he was so fast that she didn't have time to stop him. He served himself and put the open bottle of wine between them on the table.

'Bon appetit ... sorry, I don't have any parmesan.' He topped up his wine glass and poured more for Jane.

She liked being with him, he was so relaxed and easygoing, and she noticed the way he tucked his napkin into his shirt collar before twirling his spaghetti round with a fork on his spoon. He ate and talked at the same time, apologizing for his lack of culinary expertise.

'How old is she?'

'Twenty-seven. According to her CV documents at the hospital, she's an only child, owns a Mini and has given her parents' home in Brighton, well, Hove to be precise, as her permanent address. According to Barry Dawson he was not the only person she was having sex with at St Thomas'. He said she put it about and Brenda, the nurse she shared a room with, said she thought Katrina was maybe seeing a doctor at St Thomas'. To be honest, I suppose having a scene with a porter is not in the same league.'

'He's good-looking, isn't he?'

'Yes, he is, but not high enough up the pecking order. I got the feeling that Barry was a bit afraid of Katrina. We know she had previously been engaged to a doctor, had a wedding dress, bridesmaids and everything ... but she was jilted at the altar. I think she set her sights on Barry Dawson ...'

Lawrence continued '... And his wife found out ... which explains those three photographs. So why did Barry become so agitated and anxious when he couldn't contact his wife, and knew that his mother was not going to be at his flat to babysit?'

'What if Shirley was already dead, and all he was doing was creating an alibi ...'

'My God, Jane ... so far this is just supposition and we've still got no hard evidence to get another PM. Dawson could arrange for Shirley's body to be removed for a funeral tomorrow, and I'm on duty in the morning.'

'We have this afternoon so we could go and question Katrina Harcourt?'

'But she might not be there,' he said. 'Hold on.' He put in a call to ask the local CID to do a drive by and check if Katrina's Mini was parked outside the property address in Hove. When the call came back confirming it was, Lawrence looked up at Jane. 'What do you think?'

'It's up to you, but I think as this is just supposition we should see if we can confirm our suspicions.'

Lawrence was still unsure. He sighed. 'We just have to be a bit careful because we're acting without any authority.'

Marie checked the children were out playing in the back garden and went to lie down. She took two more aspirin for her headache. She climbed into bed. Even without Peter being at home she slept on the left side of the double bed as he always liked to be on the right. She lay back, closing her eyes, but she was too anxious to sleep. She had asked her mother-in-law to visit Peter and had lied that the children had been invited to a birthday party so she would have to go and buy a birthday present. Lies tumbled out one after the other because she was afraid to go and talk to him. She would have had to explain that, even though she had followed his instructions, she had only seen the young red-haired boy take the money and get into a taxi.

Marie was only just able to function, making the children their meals and washing and ironing. But any time she was alone she felt sick and sat in the kitchen crying. Afraid to answer the phone, she often let it ring and ring, scared of hearing that awful voice singing the same song over and over. She also hated speaking to her mother-in-law, who asked one question after another, telling her what a good man her son was and how lucky Marie was to have him. Even when Marie had called her about the prison visit she had constantly interrupted, eventually asking about the bank account and why she had withdrawn so much money. But Marie had said she would explain another time, and had put down the handset.

She was in a quandary as to what she should do. Then she decided that the one person who might be able to help her was that policewoman. It took a while for her to recall her name, and that she worked at Hackney Police Station. Marie thought of the note she had left and went downstairs into the hall. It was in a drawer of the hall table, by the telephone. Marie took it out and read the name, 'Jane Tennison'. Returning to bed she carried the note in her hand. She didn't know why but she felt comforted and decided that first thing in the morning, after the school run, she would come home and call her. Then the doubts surfaced again. Peter had warned her that the police officers had fitted him up, and that they could not be trusted. But even in her anxious state, Marie felt certain that the young woman might be able to give her some advice. She needed it because she had no one else to turn to.

CHAPTER SIXTEEN

Jane was waiting outside the small garage attached to the mews cottage as DS Lawrence drove out in a pale blue Austin-Healey Sprite sports car, the roof pulled down. He hopped out and opened the passenger door. He was wearing a Harris tweed cloth cap, and what looked like a dark green thick tweed shooting jacket, with a button at the collar. Jane got in and smiled saying that, like his mews house, she had not expected him to be driving a smart new sports car. He closed the garage doors and got into the driving seat.

'Well it's not exactly a smart new one, and to be honest with my long legs it's not that comfortable. But I like to drive out to the country on my days off and I got it at a very good price.'

Jane wished she had worn a headscarf as the wind was blowing her hair loose from the hair grips. They drove through London to Croydon and onto the A23 Brighton Road. It was an hour and a half before they arrived on the outskirts of Brighton.

By the time they slowed down towards the town

centre Jane's initial impression that Lawrence was a careful driver had changed. He had put his foot down on the A23 dual carriageway and appeared intent on passing every vehicle, and her hair was now a tangled mess. Lawrence drove past the ornate Royal Pavilion, which looked very Arabian to Jane, with its bulbous domes, carved walls and beautiful gardens. They headed towards the seafront, the wonderful pier and fairground straight ahead. They passed the Aquarium on their left and, turning right, continued along the seafront, passing the Grand Hotel, and headed towards Hove. Lawrence pulled over to check a street map. By now it was almost four thirty and he passed Jane the map to double check their route. Jane studied the map as Lawrence drove at fifteen miles an hour.

'Second on the right,' Jane said. Lawrence indicated and turned into the pleasant Hamilton Street, with well-kept gardens and freshly painted three-storey houses. They passed a parked Mini outside number 34 and reversed into a space a few houses back. He got out to put the hood up as Jane searched in her bag for her hair-brush. She was on the pavement still trying to untangle her hair when he took his cap off and tossed it onto the front driving seat.

'Right, we work this nice and calmly. We're just making enquiries to check on Barry Dawson's movements on the day in question. Don't bring out the photographs until I give you the nod. Let's see how much she admits to and if she's going to co-operate.'

Jane nodded, then hesitated. 'Do I look all right, or still windswept?'

'You look fine.' He stopped to run his fingers through his blond hair, and then walked up the path to the house with Jane following behind him.

There was a large pot plant at the door on a pristine black and white tiled step. The front door looked freshly painted and had a brass letterbox with a lion head door knocker. There was also a bell beside the door. Lawrence rang the doorbell and stepped back, waiting.

A pleasant-looking woman opened the door, wearing a pink house coat over a twinset and tweed skirt.

'Mrs Harcourt?'

'Yes.'

Lawrence showed his warrant card and introduced himself, saying that WDC Tennison was accompanying him and that they wished to talk to Katrina.

'My daughter ... Yes, do please come in.' She hesitated. 'Is there something wrong?'

'No,' he said charmingly. 'We'd just like to talk to her, please.'

'Do come in and I'll call Katrina. She was just making herself a coffee.'

They were led into a very spacious front sitting room, filled with nice G Plan furniture, a large gas fire and decorated with flock wallpaper and a fur rug. There were numerous paintings, and copies of well-known artists hanging on the walls, and on top of a dresser were various family photographs.

Lawrence glanced at the photos and nodded at Tennison. 'Right house.'

Jane turned to look at a line of silver framed

photographs. There were two large ones of Katrina, one in tennis shorts with a racket and another standing wearing black riding boots and jodhpurs next to a white pony. But none of them looked very recent.

'Hello.'

They turned as Katrina Harcourt walked in holding a mug of coffee. She was very attractive and slender, with an abundance of shoulder-length red curly hair. She had pale porcelain skin, which enhanced her green eyes. Her lashes were dark with thick mascara, and she appeared younger than they knew she was. However, she had a very mature and confident manner.

'Mother said that you're detectives?'

'Yes.'

Lawrence introduced himself and Jane again. Katrina sat down on the edge of a thick cushioned sofa and crossed her slender legs. She was wearing fluffy slippers, and her legs were shapely and alabaster white. She was obviously a girl who stayed out of the sun despite the proximity to the beach.

'What is this about?'

'Do you know a Mr Barry Dawson?'

'Yes, he's a porter at St Thomas' Hospital.'

'You worked there until recently?'

'Yes, that is correct.'

'Were you aware that his wife recently drowned?'

'I think I heard about it.'

'But you had already left St Thomas' by then, isn't that right?'

'Ummm, yes ...'

'So who told you about Barry's wife then?'

'Oh ... I think my old room mate, Brenda, called me ... it's very sad ...'

Jane looked up. She knew Brenda hadn't said she'd been in touch.

'Did you know Shirley Dawson?'

'No.'

'But you were well acquainted with her husband.'

'Well, I'm not quite sure what you are inferring by saying I was well acquainted. I knew him as a porter and if he was on a wing I was working then I would obviously be aware of who he was.'

'Well, we seem to have a different view because he has stated that you and he were having an affair, and that it had been going on for some time.'

Lawrence glanced at Jane, who was writing in her notebook.

Katrina shrugged, sipping her coffee. 'Well, that's porters for you. He has obviously exaggerated my being pleasant to him as something far more.'

'So you are saying that you did not have a sexual relationship with Mr Dawson?'

'If you need me to repeat it, then the answer is that I was not in any kind of relationship with him, and I am becoming rather confused as to why you are here.'

Lawrence gave a small nod to indicate for Jane to continue the questioning.

Jane smiled. 'It's just out of necessity really. You see, Mr Dawson claims that you were having a sexual relationship. He says that it was nothing more than a cheap fling. According to him you were having various other sexual encounters, in fact he spoke about you in rather derogatory terms because he was not interested in having a long-term relationship with you.'

'I don't believe this. Not that I give a shit because I have nothing whatsoever to do with him, and if he is saying those things about me then he's disgusting.'

'So are you admitting that you and Mr Dawson were having a sexual relationship?' Lawrence asked. Katrina glared at him.

'I am not admitting anything. I think you should leave ... this is very upsetting.'

'Did you know his wife Shirley?'

'No, I bloody did not! I've said this before ... I just don't understand why you are here asking me these questions about my private business. If I did see Barry, then so what? Nothing is making sense to me ... I mean, why are you here?'

'Because we have some questions that need to be answered regarding the death of Shirley Dawson. We have to check that everything her husband has told us is correct. Could you please tell me where you were on the seventh of October?'

Katrina closed her eyes.

'Seventh of October? ... What day was that?'

'Monday.'

'Oh yes ... I was here. There's a new Arts Festival in Brighton and I went over there to see if any of the paintings interested me. We have a lot of artists in this area, and at one time I quite fancied the idea of running a gallery.'

Lawrence turned and waited for Jane to finish making her notes before he continued.

'Am I correct in saying that Shirley Dawson found out that you and he were having a sexual relationship?'

'I'll tell you what is correct – he is a fucking liar! Firstly, he never told me he was married, or that he had a kid. Secondly, he came on to me and made me ridiculous promises until I found out the truth about him being married. I left my job at St Thomas', which I was really enjoying, because I wanted nothing more to do with him and was disgusted that he had blatantly lied to me. I never met his wife.'

Neither Jane nor Lawrence said anything for a moment. It was obvious that since first denying having anything to do with Barry Dawson, she had now changed her story. They remained silent and Katrina seemed unable to keep quiet. Her leg twitched as she kicked out with her slipper.

'I don't know what he's told you but I am now telling you the truth. I mean, it was virtually a one-night stand. I made a big mistake by trusting in what he told me. He said he owned his flat, that he would sell up and we would have money. I mean, please, he was promising me God knows what. I never had any intention of getting serious with him, he was just a porter for heaven's sake.'

'Did you ever go to Mr Dawson's flat?'

'No, I had no reason to go there.'

'So, when you found out ...?' Lawrence said quietly.

'I finished with him, and left my job at the hospital.'

In a quiet manner Lawrence told her that, contrary to her saying that it was her decision to leave St Thomas', they had been informed that her contract had been terminated because of her unprofessional conduct.

'That is total bullshit! It was my choice! They were always understaffed and we were constantly being asked to change shifts and work extra hours. I don't know who you are getting this information from but it isn't true.'

'We also have information regarding your previous employment, Miss Harcourt, and that you had also been sacked from care homes for unprofessional conduct.'

'Christ, if you think that washing dirty old women's shit off their bedclothes is professional. Dementia patients are never easy to deal with ... I tried to be caring but I was never cut out to be ordered around by some vicious trumped-up Matron who didn't have the qualification to run any of the care homes I worked for. You give me any details you've got and I can qualify my reasons for leaving.'

Jane stood up and asked if she could use the bathroom. Katrina told her there was a downstairs toilet further along the hall. Jane was becoming frustrated by their interview and felt that maybe Lawrence would be able to get more information on his own. They had not yet gained any further evidence or connection to the death of Shirley Dawson. Jane left the room and closed the door. She walked into the hall and at the end of the hallway she saw Mrs Harcourt in the kitchen who, on seeing Jane, came out into the hall.

'Did Katrina offer you a tea or coffee?'

'No, but we're fine – thank you. You have a lovely house. It must be so nice living close to the beach.'

'Yes, we retired here quite a few years ago now. My

husband and I really enjoy bracing walks on the beach, and they have a very good theatre in Brighton with some excellent productions.'

'I'd love to see the rest of the house, Mrs Harcourt . . . it's so beautifully furnished.'

'Oh, let me show you around. When we moved there was a lot of work to do. My husband is a real one for putting up new wallpaper. He's very accomplished, and we like to have everything clean and fresh.'

They went up the stairs. Mrs Harcourt was so sweet and proud of her flock wallpaper, and new stair carpet.

'It must be nice to have your daughter home.'

'Yes, she comes and goes but right now she's looking for a new position. So until she finds one we're happy she's here.'

'I suppose there is a very good train service between here and London.'

'Yes, but she has her own car, and she doesn't like to use the train when she needs to go to London for an interview, as they are always so crowded. She had a very important interview the other day and I had to put the alarm on to make sure she was up in time as she had to leave at the crack of dawn.'

'Oh, can you remember what day that was, Mrs Harcourt?'

'Yes I do, it was the seventh of October, because it was just two days after those awful IRA bombings in Guildford. She rang me from the petrol station on the roundabout by the A23, where my husband has an account, and she asked for permission to fill her car up because she'd left her purse at home.'

'Do you recall what time that was?'

'Well, now you're asking me ... I think it was before seven o'clock in the morning.'

Jane was very complimentary as they toured the house. She was shown the master bedroom and then Mrs Harcourt showed her Katrina's bedroom. It was a large room at the front of the house, with bay windows and fitted wardrobes.

'Oh good heavens, what a lovely room! Are those all fitted wardrobes?'

'Yes, we got a local carpenter in and he made them to my husband's specifications. He and Katrina are both very particular about things.'

Mrs Harcourt opened one of the wardrobe doors, saying that Katrina liked her clothes to be colour co-ordinated. Jane looked inside and glanced down at the shoe rack.

'She must never want to leave! I am so impressed ... I wish I had a wardrobe this size.'

Jane knew they had no search warrant, and spotting a pair of very high-heeled patent leather shoes was more than she could have anticipated finding.

As they were about to leave the bedroom Jane noticed on the dressing table a large framed photograph of Katrina in a wedding gown with a tiara and a beautiful long veil. She turned to Mrs Harcourt.

'Oh, Katrina was married?'

Mrs Harcourt picked up the photo. 'Sadly the wedding never took place. Katrina ordered this gown from Ossie Clark – he's a very famous fashion designer – and the gown was satin chiffon Botticelli print. She had seen it in a fashion magazine and ordered it to be made especially. It was very expensive. Ossie Clark also designed her shoes and the bridesmaids' gowns.'

'Good heavens, that must have cost a fortune.'

Mrs Harcourt replaced the photograph. 'It did, believe you me. My husband couldn't afford it as he's retired. So Katrina foolishly took out a bank loan. She'd ordered cars and booked a reception at the Grand Hotel in Brighton. It was just awful because she ended up in debt.'

'Is she still paying it off?' asked Jane.

'Yes, she's also paying for the lease on her car. I don't know how she manages it, because you don't get paid much as a nurse, do you?'

'Going to such lengths, a wedding gown and all the arrangements, must've been dreadful. Was it Katrina's decision not to go ahead with the wedding?'

Mrs Harcourt hesitated and looked towards the doorway as if afraid she would be overheard. She lowered her voice. 'No, it wasn't Katrina's decision, it was her fiancé's, although we had never met him. I don't even know if they were officially engaged, and to be honest I felt very concerned at the time because she'd only recently met him. He apparently just said he had no intention of getting married and didn't want to see her.'

'That must have been dreadful.'

'Yes, yes, it was.' Mrs Harcourt rubbed her hands. 'It was humiliating. I never thought she'd recover and truthfully she had no one but herself to blame. And now she's still in debt, which is why she has to live at home with us. She has nowhere to go.'

By the time Jane returned to the drawing room,

Katrina was standing by the fireplace telling Lawrence that she had been almost suicidal when her engagement to a young doctor had fallen apart.

'I was devastated. I mean, it was a bolt out of the blue ... one moment I was choosing my wedding dress and the next he had the audacity to call me and tell me it had been too much of a rush and he was undecided. Undecided? ... I had booked the church and Mummy was organizing the reception! It gave me a total nervous breakdown.'

Katrina hardly acknowledged that Jane had returned and was very tearful, acting as though she was a wronged woman. Jane picked up her notebook and jotted down *'Katrina in London 7th October – patent leather shoes in wardrobe'*, before discreetly handing it to Lawrence.

Lawrence glanced down at Jane's note and wrote a quick message before handing the notebook back to her. He watched as Katrina sat down on the sofa, acting like the bewildered, jilted bride as she shook her head and sighed.

'So you have to understand that when Barry admitted to me he was married it felt as though it was all happening again. If you consider the lies I've been told and the promises I've been made I would never want to see his common little wife, let alone want to have anything to do with her. And I really don't care if she drowned. All I care about is that nobody is ever going to betray me again.'

Lawrence stood up and quietly thanked Katrina for co-operating and for answering their questions.

'I am sorry if this has been distressing for you.'

Jane stood uncertainly and joined him at the drawing room door. She thanked Katrina and then followed Lawrence out and into the hall. Mrs Harcourt was in the kitchen, as Lawrence smiled and said they would show themselves out. They didn't speak until they reached his parked car and got inside.

'Why didn't you let me show her the photographs?' Jane asked.

'It's called "keeping your powder dry". I guarantee we will be interviewing Miss Katrina Harcourt again, and this time with a search warrant. With what you discovered in her room I think we have enough leverage for me to talk to DCI Shepherd first thing in the morning.'

Lawrence reversed in a three point turn before heading back towards the seafront.

'If it's OK with you, Jane, I think that I should talk to Shepherd alone. I don't want there to be any negative repercussions on you and how much you're investigating without his authority.'

Jane stared out of the window.

'Do you really think we have enough evidence? I feel as though we should have questioned her further.'

'Listen, you had confirmation from her mother that on the morning Shirley Dawson died, Katrina left Brighton early in the morning and drove to London. You also saw a pair of patent leather stilettos in her wardrobe. If we had continued to question her, or asked about the day she drove to London, or her shoes, all without a warrant, we could give her time to come up with an alibi, or get rid of the shoes. What we don't need is for her to hear any alarm bells ringing.'

'Well, she certainly kept changing her story. One minute denying she was having a relationship with Barry Dawson, the next admitting it. But do we have a strong enough motive?'

'We do. It was when she said that Barry had promised to marry her, and told her he owned his flat. Plus, her mother said that she was in debt, so money is an incentive, and a motive to get rid of Shirley.'

Jane sat quietly, taking on board everything Lawrence said. She still felt uncertain about whether Barry Dawson and Katrina were in on it together, or if Katrina had acted alone. As if reading her mind Lawrence turned towards her and smiled.

'I think they worked this together. If we can get that next-door neighbour to identify the shoes we can verify that at eight a.m. on the day Shirley's body was found Katrina was there. It's a question of the time line. We are told Barry Dawson was seen at the hospital after ten a.m. and there is a witness who is certain they saw him. But it could be that Barry came home earlier than he has stated, met up with Katrina, and both of them killed Shirley.'

Jane remained silent. They drove back the way they had come, and she was thankful that this time the hood wasn't down.

'Can I just ask you something? At first Katrina was very scathing about Barry, being just a lowly porter. I mean, she is quite stunning, she's obviously well educated, and her mother was a sweetheart, proudly showing me all her husband's prowess with the décor and fitted wardrobes. It doesn't quite add up that she would go to such dreadful lengths to be a partner in crime with Barry, murdering his wife?'

Lawrence immediately replied that it was obvious to him. Katrina had recently been jilted at the altar and had been dismissed for her unprofessional conduct on several previous occasions. She was desperate, in debt, and had no job.

'Yes, I am aware of that. But do you think she would really be prepared to be a party to murder?'

'Yes, I do. I think she is a very dangerous woman with a psychopathic fury – did you hear what she said about the fact that she didn't care if Shirley Dawson had drowned, all she cared about was that nobody was ever going to betray her again, or stop her from getting what she wants? In this case it was Barry Dawson. If he wasn't a pawn then they planned it together. If I am successful in getting a more detailed PM, maybe we can prove it.'

CHAPTER SEVENTEEN

Jane arrived at the station at eight-thirty the following morning and went straight to the incident room. DI Gibbs was already in his office, which struck her as unusual, and he glanced over at her as she checked for any instructions from the DCI. She presumed DCI Shepherd would already be re-interviewing the suspects. Gibbs was a mess and obviously very hungover if not still under the influence of alcohol.

'Is everything all right, Spence?'

'Can you get me a coffee, please, Jane?'

'Do you want the canteen brew, or for me to get a takeaway? There are lots of new coffee bars opening up around Covent Garden.'

'I just want a fuckin' strong black coffee, Tennison, there's no need for you to schlepp out of the station, all right?'

Rolling her eyes, Jane went up to the canteen and, as requested, brought back as strong a mug of black coffee as she could get. Gibbs pulled a face when he tasted it, saying that she hadn't sugared it, and he went out to B Relief to use their sugar bag.

'I collared the bag slasher in broad daylight, right outside John Lewis ... caught him about to rob a teenager. As I suspected, he's a junkie with a sheet as long as my arm.'

'Congratulations!' Jane said, sitting at a desk.

'Message came in for you from the duty sergeant at Hackney. A woman, a Mrs Allard, left her number for you to call her. I didn't tell DCI Shepherd that you were on a jaunt to Brighton with blondie yesterday ... I hope you're not sleuthing around on something that you have no business working on.'

Jane didn't have time to explain as DS Lawrence walked in but she made a note in her notebook, puzzled why Mrs Allard was calling her.

'Morning, Spence, sorry I woke you up early. Now we need to talk to DCI Shepherd to get a second PM done. We're running out of time as Shirley Dawson's body is going to be released today for burial.'

'So what exactly *have* you got?'

Jane referred to her notebook.

'Barry Dawson was having an affair with Katrina Harcourt – she worked at the same hospital before she was dismissed. We believe that Shirley Dawson found out about their affair, and possibly followed them to take photographs of them together to confront him.'

Gibbs scratched his head.

'Hang on, hang on. This isn't hard evidence, it's just supposition.'

'We also have confirmation from Katrina Harcourt's mother that on the day Shirley Dawson's body was found, Katrina left Brighton at six a.m. and drove to London,' Lawrence said impatiently.

Gibbs laughed.

'But you don't have any proof that she was actually at the Dawsons' flat? Even a parking ticket would be useful ...'

'She has a pair of patent leather stiletto shoes that fit the description given by the neighbour, Mrs Cook.'

'Jane, she saw a pair of fucking shoes, not who was wearing them! Was there anything particularly unusual about the shoes?'

'No, they were just plain black patent leather shoes, with stiletto heels ...'

'... Like how many thousands of pairs sold in Saxone? You would be laughed out of court if your main witness for the prosecution was a pair of bloody shoes!'

Lawrence sat on top of the desk beside Gibbs, running his hands through his blond hair.

'All right, what if I was to tell you that, on a purely gut feeling, Shirley Dawson was murdered? I've been concerned from day one about the position she was found in the bath tub, and there are other inconsistencies that Jane came up with from their flat. I think Shirley Dawson was murdered, and I think Katrina Harcourt had something to do with it.'

There was a pause as Gibbs digested what he had just heard. He looked from Lawrence to Jane.

'And you have the same gut feeling, do you, Jane?'

'Yes, Spence, I do.'

'And you reckon Barry Dawson is also in the frame for it? But he's got an alibi hasn't he? He has witnesses who saw him making phone calls at the hospital?'

Jane was about to reply when Lawrence got up from the desk.

'I think we can break that alibi, but we have to have a second PM, and I'm going to need Shepherd to give us the go-ahead.'

Again Gibbs hesitated, then walked back towards his office.

'OK ... you'd better go and find him then.'

DI Moran was feeling very impatient. He had been in to the Hackney incident room twice looking for DC Edwards. Eventually a clerk had arrived to start work and explained to Moran that Edwards had gone home early the previous night as he had a high temperature and his cold had turned into bronchitis. She went over to her in-tray, saying that she had a couple of memos that Edwards wanted her to pass on to him. Delving through the pile of paperwork she pulled out two sheets, clipped together.

'He's been making enquiries into any cases that had a similar MO to Peter Allard's, sir. I really felt that he should have gone home earlier – he didn't stop sneezing and was passing his germs all around the office. Anyway, just before he left he contacted the police division in Maidstone ...'

'Maidstone? I told him to focus on local areas.'

'Apparently that's where Peter Allard and his wife lived five years previously, sir, before he took over his father's taxi and came back to live in Walthamstow.'

'Christ! You ask these young guys to do something simple ... What the hell is he going that far back for?'

'I don't know, sir, you'll have to ask him. He's underlined the name "Susie Luna", but I've no idea what that means.'

'I'll have to wait until he gets back. Meanwhile, I've got a situation – a woman's been pushed under a bus outside the Pembridge Estate. Can you ask DC Ashton to get a squad car—'

'Sorry, sir, but he's not in today,' the clerk interrupted. 'His new baby's got a very bad rash and his wife needs him to drive her to the doctor. You see, she's not breast-feeding, she's using formula milk and they often get an adverse reaction to that . . .'

Moran raised his eyebrows.

'See if you can get a plonk to drive me to the Pembridge then.'

Jane was at her desk typing up a lengthy report on all the latest information she had gathered over the week-end. DS Lawrence had been in with DCI Shepherd for over half an hour. Edith was moaning about the stack of work she had to do, lodging the complaints that the market stallholders had passed to the station.

Lawrence rushed in and went over to Jane's desk.

'I've twisted DCI Shepherd's arm and he's given me the OK to get a second PM on Shirley Dawson. Prof Martin has agreed to come in after lunch. In the mean-time, you'd better get over to the mortuary as Barry Dawson and his mother are due there to arrange the removal of the body for burial. I have some business to deal with in the lab, but I'll get over there as soon as I'm free. Just fend them off, and don't indicate that we are in anyway suspicious until Prof Martin has done his job. I'll take it up with the coroner. No matter what we think, we might just have to walk away . . . understand?'

Jane nodded and pulled out her typed report.

'DCI Shepherd wants your full report,' Lawrence added, 'and he wants it from every angle so don't miss anything out. Cover everything – he wasn't all that happy about that trip yesterday.'

'I've just finished it, if you want to read it over?'

'Sorry, I don't have time, I'm needed at the lab.' Lawrence hurried out and Jane stood up to take the report in to Shepherd. Gibbs appeared at his office doorway.

'What's going on, Tennison?'

'Oh, we've been given clearance for a second PM on Shirley Dawson.'

Edith stopped typing and turned to stare at Jane.

'DS Lawrence instigated it, Edith, as he reckoned there were some discrepancies in the non-suspicious death report from the coroner. So he's organizing another inquiry.'

'So, what exactly is your involvement?'

'Well, I was on the scene, that's all.' Jane hurried out.

Edith pursed her lips. 'She needs taking down a peg or two ... wasn't ever like that in my day, you know ... straight from being a probationary officer into plain clothes. She's going to get a smack around the chops from DCI Shepherd – he was asking where she was earlier.'

Ignoring Edith, his head pounding, Gibbs went over to the filing cabinet to pull out the reports on the Shirley Dawson case, then went into his office and shut the door.

By the time Jane arrived at the mortuary it was almost 2 p.m. Professor Martin hadn't arrived yet, and even when he did she knew it would take a considerable while before he could gain access to the body and begin the second post-mortem. Barry Dawson was sitting in the reception with his mother. His daughter, Heidi, was asleep in her pushchair clutching a teddy bear.

'What's going on?' Barry demanded.

'I'm sorry ... I have only just arrived,' Jane replied quietly.

'We have been told that Shirley's body can't be released. We have organized for her to be taken to a funeral parlour as we are having her buried tomorrow morning.'

'I'm sorry. I am not actually aware of what you are being told.'

'Just what I said. I mean, you tell me what's going on.'

'We have been informed that a second post-mortem has been requested and there was some suggestion that the first one was not as straightforward as it would seem.'

Jane excused herself and said she would try to find out what was going on and would get back to them as soon as she could. Pushing open the door to the corridor she stopped as Mrs Dawson called after her.

'This is bloody disgusting, you know,' she said, pushing the little girl back and forth in her pushchair. 'Barry's had to take another day off work, and we got family to organize. We get here only to be told that our funeral arrangements have got to be put on hold? You tell me, why?'

'If you just wait here I'll go and see what I can find out.'

Jane hurried along the corridor and stepped back as a mortician assistant wheeled out a covered gurney from the chill room towards the autopsy section. Professor Dean Martin appeared, already wearing his rubber gown and black boots. Judging by the stains on his apron it was clear that he had already been at work. He gave a polite nod to Jane as he pushed open the doors to allow the gurney to pass in front of him, then the doors swung closed behind him. Jane was disinclined to ask permission to follow but stood waiting in the corridor until she felt it was time enough to return to the reception. Barry Dawson had gone, leaving just his mother and the still sleeping Heidi.

'He's had to go to work ... he's really distressed, and we need to get some answers. This is disgusting and there doesn't seem to be anyone I can ask.'

Jane apologized and sat down beside her. She decided to take a risk in the hope that Mrs Dawson might let something slip.

'Basically there seems to be some confusion regarding your son's statement. We now have information regarding a relationship he had with a woman called Katrina Harcourt.'

'What? I've never bloody heard of her! This isn't right.'

'I just need to double-check that I have your own statement correct, Mrs Dawson. Could you please tell me exactly what happened on the morning your daughter-in-law was found at your son's flat?'

'I've told you! I was supposed to go and look after Heidi because Shirley had a hair appointment.'

'Ah, I see. That's why you were going to babysit, because ...'

'She was going to have her hair done at nine o'clock. But I couldn't go round there because my washing machine was faulty and I was waiting for the engineer to come. I've already told you this.'

'Did you call Shirley to tell her that you wouldn't be able to babysit?'

'I rang the payphone in her house, but she never answered so I presumed she'd already gone out and had taken Heidi with her.'

'What time did you call Shirley?'

Mrs Dawson sighed.

'Be about a quarter to nine ... but like I just said, she didn't answer so I presumed she had gone to have her hair done. I don't see why you want to know all this. She always asked me to look after Heidi if she was going out. And I presume that's why Barry got no reply either, when he called her.'

'I am going to show you some photographs now, Mrs Dawson. Could you tell me if you recognize this woman?'

Jane took out the three small black and white photographs of Katrina Harcourt and showed them to Mrs Dawson, who shook her head. She sighed.

'Don't tell me that silly bugger was seeing another woman? I swear to God, he's unable to keep his ruddy dick in his pants! But he never mentioned nothin' to me about her, and he's been in a terrible state since Shirley died. So what difference does it make? He's always been a one for the girls, and I have to say that it's not easy for me neither as I got to look out for his daughter. He's got to go to work, and I mean he's still living at my place, and his dog ... I don't know what he's gonna do when he moves back to his flat.'

'Has he suggested selling the flat? I believe he owns it, doesn't he?'

'Yes, he does. He pays the mortgage, but his dad left him the money to make the down payment. Mind you, it needs a lot doing to it and the landlord is a nasty piece of work. Never does nothing about the communal areas. There used to be a general cleaner who'd collect their rubbish from the storage area by their flat and take it down to the basement. But since he got rid of her, Shirley's had to do it herself.'

Mrs Dawson rambled on, all the while pushing the buggy back and forth, until Heidi woke up and started crying. Mrs Dawson was becoming more and more agitated now, standing as she rocked the pushchair. Jane discreetly glanced at her watch.

'You tell me what I should do, will you? I mean, we've arranged the funeral and now I don't know if it can go ahead. I just don't understand why there is this delay.'

Jane stood up and once again checked her watch. She suggested that Mrs Dawson return home and said that she would call her with an update as soon as she knew the details. Heidi was now howling loudly and Mrs Dawson eventually agreed to take her home.

Relieved that she had gone, Jane sat waiting in reception. There was something about the cavernous, cold room that always had a faint smell of cleaning fluid and Dettol, which became stronger when you passed through the double doors into the chill rooms. The first time she had been in there was for the identification of the murder victim Julie Ann Collins. She remembered how Julie Ann's father, after seeing his dead daughter, had become frighteningly enraged. Nothing had prepared her, after witnessing his overwhelming grief, for learning that he had instigated the brutal beating of his daughter. DS Lawrence appeared, having arrived via the back entrance.

'It's going to take a while . . . the old boy is being very methodical and won't be hurried. So far he has made no further conclusion and is ticking off the previous PM as all being acceptable. As soon as I get anything to the contrary I'll call you at the station.'

Jane would have liked to have stayed but before she could argue, Lawrence left her to return to the post-mortem. With nothing else to do, Jane headed back to Bow Street to wait for Professor Martin's PM report.

Marie Allard sat at the Formica-topped table in the visitors' section at Brixton Prison. The noise of the waiting families always gave her a headache. The children were mostly under five, so weren't at school like her own two. The babies screamed while the mothers and grandmothers shouted and tried to keep them from running between the tables. The male visitors always seemed much older than the prisoners they were visiting, with rough, worn faces. Many of them were rolling cigarettes and the walls of the prison visiting room smelt stale and were yellowing from tobacco stains. The tin ashtrays were never emptied and the officers walked up and down between the tables as they waited for the loud clanging sound that heralded the prisoners' entry into the visiting section.

Two wardens sat on high stools surveying the room and making sure nothing illegal was passed across, or underneath, the tables. Marie waited patiently, becoming more nervous as the minutes ticked by. Then the buzzer sounded, the communication door was opened and a loud bell rang.

The hubbub of noise increased as the prisoners were led in, and the men hurried to their allocated tables and loved ones. Peter Allard wore creased and stained prison issue denims, and was unshaven. He had always been so particular about his clothes and his personal hygiene, with clean cut nails, and shiny well-styled hair. Now he looked very pale, with deep circles beneath his eyes. As he pulled out the chair to sit opposite Marie she could feel the weight of his depression.

'You all right?' he asked quietly.

'Not really . . . but I'm OK.'

He looked down at his dirty fingernails, then glanced around the room.

'So, did you sort it as I told you to do?'

Marie hesitated and then tightly clasped her hands.

'No, I never get another phone call. So I didn't do it.'

He asked if she had got the money ready and Marie replied that she had. One lie after another tumbled out. Part of her was unsure why she was so afraid of admitting that all she had seen was a young boy collecting the cash.

'I too scared to answer the phone, Peter,' she admitted. 'It's such a lot of money, and with you in here.'

'I called you last night ... you know I got to wait in line to use the payphone so I can't tell you exactly when I'll be calling, but we get time around six o'clock ... so pick up around then, as you know it'll be me.'

'OK. You heard about a trial date yet?'

'No. Bastards are just keeping me here ... I hope to God it's soon because I don't know how much longer I can last in this shit hole. You have no idea what it's like ... a ping pong ball went missing and there was a big fight so we had to have a lockup for the entire day as punishment. As if being in this dump wasn't enough.'

'The kids are fine, Peter.'

'What did you buy then?'

'What?'

'Ma said you were taking them to a birthday party on Sunday.'

'Oh yes, it was just a jigsaw puzzle.'

Peter unclenched his hands and reached over to take hers. A passing warden snapped as he passed, 'No contact, please.'

Peter quickly withdrew his hand.

'Well, maybe that bent cop has got enough of my hard-earned dough and won't be blackmailing us for our savings.'

From across the room a young thug stood up, shouting at the top of his voice, 'The law sucks! Innocent until proved fuckin' guilty, my arse! It's a shit pile!'

Two officers removed the boy, who continued yelling

and kicking out, leaving the two women at his table crying. Peter shook his head.

'That's true – I know it better'n anyone else ... I'm innocent. You know it too, don't you? All I want is a fair trial so I can prove I was fitted up.'

Marie felt ashamed that she was willing the bell to ring for the end of visiting time. She just wanted to go and collect the children from school. But for a further half-hour Peter repeated over and over that he was going to prove his innocence. At one point he was in tears, and Marie had never seen him in such a depressed state.

'I can't forgive myself for doing this to you, Marie, and to my kids. You know I love you and want to make it good when I get out. But I just get into a bad state, because it's so frustrating. I admitted what I did was wrong, but it wasn't serious, not like that other time ... you know that, and you know why ... but we'll be all right, as soon as I get out.'

'Yes, of course we will.'

The bell rang and Marie was free to go. But first she had to watch him being led out back into the prison section, as the door was bolted behind all the inmates. Once he was out of sight, Marie turned away. It was too late now, she'd lied to him. And what if there was another call from 'Angie'? She was terrified there would be another demand, and the money in their savings account was running out.

At the mortuary Professor Martin peered through his half-moon spectacles at the right side of the victim's scalp. Using a fine spatula, he moved aside the thick curly hair, bent very close and sniffed. He then carefully parted a section of hair and turned to Lawrence.

'This is interesting. Can you see that a small section of hair looks frizzy? Not the section close to the face but just behind it? And if you lean in close you can just detect a slight smell of Dettol, but also burning. It's not strong, but then she was in the bath for some time. Can you see the strands are shorter here?'

Lawrence leaned in close and agreed. He watched as Prof Martin used sharp scissors to cut away the long thick strands and then, with the hair cropped, began to shave the complete right side of Shirley's scalp.

'Well, well . . . what have we here? I would say that this is what could have caused your victim to be unconscious, not the blow to her forehead. Can you see it?'

Lawrence looked at a strange V-shaped red mark, about three and a half inches in length. Prof Martin now continued to peel back the face and remaining scalp hair to examine the skull.

'Easily missed, and I could be wrong . . . perhaps the victim was wearing a band of some kind that in part might have cushioned the blow from being that visible. And her hair was thick enough to hide the strange burnt section. But it is clear she was struck to the right side of her head.'

Lawrence watched closely.

'The wound on her forehead is not the one that would have rendered her unconscious?' he asked quietly.

'No, it would probably have been caused by her falling forward and hitting the edge of the tap, as has been suggested, but having read the reports describing how her body was found, it doesn't quite add up. She should have been face down, not on her back.'

'So you are saying that she was more than likely unconscious when she hit the tap with her head?'

'Yes, but in any case your victim was alive in the bath water, as her blood was still flowing out of her nostrils. I would say the young lady could have had a severe nose-bleed from the blow.'

Lawrence stepped back to allow Prof Martin to finish. His mind was reeling as he took in the consequences of this new information.

He was stunned.

By the time Lawrence returned to the station he was feeling exhilarated, and went straight to the incident room. Jane turned expectantly towards him as he came in and his triumphant expression told her all she needed to know. But a thrill still went through her when Lawrence said, 'Our non-suspicious death is now very suspicious. Shirley Dawson was murdered.'

CHAPTER EIGHTEEN

Two days later, after all the investigation she had instigated, Jane was very upset that DCI Shepherd excluded
her from the inquiry. DI Gibbs and DS Lawrence were
given the overall lead, with three other DCs who had
been with Bow Street a lot longer than Jane. She had
presumed that Shepherd would ask for her to be present
and had even expected some acknowledgement from
him when he had been asking Edith what DCs were
available.

'Excuse me, sir, will you want me to discuss the report
and my notes from my enquiries?' Jane asked.

He glanced towards her and then went back to
looking over the lists of available officers, making sug-
gestions of who he wanted for the briefing.

'As you will see, I have underlined sections that we
will need to discuss, so please put them on my desk
straight away,' he told Edith.

Edith scurried out of the office and only after she had
left did he turn his attention to Jane.

'Tennison, I think you have proved yourself to be very
diligent. However, I also have major issues with the fact

that you have acted, or appear to have been acting, without authority. As you have only recently completed your probationary period and joined us here at Bow Street just over a week ago, I am warning you that I do not, and will not, have any detectives working without the full co-operation of the team. Your priority should have been to inform me of any new evidence or suspicions you acquired.'

Shepherd walked out, leaving Jane shocked and confused.

Edith returned carrying a large stack of papers she had to check through and banged them down on her desk.

'My God, this has created a lot of extra work. I now have to sort out what meetings he can be available for with all this new development.'

'What exactly is going on in the Board Room?' Jane asked, watching as officers including Shepherd and Lawrence gathered round a large oval table in the room opposite.

'I am not privy to what their intentions are, dear, but this Shirley Dawson case is leaving the desk sergeant pulling out his hair.'

Jane felt awful after the dressing down from Shepherd. As she was almost at the end of her shift she went into the ladies' locker room. She sat in a cubicle and, as much as she hated herself for doing so, she burst into tears. She was loath to admit it, but after a good cry she was feeling increasingly irritated that she had not been brought onto the case, after all the work she had done on it. She was also hurt that DS Lawrence had not intervened on her behalf. She collected her bag and jacket and left the station to return to the section house. She went to the laundry room and ironed a fresh shirt for the morning, then returned to her room. Sitting on the edge of her bed as she flicked through her notebook, she came across the message she had jotted down about Mrs Allard calling Hackney Station, which had been forwarded on to the duty sergeant at Bow Street. She had not really given it much thought, having been so caught up with the Shirley Dawson situation. Glancing at her watch she saw that it was after seven, she hoped it wouldn't be too late to return Mrs Allard's call.

Jane was also intrigued to find out what Mrs Allard wanted, so she made her way down to the reception to use the payphone. It rang unanswered for a long time, and Jane double-checked that she was dialling the correct number. She replaced the receiver, waited five minutes and tried again but it still rang with no one picking up. She was about to go back upstairs to her room when DI Gibbs came hurrying through the reception doors.

'Ah! Just the person I was coming to see.'

He gestured towards her to join him.

'Come on, I'll buy you a drink over at the Warburton . . . Just want to have a bit of a chat.'

'If it's to have a go at me I'm not interested.'

Gibbs grinned. 'I think you've had enough goes. I just need a moment of your valuable mind!'

She didn't bother fetching her coat as it was just a short walk across the road. Gibbs strode ahead of her, always seeming to have an excess of energy. Even though he was striding ahead he would half turn back towards her and then move forward; he was surprisingly elegant in his movements and had a natural rhythm. He shouldered the pub door, and held it open for her to pass him before he let it swing closed behind them. He ushered her to the bar and ordered a pint and a whisky chaser for himself. Jane asked for a dry white wine, which was never very dry and was usually rather tepid but Ron, the pub landlord, always dropped in a couple of ice cubes whether you asked him to or not.

Gibbs moved around the full pub to grab a small table in the corner, at the far end of the bar. He put his pint down and lit a cigarette, heaved in the smoke and then downed his whisky in one. Jane took an unenthusiastic sip of wine, waiting for him to explain why he wanted to talk to her. His right foot twitched as he picked up his pint and took a large gulp before he placed it back down onto the soggy beer mat.

'OK ... I got to the meeting this afternoon halfway through as I was over at the Magistrates' Court with this bag snatcher. But I have to tell you that you've got a fan in DS Lawrence. He was very complimentary about your queries with the non-suspicious death. Shepherd was a bit tight-lipped and prissy about you being unethical et cetera, but he had to stand down a bit as it's now a murder inquiry. The old boy, Prof Martin, did a second PM and discovered an additional abrasion to the dead woman's head, right side on in an odd V shape. He's stated that this would have been the first blow. Anyway, I'm not here to go into that until we've done more of whom did what to whomever ...'

Gibbs spoke very fast, his foot still twitching, and his eyes darting around the pub and snooker area.

'What did you want to talk to me about, Spence?'

'Well, I need you to explain how you got the information from the suspect – this girlfriend of the husband, Katrina Harcourt – and then how you saw the shoes that Dawson's neighbour gave a statement about, saying she didn't see the woman from above the knee.'

Irritated, Jane replied, 'There was nothing unethical about it. Katrina's mother invited me to see their home décor upstairs, and took me into Katrina's bedroom. She was very proud of her husband's DIY efforts and showed me the inside of Katrina's wardrobe with all the shoes. I didn't touch them.'

'Don't get tetchy with me, I'm just looking out for you. When the judge hears that it wasn't exactly an eyeball witness who *only* saw a pair of legs and feet, it's going to be a tricky one, your Honour!'

'I'll tell you what was really interesting: Katrina Harcourt had a photographer to take glamorous pictures of her as a bride. She had the full wedding dress, veil, all designed by Ossie Clark, and because she was jilted it left her in debt up to her neck.'

'I've heard of him. In fact, I bought a second-hand pair of snakeskin shoes designed by him.'

Jane gave Gibbs a curious look before telling him exactly where she had seen Katrina's shoes, and relayed how she had asked Katrina's mother about her travelling to London on the day of the murder.

'Just need to check that you didn't mention anything

about the coincidence, or say why you were interested in the patent leather high heels?'

'I just saw them because I was shown the inside of her wardrobe. They fit the exact description ... five inch heels, pointed toes and black patent leather.'

'Well, I shouldn't think they are going to be that useful ... We might get you to parade up and down in them, but I doubt it. Anyway, we're going to Brighton with a search warrant and we have to get the local nobs on our side. God forbid you should tread on anyone's patch ... and it's imperative we don't give this Katrina any signals to do a runner.'

'So is she a suspect?'

'Yeah, and DS Lawrence strongly believes they were in it together. But we're going to bring Barry Dawson in for questioning first thing in the morning. I could do without the schlepp out to Brighton, but you gotta do what you gotta do ...'

'Was Professor Martin able to give a clearer time of death?'

Gibbs drained his pint.

'Nope ... you know these pathologists, anywhere between eight to nine hours. I love it when they say possible nearest five hours or six. They won't ever allow themselves to be on the line.'

'Well, we can put a time on it. If we take the neighbours' information, that they heard the buzzer go at eight o'clock, and we know there was no one in the basement, no one in the first or second floor flat, it would have had to have been Shirley.'

'Yeah, I know that. Prof Martin said it was possible

she'd been dead three hours. He also came out with the fact that the cut to her forehead was not that deep and would not necessarily have bloodied the water.'

'But something did, because I saw it on the ceiling of the bathroom below,' Jane interjected.

'The prof said it was a possibility that Shirley Dawson had a severe nosebleed, which could've been the outcome of her hitting her head on the tap. But due to her being in the water for however long she was, her lower nostrils were clear. He found a substantial clot up in the bridge of her nose. Apparently it was even harder with this victim because she was in the water and had drowned, but both PMs agree that she was unconscious, but still alive, in the bath, and Martin thinks that maybe she was held down.'

Gibbs didn't ask Jane if she wanted another drink but pushed his chair back. His mood suddenly changed.

'He always used to sit over there, you know.' He nodded towards a similar-sized table on the opposite side of the room.

'Most nights I'd find him eating one of those disgusting steak and kidney pies from the heated cabinet on the bar. He always said he was never going to eat another one, so when I saw him with a greasy sausage roll I said to him, "Oh, not eatin' your usual crap then?" and he grins up at me and says, "Some bastard ate the last one!"'

Jane could see the grief in Gibbs's face and knew he had yet to get over the death of DCI Bradfield. Struggling with her own feelings of loss, Jane didn't know what to say. But he quickly masked his sadness, turned back to her and thanked her for coming for a drink. He then said he was going over to the snooker section to have a game, but he didn't wait for her reply as he moved away. Jane didn't even bother to finish her wine and left shortly after.

Jane clocked in for duty early, at 7.15 the following morning. She was heading towards the incident room when DCI Shepherd approached her.

'Give me a minute in my office would you, Tennison?'

Feeling apprehensive, she popped her handbag in the drawer of her desk, picked up her notebook and hurried to the DCI's office. The door was open and he was sitting at his desk typing – he was very fast. He signalled to her to wait a moment as he finished and drew the paper out of the typewriter, removing the carbon and copy. He passed the top page over to Jane.

'I hope to have all these queries you noted confirmed before we begin the interrogations. It's imperative I have a firmed-up time line. I think perhaps I was a bit hard on you yesterday, but for obvious reasons. DS Lawrence was very complimentary about your investigative abilities, but learn from this, Tennison. Please attend the briefing meeting at twelve-thirty p.m. today, as a team of detectives have been working flat out.'

Jane returned to the incident room and sat at her desk. Edith glanced over at her, then pushed her chair back.

'Do you mind if I say something, Jane? It was obvious yesterday that your nose was put out of joint. I am very aware of how much work you have been doing when you have been off duty, because I had to break down the reports for Shepherd.'

Jane chewed her lip, not wanting to get into a discussion with Edith.

'You have to understand the pecking order, dear. DCI Shepherd accepted the non-suspicious death, so how do you think it looks when a young trainee who has only been here less than two weeks, and a female to boot, goes off and does her own investigation? And now they have confirmation that the first PM was not adequate and it is being investigated as a murder.'

'I hear what you're saying, Edith . . .'

'Good. Make moves slowly, Jane, or they will have you back in uniform for insubordination. You were lucky you had DS Lawrence looking out for you.'

'Thank you, Edith. Can I get you a coffee?'

'No, thank you, dear. But at the briefing just sit tight and listen. I've been there before you, Jane . . . they'll wipe the floor with you if you overstep the mark.'

Jane gave Edith a rueful smile and went out to go to the canteen.

Jane arrived at the Board Room on the dot of 12.30, but already there was a team of detectives, some of their faces familiar to her, sitting around the table quietly discussing their notes. She was acknowledged but no one spoke to her as she sat down on one of the vacant chairs, hoping she hadn't taken anyone's seat. She placed her notebook down in front of her, along with two sharpened pencils.

The air was thick with tobacco smoke. Everyone fell silent as DCI Shepherd walked in and sat at the top end of the table, placing a thick folder in front of him. DS Lawrence was the last to arrive. He sat opposite Jane and was very intent on placing a large manila envelope on the table.

'Right, everyone ... time is against us so let's run through everything as fast as possible before the interviews begin. Paul, what have you got for us?'

DS Lawrence laid out various black and white photographs on the table, showing the victim's head wounds and also the shaven head clearly showing the deep V indentation.

The photographs were passed around as Lawrence spoke.

'I am certain that this wound to the victim's head was as a result of being hit exceptionally hard from the right side. The weapon, without doubt, is this ...'

Lawrence pushed forward the photographs of the iron.

'As you can see, the iron was yanked out of the plug socket when the victim was attacked. Close-up pictures reveal the loose wires, and when tested the iron did not connect. As you can see from this photograph, the victim may have been standing up ironing, and there was a female's blouse on the ironing board.'

Shepherd put up his hand to indicate that he wanted Lawrence to pause.

'We can conclude what the victim was doing before being struck, but as we are bringing in two suspects I need a clearer time frame of when this attack possibly took place.'

'The neighbour Mrs Cook, from the basement next door, is adamant that she saw a woman – but only from the knees down – wearing black patent leather high heels, pacing back and forth. Then she heard a very loud click, which indicated that someone, possibly Shirley Dawson, had pressed the entry release to open the front door.'

'Time?' Shepherd asked briskly.

'It was between eight a.m. and eight-fifteen a.m. This time was pinpointed by the paper delivery as the paper-boy delivers at the same time every day, like clockwork according to his boss at the newsagent.'

'Shirley Dawson had a hair appointment, not at nine a.m. as we had first been told, but for nine-thirty a.m. Her mother-in-law had agreed to babysit but due to her washing machine breaking down she could not be there. So she called the phone on the landing at the Dawsons' flat at a quarter to nine, but received no reply.'

Shepherd flicked through his notes.

'Detective Summers, you were checking this out – what did you come up with?'

Detective Summers was a thin, balding man. He tapped his notebook.

'The hair salon, Pearls and Curls in Brick Lane, con-firmed that they had Shirley's appointment booked in the diary for more than two weeks. Shirley was a regular customer: apparently she had exceptionally thick hair which had to be straightened and thinned. The salon say that they did not receive any call to say that Shirley was unable to keep the appointment. She had never missed any previous appointments.'

Shepherd nodded as another detective held up his hand.

'I interviewed Mrs Dawson yesterday evening and

she confirmed that she had received a call from her son, Barry Dawson, at around nine a.m. Mrs Dawson was unable to confirm the exact time but the engineer had not shown up to repair her washing machine yet. Barry wanted to know why she was not at the flat as she was supposed to be babysitting. Barry told her that he had tried to call Shirley but had got no reply and Mrs Dawson suggested that perhaps she had taken their daughter, Heidi, to the hair salon with her.'

Shepherd was making notes, then looked up.

'Sir, I don't know if this is of interest but when I arrived at Mrs Dawson's house she was out walking the dog and a friend was babysitting her granddaughter, Heidi. She was quite elderly and her name was Norma Hall. She said she had been Shirley's foster carer, and that it was all very sad, particularly as Shirley had believed that this was going to be everything she had dreamed—'

'Is there a point to this?' Shepherd interrupted.

'Just that the last time Shirley had seen this foster carer she had been very depressed. Although they owned their flat and Barry paid the mortgage, he had done nothing to redecorate or refurbish it for them to resell and make a profit, which was the original intention, and he kept breaking his promises. She said that it was stressful having the dog to take care of, and having to carry the pushchair up and down the stairs. Even the rubbish had to be carried all the way downstairs into the basement and—'

'One second – is the basement used for bins?'

'No, sir, I checked first thing this morning and there's

an old coal hole where all the tenants keep their bins. You gain access from the basement.'

'Anyone checked these bins out?' Shepherd glanced round the table. 'No? Let's do it then. I think we have a picture taken of a bucket with soiled nappies, yes? DS Lawrence, check out the bins. Can anyone tell me the value of the Dawsons' property?'

The same detective lifted his hand. 'Yes, sir. The flat beneath them, which is being refurbished, is on the market for forty-five thousand pounds and the Dawsons' on the top floor is estimated at between thirty-five and thirty-eight thousand pounds. It's a good location.'

'Good God! That's a lot of money,' Shepherd muttered, then tapped the desk with the point of his sharpened pencil.

'If I could just continue, sir ... I felt that I should talk to Norma Hall, the foster carer, again as she left when Mrs Dawson returned. She has been taking kids into foster care for thirty years. She was not in the best of health but was very informative about Shirley, who was placed into her care when she was in her teens. She also said that it was via her that Barry Dawson had met Shirley. I was about to leave when Norma said something that seemed rather odd. When she had first found out about Shirley's death she went over to see Barry. She said that he was very emotional, crying and sobbing, but when she left the room he put on the television and seemed more interested in some football match ... In fact, she said she heard him cheering and laughing.'

Shepherd shrugged and looked around the table.

'I am hoping you have saved the best until last, DC Tomlinson?'

Jane looked across at the overweight detective who was stubbing out his cigarette.

'I re-questioned Mr Goncalves, the hospital porter, as we have a statement from him and from Mr Dawson regarding the calls made from the phone kiosk in the hospital corridor. You may recall that Barry Dawson said that he called home at ten a.m., and on getting no reply became very worried as he claimed Shirley was not well and had been very depressed. He appeared to be very anxious and asked Mr Goncalves for change, expressing his concerns over his wife's health and his need to call his mother again. He then claimed to leave the hospital and returned home to find his wife dead in the bath.'

Tomlinson had everyone's attention as he explained tracking down the porter and then standing with him in the corridor and asking him if he could recall the exact timings. The porter said he was unsure and thought he had been told by Barry that he needed to leave as it was coming up to his break at ten a.m. He said that he had given him some coppers and returned to the wing as he had a patient to take up to theatre.

'I asked him to be very clear about exactly what he had heard. Did he hear the coins being returned as the call wasn't answered, or did he hear the call connect? He couldn't answer, but by my calculations Barry Dawson made one call to Shirley and got no reply. The next call was, he claimed, to his mother who said she was not at his flat. Then there was a third call that the witness saw him ending when he returned to the corridor, and this time he said that Barry Dawson was very anxious. I was eventually able to get closer to the exact time because we went back to the theatre records and it showed that Mr Goncalves had brought the patient up into theatre at five past ten, so adding on ten minutes to get back to the corridor he would have seen the agitated Barry Dawson much later than he had originally stated.'

Jane noticed how Shepherd doodled on his notepad before looking around the room.

'I am just estimating this, sir, but going on the original time line from WDC Tennison, our victim Shirley Dawson could have been dead shortly after eight-thirty a.m. I made some further enquiries and then spoke with another porter in their rest room at St Thomas' and he checked over the old listings of on and off duty porters. He kept on referring to something being the "Rose Cottage" duty and when I asked him what he meant he said that it was the porters' joke terminology for the mortuary.'

Jane wrote this down and underlined it because she had never heard it mentioned before.

'Barry Dawson had a body to take to the mortuary at just after eight a.m. When I went over there, a number of bodies were actually lined up, obviously covered over. Apparently there is often a delay or backlog ... but Dawson delivered the body on time. So if we go by the time frame, he dropped off the body at eight a.m. and was not seen again until after ten a.m.'

Everyone waited as Tomlinson lit a cigarette, drew on it deeply and then exhaled the smoke before he continued.

'Along with Detective Johnston, who was with me at the hospital, we checked out the mortuary. The main doors into the mortuary are directly across a courtyard into the hospital, and there is an exit door that opens straight onto the street.'

At this point Johnston, a young, fresh-faced officer, took over.

'We decided that it would be possible for Dawson to take off his porter's uniform and leave the mortuary via the street exit without being seen. We then timed the journey from the mortuary to Dawson's address. If he got a taxi he could travel there in under half an hour. There are also a number of bus routes that he could have taken and that would add a good half-hour on to his journey. But it is possible that he could have returned to his flat, and been there at around eight forty-five a.m.'

Jane leaned forward, taking it all in. Her annoyance at not being involved was superseded by excitement. She was stunned by the amount of basic legwork the detectives had achieved, and by what they were suggesting.

Shepherd nodded his approval.

'Well done. I don't suppose you were able to find any witnesses who actually saw Dawson leave the mortuary?'

'No, sir, but at that time in the morning the hospital is very busy with breakfasts and patients waiting to go into theatre for operations.'

Again Shepherd tapped the page in front of him with the tip of his pencil.

'So, let's just walk through what we've got ... Shirley is expecting mother-in-law to babysit. She prepares her little girl's food, then puts her in the playpen. She has a hair appointment for nine-thirty a.m. and is maybe ironing the blouse she is going to wear. The door bell goes, and this might even coincide with the phone ringing, but Shirley buzzes open the front door. It is possible that it was Katrina Harcourt, but Shirley is expecting her mother-in-law so she presses the door release. Shirley was already suspicious that her husband is having an affair, and has even taken photographs of this woman. Then there is a bitter argument—'

'Could I just interrupt here, sir?' It was Tomlinson again. 'What I didn't mention was the fact that inside the porters' rest room there is a phone that connects to the wards. You can't make any outgoing calls as it's just intended for calling the porters for duties, and is an extension. If Katrina Harcourt worked as a nurse at the hospital she would be aware of the extension number and could actually call the hospital directly and ask to be put through to the porters' rest room.'

'That's supposition, isn't it? Unless you have a witness who saw Dawson take a call in the rest room early that morning?'

'No luck, sir. But Dawson was there, and was on his way to the mortuary. It's possible that Katrina Harcourt could have contacted him there to tell him his wife was dead.'

Shepherd rubbed his head and checked his watch. Lawrence pointed to the photographs of the iron and the wound to Shirley's head.

'Not dead but unconscious. We can conjecture what might have happened next ... Barry returns and he and Katrina run a bath. Maybe Shirley started to come round, struggled, hit her head on the tap ... they might even have held her down ... It's imperative we find a time frame that confirms that the pair had liaised together.'

'Of course it bloody is,' Shepherd replied. 'Did Barry and Katrina plan this murder? Or did Katrina, who may possibly have been wearing the patent leather high-heeled shoes and was maybe let into the flat by Shirley, become part of a spur of the moment attack? Because we have to be on firm ground to charge this duo.'

Shepherd glanced at his watch. 'Let's take a late lunch break, and be on standby for the interrogations this afternoon.'

Jane returned to the incident room and flopped into her chair. She was exhausted and felt completely deflated. She knew that every one of the detectives had worked from the information that she had compiled, and she had received no credit for it. It was as if she hardly existed.

DS Lawrence appeared in the doorway and gave her a rueful smile.

'Well, that was impressive in there. I have to say, when old Shepherd gets to work he really shows his experience.'

'And everything that I had reported was taken and used, but not one of them even looked in my direction.'

'Get over it, Jane – they all worked their butts off.'

'And I didn't? If it wasn't for me, Shirley Dawson would have been buried by now!'

Lawrence held up both hands in a gesture of peace.

'Look, I'm just on my way to the Dawsons' flat to check the rubbish bins ... do you want to come along?'

'Why not? Give me the dirty work ...'

Edith watched with narrowed eyes as Jane followed Lawrence out.

Jane sat in the passenger seat of the patrol car. Lawrence found a parking space a short distance from the Dawsons' building and together they moved down the basement steps, the old iron gate swinging back on its rusty hinges.

Lawrence wrenched open the wooden door into the old coal hole of the property. The bricks were coated in dusty cobwebs and the curved walled outhouse had a grid in the ceiling that, in the old days, would have been opened and filled with coal for the fires in the house. Now it only contained four large lidded bins with flat details painted on each. They opened the bin labelled 'Top Floor'. It was empty but still had a very strong odour of mouldy food and soiled nappies.

'Nothing here,' Lawrence said, replacing the lid.

'Did you empty that bucket we saw in the bathroom?' Jane asked.

'No.'

'Well, maybe somebody else did ...'

'Yes,' he said tetchily, checking the other bins. Two of them contained a lot of paper bags and rubbish.

'Mrs Dawson told me there used to be a person that cleaned the hallways, a sort of maintenance cleaner, who was hired by the landlord. But he'd got rid of her, so Shirley would have had to cart the rubbish up and down the stairs.'

'What is the point to this, Jane?'

'It's the small trapdoor by the front door. You would put your bags of rubbish inside, lock it and the maintenance cleaner would collect them on certain days and take them down to the basement for you.'

Jane sensed that she was irritating Lawrence, but couldn't really see why. As they still had the house keys they let themselves in and moved up the stairs to the top floor. They could see that the ground-floor flat had blocked in their trapdoor, and the same on the newly decorated second-floor flat. Workmen were inside painting, and from the amount of packing cases and boxes it looked as if a new kitchen and bathroom had now been delivered.

They reached the top floor, and Lawrence sniffed. He bent down and slid the small bolt across the trapdoor to remove a dirty bag full of mouldy food and soiled nappies. Without saying a word, he took the bag downstairs with Jane following quickly behind. Lawrence placed the stinking rubbish bag in the boot of the patrol car and they headed back to the station.

In the incident room Lawrence tipped the bag out onto a desk covered with newspapers. Ignoring Edith's protests, he began to pick through the rubbish. The stench was overwhelming. There were old milk cartons, clusters of rice and baby food, dirty disposable nappies, and even an old terry nappy had been thrown out. There were dog food tins and numerous soup and baked bean cans. Caught on the edge of a jagged tin lid was a small, folded, pale pink gingham headscarf, the type worn under the chin by models. On one side of the scarf was a burnt V scorched into the cotton, with strands of dark hair attached.

Lawrence glanced at Jane and carefully used a pair of tongs to place the scarf into a paper bag. It was a very important find because it meant it had to have been removed from the victim by the person that struck Shirley across her scalp. The question was who had wilfully murdered Shirley by placing her unconscious body in the bath?

DI Gibbs opened the door and instantly covered his nose.

'Christ ... what is the stink in here?'

'Rubbish from the Dawsons' bins. How was Katrina?'

'She's being held in cell one. She's refused to have a solicitor and is creating merry hell.'

He handed over the patent leather shoes in an evidence bag, and perched on the edge of the desk.

'You do know Katrina's mother has changed her statement regarding the day her daughter went to London? But we checked with the petrol station where the father holds an account – they verified that he authorized for her to fill the tank of her Mini on the seventh of October. We might be able to use this when we question her.'

Lawrence reacted. 'At the same time, we don't actually have a witness that saw her in London that day.'

'I know. Are you in on the interrogation, Paul?'

Lawrence shook his head. 'Nope, I'm down to be in when they question Barry Dawson. But I want to get this over to the lab to do a few checks.'

DS Lawrence gestured to Jane. 'Right, I've got everything I need ... you can get rid of the rest of it.' Before Jane could protest he'd already left.

Jane found it really extraordinary that both men seemed capable of not only talking across her but completely ignoring her presence. When they left the incident room Jane looked over to Edith.

'Am I invisible?' Jane asked tetchily.

'Yes, dear ... that's why I'm doing clerical work. I got frozen out of any hope for promotion and this job will pay towards my pension. You can't change anything, as I have repeatedly told you. And you had better supply this incident room with some form of air freshener. That disgusting heap of rubbish should have been taken to the laboratory, not tipped out here. God forbid that DCI Shepherd should come in – it smells like a lavatory.'

Jane began to wrap the newspaper around the remains of the rubbish as Edith continued speaking.

'Do you know why we put up with it? I'll tell you why ... DCI Shepherd may have a rather pasty face, and thin twitchy fingers, but you underestimate him at your peril. I know he's had words with you, as have I, and I can tell that you're not exactly a happy bunny, but I'm not asking you to lick DCI Shepherd's boots ... although there are some here that are more than happy to do so—'

She stopped abruptly as DCI Shepherd appeared in the doorway.

'I want you to sit in on the Katrina Harcourt interrogation, WDC Tennison. Fifteen minutes, my office.'

2

LYNDA LA PLANTE

Jane nodded, and waited for him to leave before she looked at Edith. She had two bright pink spots on her cheeks.

'Oh God, do you think he heard me?'

Jane, rolling two sheets of paper into the typewriter, answered, ' I don't think he heard you.'

'Thank God. He's got the stealth of an ocelot.'

CHAPTER NINETEEN

The door was ajar so Jane went into DCI Shepherd's office, knocking respectfully before she entered. Shepherd turned and nodded towards her as he carried on sifting through notes and statements. He checked his watch as she waited patiently, then instructed her to place a hard-backed chair up against the far wall. Sitting at his desk he motioned for her to put in place another chair directly in front of him.

'Right, you sit back there. I don't want you to be in her peripheral vision but I need to see you. If I nod my head towards you I want you to give a slight cough and I will make some kind of interaction with you ... not sure what yet ... I think it is going to take a lot of work to unnerve this lady.'

'What ... when I sit behind her?'

'Yes. I've used these tactics before – the interviewee just needs to be aware of someone behind them. It unsettles them, and by coughing you will distract her and give me the opportunity to choose my next line of questioning.'

Jane was still unsure of what Shepherd's intentions

were, but placed the chair for Katrina Harcourt as requested. She then went and sat at the far end of the room. DS Lawrence knocked and entered. He was carrying a large evidence bag containing the patent leather shoes.

'Put them on the desk,' Shepherd said, and then asked how Katrina was behaving.

'Fairly quiet; she's not said anything and is refusing to have a solicitor present. She was more irritated than emotional in the car from Hove. She's sitting in the small interview room with DI Gibbs and had been given a cup of coffee and a cigarette when I last saw her.'

'What about Barry Dawson?'

'He's in cell two, as it was empty. But he seems much more upset than Katrina. He asked us to call his mother, not a solicitor, as he wants her to know where he is.'

'Thoughtful son ...' Shepherd said, then checked his watch again.

'Right, let's have a go at her, shall we? If you get DI Gibbs to start on Mr Dawson then we can swap over, all right?'

A few minutes later DS Lawrence came back into the office with Katrina Harcourt. She was wearing a tailored green linen suit and white blouse with high-heeled leather court shoes. Her flame red hair was loose and hung in natural curls to her shoulders. Jane took a good look. She had very pale skin and yet her eyes were enhanced by thick mascara lashes and dark grey-green eye shadow. She wore no jewellery.

Jane listened as Shepherd quietly went through the reason Katrina was being questioned, informing her again that she had the right to have a solicitor present if she wished. There was a brief moment when Katrina turned around to look directly at Jane. A flash of recognition registered on her face. She then sat straight-backed in the chair, facing ahead. She spoke in a very calm, clear voice and crossed her legs as if unconcerned about why she was being interviewed.

'I declined having a solicitor present because I have done nothing wrong. I would like to know why I have been subjected to having my poor parents' home searched and why I have been brought here for questioning with regard to Mr Dawson's wife.'

'You have been told that you are under arrest for murder, Miss Harcourt, but let's hope this unfortunate situation can be dealt with very expediently so that you can return home.'

Jane noticed how charming Shepherd appeared, as if he was only interested in gaining Katrina's confidence and was on her side. He leaned back in his chair, smiling at her.

'Let's just go through the scenario, Miss Harcourt, because you have admitted quite freely that you do not want any representation. Is that correct?'

'Yes, simply because why would I need anyone to represent me when I have done nothing wrong? I have said from the outset that I have never met Barry Dawson's wife. I have also admitted, and I am not proud of this at all, that I did have a very brief affair with him because I was unaware that he was married, or that he had a young child. When I discovered this and found out that he had lied to me I ended the relationship immediately. I also left my place of work, since being there meant that I would obviously come into contact with him as we were both employed at the same hospital.'

'That was very commendable of you.' Shepherd casually glanced through the statements in front of him, then looked up.

'It must have been very distressing for you when your engagement to a doctor and hopes for future marriage were shattered, and the wedding never took place. Then to form a relationship with Mr Dawson only to discover he had lied to you about his circumstances . . .'

Katrina shrugged her shoulders.

'Yes, but then I am too trusting . . . some would call me foolish.'

'Oh, you seem to be a very intelligent woman to me. Nevertheless, you must have felt some degree of anger towards Mr Dawson, perhaps even his wife?'

'I couldn't be angry with her as I never met her. As I said previously, as soon as I found out, although I was obviously hurt, I ended the relationship.'

'I understand. Perhaps you could just clarify for me if this is you in this photograph?'

Shepherd held the three photographs that Jane had found on the film in the camera at the Dawsons' flat. He laid one down like a playing card and pushed it towards the edge of the desk so Katrina could clearly see it.

'Is this you, Miss Harcourt?'

She leaned forward and looked at the small black and white photograph.

'Yes.'

'Where was this taken?'

She sat back in her chair and looked up to the ceiling. 'I don't recall.'

'Take another look, Miss Harcourt.'

She looked again, then prodded it with one finger.

'I think it might be in Regent's Park.'

'What about this one?'

Shepherd placed down the second photograph.

'This is you again, isn't it?'

'Yes, I think it might be again . . . I mean, it is me, but it could have been in the park again.'

'But you're not wearing the same coat?'

'I don't recall it being taken as it appears to have been taken when I was unaware.'

'What about the third one, Miss Harcourt? Again you are wearing a different outfit. So it is quite possible these were taken on different days and at different times.'

'If you say so.'

'These were taken by Shirley Dawson. So it is clear that she was aware of you, and knew that you and her husband were having an affair.'

'Maybe she was suspicious . . . I mean, he is obviously a liar. As I have said, I had no idea that he was married and had a daughter.'

'So Shirley Dawson never approached you?'

'No, I never met her.'

'Did you go to their flat?'

'No, I did not.'

'So tell me, Miss Harcourt, how did you find out that Barry Dawson was not only married but also a father?'

'He told me.'

'Yes, but was there some reason why he admitted to

you that he had lied? Because it was quite serious, wasn't it? He had given you a ring?'

Jane could see Katrina's body tense as she swivelled in her chair and flicked back her long hair. Shepherd remained at ease, picking up the three photographs and stacking them together, tapping the edges of the desk. He appeared to be very calm, almost as if he was having a friendly conversation with the suspect rather than an interrogation. Jane found his demeanour interesting as she had never seen any of her other senior officers, particularly Moran, conducting an interview in such a relaxed manner.

'Did someone tell you that Barry was married, so you then brought it up with him? Or did he just come out with it and say "Look here, this has got to end as I am a married man and have a family"?'

'I don't remember.'

'You don't remember? Well, that's very strange. I mean, here we have photographs of you that were taken when you were unaware. One in the park, maybe two in the park ... one you can't recall where you were ... but you're wearing different coats. So these might have been meetings with Mr Dawson, witnessed by his wife and taken as proof he was having an affair, do you agree with that?'

'It's possible, but if you are trying to get me to admit that she approached me or that I met up with her, then prove it. I never met her ... I never went to their home.'

'Did he promise to marry you, like your previous lover, the doctor?'

Shepherd glanced towards Jane and inclined his head

slightly. Jane coughed and Katrina swivelled around to look at her. She said nothing, smirked and turned back again. DCI Shepherd changed the subject and raised his voice.

'You knew he owned his flat, which was worth a considerable amount of money, and believed he had every intention of selling it to finance your future together, especially as you were in debt due to losing a considerable amount of money paying for wedding photographs and bridal outfits that were never worn.'

Jane could see Katrina crossing and uncrossing her legs as Shepherd continued, in his unnerving, quiet way, to put the pressure on.

'So when exactly did you find out it was all lies, that he had no intention of ever marrying you, that there was no future, and no intention of selling his home because he loved his wife?'

'I do not recall exactly how I found out, but when I did I confronted him and he admitted that he had lied and was ashamed.'

'But you must have been angry. He was the second man to let you down, and this time he was, as you described, "just a porter", not even a qualified doctor.'

'I wasn't angry, just upset that I had made the mistake of trusting him.'

Shepherd glanced at Jane and again she gave a light cough. Katrina turned to glare at her.

'But you are known to have quite a volatile temper, aren't you? And you do skirt the truth, Miss Harcourt, because I am aware that you did not leave the hospital because of your emotional turmoil about discovering that Mr Dawson had lied to you. Your contract was in actual fact terminated, and this had occurred numerous times before – you were accused of unprofessional conduct, specifically towards dementia patients at—'

Katrina stood up and Shepherd immediately gestured, calmly and quietly, for her to sit down again. Then he spoke quite sharply.

'Please, Miss Harcourt, remain seated. If you refuse I will have you removed from my office. You may disagree with accusations of unprofessional conduct but we do have them from your previous employers. I apologize if what I am saying is distressing but I am trying to ascertain exactly how Shirley Dawson died.'

'If you can prove that I am lying then go ahead. I never met the woman and I was never at their flat. All I know is that she drowned in her bath.'

'Could you please tell us exactly where you were on Monday the seventh of October?'

'This is absolutely ridiculous! I have already explained where I was – I was at home, and my mother can confirm it.'

'On the contrary, Miss Harcourt. Your mother, when asked where you were on that date, recalled clearly that you had left home very early in the morning. And the reason that she remembered that you had gone to London was because you needed petrol for the journey, and asked permission to use your father's petrol account.'

Katrina laughed.

'Listen to me ... My mother is menopausal, she can't remember one day from the next. Surely it all makes sense that I had to use my father's account – I had no money on me and was therefore clearly not planning a long journey to London. I did come to London on a regular basis but I totally deny that I was anywhere near their flat on Monday the seventh of October. If you have a witness that saw me there then put me in an identity parade! I was not there, and have never been to Barry Dawson's flat ... and *I never met his wife.*'

She sat back in her chair, folding her arms and smiling. Shepherd looked at Jane and yet again she made a soft coughing sound. This time Katrina not only turned to look at her but snapped, 'You enjoying looking at my back, are you?'

Shepherd responded. 'I'm sorry if she is unnerving you, Miss Harcourt. WDC Tennison, please come with me.'

'She's not unnerving me,' Katrina said, as Jane followed Shepherd out of the room.

He closed the door behind them and said to Jane, 'Go over with me exactly what the neighbour told you about seeing the shoes. I'm not going to bring them up, but she's a hard nut to crack and I need to get her to admit to going to the Dawsons' flat.'

Jane repeated that Mrs Cook said she had seen whoever wore the shoes pacing back and forth on the pavement, and then heard the front door clicking open.

Shepherd nodded. 'She's very confident about not being seen entering or, for that matter, leaving the flat. We have no evidence she was in there but I believe she was. I also think they are going to back each other's story up. You go and talk to DI Gibbs – ask him to leave

Dawson alone and make out there is a breakthrough. Let's see if we can put the pressure on him, and I'll keep on going with her. Give it ten minutes, then return to my office and take up your seat. But pass me notes ... scribble anything on them.'

'Yes, sir.'

Jane tapped on the glass panel of the interview room door. Gibbs looked up, told the officer to remain with Dawson and stepped out into the corridor to talk to Jane.

She told him, 'So far DCI Shepherd has been unable to break Katrina Harcourt. She is insisting she didn't go anywhere near Dawson's flat, but he is certain they are both involved. He wants you to shake Dawson up and act as if Katrina is giving evidence that implicates him, to see if you can unnerve him.'

'Terrific ... he's not shown any break in his original statement, and keeps crying.'

'Apparently he can bring on the tears. Katrina, in contrast, seems to be almost enjoying herself.'

Gibbs nodded and was about to walk back into the interview room when Jane tapped his arm.

'Just a thought ... all those calls he made from the hospital – if Barry knew his mother was going to be babysitting for Heidi but then couldn't come because she had to wait for the washing machine engineer, why did he become so anxious when Shirley didn't answer the phone? Logically it would make sense that she had taken Heidi to the hair salon with her, and he knew she had an appointment.'

'I'm not following you.'

'If we are going on the assumption that Barry was contacted by Katrina and left the hospital to meet her at his flat, they could have drowned Shirley in the bath ... But they would have to leave before his mother turned up to babysit.'

Gibbs ran his hands through his hair anxiously.

'But this is all supposition ... We don't know if either of them were at the flat.'

'I know we don't, Spence, but it is a possible scenario. I remember Rita Dawson saying to me that if she'd been on time she would have found Shirley ... Do you understand, Spence? If Barry Dawson went back to the hospital to secure his alibi, he left his little girl Heidi all on her own.'

'OK, OK ... I'll give it a shot.'

Jane made copious notes to hand to Shepherd as if there had been a development and returned to his office.

'Come in, WDC Tennison,' Shepherd said curtly. Jane approached his desk and passed him the notes. Then, turning her back towards Katrina, she whispered, 'Please read these, sir ... it is very important.'

Shepherd glanced down at her notes and showed no reaction at first. He seemed to be reading every line before a tense expression slowly formed.

'Excellent. Please take your seat, WDC Tennison.'

'Yes, sir.'

DI Gibbs took his time settling back in his chair. Dawson was chewing his lips.

'I am sure you know we are questioning Katrina Harcourt. There appear to be some discrepancies in the timing regarding the phone calls you made when trying to reach Shirley.'

Dawson shrugged and said defensively that he had been worried because the last time he had seen his wife she had been very nervous, and it was a usual arrangement that he called to check on her at that time in the morning.

'What time did you leave your home to start your work at the hospital?'

'It was the early shift, so I left about six ... six fifteen.'

'You have admitted that you were worried about your wife, but did not actually attempt to call her until just after ten o'clock?'

'I was on duty so I couldn't call her before that time.'

'But you did speak to your mother, and she told you that she was unable to babysit as she had a problem with her washing machine?'

'Yes.'

'What time did you discover this?'

'I don't understand.'

'It's very simple, Mr Dawson ... if you had been able to contact your mother and knew she was no longer able to babysit, why did you not call your wife until a considerable time later?'

'I was out of change.'

'So, when eventually you did get the change to call your wife over an hour later, why did you become so alarmed ... surely she'd gone to her hair appointment?'

'Because she didn't answer.'

'But the logical response would surely have been that if your mother was no longer able to babysit, your wife would more than likely have taken your daughter with her to the hair salon?'

'I wasn't thinking that way.'

'Why not?'

'I just wasn't ... Shirley was not very well when I left.'

'At six fifteen that morning?'

'Yes, so I went back home as soon as I could.'

'Was your concern about your wife because she had found out about your affair with Katrina Harcourt?'

For the first time Barry was not quite so confident.

'No ... that was not the reason.'

'But she found out, didn't she?'

'Well, yes ... but I had ended it all. I loved my wife and there was no question that we would divorce.'

'Oh, so that had been a possibility, had it?'

'No! It was a stupid thing to have done, and I regretted it. It was just a one-night stand and it didn't mean anything to me.'

'So Shirley just accepted that you had finished the affair? What about the photographs? When did she take the photographs of Katrina Harcourt?'

'Before ... I mean, she suspected and took the pictures to confront me.'

'Sorry, can we just go back on that? Are you admitting that you did in actual fact know about these photographs?'

'Yes, all right, yes, I did know, and Shirley told me that she'd seen me with a woman. She didn't know who she was, and I admitted to her that I had been very stupid, and that I regretted it and never wanted to hurt her.'

'On the morning Shirley died what time did Katrina Harcourt call you at the hospital?'

Dawson pressed his body back into the chair and started shaking his head.

'I never received any call from her ... as I keep on telling you, it was over between us. I have told you the truth! I called home and was worried about Shirley, so I left the hospital.'

Gibbs felt as though he was getting nowhere, even with the scenario Jane had put forward. Basically they had no evidence to counteract Dawson's original statement.

DCI Shepherd was equally frustrated at going over the same ground. Katrina remained very controlled and uncooperative. She still insisted that she had never met Shirley Dawson and had never been to the Dawsons' flat.

'So you are admitting that you were having an affair with Barry Dawson, but you say that you have never visited his home?'

'Yes.'

'How did you react when Barry told you that it was over between you?'

'How do you expect me to react? I was very hurt. I would say that has to be rather obvious. He made me promises and then confessed that he had lied.'

'That he was not only married but had fathered a little girl?'

'Yes,' Katrina almost hissed.

'And you just accepted that you had been treated as a casual sex partner, and that he had no intention of leaving his wife for you.'

'That is pretty succinct ... but what alternative did I have?'

'Divorce?'

'She wouldn't consider it.'

Katrina knew as soon as she had said it that she had made a mistake and Shepherd was on to it. Jane listened intently, observing how he had cast his line and was now reeling it in.

'So you did discuss the possibility of Mr Dawson divorcing his wife?'

Katrina was on edge for the first time, patting the hem of her pencil skirt as it rested on her knee.

'I think he might have suggested it ... but I can't recall, because at the time I was shocked.'

'So, Mr Dawson suggested it but Shirley wouldn't agree? Then there would be the matter of custody of their daughter, and obviously if they were to contemplate a divorce then would Shirley agree to move out of their flat?'

Katrina was tight lipped.

'We never even discussed that as a possibility. This is really starting to be very tedious ...'

'When you were let into Mr Dawson's flat on Monday the seventh of October, did you confront Shirley regarding your relationship with her husband?'

Katrina had the audacity to laugh, shaking her head and threading her fingers through her long curls.

'This is preposterous! I was never in that flat, and I never met Shirley Dawson.'

Shepherd looked over Katrina's shoulder at Jane. She could sense that he knew he had lost his catch, and for the first time he snapped angrily.

'What time did you call Mr Dawson, to tell him that you had struck his wife? Because that is what happened, isn't it, Miss Harcourt? You rang the doorbell and Shirley buzzed you inside the building.'

Katrina lifted her eyes to the ceiling, laughing.

'I am giving you a way out to explain how it happened, Miss Harcourt, that it was never your intention to physically hurt Shirley Dawson,' Shepherd shouted.

Katrina uncrossed her legs and leaned forward with a faint smile.

'I was never there, and you have no proof that I was.'

CHAPTER TWENTY

Jane was in the CID office with DI Gibbs and DS Lawrence.

'Right now we have nothing to implicate either one of them,' Gibbs said.

Jane replied, 'Apart from the fact that one or other of them removed that headscarf, and put it into the rubbish bin after Shirley was hit with the red-hot iron.'

Lawrence was fed up. 'We know *who* was hit, Tennison, we don't know which one of them did it, and whether or not they were in it together. I've taken Katrina's fingerprints and I'll be back first thing tomorrow morning for another search of the Dawsons' flat.'

Katrina Harcourt and Barry Dawson had been taken back to the cells pending further questioning on suspicion of murder. The duty sergeant was organizing meal trays to be taken to both the prisoners who had been kept separated and not allowed to see or speak to one another. DCI Shepherd had left, true to his usual time-keeping, in order to be at home with his family by 7 p.m.

'Barry could have left the hospital at eight-thirty a.m., arrived home at—'

Gibbs interrupted.

'Please, Jane ... "could have" and "might have" is not good enough ... we have to find conclusive evidence to prove either one of them killed Shirley. Right now we can't prove it, and after this afternoon's questioning both of them will be lawyered up tomorrow.'

'What if we don't find anything?' Jane asked.

'They'll walk ...'

Lawrence headed out of the room, then paused.

'You both want a drink? I'm going over to the pub.'

'Not for me, I need to be on my toes for the next round of questioning,' Gibbs said, walking into his office.

'What about you, Jane?'

'No thanks, but could I come to the Dawsons' flat tomorrow?'

'Sure. I'll be there at seven-thirty a.m. as I want to be back for the next round of interviews as well as Spencer, but I need a beer right now.'

After Lawrence had left Jane typed up her report and filed it as the night duty staff took over. She was about to head out when, with a pang of guilt, she remembered Marie Allard. Jane took out her notebook and dialled the number she had tried to call the previous evening.

Marie jumped as she heard the phone ring. She was in her dressing gown after taking a long bath to calm herself, and the children were asleep. The sound of the phone made her shake. She walked slowly down the stairs, and in the semi-dark hallway the ivory-coloured plastic phone looked ominous and threatening as it rang and rang. Marie was afraid to answer it in case it was that awful woman singing 'Angie, Angie . . .', the dreadful sound of the grating rasping voice. Or it might be her mother-in-law who was putting her nerves on edge with all her questions. She knew it couldn't be Peter as it was too late, and lights in the cells would already be out.

Marie reached the last step and stretched her hand out to pick up the receiver and answer.

Back in the CID office Jane replaced the receiver, having let it ring for ages. Perhaps it was too late to call. She made a mental note to herself to call earlier tomorrow. Marie held the receiver up to her ear and could only hear the dead tone vibrating as the call had been terminated. She started to cry and was soon sobbing uncontrollably. She was so afraid and didn't have anyone to turn to.

DI Moran was going out for a curry with some of his team at their favourite local Indian, the Star of India. It had been a busy day, arresting two thugs who were trying to get protection money from a local betting shop. They turned out to be rather sad figures, old-time gangsters, who were still reminiscing about the Krays. Both of them were pensioners and would probably get a heavy sentence due to their previous, quite apart from the fact that they had used an old sawn-off shotgun. Moran suspected that as he was a good half an hour late the lads would already be stuck into the lager, and he had asked them to order him a vindaloo. He was just crossing Mare Street when he saw her. Janet Brown wasn't wearing her usual blue rabbit fur coat, but instead she had on a thick, brightly coloured Mexican poncho and a leather cowboy hat. She had her little boy in a pushchair, laden down with bags of groceries on the handles. Moran zig-zagged behind her.

'Not working tonight, Janet?'

She whipped around to face him.

'What're you doing scaring the effin' life out of me?'

He laughed. 'Just checking you're OK.'

Moran bent down and rested back on his heels as he touched the little boy's face.

'You got anything for me?'

'No . . . I'll be in touch, though.'

'Good girl . . . you look after yourself.' He had slipped a five pound note into the little boy's hand. Janet gave him a brief nod and hurriedly walked away.

Moran was now in the mood to get hammered. He pulled off his tie, undid his shirt collar, and sashayed down the road towards the Star of India for a good night out with the boys.

By the time Jane arrived at the Dawsons' flat Lawrence had been there for a while. She rang the bell for the top flat and heard the loud buzzer allowing her entry. She carried two takeaway coffees and two bacon sandwiches and headed up the stairs. The flat door was open.

'Hi there, it's me . . . and I've brought breakfast.'

Lawrence was bending over an upturned table, carefully brushing the black fingerprint dust around the underside of the rim.

'Great, I'm starving. Just hoping whoever did the clean-up here might have just done the top surfaces and forgotten to test the underneath of the table. The table was pushed away from the ironing board, right?'

'I think so, yes. Coffee and bacon sandwich. We got no prints off the iron, taps, bath or basin. I mean, they did quite a clean-up job.'

'Telling me,' he said, as he continued to dust the underside of the table with fingerprint powder. He found nothing, and broke open his sandwich wrapper.

'Tell me about Spencer Gibbs . . . is he all right?'

Jane was opening up her sandwich too.

'How do you mean?'

'Well, totally off the record . . . and by that I mean this is between you and me . . . he's been drinking heavily and was out of his head last night. I know that DCI Bradfield's death really hit him hard and he's not getting himself back together. What do you think?'

Jane couldn't look him in the face and simply shrugged her shoulders.

'I didn't think he was going to have a drink last night.'

'Well, he came into the pub, and he'd already had a few.'

'I think we all took it hard . . . but you know Spencer is a big character and they always backed each other up.'

'Maybe that's it, but he should get back singing with his rock band to let off the steam . . . last night he was completely out of it.'

Jane was unable to finish her sandwich and her coffee tasted tepid. She wrapped them up in the plastic bag ready to dump in the bin later. She didn't want to think about DCI Bradfield now, didn't want to feel that awful pain in the pit of her stomach. She changed the subject.

'We need to time exactly how long it takes to walk from here to St Thomas' and to get a taxi. I have a rough idea ... but then it is possible that if Katrina was here and they are in this together she could have driven him back to the hospital in good time.'

'Yeah ... Get some photos of a Mini the same colour as Katrina's – we might get lucky. But then again we might not ... we've not had much going for us on this one.'

They worked well together. Lawrence instructed Jane to check through all the family photo albums to search for any pictures that might have been taken of Katrina. She found none, but there were numerous photos of Shirley wearing the gingham scarf like Audrey Hepburn, tucked in a little bow just beneath her chin. Jane was moved as Shirley had been such a pretty young woman, her thick curly hair sometimes worn in braids and sometimes in a top knot. She wore very fashionable thick black eyeliner and pale pink lipstick. In a number of photographs she was wearing white knee-high boots and a miniskirt, and Jane thought she looked like one of The Supremes.

There were other photos that were not as glamorous, but Jane decided that Shirley was probably quite aware of her good looks as she played up to the camera and was very coquettish with her lips pursed. Even when she was pregnant she was wearing pretty smock dresses. All of the images were a far cry from that sad wretched drowned woman Jane had lifted out of the bath.

'Can you do me a favour?' Lawrence asked, making

her jump. 'I'm about ready to go back to the station but I just want you to do something for me. Act out the scenario I'm trying to piece together, will you?'

'Yes, of course. I haven't found any other photos of Katrina in the albums.'

Lawrence asked Jane to stand at the ironing board. It was positioned in the exact place they had first found it and its position meant that Jane's back was facing the front door. Lawrence spoke quietly to himself as Jane stood still and he walked around her. He stopped by the high chair and touched the playpen.

'Shirley was ironing. Maybe she intended to wear the blouse that was on the board. She had prepared the baby's bottle, dressed her and laid out the food for her breakfast on the high chair. She was expecting her mother-in-law to babysit so that she could go to the hairdresser.'

Jane turned and touched her head.

'The scarf . . . she could have put the scarf on to keep her hair back while she took a bath.'

Lawrence nodded and then turned to the bathroom.

'She could have been running a bath ready for herself, which would mean she was not wearing underwear, just the dressing gown.'

Jane agreed. 'Yes, if she had been wearing underwear it would not have been on the floor beneath the dressing gown but on top of it.'

Lawrence frowned in concentration. 'If she leaves the iron on, the doorbell rings and she clicks the buzzer, expecting it to be her mother-in-law. Then she goes to the bathroom to turn off the taps and in walks Katrina, who she knows is having an affair with her husband. So seeing her walking into their flat would be like a red rag to a bull.'

Jane sighed. Yet again there was no proof that this was what had occurred.

'Jane, listen, there has to be something in this bloody place. We've searched drawers and wardrobes but you start again. I am going to move inch by inch over that bathroom ... I won't give up.'

Jane started searching through a stack of magazines left piled up in the bedroom. They were teenage magazines and nothing glossy or expensive. She sat on the bed flicking through them but nothing was stuck inside, or any articles even earmarked or turned down. She glanced at the bedside clock. It was coming up to almost 8.30 a.m. and she placed the stack back beside the bed. She had already searched beneath the bed and on top of the wardrobe. The flat was not very clean or hygienic, and she felt dirty and frustrated. She told Lawrence that she wanted to get out for a few minutes and take a breather.

He looked at her in surprise. 'Sure, go ahead.'

'I just want to make a call.' She used it as an excuse but then decided that she had not been very professional in failing to return Marie Allard's call, so she would do it now.

'Fine by me. I'm coming up with bugger all in here ...'

Jane took her purse out of her handbag to get coins for the phone on the landing. As she headed down the stairs she heard a loud crash and hurried down to the landing to see the landlord, Mr De Silva, standing next to a builder who was chiselling the call box loose from the wall.

'What are you doing?' Jane asked, concerned.

'Having this phone taken out ... waste of bloody money as I have to pay the rental on it. I'm putting a landline in the flat below and they've got their own on the ground floor. This is hardly used up here anyway, and I want to redecorate the hallway.'

There was an ominous creaking sound as the wooden surrounds of the payphone were wrenched from the wall. Jane headed back up the stairs.

'Well, that was a waste of time ... the landlord is ripping the phone out of the wall, said it wasn't worth the rental he has to pay and that it's hardly used.'

Jane picked up her purse ready to put the coins away when Lawrence grabbed her wrist.

'Coins! If Katrina used the phone to call Dawson, she would have had to put coins into the call box and then left her fingerprints on them.'

Jane didn't really hear all of what Lawrence was saying as he charged out of the flat and leaped down the stairs. There was a lot of raised voices and unpleasantness from De Silva before the entire piece of equipment was removed from the wall and wrapped in a sheet. Jane watched DS Lawrence carry it carefully down to the waiting patrol car. He was eager to work on it in the lab and he drove off with a squeal of tyres, not even saying goodbye. Jane locked the Dawsons' flat and returned to the station.

*

DI Moran felt terrible. He was very hungover and was sick to his stomach. The vindaloo had been hotter than hell and he had had to drop his suit at the dry-cleaners on the way to work that morning. DC Edwards was back at his desk and looked over at Moran who was standing holding a glass of Andrews Liver Salts.

'I heard it was a good night, sir?'

Moran frowned. 'Ruined my bloody suit ... that idiot Ellis spilt an entire pint down the back of it.'

'So you're not feeling too good then, sir?'

'No, I am bloody not.'

'I'm feeling better ...'

'Obviously, now that you are at long last back at work,' Moran replied grumpily, as he headed towards his office.

'Have we had any news regarding the Allard trial yet, sir?'

'No, we have not. And your last report, Edwards, which you left unfinished ...'

'Yes, sir, you told me to check out any previous assaults and rapes that might match Allard's MO ...'

'Yes?'

'I didn't find any.'

'Terrific.'

'So I was about to check from when he lived in Maidstone ...'

'Maidstone? Well, how far back is that? He'd be a bloody teenager?'

'Not quite, sir, he's twenty-nine years old now. It was only five years or so ago.'

'And?'

'Well, I wasn't feeling very well ... had a high temperature ... so I had to go home, sir.'

'Yes, I know that, Edwards.'

'We need to check with a DS Victor Bethell.'

'Who?'

'I was told we needed to talk to him regarding a missing persons case ...'

'In Maidstone? What's the connection to Peter Allard, for Chrissakes?' Moran was becoming very impatient.

'Allard was questioned because the missing girl was a Filipino friend of his wife. They never found her ... her name was Susie Luna.'

Moran downed his Andrews Liver Salts and belched loudly.

'Well, let's get onto him then.'

'I wish I could be present at one or other of the interviews,' Jane said.

'I doubt it. As I keep on telling you, we are invisible, underpaid and totally unappreciated. Right, I'm going to take these files in to the boys so that they can get started.'

Shepherd walked in and Edith flushed, hoping he had not overheard.

'I want DC Tomlinson in with me. And Tennison, I want you in with DI Gibbs. We're one man down with Paul being over at the labs. Pity ... but when he gets back let's see if he's uncovered anything. Edith, if Lawrence gets a result you interrupt, but we'll be a while before we get started. The longer time we've got the better, as Harcourt is waiting for her lawyer.'

Edith handed Shepherd the files and as he walked out she turned and looked at Jane.

'Do you think he heard me having a go? But you know I am telling the truth ... you got lucky. Can you do Gibbs a favour? Get him to suck one of these – he stinks of alcohol.'

Just as Edith returned to her desk there was a call from reception to say that a Richard Blake was there to speak to his client, Katrina Harcourt. Edith walked out and Jane went back to looking over the Mini vehicle leaflets. Gibbs appeared and asked where Shepherd was, and Jane said he had just taken all the files to his office.

'Spencer, do you mind if I say something? It's just that you might want to suck one of these ... you know what Shepherd is like.'

He cocked his head to one side as she passed him the half-opened pack of Polo mints. Gibbs shrugged as he left the room and didn't appear to be at all embarrassed by her comment.

Gibbs and Shepherd worked on cross-referencing all the statements taken from Katrina Harcourt and Barry Dawson. They underlined and discussed their different approaches and made detailed notes. They were deep in discussion when Edith knocked on the door and entered.

'There's a Richard Blake here to talk to his client, Katrina Harcourt. He has asked for any disclosures to be discussed with him.'

'Disclosures? What is he talking about?' snapped Shepherd.

'Well, he has been hired by her family and he is unaware of why she is under arrest. Despite having been asked by Katrina, the Harcourts have refused to pay for any representation for Barry Dawson and he has now claimed he does not want a solicitor present.'

Shepherd smiled. 'Well, thank you, Mr Dawson ... makes my life a lot easier.'

'I think yours might as well, DI Gibbs,' Edith said. 'I ran a check on Mr Blake and his chambers are in Victoria, but they are not criminal specialists and deal mostly in property development frauds. Blake is semi-retired and lives in Hove, so he might be a family friend of Miss Harcourt's parents.'

Shepherd smiled again and thanked Edith, joking that 'The Taming of the Shrew' might not be too problematic. However, when Edith closed the office door he glanced at DI Gibbs.

'You don't have much to go on, so I suggest you kick-start the interview on a tough line. She is going to be a difficult one to break.'

CHAPTER TWENTY-ONE

Jane sat at the Formica-topped table, an empty chair beside her. The dank green walls of the partly tiled interview room smelt of stale sweat and nicotine. There were two plastic beakers of water on the table and Gibbs's thick file, with his notebook and pen beside it.

Katrina was brought up from the cells by a uniform officer. She had been allowed a twenty-minute interview with her solicitor, Richard Blake. He had subsequently had another fifteen minutes with DCI Shepherd and was brought into the room by the duty sergeant.

The two hard-backed chairs in front of Jane were close together and she noticed Katrina move hers further apart, as if she didn't want to sit too close to Richard Blake. Unlike his client he appeared very nervous. His worn briefcase was placed beside him as he took out a legal pad and pen. Without makeup Katrina was very pale, her skin translucent. Her green eyes were devoid of mascara and black liner and were red rimmed with blonde lashes. She was wearing the same suit she had been wearing when she had been brought to the station. Katrina's slender, shapely legs were clad in sheer stockings and she was wearing high-heeled pointed dark green suede stilettos that were a shade darker than her suit.

Richard Blake introduced himself to Jane but Katrina totally ignored her, and the uniform officer remained standing by the door, which was slightly ajar. Gibbs made his entrance, crunching on the Polo mint Jane had offered him earlier as an attempt to disguise the smell of booze from the night before. He patted the officer's shoulder in a friendly way and then gestured for the door to be closed. He circled around the table, then in a flamboyant manner drew out his chair and swung it round for him to sit, leaving quite a space between himself and the table. He had long legs and Jane edged further away as he stretched them out and crossed his feet at the ankles.

'I am Detective Inspector Spencer Gibbs, and this is Detective Constable Jane Tennison, whom I believe you have met before. Mr Blake is acting as your solicitor. Basically all I really need to do is make sure you understand the serious charges that are levelled against you, Miss Harcourt, and ask you to answer the relevant questions—'

'Oh, just get on with it,' Katrina interrupted him, as she crossed her legs and then ran one hand through her hair. 'I know that you don't have a shred of evidence that can prove I even knew Shirley Dawson. I never even went to her flat and this is all preposterous. I do apologize for my crumpled suit, but it is linen, which always creases, and I have been forced to wear the same underwear, and have no makeup or even a hairbrush.'

She looked at Spence hoping he'd respond, but he ignored her obvious attempt to win him over.

'According to WDC Tennison, you told her that, to begin with, you were astonished and surprised at yourself for considering having a sexual affair with an ill-educated porter like Barry Dawson. Especially after you were previously engaged to an accomplished and highly qualified doctor. Sadly you were unceremoniously dumped after the wedding banns had been read out in preparation for what would have been quite a society wedding.'

Blake leaned forward.

'I really don't see that anything in my client's past has a connection to whether or not she knew Mrs Dawson.'

'Mr Blake, I feel that there is a strong connection to the humiliating experience of being dumped by one man, and then setting her sights at a much lower level porter, who claims that not only was she just a one-night stand but that he never had any intention of marrying her . . .'

Gibbs had taken advice from DCI Shepherd to keep his questioning low key. Jane knew what he was after but it was not having the effect he was hoping for, as Katrina wasn't rising to the bait as she had done before. But her lawyer was.

'This is completely unacceptable, and purely supposition. My client would never have admitted to a relationship with a man you suggest she felt was of a lower level.'

'Oh shut up!' Katrina said. 'Can't you see what he is trying to do? If you can't think of anything better to interrupt with then keep your mouth shut ... he's just trying to goad me into admitting I was connected to that woman's death.'

Katrina crossed and uncrossed her legs, then folded her arms, glaring at Gibbs.

'Go on, Detective Gibbs, try and find some other ulterior motive that you think I might possibly have. I have been totally honest with you at all times. I have admitted that I did have an affair but I have also clearly stated that it was over as soon as I knew he was married. He also lied about the fact that he had a child, so I ended the relationship and left St Thomas' Hospital.'

Gibbs leaned forward and drew his file closer as he thumbed through page after page, all the while speaking quietly.

'Yes, this is all nice and tidy and I am sure you think totally believable. But you are a known liar, Miss Harcourt. You were fired from St Thomas' Hospital, as you have been on numerous previous occasions from various care homes, due to your unprofessional conduct. You have even been quoted as disliking having to work with dementia patients. So let's go back to just how important this so-called fling with Barry Dawson was, because I believe it was pretty desperate on your part.'

'Desperate?' Katrina snapped. 'Why don't you take a good look at me ... do you think I look like a desperate woman? You've got a bloody nerve. Take a look at yourself in the mirror. Has anybody ever told you that you stink of BO, and crunching peppermints doesn't hide your beer breath?'

Katrina then looked over at Jane.

'And as for that dull, flat footed Detective Tennison . . . I would describe the pair of YOU as being pretty desperate.'

Gibbs ignored her and continued.

'In my estimation, a woman who gets herself into debt buying a designer wedding gown and having herself photographed as a bride before the actual ceremony, and then gets jilted before getting to the altar, must be more than just desperate. Barry Dawson made promises, marriage proposals, and you also knew he owned their flat in a very nice location. All this must have sounded very enticing for a woman whose qualifications restricted her to agency work instead of full-time nursing staff.'

'Rubbish, you have no idea just how good the wages are for agency staff.'

'I am very aware; you were sharing a bedsit with another nurse, and you don't even own your car.'

Katrina pursed her lips and Jane was sure Gibbs was turning the tables as he continued.

'You have a record of unprofessional conduct and abusive behaviour working with the elderly. And to still be dependent on your parents . . . All of this would have been a very cumulative build-up to—'

'To what exactly?' Katrina interrupted.

'Getting rid of the woman who stood in your way.'

Jane was impressed as Gibbs kept going, but Katrina remained unperturbed. She crossed and uncrossed her legs again and sighed as he continued.

'You couldn't let his cheap little wife stand in your way . . . you wanted him to get a divorce. Mr Dawson says he ended the affair with you as he knew he had made a gross mistake. So he confessed to his wife about the one-night stand he had with you.'

'It was *not* a one-night stand!' Katrina spat. Jane could see that at last there was another small crack in her composure.

Gibbs was now stepping up the game, his voice louder and sharper as he leaned forward at the table.

'Shirley didn't quite believe it was over. So she followed her husband and took photographs of the woman he says was just a cheap one-night stand. Some woman ... *you* ... who worked at the hospital and was proving to be desperate and hard to get rid of. You'd been rejected and burned before by someone you rated a lot higher than a porter, so you took it into your own hands and decided you would call on Shirley Dawson.'

'I did not.'

'We have a witness. You paced up and down outside the building, didn't you? Was that to work your temper up, or in the hope that nobody saw you going inside the Dawsons' flat?'

Katrina looked at Blake. 'Why don't you interrupt?' She then turned back to Gibbs. 'Nobody saw me ... as I have said before, if you have a witness then put me in an ID parade.'

Gibbs knew he was flying by his shirt tail, but she had just slipped up and he needed to up the ante.

'The point is, Shirley Dawson was not the silly woman you wanted to believe her to be. In fact, she was quite the opposite. Let's face it, she was not only a lot younger than you, and very pretty, but she had something Barry would never let go – his daughter.'

'Heidi ...' Katrina said, in a surly and dismissive manner.

'Ah, so you know the little girl's name? So you must have been aware that Shirley was not about to agree to a divorce or let Barry bring in the "one-night stand". So, Miss Harcourt, you were going to be left in the lurch one more time and you were not prepared to take it, so you went to talk to Shirley yourself—'

Katrina interrupted. 'I know the child's name because Barry told me. I resent the way you keep on referring to me as a "one-night stand", and you ...' Katrina turned angrily and pointed at her lawyer. 'Why are you allowing this to continue? I am getting sick and tired of being shown such disrespect, when the reality is that as soon as I knew Mr Dawson had lied to me and we had no future together I ended the relationship. Whatever he has subsequently been saying about me are yet more lies. I did not wish to discuss anything with Shirley Dawson, and I never met her.'

Mr Blake nodded and then pointedly looked to Gibbs.

'I think my client does have a reasonable query as to why you persist in this line of enquiry. She has stated that her relationship with Mr Dawson was over for some time before the unfortunate incident occurred, and at no time discussed anything with the victim or visited her at her home.'

Jane wondered if Gibbs was losing it as Katrina was nodding overconfidently. Then he opened a file of photographs. He picked up an enlarged image of the shaven-headed Shirley Dawson, with the clear head wound in the shape of a V which they had matched to the iron she had been using. Next he took out the same-sized photograph of the wound to Shirley's forehead.

Blake looked shocked as both pictures were placed down side by side in front of Katrina.

'Miss Harcourt, we know you were at the Dawsons' flat on the morning of her murder. She let you in through the main building door thinking you were her mother-in-law, and you went up to the top floor. She was very surprised to see you. Whether or not you intended to, you picked up the red hot iron and slammed it into the side of her head.'

'I was not there! This is all lies!'

'You have been lying, Miss Harcourt, and Mr Dawson has given us details of exactly how the murder of his wife occurred. I sincerely think that this is now the time to start telling the truth. You have to be aware that we have enough evidence to charge you—'

'Whatever he has told you is not the truth! He is a liar! He is a two-faced LIAR!'

Jane felt her stomach lurch as she observed Gibbs's progress. Katrina's fists were clenched tight and her face was twisted with rage. As her lawyer reached out to take her hand she snatched it away.

'Don't start trying to help this situation now! If Barry is implicating me in something I did not do then I am not going to be framed and made to be the guilty one. I am totally innocent ... I never touched her, I swear on my life ... I never did that to her.'

Katrina pushed the photographs away from her, and one slid onto the floor. Jane bent down and picked it up, placing it back down on the table.

'Take that out of my sight!' Katrina shouted.

'But this was what was done to her, Miss Harcourt. Someone, either you or Mr Dawson, slammed the red hot iron into the side of her head and then—'

'I didn't do it!' she screamed.

Gibbs kept his voice low.

'So what exactly did you do, Miss Harcourt? Because now is the time to tell us the truth. Barry Dawson is so confident that he is innocent that he didn't even request any legal representation.'

Katrina's face creased into a snarl as she leaned forward.

'I'll tell you what that two-faced liar did.'

Barry Dawson had his head bent low as tears streamed down his cheeks. In front of him on Shepherd's desk were the two identical photographs of the injuries sustained by his wife.

'So help me God, I didn't do that! I swear to you. I would never have hurt Shirley! It was Katrina ... she's crazy, and because of her it was all getting messed up ... she wouldn't leave me alone. I can't lie any more.'

Up until now he had claimed that the first he knew about his wife's drowning was when he had arrived home and found her in the bath. Now he changed his story, and the tears flowed as he sobbed.

'Take me through exactly what happened on the morning of your wife's death, Barry ... get it all off your chest, it will make it easier for you if you talk it all through. Come on, son, start telling us the truth.' Shepherd spoke calmly, coaxing Barry to confess.

Barry nodded and took a deep breath.

'I was on duty, at work, and I was in the porters' rest room when they put a call in to me. That's how we get instructions to go to where we are needed, via the phone in the porters' room. It was Katrina – because she knew the extension number, she could call directly. She was hysterical ... she said she was at my flat and there had been an accident.'

'What time was that?' Shepherd asked quietly.

'Be about eight o'clock ... maybe a bit later. I had been on since six thirty and was due for a break. I took the short cut out of the hospital, going through the mortuary then across the courtyard. I left my porter's jacket in the mortuary.'

'Why didn't you just ask to leave?'

'Because of what she had said ... that Shirley didn't look good.'

'You mean she described what she had done?'

'In a way yes, I mean, I dunno ... she just said they had been fighting and she had hit out at Shirley.'

'You mean that she said she was unconscious, or bleeding, or what?'

'Yeah, that she couldn't get her to come round.'

'But isn't Miss Harcourt a qualified nurse?'

'Yes, and that's why I was so freaked out because I was desperate to find out if Shirley was all right. I mean, she would know because she is a nurse, and then I got into a panic about my daughter being there.'

*

Katrina was sitting with her hands folded in her lap. She had explained that Barry had called her very early on the morning Shirley died. He told her that he was not going to be on duty and wanted her to come round to the flat to talk to Shirley about the divorce.

'Well, I was not very willing to agree because I had finished with him and I'd left my job at the hospital to get away from him. He begged me to meet him there, so I agreed and drove to London. I think I got there about eight in the morning. I mean, I was really worried about going up to the flat and I walked up and down the road a few times outside before I rang the bell.'

Jane watched intently. Katrina spoke very clearly and without any emotion, only occasionally lifting her hands in a theatrical manner to emphasize a point. It was as though she was performing to an audience and Jane was certain she was lying.

'When I got to the top floor Barry came out, in a terrible state. He said that he had fought with Shirley over him leaving her and that she had refused to ever leave the flat, and told him he would have to pay the mortgage and all child maintenance. He was in such a rage that he had struck her with the iron, and now he thought she was dead ...'

Barry had straightened out, as if spilling out the whole story was making him less tense. He explained that he had caught a taxi back to his flat and arrived at about eight thirty. He had run up the stairs and found Katrina in a state of panic, with Shirley lying on the floor still unconscious, or so Katrina had told him.

'She was lying by the ironing board, face down and not moving at all, and Katrina was crying, saying over and over that it wasn't her fault.'

Barry had to gather himself before he could continue. He seemed overwhelmed with shame.

'She had run a bath. Katrina said that she was dead and what we should do was put her in the bath and leave her. But I said we couldn't do that as Heidi, my daughter, was there and I couldn't leave her alone. Then I remembered my mother was coming to babysit at nine, so I agreed to do what she wanted me to do.'

'I helped Barry carry her into the bathroom. She'd been running a bath before I got there and he said we should just leave her in it. He was expecting his mother to come, so the baby wasn't going to be left for too long.'

Barry lifted his arms to demonstrate how they carried Shirley to the bathroom and put her down in the water, which was overflowing. He then became very agitated.

'But she wasn't dead ... she jerked up in my arms and the next minute I lost my grip of her ... Katrina started screaming that she was alive, and then she fell forward and hit her head on the water tap, and the next minute there was blood pouring from her nose and I couldn't hold on to her.'

'Can you explain to me exactly how Shirley fell forward?'

Gibbs was making copious notes.

'Barry put her in the bath, head to the right, feet

facing the taps, and he lowered her into the water. But it started overflowing and I don't know if it was because it was too hot or what, but the next minute Shirley jerked upwards and forward. She was alive, but he lost grip of her and she fell forward and slammed her forehead into the tap. She started to pour blood from her nose and I was screaming as she flopped back. Then the kid was screeching, and the dog was running in and out barking, and Barry had to grab it by its collar and drag it out.'

Shepherd tapped his notebook.

'Just let me get this clear, Barry, because it is very important I understand exactly what you are saying. Shirley was placed unconscious into the bath, her feet towards the taps, and the bath was overflowing. Then she suddenly came round?'

'Yes, she sat up but flopped forward and hit her head on the main tap. It cut her head and then she sort of made this snorting sound as blood poured from her nose and then she slid back and went under the water.'

Katrina crossed her legs.

'It was just terrible ... I mean, Barry was totally losing it and crying, and with his wretched child screaming as well, and he had hit the dog with the leather lead so it was howling. I was trying to make him calm down because it was obvious that she was still alive, do you understand? I told him to look after her and said that I would go and see to the baby and give her a bottle.'

Barry was weeping again as he explained that Heidi had

started screaming and crying for her mummy, so he had gone out of the bathroom to settle her down and give her the bottle of milk that Shirley had left on the high chair. His dog had been running back and forth all the time, as Shirley usually took him out for his morning walk.

'I put him in his cage, but he was barking and I had to really restrain him. It was only a few minutes but Katrina came out of the bathroom and said that Shirley was dead, and we should both get our stories straight.'

He was wringing his hands.

'You see, I knew my mum was coming over because Shirley had a hair appointment, so I knew the baby wouldn't be left on her own for too long. Katrina dropped me off at the mortuary. I had to get back to the hospital and look like I had never left. I called home but there was no answer, and I knew by this time that my mother should have been there to babysit. So I called her and she said that she was waiting for an engineer to fix her washing machine. She had tried to call Shirley, got no reply, but told me not to worry as she had probably taken Heidi to the hair salon with her. But I knew she hadn't ... I borrowed some change off a mate and kept on acting like I was calling, and then I went home.'

Katrina leaned back in her seat.

'It was obvious she was dead ... there were no more bubbles from her mouth, and her eyes were wide open.'

Barry kept his eyes to the floor and his voice sounded hoarse.

'I knew she was dead. Katrina said she wasn't

breathing and there were no bubbles coming out from her mouth or nose, and her eyes were wide open.'

The two suspects had now been charged with the murder of Shirley Dawson and had been taken back to the cells. The following day they would be taken before a Magistrates' Court for the charges to be formally heard and a trial date set.

It was five o'clock when DS Lawrence had a match of Katrina's thumb and forefinger print on one of the coins from the payphone taken from the hallway. However, by the time he had relayed the information it was all over. The evidence would be used to prove that Katrina lied about not calling Barry Dawson from the flat.

It had been a long day and everyone was tired, but satisfied at the eventual outcome. Jane had heard Gibbs relaying Katrina's behaviour to DCI Shepherd, and how she had tried to put the blame on Barry. Shepherd had laughed, saying that Barry had done exactly the same with his story.

'Which one held her under?' Gibbs asked. Without hesitation Shepherd said he would put his money on Katrina. But in reality it didn't matter because they had both committed murder and would go down for it.

Jane was walking along a corridor on the ground floor as Richard Blake approached. He had his raincoat folded over his arm. Jane had watched his interaction during the interview with Katrina, and had witnessed how ill-equipped he had been to handle the situation or control his client. Jane acknowledged Mr Blake and he hesitated. His face looked grey with fatigue, and he seemed to be fighting to say something about the awful afternoon he had just been forced to sit through. When he did speak he surprised Jane because it was something so inadequate.

'I play golf with her father every first Sunday of the month.'

Jane was now officially off duty. She collected her coat and popped her head into the incident room to see Edith still there.

'You're here late, Edith? Are you coming over to join us at the pub? Everyone's celebrating.'

'Listen, with the amount of work I've got to type up from DCI Shepherd I could be here all night ... I have to say, I didn't think the husband did it, did you?'

Jane shrugged. 'I don't know. I mean, Katrina Harcourt was a real piece of work and I was very impressed with Spence ... he really handled her well and sort of cornered her. He constantly referred to her as being a "one-night stand", which she hated, but it took a long time.'

'Yes and all his notes have to be typed up. It's going to be a lot of work checking and double-checking all the statements, you know ... he did this, she did that, and they blamed each other so that's all got to be investigated ready for the trial. It'll be months of work.'

Jane nodded. 'One of them held her under the water. Katrina says that Barry held her and he says she did, but what's interesting is that they both describe the same thing about waiting until there were no bubbles ... so they both had to be in the bathroom.'

'Well, they deserve what they'll get. It'll be a big trial

with lots of publicity … there's already been a press release. Headlines will be "Murder in the Bath" by tomorrow, and with it being a twosome even more press will be hungry. That redhead'll love it.'

Jane put on her coat. She felt confused. Barry had appeared to be so emotionally distraught when she had first met him in the neighbours' basement. He had also appeared to be very honest when she had taken his statement and the tears seemed genuine when he had identified his wife's body. She remembered watching him as he walked away from the mortuary, and how bereft he had seemed … And all the time he knew what he had done. Jane realised she was a very poor judge of character and wouldn't make the same mistake again.

'Jailhouse Rock' was playing on the juke box. The CID team had pushed three tables together and there were bottles of wine and beer, and similar to the fare served at the Warburton Arms there was an array of shrunken sausage rolls, curling sandwiches and packets of crisps. Gibbs passed Jane a glass of wine as she sat down next to Lawrence.

'Well, I got there eventually! The fingerprints were confirmation that Katrina Harcourt lied about the phone call. It will be useful evidence in the trial for the prosecution – two fingerprints on the same coin. The coins from the machine at the Dawsons' building all had to be checked by eye match print. Each one had to be carefully laid out on white paper and dusted—'

Jane interrupted his overly detailed description.

'Congratulations. As you said, it was a long shot.'

'Well, it's going to be one hell of a schlepp to the trial. But we all got there in the end. It was seeing you with the coins in your hand about to use the Dawsons' phone box ... it just clicked! As you said, it was a long shot. But it paid off, and ...'

Jane realized that DS Lawrence must have been in the pub for quite a while and it sounded as if he was about to detail the entire forensic department's discovery of Katrina Harcourt's fingerprints to them all.

Gibbs pulled over a chair and took out his wallet.

'Right, everybody, place your bets. Which one of them held Shirley Dawson down in the bath?'

As the rest of the team took out various coins and notes, Jane had a second glass of wine. Gibbs nudged her.

'Come on, Tennison, who are you betting on?'

'I think they both did it.'

'No, no, no ... you've got to bet on one or the other!'

'I think it was Katrina ... I'll put a fiver on it.'

'Fiver on for Katrina!' Gibbs shouted loudly.

'Make that another fiver,' Lawrence joined in. 'I say it was Katrina too. As you know, with my scientific prowess, I was able to provide the vital evidence from the coins in the phone box ...'

Gibbs looked at Lawrence despairingly. 'Oh God ... here we go again!'

By the time Jane left the pub it didn't look as if there were going to be any winnings as the bets were all being spent on drinks.

It was already 9.30 p.m. so she decided that, as she

hadn't yet managed to get through to Peter Allard's wife, she would ring her again. She wondered if perhaps Marie just wanted to get in touch to find out if a trial date had been set. She made a mental note to be very careful about exactly what she was going to discuss as she was using the payphone in the reception area of the section house. Jane dialled the number in her notebook. The phone rang for a long time before Marie answered.

'Hello?' Her voice wavered like a child's.

'Is this Marie Allard? This is Detective Jane Tennison ... I understand you've been trying to contact me?'

'Yes ...' There was a pause.

'Are you all right, Marie?'

'I need speak with you ... but not on phone ... to your face, please. I need your help, but it private.'

Jane didn't think it was wise to go and see her straight away as she had consumed three glasses of wine in the pub.

'I'm off duty in the morning ... how about I come to your house at nine o'clock tomorrow?'

'Thank you ... thank you very much.'

Jane replaced the handset and headed towards her room. It had been a very long day, but one she had learned a lot from. She would be careful how she approached Marie, and mindful of what she said as she didn't want any repercussions from DI Moran. She had made a mistake in talking to her at the Magistrates' Court and had been reprimanded, so at the meeting she would not take any chances.

*

DI Moran still felt very queasy. He had ordered some

chicken and sweetcorn soup as he couldn't face anything too solid. DC Edwards was tucking into beef chow mein and crispy sweet and sour pork with fried rice. They were dining at the Golden Dragon, a small Chinese restaurant in the outskirts of Maidstone.

'I think this is him, guv . . .' as the bell tinkled signalling a customer entering through the door.

Moran turned to see a very broad-shouldered, ruddy faced man with grey-streaked hair, who almost filled the open doorway.

'Ahhh, Moran? Victor Bethell.' He walked over and held out his huge hand, shaking Moran's hand vigorously.

Moran gestured to Bethell to sit down with them. 'This is DC Brian Edwards. Nice to meet you. Glad you found the place.'

Bethell turned to a hovering Chinese waiter.

'I'll have a whole crispy duck, pancakes, plum sauce and fresh vegetables.'

Bethell took off his duffle coat and pulled out an old notebook from an inside pocket, tossing it on the table. The waiter took his coat to hang it up and Bethell sat his large frame down rather precariously on a small chair.

'You were lucky to get hold of me . . . I retired two years ago. I put my pension into a motor home. Me and the wife are driving to Folkestone for a very carefully planned six-month tour of the Continent.'

If Moran had had a headache first thing that morning, he now had what felt like a severe migraine. Bethell's booming voice was like a hammer in his head. A few

Chinese customers kept darting fearful glances towards their table.

'I am very grateful you agreed to see us,' Moran replied, taking a slurp of his soup.

'When your young DC contacted the station they immediately got on to me because I handled the case. It's all packed up in the cold files, and if needs be I can get one of the detectives there to get it out.' He looked at DC Edwards. 'But this youngster wanted to have a chat about it first.'

Moran took another spoonful of soup, then pushed the bowl aside.

'So what can you tell us about Susie Luna?'

The big man opened his notebook.

'Well, for starters it's such a simple name ... you never forget it.'

'She was missing?' Moran asked, wanting to get on with it.

'Yes, she was. She was a Filipino who worked as a chambermaid in one of the hotels ... pretty little thing.'

'So what was the consensus?'

'Foul play – she had one and a half thousand pounds in the bank, she left all her clothes in the room she rented, she gave no notice at the hotel, and she was liked. We had a couple of sightings around the town, but then she just disappeared off the face of the earth.'

'Do you think she was abducted? Kidnapped? Murdered ...? Did you find her passport?'

'Nope. She was last seen leaving the staff exit at the hotel where she worked, and that was it. No other sightings.'

Moran leaned to one side as the waiter brought Bethell's

order. He was impatient to get to the point of why they had asked to meet, but he waited until the various dishes had been laid in front of the retired detective before he quietly spoke.

'You never found a body. But did you have a suspect?'

With great dexterity Bethell placed a pancake on his plate, spread the plum sauce, then used his fork to shred the crispy duck and carefully laid it onto the pancake.

'His name was Peter Allard. His wife, Marie Allard, was Filipino and worked at the same hotel.'

CHAPTER TWENTY-TWO

Jane rang the doorbell for the second time, and waited. She stepped back from the porch and looked over to a side window where she saw the curtain drawn back for a second. Jane had already doubted her reasons for coming all the way to Walthamstow, and it was much further than she had calculated because the previous time she had been at the house was as a passenger in a patrol car. It really did seem such a long time ago. She had still been in uniform as a probationary WPC, and the Allard case had been her first introduction to CID.

'Who is it?' Marie asked nervously from behind the front door.

'It's WDC Tennison, Mrs Allard ... you wanted to talk to me?'

Jane waited as various locks and a chain link were undone. Marie opened the door and gestured for her to come in, then quickly closed the door and replaced the chain.

'To stop my mother-in-law from getting in. She very trying and is making my life a misery.'

Jane was ushered into the kitchen and Marie offered

her tea or coffee, but she declined both. Without taking her coat off she asked if there was anything wrong that Marie wished to talk to her about, and apologized for the delay in returning her call.

'I given up on you,' Marie said, and pulled out a chair to sit down. She pointed to the one next to her for Jane to use.

'I have no one else ... well, I not mean I not know anyone ... I not have anybody that I can talk to about it and now I am very anxious, and my mother-in-law ask me lots of questions and I am frightened to answer the phone in case it is her, and ...'

Marie started to take deep breaths and wave her hand in front of her chest.

'I sorry, I get this panic and my lungs not work properly ... I sorry ...'

It was a few moments before Marie calmed herself down, and then started to cry, getting up to fetch a box of tissues. Eventually Jane was able to ask why Marie needed to talk to her, and bit by bit she opened up about the blackmail phone calls, the money drops, and that her mother-in-law had discovered the £1,000 missing from the joint account with her husband. She was sobbing.

'I cannot see my husband because of the stress ... I had to lie about the last five hundred pounds ... he was becoming very angry with me ... He tell me what to do, but I not see who take the money wrapped in the newspaper.'

Jane had asked if she could take down some details, so as the story unfolded she made pages of notes, trying to ascertain exactly what the chronological order was, as sometimes Marie jumped back and forth as she tried to explain.

'Do you mind if I just go through everything you have told me? I need to understand clearly exactly what has been happening. First, you received a phone call from a woman, who you say sang a song to you and said she wanted five hundred pounds in cash or she would go to the police with incriminating evidence that proved your husband had committed the rape he has denied?'

'Yes, yes ... that's it. I very scared because she said that if I not pay he would go away to prison for a very long time, and I not know what to do.'

'Yes, you said ... so you went to the prison and visited your husband, and you told him that you paid this woman and she then called again for the second time blackmailing you into paying five hundred pounds?'

'Yes. She gave me time to go to bank and said she would call me again. And I told Peter ... I told him this.'

Jane nodded, and turned a page in her notebook.

'Just repeat to me what he said, will you?'

Marie nodded.

'That it was the police ... that it was Detective Moran who lied and fitted him up ... that it was him doing blackmail and that I should just pay to get rid of him as he was bent copper. That how he describe the detective, as bent copper ... because he had framed him and he did not do the rape.'

Jane showed no reaction, but it was very difficult not to be shocked by the accusations against DI Moran. Marie continued describing how she had done as instructed and left the money wrapped in newspaper but she had not seen who collected it. She continued by detailing how the next call came from the same woman, and she wanted another £500. She told Jane how Peter had instructed her to place the money in the litter bin, get on the bus and then jump off to see if she could follow or identify who collected the money.

Marie started to cry again, and Jane had to wait until she calmed down before she falteringly described the ginger-haired boy and how she had seen him getting into a taxi, but had not seen who else was inside. Jane felt herself becoming deeply involved as she was certain the boy that Marie had seen fitted the description of the young red-haired boy with the gapped teeth whom she had questioned about Janet Brown.

'Can you go over the phone call again, Marie?'

'I told you ... she sings this song "Angie" something, and she keep repeating it over and over, I don't know if she is Angie or she is singing about someone else. It horrible. That's why I not pick up the phone at night no more.'

Jane felt herself becoming increasingly tense as she was certain that Angie was Janet Brown, with her connection to the red-haired boy. She asked Marie again if the woman had ever described just what evidence she had to implicate Peter Allard in the rape. Marie said that she had laughed and said that it was enough to find him guilty.

'How did Peter react when you told him that you paid another five hundred pounds?'

'He not know ... I told you, you not listening to me ... I said the woman never showed so I never paid.

But now my mother-in-law find out and she told him that I had withdrawn it from our joint bank account. She will make threats to me about the children. She is very interfering, she tries always to dominate me. Peter will go berserk when he knows I never saw who collected it … he certain it was that police detective because he swears that he is innocent and they set him up.'

Marie was going into repeat mode, and she was becoming more and more distressed. She started gasping for breath, then weeping uncontrollably, plucking one tissue after another out of the box.

'Marie, let me go away and think about all of this and I will get back to you in the morning. I really think you did the right thing in contacting me, but for now can you keep this just between us until I can establish what should be done?'

The front door was rebolted and the chain locked behind her as Jane left. She had been with Marie Allard for more than two hours, and felt exhausted by this new development. She didn't look at her lengthy notes but leaned back in her seat on the top deck of the bus and ran it all over in her mind.

Jane had already been warned once for working solo by DCI Shepherd, and even Gibbs had given her a tough talking to and reprimanded her for blowing his cover in Soho and wasting time on what he considered a piece of lowlife scum like Peter Allard. Jane decided that perhaps the one person she could talk to would be DS Lawrence.

DI Moran and DC Edwards had returned to Maidstone Police Station and were awaiting the release of Bethell's old files on the Susie Luna case. As impatient as ever, Moran paced up and down the small reception area of the 1950s station, checking his watch.

'How much longer do you think they're bloody well going to keep us waiting?'

Just then a very neat, chisel-faced officer introduced himself and handed Moran a worn cardboard box full of files, photographs and assorted evidence.

'I'm afraid nothing can be taken off the premises without my signature, but you are most welcome to use an interview room to sort through and select what items you require.'

'Thank you very much,' Moran said curtly.

'Follow me.' The detective led them down a dark corridor, up a flight of stairs and opened a porthole-windowed door to an interview room.

'There's a canteen upstairs if you want any refreshments. I'll be in the incident room next door if you need me.'

'Thank you very much,' Moran said, eager for the detective to leave.

He placed the worn cardboard box on a Formica-topped table as Edwards pulled up a hard-backed chair. Moran looked around the sparse room, taking in the grimy windows. Even the yellowing walls reminded him of Hackney Station, and yet this was a relatively 'new' building. He shook his head as he sat down at the table.

'Do you think every police station built in the fifties and sixties gets a bulk discount on pots of crappy paint?'

Edwards pulled the packing tape holding down the flaps of the dusty cardboard box and peered inside. Face up, in a cheap frame, was a photograph of Susie Luna. He took it out and held it up for Moran.

'Pretty little thing ... Got a rose in her hair ...'

Moran stared at the photograph, then placed it to one side.

'Right, let's see what else they've got ...'

Jane had spent a great deal of time on Sunday writing up Marie Allard's complaints and accusations against DI Moran. She knew that the following morning, she would have to have a serious conversation with a senior officer, as what Marie Allard had told her was a very grave allegation against Moran. If there was any truth in it then there would be some significant repercussions. Peter Allard had accused DI Moran of planting evidence in his rape case, and now he was inferring that he was part of a blackmail scam using a prostitute to collect a lot of money, now up to £1,000.

On Monday morning, Jane was glancing through her file when Gibbs appeared.

'Penny for 'em,' Gibbs said, as he stood by her desk. He looked smarter than usual, wearing a grey suit and white shirt, with a striped tie and loafer shoes.

'I'm sorry, I was miles away.' She looked up at him as he sat on the edge of her desk. 'You look very smart.'

'Yeah, well, had to look my best as all the press were there, the tabloids are loving it. I'd say we'll all be running around like blue-arsed flies when this bitch Harcourt gets to trial ... Man, is she a piece of work. She was lapping it up in court this morning, while Dawson was on suicide watch last night. He looked pitiful in court. Apparently he was heartbroken as his mother had had his dog put down.'

Jane licked her lips, then made the decision.

'Spence, can I have a private word with you about something? I don't know who else I can talk to about it, but I really need some guidance.'

He shrugged. 'Sure, fire away.'

'Do you mind if we go into your office? It's just quite, erm, sensitive and I need your advice ... but I don't want anything spread around.'

Gibbs cocked his head to one side, then slid off the desk and gestured for her to follow him. His office was smelly and an overflowing ashtray sat in the centre of his desk, surrounded by used cups and paper plates.

'Why don't they clean it up in here? Where's Edith?'

'She was here earlier, but she had to go over to the comms room. I'm not sure she'd appreciate you thinking of her as a cleaner, Spence?'

'I wasn't! It's just that if you want to have a private conversation, she's got ears on elastic.' He shut the door. By the time he had tossed everything into a waste bin Jane was getting cold feet.

'Right, WDC Tennison, I am all yours.'

'I was going to talk it through with Paul Lawrence but, as you've said, he's very busy ... and I don't have enough confirmation to talk to DCI Shepherd.'

'Well, go on, Jane, spill it out ...'

Jane hesitated, then took a deep breath. Keeping it as succinct and direct as possible, she told him the entire story. Gibbs was rather unnerving as he didn't interrupt, but laid his head down on top of his hands on his desk.

'And I think I should question this Janet Brown ... Remember, she was the prostitute who wore the blue rabbit fur coat that Moran gave me to wear when I was being a decoy. I know she has used "Angie" as one of her aliases ... what do you think?'

There was a short pause before Gibbs slowly lifted his head and looked at her.

'Jesus Christ, Tennison ... talk about kicking over a hornet's nest. There's stuff there that'll rise up and sting you.'

'But I'm not repeating anything that I haven't given serious thought to. That's why I needed to talk it through with someone.'

'Talk it through with someone? Unfortunately, that's me,' he snapped, and turned away, folding his arms across his chest.

'Right, just let me get this straight ... I'm going from the fuckin' beginning so that I get it right. That night after the Marquee Club, I told you to forget about this whore in the blue rabbit fur coat. You pay no attention to my warning about playing solo, and you totally disobey me ... and that same night you chase after this Janet Brown, or Angie, who's singing down the phone to Peter Allard's wife. Is it the Rolling Stones song?'

'I don't know. I had no intention of following her, but I saw her getting into a taxi and this boy being paid by her—'

'Yes, yes ... so Janet/Angie goes off in a taxi and you take after the kid?'

Jane nodded. 'Yes, exactly. I saw him going into this adult bookshop.'

Gibbs held up his hand.

'Now, you said a guy wearing a cowboy outfit called Stevie ran the shop, together with a big-titted blonde whose name you didn't hear, and the boy worked in the back room?' Jane opened her mouth to interrupt and he snapped, 'No, let me finish.'

He stood up and started pacing around the room.

'What you don't know is that Stevie Bishop and his wife Ada are virtually the Soho King and Queen of Vice. They have brothels and strip joints all around the red light district. They run the dirtiest sex rackets and are making a fortune. We know that Stevie has big clout with some very senior Metropolitan police officers, and he can buy his way out of any charges ... I am talking about paying over tens of thousands of pounds ... and you walk in with your DC card because you just want to speak to some red-haired kid?'

'I had no idea,' Jane said sheepishly.

'No, you very obviously didn't. I will have to check out if you stepped into a surveillance operation because they will have been royally pissed off if you did. The drug squad are also being brought in as Stevie and Ada are not satisfied with rolling in the money from the whores – they are starting to deal with international drug operations too. But it'll take a long time to bring down the King of Soho and his dirty grubby wife the Queen of Vice. Right now they are making elephantine fortunes on their dirty book trade, so they lavish big favours on the bent cops ... and I mean *huge* favours – cars, cash, holidays abroad ...'

Jane hesitated and asked nervously if Gibbs was

explaining the Soho sex trade business and police involvement because it was possible that DI Moran was behind the blackmail with Janet Brown.

'No I'm bloody not! I am simply warning you about treading into dangerous areas that you know fuck all about. This gap-toothed kid that runs for the whores, we need to snatch and grab him without it looking like we are in any way connected to the police.'

'You'll help me? Because he has to know where Janet Brown lives, and she is who we need to talk to. Because if she does have this evidence . . .'

Gibbs opened the door.

'I doubt she has, but we need to clear up this shit about DI Moran.' He barged out, leaving Jane to follow.

Gibbs booked out a plain patrol car and he and Jane headed for Soho.

On the way they stopped at a 'Hot Tea and Pie' cabin and Gibbs bought them both a sausage roll and a cup of tea. Jane was unsure about being seen eating and drinking in a police car and Gibbs laughed.

'Don't be dumb, you're not in uniform, and I've had more hot dinners in the front seat of a car than I have at home.'

Gibbs drove erratically, his coffee balanced precariously in the seat divide between them, while he held his sausage roll in a napkin in his right hand. They drove down Wardour Street, then left into Old Compton Street before doing the loop again as they passed numerous strip clubs. They crossed Berwick Street, which was filled with fruit and veg stalls, then into Beak Street and did yet another slow loop around into Shaftesbury

Avenue where there was bumper to bumper traffic. Returning to Wardour Street, Jane suddenly spotted the red-haired boy, this time with a very young blonde girl who was carrying a bag of feather boas.

'There he is!' Jane said.

Gibbs stopped the car.

'OK ... take over the driving and park up in that wasteland car park opposite the Windmill Theatre, and leave the back passenger door open.'

With his hands dug deep into his overcoat Gibbs got out of the car and took off down Berwick Street. His head was lowered as he gained momentum to walk directly behind the boy, who was laughing and chatting with the blonde girl who looked no more than fifteen or sixteen. They stopped outside 'Pretty Pussies' and the girl turned to go inside. As the boy was about to follow Gibbs used his right finger and thumb to snap a tight, painful hold on the nerves in the back of the boy's scrawny neck.

'You walk quietly along with me, son, or I cuff you and make out you're my informant and you're squealin', and everyone is gonna know ... I'm a Vice copper, sonny.'

The boy was in agony but he could only shrug his shoulders higher to relieve the pain in his neck. To anyone watching it looked as if Gibbs just had a friendly hand on the kid's neck. They continued down the road and then took a side turning to come out by the Windmill Theatre's stage door. Crossing the road, Gibbs could see Jane waiting in the patrol car.

The car park was an old bomb site that had been

developed as a parking facility. It wouldn't be for much longer as all the land in the West End was being used for more and more office and retail building. There was an elderly man sitting on a camping stool outside a crumbling wooden sentry box. In front of him was an upturned wooden wine crate with a tin box for selling day-long parking tickets. When he had glanced towards the open car Jane had shown him her ID and he gestured for her to park by a crumbling brick wall on the far side of what had been a crater. She watched Gibbs walking towards her, guiding the red-haired boy. It looked as if they were simply having a chat. Gibbs was smiling, and then as they reached the rear open passenger door he kept his hold of the boy's neck with his right hand but took out his handcuffs with his left. He pushed the boy forward, face down, into the back seat and drew his arms up painfully high to cuff his wrists. He kicked out at the boy's legs as he wriggled and swore and said that if he didn't pull his knees up he'd slam the door on his ankles and break them.

Jane was not exactly comfortable with Gibbs's heavy-handedness, but she had seen it all before when they had been at Hackney together. He had the nickname of 'The Slapper'. But as he was doing her a favour she sat silently watching as he slammed his fist hard into the boy's head, warning him to stay very quiet. She was now sitting in the passenger seat of the plain patrol car.

'Right, we have Philip Jackson, aged twelve. Lives on the Kenworth Estate, and his mother's a junkie called Wanda. Have I got this all correct, Philip?'

'Yes, sir.'

'You'd better not be bullshitting me ... I know where you work and I'll come back and beat the living daylights out of you. I could get you locked up and let Stevie and his wife know you're my informant, so ...'

'I don't fuckin' know nuffink. I just earn a few quid from the girls when I look after their gear backstage. I swear before God, I'm not running drugs.'

Gibbs leaned over the front passenger seat and slapped the boy's head hard, and he moaned.

'Right, this is what's going to happen. I'm going to ask you a few questions and I need you to answer honestly. If you don't, you'll be arrested for living off immoral earnings, you'll be held in the cells overnight to await transportation to a Borstal institution, and this lady here will contact social services to arrest your mother, and any other kids she lets work the strip joints.'

The boy started sniffing and Gibbs slapped him again. He then began asking Philip quietly about Janet Brown, wanting to know where she lived. At first he denied knowing her, but as soon as Gibbs mentioned the name 'Angie' it was obvious that he did. Gibbs waited as he muttered that he didn't know her address as she just worked the strip clubs in the afternoons, and other times at night, and all he did was look after her handbag as the other tarts were known to steal each others' belongings.

'I need her address, Philip ...'

'I dunno it! I never been to her pad, honest!'

'So, tell me about the time you picked up a bundle for Angie from the bus stop by the Grosvenor Hotel on Park Lane.'

Philip hesitated, then blurted out that Janet had asked

him to come with her one afternoon after she'd done a gig at the 'Dirty Girls' and he had got into a taxi with her. He had to get out and go to the bus stop and wait to see an oriental-looking lady. When he saw her put a package into the litter bin and get on the next bus he had to retrieve the package and take it back to Janet in the taxi. He said she gave him a ten pound note, then drove off in the taxi while he went and bought some shoes in Carnaby Street.

'Did she tell you what was in the package?' Gibbs asked.

'No, but I knew it was cash ... I saw it in the envelope.'

'Did she tell you why she was getting it?'

'No, just that she was owed it by some piece of scum.'

'Where does she live?'

'I dunno! I honest to God don't know!'

'Does she have a pimp?'

'No ... well, I never seen one with her. She's very tough and I just sometimes work for her, but she don't work for Stevie. He calls her dirty black trash ... she's got a weird accent, you know, like it's a made-up one ... like American.'

Gibbs sighed, then after a moment he turned and rubbed Philip's head.

'This is important, son. Do you know if Janet or Angie is used by the CID?'

'I don't understand what you mean.'

Jane turned to look at the boy, whose face was now pressed down into the back seat.

'Well, does she give a freebee once in a while, to uniforms or detectives? You know anything about that?'

'What you sayin'? She's a grass, like a tipster?'

Jane wanted to ask the boy a few questions but Gibbs wasn't allowing her to say a word, and in some ways she felt as if he was protecting Moran, never mentioning his name.

'No, I am asking if she screws around with the Old Bill.'

'No. She don't talk much. She knows what she wants me to do and I just look after her gear. She's a got a kid, I know that. He's brown like her, but I never seen him ... she had pictures of him in her wallet.'

'How do you know that?'

'Cos she takes it out and counts the money in it, in case I filch any. Like I said, she's tough and knows the ropes ... and she don't mix with the other slags.'

Gibbs climbed out and walked round to the rear passenger door behind Jane. He opened the door and Philip cowered away, but Gibbs just yanked him out by his legs. He unlocked the cuffs and then pushed the boy to stand upright, leaning towards him.

'I'm letting you go, son, but you had better not be lying to me because I will come back to get you.'

Jane looked through the window of the patrol car as Gibbs gripped the boy's chin, making his mouth purse open like a goldfish. They had words, then the boy scuttled away, passing the sleeping parking attendant who would get more customers later when the shows started their evening performances. Gibbs climbed in beside Jane and started the engine.

427

'OK, we need to find this bitch. So far Marie Allard's story that she was being blackmailed pans out, but it could be a load of lies. Or this Angie, or Janet, might have something that could prove Allard was the rapist. I don't think DI Moran is involved . . . he wouldn't be that crazy. The kid's just said that Angie is often around the clubs later when it gets dark . . . she collects the money for the numbers game and takes it over to the big man in Chinatown. So tonight I think we should check out the strip clubs. You up for that?'

Jane didn't reply. Deep down she began to feel that perhaps Gibbs wanted to keep on trying to trace Janet Brown because he was also unsure about Moran.

'Why don't we leave the car here and get something to eat, until this place hots up? Do you fancy some Italian? Luigi's is around the corner from here. We can have a pizza, kill a few hours until the strip clubs get going?'

Moran was sitting in the CID office at Hackney Station. DCs Ashton and Edwards, alongside two other detectives, watched as Moran pinned up the photograph of Susie Luna, which he had taken out of its frame. He proceeded to put up various smaller photographs, some black and white, and numerous Polaroids. He then chalked on the board 'Susie Luna – Aged 17, Filipino, Chambermaid/Waitress/Barmaid, Majestic Hotel, Maidstone. Missing since 15th March 1969.' Two more officers came into the office and perched on the edge of a couple of desks, eager to find out what was going on.

Moran tossed the chalk aside and stuffed his hands into his pockets.

'Brian here was doing some checks into previous possible assault cases in connection with the Peter Allard case. The reason I'm questioning this is because there have been a few queries from Allard's defence counsel about his confession. It might stand firm, I bloody hope it does, but in the meantime Perry Mason here came across this case.'

Moran pointed up to the board.

'Susie Luna, the girl with the rose in her hair. Her body was never found. We have four statements from the officer leading the inquiry ... Guess who he was questioning?'

'Peter Allard!' Edwards exclaimed.

'Well, I know you know that, you bloody idiot, but these lot didn't. Allard was living in Maidstone – pin that up, Edwards.'

Moran pointed to a photograph of a two-up, two-down terraced corner house. 'Right, we know Allard rented this property with his Filipino wife, who had also worked at the Majestic Hotel and was close friends with the victim, Susie Luna, so the two women knew each other.'

Looking over the information board, Ashton reacted.

'Bloody hell! You think Allard killed her?'

'He has a watertight alibi, provided by his wife. He wasn't arrested because there were three sightings of Susie Luna: on a bus, at a bus stop, and outside a fish and chip shop.'

'So he's not connected then?' Ashton asked.

'No ... on the contrary. I think he *is* connected, and I need to find more evidence that'll get me authority from the Kent Constabulary to have the garden in Maidstone excavated,' Moran replied.

Jane had ordered a *salade niçoise*, having already had a sausage roll on the way to Soho. Gibbs, however, was wading through a very large dish of lasagne and had already consumed two glasses of Chianti.

'Did you always suspect that Barry Dawson had murdered his wife?' Jane asked.

'Not to begin with. I mean, I was there when it was recorded as a non-suspicious death. But later, you know, when suspicions were flying I remembered something about him.'

'Like what?'

'The dog ... he was snapping and growling at everyone, and was shut in his cage. I wasn't that keen on it being brought in the car with me. His mother kept going on about it being nice tempered, then when Barry got the lead and opened the cage the poor thing cowered back and was terrified of him.'

'Yes, I remember ... and I also recall his mother saying that it was a sweet-natured dog.'

'When those two were carrying Shirley's body to put it in the bath they said the dog was barking and running around, and it woke up the little girl. In a statement to DCI Shepherd Barry admitted that he had whipped the dog to be quiet and had put him in the cage.'

Jane glanced at Gibbs. He never ceased to fascinate her because the more she got to know him the more sides of him he allowed her to see.

'I knew something was bad about Dawson then – a

dog only cowers in fear for a reason, especially as it was normally well behaved.'

Jane nodded. She wondered at what point she herself had been suspicious and was concerned that it hadn't been for a considerable time.

'I didn't immediately think he had any connection as he was obviously so emotionally distraught ... I felt that he was very genuine. To see him cradling his little girl in the neighbours' basement, having just found his wife, was deeply distressing for me to witness. It wasn't until there were small pieces of the jigsaw that didn't match up ... his lies about Katrina, and his attempts to give himself an alibi with the phone calls. He suddenly transformed from being a compassionate, loving husband to a weak, blubbering man.'

Gibbs interjected. 'But he wasn't bad-looking, and Katrina obviously thought he was a good catch ...'

Before Jane could respond Gibbs signalled to the waiter for the bill and glanced at his watch. It was almost 9.30 p.m.

'Right, the tarts should be out, and we should go and find your girl ...'

CHAPTER TWENTY-THREE

Jane and Gibbs had walked along Wardour Street twice and were now heading towards Berwick Street.

'There she is!' Jane exclaimed.

The blue rabbit fur coat stood out in the neon lights from the various sex shops and strip clubs. Jane was very mindful of the red-haired boy appearing, but there was no sign of him, and maybe they had scared him enough not to get back to work straightaway.

Suddenly there were large groups of men standing outside the strip clubs, as the hustle and bustle of the seediest part of the West End kicked in. Heavy muscle men stood outside the strip joints stopping any customers they didn't like the look of from coming inside. Deafening music played loudly from every doorway, as if in competition with each other.

Gibbs stopped. 'Where the hell did she go?'

Jane shrugged and shook her head.

Taxis dropped and picked up girls and customers, and the hookers moved along the street showing off their figures and backcombed beehive hairstyles. They wore an assortment of red plastic macs, high-heeled patent shoes and miniskirts that were so small they looked like curtain pelmets. Some had on silver and gold hot pants, showing off their bum cheeks in fishnet stockings. They wore glittering earrings, bracelets and necklaces, and many of them revealed too much cleavage to be decent, in skintight boob tubes. These were the street girls, and hurrying from one venue to the next were the strippers. They carried their costumes and wigs in tote bags, their faces plastered with thick makeup and false eyelashes, as they ducked and dived between the strip joints. Many of them were doing three to four shows a night.

Incongruously, as Jane and Gibbs moved nearer to the high-priced revue bars, smartly dressed men and women mingled with the crowd. The most famous club, the Raymond Revuebar, was very popular. The narrow road was filling up with classy cars, while women in glamorous long dresses and furs were escorted by men in evening suits. They were greeted at the entrance of the bar by a suitably attired doorman.

Gibbs was getting pissed off. 'Well, she must be around here somewhere . . . I need a leak, so I'm popping into the pub.' He went into the Queen's Head, leaving Jane waiting outside.

Having done the business, Gibbs ordered a bottle of Coke, and drank three quarters of it before asking the barman to fill it up to the neck with vodka. He then went back out to Jane, who was clearly very frustrated that Janet had disappeared.

'We lost her,' Jane said.

'Terrific! Listen, the kid, the red-haired boy, he said

she hangs out in Chinatown. Let's go back and get the car and head over there.'

Gibbs started up the engine and they began to reverse out of the car park. The old parking attendant removed the rope from the cratered area, hoping for a tip, but he didn't get one.

'It's unbelievable watching the real lowlife cheek by jowl with the fancy people getting out of their flash cars, all dressed up to see the fan dancers and sequinned strippers,' Jane commented.

'Grow up, sweetheart ... most of the hostesses in those swanky places are on the game and charge a fortune for a glass of cheap fizz and a feel up. But I doubt your Janet is in their league, or she wouldn't be working that patch over at London Fields. She might be working in one of the brothels ... hard to know. They use plain white, nondescript doors and the girls are out the back in all the shitty little partitioned bedrooms. The entrances are more'n likely in Wardour Street. You'd be amazed how many smart-looking Private Members' clubs are fronts for seedy brothels. I can do a drive past, but then I'm calling it quits for tonight.'

They drove up the entire length of Wardour Street and right onto Oxford Street, before heading back south around Soho Square and into Greek Street, but there was no sign of Angie. Determined to keep looking, they crossed over to Dean Street and back up to Oxford Street, before returning down Wardour Street. Reaching the end of the road they were about to turn left into Shaftesbury Avenue when Jane was sure she saw the blue rabbit fur coat. Directly across the road was the start of Chinatown, with all the lanterns swinging on ropes across a pedestrianized area. There were numerous small, lit-up restaurants and noodle bars, with flashing lights and throngs of customers. The streets were filled with people buying Chinese food in takeaway cartons, and there was a strong, slightly sickly sweet smell of frying chicken and fish.

'It's her, I'm sure of it! D'you see her, Spence? She's outside the restaurant with a blue neon sign above it ... her blue fur coat's obvious.'

Jane started to open the car door and clamber out.

'Hang on, just hang on. You don't go out here alone.'

An irate driver behind them sounded his horn as Gibbs made a hand signal for him to overtake. He then mounted the pavement and reversed a few yards. As soon as the engine stopped, Gibbs and Jane were both out and running beside a theatre with huge posters advertising the big hit musical *Joseph and the Amazing Technicolor Dreamcoat*. The main entrance for Chinatown was now a few yards ahead. Gibbs was moving faster than Jane, turning out of her sight for a moment. As she caught up he held out his arm for her to stop beside him.

'Stay back a minute, Jane ... she's heading straight towards us ...'

Gibbs stepped forward, saying Angie's name. Jane, almost directly behind him, moved to try and block her from passing saying, 'We just need to talk to you.'

Without missing a beat Janet side-stepped and made a run for it, heading straight into Shaftesbury Avenue.

A bus missed her by a terrifying few feet and, with traffic moving both ways beside her, she tried to make it across the road. Gibbs was dodging oncoming vehicles and held his hand up in the air as if it was some kind of warning that he was a police officer. Janet made the mistake of turning back to look at him. The oncoming green Mini estate screeched to a halt as it clipped her left hip and she flipped up into the air and sprawled over the bonnet. Jane made it to the pavement as the distressed driver climbed out, shouting that the woman had run directly into him. Gibbs dragged Janet up onto her feet and gripped both hands on her fur coat, hauling her away.

'She's fine ... just get back into your car and drive off. Move it.'

Jane picked up Janet's tote bag, which had fallen from her hand when she was flung over the bonnet, and she was beside Gibbs as he dragged Janet to their patrol car. She didn't scream and seemed to be in a state of shock, heaving for breath. As Gibbs opened the passenger door she started kicking and punching, and then snarled as she tried to bite his hand.

Gibbs backhanded her hard and, shoving her into the car face forward, he chucked the keys to Jane and instructed her to drive. He had his whole weight on Janet as he pushed her face down and told her she was under arrest, and that they were CID. She seemed to deflate like a punctured rubber tyre, then swore at him.

'You fuckin' arseholes! I need a doctor ... you bastards ...'

Jane was shaking badly as she drove through the West

End and headed towards a multi-storey car park that Gibbs suggested they use to ask Angie some questions. The car park was regularly used by the Met and the attendant lifted up the barrier and asked no questions. They went up to the fourth floor where it was partly open, with only a few cars parked. Gibbs gestured for Jane to drive to the furthest corner, then instructed her to reverse and park up.

Janet had grown quiet and Gibbs allowed her to sit up beside him. She was complaining about the pain in her hip and had rubbed it, then pulled down her elastic skirt waistband to check it out. Only as they parked up and Jane switched off the engine did Janet show she was scared. She had a deep, rasping, husky voice that sounded part cockney and part American.

'I don't like this . . . I want to know what you two are after. You got to show me some fuckin' ID cos I don't believe you are coppers.'

Gibbs took out a packet of cigarettes and offered her one. She shook her head, and he lit one for himself. He gestured towards Jane who turned to face her.

'That is WDC Jane Tennison. She was stationed at Hackney until recently, and was part of the investigation into a series of sexual assaults. She was subsequently on the arrest of the perp, who is also being accused of rape. WDC Tennison was given your coat to wear. Why was that?'

'I dunno'

'Why did she need to wear something that made her look like you? It's a very distinctive coat, Janet, or do you prefer to be called Angie?'

LYNDA LA PLANTE

She shrugged and gestured for Gibbs to open the
window as the smoke was wafting in her face from his
cigarette.

'The arresting officer was DI Nick Moran ... you
know him?'

'No.'

'You know anything about the rapist?'

'No.'

'He was caught trying to assault WDC Tennison in
your coat, so shall we start again?'

'They sell 'em in Brick Lane. They also come in pink,
and three different sizes ... small, medium and large,
and you can call me any name you like, you bastard.'

'Don't make me angry. I am going to give you one
last chance to give me some answers. Firstly, about the
severe beating you took; secondly, about DI Moran's
relationship with you; and thirdly, how your coat was
used in a CID covert operation and then you got it back,
as you are still wearing it.'

He slapped Janet hard on the back of her head and
she jolted forward and then rocked back. Jane decided
that enough was enough and leaned over from the front
seat.

'Please, Spence, will you let me talk to her? There's no
need for you to get physical ...'

'Oh, I see ... we're going to play good cop, bad cop,
are we? You lot make me sick.'

Gibbs gave Janet another hard slap, took out his
handcuffs and gripped her wrist. He clicked them on
and then attached one end to the door handle.

'She's all yours, for ten minutes.'

Gibbs reached into the front seat shelf and pulled out his Coke bottle, then opened the door and slammed it shut. Jane turned her body round in the front seat and pulled up her legs so she was raised higher and was able to lean towards Janet.

'Please don't make him angry ... we're trying to get to the truth. It is a very serious offence to withhold evidence, and for an officer to be connected to that offence will have severe repercussions that will give us reason to arrest you.'

'I haven't fuckin' done anything wrong! I don't know what you are bloody talking about. Just what offence am I supposed to have done? I tell you what is an offence, you two almost getting me bloody run over and then kidnappin' me, and bringing me to this shit-hole.'

'A bigger offence will be you leaving your son on his own while you are in Holloway, because that's where you are going to be sent for a long time.'

'Pleeease don't try that one ... you're fishin' and you ain't gonna catch me, because I've been around far longer than you ever had hot dinners. If you had anything on me I'd be down the station banged up, instead of being handcuffed with an amateur DC who looks like a teenager let out by Mummy and Daddy for the night.'

Jane felt her hackles rising.

'You listen to me ... I was the officer that got attacked, wearing your coat stinking of your perfume. He tried to rape me, split my lip open, but it is nothing compared to what he did to that poor kid he raped and left for dead. I have to be honest that I was not sure about him committing the rape of that seventeen-year-old, but if you have evidence to prove he is the rapist then you are letting him walk free ... Why? Just tell me why?'

'Money.'

'What?'

'He owes me, that's why.'

'Owes you? But that doesn't make any sense ... You would let him off the hook because he owes you?'

'He did this to me ...'

Janet pulled open her shirt and there was a deep scar just below her throat and across her breasts. It was shocking and Jane couldn't think of anything to say as Angie did up her blouse.

'Screwed me up for stripping in any decent club. Besides, I just wanted to get some compensation. I'd have given it up in time, before his trial anyway.'

'Given what up? I mean, do you really have incriminating evidence? Come on, start talking to me, I know about the phone calls to Allard's wife, I know you were blackmailing her into paying you a lot of money and I am asking you now to be honest with me.'

'Yeah, I admit it, and I reckon that piece of garbage knows I could get him on the rape, otherwise why let his slitty-eyed wife pay up the cash? He knows I'm Angie, but he doesn't know my real name. I've got him by the short and curlies.'

'What evidence do you have?' Jane asked.

'I had the knife that he cut me up with.'

Jane took a deep breath.

'Did you give the knife to DI Moran?'

'Mind yer own fuckin' business.'

'It *is* my business. It is very important – was the flick knife in your possession after he attacked you?'

'Maybe it was, maybe it wasn't.'

'I wore your coat, and I was attacked because of it. He thought I was you, didn't he, *Janet*?'

Janet laughed and leaned back.

'Just goes to show, doesn't it, darlin'? In the dark all cats are grey. He had such an adrenalin buzz, he was stinkin'. Let me tell you something else ... there's no way that little slitty-eyed bitch of a wife didn't know what he was getting up to. He must've gone back to her reeking of sex. He's hung like a horse!'

Jane almost recoiled.

'The only person that's been half-decent to me is Nick Moran. After Allard cut me up I couldn't work. I was badly in debt and I needed money for my son ... I'm not making excuses.'

'Take me through exactly what happened when he attacked you.'

'I was up by the Lido, waiting for a punter. It was about eleven p.m. and I was getting cold. I was passing under a load of big trees, and the next minute he's behind me, grabbing me by the neck and saying that he was going to kill me.'

'Can you remember the exact words he used?' Jane asked.

'"You thieving whore ... I'm going to kill you." Next minute he's lifted me off my feet. I fight him off, punchin' and kickin' him, and I grabbed his bala- clava ... I was trying to pull his hair, but the hood came off in my hand. I spat at him, but he was too strong. He pushed me down on the ground, ripped open my blouse, and slashed at my neck and my breasts with the knife. I thought I was gonna die, so I kneed him in the balls and he dropped the knife. Then he heard the uniform copper shouting, cos he heard me screamin'. By the time they got to me Allard had jumped up and run off.'

'You had the knife?'

'Yes, in me pocket.'

'And as you had taken his balaclava it meant that you could recognize him – did you also take that?'

'No, I fuckin' didn't.'

'But you saw his face?'

'Yeah, of course I fuckin' did!' Angie shouted.

'And that was all you used to blackmail Marie, that you could identify him and you had no other evidence?'

'For Chrissakes, I've told you now. I wanna get out.'

At that moment Gibbs opened the passenger door and peered in.

'Are you all right, Tennison?'

'Yes, I'm fine ... close the door, please.'

Angie continued. 'Anyway, they took me to hospital, stitched me up, but my face was a mess, I mean, I was in a bad way.'

Jane leaned closer to her. 'You made out a report at Hackney Station, didn't you?'

'Yeah, I did ... they photographed my injuries and took a statement after I'd been to the hospital.'

'Let's just go back. I need to know when you knew that earlier that night a young teenage girl had been raped in that same area.'

'I heard about it when I had to make out the report.'

'Who interviewed you at Hackney?'

Janet turned away. 'I don't remember, I was in bad shape, I just wanted to get home. I had to go back cos I didn't want to take it any further.'

Jane leaned closer. 'When you went back to Hackney Station did you give the knife to DI Moran? It's very important you tell me, because the young rape victim remembered her assailant held a knife to her throat.'

'Yeah, I did . . . but if it gets him into trouble I'll deny it.'

Outside Gibbs got to the butt of his third cigarette and tossed it down on the ground impatiently. He had seen that Janet was talking so had kept his distance, his back towards the car. He turned as he heard the car door open and saw Jane getting out of the patrol car. She walked towards him, pulling the collar of her jacket up as the wind was whipping around the open section of the car park.

'Moran is in the clear for the connection to the blackmail. That's all down to Angie, aka Janet . . . but we need to talk to him as soon as possible.'

Gibbs glared at her. 'Really?'

'Yes. She was attacked later on the same night the young girl was raped. She was almost killed and fought like a wild cat. She would have been dead if a uniform officer hadn't found her. The rape victim wasn't discovered until early morning as she was unconscious and hidden in bushes.'

'How much longer is this gonna take? I'm freezing my bollocks off up here.'

'Don't you understand, Spence? The two cases were not connected straight away. The rape victim is an innocent seventeen-year-old. It was Moran who sifted out the possibility that the attacks were both committed by the same man, but it took him two weeks before he brought "Mary Kelly", Angie, who we now know to be Janet Brown, in for questioning.'

'What evidence has she got, Jane?'

'She snatched the balaclava off his face ... she recognized him.'

'And that's it?' Gibbs asked.

Jane hesitated and decided against repeating to him that Janet had admitted giving the knife to Moran to use as evidence. If, as she had said, she were to deny it, it could create even more of a problem for Moran.

'So she admitted the blackmail?'

'Yes, she lied about having evidence so that she could blackmail Marie Allard.'

Janet began banging and shouting for them to let her out, and they both started to move towards the car.

Gibbs stopped and turned to her.

'Listen, Tennison. This is not my case ... I've already done my part tonight. I was only interested in checking out Moran, and that's what I've done. He's not a bent copper, as I knew he wouldn't be. I'm not involved, all right? You were on this business at Hackney, so now it's down to you to do the run around and report to Moran in the morning.'

Jane was in a quandary. She really hadn't expected Gibbs to just leave her to handle all the new information, but she had no option. They drove Janet to a high rise council estate, where she was staying with her mother-in-law who was caring for her little boy. She had grown very quiet in the car and moaned about her hip hurting. Gibbs helped her out of the rear passenger side and she walked very slowly towards the entrance of her block. He stayed with her as she got into the dirty lift, which stank of urine, and the floor was littered with cigarette butts.

'Which floor?'

'Six ... the button someone has stubbed a cigarette out on.'

He watched her press the button, and as the gates started to close he stepped out.

Gibbs was silent as he drove Jane back to the section house. She had attempted to be a team player, but she really felt as if she was on her own again.

He parked up and decided to go across the road to the Warburton Arms, where he knew he could get a drink even after closing time. The first person he saw, playing snooker, was DI Nick Moran.

CHAPTER TWENTY-FOUR

The following morning Jane was in the ladies' locker room and hadn't even taken off her coat when Edith walked in.

'You'd better get over to Hackney – DI Moran has called three times. He says he has an update on the Allard trial. I'll make a note in the schedule that that's where you'll be.'

'Is DI Gibbs in?'

'He's in, but he's having a meeting with DCI Shepherd and left instructions that he didn't want to be disturbed.'

Jane had a terrible sinking feeling as she left Bow Street. She was sure that Spencer Gibbs had gone behind her back and spoken to Moran. Her fears were confirmed when, on arriving at the reception in Hackney Station, DC Brian Edwards told her that DI Moran was waiting to see her in his office, and he wasn't a happy man.

Moran was perching on the edge of his desk, his office door open, as Jane approached.

'Sir . . .' Her stomach was churning.

'Shut the door behind you. You know, Tennison, if you were a bloke I would grab you by your collar and throw a punch at your smug little face. I don't know what you think you've been playing at, but I am going to hear what you've got to say before I get you back in uniform directing traffic.'

'I am not in any way smug, sir, I'm just very nervous. I never had any intention of acting on my own, it was just circumstances and my need to double-check before I brought my findings to anyone's attention, especially yours.'

Moran leaned forward, pulling his loud tie loose from his shirt collar.

'I'm all ears . . .'

'May I refer to my notes?'

Moran gave the go-ahead with his hands. Jane opened her bag and took out her notebook.

'You can obviously verify the dates, sir. On the night of the twenty-third of August uniform officers brought in a prostitute called Janet Brown. She had been badly beaten and had a deep knife wound to her chest and left breast, which required hospital treatment. She was photographed and a report made out but she refused to press charges, claiming that she was unable to identify the man as he had worn a balaclava.'

Moran stared at her, his blue eyes holding hers, and acted as if what she was saying was obvious.

Jane continued.

'The CID were brought in to investigate the rape of a young girl who was found semi-conscious on the morning of the twenty-fourth of August. She had suffered a terrible beating and was unable to identify the rapist as he had worn a black woollen mask covering his entire face. But timewise it was possible that she had been raped earlier the same night as Janet Brown. But the two cases were not, to begin with, linked as having the same perpetrator.'

He banged his chair to sit forward. 'I linked them.'

'I know you did, sir, because you brought in Janet Brown, under the assumed name of Mary Kelly, and re-questioned her. But this was two weeks later, when you organized a CID operation and used me as a decoy. I believe you gave me the blue rabbit fur coat as it was probable that the rapist intended Janet Brown to be his victim, and not the young girl.'

Moran leaned forward, and flicked through a statement, not looking at Jane. He then sighed and picked up a pencil.

'The prostitute – Janet Brown, Mary Kelly, Angie – was unable to identify her attacker and refused point blank to assist my operation, which was why I held her in the cells. She was released the following morning after we had arrested Peter Allard.'

'I know that, sir. I also know that she is capable of identifying him. She pulled his balaclava off when he was attacking her.'

'Perhaps what you don't know, Tennison, is that Janet Brown, aka Mary Kelly, aka Angie, had stolen a bag of takings from a taxi around about a month before-hand . . . it was a lot of money, nearly four hundred quid as he had been doing airport runs. He had argued about paying her after sex, so she stole it and did a runner. So now we have a known hooker who steals a load of money from Peter Allard. When he did catch up with her he beat the shit out of her, because she was a thief. Are you following me, Tennison?'

'Yes, sir ... I didn't know that it was Janet who had stolen Allard's money ...' She swallowed and took a deep breath.

'No, you didn't know ... but I did. So you tell me what a jury are going to believe? A known tart with a long list of previous arrests for prostitution, or are they going to say she deserved what she got and that he didn't rape her? He's a hard-working man with a wife and two kids. It was the first time he had ever been arrested ... look at how he behaved in court, head hanging down and weeping, all innocent. He even admitted that he did fondle a few women, but he denied rape.'

Jane couldn't look at him.

'I wanted him for the rape of that seventeen-year-old innocent girl. I wanted him charged with sexual assaults that I had no evidence to prove he did, but I knew he did them. Look at the way he attacked you and how he acted in court and what you were subjected to by his defence counsel. So you tell me, why would I not use Janet Brown as a witness?'

'I don't know, sir?'

'She is a tart ... but she's also an informer and has been for years. One court appearance and she's no use to us. You have no idea just how useful she has been. And you think after one conversation with her that you know her?'

'But she was blackmailing Marie Allard, sir.'

Moran threw up his hands and laughed, becoming increasingly impatient.

'That's how she survives, Tennison! Allard cut her breasts and scarred her . . . he would have killed her if we hadn't stopped him.'

Jane was unable to hold back.

'So you *knew* what Allard had done to Janet Brown, and yet you made me wear her blue fur coat and planted me as a decoy, *knowing* that he had almost killed her?'

Moran lifted his arms up again.

'Yes, I own up to that. We lost sight of you for a few minutes. But it was only a few minutes . . .'

'So, I'm wearing Janet Brown's blue fur coat . . . you want Allard to think I am her and for him to attack me, so that you can arrest him? Because you already had the knife he used in the rape, and when he slashed Janet.'

Moran folded his arms. After a long pause he spoke. For the first time she could see he was uneasy, eventually choosing his words carefully.

'What choice do I have? I'm pretty certain he may be connected to a murder that occurred five years ago. If I don't put him away he's going to kill again.'

Moran stood up and opened his office door. Jane didn't know how to react to the fact that he had just virtually admitted to planting evidence. As if he was reading her mind Moran gently touched her shoulder.

'It was all on the level, OK? Now, come with me. I want to show you something.'

Moran walked ahead of her and went into the incident room. DC Brian Edwards was standing in front of the information board.

'It's not positive news from Maidstone, guv. The Chief

Superintendent there said we would need a lot more incriminating evidence to excavate the garden at the house the Allards used to rent.'

Moran sighed as Edwards moved away from the board. Pinned up were the photographs they had pulled out from the cold files at Maidstone. Moran tapped the board with his pencil.

'This is what we're looking into, Tennison, and we need to question—'

Jane interrupted as she saw the photograph of Susie Luna with the rose in her hair.

'Marie Allard?''

Moran hesitated. 'What did you just say?'

'That's a photograph of Marie Allard.'

'No, it isn't, it's the missing girl from five years ago. Her name is Susie Luna.'

'Oh, sorry ... they look so similar.'

Moran glanced at Edwards, then back to Jane.

'Marie Allard gave her husband a cast-iron alibi for the day Susie Luna went missing. I think we need to go and have a chat with her.'

'I would really appreciate it if I was allowed to accompany you – Marie Allard trusts me. In fact, she called me personally to tell me she was being blackmailed by Janet Brown who referred to herself as Angie and sang a song and—'

'Did she now?'

Edwards raised his hand. 'Can I have a quiet word, guv, in your office?'

'Sure. DC Ashton, show Tennison the files we've got on Susie Luna.'

Edwards closed Moran's office door behind them.

'Did everything go all right, guv?'

'Yes. Just a misunderstanding. What did you want to talk to me about?'

'Two things ... we received confirmation this morning of a trial date for Peter Allard, in two weeks' time.'

'That doesn't give us much time to investigate the Susie Luna connection, does it?'

'I'm afraid there may be another problem, sir. Apparently the barrister who represents Allard has raised doubts about his confession and has requested an independent forensic examination of the interview notes. In particular, the confession that Allard supposedly signed.'

'Shit ... that's all I bloody need. I'm going to take Tennison with me to interview Marie Allard. The last time we were there with SOCO we pulled the bloody house apart, so I'm taking Tennison along to give the gentle touch ... maybe have a woman to woman chat with her.' Moran smiled.

'I wouldn't mind coming along after all the new information we've uncovered ...'

'No, I want you to man the fort here, Edwards. I'm only taking Tennison with me to keep her sweet.'

'Gone sour on you, has she, sir?'

'You could say that.'

CHAPTER TWENTY-FIVE

Moran parked up outside the Allards' house.

'She's very nervous, sir. It might take a while for her to come to the front door.'

'Take as long as you like, I'll be here.'

'Thank you.'

Moran watched Jane walk away, then down the small pathway leading to the doorway where she rang the bell. He saw her step back and look up at the first-floor window, and then move closer to the door. It was another few minutes before the door opened and Jane stepped inside.

Marie replaced the chain lock. Jane waited for her to turn, and was taken aback by the way she looked. Her hair was lank, she had lost even more weight and seemed shrunken and shaking with nerves. Jane dropped her bag to the floor and held out her arms, hugging Marie.

'I am so sorry not to get back to you before now, but it has taken such a long time and I wanted to come to see you personally as I didn't want any of the officers here when I tell you what I have found out. I know how much it will affect you.'

Marie stepped away, her eyes wide with anxiety. Jane put an arm around her shoulders and suggested that they went into the lounge to sit down. Marie seemed to calm down as Jane sat on the sofa opposite her.

'I am so sorry to be the one to tell you, but the woman that was blackmailing you is not connected to the police. She was attacked by your husband and suffered a terrible beating that has scarred her for life. She was not prepared to identify him before, but she is now prepared to go to court.'

Jane was surprised at how easily she was able to lie, because in reality she knew that Janet Brown would not go to court.

Marie pressed her body back in the easy chair and clasped her hands together.

'He has lied to you, terrible lies ... the rape victim was just a young, vulnerable teenager. She won't ever recover from the ordeal, and you know that he also attacked me, and if the police officer hadn't been there ...' Jane's performance was getting better by the second as she lowered her head and ran her fingers over her lips, reminding Marie about when she had first seen her with her lips cut.

'Oh my God,' Marie said, clasping and unclasping her hands.

Jane left a long pause, taking out a handkerchief from her pocket and blowing her nose. Marie seemed unable to look directly at her; she was so tiny and vulnerable and trembling, but even though Jane felt sorry for her she had to use that to get some answers.

'How long did you know, Marie, that he was leaving you and your two children and going out to attack and rape women? How long have you known he was evil? Do you realize that you made the reality invisible to yourself, refused to smell the sex? You could smell them on him, couldn't you?'

'No ... no ... that's not true.'

'Yes, it is, Marie, don't lie. You kept that room upstairs locked. You said it was to protect your children but you knew what was in there, and you used to go into that room when you were here alone ... didn't you?'

'No ... no, I did not. He would never ...' She stopped.

'What did he do to you when he found out you were looking in that room, seeing those disgusting porno-graphic magazines? You knew when he was on steroids and behaving like a crazy man ... you knew and you kept quiet because you didn't want to know the truth. But he will be out soon, Marie, and he will come back here, and you will have to live with it all over again.'

Jane knew that some of what she was saying was get-ting through, as Marie bent forward, clutching at her stomach.

'He will get out, Marie, he will come back unless you stand up and face the truth. You said to me that you couldn't have sex and that was the excuse ... that is *his* excuse. He blames *you* – it's all your fault that he went with those women and raped and assaulted them. It's your fault because he says you couldn't have sex. You lied about it to me, but it isn't true, is it? What did he do to you, Marie?'

Her face crumpled and she began to sob uncontrol-lably. Jane felt for her but she knew she had to plough on because Marie had not yet admitted knowing the truth about her husband or if he had, as Jane suspected, abused her.

'Why don't you tell me, Marie, because I am really trying to understand why you appeared to be adamant your husband was innocent, when I can see the pressure you have been under with the blackmail and the threats . . .'

'I been frightened of him, always frightened. He made me do things, always he threatened to take my children from me, so I stay, but if I make him happy he would not beat me. If I not do what he want he would lock me up and take children to his mother. Always he threaten me so I do what he wants.'

Jane got up and gently laid her hand on Marie's shoulder. As she turned back she noticed a photograph of Marie with her eldest child as a toddler. Jane pointed to it.

'Was that taken when you lived in Maidstone?'

Marie seemed relieved to be changing the subject. She wiped her eyes.

'Yes . . . yes.'

'And you worked at the Majestic Hotel when you were there, didn't you?'

'Yes, I did,' Marie replied.

Jane waited a moment before saying quietly, 'I need to ask you about your friend, Susie Luna.'

Marie reeled back in her chair, visibly shaken by the reference to Susie Luna.

'Five years ago you gave your husband an alibi, confirming that he was at home with you on the afternoon and evening that your friend went missing. If you lied about that, and we find out, do you know what that means ... committing perjury? You could be sent to prison for six years. But if you want to tell me the truth now, I might be able to help you. Did you lie for him, Marie?'

Marie was expressionless. Very slowly she stood up, and with no emotion she began twisting strands of her hair through her fingers. It was strange, but it seemed to calm her.

'He says he will take my children if I not do or say what he want me to. But I have plan now ...'

Jane was confused by the complete change in Marie's demeanour.

'I have something for you,' Marie said calmly. She started walking towards the door as Jane stood up.

'Where are you going, Marie?'

She walked out of the room. 'Follow me ...'

Jane hurried after her, down the hallway and into the kitchen. She was horrified as she watched Marie pulling a large knife out of the knife block on the counter. Marie knelt down, opened a cupboard door, and used the knife to release a worn envelope that had been stuck to the inside of the cupboard with Sellotape. She then stood up, put the knife back in the block and laid the envelope on the kitchen counter, placing her hand on top of it.

'This is proof ... but you not send me away from my children.'

Moran looked up as Jane came out of the house and gestured for him to come inside. He hurried from the car and followed Jane into the lounge. Marie was sitting calmly on the sofa, staring into space and twisting her hair between her fingers.

'Marie has given me this, sir. It's Susie Luna's passport. She has also admitted that she posed as Susie, wearing a rose in her hair, at a few locations, including a bus stop and outside a fish and chip shop.'

Moran took it, then flicked through the old, dog-eared passport and glanced over at Marie.

'So when you were posing as your friend, where was your husband, Mrs Allard?'

'I don't know ... when I go home, Susie had gone. I never saw her again.'

Moran held up the passport. 'So where did you find this?'

'It was in her handbag,' Marie replied.

'We're going to need a statement from you at the station, Marie,' said Jane gently. 'I'll stay with you throughout.'

Jane stayed with Marie for two and a half hours as she gave a statement. She admitted that she had introduced Susie to her husband. Their son was three years old, and Marie was pregnant with their daughter. Under pressure to recall how well her husband had known Susie Luna, Marie became very distressed and said that he had sex with her, but he made Marie deny it when the police in Kent questioned them both as being the last people to see Susie Luna alive.

Marie admitted that, because of her pregnancy, she had felt very sick at work and had returned home early, walking in on Peter raping Susie. He was very angry and

Marie had run out, afraid that he was going to beat her up. Marie never saw her friend again. Susie Luna had always worn a red rose in her hair and Peter had told Marie to put it on and walk around obvious places for two hours. Marie went and stood for twenty minutes at a bus stop and then outside a fish and chip shop for a further half an hour, eventually standing outside a pub. When she returned home, Peter was working out with his weights and never mentioned Susie Luna again. A few weeks later, Marie found Susie's handbag, went through it and took out the passport. Peter used a leather strap to beat her, snatching the handbag from her, and she thought he must have thrown it in one of the industrial bins outside the hotel. Marie kept Susie's rose and used to always have it by her little statue of the Madonna. She looked at Jane.

'I saw it every day when we move here, so I never forget her, but Peter, he sometime frightened the children, and Kim, my little boy, when they arrested Peter, he ask me if he was bad boy, would he be punished like Susie Luna? I could not believe my boy even remember her, because he was only three year old. But Susie was always so sweet and kind to him. I took the rose as my daughter want to put it in her hair. Susie Luna has been a ghost in my heart.'

Jane was exhausted and remained sitting in the interview room with Marie. 'You have been very brave, Marie. And you know if you ever need to talk to someone, please call me.'

Marie nodded.

'Today I feel better than I have for as long as I remember. I won't go and visit him but if he call me, Detective

Moran said I not mention Susie Luna and I won't. I will keep secret until he pay the price for her murder.' By mid-afternoon Marie was taken home. Moran knocked on the open door, and leaned against the door frame as she turned towards him.

'She will make one hell of a witness for the prosecution ... well done, Tennison.'

'Thank you, sir. You were always right about Peter Allard and hopefully we will now have enough to legally make sure he gets a long sentence.'

Moran watched Jane pick up her bag, put away her notebook and walk past him. He had previously thought of her as a waste of space. A female probationary officer of no consequence ... but he now knew she was a force to be reckoned with, and not to be treated lightly.

CHAPTER TWENTY-SIX

Jane was off duty at the weekend, and she had agreed to go home to visit her parents. Mrs Tennison had made roast chicken with all the trimmings, roast potatoes, carrots and broccoli, and her usual gravy from the roasting tin. Jane's sister Pam and her brother-in-law were at some hairdressing function in Birmingham as Pam had been doing a special hair tinting course and wanted Tony there for the weekend.

'That's good news. Is there anything I can do to help with lunch?' Jane said.

'No no, dear, everything's done but the dessert. Pam's back at work and might even win the colouring competition as they have to cut and recolour and style with models. I doubt Tony will be all that interested, but they have a double room at a very nice hotel,' Mrs Tennison said proudly.

'That's good,' Jane said, as her attention was drawn to a newspaper placed on the sideboard while her mother added the finishing touches to lunch. She picked it up and took it into the sitting room, never having time to read the newspaper while at work. She was shocked at the headline, 'Murder in the Bath accused couple to stand trial', and the press coverage was extensive, with photographs of Katrina Harcourt being led into the court. The redhead was smiling as if enjoying the moment, unlike the photographs of Barry Dawson who had a blanket covering his head. By the time Jane had finished reading the article her father had opened a bottle of wine.

'That's a shocking case, isn't it?'

'Yes, the CID at the station investigated and it was a very complicated case as the young wife in the bath was wrongly diagnosed as being a non-suspicious death, but when we had a second post-mortem it revealed another wound had been inflicted. The suspects were having an affair and it was a very complicated inquiry to be able to charge them with murder. The trial will not go ahead for months.'

'Good God, and she looks such an attractive woman! So were you involved in the investigation?'

Jane hesitated and then nodded, but not wanting to go into details she collected the newspapers and stacked them ready to be thrown out.

Her mother, who had overheard the conversation, found it difficult to ask Jane about her work as a police officer. She gave her husband a shake of her head as a warning not to continue. Her father steered the conversation back to safer waters, but after a couple of glasses of wine, while Mrs Tennison tried to make a crème brûlée, her father topped up her glass and asked quietly, 'So it must have been quite a time for you at Bow Street?'

Jane raised her glass and took a sip. How could she even begin to explain about the tragic murder of Shirley Dawson, or the forthcoming trial of Peter Allard? To tell him about the time spent in and around the sex shops and strip joints of Soho, or even the interaction with the beautiful Janet Brown? It was all so far removed from the warmth and normality of being at home with her family.

They sat down together and enjoyed the main course but her mother was in a state of anxiety as the toffee crisp on top of her crème brûlée had hardened like cement and her father was worried he'd break the denture plate in his mouth.

'I must have used too much sugar; it's not that bad is it, Jane?' her mother asked.

'No, it's fine,' she said with clenched teeth.

'It's supposed to just crack when you tap it with a spoon.'

'You should have used a hammer!' her father said.

This made Jane smile, and as they were trying to chew through the very hard topping, all three of them suddenly started laughing.

'It's so good to be home,' Jane said, feeling emotional.

Her father screwed up his face again as he chewed and then swallowed.

'Well, it's perfect for us to have you safe and sound, because we miss you.'

The phone suddenly started ringing in the hallway. Mr Tennison stood up and went to answer it. A moment later he called out to Jane.

'It's for you, Jane.'

'For me?' she asked, surprised. She walked over and took the receiver from her father.

'Hello?' she said into the mouthpiece.

'Jane, it's me, Spence. I'm in a callbox at the end of your road ... I need to see you. Can you come and meet me?'

Jane laughed. 'Are you asking me out on a date, Spence?'

'No ... we've got a nightmare on our hands, Jane. Peter Allard's been released.'

'Give me five minutes, all right?'

Jane didn't want to show her parents how disturbed she was by Gibbs's phone call.

'I'm sorry, but I have to go in to the station. There's some confusion about one of my reports.'

'Oh, don't you have time for a coffee?' her mother asked.

'No, Mum, I'm sorry but if I can I'll come back later.'

She walked down to the end of the road and found Gibbs standing beside a patrol car parked next to the callbox.

'Is this a joke, Spence?'

'No, it's deadly serious. Moran is going crazy. Apparently Marie got a call from him from the prison, and even though she was warned not to mention anything or refer to the present inquiry about Susie Luna, she told Allard she wanted a divorce, that she knew about Angie.'

'What?'

'Yeah, her idea of revenge, but the stupid bitch has really screwed up because he's fucking got compassionate bail until his trial.'

'I don't believe it, not after what we uncovered about his connection to Susie Luna.'

'You don't understand, Jane ... that's an entirely separate investigation, and if they find a body they can arrest him straight after the trial.'

'But you're not even working on Allard's case. What do you want me to do?'

'I know I'm bloody not, but Moran wants protection for Janet Brown. He contacted me because he knew that we had taken her to her mother-in-law's flat at the council estate. So I need you to come with me to go back there again and get her into protective custody.'

When DI Moran found out, he was apoplectic with fury. He had only just returned from Maidstone where Scenes of Crime officers were waiting for permission to lift the paving stones from the small patio garden of the property that had been rented by Allard. They had run into a problem as the actual owner of the house had sublet it and they would require his permission to begin working. DC Edwards had also discovered that the garden had only been paved over during Allard's occupation. They had no option but to wait for permission to start digging.

Moran's blood pressure was going through the roof. He had contacted Detective Chief Superintendent Metcalf and wanted to update him on the Susie Luna case and he had agreed to come into the station, but he had to wait for over an hour.

'Sir, all I was told when I was at Maidstone was that a trial date had been set for two weeks' time. I've now been informed that they have released Peter Allard on compassionate grounds. They've just let a killer walk out, sir.'

Metcalf gestured for Moran to calm down.

'I can't do anything about that, because this is a very complex situation, Nick. I don't want to have to underline this to you but it is the inconsistencies in Allard's confession that have given the barristers and the judge the opportunity to release him. Apparently his wife wanted to divorce him and take his children and he begged to be given the opportunity to see her.'

'Yes, I know that, sir, and I want her and their two children put into protective custody, because if he is on the loose God knows what he is going to do. And we now have a strong witness that has agreed to identify him with evidence on the rape charge and in my estimation he's going to go after her.'

Metcalf flicked through the statements and notes.

'The prostitute Janet Brown?'

'Yes, sir.'

'She used the name "Angie", among others, but he must now know she is a valuable witness if his wife told him she knew about her.'

Metcalf continued to read the reports as Moran waited impatiently.

'This Susie Luna situation, you don't have enough evidence. She was reported missing five years ago, and these accusations from an aggrieved wife are not enough. But if you want them protected, go ahead ... and just keep your powder dry. I'll leave you to handle it.'

'Thank you, sir.'

*

Peter Allard, carrying a small overnight bag, stepped out of the prison gates. Unshaven and already over-anxious because of the wait he had been subjected to before he was released, he hurried to get to the nearest phone kiosk. He had only a small amount of change which had been taken from his pocket when he was brought in to the prison.

DC Edwards drove DI Moran in a patrol car to the Allards' house. They parked up outside, and DC Ashton approached the car and opened the back passenger door.

'He hasn't shown yet, guv ... We've got her and the kids in a safe house. When I told her he had been released, she was terrified. I thought she was going to collapse.'

'This is bloody unbelievable, isn't it? They let a killer out on the loose, they don't tell his wife, and even I wasn't told until this morning.'

'We don't yet know for sure if he is a killer.'

'Yes, thank you, Edwards. Either way they've bloody released a man accused of indecent sexual assault, a man who's also been told the name of the key witness in the case against him.'

'How did Allard manage to get out?' Ashton asked.

'His confession was thrown out due to inconsistencies, and as he has been on remand for some time, and the only firmed-up evidence we've got is sexual assault, he was granted bail. He just needs to go back for his trial in two weeks. If he finds out that we're on to him regarding the Susie Luna case, he'll do a bloody runner. You go back to the station and keep in contact on the radio if you hear anything.'

'Yes, sir, I'll get the Underground then. I've been here since early this morning.'

'Get back any way you can, go on, but stand by as we might need you, I've only got a handful of officers.'

Ashton, rather disgruntled, walked off down the road as he was also supposed to have the weekend off. He was tired out having been up all night with his new baby girl and his wife was exhausted. She would be really pissed off with him as he was now on standby at the station.

Moran lit a cigarette and checked his watch. Edwards saw a black taxi pull up in front of the house. Peter Allard stepped out of the passenger door.

'Shit, here he is, guv,' Edwards said.

'Let's see how he reacts to an empty house.'

Allard was wearing a pair of jeans and a denim shirt. They saw him leaning into the taxi driver's window, and he appeared to be having a conversation. He then went up the path to the front door and rang the doorbell. He stepped back and looked up at the windows, then rang the bell again. When there was still no answer they saw him reach up to the top of the door frame and take down what was obviously a spare front door key.

Allard opened the door and replaced the key before he slammed the door behind him. Moran gestured to Edwards.

'That's Allard's taxi cab, isn't it? Go and check the driver out and get rid of him.'

Edwards climbed out of the patrol car, crossed over to the taxi and tapped on the driver's window.

'Are you waiting for someone?'

The driver answered, 'Yes, I'm booked.'

'No you're not. This cab registered to you, is it? You got your cab driver's licence?'

Moran saw the driver move off as Edwards returned to sit beside him.

'He moved off fast but it's Allard's taxi, didn't even have to show my warrant card.'

Allard stood in the neat and orderly lounge. He went out into the kitchen and immediately became suspicious as a meal had been left half-eaten on the table.

He headed up the stairs and saw the wooden slats nailed across his gym door. He placed one hand on either side of the door frame and kicked the door open. The room was in the same state of disarray as it had been when Moran and the SOCO had searched his house. The knives were all gone, but he picked up a nunchuck, swinging it by the chain. He then went into the children's bedroom. The beds were unmade and the floor was strewn with toys.

'Bloody untidy,' he muttered, as he made his way to the master bedroom. It wasn't like Marie to leave the house in such a mess. If nothing else she had always kept the place spick and span and even his mother had agreed with that.

'Bitch!' he exclaimed, as he saw that the wardrobe doors were wide open. Some of the clothes were lying on the bed and it was evident that Marie had packed in a hurry. He twisted the chain in his hand and swung the nunchuck down hard on the bed.

Gibbs and Jane stepped into the stinking lift of the council block and went up to floor six.

'Which flat did she go into?' Jane asked.

'I dunno ... I just saw her into the lift and she asked for the sixth floor. I didn't go up with her, so we'll have to try them all. I'll start at 600, you start at 640 ...'

Moran looked at his watch. 'He's been in there over an hour.'

Edwards yawned. 'Maybe this is a waste of time. It doesn't look as if he's going anywhere.'

'Yes, he was. He asked that taxi to wait for him.'

Inside the house Allard pulled on a black tracksuit and a pair of Adidas trainers. He looked out of the window and swore when he saw that the taxi had gone.

'Bastard!' he muttered. He then put in a call using the phone in the hallway. He needed cash, as he'd not found any in the house.

He went into the kitchen, put two slices of bread on a plate, buttered them, and opened the cupboard to take out a jar of Marmite.

Gibbs and Jane had no luck with their door to door enquiries. Nobody had heard of Janet Brown, Mary Kelly or Angie, and no one had seen a black girl with a toddler. By now they had knocked on every door on the sixth floor. Two flats had not answered so the residents could be out. In most cases the occupants were abusive, slamming their doors shut. No one wanted to admit to knowing anyone when the police were involved.

'Well, that's it then,' Gibbs said.

'You know who I think might know where she is, and if she's working one of the clubs? That ginger-haired boy, Philip.'

'Christ! Does that mean another trek into Soho?' Gibbs moaned.

'You don't have to come with me, Spence. I'll find her on my own,' Jane said tetchily.

'Listen, Jane, I've already explained about Moran. I just covered my arse, all right? I didn't drop you in it, but you have to learn you can't just hurl dirt at a good officer like Moran without severe consequences. I was looking out for him, OK? I didn't even intend talking to him but he was in the pub and asked what was going down ...'

'All right, all right. Are you going to come with me, or not?'

'Yes ... but it's my day off, as well you know,' Gibbs said, reluctantly.

They returned to the patrol car and Gibbs radioed in to Moran to say they had not been able to warn Janet Brown so they were now going off to see if she was working one of the strip clubs.

Moran was becoming impatient. After receiving the call in from Gibbs he had hoped they would be able to follow Allard and see if he led them to Janet Brown. As there was no show, he was not going to wait any longer but would go into the house and check it out. He slammed out of the car, and Edwards hurried after him. He kicked the door in and shouted, 'Police ... POLICE!'

They moved from room to room, unsure if Allard was in the house. Not finding him downstairs, Moran went cautiously up to the landing, while Edwards looked in the cupboard under the stairs. The door to the room used by Allard as a gym was half open, the splintered wood all over the carpet. Moran eased the door open wider with his foot before entering but it was empty; he then went into the bedroom. All the wardrobe doors were wide open, and disturbingly there was an array of women's clothes left torn and shredded over the bed. Moran then hurtled down the stairs as Edwards yelled from the kitchen, 'He was onto us, he's just legged it.'

The kitchen window looked out over the small back garden. It had a low fence; each property had a similar type, and the end of terrace had a high brick wall. Edwards and Moran watched Allard climbing up and taking two attempts to make it to the top.

'Get out, cut him off,' Moran shouted.

As Edwards raced down the road, Moran hurtled out of the front door and threw himself into the patrol car. He started up the engine and did a fast U turn, the tyres screeching as he drove to the end terraced house.

Edwards was bending over, panting and gasping for breath, and they could both see the black taxi disappearing down the road.

'Shit.' Moran hit the steering wheel with his hand as Edwards got in beside him.

The numerous small turnings up ahead gave no sighting and Edwards radioed in to Gibbs to inform him they were following a black taxi with Allard as passenger.

Moran shook his head. 'We're not following, we've bloody lost him.'

'There it is, up ahead,' shouted Edwards. Moran put his foot down and at speed overtook the taxi and swung the car to stop directly in front of the vehicle. There was no passenger, just a very startled cab driver who put his hands up in the air, terrified.

Gibbs and Jane were walking down Berwick Street. They had stopped by various strip clubs, some closed and not opening until the evening. At one small dingy club, Gibbs had removed a photograph of Janet, and the bouncer was very unpleasant and abusive, saying she had not worked there for weeks, that she was black trash and a loud-mouthed bitch.

Armed with Janet Brown's photo, they continued moving along the road, and stopped at the adult bookshop. The blinds were down, and the 'closed' sign in the window. Gibbs hammered on the door but no one answered as it was too early in the afternoon, and Berwick Street was almost empty.

'Let's do another round of the clubs,' Gibbs said, as they moved off. They were just turning into Wardour Street when Peter Allard got out of the Underground station in Oxford Street. He did not go via Wardour Street but walked down Regent Street, turning left into Argyle Street and passing the Palladium Theatre, then Liberty and the Magistrates' Court to head into Berwick Street from the opposite direction. He was very tense, constantly looking over his shoulder.

He got to the adult bookshop, but made no attempt to try to gain entrance by the shop's front door; instead he eased warily towards the small white door beside it.

It was chipped and peeling and had no number or door knob, but a substantial key hole, and just above it was a small eye hole for anyone on the other side to check who was at the door. He gave two bangs of his fist and waited; he then repeated it, and pressed closer.

He heard the key turning, and the door was inched open by Stevie, the pot-bellied owner, who was wearing a pyjama top, stained trousers and slippers.

'Hello, Stevie, lemme in.'

'Shit, we're not fuckin' open.'

'Yes you are, lemme in.'

Stevie begrudgingly unhooked the chain and opened the door. He knew Allard because he was a regular customer and bought his porno magazines and steroids from the shop, but he didn't like being bamboozled to open up. He walked along a dirty, bare-boarded narrow hallway, passing the door that gave access into the shop, Allard following behind. Above were the rooms the girls used for their clients and where Stevie had been sleeping. They continued into a small back room with racks of stacked magazines, some of them still boxed and some in an old locked cabinet as they were obscene adult pornography with graphic content. There were also drugs bagged and tagged, and bottles of extremely potent steroids.

'What you want? Take your pick, but make it fast.'

Allard said he wanted the pills, not any magazines, and Stevie unlocked the cabinet, selecting the usual container and held it in his hand.

'You got the cash?'

Allard dug into the deep pocket of his tracksuit jacket

with his left hand as if he was about to hand over the cash, but he used his right to bring out the nunchuck he had tucked into his waistband at the back. He was so fast, Stevie didn't see it coming, and the crack against his scalp was so vicious he sank to his knees. He tried to grab hold of one of the racks containing the magazines and it toppled over onto him. Allard stepped over the unconscious man, and picked up the container, before turning back and out into the small corridor.

He knew this area, knew the girls rented the upstairs squalid rooms. This was where he had first met that tart Angie, and this was the place the red-haired kid worked – the kid Marie had described, that took his money. Just thinking of his wife made him tense with rage. He'd find her and when he did, he'd beat the living daylights out of her.

He went up the stairs and checked each dingy room before he sat on one of the dirty sheets, opened the container and took a fistful of small yellow pills.

It was getting dark and Soho was coming alive. Gibbs and Jane met up with Moran in the car park they had used previously. By now Moran had assigned a few uniform officers to search for Angie as well as Allard. There was one positive piece of news, and that was they had now been granted permission to start lifting the paving stones at the Allards' previous residence. As they had his passport they knew he could not escape abroad.

'Allard will be looking for Janet, and as we've not been able to trace her, maybe he's having the same problem.'

Jane said nothing. They were sitting in Moran's patrol car and the smoke was making her eyes run as the men were all chain smoking.

'She's a wily lady. I mean, she took me inside that estate, I saw her get into the lift, and she was lying. Press the sixth floor, she said, it's the one where someone stubbed their cigarette out. I saw her do it and then left. I never went up with her . . .'

Jane agreed. 'We knocked on every door on the sixth floor, apart from two. Maybe we need to go back. None of the residents were that helpful, they just slammed the doors in our faces.'

Gibbs sighed. 'Listen, this is not my case, pals. I've been legging it around all afternoon and it's now getting dark; the tart could be anywhere, and so could Allard.'

Moran stubbed out his cigarette and turned to Jane. 'You want to give it one more try at that estate, and I'll do another round of the clubs? Spence, just drop her off, and Jane, radio in if you find her.'

Gibbs drove Jane out of the car park as Moran and Edwards started to head towards the red light district. They stopped to buy a hot dog each and then heard the ambulance approaching with the lights flashing and bell ringing. A uniform officer approached and said that there was an altercation in Berwick Street at the adult bookshop and the woman who owned it had called in the police.

Moran watched as the still unconscious Stevie was carried on a stretcher into the ambulance and the paramedics began to try to resuscitate him. His wife was sobbing and swearing at the same time as she said she would find the bastard. Her husband had only one dried wound to the side of his head; apart from that there was no other physical sign of violence. She said it had to have been some pervert after money but she had already locked up the cabinet of drugs.

Moran was standing in the corridor where the rack of magazines still lay on its side as Stevie's wife became very agitated and wanted him to leave as she was going in the ambulance.

'I got to lock up . . . you can come back another time.'

'Shut up,' Moran snapped.

'I am not leaving without locking the doors, it'll be an open bloody invitation, there's stuff in here worth a lot of money.'

Moran turned on her and told her to be quiet again, when he saw a trail of blood, not from beneath the rack but closer to the small staircase. She tried to interrupt him again but he ordered her to go and get in the ambulance.

'I can't leave this place open,' Ada wailed.

Moran ignored her and began to slowly move up the stairs. Spots of blood could be seen, and then as he reached the landing there were blood splatterings against the wall. He pushed open the door and could see the small figure curled on his side, his red hair matted with blood, his face badly beaten, blood bubbles gathered at his open mouth. Moran went over to him. The poor kid was terrified, his eyes wide, and he even tried to ward off Moran.

''S'all right, I'm not going to hurt you. Do you know who did this to you? Look at me, come on, I've got an ambulance outside. You know who beat you up?'

Ginger started crying and then nodded his head. 'Big guy ... he hit me wiv this thing on a chain. Oh God, he done me head in.'

'Listen, you are going to be looked after, but tell me why he did this to you.'

Ginger spat out blood as Moran held him upright in a sitting position.

'Angie, he wanted to know where Angie lives.'

'Did you tell him?'

'What you fuckin' think, he was crazy. I told him.'

It was another few minutes before the boy was able to give Moran the address.

Moran picked the injured boy up in his arms and carried him out.

'Oh Jesus God, that's Ginger. Ginger, who would want to do something like that to him, he's just a kid?' Ada began screaming in hysterics as Moran carried the boy out into the street to the still waiting ambulance. He spoke urgently to Edwards.

'We get the car and get over to Janet Brown's estate. It has to have been Allard. Radio in to Gibbs that we're on our way.'

Jane got out of the car and slammed the door.

'I'm going,' Gibbs said.

'Fine, Spence, you go, or just wait until I come out and you can take me back to the section house. It's my day off as well, you know.'

'It's not my bloody case,' he moaned.

He watched her heading up the pathway to the estate entrance. She had the photograph of Janet Brown in her hand. She turned back and gave him a smile as she went in through the main doors. He felt a bit guilty. He knew he wouldn't drive off and leave her, he was just pissed off at losing almost an entire day off.

Inside Jane stood in the lift and looked at the floor numbered buttons. Floor six did have a burn mark, as if someone had stubbed out a cigarette against it. The lift was rank, smelling of urine, and dried white chewing gum covered the filthy carpet. It moved slowly upwards, clanking and grinding. Once it lurched and she thought it was going to stop, but it continued upwards.

The lift door opened, and Jane stepped out. She headed for the two flats where previously there had been no answer. She rang 615 and waited but there was still no one at home. She moved to flat 620 and was about to ring the doorbell when a thin-faced woman with a trolley bag came towards her.

'Excuse me, I am trying to contact this woman, she has a young child. Can you look at the photograph? I was told she lived on this floor.'

The woman moved closer and stared at the photograph of Janet Brown.

'She's round the corner by the stairwell, go through the doors.'

Jane smiled. 'Thank you very much.'

'That's all right. I live here.' She took out her keys to flat 620, and Jane moved down the corridor. They had made a mistake, presuming all the flats were located along the landing. They had not considered there was another flat by the stone stairwell.

Jane, annoyed at all the time they had wasted, pushed

open the double doors. They had cracked panes of glass and graffiti on them, and where the old carpet stopped there was a stone floor leading onto the stairwell. The flat's front door was painted green, chipped in places, and the brass letter box was in need of a polish. Jane had her hand on the old bell cemented into the wall. It also had brass surrounds but the button was missing. She put her hand out to push the letter box flap instead of knocking, but the door slowly opened a few inches. She hesitated and gently laid the flat of her hand to open it wider.

Still being very cautious, Jane moved a few steps into the hallway. A child's pushchair and toys were left on the floor. A large red tin toy double-decker bus lay on its side. The carpet was threadbare but the hallway was clean, an old upright hoover was propped against a wall with a full basket of laundry beside it. Hanging on a hook was the blue rabbit fur coat, and with relief Jane knew she was in the right flat, so she walked more confidently towards an open door that led into the sitting room. It was worn but comfortable, a sofa and an easy chair with a big throw rug in front of an electric three bar fire. Jane was about to call out for Janet, but stopped as she could smell a strong sweet unpleasant smell of body odour.

Allard had seen Jane enter. He was in the kitchen at the far end of the hall, the door open just a crack. He'd beaten the hell out of the ginger-haired kid to get the address and he'd been waiting for Janet. By now, Allard was sweating and hyper, and he eased back towards a cabinet to open a kitchen drawer. It made a scratching sound as it opened and it contained dishcloths and tea towels. He tensed up, listening, and then eased back another drawer that contained kitchen knives.

Jane heard the noise as her heart began pounding. She was sure that someone was in the flat and the fear made her freeze, because she was certain it was Allard. She tried to control her nerves and think where the sound had come from, but as she didn't know the layout of the flat, she couldn't be sure. It felt as if she was trapped in the room. She took deep breaths, telling herself that the sound had to have come from the left at the end of the hallway, and she would have to get out of the room and run to her right to escape.

Gibbs lost his attention on the road for a moment, as Moran was on the radio saying they would be there in minutes, so he missed Janet Brown walking into the estate with a bag of shopping, only catching her as she walked into the reception area.

'Nick, I think I've got her, she's here at the estate,' Gibbs said into the radio, getting out of the car. He ran into the flats' entrance as the lift began to move upwards. He looked at the old dial, which didn't work, unable to tell which floor it was moving to. He pressed the call button again and waited.

Jane had looked around the room for anything she could use as a weapon, but there was nothing. She decided to run for it, and as she got to the hall the kitchen door flew open and Allard came at her, holding the knife up above him, making stabbing motions, and then slashing down towards her body. As she backed into the room, the knife wedged into the wooden door and he began dragging it loose.

When Janet got to her front door she was immediately suspicious as it was half open. She kicked it wider as she heard Jane screaming, and hurled the bag of groceries aside. Allard had his back to her and, turning to face her now with the carving knife free, he switched from attacking Jane and went for Janet. She picked up the old hoover and swung it at him. She didn't release it, but swung it again and this time it knocked him into the door frame. He was screeching like a crazed animal and Jane came out, kicking at his legs, but he got back up on his feet screaming with rage. Janet now rammed him hard in the groin with the folded child's buggy. He dropped the knife and yelped in agony. She grabbed the knife and was on top of him, holding it at his throat.

'You want to know what it feels like, you scum. I'm gonna cut your throat, you bastard.'

Gibbs had done a frantic run, unaware as Jane had been about the flat by the stairwell; he now heard the screams, hurtled through the double doors and ran into the flat. Janet was losing her fight as Allard was able to push her aside – his strength was frightening. It took the three of them to get him down. Gibbs was punching and stamping on his prone body but Allard still attempted to get up. He was clawing at Gibbs and then punched him in the chest and he was by far stronger and starting to stand.

Jane was gasping for breath as she picked up the little boy's tin bus and rammed it down on Allard's head, knocking him face down and giving Gibbs the chance to drag his arms up and cuff him.

Janet was crying and laughing at the same time. She slumped against the corner and then started to sing in a screeching voice 'The wheels on the bus go round and round, *round and round*.' She picked up the knife wanting to have another go at Allard. 'He could have got my boy, he could have hurt my boy.'

'Just knock it off, will you. Gimme that *now*.'

Gibbs had tied a towel around Allard's head, so he was disoriented and cuffed, but still using his body like a ram and kicking out at anything as Jane and Gibbs hauled him into the lift.

Moran and Edwards screeched to a halt beside the patrol car. Edwards immediately went to assist Gibbs and get Allard in the car. Moran went directly over to Jane, and held her, asking quietly if she was all right. She nodded, and he gently touched her face.

'You come back with me, Edwards will go with Gibbs and lock the bastard up. Come on, let me put you in the car. I won't be long.'

Jane sank into the passenger seat, and closed her eyes. Moran had a few words with Gibbs and Edwards and then headed into the estate.

Moran found Janet sitting on the sofa, shaking and drinking from a bottle of brandy. 'If she wasn't here, he'd have killed me, I just thank Christ my mum took the kid to a friend's cos I got to work and . . .'

'Shush, shush,' he said, sitting beside her. 'We got him and you're safe.'

She nodded. 'You want me in court, Nick, I'll do it,

do whatever you want. She knocked him for six with the double-decker bus.'

'Will you be all right?'

She nodded, taking another swig of brandy. 'You make sure she's all right because she was in here alone with him.'

'I will, but you muddied the waters, Janet. What the hell were you doing blackmailing the bastard?'

'I couldn't work, I'm still red raw from where he sliced me, an' I wanted to get something out of it. I had to get my mother-in-law over from Jamaica to look after my son, I was broke, Nick.'

He sighed. 'Is it true you have evidence, I mean apart from being able to identify him?'

She took another mouthful of brandy.

'Tell me, I am looking out for you, for Chrissakes, and I always have, but this is you pushing the limit ... was it a lie?'

She hesitated and then slowly got to her feet. 'It might mean nothin', but when those coppers found me, I stuffed it into me bag along with you know what.'

Janet went to a cabinet and opened a drawer. She took out something wrapped in newspaper. 'You can smell him on it, and I know he raped that young girl because he thought she was me, and I know you used that blonde copper in my fur coat because it was me he was always after.'

Moran frowned as she slowly placed the newspaper-wrapped parcel on the coffee table. As he reached over to open it she put her hand over it.

'It's all been my fault, Nick, cos I stole his money out of his cab and I know you was protecting me and couldn't use me as a witness, and to be honest you have always been about the only person I could trust.'

'You've certainly screwed me over, so what is it?'

Janet slowly opened the newspaper. It contained Peter Allard's balaclava that she had ripped from his head. He didn't touch it but rewrapped the newspaper around it. He knew it could not be used as evidence as it was too long after Allard's arrest.

'Will you still look after me, Nick?'

He got up and smiled, saying he would make sure she was taken care of. He had no idea what she had meant by the double-decker bus but he would find out.

CHAPTER TWENTY-SEVEN

DS Gibbs drove Jane back to the section house and as she attempted to get out of the car he had touched her arm.

'Listen, I need to apologize to you, I behaved like an arsehole, and I just want to clear the air between us. To be honest when I did that run into that estate I had a few seconds when I didn't think I would be able to deal with stuff, you know, the tension and all that crap. I've had these recurring sweats and panicky feelings, but when I saw you with that bastard I never felt for a minute I couldn't cope. Maybe it's over, you know, I've come through it.' Jane was taken aback when he leaned towards her and kissed her cheek, before he gave an embarrassed wave of his hand for her to get out of the car.

Jane was back on duty on the Monday morning. DCI Shepherd had been informed of the arrest of Allard, and told her that she was to be at Hackney Station to make a formal report. He didn't appear interested in discussing what had occurred, having already had a lengthy conversation with DI Gibbs.

Jane was not disappointed. In fact, she was partly relieved as she had been very traumatized, and had hardly slept after she had left Gibbs. However, like Spence, she had been somewhat comforted by the fact that she had remained in control and had not suffered from nerves.

Peter Allard had been charged with assault and battery and held in the cells at Hackney. On his arrival at the station, Moran had received a call from Maidstone. The stones from the patio had been lifted, and using arc lights, as the soil beneath was being carefully sifted, they had partly uncovered a roll of carpet.

The body was inside the carpet, covered with plastic, and thick duct tape bound her from head to toe. As a result of the tight bindings there was little decomposition. It was without doubt Susie Luna, as in the pocket of her overall was a name tag from the Majestic Hotel where she had worked.

After clearing her absence with DCI Shepherd, Jane arrived at Hackney Station and went into the incident room where DC Edwards gave her the update on the discovery of the body. Moran was waiting for the formal identification but it was pretty conclusive. 'He wants to see you, and he's had DCI Shepherd on the phone, so he'll no doubt fill you in.'

Jane felt nervous, wondering if this was going to be a severe reprimand over her suspicions about Moran. She was not that eager to go and see him, but she had no option. She checked her appearance in the ladies' locker room and then went to his office, which she still thought of as Bradfield's. She knocked on the door, and it was a moment before she heard Moran say 'come in'. He gave almost a curt nod of his head, to indicate for her to sit in the chair opposite his desk.

'We need to discuss a few things just to clear the air a bit. I have given DCI Shepherd a rundown. He started off being a bit tetchy about your professional conduct, saying that you were not a team player – he already seems to think you were acting without backup on the Shirley Dawson case.' Jane chewed her lips.

'Shepherd said he had discussed this with you previously, about some unethical procedure. Apparently, despite the coroner's report that it was a non-suspicious death, you and DS Lawrence continued to investigate. You went without authority to question Katrina Harcourt and introduced evidence of the black patent leather shoes but—'

Jane interrupted. 'It was a good job we did.'

'Hang on, Tennison. Although he disapproved of what he described as unethical procedure, he did express his admiration for the way you triggered the investigation into the murder of Shirley Dawson. What was it that made you suspect foul play?'

Jane hesitated before answering. 'I found it very distressing because I was alone in the flat with the victim, her eyes were open, and I had to lift her out of the bath to be taken to the mortuary. Something just didn't feel right. She was the same age as me, and she had a small child, and it was seeing the baby food, her bottle ready to feed her.'

'As a detective, you're going to find an awful lot of cases of non-suspicious death and of victims as young or even younger than you. What was it that made you believe Shirley Dawson's death was suspicious?' he asked her again.

'It was an intuitive feeling that something didn't add up. I think the position that her body was found in, in the bath, was not quite right. That was all really.'

'But at that point you didn't have the evidence. Would you have ever considered the need to find something that would implicate them?'

Jane knew he was testing her with regard to the fact she knew he had planted the knife. She looked at him directly. 'There was no need to uncover evidence that wasn't there because my finding of the photographs was enough.'

'What did you feel when you were proved right?' Moran asked quietly.

She turned away, unable to answer.

'It made you feel good, didn't it?' he asked, and she nodded.

'And how did you feel about the two suspects being charged with murder?'

'Good, they deserve to be given life sentences.'

'How would you feel if they had got away with it?'

'That I had failed.'

'I suppose you know why Allard was given bail and was let out of prison?' Moran stood up and put his hands in his trouser pockets, and moved from behind the desk.

Jane was becoming more uneasy, suspecting he was going to bring up the fact she had been suspicious of him doctoring the confession and planting evidence of the flick knife, which she now knew had been given to him by Janet Brown.

'Allard will be put away for the rest of his life. He hid the murder of Susie Luna for five years, hid his disgusting perverted sexual urges and appeared on the surface to be a decent honest husband and father. The current trial will go ahead because the other criminal offences, the assault on the owner of the adult bookshop, the kid Ginger, the attack against you and Janet Brown, and even the murder of Susie Luna, are not what he is on trial for, they will be a completely separate arrest. Do you understand? The law let him loose, and we got him back, and we won't let him out of our sight, but it's all down to the legal boffins' correct procedure in the courts, understand?'

'I find it hard to believe,' she said and he nodded. He began to unnerve her even more as he moved behind her, still with his hands in his pockets. She was sure this was now going to be a reference to the knife.

'Make you feel positive, does it?'

'On the one hand, yes, that we caught him. On the other, very confused that the trial will get him on one set of charges and that he could then be free unless we have the evidence to get him on something else.'

'Right, because his legal team will not allow the new charges to be read at the same time, so the jury will not be privy to them. There will have to be a completely new trial.'

She swivelled her head round to see him because it sounded unbelievable.

'What do you feel about Janet Brown? Or Angie as she calls herself?'

She was taken off guard and shrugged. 'I don't know what I feel about her.'

'She saved your life?'

'Yes.'

'She has agreed to give evidence at Peter Allard's immediate trial, but I am unsure if we will need her. What do you think about that?'

'If it will jeopardize her as an informer, and it is possible to keep her identity safe ... then she should not be called.'

'But you know she blackmailed Marie Allard?'

'Yes, but in reality if she hadn't we might never have got the details and information about Susie Luna.'

He nodded and moved back to the desk. 'So that is something you would not deem necessary to expose?'

'Yes, sir.'

'Good, OK, WDC Tennison. I think we've cleared up a lot, apart from ...'

Oh God, she thought, now it's coming, but he leaned down behind the desk and brought up a large package wrapped in a Hamleys carrier bag. 'This is for you. I don't think it is necessary to put it in the report. DC Gibbs organized it, and we all chipped in.'

He swung the handles in his fingers. 'WDC Tennison, you are one of us. So take it and we'll see you tonight for a good knees-up.'

Jane left with the carrier bag, and went into the ladies'. She opened it up and took out a very large, very expensive replica of a red double-decker bus. She couldn't keep the smile off her face, tucking it under her arm, loving the fact he had said that she was one of them. It made up for everything she had been through. She'd make sure Peter Allard was put away when the time came, and if that failed, she would make sure that she would be the one to arrest him for murder.

Shortly before the trial of Peter Allard began, DS Lawrence had a meeting with Moran. The newspaper was still wrapped around the black woollen balaclava, and as he carefully opened it to reveal the hood, he placed it onto a sheet of white paper on the lab table.

He leaned in closely and sniffed, as he could detect a strong sweet smell.

'I can smell some kind of aftershave.'

Moran nodded. 'Yeah, I know, it's Aramis ... I use it, but I won't be as from today ... Anything else? Any bloodstains?'

Lawrence used a spatula and took his time examining it, turning the hood around, pressing it down and checking every inch. He detected that on the area where the assailant's mouth would have been, the wool was in part stuck together.

'This could be his saliva, but I can't detect any blood. I can test if there is a residue but I doubt it, and with it being black nothing shows up. Your rape victim wasn't cut, was she? Besides, you won't get it into the trial now – how long ago was this found?'

'He was wearing it on the night of the rape, so it's quite a substantial time, although it was kept wrapped in that newspaper. But I'm certain his defence counsel won't accept it ... I just needed to know for certain.'

'Sorry, but like I said I can do some tests ...'

Moran shrugged and checked his watch.

'I got to go. Thanks for your time, Paul.'

Just as Moran reached the double doors leading out from the lab, Paul called out to him.

'Hang on ... come back.'

Moran hurried to the table. Lawrence was using a pair of fine long tweezers and had placed onto the white paper a thin, pale blue woollen strand. He now teased out a second strand and held it up.

'Is that blue rabbit fur?' Moran asked.

'No, it's wool, just caught inside the rim of the hood. What was your rape victim wearing?'

Moran took a deep breath. 'A shaggy blue mohair jacket.'

'Shit ... it's a pity this wasn't brought in earlier because I could have checked it out with the actual jacket.'

'Thanks, Paul, but I don't hold out much hope that we can use it.'

By the time Moran returned to Hackney he was anxious to discuss the findings from the balaclava. He felt that the results confirmed, without doubt, that Peter Allard had committed the rape. But he was concerned about the late discovery of the vital evidence and after a heated discussion with the defence lawyer they were refused permission for it to be used in court.

Disappointed, Moran put more pressure on confirming that the body found at the Allards' rented house was Susie Luna. The body had still not been formally identified when the trial began. All he knew was that they were hoping to gain a result from dental checks, and there had been delays caused by trying to trace a dentist in Maidstone who had had Susie Luna registered as a patient.

As the trial commenced Jane witnessed the hidden depths of Peter Allard's sick mind. He constantly made direct eye contact with the jury and said very clearly that he pleaded guilty to the assault charges. When the rape charge was read out he said loudly, 'Not guilty.'

Jane held her own in the witness box. She was controlled under questioning by the defence counsel, who accused her of deliberately encouraging the defendant by wearing sexually suggestive attire that would have been an attempt to lure the defendant into making a sexual approach. Jane denied the allegations and said that her intention was to safeguard any other women from being attacked. It was all very uncomfortable and by the time she returned to sit in the court to listen to the rest of the trial she could hardly contain her anger. Moran winked at her to indicate that she had held her own. He then sat with his head bowed, refusing to look at Allard who stood in the witness box looking very handsome, wearing a suit and a pressed shirt his mother had brought into the prison for him to wear for his court appearance. Allard had the audacity to keep his head held high, and then lower it in a gesture of submission when he said softly that he was ashamed of having assaulted the women but he was under such stress because of his wife's medical predicament.

The defence were able to argue that his confession was taken under duress and was therefore not admissible evidence. They argued that his signature and that of WDC Tennison were also not acceptable.

The prosecution asked why, as innocent as he professed to be, he was wearing a stocking mask and Allard bowed his head.

'Because I am a foolish, stupid man. I was desperate for some kind of satisfaction, and I am deeply sorry.'

The jury filed out as DC Edwards approached Moran and passed him an envelope. He ripped it open and then leaned back, closing his eyes. Jane was sitting directly behind him and he turned to face her whispering, 'We just got confirmation ... Susie Luna's dental records match the body found at Allard's house. We bloody got him!'

The jury returned half an hour later. The foreman handed the judge the result and there was a palpable tension in the courtroom. When the judge read out the verdict there was an audible murmur from everyone present. Peter Allard was found not guilty of rape and, as he had pleaded, guilty of the assaults. As he had already spent time in prison on remand he was released and free to leave the court.

Allard walked out into the marble reception area of the Old Bailey. He was smiling as he shook the hand of his barrister. It was extraordinary and it felt as if he was in total denial about the second knife attack on Jane and Janet Brown, and the brutal assault of the young boy Ginger. But he suddenly straightened and looked afraid, his eyes like a trapped animal.

DI Moran was clearly enjoying the moment, and he made a point of having WDC Tennison by his side. He looked across at Jane.

'He's yours, Tennison ... it's your arrest.'

They approached Allard and Jane's voice echoed around the old courthouse reception.

'Peter Allard, I am arresting you on the suspicion of the murder of Susie Luna. You do not have to say anything unless you wish to do so, but what you say may be given in evidence.'

It was as if everyone was caught in time, moving in slow motion as Allard stepped back. But an officer had already moved in behind him. Moran handcuffed him, then stepped to stand beside him as Jane moved to walk on the other side. As DI Moran and WDC Tennison escorted Allard out of the court, the press photographers suddenly realized that something very newsworthy was happening, and the flash bulbs began popping as the cameras clicked in quick succession.

Allard was still handcuffed as he was pushed into the waiting police van and the caged doors locked behind him. When the doors slammed shut he let out a howl like a wolf.

Jane and Moran got into a patrol car together. She had expected him to show some kind of emotional exuberance but instead he was quiet. He eventually turned towards her.

'It's over. I'm going to give you a nudge for a commendation, because you've shown persistence and good team work as a trainee CID Detective ... surprising for ...'

She was about to thank him when he added, '... a young woman.'

Jane laughed. It was a backhanded compliment but she was now more determined than ever to move up the ranks in this, her chosen career.

Lynda La Plante

Tennison

From the creator of the award-winning ITV series
***Prime Suspect*, starring Helen Mirren, comes the**
fascinating back story of the iconic DCI Jane Tennison.

The Kray twins are behind bars, but the streets of London
are still rife with drugs, robbery and murder.

It is 1973 in the East End of London and a young WPC,
Jane Tennison, joins the toughest ranks of the Hackney
police force as a probationary officer.

When her first case comes in, a woman savagely beaten and
strangled to death, Jane is thrown right in at the deep end.

The victim's autopsy is just the beginning of Tennison's
harsh initiation into the criminal world ...

**'La Plante excels in her ability to pick out details that
give her portrayal of life in a police station a rare ring
of authenticity'**
Sunday Telegraph

PAPERBACK ISBN 978-1-4711-4052-5
EBOOK ISBN 978-1-4711-4053-2

Lynda La Plante
Prime Suspect

**The sensational thriller behind the
hit TV series *Prime Suspect***

When a prostitute is found murdered in her bedsit, the
Metropolitan police set to work finding the perpetrator
of this brutal attack. DNA samples lead them straight to
George Marlow, a man previously convicted of attempted
rape. Everything appears to add up and the police think
they've found their man, but things aren't
quite what they seem . . .

Detective Chief Inspector Jane Tennison came through the
ranks the hard way, opposed and resented at every step
by her male colleagues. So when DCI Shefford falls ill,
the opportunity for Tennison to get herself noticed finally
arrives. But the boys are not happy and every one of her
colleagues is willing her to trip up.

Desperate to remove all doubt around her suspect, Tennison
struggles to make the charges stick. And then a second
body turns up. With the team against her, and a dangerous
criminal still on the loose, DCI Jane Tennison must fight to
prove herself, now or never.

'The mistress of suspense'
Daily Express

**PAPERBACK ISBN 978-1-4711-0021-5
EBOOK ISBN 978-1-4711-0023-9**

Lynda La Plante
Above Suspicion

**The first instalment in the bestselling Anna Travis series
from the BAFTA-winning writer Lynda La Plante**

Young Anna Travis has been assigned to her first murder
case – a series of killings that has shocked even the most
hardened of detectives. The method of killing and the
backgrounds of the girls are identical:
all drug-users and prostitutes.

Then a new body is found and the profile of the murderer
changes dramatically. The modus operandi is the same, but
the victim is a young student with 'the face of an angel'.

Anna stumbles on a vital piece of information which links
one man to the killings, a much-loved actor on the brink
of international stardom. His arrest would create a media
frenzy. But if he were found innocent, his wouldn't be the
only career over . . .

'Above Suspicion blew me away – it grabs you
and doesn't let go until the last page'
Karin Slaughter

**PAPERBACK ISBN 978-1-84983-433-9
EBOOK ISBN 978-1-84739-509-2**

Lynda La Plante
Cold Shoulder

**The first in the thrilling Lorraine Page series,
from TV's most successful writer, Lynda La Plante**

Lieutenant Lorraine Page had everything – a devoted
husband, two beautiful daughters and an impressive
career with the Homicide Squad. It's impossible to
believe that she could be thrown out of the police force
and end up on Skid Row.

Lorraine's ex-colleagues soon forget her, as the hunt for
a nightmare serial killer spirals into an all-out search
for a missing witness: a victim who escaped.

Lorraine Page is that witness. Against her will she is
drawn into the investigation, and forced to face her past
and her overwhelming guilt ...

**'Lorraine Page, officer, wife and mother,
is as tough as they come'**
Sunday Telegraph

**PAPERBACK ISBN 978-1-84983-262-5
EBOOK ISBN 978-1-84983-263-2**